STARMEN

A Novel by **Francis Hamit**

Written by Francis Hamit

Edited by Leigh Strother-Vien

BRASS CANNON BOOKS

This book is dedicated to my maternal cousins

Joan, Priscilla, & Mozelle

who have always been there for me.

ACKNOWLEDGMENTS

This book would not have been possible without the help, encouragement, and companionship of Leigh Strother-Vien, another Army veteran who has shared my foxhole for more than 34 years now, and has edited all of my work as well as being my business partner, sounding board, and best friend. She has seen me through more than one long period of near catastrophic ill health with good humour and extreme patience. I love her very much.

The cover image was donated by **Markee Book Cover Designs** and developed in collaboration. The team there has been quick, responsive to suggestion and feedback and entirely professional.

Three old friends served as beta readers and provided valuable feedback on earlier drafts. **Jacqueline Lichtenberg** also provided great encouragement and a nice blurb for promotional purposes. **Mike Glyer**, the founder and editor of the science fiction and fantasy fandom newszine **FILE 770**, and novelist **Glen Olsen** provided valuable feedback about where I had gone wrong with the narrative flow. Leigh, as always, had a lot of questions.

We raised some money on **Kickstarter** to pay for e-book formatting. 35 people contributed. Under Kickstarter's rules I am not allowed to disclose their names, but I am grateful for their support and encouragement.

I am also extending thanks in advance to the many book reviewers, book bloggers and influencers who will help spread the word about this book to others.

INTRODUCTION

Hello everyone:

Our first job as writers is to entertain our readers. I hope you will enjoy the adventure.

As you may know I've just completed a successful Kickstarter campaign to buy proper formatting for my new novel **STARMEN**. All part of the process now, especially if you create a wildly experimental novel that is too big and complicated to jam into a standard genre category (and for those who think genres are a lesser form, "Literary" is also a genre).

I started this novel during the COVID lockdown after my first operation for spinal stenosis. My doctors said to keep writing to keep my mind alive and prevent dementia. "No problem," I said and took an old unsold screenplay and used that as a premise.

Then I asked the question(s) inspired by Dr. Howard Stein's Playwriting class, Spring 1966. "What would happen if...? and fill in the blanks. I was also filling time with some of The Great Courses. New facts inspired new writing. Courses on everything from The Transcendentalists to Native American anthropology to Quantum Mechanics and String Theory.

I was already familiar with the Pinkerton National Detective Agency from the research for my Civil War novels. And with British spying and influence operations in the 19th Century. (They invented the science of Anthropology as an intelligence collection discipline.)

A new premise arose in my fevered mind. What would happen if the famous Anthropologist George James Frazer went to El Paso, Texas, as a young man in 1875, fell in with Pinkerton operatives and was able to study Apache myths and culture in a very intimate way? New characters showed up and demanded to become part of the story. Witches who are also detectives and young girls with romantic problems, Alien creatures on a Western Cos-Play holiday, Apache Shamans who manipulate time and space and can fly by turning into birds. The list goes on.

This book is very big and crosses over from Historical and Detective/Espionage fiction into Science Fiction, Fantasy, Mystery, Political, and Romance narratives.

This is called Magical Realism.

To give you a big, improbable, but very enjoyable story.

A note for nitpickers and fact checkers:

This is set in an alternative universe much like our own, but not the same in all respects. Research to your heart's content. You will be surprised how many real world anchors there are. But some parts will not match, and that is as I intended.

Some readers may be upset or put off by parts of this story. It is set in 1875 in A United States of America recovering from a devastating Civil War when Reconstruction is failing and the threat from unreconstructed Confederates and their British friends are a concern to the Pinkerton National Detective Agency, a forerunner of the F.B.I.

The Demimonde, that floating world of prostitution and vice, is one of the few paths to prosperity available to women. Native American tribes were losing their 400 year war with White domination. Slave and other narratives about the Civil War were being rewritten, and the Gilded Age of greed and corruption was well underway. But that is the way it was. The Pinkertons tread a delicate path: always trying to what was right, even when it wasn't entirely legal.

There is a strong moral center. Read and you will find it.

CHAPTER ONE

One day early in 1875, over the city variously known as El Paso and Ciudad Juarez, appeared a remarkable thing that looked like a large floating whale.

It was a hot air balloon, and such had been seen there from time to time, but never of such size. The woven basket carried below showed half a dozen heads looking over and down at the ground below, where a large wondering crowd gathered. It was mid-morning, bright and clear, with the last of a morning mist quickly dissipating. The large open square below the slowly descending balloon was bordered by two and three story buildings on three sides. Some of them, faced in yellow or tan adobe, went back to the first Spanish incursion hundreds of years before. Others, mostly painted white or brown, were more recent, erected by settlers before, during and after that brief period that Texas was a nation rather than just a state of two different North American national governments. The square was far, far older, tinged with ghosts and ancient ceremonies. As the balloon got ever closer, almost everyone stopped to stare.

One man in particular, sitting on a chair on the veranda of a small hotel, looked up and smiled ruefully. In the chair next to him an older man, about fifty years old, inspected the end of his cigar, struck a sulphur match to relight it, and asked, "So, this is she?"

"Indeed, it is," the young man said.

"When you told me about her last night, I thought you the most prodigious liar I had met in many a moon, and in my line of work

I meet a fair number of them." The older man subconsciously tapped the brass badge over his heart on his vest, puffed on his cigar and then used it to point at the balloon slowly descending. "But now I see I will have to take it all back. I humbly beg your pardon for doubting you, Jim."

The younger man smiled. "You never said, Harry, so I am not sure an apology is necessary."

The older man, who sported greying muttonchop whiskers that ran over his cheeks, but a bare chin, and wore an expensive, well-tailored brown broadcloth suit that no longer quite fit over an expanding belly, took off his bowler hat and tilted his head back, staring upward at the balloon, trying to get a better look.

"Augh. You could tell. I could not hide it entirely, not from the likes of you. You're too sharp, too close an observer. What is your trade again?"

"Ethnographer. The study of native cultures."

"Ah, just so. So you're, like me, a detective. You should think about my offer."

"Very kind, but quite impossible. I must continue my studies at Cambridge next fall."

The older man looked upward again at the huge balloon. "How long will it take?"

"About an hour. The gas has to be released, very slowly, through valves. Otherwise there could be an explosion."

"So we wait?"

"We do."

The two had met the day before at a local photographer's establishment, when the younger man, Frazer, had handed over a box of glass plates to be developed, and Harry, hearing him speak, said, "I'd know that accent anywhere! You're from Glasgow!"

" I am." The young man smiled pleasantly, held out his hand and said, "I'm James George Frazer."

The older man threw his head back and laughed. "And I'm Harold Elliot McLean, but everyone calls me Harry. Really, son, that's too grand a moniker to use here. This is the West. No one has two first names except lawyers, preachers and con-men. Pick one and stick to it. You'll do better."

Frazer tilted his head to one side and smiled. His new friend was overbearing, but likeable, and reminded him of an uncle of his who lived up by Dundee. He also noted the brass six-pointed star inscribed with the legend "Pinkerton National Detective Agency" and next to it a small Masonic pin. He turned his lapel to reveal his own. McLean's eyebrows raised slightly and he put his right forefinger next to his nose in recognition.

"You look like a likely fellow. Why don't I buy you a wee dram and we'll see if we can chase up a connection between us... if you have nothing better to do?"

Frazer was pleased by the offer and nodded. He found Texas strange, with its rich mix of cultures and influences, and the casual violence that seemed to pervade the town... and had yet to speak with a native savage. He had been distracted and pulled away from his purpose by Mademoiselle Fifi Pompadour, aeronaut, who'd captured his heart with a single smile.

"I have some arrangements to make, but give me two hours."

McLean nodded and named a saloon, which he said, "Serves a fine single malt and not just that horse piss the Americans call Bourbon or that the Mexicans call Tequila."

Frazer smiled at that. He had sampled both... in the interests of science of course... but was gratified that McLean's opinion reflected his own. He went off to arrange hotel rooms for Mlle. Pompadour's crew, as well as a suitable greeting for her arrival. In need of money, he had answered her advertisement for an 'advance man'. The position carried duties he had not imagined at the time. And some secrets that he would not reveal even to a newly met Masonic brother. One was that her name was actually Rose Green, from Liverpool, and that her 'tour' of the Texas/Mexican Border was financed by a British government office in Whitehall. It was exciting, and so was she, but somehow in the midst of all of the commotion he must contrive to get some real work done. So far, he barely knew where to begin.

So at one point in their drinking and endless wandering conversation full of hidden probes, Frazer asked for advice from his new friend.

"Well, how much Mex do you speak?" McLean asked.

"I have some rudimentary Spanish."

"Learned in Spain?"

"Yes."

"Well that won't serve you here. Mex is a blend of Spanish, Cajun French, and several Indian dialects. The Conquistadors intermarried. So did their language. After 400 years it can no longer recognize itself."

"You're very well informed."

"It's what I do, Laddie. Go to strange places, see what's happening and report back. And this is a promotion for me. I'm the Branch Manager for our new office."

"Congratulations."

"Not sure those are in order just yet. I've got to set the whole thing up myself, y'see. Got one senior man who came in from the New York office. Him aside, everything else is local hires, and we already have requests for service. Even before we hung out our shingle. So it's an embarrassment of riches. It's easy enough for the standing guards for the railroads. Put up a notice for any man over thirty who served in the late unpleasantness and is clean and sober, offering two dollars a day, and I almost have to beat them away with a stick. We bill them out at three to four dollars a day. I've got a defrocked minister running that bit so's I can attend to what we're known for, the detectives. Finding men... and the odd female... who can master that craft is not so easy. You might think about joining us." Harry smiled genially.

Frazer smiled back. "Sorry, friend. I'm previously engaged and I need to find a way to connect to the native culture. Everyone professes ignorance about that. Have you any ideas?"

McLean sipped his single malt and considered carefully. "Well," he said after a moment, "You can hire a so-called 'native guide' to lead you around by the nose and pick your pockets by degree. And gain nothing. Those are con-men and fantasists who tell the most remarkable lies. One tried to convince me that his ancestors were living gods and could fly."

Fraser perked up. "Exactly the kind of tale I'm looking for. Mythological creatures with superior powers, like the Greek and Roman gods of old."

"You mean there might be something to it?" McLean looked scornful.

"If there are artifacts or records. We have the Greek and Roman structures and even older artifacts all over Mesopotamia. Hundreds of years of history. Legends from Homer."

"Fairy tales," McLean poured another drink from the brown bottle sitting between them and then one for Frazer. Frazer left it untouched. He was at a point where he felt very warm and that his mind was clear.

He shook his head slowly. "But where do those come from? My father told me, and his told him, and so on to the beginning of time…or at least of history."

"Well, none of that here. All rocks and desert, and some very unpleasant natives."

"There is more to it than that, Harry. Flying over the desert we saw a large circle of stones on top of a mesa. All by itself."

"So?"

"What does it mean? Out there all by itself? Stones do not naturally arrange themselves in a circle, Harry. Someone had to carry them there, and it's almost a perfect circle, of white stones, all alike. Big ones. Bigger than one man could carry, on top of a mesa about two miles long that is four hundred feet above the desert floor. Why it there? Who made it? And why?"

McLean was staring at him, transfixed. "No idea. What do you think?"

"Well, Religion is the second phase of a civilization. Some sort of ceremonial place?"

"Beats me, son. What's the first phase?"

"Pardon?"

"You said Religion is the second phase. What comes before that?"

"Oh, Myth. Stories."

"Sure they're not one and the same?"

"Not at all," Frazer admitted; "It's something for later study."

"I'd like to see that circle some time," Harry McLean said.

"Oh, you may. I took photographs. That's what I had developed. I want to do an article for one of the journals eventually, and, as they say..."

"A picture is worth a thousand words."

And that morning, young Jim Frazer boyishly produced a print from his large notebook of the white stone circle, surrounded by.... nothing at all! Just desert.

. . .

McLean laughed. And stared upward.

"And now we have an angel from above," he said.

"She calls herself an aeronaut," Jim said.

The balloon floated lower, and now weighted ropes were unfurled over the side for some of the men below to catch and pull the balloon further down. A very attractive woman with blonde hair wearing pink tights stood at the edge. She grabbed one of the ropes and slide slowly down it to the cheers and applause of the crowd. A photographer, in the midst of setting up his camera, hurried to capture the moment.

"She does know how to make an entrance," McLean said, grinning.

"That she does," Frazer replied. "As a boy, I often dreamt of running away and joining the circus. Now I've done it."

They watched as the crowd, almost entirely men, made a circle around the young woman. From a side street a Mexican band emerged, playing a cheerful Mariachi tune of welcome. Suddenly it was a fiesta, and vendors walked in selling tamales and ears of roasted corn and beer.

McLean turned to Frazer with new respect.

"Is this what you meant by arrangements?"

"Only that I made sure everything was ready and paid for. Most of it was done by others. I just gave the cue."

McLean looked thoughtful. Frazer was a very young man, but there was a toughness about him. His sharp angular face and bright blue eyes were softened only a little by his neatly trimmed dark red-brown beard. McLean knew too well that British ethnographic studies were often a cover for spying and imperial mischief. In a previous life he had been part of that service. But what was the purpose here? Why float, in the most literal sense of the word, such a large 'cover' for the surveying of an insignificant border town? He smiled again as Madame Fifi, now wrapped in a black wool cloak, strode towards them, paused, threw open her arms and embraced Frazer. This was followed by a kiss that left the younger man squirming, his face growing red.

"Please, Mademoiselle...."

"Oh, *Cherie*, you have done a wonderful job arranging such a greeting," she said and then turned her gaze towards McLean. "And who do we have here?" Her intelligent blue eyes surveyed him cautiously.

McLean smiled and bowed slightly, "Harry McLean. Pinkerton National Detective Agency. At your service."

Madame Fifi suddenly frowned, and focused on the brass badge on his vest and the Masonic pin next to it. She smiled brightly. "You're from the Government?"

"No, ma'am. Despite the name, we are a private agency. That is an artifact from our Civil War service, when we protected President Lincoln and worked for the Army. These days we serve railroads and similar enterprises."

Madame Fifi nodded and looked surprised. "Are there railroads here? I saw none as we flew over the land."

"No, ma'am. Not yet. There will be. There's quite a bit for us to do, protecting supplies and equipment. Standing guard as it were. Not glamourous work, like you read about in the dime novels, but it pays the bills."

"So nothing for the Government?"

"Just the Courts. We are Bail Agents for some. We do go after murderers and thieves and investigate frauds of all kinds."

Madam Fifi smiled very graciously. "Fascinating. I want to hear more. You must come to dinner tonight. Georgie!"

Frazer stood a little straighter. "Yes Fifi?"

"Make those arrangements, will you? And take me to our hotel."

"Yes, of course."

He offered his arm and she took it, holding the cloak tight about her. Her pink tights gave the illusion that she was wearing nothing at all beneath it. Her performance was over. Now McLean saw only a tired-looking woman in need of comfort.

"Where will I find you?" Frazer asked McLean.

"At my office. Address is on my card. Come about two."

"I will." Frazer solicitously walked away with Fifi on his arm, his hand over hers.

McLean stared after them a moment, trying to read them and what that closeness meant. Were they lovers or did the younger man simply aspire to that intimacy? Was he serious about his studies, or was that, too, some sort of cover?

McLean looked past the fiesta to the huge hot air balloon, now secured to the ground and guarded by several tall men in the uniforms of French sailors, carrying new Winchester carbines and wearing Colt's revolvers on their belts.

No business to be had there, he decided, and walked away, his curiosity aroused. The entire enterprise seemed off. And young Frazer intrigued him even more. He found himself wanting to help the younger man. Obviously very bright, and full of knowledge, he was. And with an easy ingratiating manner. Wary of his own sudden affection, he reminded himself that he'd met many likely young men over the years and that few of them were truly honest. Sharpers, most of them, out for any advantage.

He walked through the fiesta, skirting around the huge balloon to get a better look. Almost a hundred feet long and thirty wide, the fabric of the balloon seemed to be too fine to be canvas and was stretched over a lattice of thin wooden spars. Slack now that it was at rest. The weave of the basket that carried its crew was tight and thick, painted a dark uniform brown. In the rear he spotted a brass telescope and something that might be a camera. Other instruments he could not put a name to, and a brass mount for something large. It's U-shaped yoke caught his eye. It looked like something military. He walked on out of the square and towards his office. It was growing warmer and he looked around, taking in the scene. The women in their bright flowered dresses, spinning a riot of color as they danced to the loud, strange, but, he decided, not unpleasant music. The combination of brass and stringed instruments was a novelty he had encountered only here.

The locals seemed to embrace any excuse for a celebration, at least the locals who were not from Back East: White, Christian and all too proud of both. He felt his steps quicken to the music and felt like dancing a bit himself, but he had business to attend to. He looked at the huge balloon now under heavy guard. This excited his curiosity most of all, but he would have to contain it. No one had paid for an inquiry, and these days the Pinkertons were strictly 'work for hire'. Allan Pinkerton's volunteerism for Lincoln and McClellan in the early part of the Civil War had nearly ruined them all. It had taken years to get paid, and that only after they had rescued President Johnson from certain disgrace by stealing La Fayette Baker's huge, overstuffed briefcase just as he was about to lay a pile of damning evidence before a Senate Committee. So, no. Thank you very much, they did not work for the Government, the worst of all possible clients. But McLean could not shake the balloon and its strange crew from his mind.

Why are they here? Why here? This place, at this time? What are they looking for? He sighed. He knew he would ponder this until he found an answer. Perhaps young Mister Frazer would provide one.

He walked on, until he reached a modest two story building on a side street. A freshly painted sign with the Pinkerton logo of a single eye and the words "We Never Sleep" painted black on a bright yellow background, hung over the street. Waiting for him at the bottom of the stairs was a thin Mexican boy about twelve years old, dressed in a ragged white cotton shirt and pants. His feet were bare.

"Hello, Hey-suess," he said gravely. "How are you today?"

The boy nodded shyly and didn't say anything.

"Come to clean, have you?"

Jesus nodded again. McLean and he had a set arrangment. The boy came every day except Sunday, to dust, sweep, and wipe the grime from the windows with a wet rag. This took about an hour. At the end, McLean would inspect the work and then present him with a shiny new US Quarter, after making him sign a line in the petty cash ledger where the expense was recorded. The process fascinated Jesus, whose other clients were not so particular.

"Why have you not begun?"

"Mister Johnson is there. Sick again."

Drunk again, McLean thought. Hiram Johnson was a failed Baptist Minister who had lost more than one church for his habits, and was not likely to find another unless he came to Temperance and stopped drinking entirely. Not that he had not signed the pledge more than a few times. He simply lacked the resolve to follow through. He was a mean, often violent and very frightening drunk, since he stood six feet, eight inches tall and weighed well over 200 pounds. When sober he was just the man to supervise the rough men who worked, at two dollars a day, as standing guards and night watchmen for Pinkerton's. There he was a dignified presence and strict disciplinarian.

"Well, you could have worked around him," McLean joked. "He don't take up much space. You might even dust him off."

Jesus's eyes went wide at the thought. He shook his head slowly. "No. I don't like him. He scare me."

McLean had to think about that for a moment. It was prudent to never poke the bear. He liked the boy and did not much care for Johnson. A suspicion nagged at him. Was the boy scared because Johnson was sometimes a violent drunk, or was there a darker, more unpleasant reason? He shook the notion off. In the absence of evidence, such things were not even to be thought of. That was the problem with being a detective. You knew too much, saw too much, and, at the same time, never knew enough. Something always got by you. And it was not what you didn't know but what you didn't know about what you didn't know that did you in.

"Well, come on," he said, and he and the boy went up the stairs together. Johnson was asleep, head on the table in the center of the room, snoring. McLean pushed him off his chair and on to the floor. Johnson jumped up, ready for a fight, fists cocked, and then saw who had assaulted him. He dropped his hands at once, hung his head and said, "I'm sorry, Boss."

"Yep. You sure are. Look, Hiram, this simply will not do. What if a client had come in and seen you like that? People talk. It would hurt the business. This happens again, and I will discharge you. This is your only warning. Go get some coffee and come back later."

Without a word, Johnson edged his way out of the huge room and went down the stairs with a shambling gait. McLean sighed. He found his chair, took a key from his vest pocket, and opened his rolltop desk to reveal several neat piles of paper. Jesus began to clean the office.

Promptly at two, Frazer climbed the stairs and opened the door. The middle step of the stairway creaked loudly as it always did. McLean was standing, ready to greet him.

"Hallo, Jim," he said, his face and manner genial. Jesus stopped and stared.

"Harry, how are you?" The two men shook hands.

"Oh, let me introduce our very able apprentice, Hey-suess Martinez."

Frazer nodded gravely and held out his hand. Jesus shifted the feather duster he was holding and took it.

"Señor."

Frazer said something in Spanish. Jesus looked at him, puzzled.

Frazer tried again. The boy smiled and then repeated the phrase.

Frazer repeated the phrase, trying to get closer to what the boy had said. The boy cocked his head and looked puzzled again. "Why are you talking so funny?"

McLean laughed. "Told you! The language don't recognize itself any more."

Frazer smiled. "Let me try again. In English. I said 'I'm very pleased to meet you, Jesus' ".

"Hey-suess," McLean said. "That's the name in Mex. Say the English version too often and you will have some folks looking around for the Second Coming."

"I see." Frazer smiled again. McLean motioned for him to take a chair. The two men stared at each other for a moment.

"So," McLean said after a moment, "She calls you Georgie?"

Frazer blushed slightly. "She does. But Jim or George or Georgie, I answer to them all."

McLean smiled. "She seems quite fond of you."

Frazer shook his head. "She's like that with many. Very extravagant in her manner. I wouldn't read too much into it."

"So she and you aren't..."

Frazer blushed harder this time, as good as a confession to McLean's eyes. He frowned. "They say a gentleman never tells, but I can't even say that can I, lest you take it for confirmation, so I will say nothing." He looked quite put out.

McLean leaned forward and patted him on the knee. "There, now, Laddie, I meant nothing untoward by it. Just making conversation." He leaned back.

Frazer was looking away from him and seemed angry.

She must really have her hooks into him, McLean thought, and tried to restore the good will between them. "So, what can I do for you, Jim?"

Frazer let his breath out, turned and smiled at him.

"I need a contact with someone who knows the local culture well."

"Well that's not me," McLean admitted. "I'm a stranger here myself, came down from the Denver office three months ago. Perhaps my young associate here can help."

Jesus looked up alertly, like a hound on the hunt, but he stood very still, waiting for McLean to finish the play.

"Hey-suess. Do you know anyone who tells stories of the old time?"

The boy pretended reluctance to jump in. Harry McLean had a fish on the line, he saw, one that would need to be led carefully. So he cast his eyes towards the heavens as if thinking the matter over, and then said, "My grandmother is a Bruja. She's always telling those stories."

"Bruja?" Frazer took out his pocket notebook and wrote the word down. "What does that mean?"

"She's a healer, or medicine woman."

"Just the thing!" Frazer was excited now. "She will know all the ceremonies."

Jesus looked doubtful. "She never talk about that. That's sacred, and a secret."

Frazer looked disappointed for a moment, and then brightened. "Well, we have our secrets, too, but I would love to hear the myths— er —stories."

McLean leaned back. "Go easy here, Jim. You're acting like a White man."

Frazer was puzzled. "How should I act?"

"Don't talk so much," Jesus said urgently. "Listen instead."

Frazer blinked, taken aback.

"Good advice," McLean said. "Now, let's get down to cases. What is this worth to you? And before you answer, take note that Bruja also means 'witch'."

Frazer looked slightly amazed. "Really? Does she fly?"

"Of course," Jesus Martinez said, as if he had never heard a more stupid question. "They all do."

CHAPTER TWO

Frazer momentarily looked surprised. *Witches can fly*, he thought. *Well, of course they can. The same was said back in Britain before we began burning them alive. My, my, can these be the same myths and how did they come here, or were they part of the culture all along?* His mind raced as he examined the possibilities.

All that Harry McLean saw was the young man's face freeze into a mask. And then he smiled politely, like a bartender greeting an old customer, while his eyes were as skeptical as a pawnbroker's.

"Fascinating," Frazer said, writing something in his notebook. "How would I meet your grandmother?"

"She has a stall in the *mercado*. I can take you."

Frazer got to his feet. He could barely contain his excitement. His face flushed a light pink. He closed his notebook and looked towards the door.

"Hold on," McLean said. "This is a place of business. Do you propose to interview the old woman?"

"I do." Frazer looked from one to the other.

"And you propose to use my young associate here as an intermediary?"

"If he would be so kind?"

"Kindness has nothing to do with it. He's a hard-working lad, and, as you can see from his appearance, in need of funds. What is that introduction worth to you?"

Frazer shrugged, and looked at the boy. "A dollar?"

McLean looked over to where Jesus stood, absolutely still, his face as hard as a stone idol.

"Hey-suess?"

The boy took his time. Looked away as if thinking hard and frowned. "Two," he said at last.

Frazer searched in his pocket and came up with two silver dollars. "Done."

McLean leaned back, beaming at them both like a benevolent uncle. "Very good. You have the services of Hey-suess Martinez at the rate of two dollars a day for the purposes of gathering information on native cultures. Paid in advance."

Frazier placed the two silver dollars on McLean's desk. McLean took a preprinted invoice, carefully wrote down the bargain and handed it to Frazer, who carefully put it in his notebook. Jesus stared, wide-eyed, taking in the ceremony of it. He started to reach for the coins.

"Not yet," McLean said. "After the job is done." McLean eased back in his chair, entering the amount and details in the daily journal. He nodded to Frazer.

"Show him that photograph you showed me."

Frazer pulled out the aerial picture of the stone circle and passed it to the boy whose mouth fell open in surprise. He looked suddenly scared.

"How did you take this? Are you a Brujo?"

"A what?" Frazer was confused now. He opened his notebook and scribbled something.

"A witch. Man-witch."

Frazer looked very confused. "Not that I know of. Why would you ask that?"

McLean interceded. Jesus was suddenly standing as far away from Frazer as he could get without running down the stairs and into the street, something he would never do because it would be unmanly. McLean spoke softly: "It's all right, son. Mr. Frazer is with that big balloon that landed in the square this morning. The photograph was taken from there. As they flew over."

The boy let out a sigh of relief. He edged closer. Looked again.

"Arapaho. One of their prayer circles. Young braves use it to start a vision quest." He looked at Frazer with new respect. "North of here?"

"Just so!" Frazer was openly excited now. "How did you know?"

"They're sort of cousins of ours. I must have heard it at a pow-wow."

Again Frazier was scribbling in his notebook. "Pow-wow? What is that?"

"Something you read about in bad dime novels," McLean said, shaking his head.

Jesus sniffed, "Don't mean it's not true. They happen. I go there."

The two men saw that the boy was offended. That the whole thing was about to fall apart, and that would never do. *Once more,* thought Harry McLean, *it's not what you don't know, but what you don't know about what you don't know that does you in.*

"I'm sorry, Hey-suess. I apologize for doubting you. We're just a couple of stupid ignorant White men."

The boy shook his head, his jaw set. He was angry now. As he stood profiled against the sunlight streaming in from the window, McLean saw what he had never seen in him before, the face of a an Indian warrior, the warrior he might become when he got his full growth. It took his breath away. How could he have missed this? And the answer was easy. He had been looking down at a ragged boy looking for work, for some of the White Man's bounty. He had been fooled because he'd fooled himself.

Frazer was also looking at Jesus strangely.

"I thought you were Mexican?"

"Because I have a Mexican name? That don't signify. Lots of Americans have such names. I have Spanish blood because somewhere in the past a Conquistador raped an Indian woman – or married one. But my family goes back way before that, and we used to own all this, or so my grandmother says."

"Family?" Frazer was blinking, trying to take it all in.

"Maybe 'tribe' is better. Hundreds of families."

McLean leaned forward. "And which tribe would that be?"

"Apache. I'm an Apache."

McLean and Frazer looked at each other. Frazer was excited, but McLean wondered if he'd made a mistake in hiring the boy. Jesus was suddenly too damned smart and able for his taste, and he suddenly remembered that the U.S. Calvary hired Indian scouts to hunt Apaches, reputed to be the fiercest warriors on the Plains now that the Comanches had been subdued. His growing affection for the lad tugged against his common sense. He should fire the little rascal at once, and bar him from the office, but what good would that do now? Anything in the files was already exposed. If the boy could read and write? No doubt he could – in English and Spanish both.

Frazer smiled and said, "Well, Mr. McLean and I are also members of a tribe. Scots! We're both from Scotland."

Jesus relaxed a bit and smiled, suddenly a boy again. McLean took note of the transition.

"I've heard of Scots," Jesus said, "You're fierce warriors, right?"

"We are," Frazer replied; "The best regiments in the British Army are Scottish, and we wear our tartan colors and kilts proudly with pipers sounding the call to battle. A kilt is a kind of skirt that allows the men more freedom of movement. Our opponents call us 'The ladies from Hell'. We lead the charge."

Jesus thought about this a moment and then said, "But it's the British Army, not the Scottish Army?"

Frazer's smile faded. "True. Very true, but it came about because the Scottish King became the English king as well, about two hundred years ago, and combined the two."

Seeing that his young friend was floundering, McLean intervened. "Say, why don't you do your duty, Hey-suess, and take Mister Frazer to meet your old granny?"

"Okay," the boy said. "What about the cleaning?"

"Come back later. This is more important."

Frazer got to his feet and closed his notebook.

"Say, Harry. Don't forget you are invited for dinner tonight."

McLean smiled warmly. "Wouldn't miss it for the world. Where and when?"

"Hotel Excelsior at Eight. The name is 'Green'."

"I will be there. Now, shoo, both of you. I have some billing to do."

Jesus and Frazer went out the door, looking very young and enthusiastic. McLean shook his head. He made a small entry in the daily journal. He would have to work out with the boy a fair commission for his new duties. Business was business. He also pondered the amazing transformation when the boy, who was thin and wiry, but hardly starved, revealed his true identity and nature. Capable of mischief, perhaps much more, even murder. That did not trouble McLean in the least. He hired killers all the time to pursue those wanted by the Courts of various jurisdictions, for a fair split of the reward money. Most of the offenders were wanted 'dead or alive'. Pinkerton's made it clear that either outcome was possible and that 'dead' was much less trouble than 'alive'.

This boy was too young and too smart for such duty, but might be useful in other ways. But he would have to be careful with him. Very careful. He sighed and went back to writing out bills. It was a day of mysteries, but for the moment he sought refuge in the certainty of numbers and accounts to clear his head.

The Excelsior was the newest and grandest hotel in El Paso. It stood four stories tall and aspired to an elegance previously only seen back East. Fine china and crystal and silver was present on every table in the common dining area. The 'Green' party had reserved a private dining room. There the walls were hung with fine dark red velvet curtains and oil paintings from the best artists in France. One was rather large, of a naked woman laying on a couch. A very beautiful woman. It looked like a Goya but was likely just a copy. *It did add tone to the room,* McLean thought.

McLean suspected that most of the patrons in this space were men of substance, and not usually accompanied by their wives, although younger, more nubile young women might be present. Work for hire was the coded explanation for this outcropping of the world's oldest profession. Also called 'nieces' to add the gloss of respectability. It reminded him that he needed to hire one or two such beauties to train as detectives. They could go places men could not. His mind wandered to his two oldest daughters, both Pinkerton detectives in Denver. In a frontier town few occupations were open to them, and neither wanted to rush into marriage and child-bearing. They'd read too many novels and wanted true love. Whatever that was.

Frazer came out into the hallway and warmly shook hands.

"Hello, Harry. I'm very glad to see you. I've had an amazing afternoon."

"You must tell me about it later," McLean said kindly. "Right now, I want to meet your friends."

"And they want to meet you. They've never met a detective before."

Oh, I doubt that's true, McLean thought.

Frazer led him to where a long table was set and four people waited. One, a tall slender man in his forties looked oddly familiar. The only woman was Mlle. Pompadour, dressed in a flowing yellow-green silk gown that did nothing to hide her figure, and left her shoulders and part of her bosom bare. She stood, extended both hands in greeting, and said, "Mister McLean, how good of you to come. I appreciate having someone new to talk to."

"You're hardly starved for conversation, Rose," said the tall man, smiling. "Given that you initiate most of it."

The other men all laughed at once and she dimpled a smile, blushing just a bit. It was charming but McLean had daughters and recognized it as a tactic deployed to win him over. *To what?* he wondered. Frazer led McLean to a chair opposite her. The detective pulled it out far enough so that it could not be used to trap him and carefully lowered his bulk. He put his hat under the table. His coat slid open just enough to reveal the butt of the grip of the small Colt's revolver he habitually wore in a holster under his left shoulder. It was such a part of him that he had forgotten it was there.

Mlle. Pompadour, pretending not to notice, leaned forward to expose two of her most obvious weapons further. They moved slightly and the edge of a pink aureole briefly appeared. Her skin was very white, almost translucent. He poured himself a glass of water as a waiter appeared, seemingly from nowhere, to pour glasses of red wine. He sipped the water, and then, so as not to be rude, sampled the wine.

"I am a chatter box, ain't I? Let me introduce everyone. You've met our young apprentice, Mister Frazer. This is Francois Gilbert, our Engineer, and Paulo Marconi, our scientific advisor. He takes measurements – of what, I do not know. And Justin Richards, our surveyor. And the tall, sarcastic fellow is our pilot, Colonel Wyndham."

McLean sat up as if he'd been given an electric shock. He knew him now. "Sir Percy Wyndham! I thought you were back with Victor Emmanuel in Italy?"

Wyndham studied him carefully and then smiled. "On detached service, sir, doing my bit for Queen and Country. Have we met?"

"During the War, several times."

"Oh, of course. You delivered reports about enemy spies."

McLean nodded. *And had you listened*, he thought, *you would have not been caught short when Mosby raided your headquarters ... unless that was your purpose all along.* He looked carefully at Wyndham and the other men, all elegantly attired for a formal occasion. Why? Certainly not for him. For the overly gracious young lady, holding court? It was almost like a play with every gesture carefully planned. He decided to cut to the chase.

"So is this a British expedition?"

Mlle. Pompadour smiled even more. "Why would you think that?"

"Only because I know what the Ethnographic Survey actually is, having once been a member. Young Frazer gave the game away the moment he said it."

Wyndham chuckled. "I told you so," he said to Frazer, who blushed and looked downcast.

"Don't be too hard on the boy," McLean said. "After all, I am a detective."

There was general laughter. Everyone relaxed.

"Say, Sir Percy," McLean asked. "What became of those extravagant mustaches you normally wear that stick out a foot on either side?"

"Had to cut them off for this party. Not exactly incognito, not using false names and all that, but not looking to draw attention to myself, either. I'm sure you understand."

McLean did, all too well. The very expensive airship they flew was gathering intelligence, but for whom? Cameras, survey equipment, and other scientific instruments told the tale. Young Frazer was a tag-along to acquire better understanding of the indigenous peoples, who were still a military force to be reckoned with even as they chafed under the White Man's boot. He took another sip of the excellent wine. *Just one and no more*, he cautioned himself. *You need a clear head for this party.*

"What are you looking for, then? Gold?"

Wyndham shook his head. "A game for fools, that. I think the Spanish got most of what can be easily had. And what can you use it for? Pretties for the ladies? No, we're after other minerals. Copper, iron, coal, things like that. That can be used to build things like bridges and railroads and telegraph lines. As the West opens more, there will be great need for these."

"And the British Government is financing this?"

"No," said Mme Pompadour, "They will deny it most strongly and our airship was built in France and Italy. No, it is a private syndicate. King Victor Emmanuel took a part. So did a syndicate of French and British banks, and the Queen may have some of it. From her private fortune, not government funds. Judah Benjamin organized it. He's always been more than just a lawyer. A true entrepreneur. He wants us to try and find another route for a transcontinental railway."

McLean's mind raced. He could hardly take it all in. The former Confederate Secretary of State, and head of its Secret Service, was behind this? He was amazed, but tried not to show it. Judah Benjamin might be a well-respected barrister now in London and Paris, but here he was a wanted traitor, the only member of the Confederate Cabinet to escape at the war's end.

"And why tell me?"

Mlle. Pompadour leaned forward, staring into his eyes so intently he had to blink and look away. "We were hoping you would join us."

McLean's facial expression told her that was a non-starter. "Oh, not on the survey. We simply want to have some copies of land records retrieved. In case we find anything we want to buy."

McLean nodded. "That we could do. No harm in that."

She smiled. "Don't be so sure. My father was investigating land claims in San Francisco when he was killed. In 1853."

McLean was puzzled. "Excuse me. Who was your father?"

"Robert Greenhow. You may have heard of the Limantour case?"

McLean had to really search his memory now. Then another thought came rushing in.

"Greenhow? He was married to Rose Greenhow, the Confederate – " he stopped himself from saying the word 'traitor'.

She smiled and nodded. "My mother. I had a taste of Federal prison when I was eight. They tried to break her spirit by putting me in with her. So, everything is on the up-and-up, so I can return to my quiet life in Liverpool. No more of that for me."

Little Rose, McLean thought. *Amazing!*

"Well I'm very pleased to meet you," McLean said. "So you're not really named Pompadour?"

"A theatrical device to amuse and attract people. Otherwise someone might see us as a threat. It's just plain Rose Green when I'm at home, sir. Had to shorten it a bit to avoid all the idiots in the world who either want to worship me or destroy me."

"I would worship you," Frazer blurted out.

"We've had our fun, Georgie. Don't spoil things by going all Scots on me."

There was general laughter around the table. Frazer's face turned bright red. Rose held out her hand and took his before he could pull it away. She smiled kindly. "You never want to give your heart to a woman like me, Georgie. We're rude and careless and break things."

McLean was taken aback at such honesty, but Rose Green obviously felt no need to dissemble and lead the lad on. She would be cruel now, to be kind. She smiled brightly at the others. "I'm famished. Where is our dinner?"

"The first course is the duck," Wyndham said smoothly and motioned for the waiters to start serving. Everyone settled in and paid due homage to the gourmet dish before them. It was delicious and soon followed by venison. McLean wondered briefly if they always ate so well, or if this was just pretense to make a good show for him.

As if he had voiced this aloud, Wyndham raised a glass and said, "Always eat as best as you can on the company tab, eh? For who knows what tomorrow may bring...or even if there will be one."

"Spoken like a true soldier," one of the other men said, joining the toast.

"I am a soldier," Wyndham said; "Born and bred. I've been miserable in the field, starving on short rations, up to my arse in mud and cold rain, and will be again. That makes moments like these all the more precious."

"Here, here," said someone else.

McLean saw that Rose was leaning over, whispering in Frazer's ear. The young man was nodding, his face unhappy. McLean looked away, thinking that Frazer might be experiencing the heartbreak of first love, and the disillusionment that the object of his desire felt only the need for a little fun. *At least*, he thought, *she is kind.*

He turned his gaze on Wyndham, who was mopping up the last of the gravy on his plate with a bit of bread.

"So, Sir Percy, how did you become a balloonist?"

Wyndham laughed. "That was courtesy of the U.S. Government. You may recall that after that peerless horseman General Ashby captured me, it took a few months for me to be exchanged. And since I am a mercenary, a wild goose as it were, suspicion fell upon me that I had surrendered my men far too easily, that I should have let them all die gloriously in battle. Which is not how we do things in Europe. Some civilian's juvenile idea of combat. But, my patron McClellan intervened, and I was given command of the First New Jersey again, but assigned garrison duty at Fairfax Courthouse, where I suffered another disaster when the charming Miss Antonia Ford collaborated with Colonel Mosby to capture my commanding general and several staff officers, while I was in Washington at a reception at the British Legation. Spectacularly bad timing for me. Ironically, I stayed at Willard's Hotel that night and Joe Willard was the Provost who arrested dear sweet Antonia after Stoughton confessed he was plucked right out of her arms after Mosby slapped him on his bare buttocks with the flat of his sword."

Wyndham laughed and the others joined in, even McLean, who'd never heard that part of the story. Wyndham had famously complained about his 23-year-old Brigadier at the time, calling him a 'young pup'. The young pup, like Custer, was a West Point man. His appointment was political, and Wyndham's discontent had been mentioned in the newspapers. A mistake he now cheerfully confessed.

"After that, I was encouraged to serve elsewhere. And after Lincoln was re-elected, and Little Mac did not replace him, I went back to Italy, where, after all, I have endless opportunities."

"What became of Miss Ford?" Frazer was now taking this in, his own troubles forgotten. He was listening so intently that McLean suspected he was making a study of Wyndham, who was certainly one of the more colorful characters McLean had ever met.

"Oh, prison, of course. Willard arrested her himself, and then began visiting her. He finally persuaded her to come over to the Union side and married her."

"Now, that *is* a love story," Rose said. "True devotion."

McLean nodded gravely. "It was a truce, not a defection. He resigned his commission and she stopped spying for the South." He turned the conversation back to the balloon. If Wyndham was not a British agent then, he likely was now. But he kept his face open and friendly. Nodding agreeably. "So you're doing some prospecting. How does that lead to a career with balloons?"

"Professor Lowe. Thaddeus Lowe. You may recall that he raised one over the lines in Virginia with a telegraph line to the ground so a scout could report all the positions. Worked a treat until someone on the Confederate side shot it down. Everything laid out like a sand table model, except you could see the units moving. He took me up one time, and I saw immediately how important an advantage it was and is. Better than any number of scouts on the ground in fair weather. So I became his most fierce advocate with the high command, but it was too novel an idea, and not well received from an Irish Italian mercenary already under suspicion. But King Victor Emmanuel thought the idea had merit, and encouraged me to develop it further for our own army." Wyndham smiled again.

"And your airship is the result?"

"One of many planned. Ours is a shakedown cruise. We have these scientists to help us."

McLean looked back at Frazer, who had now recovered himself. He was not looking at Rose, who had turned her attention back to what Wyndham was saying, apparently fascinated, as if she had not heard it a dozen times before or more. McLean admired her skill. Whatever Little Rose had been before, she was something now that no one should mistake for a child.

"And you flew it here from Italy?" he asked.

Wyndham choked on his wine, recovered himself, and shook his head. "My, that would be a remarkable accomplishment! No. Sorry to disappoint. It came over on the deck of a steamer from Liverpool, and was offloaded at Matamoros, assembled, and then we brought it north over the border."

"And the Mexican Government approved this?" McLean thought that unlikely, since the collapse of the French occupation resulted in the subsequent chaos of several revolutionary governments, each worst than the one before.

"As it happened," Rose said, "It was easy. I wrote to my mother's old friend, Jose Limantour who is now the Minister of Finance."

McLean's jaw dropped open. Rose laughed. "The perfect job for such a rascal isn't it? But you must not be too hard on my Papa Jose. He's always been very kind to me, as if I were one of his own." Her words turned bitter. "He paid for my stay at that very expensive convent school in Paris. Some say I have the Limantour jaw." She turned her head to show her profile. "And that accusation, that I'm a bastard, was enough for my Greenhow relatives to deny me and leave me in the Old Capitol Prison. Little Rose, the Rebel. And I'm a Rebel still."

She took another sip of her wine and with no one to dissuade her, continued on. "Shall I tell you about that school? It is a convent, and you can be a novitiate and enter the Church as a Sister of Mercy, but you may also be trained in all of the arts of being a Lady, and taught French, English and Spanish and another language of your choice. You are taught Literature so you can hold your own in conversation, some mathematics, and also drawing so that you may have an avocation. All the arts of being a Lady, including those needed to please a man. Very French, that course, and very enjoyable. With other girls, and then with young men selected from the ranks of military cadets who think they are patronizing the Demimonde, which of course, they are."

McLean, despite all he had seen and done, was shocked. It showed on his face. *Trust the French*, he thought; *steeped in vice, the lot of them.*

"Most girls quickly find husbands," Rose said, her voice merry, "But only those from respectable backgrounds. And I not just liked those lessons, but became a teacher in that school; a total and complete whore. I was certain I was destined to become part of the Demimonde, or have to find a man to rescue me from sin, or become an actress, which is *almost* respectable now. Well, I need not have worried. I have another older man who is like an uncle to me. Judah Benjamin. He found me a place in Service."

"Secret Service," McLean shook his head.

"Did I say that? Have you ever met a more unlikely spy? I talk far too much." She looked at her empty wineglass. "Well, this is all under the Rose, ain't it? Not this one, but the big one."

McLean looked around. A prospecting trip could run cover easily for a military reconnaissance, he thought, and these other men all have the look of soldiers. Smart soldiers. Mercenaries for the Money Power? Or 'the South shall rise again' renegades? Who could tell? And the entire unlikely affair seemed to be under the direction and control of a charming 21-year-old woman who had no reason to love the United States. All of the men looked to her for their cues, even the arrogant Wyndham, who seemed to accept his subordinate role with ease.

The U.S. government might be the worst of all possible clients, but perhaps a private letter to his old friend Elmer Washburn, the former Superintendent of Police in Chicago who now headed the U.S. Secret Service, would be prudent. And another to William and Robert Pinkerton as well. His cousins and bosses would want to be in the loop on this one!

The waiters cleared the dishes away and brought coffee, brandy, and cigars.

McLean waited as everyone silently sipped coffee and then the brandy.

"This is the point when the ladies are supposed to withdraw," Rose said. "But I'm the only female here, and I'm not really a lady, am I?"

"What are you, then,?" Frazer asked. He sounded a little angry.

Rose passed the cigars around and took one for herself. She lit it, drew in some smoke, puffed out a perfect ring of it and smiled. "I'm a courtesan."

"Just another word for whore," Frazer said, his voice bitter.

Rose's smile faded. "Here's one for your notebook, Georgie. I'll ignore the insult and contribute to your education. A whore is work-for-hire and does whatever her paramour desires. She is his slave for a time and must endure any indignity that does not threaten life and limb. She has a bag of tricks that his respectable Christian wife never dreamed of, and would never consent to, because she thinks such things sinful. That novelty is how she earns her money."

"A courtesan does not consent to anything. She dispenses favors from that same bag of tricks, but she holds all the power, and makes men her willing slaves. They do as *she* commands in private, or suggests softly elsewhere. You are halfway there, and this is why our tryst must now end. You are destined for finer things. Cambridge University awaits and, I am sure, a brilliant career which I never could be part of. So let it go."

Frazer looked on the verge of tears, but simply looked away, nodding. McLean rose to his feet. "Well this has been very interesting. I will have to write to our headquarters in Chicago about accepting your offer of work. It's a bit outside our normal course of business, and probably involves some trips to Mexico. This is a new branch for us, and we may not have the capacity." McLean reached under the table for his hat and stood up. Frazer came around the table and took his elbow. The two of them moved into the hallway.

"How did you get on with the grandmother?" McLean asked.

"Oh, famously. Hey-seuss was very helpful."

"And you listened rather than talked?"

"I did, and wrote it all down later. Following your good advice."

"You have a very keen memory, I suspect. I'd like to hear more, but now must get some sleep." McLean patted him on the shoulder.

"May I call on you in the morning?" Frazer asked.

"Of course. Come to my hotel and we'll hash it out over breakfast."

Frazer looked very pleased. "I will. At seven?"

McLean looked at him, at his youth and possibilities, and said, "She's right, you know." He felt great sympathy for the lad.

"Rose?" Frazer winced. "I know. It's just hard to hear."

McLean put a hand on his shoulder. "We've all been there, Laddie. At least she is kind and, in her own way, honest. She could have ruined you."

Frazer, his head down, simply nodded.

"See you in the morning," McLean said, and walked down the stairs into the square where the huge airship sat, softly lit underneath by the small fires its guards had lit for comfort. There was a bright reddish moon shining down. That gave the entire bulk of it an eerie glow. He decided to engage the local photographer to take some pictures of it in the morning. Perhaps he already had some. *So much to do*, McLean thought. Life in El Paso was never dull.

CHAPTER THREE

Promptly at seven the next morning, Frazer knocked, and then came into the tiny third floor room that McLean rented for his El Paso stay, which he still hoped would be brief. McLean was still shaving the tiny white whiskers around the edges of his muttonchops, tilting his head that way and this, taking his time, so as to not cut himself with the straight razor in his left hand. He was still in his undershirt, but already wore his small Colt's revolver in its shoulder holster. His suspenders draped down over his pants legs. The wash basin on the vanity in front of him held hot soapy water which he used to rinse the blade before drying it with an unused washcloth. Staring at his face in the mirror, without turning around, he said, "Hallo, Georgie. You're very punctual."

"How did you know it was me?"

"Well, Laddie, that's not hard. You were expected, and this mirror is curved so that I can observe the entire room." McLean shucked off the shoulder holster, put it and the revolver on the narrow bed, and put on a fresh white linen collarless shirt. As he did so, he inspected Frazer, who looked unexpectedly cheerful. Frazer looked around the room.

"Rather austere, this." The room had painted wooden clapboard walls rather than lathe and plaster, and had only a single well-used armchair with chintz upholstery and a small table with an oil lantern on the wall above it for illumination. On the narrow wooden table were small framed sepia-toned photographs of an older, rather beautiful woman, and three girls of various ages. That sparked Frazer's curiosity: McLean had a family?

McLean smiled. "Not everyone goes high cabin on the company dime like your friend Sir Percy. The company gives me a per diem for my expenses here. How I spend it, and where, is my decision. That way there are no tiresome arguments about whether or not something was a necessary expenditure with some bookkeeper in Chicago who never spent a day in the field. And I'm still a Scot at heart. Thrifty."

"Must be hard to work in here." Frazer looked out the dusty window to the alley below.

McLean looked at him sideways, suddenly conscious that he was being led into revealing a lot of information to someone he hardly knew. *Augh*, he said to himself, *let's see where this goes*. "I have an office for that. Never bring work home with you. It annoys your wife and children. Conflict results."

"You have a family?"

McLean motioned towards the pictures. "I am so blessed."

Frazer smiled. "But they are not here?"

McLean brushed his thinning hair and inspected the black bowler hat that was practically a Pinkerton uniform, and tilted his head slightly as he put it on. His smile faded.

"In Denver. Moved there four years ago to run that branch after we got burned out in the fire. William runs the Western branch now and asked me to come down for a few months, set this one up and get it running. Sophia didn't want to move again when we're just getting settled in. She likes Denver and thinks that Texas will be too hot. So I'll be handing this off to his son Billy, I suspect. Or Bill as he likes to be called now that he's married. Allan retired to write his memoirs, which are selling very well and bring us a stream of new business."

McLean spoke casually but all the time from the corner of his eye was watching Frazer who was as attentive as a ferret and whose short red beard made him look somewhat like one.

McLean finished buttoning his shirt and attached a paper collar. Looking in the mirror again, he pronounced himself satisfied, donned the shoulder holster and revolver, and added a string tie at his throat. He turned to see Frazer making a note in his notebook.

"So, am I an object of study now?"

The young man looked embarrassed. "Sorry," he said; "I find the entire idea of detectives very interesting. It also seems to be a culture, a thing apart from the norm."

"Every business has its ways and means," McLean replied, "And I've told you nothing that might not be read in a newspaper somewhere. We give interviews to reporters just to correct all those dime novel fantasies that float everywhere. Little good it does. The ideas persist anyway, leading to all sorts of untoward requests."

McLean put his coat on and checked his pockets. Frazer looked at him intently.

"Such as?"

"We don't break the law, nor do we collaborate with those that do, and we never touch divorce work."

Frazer blinked. "My word, I would think not. You are lawmen, are you not?"

McLean moved towards the door. "No. Not unless we are acting as bail agents. Then we have a warrant to pursue the malefactor and bring him to be held to answer. Sometimes 'dead or alive'. We can kill them if they leave us no choice, but we are not assassins, we do not do murder."

Frazer's hand went involuntarily to his throat. "Goodness," he said, his smile quite gone.

McLean looked at him carefully. *You're very green*, he thought, *but you learn fast*, and managed a wide, generous smile.

"Come on, let's continue this over breakfast," McLean said, as he looked at the silver Raymond Railway pocket watch he kept in a vest pocket.

They went out of the room and down the hall and down two flights of broad wooden stairs to the big dining room on the first floor where Mexican waiters moved swiftly to deliver plates of food to the tables filled with men of every variety seen in the West: drovers, workmen, drummers, lawmen and rangers; hard men for the most part, with Black, Mexican and even a few Chinese and Native faces mixed in with Whites. Indeed, Whites were a minority population. But all had a common purpose. There was work to be done and done together. Frazer thought that, outside of a Masonic lodge, he'd never seen such democracy. But it was only breakfast. No great events occurred here.

He noted that most of the men wore one or more revolvers and a large knife on their belts and wondered if he should get a gun too? Should he buy new clothes more like theirs to blend in? There was a fine line between observer and participant he was reluctant to cross, but if everyone was always looking at him, then how much could he trust what they told him? Tall tales were a well-established sport here.

He wondered if there was a Masonic lodge here. Masons were bound by oath to assist each other. He suspected that McLean's kindness was as much Masonic principle as any kind of affection, and recognized it created obligations for him that would have to be repaid.

As they found a table in the back and settled in, McLean saw Frazer looking carefully at everyone. Again he had his notebook out.

"Don't stare," McLean said quietly.

"Excuse me?"

"Don't stare at people. Some of these roughs may see that as a challenge and confront you. Bully boys always looking for a fight, for an excuse or opportunity for one. So write that in your notebook."

To his amazement, Frazer did so. McLean laughed out loud as a waiter delivered two plates of hot food and a pot of coffee. Metal mugs already sat before them along with a knife, fork and napkin each. McLean immediately began to eat. Frazier hesitated.

"What's the problem?"

Frazer said, "Normally, I have a buttered scone and a cup of tea. My word! What is all of this?"

"Fried ham, potatoes, biscuits – there's your scone – and coffee. This is a workman's hotel. Food gives them strength for a day of hard work. Breakfast is included but it's Hobson's Choice. This or nothing, and before you ask, there is no bloody tea."

Chastened, Frazer began to eat cautiously and then with some enthusiasm.

"It's quite good, actually," he said, before putting his knife and fork across the plate to indicate he was done. Most of the food was uneaten and would go to the hogs.

"Glad you like it," McLean said ironically, having cleaned his own plate, and leaning back to enjoy his coffee. "But now it's my turn to ask questions. How did you leave it with your lady-love?"

Frazer smiled. "She gave me quite a send-off last night. Memorable, with things I had never dreamed of. I will treasure the memory. And furthermore, deponent saith not."

McLean laughed. "I did not ask for chapter and verse. Keep those details to yourself for decency's sake. What else?"

"This morning, as we were dressing, she burst into tears and cried. Wouldn't say why. I do not understand women or how they think."

McLean grinned from ear to ear. "Well, don't look to me, Laddie. No man does, and any that say they do are liars or fools, or both. My wife and daughters are a continual mystery to me. So are you still part of that crew?"

"No. I resigned. Colonel Wyndham said it would be best."

"So, he's in charge?"

"Only for appearances' sake. Rose holds the whip hand. He is very attentive to her every wish, but there is no romance there. She commands. He obeys."

"Interesting." McLean looked up at the rough plank ceiling, searching his memory.

"There wouldn't be. Sir Percy is a sodomite. It got him into trouble a few times during the war when he'd had too much to drink. His aides all seemed to be slender, blonde young men with beautiful faces."

"Well, I saw none of that. On his best behavior."

"Yes, he would be. He's on the job, and he's a professional." McLean thought briefly how great an addition Sir Percy Wyndham would be to Pinkerton's, were it not for his very large public profile. That made him too noticeable. He discarded the idea, and said to Frazer, "Now tell me about your interview with Hey-suess's granny."

Frazer smiled. "She looked at me like she'd been expecting me for years. Big smile. She looks older than time itself. Apparently, being associated with the balloon makes me special in her eyes. If Hey-suess translated correctly, there is an old legend about men from the stars who helped the Apache people. She gave me this." Frazier reached in his coat pocket and produced a round white ceramic object with a black and red fearsome face. He put it on the table carefully.

McLean picked it up, stared at it a moment, turned it over and shrugged. "It looks like a cat. Those look like fangs."

"Jaguar, she said. I don't think there are any of those here?"

McLean shook his head. "That's South America, in the jungle. We have pumas here. I've heard of rich dudes from back East coming out here to hunt what they call 'big game' but those are tan. This fellow seems to be black. I think she may be mistaken."

Frazer slowly shook his head. "It's very old, she said. From before the Spanish came. She wants me to carry it with me for protection on my vision quest."

McLean raised an eyebrow. "And are you on a vision quest, whatever that means?"

"Hey-suess used those words yesterday when I showed him the picture of the stone circle. I suspect it's the usual coming of age ceremony common to many cultures. Young men try themselves against fate. The Arthurian legend is an example. Hey-suess expects to make one himself. He told me a bit about it. Sounds dreadful.

Starvation, sleep deprivation, and some ceremonies that seem akin to torture. Takes days. Some die of it."

McLean leaned back, studying him. He liked the young man, and didn't want to see him come to harm. "You're not thinking of trying it yourself?"

Frazer grinned. "I might, in the interests of science. It would be a spectacular paper for The Transactions of the Royal Society, and might hasten my Fellowship at Trinity. There is precedent. Sir Richard Burton penetrated the mysteries of Mecca that way, and produced several books about the Muslim culture. Had to become one himself."

"Sounds like just another damn fool from abroad trying to get himself killed."

"Well, he's a soldier. Captain in the Royal Army and the scandal of his regiment because he lived in the Bazaar and acquired first-hand knowledge of native cultures for the Ethnographic Survey. Speaks dozens of languages that he claims were mostly acquired in bed. And his translations and papers deepened our understanding of those parts of the Empire. Some of his books are quite scandalous, like 'The Arabian Nights'. I confess I quite enjoy reading that one."

McLean studied him carefully. He sighed. "I was on the Ethnographic Survey myself when I came here. That was in fifty-five." Frazer looked very surprised. McLean shook his head. "It's all spying and mischief, Laddie. Dress it up with all the high sounding honours you want, that's all it is."

Frazer looked at him, smiling, waiting for more.

McLean sighed and continued. "I was sent to assist the Abolitionists. Become part of them, work with them and feed them enough money to keep that 'Underground Railway' going, so more slaves would flee the South. Reported to a couple of comedians at the British Legation named Anderson and Clay. They were also feeding money and intelligence to Rose Green's mother, the infamous Rose Greenhow, who was working with others to set up what became The War Between The States. Rose Greenhow had a pretty effective network in Washington. That war was going to happen unless men of sense came together and worked out a permanent solution. Whitehall did not want that. It wanted that war. They wanted the country broken up so there would be a steady supply of cotton for the mills in Manchester and Leeds. And they are ruthless bastards about getting what they want. Look what they did in China and India. The South was to be another British plantation colony, *de facto*, and Mexico a French one. It was all arranged. Judah Benjamin, Rose's sponsor, was a British agent from the start, even before he was the Junior U.S. Senator from Louisiana. He worked with her father on those Spanish land claims in San Francisco."

"How do you know all this?"

"There are records. Rose's natural father, Jose Limantour, pulled off a massive scheme there, stole millions of dollars, and seduced her money-hungry mother at the same time. An infamous scoundrel. Having him as the Mexican Minister of Finance is very much the fox guarding the hen house.

"It's the nature of my trade. People talk. I listen. And I remember it all. You'd be wise to do likewise. Learn a little deceit yourself, and try to stay clear of the likes of Rose and her crew. Keep your own counsel. There are Southrons here that still have not accepted that the war is over and decided. For safety, they reside on the Mexican side of the Border. Many are Masons." He picked up the ceramic object and handed it back. "This might be as old as you were told, or just something they make to sell to tourists. Like slivers from the True Cross in Jerusalem. I can't tell."

Frazer, his face grave now, took the white token and put back in his pocket. "I know. I can't tell either. It's a matter for further investigation. How would you proceed?"

McLean laughed. "You're going to lay that at my door? I should give you an invoice first."

Frazer looked abashed. "Sorry," he said; "I didn't mean to overstep."

"Oh, you bloody well did. You've been pumping me from the start. A nibble here, a nibble there." McLean laughed out loud. "I don't mind. I like you Mister Frazer. Maybe you're as honest and naive as you make yourself out to be. Maybe not. I'm reserving judgement on that." He reached over and patted Frazer's hand. "It speaks well of you that you are sticking to your purpose, whatever the cost. You turned down my offer of employment, an easy path to penetrating our operations. So I will give you the benefit of the doubt and share some tradecraft."

Frazer relaxed and smiled. "Yes, please. I'm all ears."

"When I interview people," McLean said, "I pretend to be a little dull and stupid, so I can ask the same question several different ways. Little by little I get to the heart of the matter. And I sometimes am able to go back and repeat the process. I am never eager. I wait for them to tell me and then follow up."

Frazer was scribbling in his notebook, taking it all down.

"And, let me say it again, get rid of that bloody thing! Cultivate your memory so you can write it all down later. Taking notes just puts people off. It intimidates them. They fear what they say is going to come back and bite them. Pinkerton detectives testify from memory in courts all the time. We win most of our cases. We are famous for it, in fact."

"I should organize my notes," Frazer said. "Write everything out again."

"Well, there's an extra desk in my office. Haven't found the right man to fill it. So come along after we're done. I won't even charge you for the paper. Call it my contribution to science."

"It is science, you know," Frazer said. "That's the third stage."

"Of what?"

"Of my theory of human development. I told you about it the other day. First myth. Then someone organizes society, and uses the myth to create religion to provide a common purpose, and finally we arrive at science, where only facts matter, not pagan superstitions."

"Pagan? As in 'witches'?" McLean was suddenly uneasy. "I know a bit about them."

The way he stared at Frazer made him wonder if he'd suddenly given offense where none was intended. Religion was always a delicate subject. Especially when heresy and Magick was involved. His throat was suddenly dry. He licked his lips and began again.

"Oh, I do not mean that in a perjorative way, Harry. Christians are as pagan as they come with our elaborate ceremonies and rituals, and the King James Bible is another collection of myths that cannot be proved. Now, that I hold that view is a secret between you and me, because it would not go down well at Trinity. It's heretical, the kind of statement that other men were drawn and quartered for three hundred years ago. I must have evidence. The token the old woman gave me could be that. There are records in Madrid that I can consult again. But I really need more, and the religious practices of today are rooted in the past. Certain things persist down through the ages. Was Jesus Christ a carpenter? Probably. It's an honest profession. Did he walk on water or turn water into wine? Very doubtful. I don't see how he could have managed either feat. Do Apache witches fly? Yet to be determined. I'm keeping an open mind. Hey-suess said there is a place over West of here where there are images of that. Paintings from 'the people before us,' whoever they were. Now, *that* is evidence. Of what, I'm not sure, but I will have to go look, and find a way to record it. Sketches, or maybe photographs, if they allow that."

McLean pushed his chair back from the table and got up. "I'll say this for you, Georgie, you've got quite a mind. You'd make a great detective."

Frazer blushed a little at the compliment. "Thank you. I'll keep it in mind if Trinity throws me out, but I doubt they will. They've had many heretics there, going back to Christopher Marlowe."

"Now where do I know that name from?"

"Playwright. Wrote a play about a man who sold his soul to the Devil. Reputed to have been a spy for the first Secret Service."

McLean snapped his finger. "Of course. I saw it once. Starred John Wilkes Booth."

Frazer knew that name. Who here would not? He looked closely at McLean's face, trying to read his expression. But McLean gave nothing away.

"Not a fan?"

"Oh, it was a masterful performance, but his killing Lincoln spoils the memory. No one wanted that. Drunken wretch – the War was over. What was the point?" McLean sighed. "I'll tell you sometime how we ran him to ground, but there is work to be done." And with that, McLean moved towards the door, threading his way through the crowded dining room to the hallway that led outside to the square. Frazer hastened to follow.

Outside the sun blazed down, temporarily blinding them as they went out the door.

The crew of the huge balloon was making preparations for something. McLean could see Sir Percy and another man consulting a chart of some kind. Frazer stopped and stared as well.

"They are leaving," he said.

"You sound surprised," McLean said, looking sideways at him. "Where are they going?"

"West. Along the border."

McLean looked to his right where, in the distance, dark clouds were forming.

"They may want to put that off. Looks like rain that way and that always implies thunder and lightning."

"Not to worry. They have a system of copper cables that passes lightning right around and to a chain that passes it to the ground. They do quite a bit with electricity. Very scientific. Batteries to store it, little motors to power the sails they use to maneuver, even some kind of light they can use at night."

McLean stared at him, trying to take this all in. It sounded like something from one of Jules Verne's scientific romances.

"Is that what that brass u-shaped thing that looks like a gun mount is for?"

"No. It is a gun mount. In case they have to set down in the desert and meet unfriendly natives. Gatling gun. Electrically driven. Strictly for defense, and not to be displayed in civilized places where they do exhibitions. They have two."

McLean chewed on that for a moment. Now he had to write those letters. "No, of course not. That would give the lie to the whole thing." McLean looked at his young friend. "You're not going with them, Georgie?"

"I am. To see those old cliff paintings. Hey-suess has arranged for some of his tribe to meet me there so I can do interviews. Sir Percy and Rose and the rest will sail onward."

"That sounds very dangerous."

"Not at all. My work is here, and while we're on the subject, I'd prefer if you called me Jim." He felt lonely and wondered if there was a Scottish Ceremony Masonic lodge here. Frazer stared longingly at the balloon for few seconds, and then his face hardened.

McLean saw he wanted to put the encounter with Rose Green behind him. He'd been young once himself, and known heartbreak, so he said no more about it. There was no comfort in words from a stranger.

"Jim, it is then. Come along."

The two of them walked towards the Pinkerton office and did not look back.

CHAPTER FOUR

Rose Green put down the field glasses as Frazer and McLean disappeared around a corner. From the set of his back and determined stride, she gathered that Frazer felt no regard and no regrets where she was concerned. He was done with her.

She smoothed the top of the fawn-colored dress she was wearing with both hands and looked upward at the slack fabric of the balloon resisting on its framework. The slow motion of her hands on her bosom awakened fresh feelings of desire. She bit her lip.

Not now, she thought. *Have a little self-control. Still...*

"I want him back," she said. She dabbed at the tears in her eyes with a white silk handkerchief. Sir Percy Wyndham took the cigar he was about to light from his mouth and laughed. He shook his head and spoke sharply.

"Of course you do. Inconstancy, thy name is woman!"

"I have good reason."

"With all due respect, mum, I think that you have toyed with him enough. More would be cruel. I don't see the need of it."

Rose looked up at him. Wyndham was unconsciously at attention like a good Sergeant Major in a military campaign, trying to tell a young Lieutenant why his daring plan would not work. Rose sighed.

"You're right about that. I need to leave him alone, and I will. A man like that... and he is one, of considerable parts... can become a drug as bad as opium. Wicked smart, charming, and just a little cruel. He fogs me mind, he does. So, I will lock my door against him and preserve my power over him. I was trained to be a nun as well as a whore, so I will draw on that now. Besides, I need a rest. I'm quite sore."

Wyndham couldn't help himself. He laughed out loud, doubling over, as the rest of the crew looked up, wondering what the joke was. Rose managed a smile and then laughed a little herself. She shook her head ruefully.

"No, it's something he said. When we were sitting up in bed, naked, between engagements as it were. I'm sipping champagne, and he's writing in his notebook, telling me about his conversation with the Apache boy and his grandmother, who, he says, is some kind of witch. Known as 'the old woman who does not die'. The giver of life who brings forth the corn maiden every year so that the crops grow."

"In the flesh, as it were?"

"I don't know. Maybe it's just a title or a name. Of course, being a young man himself, he's more interested in those dreadful coming-of-age tales you all like and emulate. What is a man? A bloody idiot intent on getting himself killed most of the time."

"Someone should write that down."

"Someone has. Many times. I spend a lot of time reading between assignments. Sir Walter Scott and the old legends about King Arthur. It takes me out of myself to a different world."

"How does that signify with young Frazer?" Wyndham reached to stroke the long mustache he no longer had, and caught himself. He shook his head in irritation.

"Frazer is a scientist at heart. A shifter and sorter of information," Rose said; "So he wants to know the source of everything, and he's quite a skeptic about the Bible. Says the whole thing does not add up, that the Church has it all wrong when it says that the Earth is only a few thousand years old. Now, this old woman says that what is now El Paso has been here all of that time, and much more, and that there were people before, long before, that left paintings. Enormous ones on the sides of canyons not far from here. Well, now that is proof, ain't it? And maybe those canyons have other proofs as well."

She turned and looked over her shoulder and called out, "Paulo! A moment of your time?"

Paulo Marconi looked up from the instruments he was checking, waved and made his way forward cautiously. With the balloon deflated and on its struts, there was not much headroom. He stood up as he reached the pilot's cabin and spoke in Italian.

"How may I help the beautiful signora today?" He was about forty years old and wore a cheerful face most of the time. He was rotund, and could have easily been mistaken for a chef in a trattoria rather than a former professor from the University of Milan, who specialized in geology, chemistry, and physics. He and Wyndham enjoyed long arguments about Italian opera. Rose suspected that he hoped to replace Frazer in her bed. She was charmed, but far from convinced that it was a good idea. She needed to stay aloof and in command of these men.

Unconsciously, Rose replied in Italian. "Did you not say that the best way to find minerals was in the canyons?"

"Of course. The Earth is laid down in layers. You look for outcroppings of colors. Sulfides and oxides. An outcropping or stripe of greenish blue might be the oxidate of copper, and red that of iron. That is the easy part. Getting them out and someplace they can be used is the hard part. That requires water. Lots of water."

"Looks pretty dry out there," Wyndham replied, also in Italian.

"There is water. That's how the canyons are made, when water cuts into the earth. Drill down and you will find it."

"And then what?" Rose looked at the Italian as if he were the most fascinating man in the world. Dazzled, he paused. He stammered, trying to think.

"Rose!" Wyndham was immune to her charms and saw what was happening.

"Oh. Sorry," she said and looked away, allowing Paulo to recover himself.

"Uh, pumps. You bring it up with big pumps and create an infrastructure. If you have water, you can grow crops. You grow crops, then you have people to do the work. Or you can use the water to extract the ore and build railroads to carry it away. If you have the right kind of coal you can make iron here. The possibilities are endless."

Rose pursed her lips. "Sir Percy."

"Mum?"

"I think we will tell Georgie that if he can get someone to guide us to those paintings, we will help him make pictures of them. In the interests of science, of course. This will give us a chance to see if Mister Marconi can find some minerals that can be extracted."

"Your wish is my command, milady."

Rose looked up at him, still at rigid attention, and smiled. "When can we go?"

"Not today. There's a nasty storm brewing up."

"No," said Rose, "Not today." She sighed. "You ever have the feeling that you've met your soul-mate, but that the whole thing is just impossible and wrong, that you are from two different worlds that can never meet?"

Wyndham smiled sympathetically. "Like Romeo and Juliet? Star crossed-lovers?"

"Yes!"

"I did once. Long ago. He was killed at Crimea."

Rose, shocked, stared up at him and then said softly, "Oh, Percy, I'm so sorry… "

He shook his head. "Don't be. This is the trade we chose. He died the way he wanted. Victoria Cross. It was his fate."

"And is that the fate you sought when you became a soldier?"

"I accepted the possibility, but medals don't mean much to a dead man. And then I got involved with you lot, and the matter was taken out of my hands. I am too useful."

He stared straight ahead, unreadable, and Rose Green for once had nothing to say.

· · ·

As they began up the stairs to the Pinkerton office, Harry McLean noticed that the door was already open and slightly ajar. He stopped, standing upright, and reached for his revolver. He used his free hand to motion to Frazer and the younger man took two steps back down the stairs to the ground. McLean stepped over the creaky step and bounded up to the landing, shoving the door violently open as he drew down on the man sitting at his desk looking at his journal.

"Hello, Harry," said William Pinkerton.

McLean let out his breath, thumbed down the hammer on his revolver, slid it back into its holster, and tried to think of what to say. He felt his face flush red with sudden rage. He took a step into the big room and looked around. Nothing else looked out of place. Of course, William was a skilled operative, trained by his father, so nothing would be if he had searched. Obviously, picking the locks had not been problem. He took a deep breath and let it out slowly to regain his composure as he studied the dust motes dancing in the yellow sunlight streaming into the windows that looked over the street below.

"Hello, William," he said at last. "What an unexpected surprise. Been in town long?" There was an edge in his voice. Pinkerton and his older brother Robert ran the agency now, and he had every right to be there, but McLean thought a little prior notice might have been his due. He'd been a Pinkerton much longer than William. Since before the now-President of the Pinkerton Western Region had been born. That made it hard for him to take the younger man seriously.

"I got in this morning. I looked for you at your hotel, but they said you'd already gone out." He looked down at the journal. "What is this two dollar item? Research for Mister Frazer?"

McLean heard the middle stair creak and felt Frazer come cautiously in the door. He turned, smiled at him reassuringly, and then said, "This is Mr. Frazer. Jim, meet William Pinkerton, the President of our company. William, Mister Frazer is a scholar from England with the Ethnographic Survey." He raised his eyebrows significantly, but William did not catch the meaning behind those words.

"Really?" William stood up and offered his hand. "And where do you study?"

Frazer looked from one to the other, slightly confused. "Well, for the moment, here. I'm collecting tales of native cultures. But I read at Trinity. Cambridge."

William looked suitably impressed. "I'm a Notre Dame man myself."

McLean decided to jump in. "Jim needed a connection to someone in a local tribe. We have a young lad helping us who was able to help, and settled on a price for that service. It's a per diem."

William Pinkerton, who was stout, with a big square head crowned with black hair, accented by a small mustache, and bright blue eyes, nodded. "How much are you paying the boy?"

"Yet to be determined," McLean said. "It depends on the client's satisfaction."

Pinkerton nodded. *Was it worth asking further?* He decided not. *Harry McLean was already irritated enough. And could simply take his pension and retire to a comfortable life in Denver if pushed too far.* Fortunately, William knew, he loved the work too much to do that.

"Well, I'll leave that to you. Are you satisfied so far, Mister Frazer?"

"Jim, please. Yes. It's going very well. Harry has also been very helpful."

William Pinkerton smiled. "Glad to hear it."

McLean nodded. He cleared his throat. "Uh, Jim, I think we will have to pick this up later. William and I have agency business to discuss."

Frazer looked slightly surprised. "Of course," he murmured. "Perhaps tonight?"

"I will find you," McLean promised. Frazer was quickly gone.

The two detectives stared at each other.

"What the Hell are you playing at, William?" McLean finally exploded. "This is one diabolical liberty, just showing up like this!"

"Why are you surprised?" Pinkerton leaned back. "I do the same with other branches now. It keeps people on their toes. And with the current political and economic situation, we need to be sharp. Got the big Centennial celebration next year, and the election."

McLean stared at him, and then sighed. "Working as hard as I can, Boss. You don't like it, then send me back to Denver and my wife and kids. Run this yourself."

Pinkerton held out both hands before him as if pushing back an invisible wall. "Now, Harry, I meant nothing by it. You know that we miss you in Chicago, and we need someone we can trust here. This is a great location. It gets us into Mexico."

McLean began to make a pot of coffee. "Not sure we want to go there, myself. Different system of law. Napoleonic Code. Different language, and, by the way, about a hundred thousand Indians in various tribes that don't recognize that border or any White Man's authority."

"We go where the business is." Pinkerton looked at the journal again. "Explain this bit of correspondence. Why are you writing Elmer Washburn about a balloon?"

McLean's face relaxed into a smile. He chuckled. "Now that is a mystery. You've not been over to the *Mercado*? The big square near the cathedral?"

Pinkerton shook his head no. McLean set the coffee pot on top of the pot bellied stove, lit the fire and sat down in the chair at the next desk.

"Yesterday, a big hot air balloon appears there and lands. Bigger than you have ever seen. Now young Frazer and me, we'd struck up an acquaintance the day before, and he's told me about Madamoiselle Pompadour and her traveling show. I thought he was having me on until I saw this prodigious balloon appear, and this very attractive blonde lower herself over the side, wearing pink tights that did nothing to conceal her figure. Quite an entrance."

Pinkerton stared at him, and then nodded.

"Young Frazer has been hired by them as an advance man, and there is a big greeting with a band, and he introduces me to the lady. She sees my badge and wants to know, right away, if I'm from the Government. I explain that we are and always have been a private enterprise. She says you must come to dinner. So I do that." The coffee was ready and McLean got up and poured two cups.

"Be careful not to burn your hand," he cautioned.

Pinkerton took his cup and set it on the desk to cool. "And?"

"They are staying at the Excelsior. Best hotel in town. And the name of the lady is actually Rose Green, and she's from Liverpool. And the pilot is Sir Percy Wyndham, who does not have his trademark mustaches that he wore when he commanded the First New Jersey during the War. The others are a mixed lot, Italian and French scientists. The crew are dressed like French sailors, but King Victor Emmanuel is the sponsor."

Pinkerton nodded slowly. "I am going to have to read up on this, because I'm understanding only about half of what you are saying. Cut to the chase, Harry. Why write Washburn about this?"

McLean shook his head. "Come on, William. Ethnographic Survey? That's a British Secret Service cover most of the time. Jim Frazer's research may be on the up-and-up, but the rest of it stinks like fish that's been left out too long. And why the big show to cover what they are really doing? Rose Green's real name is Rose Greenhow."

Pinkerton was startled. "Like the famous Confederate spy?"

"Her daughter. And reputedly the bastard child of her and Jose Limantour, the current Minister of Finance for Mexico. As crooked as they come, and Rose's paterfamilas in England is Judah P. Benjamin. She was a little drunk and feeling sorry for herself, and just babbled on. Or so it seemed."

"You think it was an act?"

"They were trying to recruit me, William. Pull me back in. I came here for them before the War. Your Dad knows all about it. He worked for them, too."

"What?"

McLean sighed. "You ever talk politics with Allan? Back then, we were Chartists, rebels against the Queen. We got caught. Given a choice between a rather grisly traitor's death and working here for Percy Anderson at the British Legation helping the Abolitionists. Well, that suited us just fine, and we joined the Chicago Police and became detectives, and then Allan set up the agency, and then found another lost cause, the Presidential campaign of a railroad lawyer by the name of Lincoln. Railroads made us what we are today, but Lincoln, and Judah Benjamin, who was, back then, one of his law partners, got us started."

William Pinkerton shook his head. "Dad is writing his memoirs, but he's left that part out." He took a sip of his coffee. "So, how did you get out of it?"

"Helping run the Underground Railroad helped, and then we spied against the South. Had to take the Oath of Allegiance, and become American citizens. With Judah Benjamin running the other spy service, the, as we called it, 'adversary party', we had to make a choice. In 1862 you were either a patriot or a traitor. Traitors got hung. It helped that we suddenly had money, lots of money. Our fortune was here and we cannot go back, on pain of death. I'm sure that warrant is still valid. And we saw how England was trying to break up the country and wanted no part of that. So we're Americans now. And you and your brother and sister were born here. Natives. So I never considered it for a moment."

Pinkerton nodded. "You are right, of course. What else bothers you about the balloon?"

McLean looked upwards, trying to remember something.

"Ah! Something Frazer said. They are armed. Gatling guns. In case they set down and have to defend themselves from unfriendly natives. They don't display them, but they are there. And the crew has the new Winchester rifles."

"That is troublesome. You might call it 'overkill'."

McLean laughed and nodded. "Think about it, William. It's a massive craft for what it is, and, aside from having a 21-year-old woman in charge, seems to be very military. Or maybe naval. Sir

Percy Wyndham is a star soldier, a mercenary, which means while his title comes from King Victor Emmanuel, he's also British Secret Service. He said he was on 'detached service'."

"And if it traveled on the water instead of through the air as some kind of amusement, it would cause alarms to be sent up. Have we been invaded?"

McLean shook his head. "I think it's more in the nature of a reconnaissance. They say they are searching for minerals and land to buy. But the Confederate government angle troubles me. The Confederate Treasury had four million in gold that's never been found. Judah Benjamin burned all the Secret Service records in Richmond as they evacuated the government. There's a whole network of traitors in the North that's never been found out."

"And an amnesty in '72. They can't be prosecuted."

"That don't matter. Exposure would bring social and financial ruin. They can be blackmailed. James Buchanan was."

"The President?" William looked shocked. "How?"

"He liked men, not women. This was well known before the war, and tolerated because he was a very able politician. Yet he sat on his hands and did nothing as the nation came apart, and we had the worst war in history. Rose Greenhow was his beard. He visited her at night so everyone drew an obvious and wrong conclusion. She worked for the French and the British and anyone else who'd help finance those elaborate balls she put on. Senator Judah Benjamin was one of them. Seems the Confederate Secret Service was operating before there was a Confederate government. The Brits again. Ol' La Fayette Baker was right, the treason was years in the making. 'The South will rise again?' Reconstruction has not really pacified the South. Imagine those balloons coming against what's left of the Union Army now, invading Texas and rallying all those poor bastards who saved their Confederate money to the cause. Throwing down grenades and Greek fire in bottles? Percy Wyndham was a Brigade Commander during the Italian War. Just the man to make it happen. He could be making military maps with that crew of his. Planning a march in from Mexico of a mercenary army."

William looked very grave. "So this is why you are writing to Washburn?"

"Yes. If we are Americans, then I think we have a duty. It's not a pitch for business. He has his own detectives. Leave it to them."

William smiled. "Write the letter and I will sign it. It will have more weight coming from me."

"How do you make that out?"

"I'm the President of this agency."

McLean smiled kindly. "And he remembers you in short pants, getting caught stealing apples from a neighbor's tree when he was a beat cop in Dundee. You're new, and haven't proven yourself in his eyes."

Pinkerton blushed and looked offended. He looked away and murmured, "Have it your way. We both can sign."

"Whatever you like, Boss," McLean said, twisting the knife a little.

CHAPTER FIVE

Several days later, at a cantina just across the border that only governments recognized, Harry McLean watched with amusement as Jim Frazer, coughing, with tears streaming down his face, suddenly reached for and drained a glass of beer. William Pinkerton and another Pinkerton detective, Blake Tilman, looked on, also highly amused.

Jesus looked from one to the other to the other, silent, watchful. He was not part of this tribe but recognized that what appeared to be a crude practical joke was actually a test. The kind that young Apache braves were tried with to define their character.

It was slightly after noon, and the simple wooden tables, covered with bright red and white checkered cloths, held several plates of Mexican food in the center with each man having a bare plate to fill as he wished. Pitchers of beer and water were handy. The water went untouched because everyone knew that only the beer was safe to drink, but now Frazer reached for a pitcher, while fanning his mouth.

"Hold on," McLean said, reaching out to stay his hand, "That will only make it worse."

He slid his own glass of beer towards the young man. Frazer took it, gulped some down and then sipped.

"Bloody Hell! What was that?"

"A pepper," said McLean.

"A *habañero*," Jesus said.

Frazer pulled a clean white handkerchief from his pocket and wiped his face.

"And people eat those?"

"All the time," Jesus said.

Frazer looked around, suspecting that he was the victim of an elaborate joke, but then McLean took another of the small, dark green pods from the plate of multi-colored pods in the center of the table and bit off a tiny bit of the tip. He poured more beer and then drank a bit.

"Your mistake, Jim, was eating the whole thing at once. You should have investigated. Try a red one. They are far milder."

Frazer shook his head. "Once is enough, thank you." He looked at McLean resentfully. "This is another lesson, I suppose?"

"Not by design. I would have warned you if you had asked, but you just dived in."

"Haste makes waste," Pinkerton added, cautiously looking at the unfamiliar food. "What is this?"

"Chili. Also very spicy. Have a tortilla with it on the side. That flat corn pancake there."

Jesus shoved a plantain towards Frazer. "Eat some of this, it will make the burning go away."

Frazer ate some and nodded. "Much better. Thank you, Hey-seuss."

"*De nada.*"

Frazer looked at McLean again. The older man was eating something brown that looked very dubious to him. "You like this food?"

McLean paused and patted his belly, which was straining the buttons on his vest. "Too much so."

William Pinkerton stopped eating for a moment, used a napkin to pat off his lips, and said, "I shall have to be cautious. It's very good. I don't think we have anything like this in Chicago." He stared at Frazer for a moment. "So you are going forward with your quest?"

Frazer smiled. "I rather have to. My sponsor expects it. Cambridge University expects it." A young and very pretty Mexican girl with long dark hair and green eyes, one of the cantina's waitresses, walked over with a pitcher of beer and put it in front of Frazer. He looked up and smiled at her and, smiling back, she modestly ducked her head and slowly walked away, her hips moving side to side with an invitation that was as old as time. Frazer was thoughtful for a brief moment and then turned back to the conversation.

"And your lady-friend?" McLean asked. "What is Miss Green's opinion?"

"Said 'what is a man? Some bloody fool trying to get himself killed most of the time'."

Everyone laughed. Even Jesus joined in.

"So, Mister Tilman," Frazer asked suddenly, "How did you come to become a detective?"

Tilman looked up from his food. His dark brown eyes looked at Frazer in a measuring way. His face took on a thoughtful expression.

"I warned you," McLean murmured.

"That's a rather personal question, isn't it?" Tilman was stone faced now, severe.

"I s'suppose it is," Frazer stammered. "I meant nothing by it."

Tilman looked over to McLean. "You're right. He's very good."

Both men laughed. Pinkerton nodded in appreciation.

"By God, sir. You'd make a brilliant detective. I'll double whatever offer Harry made you. Triple, even."

Frazer shook his head. "It's not the money, sir. It's about my place in life, which I have struggled hard to attain, and cannot give up now without being a traitor to myself."

The other three men slowly nodded. They understood that declaration perfectly.

"Yet you seem to be part of a reconnaissance operation that has military as well as commercial implications," William Pinkerton said mildly.

"Not by intent, I assure you. That is not my purpose, nor why I am here. Sometimes the Ethnographic Survey does survey ethnographies," Frazer replied lightly.

Jesus looked from one to the other, taking it all in. White men were always so devious.

"To answer your question, Jim," Blake Tilman said, "I came to the work by degrees. And luck. It engages my mind as nothing else has. I grew up in a fishing village on the coast of Maine. The sea had taken two of my brothers and my mother begged me, over my father's strong objections, to find other work. The War came along and I joined the 20th Maine Regiment. Not what she had in mind, but we were patriots, and firm abolitionists. The Underground Railroad stopped in our village. Our commander was Joshua Chamberlain, the President of Bowdoin College. I was a runner at his headquarters, and he saw something in me, and made me a clerk. Then I discovered a crooked supply officer was stealing, and doing other crimes. He was very glib and clever and went undiscovered, until I proved the case. This was right before Gettysburg and our defense at Little Round Top. He tried to kill me but I subdued him. He was tried and sent to prison. He had friends who wanted revenge. So to protect me, Chamberlain sent me to La Fayette Baker in Washington. First District Cavalry, which was a spying and provost martial operation. We caught John Wilkes Booth and the other traitors. Then the whole thing was broken up and Mister Pinkerton's father offered me a job. That's the short version."

Tilman reached into an inner coat pocket. "I have something for you, Jim." He produced a book covered in brown leather. " 'Life Among The Apaches'. Written by a man who was their Reservation Agent and studied them at length."

Frazer took it and examined it. Then opened a few pages. He read a bit of it.

"Hey-seuss? Have you read this book?"

The boy looked resentful. "No. I've heard of it. Full of White Men's lies."

"Really? None of it is true?"

"Some. Some not. He makes us out to be ignorant, superstitious people."

McLean watched with amusement, as the realization came over William Pinkerton that Jesus was more than just a simple Mexican kid that he was indulging. Tilman, on the other hand, looked not at all surprised.

You need to get out in the field more, William, McLean said to himself.

"Superstition?"

"You Whites call it that. We call it religion."

Frazer nodded, looked around the table and said, "Precisely. Tainted by prejudice and unconscious bias, but not without merit, no matter how flawed, if his intent was to understand that tribe. You see, Gentlemen, this is why I must undergo a vision quest of my own. My study cannot rely entirely upon the opinion of others. Exaggerations abound and cloud the truth."

"That's simply good science," Tilman agreed.

"The old Spanish records from 300 years ago have all sorts of fabrications. Lost cities made of gold and all that. The Conquistadors were obsessive looters. Grabbed everything they could, and just melted it down. From what survived, those who study this assume that much beautiful art was lost, and a lot of historical material incorporated there-in. It's a tragedy."

Tilman looked at him a long moment. "Incorporated there-in? What does that mean?"

Frazer looked up from the food he was cautiously tasting. "Gold is the most permanent of metals. Lasts for centuries and does not tarnish. And it is rare and valuable. So, if a gold object has a figure or a symbol, then that's a message from the past we should try to read. It may be important. History always is, no matter how much some may try to obscure it."

Pinkerton nodded. "That's already happening with the late War. Jubal Early, one of the South's less distinguished generals, has created something called The Southern Historical Society to tell 'their side of the story'." Pinkerton made quote marks with his fingers.

"Really?" Frazer reached for his notebook, opened it and scribbled a note. "How is their version different?"

"Too many ways," Pinkerton replied. "They blame the war on us. now, when they fired first. Said the slaves were happy and content before we interfered and started stealing their property, and on and on and on. One lie after another. A cacophony to overwhelm truth. Which I fear will happen. This next election will be the decider."

William Pinkerton sipped his beer and then smiled at Frazer. "Of course, we have our own view of all of that. My father helped the Underground Railroad as much as he could within the bounds of the law... "

McLean coughed, and Tilman laughed outright. Pinkerton stopped and stared at them.

"Come on, Boss," Tilman said, "We may not have broken the law but we bent it pretty hard. We ran spies against the South. One of us was hanged for it."

Pinkerton nodded gravely. "Uncle Tim, and we almost lost Kitty as well. It was a very bad business." Seeing the look on Frazer's face, he added, "Timothy Webster, one of our top operatives, was caught in Richmond, tried for spying and executed. He was Dad's best friend. Kitty Lawton was with him, our top female operative. She was facing a similar fate. Then Abe sent word to Judah Benjamin that we'd hang Belle Boyd in retaliation. So that was that, and we got her home and safe. Kitty was also close to Dad."

"You might say that," McLean said drily. "I'm surprised your mother put up with it."

"She had her own interests. And she liked Kitty." Pinkerton leaned back and stared at him. "We are not like other people, Harry. So shelve that and never bring it up again." His voice now had considerable steel in it. "Kitty was one of our own. She's buried in the family plot."

McLean realized he had overstepped. "Sorry, William. She was a good woman. One of our best." He sighed, "I still haven't found any women here to take up the work. I even ran an ad in the local newspaper. So far no takers."

"You ran it in English," Jesus said. "Try it in Spanish. You'll be surprised."

The three detectives stared at him, while Frazer made another note.

"Damn me. I forgot you were sitting there, Hey-seuss," said Harry McLean. "You sort of disappeared."

"White men never see us. Even when we are right in front of you. You think we are not there, but you are just too blind to see." There was no resentment in his voice. "With women you only notice the young and pretty ones, but even them, you hold to be no account. It's a mistake. You could hire one of the women here and train her. Who would suspect her? She's just a stupid Mexican."

Damn! Thought William Pinkerton, *who is this kid? Harry is right. As young as he is, we have to bring him into the work.*

"So, Hey-seuss, how would you proceed?"

"What do you need?"

"Someone who, as you said, disappears. Who can see without being seen. Who both understands and reads English and Spanish. Who also knows some mathematics. And is also something of an actress."

"And of legal age," McLean added, "Because she must be able to testify in Court."

Jesus shrugged. "And will sleep with a man she does not love?"

Tilman laughed. "Unfortunately, no. Not for us. We can't allow that. It would taint the entire case in an American court. We can use them only if we have not paid them for that."

Jesus shook his head. "I can ask around. Maybe a *puta.*"

The three detectives looked at each other, unable to say what they were all thinking. The Pinkerton Agency was still a path away from the degradation of prostitution for more than one bright young woman, but this was something never mentioned nor discussed. Others had been recruited from other walks of life. The ones from the demimonde were more ruthless, able, and courageous, however, willing to do anything that would keep them from returning to that life.

Frazer sensed something afoot. "Well, Harry, at that remarkable dinner with Miss Green last week, we did get a startling dissertation about female seduction." Frazer's eyes followed the young waitress who was standing nearby, still not looking directly at him, but in such a way as to command his attention. He shook his head in irritation, and looked away.

McLean saw this, but then Jesus spoke up. "Mister Pinkerton, am I working for your agency now? I want to learn how to be a detective. And I helped Mister Frazer with his pictures."

Pinkerton glanced at Harry McLean who nodded slightly.

"Well, that's up to my Branch Manager, Hey-seuss. Mister McLean there. Talk to him about it."

"See me tomorrow," McLean said. There were problems because the boy was so young, but he was certainly an asset. "How old are you?"

"How old do I have to be?" Jesus asked innocently.

The men all laughed. It was the perfect answer.

Frazer got up and brushed himself off. "Thank you for a delicious repast," he said, "But I must go pick up my photographs, and organize my notes before mailing them to The Royal Society." He looked at the young waitress again and put some coins on the table. She smiled at him and then slowly licked her lips, like a cat with cream.

McLean also rose. "I'll go with you. I have some work to do at the office and you'll need a desk. You can use one of ours."

"You're very kind."

"All part of the service," McLean said. He was worried about the young man walking alone. Even in broad daylight, this was a rough part of town, and robberies, sometimes with violence, happened. Frazer carried neither knife nor gun. He was better dressed for the town now, but the boots were too new and gave him away as a stranger, and possibly a lamb to be led to the slaughter. As they reached the door, the young waitress called out in Mex. She was smiling. Frazer looked at her, his mind racing. She was very pretty and obviously very available, and he had read the part of the

Kama Sutra that said that a man may resort to a 'public woman', but the encounters with Rose Green had bruised his character. Part of him wanted to take the wench and throw her to the ground to be ravished, but his upper mind said no. Such a thing was below his station in life. His dignity would not permit it. There was nothing there that an ice-cold bath would not fix. He shivered slightly and turned toward the door.

"Yes, thank you. Cheerio," Frazer said.

Outside as they walked away, McLean looked sideways at him. "Cheerio?"

Frazer blushed slightly. "I didn't know what else to say. What did she say?"

"Come back anytime." McLean laughed. "I don't know if that means she wants you to court her, or just wants to spread her legs for you and have bit of fun. It's a matter for further investigation."

Frazer sighed and shook his head. "I am quit with that."

"Still carrying a torch for Miss Green?"

"I am quit with that, too."

"But there is still a slight glow from the embers?"

"Perhaps. But I must focus on my work now."

"I don't suppose you could give me a sketch of the interior of that balloon?"

Frazer stopped and stared at him. "No. And please do not ask again."

McLean regarded him coolly. "Why not?"

"No man can serve two masters, Harry. You know that. So let's drop it and remain friends. I've said too much already."

"Fair enough."

They walked on to the photographer's. There Mister Deets, the photographer, a thin, weedy man with sparse thinning hair and hands that were cracked and red from the chemicals he used, greeted them, quite excited.

"Mister Frazer," he said, "Where did you take these remarkable pictures? I've never seen anything like them? How tall are these paintings?"

"More than a hundred feet." Frazer looked at the enlarged prints Deets was laying out on the counter before them. "See that fringe at the top of the cliff? Those are poplar trees, each taller than a man."

"But how were they done? Did giants walk the earth?"

Frazer considered a moment, as McLean picked up a print and then whistled softly in amazement.

"It's a mystery, like the pyramids in Egypt," Frazer said at last. "During what some call the Dark Ages, most knowledge was lost or hidden away. If I were to speculate... "

"Oh, please do!"

Frazer smiled, flattered by the admiration in Deets's eyes. "Scaffolding, possibly, or perhaps just rappelling by ropes over the top of the cliff. It's a matter for further investigation. I will tell you this much: we had to hike across the valley floor about half a mile to take it all in."

"What lens and exposure did you use?"

Frazer blinked. "Is that important?"

"Very. People will want to know."

Frazer shook his head. "I do not know. Mister Richards, the expedition's surveyor, took them. He also made measurements and calculated the size, using trigonometry. I have his notes. Miss Green and Colonel Wyndham were also very interested in some of the striations running through the rock face. Apparently there may be quite a bit of copper ore there."

McLean looked up from his own examination of the images which he thought might be of a buffalo hunt, and asked, "Who owns the land?"

"No idea," Frazer replied, a bit uneasy now. "They propose to take it all down to extract the ore if it proves out. That much I heard."

"That would be a shame. People should see this. There are magazines back East that would pay a pretty penny for copies of these." Deets was quite excited. "I must go there and make some myself."

"That could be very dangerous," McLean said. "It's in Indian country and, according to our source, a sacred site. Visitors are discouraged."

"Well, how were you able... "

"We flew there in that big balloon. I was part of that party," Frazer said.

"And a Pinkerton associate made an agreement with the tribe on Mister Frazer's behalf." McLean added. *Damn me. I've just given that little savage a promotion, haven't I?* He thought, *But he's becoming very useful and worth more than we are paying him. Time to put that right.*

Deets was suitably impressed. "Perhaps you could do the same for me? I would need to take a wagon... "

"Well, let's not get ahead of ourselves," McLean said heartily. "Mister Frazer must be allowed to deliver his paper to the Royal Society first."

Deets looked slightly stunned. "Oh, well, of course. If you could write, and let me know when... "

Frazer nodded agreeably. "I can do better. Make some more copies from my negatives and entrust them to Mister McLean. When I can release them, I will write to him and he will deliver them back to you. Is that agreeable, Harry?"

McLean nodded. "Perfectly. The Pinkerton Agency is always in favor of science."

Deets looked crestfallen. "But I really wanted to see them for myself," he said, like a disappointed small boy denied a treat.

"That's the problem. Everyone will. And that is Apache territory. They don't take trespassing lightly."

Deets turned pale. "No, I've heard that."

As he and Frazer walked away from Deets's shop towards his office, McLean asked, "How did you manage it? For that matter how did you manage to get back to El Paso with your scalp still on?"

"We rode. There was a party of Apache warriors waiting for us. Hey-seuss knew them and they had two extra horses with them. Remarkable fellows, wearing nothing but breechclouts and war paint. Very well formed, like living statues, and faces that remind me of pictures of ancient Roman soldiers. We camped after the balloon left, ate, smoked tobacco together and I, following your good advice, listened carefully to what they said as Hey-seuss translated. I am eager to write it all down before I forget it. I'm practically a member of the tribe, now. They are quite excited that I will tell their stories in a true and unbiased manner without the usual Christian distortions and hypocrisy."

Frazer looked sideways at him for a reaction.

McLean nodded. "A Scot might manage it. What are we but a coalition of tribes ourselves? And we are also a savage, proud people. So you are an Apache warrior now?"

"Not yet," Frazer replied. "That's what the vison quest is about. Finding that within myself. I'm quite looking forward to it."

McLean shook his head and laughed. "You are quite mad, you know?"

"I do. I do know that," said James George Frazer.

CHAPTER SIX

Frazer worried that McLean's almost parental concern might cause the detective to go beyond the joke of his madness and have him committed as a lunatic if he told him everything that had happened, and he was unsure, now, of what exactly had transpired, and what might simply be a dream or hallucination inspired by the herbs that Jesus's grandmother had provided to be made into 'tea'. He had drunk very little of the bitter brew, but felt its aftereffects even now.

He felt very unsure about the state of his mind. He needed time to sort it all out. And the magical charm or disk that he wore around his neck on a leather lanyard suddenly felt too heavy. At the office he sat at the empty desk, took some loose sheets of foolscap, and began to write a few notes.

He would have to be careful not to write down any of the many unusual characteristics of the huge balloon. Obviously some kind of covert government project, but which government, and for what purpose? Harry McLean also had a sharp curiosity about this, but even without the veiled threats from Rose Green and her fellows, he knew better than to even discuss it with the detective. The lines were drawn, and he wanted nothing more than to continue the research he had come to do among the American Plains tribes.

This, as much as his experience in the canyon where the ancient paintings covered the sheer rock side of the Eastern wall, made everything seem like a dream. What had he seen? And how could he be sure? Rose's voice intruded in his thoughts.

. . .

"You be careful, Sunny Jim, not to tell anyone how you got out here. We have a larger purpose than some pictures. So keep that under your hat, and stay safe."

She had whispered this in his ear as they stood at the front of the basket under the balloon, watching the ground race by underneath. The huge shadow's movement told him that they were moving at an impossibly brisk pace. Side sails had been deployed to catch the wind. But there was a low-pitched hum as well that penetrated the sound of the rushing wind that blew Rose's hair about and made her look more desirable than ever. What was that noise from?

While Frazer felt very surprised and confused by it all, the boy Jesus seemed to take it in stride, sitting midway back as Paulo Marconi consulted his instruments and wrote down readings in a ledger. There were screens that could be lowered to cut the amount of wind coming through the basket, and some of the crew of silent men sat in seats along each side, each holding a Winchester rifle between his knees. One checked the action on a new Colt's revolver. This was, Wyndham said, 'Indian Country' – and they had to be ready for anything. Once they were well away from El Paso, he ordered the Gatling guns brought out of hiding and deployed. Frazer thought such preparations overblown, but it was not his place to say. Wyndham was the pilot and *de facto* military commander, a role he obviously relished. Like all such men, he was also an engineer and geographer with sharp eyes for terrain. And he was enthusiastic about the tactical advantage.

Earlier, as they rose over El Paso, he pointed out how far one could see from just a few hundred feet above the ground.

"The first time I went up in Professor Lowe's invention, I could see a hundred miles into Virginia and discern exactly the route the Southern forces could take to capture Washington. I could see their weary regiments on the turnpike coming from Winchester. It was amazing. Lowe had a telegraph operator with a telescope and that lad was tapping out Morse code at such a rate that I could not keep up. I knew then that this is the future of observation. Of course, that was tethered to the ground. and some smart Rebel officer eventually had it shot down." Wyndham shook his head ruefully. "I tried to persuade the Union High Command to make more of them, but, since they hadn't been up in one, it was hard for them to credit the notion. Even photographs did not persuade them."

Suddenly he picked up a brass telescope and extended it. He swung it away from the city below towards a plume of dust. Then he handed the telescope to Frazer who looked.

"What is it? I can't make it out."

"A group of men riding hard. About forty of them. In somewhat of a hurry. Some kind of posse? Perhaps a platoon of cavalry? You see what I mean about tactical advantage?"

Frazer nodded. "Yes. Forewarned is forearmed."

As they approached the sacred canyon, he again motioned Frazer forward to the bow. Pointing downward he said loudly enough to be heard. "There's something that is very interesting. Might support your notion of an ancient civilization."

Frazer looked down and saw what seemed to be a ribbon of green running across the bottom of the canyon. Wyndham was consulting a pocket compass.

"Remarkable. It runs directly from North to South in a more or less straight line. And the edges are parallel to each other. We'll have to drag a chain, but that looks like something that might have been a military road."

"Military?"

"Sixty-six feet wide. Hardly a trail or pathway dictated by nature. This might be wider, and it's overgrown, with trees and scrub in the middle, but that is engineering down there, not nature, the same as your stone circle. Who put it there and when? Your guess is as good as mine."

Frazer was writing in his notebook.

"Why do you say 'military'?"

"I thought you had a classical education," Wyndham said, smiling. "From ancient Rome. It's wide enough so that two chariots can pass each other and strong enough that the footsteps of thousands of marching men will not destroy it. You dig down and you'll find some kind of hard surface. Be quite a job to clear all that away, and you will not be able to see it up close. But some of the Roman roads, such as the Appian Way, are in use to this day. They knew how to build things, those fellows."

"Can we get a picture?"

Wyndham shook his head. "Not if you have to explain how and where you got it. Besides, the light is bad. It will not come out clearly."

The basket under the balloon was rocking back and forth, buffeted by a heavy wind.

"You'll have better luck with the cliff pictures," Wyndham said. He motioned with his hand, and the balloon began to slowly descend. Jesus edged up to the front and looked over the side. Again, he seemed not to be surprised by anything he saw.

Suddenly, seemingly from nowhere, a large white owl, wings fully spread to about six feet, flew at the front of the basket. Wyndham and Frazer involuntarily took two steps back as the huge white bird landed on the railing, folded its wings, and stared at them with huge golden eyes. Frazer found this quite unnerving. And looking sideways at Wyndham, he saw the Colonel swallow hard, and start to reach for the Colt's revolver in the military holster at his right side.

"Don't," said Jesus. "It's just Old Man Owl. He guards the canyon."

"Oh, what a pretty birdy," Rose exclaimed from behind them. "Such a magnificent creature."

The owl turned its head so it was gazing directly at her, opened its beak and uttered a impossibly loud penetrating screech. So loud that Frazer and Wyndham clapped their hands over their ears. Rose froze. Jesus just turned and looked at them, and then at the others behind them, his face very still.

"What was that?" Wyndham muttered, "A challenge? 'Who goes there'?"

Jesus lifted both of his arms, extending them wide. The owl flapped its wings and then disappeared upward into the sky. Frazer turned to him in amazement.

"What did you do?"

"Nothing. But he knew me. Now everything will be all right."

Wyndham, slightly unnerved, began to issue the orders needed to get the balloon to the ground. The crew quickly complied. Frazer looked over the side and saw a small group of Apache warriors mounted on horseback waiting below. They were staring upward, obviously amazed by the huge balloon. But they simply moved off a little as it got closer, to avoid the anchors tossed over the side. They did nothing to help secure it and there was no wind at that moment in the canyon to pull it off its targeted landing ground.

Once grounded and secured, most of the crew dismounted and walked about. Rose Green carried a parasol over one shoulder, parading as if she were on the boardwalk at Brighton. Her attire was modest, a long dark green cotton frock that ended at her ankles, and a loose white lace over-bodice. Her blonde hair was now tied up in a bun. Some of the silent men of the crew lifted woven baskets over the side, and Richards, the surveyor, soon had a transit set up and was taking some distances.

The Apaches watched impassively from a distance. The ground across the canyon floor was gently rolling, covered with tall, sweet grass that the horses were enjoying. It was very peaceful, but Wyndham remained wary, and his crewmen alert. One of the Apaches called out something to Rose Green and his fellows laughed.

Rose turned to Jesus who was nearby. "What did he say?"

The boy blushed a little. "He asked if you would like to be one of his squaws."

Rose turned and stared at him. He was a young warrior, about six feet tall, and naked except for a breechclout. His muscular body shone with a coating of oil. His long hair was braided, and he had war paint on his face and chest. Rose smiled brightly at him.

"He does not look like a man in need of a wife."

Jesus called out to the warrior. The Apache laughed and shouted back.

Jesus translated. "He has six, but there is always room for one more, if she is humble and willing to work hard." The other warriors and some of the men in the crew broke into laughter.

Rose dipped her head, smiling. "Not my strong suit," she murmured. "Tell him that I thank him for his kind offer, but I must decline. Ask him if he would like to be one of my husbands?" When this was translated, the Apache sat very still as his fellows almost fell off their horses, convulsed with laughter. He turned suddenly and rode away, stiff with anger.

"Was it something I said?" Rose asked innocently.

Jesus smiled. "You turned his own words against him. The others will not forget this. He will hear of it for many moons, and so will others, of how he was bested by a White woman. Are all of these men really your husbands?"

"Only if I want them to be. Ask Mister Frazer."

Now she was a little angry herself. She walked off, defiantly twirling her parasol.

The sunlight began to fill the canyon, and edged down the East wall, revealing the paintings. Frazer gaped in amazement. So did Wyndham and the others from the balloon's crew. Everyone was silent now, even the Apaches, and for a few moments the figures on the wall even seemed to be in motion, as wispy clouds overhead made the sunlight flicker across the images. Frazer was just stunned by the beauty of it.

"What is it? What does it mean?"

Jesus screwed up his face in concentration. "Some kind of battle. Maybe a big hunt. It's hard to make out. This is not Apache. The tale has not come down to us that might tell us what it means. It is from the people before us. Perhaps even the people before them."

"So it's hundreds of years old?"

"Thousands."

Frazer turned and saw that Jesus was perfectly serious when he said this. This would indeed make his mark with the Royal Society, but he needed proof.

"Mister Richards!" he shouted.

The surveyor looked up from his transit. "Sir?"

"I'd like some pictures, please."

"Yes, sir. Give me the quarter of an hour to finish what I'm doing here."

Wyndham was standing next to him holding a sextant and a compass.

"You are right, Percy," Richards said. "Straight true North and eighty feet wide, not sixty-six. And it goes on for many miles. Must have been a major trade route at some time."

"It is a mystery," Wyndham agreed; "But not one we'll solve today. Let Frazer publish his findings. It's been here a long time. A few more years won't matter."

"There is something else," Richards said. "Look to the base of the cliff. There are structures of some kind. About twenty feet tall. Square walls, flat roofs, except for the one in the center which curves outward."

"Maybe it was giants that did all this?"

"Maybe." Richards shrugged. "I think I will make a few pictures for us as well." Seeing Frazer approaching with the Mexican boy, he called out, "Coming now, sir." He handed Wyndham a heavy object about the size of a fist. "There is also this."

Wyndham looked at it, weighed it in his hand and said, "What is it?"

"If you take your penknife and scrape off the dirt, you will see that it is the very thing we are supposed to be looking for. That's a copper nugget. Likely more where that came from."

Wyndham stared upward at the huge painting on the cliff. "What a pity," he sighed, "They will want to take it all down."

"Most likely," Richards replied. "Art seldom wins out over Commerce."

He walked off, calling out to some of the crewmen, and was soon leading them to a position several hundred feet away to set up a camera with a wide angle lens that could take in the entire painting. Frazer went with them. Jesus lingered behind, watching Wyndham, who had a few tears running down his cheeks.

"Sir, are you crying?" the boy asked.

Wyndham took a handkerchief from a pocket, and wiped his eyes. "I suppose I am. It's just so beautiful," he said, and then smiled gently at the boy. "Don't tell the others."

"Why?"

"Why is it beautiful? It tells a story of a battle long ago, of brave men testing themselves against others or against Nature. It sings to me. The practice of arms and warfare is not just my profession, it is my calling." He looked very sad for a moment. "At least it was."

Jesus nodded. "You are a warrior."

"Oh, more than that, my young friend. I am a war chief. In battle, I commanded a thousand men or more."

Jesus walked away suddenly.

"Say! What are those buildings at the base of the cliff? Who lives there?"

Jesus, still walking away, replied, "No one lives there. They are the houses of the ancient ones. The dead inhabit them. We do not bother them."

Wyndham felt a chill go down his spine at those words. He was a rational man, well read, and thought himself immune to such superstitions, but still...

An hour later, the photographs were done and Richards was handing Frazer a package of glass plates. "You want to leave these alone until you can get them developed," he advised. "I've wrapped lead foil around each of them, so no more light can creep in and spoil them, and cotton wool around that so they are hard to break, but treat them delicately until you can get them safe home."

Wyndham came up and offered his hand. "Good luck to you, Frazer," he said. "I think you're on a fool's errand, but I've done worse myself."

"Thank you, Colonel. For all your kindness."

Rose, her parasol now folded, came up, threw her arms around his neck and kissed him passionately. "Don't forget me, Georgie."

Frazer pushed her away gently. "Never. See you in Liverpool sometime."

"You and your new friends want to stand away a bit," Wyndham said to Frazer. "I'm not sure hot air alone will be enough to lift us out of here. May have to use something else as a booster."

There was an urgency in his voice that made Frazer take heed, and Jesus signaled something to the others in the Apache war party that made them ride off a hundred yards or so, as the huge balloon began to emit a curious low humming song, and Wyndham, Rose, Richards and half a dozen crewmen scrambled to get aboard. He walked away quickly.

Then a bright light came from the bottom of the balloon's basket and it jerked upward. Frazer ran, suddenly feeling the danger, and saw the huge white owl fly at it from above, accompanied by a flock of black birds.

Still the balloon rose, and disappeared into a bank of white clouds, now illuminated from within by the lights from its bottom. Or was it merely lightning? He heard thunder crack, and rain began to fall.

One of the Apaches led over a small grey mare and spoke in Mex, which he understood enough to realize that he should mount her and ride with them. There was no saddle but enough of a mane that he could grab it and hoist himself up, his legs straddling her bare back. Muscles rippled below him, and they set off at a gentle trot. He looked around for Jesus but the boy was nowhere to be seen.

CHAPTER SEVEN

111

"Where the Devil are we?" Sir Percy Wyndham shouted as the injured balloon fell through the white mist that surrounded them, and the scientists worked frantically at the controls on the port side of the basket.

Below he could see the dark green of a triple canopy jungle quickly rising to meet them. Then their descent slowed, and then stopped, as they simply hovered. Rose Green's face was frozen with fear. She was so pale that Wyndham thought she was about to faint. Her body was rigid.

"Ease up," he advised her. "If we crash, you need to be relaxed, fluid, tuck and roll, ya know. Ya don't want to break anything."

Rose nodded and swallowed hard. She turned her head, smiling nervously.

Wyndham looked about, trying to find some point of reference.

It was very quiet. Marconi and Richards were absorbed with trying to read their instruments, and the crewmen were huddled on the bottom of the basket. Some of them were vomiting.

This will never do, Wyndham thought. "Steady on lads," he said with a calm he did not feel, wondering if he needed a change of linen. He had felt fear before, but never quite like this. He looked towards Rose Green. She was once more staring fixedly into an unknown distance.

"Miss Green!" he said loudly and repeated it twice more until she raised her head to stare at him. *Get a grip you little bitch!* He thought. Aloud he said, "Madam! What are your orders?"

Green finally came to herself. Her eyes blinked and she took a deep breath. She looked around, stood up and looked over the side. "Where are we?"

"Damned if I know," Wyndham said. "Not where we were. There's no jungle in that part of Mexico. Richards?"

The engineer hit something with his clenched left fist. "Everything is foxed. I can't find our position." He looked upwards. It was twilight and the first stars began to emerge in the night sky. Richards gaped.

"What is it?" Rose demanded

"Ever been South of the Equator?"

"Never had the pleasure or the occasion," she replied.

"Well, you have now."

"What do you mean?" Wyndham looked wildly at the stars.

"What do you see, Colonel? Unless I've gone mad, we are an impossible distance from where we were. South America rather than North. Or perhaps Australia. That constellation is called The Southern Cross."

"I think we are all mad," Rose Green said. "Find a place to land so we can sort this out."

"Yes, Ma'am," Wyndham replied, comforted that an order was given.

"Paulo!"

"Yes?"

"Do we have power and can you navigate?"

"Limited power. Pick a direction," the scientist said.

"I see a glow on the horizon," Rose said and pointed.

"Go that way," Wyndham said. "Watch out for trees."

They flew on for about an hour towards the light. To counteract the crew's fear...and his own...Wyndham had one of the men take charge of a clean-up and repair crew, and then had sandwiches and bottles of beer passed out from the large hampers they had filled in El Paso. Giving everyone something to do restored order, and distracted the men from the port side controls where Marconi and Richards conferred in worried tones, shaking their heads.

Rose Green looked around. "Where is that Mexican brat? He brought that huge white bird into...."

Marconi looked up. "He flew away."

Rose Green and Percy Wyndham stared at him a long moment.

"He flew away?" Rose said in dead tones.

"My hand to God," Marconi replied. "Turned himself into a big black bird and went over the side into the clouds." He looked thoughtful for a moment. "When we return to civilization, I shall, of course, commit myself to a lunatic asylum."

"You might have to take me with you," Wyndham said. "I saw it, too."

"None of that," Rose Green said sharply. "Attend to the task at hand."

"Yes, Mum," Wyndham said, and pointed to a clearing suddenly apparent below.

They felt moisture on their faces rather than rain. It enveloped them so much that rivulets of water ran down their bodies under their soaked clothing. Those became cold and clammy, encasing them so that movement became almost impossible. The men began to tear open their collars and open their pea coats and blouses and strip them off.

Wyndham reluctantly followed, and Rose Green, trained to discard all inhibitions, left her gown and then her flannel underthings in a puddle at her feet. Her skin lost its normally rosy tone and became shrunken and grey.

Richards and Marconi continued their work, but to no avail. The balloon continued to sink until it hit a surface, but rather than a crash and a shock, there was a loud sucking sound. The smell of rotting green vegetation assaulted them. Slimy liquid flowed over the top edges of the basket. Among the screams of alarm Wyndham heard Marconi give a cry of despair.

Richards pointed. "Shelter over there," he shouted, straining to be heard over the hissing rush of water that enveloped them. Wyndham jumped up on the rail, felt his feet slip, tried to regain his balance, and fell face first into the muck. His body was rigid. He did not tuck and roll and felt himself starting to drown in something that smelled like horse dung. *What a shitty way to die.* That was his last conscious thought.

But he was not dead. He woke to the sensation of water; warm water now, being drizzled on his face and blinked. He tried to move, but found himself restrained. Then strong hands gripped his shoulders, and he was sitting up. A short distance away, he saw Richards, still in his sodden uniform. He looked quite dead. Wyndham feared the worst but then the engineer's eyes popped open, and he sputtered, spitting out some dark matter.

Wyndham could see small cold white lights and an elongated cave's mouth that showed the ruined balloon, now half submerged under the rushing rainfall.

"What happened?" he asked Richards.

"Long story short, we crashed. You fell into the muck. Rose got the lads organized and rescued you, carried you in here, and sent Paolo and half of them back to do salvage. Food hampers first, then the gear. A proper little general she was. Thought you were dead."

Wyndham tried to crane his head around and provoked incredible pain. He gasped. "I might have been," he said and felt something soft dab his face again.

"Open your mouth" said a soft feminine voice. "We need to see if you have any broken teeth." Wyndham did so. A cold white light blinded him a moment.

"Nothing untoward." Something touched his neck and he felt a rush of momentary bliss as his pain went away.

"Now look at me."

Wyndham could now turn his head and did so. He saw a strong-featured but attractive woman who favored him with a becoming smile.

"Do you know where you are?"

"No," Wyndham replied. "No idea in hell...unless this is it."

"Hardly the time for theology," the woman said. "You are in a province of the Inca Roman Empire. I am Colonel Doctor Koh. I'm from the government and I'm here to help you."

Wyndham grimaced. "What government was that again?"

"The Inca Roman Empire."

"Never heard of it."

Dr. Koh nodded. "Be very surprised if you had. Unless you read Jules Verne's scientific romances."

"I'm a busy man," Wyndham said. "I've no time for fiction."

"There are places where they pass as history or journalism."

"Ha!" Wyndham felt his blood rising. "Journalism! I've no time for reporters either, Pack of lies, most of it."

"But not all?"

"No. The *Times* is usually reliable."

Wyndham tried to remove some of the muck with his hands.

"See here," he demanded. "Who are you and where are we?"

Dr. Koh sighed. "Not much of a listener are we? The Inca Roman Empire. Under the beneficent control of Don Carlos Acu Tucan."

"Who?"

"The provincial governor."

Stop talking nonsense, Wyndham almost said, before a nudge from Rose Green's sharp elbow reminded him that what was needed here was diplomacy, not force. He turned and looked at her, at her calm face now stripped of any cosmetics.

"You have us at a disadvantage," Rose said. "We have obviously wandered far off our intended course. How can we make amends?"

Dr. Koh's kind face took on a glow. "An interesting question. You are not of this world. Through no fault of your own, you have fallen through a rift in the firmament. But your vessel seems to be loaded with maleficence."

Dr Koh made a sweeping gesture. "What do you see there?"

"Mud. Decay," Wyndham said.

"And beneath the surface?" Koh asked.

"Nothing. It's all rot," Wyndham grumbled.

Suddenly the surface roiled, as some large beast slowly broke through the muck. It looked like a very large white grub. It had an oily sheen. Rose Green laughed nervously.

"What is that?"

"Your salvation," Dr. Koh said. "They have no mouths or eyes. They have very little minds. And they are not of this place either. You must lead them to the next level where they can acquire hands and feet. Only in that way can the Rift begin to heal."

"And how are we to do that?" Rose demanded.

"How indeed?" Wyndham sighed.

Koh laughed. "Have you ever heard the expression, 'It's a dirty job but someone has to do it?' Fate has cast you all in that role. Get in the muck and become like them. Find a path."

"But we'll die!" Richards said.

"Oh," said Koh. "Actually you already have." Her kind face became terrible. "Welcome to Hell. Or something like it. So the choice is simple. Stay here or choose rebirth and redemption."

Wyndham, always the officer, stiffened with resolve. He looked about at his sodden, naked, miserable crew and then at Rose, whose face had hardened.

"Right," he said, "In we go."

"Me first," Rose said, and dived over the side into the stinking morass. Wyndham was suddenly filled with dread. This would not go well. He looked at Koh who was now hidden behind a bright white light that blinded him. *What a cheap trick*, he thought.

"Is this necessary?" he muttered.

"Not at all." Doctor Koh said. "You can just die."

III

"Where the Devil are we?" Sir Percy Wyndham shouted. He was immersed in a dream, flying slowly through white clouds as pretty red rose explosions rocked him.

Wyndham felt his batman's gentle hand shake his shoulder. He startled awake.

"Where the Devil am I?' he groaned again. His whole body was filled with agonizing pain, with every joint in his limbs and back signaling their displeasure. A square glass bottle was in his hand. He took a swig and a pleasing elixir abolished the pain. He started to take another drink when the bottle was removed from his hand.

"That's enough, sir." He looked and saw a man about 40 years old, wearing a brown wool military uniform, smiling at him. He looked down and saw he was wearing the same uniform.

"Time for breakfast, Sir Percy," Harlan Koh said, his voice soothing.

"Oh, all right!" Wyndham sat up and swung his long legs over the side on the wooden bunk and tried to stand up. His head felt like it might explode. Koh, a former miner with a stooped posture and ragged black teeth, looked much like a children's book illustration of a troll but his gentle voice and kindly manner left Wyndham to fight through the after-effects of too much good Napoleon brandy the night before, and even smile.

He sipped the cup of hot black tea Koh had placed in his hands.

"What? No more 'hair of the dog"?"

"No, sir. Sorry, sir. Doctor's orders."

"Bloody flight surgeon!" Wyndham grumbled. "What does he know?"

Koh offered him two white pills. They rested in the palm of a calloused hand.

Wyndham took them, examined them critically, put them in his mouth and swallowed. He washed them down with a mouthful of the bitter black tea.

"And what were those?"

"Better not to ask, say I. Orders is orders. Briefing in five minutes."

Wyndham began to dress. The flight suit was a padded canvas overall. Koh, to hurry things along, helped him tug it into place. He ran a comb through Wyndham's hair and handed him the brown leather flight helmet, and then the goggles.

"How's the weather?"

"Bright and clear, sir."

"Damn. I was hoping for rain," Wyndham joked. The bombers flew poorly in rain and missions were scrubbed accordingly. "What's the target?"

"I couldn't say, sir. Above me pay grade."

"Hazard a guess."

"The submarine pens at St. Lo?"

Wyndham laughed and clapped him affectionatley on his back. "The American's call that target Flak City. So I hope you are bloody well wrong."

The older man laughed, too. Wyndham knew he was tempting Fate with the question. If his batman knew the real target, then everyone at Grafton Underwood RAF did as well, including the inevitable Nazi spy with the concealed short-wave radio.

He pulled on his boots: American cowboy boots sent by his American counterpart at the 97th USAAF Bombardment Group as a joke the month before, but much more comfortable than the British Army version when wearing electrically heated socks.

He went to a breakfast of eggs, sausage, and fried bread. Everyone was quiet and thoughtful. Two of their twelve crews were absent, their aircrafts shot down the day before. The usual joking and horseplay had also disappeared. At the appointed time, the remaining hundred men who would fly the remaining ten B-17E Flying Fortresses in their squad trooped into the briefing room. Officers sat in the chairs up front and enlisted men crowded into the rear of the tiny wooden hut. A khaki canvas was draped over the briefing chart. When the briefing officer flipped it back over the easel a collective sigh that sounded like the death of some huge animal escaped from the assembled men. An undercurrent of muttered curses ensued.

Wyndham saw the map and aerial photographs of St. Lo and his blood ran cold. He walked to the runway feeling numb. Just before he climbed into the B-17, he bent over and vomited. After making his way to the cockpit he swallowed some coffee and then turned to greet his co-pilot, Richards.

"Mixed crew today, sir." Richards said. "New Navigator. A woman."

Things had become that desperate. Women were being allowed to fly on combat missions. Most were fighter pilots and acquitted themselves well, with faster reaction times and as much or more daring than their male counterparts. On bomber crews they were still a novelty.

"What's she like?" Wyndham asked.

"Very pretty but all business. Put the top gunner in his place for saying something nasty. An officer and a Lady. A real one. Countess, no less. To the manor born." Richards grinned.

"Will she be... well, you know?"

"Not her first mission, sir. But she does have a First in Mathematics."

"Should be alright. What's her name?"

"Rose."

A Rose by any other name... he thought. Wyndham went through the checklist with Richards. They were on their 21st mission together. Four more, and they would be relieved and sent to other duties... or would they? Rumour had it that the number of required missions was about to be raised.

Wyndham, who'd once lived for danger, felt his gut clench at the thought. He tried not to think about what lay ahead. It was not one mission, but mission after mission, day after day. They had a way of piling up, and repeated dives into bottles of good whisky or brandy every night provided only temporary solace. Grim reality was still there the next day. Day after day.

The checklist completed, Richards started the interior starboard engine. It roared to life, followed by its companion on the port side. Slowly, the huge silver beast lumbered onto the runway like an ungainly elephant, turned into the wind, and started to move as the other two engines roared to life. It sped over the long paved asphalt strip, caught the wind and began the climb to twenty-five thousand feet. He checked his black rubber mask, making sure it fit tightly over his mouth and nose, and pulled down the tinted goggles that would protect his eyes from flying debris. The radioman's voice came in his ear.

"Sir. The major sends his apologies but he has a bad engine and has to abort. You are now the formation leader."

"Acknowledged." He turned to Richards. "What do you say, Dusty? What's the best formation for nine of us. Three echelons?"

"Three above, three center, three below," Richards's voice came over the intercom.

"Sort it so the best gunners are on the corners, five hundred feet intervals and no stragglers. Keep it tight."

This was the new American tactical doctrine worked out by Major Curtis LeMay. RAF guidance differed because the RAF didn't care for the mutual defense aspects, but Wyndham saw the science behind it, and figured that Americans should know how best to deploy bombers they had invented. Strategic bombing was very much a work-in-progress when German countermeasures changed the equation constantly. Thinking about how to outwit 'Fritz' kept the fear at bay.

But Fritz had a new tactic: a head on approach that closed so fast that the forward guns did little good. And there were rumours of a Nazi secret weapon, a projected force that... Wyndham saw a black dot in the white cotton clouds ahead that became an expanding circle that looked like a bottomless well. He felt his gut clinch again.

"What the Devil is that?" he said softly as he tried to turn the yoke and turn the B-17 away, but he knew it was already too late. The plane, the entire formation, began to slowly spiral into the hole like water down a drain.

III

"Where the Devil are we?" Sir Percy Wyndham yelled, shocked and surprised at the sudden heat that produced sweat from every pore. He looked around to see his men wilting and close to collapse. Rose Green had a bottle of beer in her right hand and was tilting it into her mouth, swallowing it. Wyndham looked at her reproachfully. Her fair skin glistened with sweat.

"Care to share, Mum?" he growled.

"Oh, right!" She reached into the woven hamper at her feet and produced another tall brown glass bottle with a narrow neck, and popped the metal top off against the brass gunmount, She handed it to him.

"It's cold, so have a care," she said.

Wyndham resisted the impulse to chug it down. Taking a long draft, he said, "The men come first. Pass some more around."

"Yes, of course," Rose said, "Please help yourselves."

"Just one each. Then just water," Wyndham used his command voice. "Can't have them getting tipsy."

"Is that what you call it?" Rose laughed. "Like a little girl?"

Wyndham stared at her, and saw her dilated pupils. He took a swig of his own beer. It was dark and bitter. Perhaps contaminated with some drug? Rose sober was a force to be reckoned with. Rose tipsy was another matter.

He looked around and saw that they were not where they had been just seconds before. Not at all. This was another world. Below was not a jungle set on rough terrain but a flat desert stretching endlessly to the horizon in various shades of yellow, red, and brown sand, with touches of grey and black. The air around them was incredibly warm, like the draft from a furnace. Unconsciously, Wyndham unbuttoned his tunic. His men saw this and, taking it for permission, began to do the same. Richards and Marconi were already in their shirt sleeves.

Rose reached for another bottle.

"No Miss Green. Water only." Richards said kindly. "Beer will dry you out. Too much will kill you. Drink water only."

Rose looked at him defiantly for a moment, and then at Wyndham who put his own half-finished bottle down. "Is this mutiny? Who are you to...."

"That's enough, Rose!" Wyndham said sharply. "Look around. We have a problem."

"Oh, right." Rose laughed. "What have you done now, Boys?"

The two scientists worked frantically at their instruments. Richards shot her a dirty look.

The damaged balloon was rocked by a strong gust of wind. Parts of the woven basket cladding fell away hitting below with enough force to send up spurts of sand. The rocking gradually stopped. Rose pulled a spy glass from its brown leather holster on the front railing and scanned the horizon.

"Anything?" Marconi asked, as he wrote mathematical formulae in white chalk on a black slate tablet on his knees. Richards was turning little dials whose purpose was a mystery to Rose. Wyndham, with another spyglass, was looking behind them.

"There is nothing but miles and miles of miles and miles," he complained. "Flat, desolate, and no sign of that canyon where we saw that painting and left Mr. Frazer with the Apaches."

"Speaking of Apaches," Rose said, and pointed.

A man in Native attire was floating through the air towards them at a leisurely pace. He wore a silver breast plate and a short leather and metal covering that protected his genitals. His buttocks, legs and arms were covered with tattoos and he had on silver boots that rippled with lights. His face was painted white and red and his long hair was braided with black feathers. He seemed to be about forty. As he got closer he took a small box from a leather pouch on his hip and stared at it.

"Who the Devil is that?" Wyndham asked softly.

"Some kind of official, I'll be bound." Rose waved cheerfully at the flying man, as if she had unexpectedly met an old friend on holiday.

The man flew closer and made gestures with his hands.

"What is that?" Wyndham asked; "Some kind of sign language?"

The flying man pointed at him and then crooked his arm so his hand pulled up and back.

"He wants us to follow him, I think," Rose said.

"Impertinent rascal," Wyndham said. "Should we fight or should we go? What are your orders, Mum?"

Suddenly, seemingly from nowhere, dozens of other flying men appeared. They carried staffs about four feet long with blue lights at the end. A sudden bolt of electricity crackled in front of them.

"Ya know," Rose said in a dry tone, "I think those are soldiers. With weapons better than ours. And that was a shot across our bow. But you are the military expert. What do you think?"

"I refuse to die until I know who's doing the killing. Follow them, Richards," Wyndham said loudly. He looked sideways at Rose who seemed to be smiling.

"It will be all right," Rose said. "I know it will."

"Where the Devil are we?" Wyndham said.

The balloon moved steadily along under escort. A pyramid appeared in the distance and they flew towards it. As they got closer a plaza and the low buildings of a well organized small city appeared. It was laid out geometrically. On the plaza below were assembled several groups of people in orderly ranks. As they grew closer, Wyndham chuckled.

"Damn me if they aren't all stark naked," he said.

Rose Green took a spyglass and looked. "You are correct."

A chanting sound reached them. The balloon began to descend.

"What are you doing, Richards?" Wyndham asked sharply.

"Nothing to do with me, Guv," the engineer shouted, as everyone turned to look at him and Marconi. "The controls are suddenly too hot to touch. We've apparently lost control."

Wyndham looked sideways at Rose. "Any orders? We can fight."

One of the crew suddenly dropped his carbine. He shook his hands and then poured water on them to cool them.

"Always looking for that glorious death in battle, Percy? Not today," Rose said, as she pulled her dress over her head. "Get naked, the lot of you."

Wyndham was confused. "Whatever for?"

"Basic diplomacy, you fool. When in Rome, do as the Romans do. If we observe their customs, they are less likely to torture and murder us."

Wyndham, always the obedient soldier, began to peel off his sweat-soaked woolen uniform. Soon he was naked along with the other men. A breeze came up and cooled him. "Actually that's quite refreshing."

"Everyone drink some beer or water." Marconi said loudly. "Stay hydrated."

Down the balloon went until it touched ground. Off to one side a small party of nude people came, their heads down except for the one in the lead. This was a large rotund woman who wore a colorful feathered headdress and some jewelry. She had a becoming smile that Wyndham immediately distrusted.

"Welcome," the woman said. "Your coming was foretold, and we are at your service! I am Koh, Chief Minister." She raised her hands skyward and a great shout went up from the multitude. Oven-like heat beat down from the blazing sun overhead.

"Now what?" Wyndham whispered. "Where the Devil are we?"

"No idea," Rose answered. "Play along until I figure it out. Let me do the talking."

III

CHAPTER EIGHT

Frazer looked upwards, but the balloon had disappeared into the bank of white clouds. There was now a darkening edge and flashes of lightning crackling across. More rain came pouring down, and Frazer felt himself getting thoroughly soaked. The Apaches took shelter under a canopy of cottonwood trees, dismounting and passing a canteen of water around.

"So, Mister Frazer," one of them said in perfect English, "You are on a pilgrimage?"

Frazer was caught so off-guard he nearly fell off his horse. He recovered and looked closer at the man, who looked to be in his early forties, and, like the others, tall, well-muscled, and decorated with war paint. Frazer noted that he had a full head of red hair in two long braids that hung down to his navel. *Red hair.* **Red!** Frazier felt his mouth fall open, and quickly closed it. The old woman had told him not to be amazed by anything he would see here.

He could not help himself. He had to ask. "You are an Apache?"

"Not by birth, if that's your question. I was taken in a raid as a small child. Raised Apache. Recaptured by White men, forced to learn their ways— and when I came of age I returned to my tribe. I am known as Lone Eagle here."

"And elsewhere?" Frazer could not stop himself from asking.

"As a renegade," Lone Eagle replied. "Why are you here?"

"To learn."

"You are on a pilgrimage, a religious journey? We Apache call it a vision quest, but it amounts to the same thing. A journey of the soul."

Frazer, his mind racing, said, "Your English is very good."

The Apache favored him with a cruel smile. "It should be. I was a captive in a Jesuit school for six years, and then became a scout for the Army. Hey-seuss told us you would be more comfortable if one of us spoke in your tongue while you try to learn ours."

"That's very kind of you... Call me Jim."

The Apaches were making camp near a small pool, fed by a spring. Frazer was walking with Lone Eagle now, towards it. "Have you camped in the wild before, Jim?"

"I have. In Scotland. I have uncles who take poor city boys out to the Highlands in the summer for clan reunions, so we do not forget our Highland heritage."

"So you know where not to shit or piss?"

Frazer felt suddenly at ease. "I do know," he laughed.

Lone Eagle shook his head. "Not all Whites do. Especially green ones from West Point."

He looked sideways at Frazer. "You should get out of those wet clothes so they can dry properly."

Frazer looked at him doubtfully. "What will I wear then?"

"Why wear anything? It is a pleasant day. Aside from a breechclout to protect his manhood, what Apache needs more?"

"I see," Frazer said. *What would Sir Richard Burton, the great explorer, do?* He began to unbutton his shirt. "I will need them again when we return to El Paso."

"Of course," Lone Eagle said. "We dress up, too. Seeing us naked upsets the Christians, especially the ladies. They call us savages and complain to the newspapers."

When in Rome, Frazer said to himself. The rain stopped and it became sunny and warm again. Soon he was naked. Lone Eagle handed him a soft light brown leather strip. "You can wear this."

Frazer tied it up and around, and found himself comfortable. His boots had chafed him and had come off first. Lone Eagle put them near the fire that had been started, to dry. He looked at them first. "These are new. You need to break them in. Where did you get them?"

"At a sutler's in town. He told me they would be high enough that no snake would bite me."

Lone Eagle shook his head. "No self-respecting snake would, I suppose, but you really need not worry about that. Brother Snake is a peaceful creature and a bit of a coward. If you leave him alone, he will do the same for you... and most of them have no poison."

"And if I am bitten by one that does?"

"Then you will likely die, but if you do not, then people will think you are a Brujo and have magical powers." Lone Eagle looked at him closely. "Is that what you seek?"

"I seek only your old tales and legends. For science."

"Not for amusement of ignorant White people who do not accord us respect?"

"Not at all."

"Then you must give us something in return."

"Money?"

"Do not insult us," Lone Eagle replied. "You must tell us the legends of your people, the Scots. They are mighty warriors, I am told."

"They are. And I will. When?"

"Tonight, after we eat and it is dark. I will translate for you."

"What about Hey-seuss?"

"He flew away."

"What! On the balloon? That's very bad. He's not safe."

"It's your friends you should worry about. Hey-seuss can take care of himself." Lone Eagle changed the subject. "So, you were really married to that yellow-haired puta?"

Frazer stared at him, wondering if he should take umbrage in Rose's behalf, but the lady had defined herself. So he simply said, "I was, very briefly."

"What was that like?"

"Intense. She wore me out."

Lone Eagle nodded. "I had one like that once. Traded her for two horses to a White man. Now she lives in town." He shook his head. "Women."

"Women," Frazer said ruefully, cementing at least one bond between them. He wondered what tales he could offer in exchange for theirs. Whatever they were, they had to be good. These men might be savages, but they were far from simple.

Suddenly there was a caw from above. Lone Eagle looked up. He answered with two caws of his own. An impressively large black raven landed nearby. It disappeared, and suddenly Jesus was standing there. Frazer felt his jaw fall open in astonishment.

Jesus smiled, and said, "Why are you so surprised, Jim? Did I not tell you that all Apache witches can fly?"

As Frazer later recalled, the other Apache braves did not applaud this act of prestidigitation, but rather looked away as if Jesus had committed some public indiscretion. Lone Eagle growled something in a tongue that Frazer assumed was the Apache native language and Jesus, like any other boy suffering a parental reprimand, blushed and looked downward at the ground. A single tear appeared in one eye.

Frazer did not want to compound his friend's embarrassment, so, after a moment, said, "I can tell you the legend of Finn McCool and his son Ossian."

Lone Eagle tilted his head and said, "That sounds more like an Irishman than a Scot."

"Ah, yes. Well, long ago in the distant reaches of time the Irish and the Scots were part of a larger tribe called the Celts, and they were also a powerful tribe of warriors who fought the Romans."

"Romans? As in the Roman Catholic Church?" Lone Eagle spit on the ground. "Any who took those bastards on is worthy of consideration. You can tell us later." Lone Eagle looked at Jesus severely. "First we must make camp. You can help my son gather wood for the fire."

Frazer decided this was not the time to explicate the complicated relationship between Rome and its most prominent surviving cultural institution. He trudged off with Jesus and discovered what the term 'tenderfoot' really meant. And discovered as well a species of dark green plant close to the ground that seemed to be made of very sharp knife blades.

Feeling the eyes of the Apaches watching his every move, he made no complaint. He focused on the task at hand and did as he was told. The arrangements were not that much different than those his uncles made in the Scottish Highlands. A meal was served in a large common brownish red earthernware bowl with everyone dipping with tortillas to claim a portion of a savory stew of antelope meat and corn. He felt enormously hungry, but was careful not to take too much. The lesson of the habañero was fresh in his mind.

Later, having been assigned to clean the bowl, he examined it carefully, noting the precise patterns of black and red triangles beneath the glaze in its center. They were encompassed by a clear border at the rim. He turned the bowl over and looked it. Regular markings and shapes that looked like dancing men greeted his eye. He wondered what it all meant and wanted to inquire further, but Lone Eagle had made it clear that he would have to give before he got.

As the evening became darker he found himself, his clothes now dry and restored to him, seated at Lone Eagle's right hand. A place of honor without doubt. And then everyone was watching him with rapt attention.

"Ah, yes. Finn McCool, or as he was known in his time 'Fionn mac Cumhain'."

Lone Eagle held up his hand. "How would I say that in Spanish?"

"Finn of the Cumhain tribe?"

Lone Eagle pursed his lips and shook his head, and Frazer tried a bit of his own Castilian Spanish. Lone Eagle laughed. "Between the Scottish burr of your English and that old tongue used by the Conquistadors, I can barely make it out. Perhaps we should use Latin?"

"I read it well, but don't really speak it. The Anglican church discarded it some time ago." Frazer was perplexed. Latin? An Apache who spoke Latin?

"It was beaten into me for six years by the Holy Jesuit Fathers who tried to 'civilize' some of us. A lamentable failure in my case, as you can see." Lone Eagle repeated what he had said in Spanish, and there was the sound of quiet laughter from the other braves.

"Everyone here speaks Spanish?" Frazer looked around the circle. There were murmurs of agreement and a chorus of, "Si, señor."

Frazer shrugged. "Let us adventure together," he said to Lone Eagle; "I will speak, and if you don't understand, I will say it again, and you can tell me the way you would like to hear it. That way I can learn the proper way to say it. And I can also tell my stories to your satisfaction."

One of the older braves, Kicking Horse by name, challenged him, "You do not say your way is best? What kind of White man are you?"

"One who seeks knowledge. I am here to listen to the Apache, but if you want to know my truth, I will tell it to you, and the legends of my people."

There was a loud murmuring sound around the circle, and Frazer watched the flickering light from the flames of the fire dance across the features of the Apaches. What he had said had to be repeated several times by Lone Eagle in Spanish and the Apache tongue. Eventually they were all looking at him again.

"We have decided to give you a name in Apache," Lone Eagle said. " 'He who speaks strangely'."

He began to feel less a stranger and more of a companion now. Not yet a true member of the tribe, but his path had begun. He raised his hands and began again.

"Finn McCool was a mighty warrior and hunter, who lived eight hundred years ago. His son, Ossian, was a poet who left a written record of his tribe's deeds. Ossian's mother was Maurine

MacCaine, the daughter of the chief of a rival clan – er, tribe – and the granddaughter of a high priest or Druid, what you would call a Brujo. Finn wanted to marry Maurine but her father refused. So he abducted her... "

"With her help, I bet...," said Kicking Horse. Everyone laughed. It was an old story. Some of them had wives who'd come to them just that way.

Frazer, comfortable now, got back to his tale. "The father appealed to the High King; the chief of all chiefs, and Finn was made an outlaw, and gathered his tribe around him and went into the wilderness.... "

. . .

"They ate it up," Frazer told Blake Tilman a few days later, as they sat having real English tea at a new establishment called Mildred's Tea and Crumpets. "When I got to the part about the son, Ossian, meeting his love while hunting, they were open-mouthed with amazement."

Tilman smiled as he poured them each a second cup. "Why was that?"

"Well, the young lady had been turned into a deer by a Druid, or, if you will, Brujo, because she had refused to marry him, and placed in the forest to be killed or savaged by the hunting dogs, but what Ossian did not know was that his hounds were also bewitched, men who'd offended another Druid, and they placed themselves in front to keep Ossian from killing her. When he realized what she was, he took her in his arms and she became this beautiful young woman. In gratitude, she married him instead. The Apaches agreed that this was a very bad business, and that a powerful Brujo should not act so badly. But Ossian was called by the High King to defend the country against a rival clan, and while he was away that evil dark druid, came to her, and turned her back into a deer. She disappeared. Ossian spent many years looking for her, but never found her again."

"Ah," said Tilman. "A lost love. Always a romantic theme."

Frazer smiled. "You read romances?"

"I read everything." Blake leaned forward, "I was named after William Blake, the poet. My mother was very taken with his verse. And my father had literary ambitions. They were involved in the Transcendentalist Movement. Emerson, Thoreau and that crowd. My father taught school in a Maine fishing village and sent poetry to The Dial."

"My father is also a teacher," Frazer said. "So you're a transcendentalist detective?"

Tilman laughed, and shook his head. "Not really. I am an individualist, but I never studied religion and have no opinion about God, beyond that there may be something to it, but I have no idea what."

"A Deist, then?"

"If you like. Tell me more about your adventure with the Apaches." Tilman thought that Frazer was holding something back. What it was, he had no idea. Harry McLean was suddenly quite interested in Frazer's work. He suspected the charming young man had a hidden agenda connected to that enormous balloon Frazer had left with, and now professed no knowledge of.

He tasked Tilman with finding out about it.

Tilman was starved for intelligent conversation, and here was a Cambridge University don who could feed that hunger. His mind was never far from his New England intellectual roots. He looked the young Scot over carefully. A few days in the wild had dramatically changed him. He'd acquired a deep tan that made him look much less like a White man, and he'd shaved his beard as well. Apache men did not usually have facial hair. There was a stillness and strength about him that had not been there before. And he had an open collar now and wore the white emblem with its fierce red god openly.

Frazer deflected his gaze for a moment and looked around the room. It was well appointed with homey touches, such as lace doilies, linen napkins, fine china bread plates with pastries. There was a smell of jasmine in the air. This was a place for the fair sex. They were the only men in the room, and the subject of covert glances and whispered conversation among the women seated at half a dozen other tables, being served by two large, handsome Negro women in their forties.

"Why come here?" Frazer asked.

"My landlady recommended it. Perhaps as a joke. I'm Temperance, and complained about people always trying to force alcohol on me. They serve none here." Tilman laughed. He leaned forward and lowered his voice. "The church ladies have come to El Paso to shellac a thin veneer of Western Civilization upon its pagan past. This is their own 'den of iniquity' where they can whisper to each other their shocked disapproval. We had them in Maine. My mother crossed swords with them more than once, for refusing to teach the Bible, and for telling the girls they need not be subservient to men and could find their own way. She had the lower grades. They also suspected her of being part of a circle of women who danced naked by the light of the full moon from time to time."

"And was she?"

"She never said, and I never asked," Tilman replied. His smile became a frown.

Frazer blinked and changed the subject. "I have to say, while I enjoy a good single malt, I had nothing of that kind offered me by my Apache friends. I didn't miss it much."

"So what else did you tell them?"

"Scottish creation myths. How the terrible giant hag gathered rocks and earth from the sea and heaped it up to make the hills and deep valleys of the Highlands. I had to act that out. Took a blanket, pretended to fill it and dump it. They drummed and chanted as I did it, so I may have tapped into some religious ceremony of their own. And I told them about the terrible winter hag, Beira, who always fights the coming of spring with storms and snow and cold rain coming down in sheets. She sends her eight powerful disciples in all directions to resist the coming season, but the sun and the moon overrule her and Bridee, the beautiful maiden who brings the world back to life is born, flowers to womanhood, and marries Angus, the Summer King, who comes riding in on a silver steed.

The land prospers, the harvest comes, and then Bridee and Angus ride away to prepare for the next rebirth, and Beira begins to sneak back in."

"Interesting. There are festivals about that, I suppose. We had some of that back in Maine. Very toned down because of the Calvinist and Puritan influences. Sinful. Transcendentalism was a reaction to that. 'Let he who is without sin cast the first stone.' "

Frazer was still following his own line of thought. "The Apaches have a similar myth. The Old Woman Who Does Not Die and who brings forth the Corn Maiden. Think of that! Thousand of miles and thousands of years apart and the basic theme is the same. Almost the same religious aspects. Reverence for nature and a keen appreciation of the moon and the stars. They do not measure things the same way White men do. Not miles, but the number of days needed to ride somewhere. And measure time not with a watch but by where the sun is in the sky. Maps are foreign to them, as are writing and numbers."

"Emerson commented on that in his essay about Nature," Tilman interjected.

Frazer nodded and continued on. "White men are a malevolent force of nature sent by enemies from the other world."

"The other world? Like heaven and hell?"

"Somewhat, but different. It is hidden knowledge, both sacred and secret. Brujos can travel there, albeit with great difficulty. But they want the knowledge preserved. Written down, which is why they are showing me such tolerance and regard. They know what the Conquistadors did to the Maya."

Tilman looked surprised. "Speaking of years and miles apart."

"You know the story?"

"A little. Burned their archives?"

"Put everything in a room, declared it all the work of the Devil, and burned every manuscript and religious idol they could find. Wiped out their entire history. Gave them a clean slate for teaching the new religion."

" 'No Gods before me.' This is why I'm not a Christian."

"Reading that book you lent me gave me some perspective. The author has a grudging respect for the Apaches, and describes them in great detail along with the other tribes. He is an honest broker and pinpoints the folly of trying to 'civilize' them. It boils down to 'do it our way' or die."

Tilman nodded. "God save us from True Believers. That's a Unitarian prayer from my youth. But we had our own True Believers. Very keen about Abolition and freeing the slaves and willing to ignore an evil law like the Fugitive Slave Act. We created the Underground Railroad, you know."

Frazer stared at him a moment, very surprised. "I always thought of Transcendentalists as a literary movement, rather than a political one."

"It is political up to its collective necks. Free the slaves, let women vote, free and open education for all, that was us. And Mister Emerson was wealthy and willing to put his money where his mouth was. My brothers and I bought a fishing boat with money he provided. If you lived in that village and wished not to be considered idle and useless, you learned to fish, not with a pole but with nets to harvest cod. The nobility of labor was preached to us by our parents, but it was hard, dirty, dangerous work. No one thought anything about it when the three of us got our own boat. They admired our enterprise, and found us all wives. Our true purpose was hidden. We took fugitive slaves to Nova Scotia, sometimes as many as twenty at a time, concealed in the hold where we put the fish we caught. That could be dangerous as hell. Most of them had never seen the sea, much less been on a boat, and if we encountered rough weather, they could become quite alarmed. Panic could sink us. My brothers and I all carried Colt's revolvers and tried to keep them calm. Failing that, we told them to stay below, and if they did not, we would shoot them and throw them into the sea."

Frazer was taken aback. "And did you?"

"Only once. Never had to do it again. Word traveled fast. Harriet Tubman used a similar threat to keep people in line when she was bringing them North."

"I am a stranger in a strange land," Frazer said. "I had no idea that idealists could be so brutal. You are a bit of a contradiction."

Tilman nodded. "As Walt Whitman said, 'do I contradict myself? I contradict myself and contain multitudes.' My work requires me to start every day anew, without prejudice or reference to what has gone before. I float as light as a feather and as heavy as a boulder."

He looked over Frazer carefully, thinking that that sentiment might end up in his notebook. *Was he brave, foolhardy, or simply insane? Who could tell?*

"You are still intent on the vision quest?"

"I feel that I must try if I am to truly understand them. I must go deep into the Apache mind to truly write their stories."

Tilman drank the last of his tea and considered his next words carefully. "Don't go so deep that you can't come back. They have a word for that here."

Frazer's head came up like an animal, suddenly alert to a danger unforseen.

"And that is?"

"Renegade. Outlaw."

"Oh."

Tilman added helpfully, "Pinkerton's does not abide outlaws. We catch them or kill them."

Frazer nodded slowly. "I will be careful."

"You should read Mister Cremoney's book again. In the first part of it, he is quite a young man, full of vigor, like you, and armed to the teeth as part of a group sent to determine the new boundary between the United States and Mexico. And the first Apache he meets has one question."

"What are you doing on our land?"

"Precisely. The treaties that established the boundary commission are something they had no part of. Had not even been invited to, because they were savages, and therefore dismissed as lesser men. The result was desolation and terror for decades. They and the other tribes hold their land to be theirs, and theirs alone: a vast expanse that includes much of Northern Mexico, where they already terrify the locals. Turn the proposition around, and you have a people whose land and culture have been invaded, and who are fighting a rear guard action with every means at their disposal. They were not consulted because they are demeaned as savages. Ignorant people try to elevate them to 'civilization,' which is anything but civilized in its application, and excuses all sorts of crimes against them. We need a new ontology to understand them, by looking at it from their point of view. When a leader of the country says things like 'the only good Indian is a dead Indian,' then we have failed to properly apprehend the Apache mind. They are a proud people who merely want to be left alone. The White Man is seen as an existential threat. They will not yield, and will go down fighting. Cremoney never said it that plainly, but it's there in every line of that book." Tilman became uncharacteristically excited as he said this.

He leaned forward lowering his voice. "The quest for domination ventures on the obscene. Consider the plight of the Comanches. Fiercest tribe on the Plains. Even more feared than your Apache friends. Greatest horsemen. And horses were their passion and their wealth. Great breeders. Everyone wanted a Comanche bred and trained horse. Hard to come by and they scorned money. No use for paper or the White Man's banks. Trade goods only. Weapons, blankets, food, and, regrettably, whisky."

"You want to impose Temperance on savages?" Frazer felt like reaching for the notebook he no longer carried everywhere.

"It's not a moral position. They can't handle strong drink. It destroys them. There are laws against selling them whisky. Makes them quite excitable and even more dangerous. They act like wild beasts. Their Chiefs discourage it, to maintain discipline." Tilman shook his head. "No, what destroyed the Comanche's resolve was a military campaign in Texas. The Army was having trouble getting the battle they wanted: a modern one like we had during the 'Late Unpleasantness'. They were never going to stand and fight. It's more of a game for Indians. Individual encounters on horseback. En masse, they simply melt away if outnumbered. The Army don't like that. They consider it cheating. So they cheated back. It was disgusting."

Frazer saw that the normally cool-tempered Tilman was getting angry now.

"What happened?"

"They killed all their horses."

"Surely not all?"

"All of their breeding stock and yearlings. All of their mares. Every stud. A hundreds of years of breeding, there. All that they could find. Shot them all and left them to rot. One newspaper put the number at twenty-two thousand."

Frazer did not feel the shock that Tilman expected him to feel. He did not share the detective's outrage. He thought it uncharacteristically naive. "Sounds like a very good military tactic. The kind of thing that Britain does all the time."

Tilman nodded. " 'War is Hell,' as General Sherman said. But the line has to be drawn somewhere. The horses were innocent. Why kill them?"

"Why, indeed?" Frazer knew no rational answer would dampen Tilman's temper. Therefore he offered none. Frazer was impressed by his passion. Other people in the room were staring at them. "That's quite a radical viewpoint for someone who does what you do."

"Which is why I ask that you keep this between us. Harry McLean would not be pleased and would have questions. Questions I have not yet decided myself."

"Does a Transcendentalist have any business being a detective?"

Tilman sighed. "The essence of being a detective is to have an open mind. Pinkerton's is a big agency now, and Allan's sons are taking over. As they should. But they forget our roots. Harry and

Allan were Chartists back in Scotland, in the Low Country, and exiled for it, and they were as radical as Emerson and Thoreau were in the John Brown era. Also part of the Underground Railroad, and provided the detectives who protected Frederick Douglass and kept the slave catchers from bothering him on his lecture tours. I was one of them. Anything to get away from the stink of cod." Tilman laughed again bitterly. "We do not enforce the law, except for clients. We are not from the Government. Our clients are larger than it. And sometimes opposed to it, in their zeal for power and profit. I liked the business better when we still had a moral center, and wanted to do good. Now we seem to be losing that. Money trumps Honor."

Frazer stared at him trying to take it all in. There was a contradiction here he felt compelled to explore.

"Have you killed many men?" he asked.

Tilman stopped, stared at him, suddenly red with anger. "That is a very rude and juvenile question, Jim. I am a soldier. I was at Gettysburg, and killed more on those three days than I could count. In the service of the cause that John Brown started, to end Slavery. A noble cause most say, but they were not there, and can't grasp the horror of it. Now, my work sometimes requires me to kill a very bad man under the color of law. 'Dead or alive' is on the warrant. So, yes, I am a killer, but I prefer to think of it as being a hunter. I do not do murder. I get no satisfaction from the deed. You might tell that to your Apache friends, so they understand that our quarrels are not with them. In fact, there are times we would welcome their assistance, and pay handsomely for it."

"Money does not interest them, as you said. I made that mistake myself." Frazer watched Tilman signal for the bill. "I hope I have not offended you. I humbly apologize if I have."

Tilman shrugged. "*De nada*. We're still friends, and it's partly my fault for having brought the matter up. Read the Cremoney book again. As prejudiced as it is, there is a lot of good information in it."

One of the Negro hostesses approached, a pot of hot water in one hand, and a look of concern on her face.

"Will you gentlemen require anything else?"

Tilman smiled at her. "I think we're about done. Jim?"

"Certainly. Thanks for the tea. It was a touch of home."

The hostess leaned over and spoke softly. "Do you really know Frederick Douglass?"

"I had the honor of attending to his safety before the War, along with others from my agency. I would not say I actually know him."

"Well, bless you, Sir. We try to discourage political talk here, since we are new, and need all the custom we can get, even from rough men like yourself, but those ladies come every afternoon to gossip and drink tea by the gallon, so next time, please restrain yourself."

"I will," Tilman said. "I apologize for the disturbance."

The hostess turned to Frazer. "And you, Sir, please put that heathen icon away and do not show it again. We are Christians here, even if you are not."

Frazer tucked the medallion into his shirt. "I also apologize. I did not mean to offend. This is part of the ethnographic study I am engaged in. An older god."

"Call it what you may, Sir. I know the Devil when I see him."

Outside the tea shop they shook hands to reaffirm their friendship and parted. Frazer walked back to clear out his room at his hotel and decided to place his White Man goods in safe keeping with Harry McLean at the Pinkerton office. Then he would ride away, clean shaven, and in buckskins to begin his vision quest with Lone Eagle and his fellow shamans.

At the Pinkerton office, Frazer was slightly surprised to see Jesus, now in the more respectable guise of a White youth, wearing a collarless shirt, black broadcloth trousers held up by suspenders, and brogans, going over a hand-drawn floor plan with Harry

McLean and Blake Tilman. They were absorbed in planning an operation, so he simply dropped his gear in a corner and bid them goodbye. In the street below, Lone Eagle and Kicking Horse waited with an extra horse for him. He mounted easily and they rode away, with Frazer thinking of a character from Apache myth he had recently learned of: Coyote, the trickster god.

CHAPTER NINE

Harry McLean later regretted not giving Jim Frazer more than a cursory wave as he left. Against his better judgement, he had grown fond of the boy and wished him well, but the transformation after a few days with the Apaches was startling, to say the least. He had become a completely different person, a hazard not unknown in the Ethnographic Survey: falling in love with the subject of your research, and 'going native', Captain Sir Richard Burton being the most obvious example. Still a Muslim after all these years, despite the great and public distress of his equally convinced Catholic wife, who also abhorred some of his most popular books and saw "The Arabian Nights" as little better than pornography.

During his own service before the war, McLean himself had become an ardent Abolitionist, despite the fact that he found most Blacks strange and unknowable. But John Scoville, the first Black detective Pinkerton hired, was still a close friend. They'd worked many cases together. That was the essence of being a detective: standing apart from your own emotions and considering each case with cold objectivity.

A few days before, just after the big balloon had flown away, a troop of cavalry had come thundering into the square. Forty seasoned troopers of the Ninth. All Black, except for their leader. He was short, blonde-haired, and sunburned, and at the age of twenty-two already a Captain, proving that unlike most graduates of West Point, he had no reservations handling Negro troops. The soldiers dismounted and refreshed themselves from the offerings in the market stalls, being careful to pay for everything they took, while their leader made inquiries.

Soon he was walking at a brisk pace towards the Pinkerton office, where Harry McLean and Blake Tilman were sorting the day's mail. His First Sergeant went with him. A very tall muscular man of forty with a stern face that befitted his office, and kept the more rambunctious troopers in line, he had a deep powerful voice to match. But he stood silent and two paces behind as the young Captain pulled off his thick leather riding glove and offered his hand.

"John Pershing, Sir. I've been sent to find some people in a hot air balloon. Some sort of circus performers? The telegram from Washington was not very clear. People in the marketplace said you might know something about it? Are you Mister McLean?"

"I am," McLean replied, and stepped forward to shake his hand. "I had no idea that the response would come so quickly. I only wrote to my old friend Elmer Washburn last week. I'm afraid that they have moved on. Flew away just hours ago."

Captain Perishing frowned. "I'm not sure I understand the urgency here. How much of a threat can some circus performers in a hot air balloon be?"

"Well," McLean drawled, "When the performers all have new Winchester rifles and Colt's revolvers, and are very intent on keeping people away, it's interesting. The fact that their pilot is Sir Percy Wyndham is even more interesting, as is the fact that Rose Greenhow's daughter, who now resides in Liverpool, is the star performer, and also seems to be giving the orders. That young woman is no friend of the United States." McLean turned to Tilman. "Have I left anything out?"

"The Gatling guns. You didn't mention them."

Pershing's head turned as if he had heard a rifle shot. He looked back over his shoulder at the huge Black First Sergeant. "What do you think?"

"That it was a hard ride, and that the men need to rest and eat, Captain. And that Gatling guns change the tactical situation." His deep melodious voice filled the room like a hymn in church, and gave everyone a moment for reflection.

"Yes," said Captain Pershing after a moment. "Go see to that, while I collect further intelligence." The First Sergeant saluted, turned, and went out the door and down the stairs. The loose, noisy one groaned, as if it might break under his weight. Pershing turned back and asked, "What ese can you tell me?"

Which put Harry McLean in a bit of a fix, because he did not want to betray the confidences of Jim Frazer, who was now a Pinkerton client, nor mention that he had placed an agent of unknown and dubious reliability aboard, in the person of Jesus Martinez.

"Well, we did not actually see any Gatling guns," Harry McLean said, as he motioned for Pershing to take a chair, and poured him a cup of coffee. Tilman went back to sorting the mail while listening carefully to every word.

In the end, Captain Pershing decided to wait a few days for further reports of the balloon and its location. This would give him time to rest his men. He took his troop a few miles outside of town and bivouacked them there.

After he left, McLean turned and looked at Tilman, who was deciding which wanted posters would be placed on the corkboard near the door.

"What did you think?"

"They seem very capable. The officer is no political hack to be here, working with Blacks, and to have attained that rank so young. Not given to displays of pride, and he listens to his Sergeant, who is also very professional. Of course, I was a Sergeant myself, so I have a bias."

"Anything interesting in the mail?"

Tilman looked for and found a gray envelope, which he handed to McLean.

"There is this."

McLean looked at it, turned it over in his hands looking for a return address and found none, saw that it had been slit open with

Tilman's pen knife and pulled out the contents. There was a wad of new greenbacks and a note.

"Gentlemen: Please contact Captain Pershing and no one else at Fort Bliss should you need assistance. Otherwise, a retainer for secret service is enclosed. E. Washburn."

McLean looked at it unhappily. "Seems we will be sucking on the Government teat once more."

"You do not seem pleased."

"The U.S. Government is the client from Hell. Very demanding, and slow to pay. We let them go after the War. It's usually not honest work. Very political. The last job we did for them was to snatch La Fayette Baker's briefcase during President Johnson's impeachment trial."

"What was in it?"

"Enough evidence to sink him and maybe even get him hung. Johnson was immoral and corrupt, and had the bad taste to let a woman of the town do her business with him on Dolly Madison's furniture, but that's not a high crime or misdemeanor. Baker had proof of dealings during the war involving him in smuggling cotton from Southern ports to England. He secretly invested in blockade runners. The price was sky-high, and fortunes were made. The South used that money to keep the war going after Gettysburg, and sold millions of pounds of so-called 'cotton bonds' to speculators in England and France. Those would only be good if the South won. Without that money, they would have gone under in sixty-three after Gettysburg."

Tilman, never one to express his emotions, looked angry and disturbed. "That's treason. Why not bring the matter forward?"

"Because Johnson was not the only one in the plot. Several Senators and former Senators were involved, all pigs at the trough. One of them was Judah Benjamin, who could corrupt a saint. Before the War, he was the junior senator from Louisana. He knew them all, and all their dirty little secrets and sins. And from his safe place in England, where he is now a leading barrister, he was manipulating the other side to push for the impeachment. Baker was a hard man and no fool, and a half-way decent detective, but he was also a fanatic about fraud and corruption."

"I know. I served with him."

"Did you now? Were you there for this debacle?"

"By that time, I was working at a coal mine in Pennsylvania, looking for radicals. I only know what I read in the newspapers."

"Ah. Well, Allan took on this mess with great reluctance. Several of our railroad clients 'suggested' it. Said if it got out, it would bring down the government."

"And land several of them in prison?"

"I have no doubt. Anyway, the briefcase was snatched out from right under Baker's table as he was about to testify, and he was left gibbering like a fool, 'I have it not about me, I have it not about me... Where did it go?' It was pathetic. He was in tears."

"Where did it go?"

"Into a big bonfire outside. We made sure of that."

" 'We?' So you were there?"

McLean looked at him coolly. He and Tilman had never worked together before. Pinkerton's was now like the Army. Too large and diverse. It was impossible to know everyone in a way that automatically inspired trust. Tilman had left New York under some kind of cloud that William Pinkerton had not bothered to confide. This aggravated McLean, who as Branch Manager was responsible for the conduct of the men under him. So he leaned back in his chair, sipped his cold coffee and said, "I'm not saying that. If I did, I would be admitting to the crime of destroying evidence, and of interfering in a Congressional investigation. And a Pinkerton agent would never do anything so vile. It would be against everything we stand for."

"It would. We would never do that."

"Of course, we do not always walk with the angels. Baker had his flaws. He was hard on whores and Washington was full of them. Real and political. He would go on crusades against vice and raid those houses, shutting them down."

"A labor worthy of Hercules," Tilman commented.

"Yes, when a thousand red lights burned every night in Washington, and any housewife could join the throng by putting one in her window. And did. The money was that good, and the source anonymous, with so many troops passing in and out. It was a bacchanal."

"I assume these were the same women who went to church, prayed aloud to defeat the shameful spread of vice everywhere, and urged that Annie Jones and her sisters in the demimonde be driven out of town?" Tilman's tone was ironic.

"Of course," McLean replied. "With their own men away, they got lonely. Where was the harm, really, and who would know, with every grass widow within a mile doing likewise?

Eliminating the competition allowed them to raise the price."

"Basic Capitalism. Except they did not have the skills of girls from the demimonde. Didn't know anything about how to be a whore, and considered such things degredation and sin. Not that it mattered."

"Why not?" McLean said with a grin. He was tickled by Tilman's didactic style of speech. It was like that of a college professor or touring lecturer.

"The enlisted men could not afford the likes of Annie Jones. The parlor alone intimidated them. They were not of her class, and knew it. The housewives were like a visit home. Simple and easy to love. They could stay the night if they paid extra."

"And Baker thought he could break Belle Boyd, Antonia Ford, and Rose Greenhow, by holding them in prison in miserable circumstances. They were very tough, willing to die for the cause, and be whores themselves if they had to. What he did to Rose Greenhow and her daughter was beyond decency. That little girl was only eight. Held in the midst of the Negro prisoners, men and women together, who were very free in their affections for each other. People told him it was too much, but he was determined to succeed, where we had failed. Baker would not relent. No wonder that little girl hates us, and is here to do us harm. I am sure of it. The apple don't fall far from the tree.

She has 'spy' written all over her. And then he had his own downfall."

"Janeta Valesques," Tilman said.

"So you know about that?"

"I was there. She was working from Annie Jones' house, but never available to the ordinary clientele. General officers and high Government officials only. Very attractive Cuban minx. Sometimes passed herself off as a man to get information. A top Confederate operative. Baker tried to turn her, but she turned him instead. Not to the South's cause, but to her bed. She fooled him completely."

"As she did so many. She's working for England now. We'll have to keep an eye out for her. If she shows up, we'll know England is once more interfering."

"There is a Presidential election next year. It's a matter for further investigation," Tilman said, and turned back to the wanted posters.

McLean cracked up. "You should take this talk on the road. You sound like a college professor."

Tilman looked skyward, then shook his head, and smiled. "Were it not for the War, I might have been. Joshua Chamberlain offered me a post at Bowdoin. I'm a Doctor of Philosophy."

McLean stared at him, trying to find the lie, and saw none. "Good lord, man, what are you doing here in this grubby trade?"

"I like it. It is more real. I like the puzzles and the danger. When I took the job, I made Mister Pinkerton promise not to hold it against me. And not to promote it. Most detectives, even ours, are brutal and stupid men. Hiding it gives me an advantage, because it allows me to see what others cannot. And teaching has no appeal. I do envy your friend Frazer, whose government will support his research without promise of results."

"I was part of that service before the War," McLean confessed. "It's how Allan and I became Abolitionists. We were sent to help, saw the right of it, and did our best."

"My family was also Abolitionist," Tilman said, but did not elaborate.

McLean suddenly reminded of his own pretty, much younger wife in Denver, said, "Say, can you take over the Branch while I go back to Denver and take care of some business?"

"How long?"

"A week or two. My wife has been complaining about how much she misses me. If that's the case, then she and the childen will have to move here, where my work is. I can stop living in that dreadful hotel, and find a proper house."

"I don't want to be stuck with it," Tilman said. "Administration is not my strong suit."

"No. If you worked for L.C. Baker at the end of the War, I can see how you caught the action bug."

"More like it caught me. I was part of the posse that arrested John Wilkes Booth. I discovered something unpleasant about my character."

"What was that?"

"I don't mind killing a bad man. I do not enjoy it, mind. I'm not that depraved, but I will put a murderer down like a mad dog, without hesitation."

"Hell, son. That's part of what we do. We re society's trash collectors. As long as you don't grow to like it, that's fine. Then you become a mad dog." McLean grinned.

"Harry, I've got to get back in the field soon."

"With a partner who can watch your back. I won't send a man out alone. We've lost too many, that way. And it has to be the right sort of man. A soldier like yourself. William would send his son Billy, pardon me, Bill now, to get some experience. But he's just married. I like his wife, and don't want to make her a widow. Young Bill is eager to prove himself to his father and grandfather, and he grew up in the business, but he doesn't know the hard parts."

"Such as what it feels like to kill a man, or what it takes to summon that will?"

"Precisely. Go slow, I told his father. His day will come."

They were silent for a time.

"Anything from Mister Frazer?"

"A note arrived this morning, carried by hand. Alive and well as of six days ago. Learning many things and making new friends."

"I will pray for him," said Tilman.

"As will I."

. . .

At that moment Jim Frazer was in conference with Lone Eagle, Kicking Horse, and other elders of the tribe in a place far below ground. It was dark, lit only by a small fire, yet the air was not overwhelmed with smoke. The men passed a pipe around, and Frazer took his turn, drawing that smoke deep into his lungs and exhaling slowly, as the others did. There was silence, and then murmured conversation, and at one point, Frazer's head turned at something he heard. Lone Eagle and Kicking Horse stopped and stared at him, and the others did as well.

"How much of our tongue do you understand?" He said this in Apache, not Spanish.

Frazer hesitated. "Enough" he admitted.

"How is this possible?" Lone Eagle demanded. "You have only been here ten days, and were innocent of it before."

"By deductive reasoning," Frazer said. "I see what things are, and what they are called and have learned many other languages before. Adding another is not that hard."

The other men sat silently, considering this carefully. "This is true," Lone Eagle said at last. "In the Jesuit school I was taught Latin, French and Spanish. These were easy, because they are much alike. English was harder. The language of the yellow-skinned men, the Chinese, I do not make out at all."

"They sing it rather than speak it," complained another brave.

"They are not from Europe, but the other end of the Earth, across the great water to the West," Frazer said, helpfully.

"How do you know this? Have you seen this 'great water' or been to China?"

"No. Not yet. Perhaps someday I will go," Frazier said.

"Then how can you know what you say is true?"

"It is the received wisdom of my tribe. I have seen photographs and maps. More importantly, the yellow-skinned men are here. They must have come from somewhere."

All of the men nodded. "Why not from the other world?" asked one.

"The other world?" Frazer felt himself relax. "There is another world?"

"Many more," said Kicking Horse, "But crossing over to it is not easy, and usually paid for with a death. The spirit must leave the body. For the body to also go requires secret knowledge. Knowledge that has been lost to us, because the Conquistadors burned our books and idols. The ceremonies are incomplete now, and it is not given to all men to be admitted to these mysteries."

Frazer felt sudden excitement. Here was an Apache theology or cosmology previously unknown to the scholarly world he came from. He started to speak. Lone Eagle held up his hand.

"Speaks Strangely, take a mouthful of water and hold it."

This was something that the Apaches did to prepare young men for the harshness of the desert they lived in, and make them tougher. They were told to do this and then run to the top of a nearby mountain. They could not swallow, and could not spit it out until they returned. This forced them to breath only through their nose. Frazer had been made to do this twice, running behind Horse Woman's 13-year-old son, Little Bear. The boy, in kindness, set a moderate pace, and Frazer had been give moccasins to replace his stiff boots, but it still was extremely difficult. He'd gotten into the rhythm of it at last, and his body, fueled by antelope, corn, and potatoes, had adjusted, and pumped new strength into him. He'd embraced the pain and made it go away, and completed the run, which took several hours, only spitting out the water when told to do so. It had been a test, and now he was facing another, his mind eager and thirsty for the new knowledge it would bring him.

"I require this of you, Speaks Strangely, because you often talk when you should listen. You have too many questions, and you jump ahead. You have been here ten days, and have learned many things, some so quickly that it is hard to credit that you'd never done them before. But let us say that you speak true – let us review. You can answer with a nod or shake of your head. You were part of the antelope hunt yesterday?"

Frazer nodded.

"And took two of them with a bow and arrows you made with your own hands?"

Frazer nodded again.

"On a horse you caught and tamed yourself. Horse Woman said you were awkward at first, but learned quickly."

"Perhaps we should change his name to 'Learns Quickly' ", said Kicking Horse.

All of the men nodded and passed the pipe around again, skipping Frazer who still had his mouth full of water, as he inhaled the smoke all around. It made him dizzy.

The hunt was exciting, but routine, as twenty riders, some of them women, had encircled a herd of antelope in the tall grass, and taken about half of them, letting the rest escape. He was naked. So were the others, including the women. He was able to control his new horse with his knees, as Horse Woman had taught. She had also taught him the hunting walk, how to move stealthily on the trail, and leave no trace of his passing. The bow and arrow was not that hard to comprehend. He merely had to see one to discern its mysteries. Simple geometry and physics: force and motion at the proper angle drove his arrows home. He was still clumsy with the quiver, and had only managed to take two. There was a lot of war whooping, which he was allowed to join in. He had helped skin and butcher the take, noting how almost every part of an animal was useful to the tribe for some purpose. It had its own political economy, and was a complete system. That gave him insight.

He saw now why the Apache resisted the White Man's incursions, and only took from them what was useful. Their written language, strange clothes, and other artifacts were not useful. A new Winchester rifle was useful, but not really needed except for times of war. They had been at war for more than fifty years. An ugly no-holds-barred kind of war, whose first tactic was deception and stealth, and in which any outrage including rape, murder, and kidnapping was excused. 'We were here first', the Apache said. 'You were not invited, and this is our land, our home, our domain.' He felt great sympathy for them. Who would not love it here and want to keep it as it was, with all of its simplicity, with the clear air unmolested by the White Man's industrial stinks, and the quiet purposes of just living according to the traditions handed down for centuries? What was 'progress' but a disruption of how things had ever been and would always be? *But what now?*

Lone Eagle spoke again. "To make a vision quest, one must have a vision, a dream to be interpreted. Has one come to you yet?"

Frazer shook his head slowly.

Lone Eagle added straw to the fire, which caused it to flare up, illuminating the entire cave. He pointed upward. "Perhaps you will find one there."

Frazer looked up, and was hard put not to spit out or swallow the water in his mouth.

Lone Eagle took pity on him. "You may swallow," he said.

Frazer did so, still staring at the wonderful, intricate painting above him. His mouth was now open in astonishment. Mindful of Lone Eagle's previous command, he did not speak.

"We do not know much about it ourselves," Lone Eagle said. "Just what has been passed down. It is thousands of years old, and tells the story of the Starmen who came to help the Apache in a difficult time. Taught some of us to grow crops, and those became the Navajo, whose language we still share. But the real Apache, the warriors, are what we are now. We have not been defeated and driven to the Reservation like the rest. We fight on, knowing the White Man will prevail through sheer weight of numbers, unless the Starmen return to help us. The Starmen could fly, and had huge star wagons that threw lightning at their enemies. Look there, and there, and you will see them, and see the Starmen also flying alone. That big hot air balloon you were part of in El Paso looks like a star wagon to us. Is it? Are you from the stars, Mister Frazer?"

Frazer shook his head. "Actually, I'm from Glasgow. And before they hired me as an advance man, I had never seen them. Perhaps you should ask them?"

Kicking Horse said, "We have looked for them. Their actions at the cliff painting alarmed us; measuring the land, disturbing the Old Ones. But we cannot find them. They have disappeared. They may have slipped into the Other World."

"Which cannot be done without upsetting the balance of things. We must find them, and bring them back. You must help us look."

"How am I do that?" Frazer asked.

"Perhaps your Vision Quest will take you there. You are an unusual man with strange powers. The Starmen also had the gift of tongues. When you are ready, we will guide you."

No pressure there, Frazer thought. *It's desperate and impossible.* But that night, as he lay in Horse Woman's arms, he had a dream.

Horse Woman was a complete surprise. Lean, lithe and treated by other members of the tribe as if she were a man. She was a warrior woman, one of several in the tribe, but the only one without a husband. This was accepted without notice or critique, because she was the best horse breaker and trainer by far, and the best horse thief. This allowed her to do as she pleased, and to sleep with whomever she pleased. She often initiated sex with young men coming of age to instruct them in the proper ways of lovemaking, so that their inexperienced brides would not be disappointed during the honeymoon and reject them. No Apache was truly married, not in the White Man's way. Some men had many wives, and some stuck to one, as had been the tradition many years ago. Kicking Horse, of that generation, had only one, and held her in high esteem. He wanted no other. Younger men took multiple wives.

"These fools think they have struck gold, and don't realize that they have to feed them all, and buy them things, and fuck them regularly to keep them happy. The first wives command the others, who share work. All have an easier life, and never stray. As long as their brave satisfies them. Our women are noted for their chastity, but all that means is that they never do anything with someone outside the tribe. Wives are traded all the time."

Kicking Horse stopped to consider his words. "Of course," he said at last, "We lose many men in battle and on raids. Some are hunted like animals by White Men. So there are always more wives now, than men to love and care for them. Otherwise, they might marry outside the tribe. They are prized for their beauty. But what then? They are no longer Apache, but Mexican or White, and we also lose the children they would give us. Someone has to take on that burden." He chuckled, "Better them than me."

Horse Woman had very little to say on the matter. After the antelope were slaughtered and butchered and packed, the entire hunting party, covered with blood that attracted viscious flies that bit, went to a pool under a small waterfall and took turns washing themselves, completely nude. As Horse Woman stood under the falling water, he admired how beautiful she was, with long hair and a strong shapely body that could almost be a sculpture. During the evening meal, the hunt was retold, with younger braves acting out the choice parts. His kills were acknowledged, and no one seemed to think it worthy of comment when Horse Woman led him to her teepee.

Now here he was, deep in thought as she took him deep into her loins and his seed shot into her. It was a tender moment, but she would make no claim on him afterwards. That was not her way. She sought only to preserve his essence for the tribe, where there were no longer enough men, and it was thought he might be a Brujo or a Starman himself, and not know it. He had flown in the air, hadn't he? For her, that was proof enough, and worth the trouble of another child. She hoped for a son, but only the Great Spirit could decide that. Her mumbled prayers were mistaken for love talk, and he tried to kiss her, but she shoved him away. Only Whites did that. She was forever an Apache.

Falling asleep in the afterglow of their coupling, Frazer had a dream about Rose Green. He saw her seated on a dais, almost completely nude. Below her was a throng of people, also mostly nude, staring at her with an adoration, which she took as her due. She was the Queen of this place. Next to her on either side, stood Wyndham and the other men of the crew. Wyndham, ever the soldier, stood proudly erect, a formidable presence. He wore a crested military helmet made of gold and copper. It shone brightly, as did the ones on the crew of acrobats and jugglers who'd flown with them on the balloon. All also almost naked. except for the knee high boots, breechclouts and gunbelts with their Colt's revolvers. They were ranked behind Rose and her executives. Each held a Winchester rifle at port arms.

Pizarro had taken over an empire with a few men on horseback wearing armor, and armed with steel swords. What could Rose and her crew accomplish with a dozen Winchesters? None of it seemed familiar, except that it must be very hot, and no place in this world, and therefore in the other. Unless Rose Green and her companions had landed in Hell itself.

When he told this to Kicking Horse and the other shamans, they whispered together, shaking their heads. "It may mean nothing," Kicking Horse said at last. "It may mean everything. You must try to find them. Direct your attention to her, your lover, and the rest should follow. Embrace the Great Spirit. Tonight your Vision Quest begins."

That night there was a feast, with much antelope put before him to eat, and a drink called *pulque* which made him feel relaxed and happy. That night Horse Woman once more took him into her arms.

In the morning, his head pounding from the after effects of *pulque*, he once more ran to the top of a mountain and returned, his mouth still full of water, but breathing regularly.

He was given another drink to purge his bowels, and once that was accomplished, taken to the sacred place reserved to such ceremonies, where he sat cross-legged, naked, and exposed to the elements. He tried to pray but found no words. Shamans kept up a constant drumming and chanting, and Little Bear and other young boys were nearby, tasked with seeing to his safety, but enjoined from approaching him or saying anything. They hid themselves under the grass.

This went on for three days under the sun, rain, and stars. He broiled under the sun and was washed by cold rains. On the morning of the fourth day, not having had a drop of water, he was given a long draught of *pulque* infused with herbs. It was poured down his throat until he could drink no more.

Gradually, he felt himself become transparent.

Looking down, he could see past his skin to the organs and muscles underneath, and then to the veins and arteries where his blood flowed, and beyond that to smaller things he had no name for. And saw below himself into the Earth itself. To the dirt that caressed the roots of trees and smaller plants, and the small animals and creatures that lived there. He felt something fill him, and lift him up, although his body had not moved. He looked around and saw that he was among the stars, and that there were more than could ever be counted, and that they went on and on and on beyond the ability of any man to see, but he could now see them all, because he was becoming more than a man – more like a god. Rather than make him proud, the thought humbled him, because he knew he was not worthy of such power. No mere man was.

He examined it all again, from the things too small for a man to see, to the vastness of the stars, saw that it was all connected and sought his place in it. Who was he, and where did he belong? The Great Spirit enfolded him, and he realized that, at that moment, he was exactly where he was meant to be, but that he would soon move on. He could no more be an Apache than he could be a Detective. He was a collector and teller of tales. A bard. A poet. A keeper of such truths as might come his way.

He comprehended then the minor spirits that were part of every living thing, and some that did not live but simply were. And then directed his attention to the task Kicking Horse had given him: to find Rose Green and her companions.

She was nowhere in this world. That he knew from his dream. Finding the other world baffled him, for there was more than one. Multitudes beyond counting, each a little different. But they had traveled in a vessel that was unique, and by focusing on that, he found her, and it was as he had dreamed. She was the Queen of that place, and High Priestess as well, her sexuality radiating her power over all. She had become immortal. There was no hope of pulling her back to this world. The cosmic imbalance must be addresssed in other ways beyond his ken.

And his own path also became clear. He must return to Cambridge and continue his work there. That was his place, and that was his purpose. So he would.

But first he spent time, as those who survived a vision quest were wont do, simply sitting alone, and contemplating the peace that lay upon that great desert, and feeling the spirits of every being within. He had attained, briefly, a cosmic, almost Godlike, comprehension of the universe and its components, and seen the underlying structures that held it all together. It scared the Hell out of him. What was he to do with such knowlege? How would he tell it, and be believed, rather than taken for a madman and put away?

Little Bear brought him food and drink so he did not perish, and Horse Woman continued to welome him into her arms, but she was growing indifferent to him now, already feeling the child quickening within her, and ready to return to her task of initiating young braves into the mysteries of sex. Sensing his departure before he did, she made him a fine set of buckskins.

When he went to consult Kicking Horse, the old man said simply, "You have done well, Learns Quickly, but this is not your place. It is time for you to go."

Some in the tribe grumbled. Everyone enjoyed his tales of Scottish warriors and their valor, even as he dipped into tales of King Arthur and the Round Table, and wondered when that cheat would be discovered. He was now respected as a poet, a bard, a teller of tales, and considered a wise man.

And so he returned to El Paso, wearing his new finery and moderate red and white war paint that helped keep the sun from his eyes, two feathers of rank in his headband, riding with Lone Eagle and three other Braves as a guard of honor.

At the bottom of the stairs to the Pinkerton office, he bade them goodbye, and started to climb the stairs using the hunting walk. His boyish intent was to surprise and amaze his friends.

A loud argument was in progress, and he opened the door to see Hiram Johnson, drunk again, about to attack Harry McLean with a hammer. He notched an arrow to the string of the bow in his hands and sent it flying next to Johnson's head and into the wall beyond.

"I have another!" he announced loudly. Johnson froze, confused and frightened out of what wits he still possessed, turned and stared. Frazer drew the string again, pointing another arrow at the drunk.

"Put it down," Frazer said, indicating the hammer. Johnson slowly did so, kneeling carefully. Frazer, keeping the bow drawn and the arrow pointed at his heart, said, "Now get out." He moved into the room, allowing Johnson to pass and stumble down the stairs.

McLean, slightly amazed, said, "Is that you, Jim?"

Frazer turned and smiled. "Oh, Harry, who else would it be? I told you I'd be back."

McLean laughed for several minutes, coming close to tears. Finally he drew breath.

"You fooled me completely. Such a fine joke! You made a perfect impersonation of those savages. You sure scared Johnson. And saved his life. I was going to have to shoot him. Pinkertons don't miss their marks." McLean revealed the little five-shot Colt's revolver in his hand.

"I think he heard me well enough. He must be very drunk to look so confused."

"Well," drawled McLean, "You did speak in Apache."

"Did I?" Frazer shook his head. He had 'gone native'.

"No matter. Your meaning was clear enough." McLean walked over, looking him over. "So are you one of them now?"

Frazer shook his head. "I declined the honor, and I was running out of new stories to tell."

"Did you make a vision quest?"

Blake Tilman came tromping up the stairs and entered just in time to hear this.

He stopped at the door, all attention. "Did you?"

Frazer looked at both of their eager faces, hesitated, and then said. "I did. Not sure what I can say about it."

"Well, get out of those clothes and into your regular duds, and get that paint off your face. We'll go have a drink so you can tell us about it."

Frazer foresaw another gentle but persistent Pinkerton interrogation in the wind.

"Actually," he said, "What I would like most is a good cup of strong tea."

CHAPTER TEN

"I can not tell you everything, but I will tell you what I can," Jim Frazer said to Blake Tilman as their tea arrived, carried by one of the Negro hostesses, who regarded Frazer, still attired in buckskins, war paint, and other Apache regalia, with ill-concealed concern.

She looked at the bow and quiver of arrows hanging from the back of his chair, pursed her lips, and asked, "Would you like me to check those items for you, sir?"

"Please do not trouble yourself," Frazer said. "They are fine as they are."

The woman nodded, glanced at Tilman's Colt's revolver in its cross draw holster, and nodded. "As you wish, sir."

These were Hard Men and not to be trifled with. She moved away slowly.

The appearance of a red-haired Apache Brave, accompanied by a Pinkerton detective, sent the female customers of Mildred's Tea Room into a mild tizzy, with whispered conversations rising to a cicada-like buzzing. Two women rose and bolted for the door, but the rest, twenty or so, ordered more tea and sweet things to eat, promising Mildred's its best day ever. The women did not stare openly – that would be rude – but did continue to observe and comment to one another.

Tilman looked ironically at Frazer, who was savoring the Irish blend in his cup. "You were saying?"

"Oh, yes. Well, my trip here is sponsored by the Ethnographic Survey, and there is the matter of 'The Transactions of the Royal

Society,' where I am enjoined to publish first. That will assure my place at Trinity College."

"You could make quite a bit from American newspapers," Tilman said. "In fact, you could do a lecture tour in that get-up, and make a small fortune."

Frazer shook his head. "That I will never do. It would be the end of my academic reputation. I would be seen as a grasping money-grubbing showboat, rather than a true scholar. I do not need a small fortune, nor, for that matter, a large one. To be successful, I would be required to distort the Apache, and their society, to serve the White Man's narrative that they are savages, rather than one of the most civilized races on the American continent."

Tilman smiled. "There is that 'renegade' thing I warned you about. You have gone over to their side. Some would call that treason."

"How? I am not an American, but a Scot from Glasgow, who lectures and teaches at Cambridge in Natural Philosophy, or, as it called now 'Science'. I have pledged no allegiance, save to Queen and Country."

"Precisely our difficulty," Tilman said. "You are here, and have been among them, an infiltration no Pinkerton detective has ever done."

"Exactly. I know where my loyalties lie. This is why I refused your firm's many generous offers of employment. No man can serve two masters, save for an evil and corrupt purpose."

"Or to bring an evil-doer to justice," Tilman sounded slightly defensive. "At least that's what we tell ourselves."

"It's more than that, isn't it?"

Tilman nodded slowly, looking into his own tea. "That is the game. The satisfaction of detection and the chase: the thrill of the hunt."

"Having participated in hunting antelope, I now understand that better. Working together for the good of the tribe. Seeing your arrows strike home and true."

"By, God, sir, we are going to miss you," Tilman smiled.

"And I you. It has been a singular adventure. I was tempted to stay and become one of them. Take on a wife or two and live a simple life, with no clocks or calendars beyond the seasons. But Kicking Horse, this old shaman, said it was time for me to go. He may be the same man mentioned in Cremony's book."

"Really? He would be very old."

"He is. It's a perfect society in many ways. No kings or wealthy people, and everyone takes only what he needs. Thoreau barely scratched the surface in 'Walden Pond' about becoming one with nature."

"So Cremony got it wrong?"

Frazer shrugged. "He got much of it right, about the customs and such. Very good as a work of Anthropology, if you take away the White Man's prejudice. But if you did that, you would have to admit what has been done to the Apache and other tribes is nothing less than a great crime, far more barbaric than any they ever conceived."

Tilman was silent for a long moment as he mulled this over. "Will that be in your articles for The Transactions?"

Frazer smiled and shook his head. "In theory, a member of the Royal Society can put anything he wants there. I once found an excellent recipe for mulberry wine. But there are editors, and it will be impolitic to say so. Simply providing accurate descriptions of ceremonies and customs will be quite enough, and should be well received. Grants will be bestowed for other projects, and I will shift my focus elsewhere, trying to determine why societies so far apart all have the same myths."

Tilman was startled. "Do they?"

"The old Scottish tales match those of the Apache in several respects."

Frazer was looking for a way to change the subject. *Tilman is a very skilled interrogator. I am being led by degrees to that which I do not wish to discuss: his Vision Quest. How would I explain that, without sounding like a lunatic? Dare I even write down notes of that singular experience, that I found beyond understanding? I must, of course, while memory was still green.*

But Starmen in huge flying wagons coming from some other world? Where is my proof, save in that sacred cave no White man before him had penetrated? And it is sacred. The history of Europeans in search of wealth when it came to such was not an encouraging one. They would profane it by making it an attraction; a mockery.

Then his rescue appeared at the door in the form of Harry McLean shepherding his wife and daughters into the room. He spotted Frazer and Tilman and waved. Tilman returned a slightly ironic salute, and they came over, taking the empty table next to his. Harry's wife was a mature beauty with Italian features, and the daughters, three in number, ranged in age from twelve to eighteen, and were also very pretty. Tilman was bemused, as the wife presented her hand and, recalling his manners from another life, he stood and graced it with a brief kiss. She accepted this as her due, and favored him with a brief smile. Harry McLean got them all situated and said, "My wife Sophia, and my daughters Faith, Hope and Charity."

"Oh, Daddy, please!" said the oldest. She smiled at Frazer, taking his measure: not unlike a cat regarding a bowl of cream. "My name is Molly. That's Emily, and the brat on the end is Katherine, or, as we call her, Kate. She has about as much charity as a brick."

Kate stuck out her tongue at her eldest sister, and turned to Frazer, smiling. "Pay her no attention. She's not real kind herself. Daddy said that you'd gone rogue, so I had to come along to see for myself. Is that a real Apache bow and arrows?"

Frazer smiled. He felt charmed by them. "It is," he said.

"How did you get them?"

"In the usual way. I made them."

All three girls laughed, and then saw he was perfectly serious. Then they were open-mouthed in astonishment.

"How?" asked Emily, the middle daughter.

"I was taught how. I suppose it was part of my initiation to the tribe. I later used it on an antelope hunt quite successfully."

"You ate antelope?"

"Among other things. It takes quite a bit of strength to live that way. You eat meat every day, just to survive. White men have killed most of the buffalo, so antelope is the next best choice."

"How does it taste?"

"It's delicious. Like venison back in England."

The girls all looked at each other, unsure now. Harry McLean beamed at them with pride, and their mother smiled indulgently as she consulted the bill of fare. Kate looked him over.

"Are you going to wear that get-up all the time now?"

Frazer looked down and uttered a short barking laugh. "I think not. I like to be an observer, not part of the parade. It's part of the accepted method of observation when examining another culture. Submerge and listen, rather than make yourself known. Learn everything you can that way."

"And what did you learn?" asked Molly, very serious now.

"A great deal. It will be in the papers I present to the Royal Society."

"So you are leaving?" Emily's disappointment was obvious.

"Well, I have to. I have lectures to give, and students to tutor in the Fall. But I will stay a little time to organize my notes and write some first drafts. I also need some new clothes."

"What happened to your old ones?"

"They no longer fit. My time with the Apaches has changed my body. I am much bigger now. Thicker arms and legs, a much larger chest, and I seem to be taller."

"That's true," Tilman said. "We kept them at the office for him. He could barely get into them. Quite a transformation. We hardly recognized him."

"So what will you do?" Emily said.

"I don't know. Is there a good English tailor in El Paso?"

Tilman and McLean looked at each other.

"The matter has never come up," Tilman said.

"It's a matter for further investigation," McLean added, puzzled now. "Of course, you can buy a ready-made at any dry goods store."

"I'd rather not."

"Why not?"

Frazer leaned back, thinking for a moment. "Well, it is also anthropology. You may have heard the expression 'clothes make the man'?"

Everyone nodded.

"That is never more true than in England, where a well-tailored, bespoke suit defines your caste and position in life. And that goes back to Queen Elizabeth's time, when there were laws about it. I think you will find that true almost everywhere."

"See," Sophia said in an aside to her husband. "Now stop complaining about the expense of new dresses. We must make a good appearance, or it will bring shame on the family."

Harry McLean rolled his eyes. "See what you've done?" he said to Frazer.

Frazer chuckled. "I apologize. I was simply saying that my position, if I wish to hold it, requires me to 'look right'." He made little quote marks with his fingers.

"When you leave, may I have your bow and arrows?" Kate asked suddenly.

Frazer shook his head. "I may still need them."

"In England?" Kate looked skeptical.

"We have deer there. Some Lord of the Manor may invite me to hunt. It's a popular sport there." He saw the disappointment on her face. "How about this? I will teach you how to make your own. Then it will be yours forever."

Kate's face lit up. "That would be super! Are those hunting clothes?"

Frazer blushed. "I must confess that when you hunt the Apache way, from horseback, you are almost naked. Hunting is a rehearsal for battle, and that is the way Apache fight."

Everyone at the table stared at him. Frazer hastened to explain. "It's better tactics. Clothing slows you down, and might give an enemy a hold on you that can be used to drag you from your horse.

It's very close quarters at times. And if you fall, your enemy has a better chance of killing you."

The women were shocked. It showed on their faces. Except for Emily. She merely smiled slightly, and looked at Tilman, taking his measure.

"Could you not surrender?" Sophia asked after a moment.

"Surrender is worse than death. You would never escape the shame of it. Better to die than to be a coward and have to leave the tribe." Frazer looked skyward. "I think that is the reason I was never invited to go on a raid. They knew, being a Scot, I would do as they do, for the honor of my tribe, Clan Lovat."

Here Frazer was indulging in the lie polite. He had done so. It was one of the requirements to become an Apache warrior. It had been an exhilarating experience, but mindful of Tilman'a previous advice about renegades, not one he ever planned to share.

Looking at the avid look on his daughters' faces, McLean did not like the turn the conversation was taking. They read novels and had too much imagination as it was.

"Almost naked?" Molly looked at him and licked her lips, imagining him that way. She was transfixed, blushing at the idea.

"Just a breechclout and some war paint," Frazer admitted.

"The women, too?" Tilman asked.

"Oh, yes," Frazer said; "But people in the tribe often appear in public in a state of nature. They have no sense of shame about this. That's a Christian strategy used to repress them. Shame. You might call it indecent, but they will not understand what you are talking about. They ride that way, no saddles, to show they are not afraid, to show their power. I must say it's a very comfortable way to ride."

"The women, too? Like the warriors?" Emily suddenly spoke up.

"Some women are warriors. Among the best."

"Do not the men resent it? Taking their role?" Emily was very serious now, and Tilman saw a budding advocate for the Rights of Women. So serious.

Frazer again shook his head. "No. And for the same reason that the men have several wives. There are not enough of them now. White men have killed them off. It's all one. Survival. The same reason they made me welcome, to hear their stories and study them. So that it's all written down and will survive, even if they don't."

That sobered everyone for a moment.

"I never thought I'd find sympathy for those murdering savages," McLean said; "But that is a sad tale, indeed."

"Well, how will you proceed?" Tilman asked.

"I need to find a place where I can think and write. Someplace quiet. Just for a week or so. There is so much to sort out and to write down."

"You will refute Cremony's book?" Tilman asked.

"Only in part. Most of it is good. The politics are bad."

"Well, keep that to yourself... ," McLean said.

"You could stay with us!" Emily said suddenly.

Everyone stared at her.

"Well, why not? It's a big house. All those extra rooms, and it's almost in the countryside. Plenty of space and plenty of quiet."

McLean, to his horror, saw his other daughters and his wife warm to the idea. And what could he say, after having praised Frazer in letters and talk for so long? He was trapped by his own enthusiasm for the lad.

And so it was that McLean, a thrifty Scot who'd hoped to defray the cost of his new house with a few roomers, came to be, briefly, landlord to James George Frazer, Fellow of the Royal Society and Lecturer of Trinity College at Cambridge University. Jim to his friends.

. . .

Once he settled in, assigned a room far from the girls', with an attached parlor that held a large table, Frazer set to work. Piles of notes were written and assembled into folders. Drawings were made. Frazer also spent a lot of time staring into some middle distance, just remembering everything he had seen or heard.

A tailor was found: a former slave named Moses Gridley who had made dozens of fine suits for the Gentry in Virginia and Washington, before moving West, and who now found customers not just in El Paso, where his name was known to former Confederates, but across the border as well. Frazer had been measured, found two styles he admired from Gridley's catalog, and soon had two new suits, and something more casual for everyday wear. He wanted to fit in. He did not quibble about the price. The work was first rate, as good as anything from Savile Row in London. His old suit was sold to a used clothing shop.

And there was one other thing. Deets, the photographer, was engaged to take a portrait of Frazer in his Apache persona, on horseback. Molly and Emily were stunned when they saw him, all new muscles and not a bit of body fat, like living sculpture. It made them weak in the knees, and sent impure thoughts to their minds. But Frazer in one of his new suits, brought them back to reality. He was leaving, and they were good Catholic girls.

Or so they pretended.

Actually, both were vetted Pinkerton detectives. They had worked cases in Denver that brought them unwelcome notoriety, and were glad to get out of town and start fresh. Each owned a badge and a small Colt's ladies revolver but, for the moment, kept them out of sight. Molly had a dagger strapped to her thigh. One had to be prepared, they told him, lest she might be taken unawares.

Frazer was secretly amused when he learned this, and was careful to maintain his distance. Rose Green and Horse Woman were both fresh memories, and these girls could not compare. And he was a guest. He valued Harry McLean's friendship. Nothing improper would happen. Emily's longing looks went for naught.

Frazer found he could only apply about four hours of a day to academic work, and would ride into town in the afternoons to visit the Pinkerton office, and perhaps have tea and discuss philosophy with Tilman. He wondered if the editors of 'The Transactions' might accept an article entitled 'Among The Detectives.' When he broached the idea to Harry McLean, the detective said, "Already been done, Laddie," and handed him a copy of the book Allan Pinkerton had published the year before about the agency's "Greatest Cases."

Frazer read that, and then the book La Fayette Baker had published about his time with the Union's secret service. Much of that was about pure detective work against frauds on the Government.

"Take that one with a grain of salt," Tilman advised. "Baker was not one eager to share credit for those arrests. He did not do everything alone. Far from. His cousin Luther led the posse that arrested John Wilkes Booth."

"Really? How did you learn that?"

"I was there. A Sergeant in the First District Cavalry."

Frazer looked at him for a long moment. *What an unusual man,* he thought. *He looks so ordinary, yet has been on the cusp of history more than once. And he never brags, but throws out these episodes casually, as if anyone might have done likewise.*

Frazer was also disturbed when he learned that Emily had taken a part-time position under the name. "Emily McGraw" at a big dry goods emporium in the center of El Paso. Just another floor person among many, there to assist customers, and to discover which of the others was stealing fabric and money. It wasn't hard. When Frazer expressed some shock that McLean would use his own young daughter in a case, McLean shrugged. "She was the perfect person for that job. Too young to be suspected. And very quiet, so the information flowed to her. She wasn't there for the arrests, so is still not suspected of being a detective. It is the family business."

Sophia added, "How do you think Harry and I met? It was on a case." She smiled, and served him more of the delicious pasta she had made for the evening meal.

"It was interesting," Emily said. "I might do it again."

"But it sounds very dangerous... "

"Not as much as you living with the Apaches. Surely having consorted with warrior women, you will not tell me that I am too weak and frail for such work?"

Frazer shook his head. "I suppose not."

"I am named after the greatest Pinkerton detective that ever lived," Kate said. "Kate Warne. And she was very tough." Kate stared at Frazer a moment. "When are you going to teach me about the bow and arrow?"

Frazer held up his hands in mock surrender. "Tomorrow afternoon work for you?"

Kate concealed her excitement. "I don't know. I'll have to check my schedule."

Recognizing his own limitations, Frazer asked Jesus Martinez to join them.

"The Mexican boy from Daddy's office?" Kate objected. "What would he know about it?" She looked quite put out.

"You'll be surprised," Frazer promised. "Boys that age know a lot."

Kate came dressed in boy's clothes. And rode her horse like one. Frazer noticed she had a large knife on her belt and a small pistol. A two-barreled Derringer.

"What's that for?"

Kate shrugged. "Daddy gave it to me on my twelfth birthday. Said sometimes you get into dangerous situations through no fault of your own. Denver's a rough town. So is El Paso."

"I see."

"He told me that if I ever have to use it, to aim low for the nads and fire both barrels."

Before Frazer could answer, Jesus rode up on a beautiful brown and white pinto pony, wearing buckskins and a headband. "How are you, Learns Quickly?" he asked in Apache.

"I am well, Little Crow," Frazer replied in the same tongue.

Kate looked from one to the other, her mouth open in astonishment.

"You tricked me," she said to Frazer.

"How did I do that? I said you would be surprised. Are you?"

Kate nodded. "I had no idea you are an Apache," she said to Jesus.

"Not something Harry wants advertised. He does better with me as a Mexican."

"I see."

"I am Coyote, the trickster god," Jesus said, his face serious.

I think I already knew that, Frazer thought.

The afternoon went by quickly, and was long a golden memory for Jim Frazer. By the end of it, Kate had found willow wood for her bow and arrows, and, with a few materials Jesus had brought with him, made them functional. Jesus taught her the Hunting Walk, and how to use the wind as cover. She was able to take down a large jackrabbit. Jesus taught her how to skin it, claiming the pelt for himself. As the sun set, Kate proclaimed it her best day ever.

"So nice not to be treated like a girl who is incapable of anything," she said happily, and went to present her catch to her mother, who praised her and said that rabbit stew would be on the menu tomorrow. Jesus was all smiles when she hugged him.

Before he rode away, he leaned over and said to Frazer, "When you leave, you must be sure to return your horse to me. I will take it back to Horse Woman."

"Of course," Frazer heard a subtle reminder that he had to get on, and return to England. That his time in El Paso was done. So, a week later, he left, promising to return someday.

CHAPTER ELEVEN

About three weeks after Jim Frazer left El Paso, Emily McLean came to Blake Tilman's boarding house carrying a thick folder of papers. It was about three in the afternoon. The day was hot and dry despite threatening rain clouds overhead. Emily's demeanor was prim except for a hidden half smile. Her hair was wild and uncombed, made that way by the winds.

They met in the parlor under the watchful eye of Sookie, the Negro woman who was the cook and housekeeper. Emily had the advantage of looking older than she was, with a long face, narrow nose, very full sensuous lips, and dark brown eyes curtained by long lashes. Her body was strong and slender.

Tilman rose to meet her, somewhat annoyed that his day of study and reflection was interrupted. But he was gracious. It was hardly her fault that Harry McLean was no respecter of boundaries, and considered all Pinkerton detectives in his branch always 'on call'.

Emily got right to the point.

"These seem to be papers that Jim Frazer left behind, Uncle Blake. Daddy did not know if they have any value or should be sent on to him. He told me to ask you about it."

Tilman examined the loose pages. All seemed to be drafts of papers that Frazer planned to submit to The Transactions of The Royal Society. They were written in pencil with scratch outs, words crowded in to make a thought or phrase more clear, and erasures. A few seemed to be in some kind of code. One was a large sheet folded to a fourth of its open size, a diagram or drawing, its borders an almost perfect circle. He smoothed it flat on the brown wooden table he was using as a writing desk. Then turned it around. Emily stood up and looked at it, too.

"What is it?" She leaned closer, their bodies not quite touching.

"Some kind of chart. Probably of the night sky." He pointed at one six-pointed symbol. "I think that might be the North Star."

"Really? How do you know?"

"I was a sailor when I was your age. You learn to navigate by the stars. It's how you get home if you are out of sight of land. Otherwise, you are lost, sometimes forever."

Emily nodded. "Daddy said you would know what to do."

Tilman felt very unsure about that. Frazer had been reticent about the details of his vision quest, as he had been about the big balloon and its details, implying an obligation to keep secrets, but for whom, he did not say. Some part of the British Government, obviously, but which? The so-called Ethnographic Survey, or that never mentioned secret service that sometimes used it as cover?

Who was honest, open, cheerful – yet so secretive and hidden – Jim Frazer, anyway? It was, as was said so many times in the Pinkerton office, 'a matter for further investigation'. That catch-phrase was becoming something of a sour joke among the detectives.

Tilman touched the chart again. Drawn from memory, that most unreliable of narrators, yet very significant. And leaving behind a copy and the other notes was very careless of Frazer, who was not a careless man. There were fireplaces everywhere in the McLean house, where they could have been burned in a few minutes. Was that omission an accident? Perhaps not.

Regardless, he had them now, and must do something with them. Funds had been received from Elmer Washburn, the Chief of the United States Secret Service, for unnamed purposes, after their diligence in reporting the visit of the big balloon with Rose Green in charge of an expedition with dubious intent. The Pinkerton Agency was diligent and made inquiries after it had left

El Paso, but it could not be found. No trace on either side of the border, despite the efforts of the Army's Apache Scouts, and their counterparts similarly employed by the Mexican Government, not even a crashed vessel with the bleached bones of its crew, much less the traveling circus used for cover.

Now Jim Frazer, who might or might not be a British secret agent, had left behind documents that might or might not be another part of the puzzle. Tilman, feeling a headache coming on, groaned softly, looked up and saw Emily staring at him. He collected himself.

"Of course, you can also use a sextant to find your latitude and tell the time by the position of the sun, but that's no help if you are in the midst of a raging storm, hanging on for dear life, trying not to let the next wave sink you. Then the stars are the only friend you have."

Emily fluttered her eyelids and clasped her hands theatrically. "My, sir, you do have a way with words. You should write poetry."

Tilman rolled his eyes. She laughed.

"Seriously, Uncle Blake. What am I to do with these? Daddy say postage is too expensive. And it's not really trash, is it?"

"Leave them with me, I will see what I can make of them." Tilman rose and escorted her to the door. There he leaned over and whispered, "Uncle Blake, is it? Where does that come from?"

Emily smiled, "Well, sir, a respectable young lady would never visit a man alone, who is not some kind of relative. It would be a scandal at my school. So Uncle Blake you are, outside the office. Just a bit of cover." She reached out and touched him briefly, her eyes gone suddenly serious. "Be well, Uncle. I will take my leave," she said and nodded politely towards Sookie Grimes.

Tilman smiled. She knew the arts of deception needed by a good detective. He opened the door for her and saw her horse waiting in the street. Its reins had been dropped and touched the ground but it did not wander. Jim Frazer had trained it for her, another skill he'd acquired during his time with the Apaches. She grabbed its mane, lifted herself into the saddle, waved, and trotted off. It was not the sidesaddle polite society demanded that respectable women used and which was more hindrance than not in an emergency. Emily's long divided skirts allowed her to straddle her mount for better control. It was a small scandal at her school, but catty talk from schoolmates simply rolled off her back. McLean's daughters were the talk of El Paso. That was something that would pass. And McLean did not care.

He thought about what she had said, and wondered once more about the wisdom of Harry McLean bringing his daughters into the work. They did need female detectives, and Emily, at just fifteen years of age, was now fully vetted, with a solved case under her belt, and a Pinkerton National Detective Agency badge and a-five shot revolver in her handbag. Not an indulgence on Harry's part, nor an act of desperation. Young girls like Emily were excellent detectives because they were close observers and saw everything. Regarded as slow and somewhat stupid by most men, they disappeared from view into the background, and could go where men could not without notice. Her mother had trained her well. There was a hope that Emily could be used to assure other young women seeking employment with Pinkerton's that they would be respected. If the Branch Manager's own daughter was so employed, it had to be respectable work.

He came back to see Sookie staring at the chart, puzzled. She turned and flashed a big false smile at him. "She really your niece?"

Tilman, deciding that honesty is always the best policy when silence alone will not serve, said, "Not really. Pinkerton's is much like a family, and I'm fond of her, but she's one of Harry's daughters. Emily, the middle one."

"Thass good, 'cause she look nothing like you. More Italian than Scot."

"Her mother's Italian. Born in Milan, I believe."

"Oh. I think I know who you mean. I maybe met her at the *mercado*? Sophia? Fine looking woman. Very elegant. Surprised she do her own shopping."

"She's particular about food. Does her own cooking, too."

Sookie tilted her head, pursed her lips, and said, "You want to be careful with that one."

"Why do you say that?" Tilman thought he knew the answer.

"She flirting with you. Got eyes for you."

"She has eyes for anything in pants," Tilman said. "She's at that age."

The woman laughed long and hard. Tilman joined in.

"Seriously, I had a daughter. She would be about that age now. So a girl that age has no appeal for me. I am 'in loco parentis' with her. Some lines you never cross."

"Never, eh? Many men say dat but cross anyways. But not you." Sookie flashed her big white smile again.

"Of course not. I'm a Pinkerton."

Sookie nodded, pretending to believe him, and pointed to a symbol on the chart to change the subject. "What dat?"

Tilman bent over and looked. There were several such, aligned like a flight of birds. "They appear to be men. Warriors. Flying."

"Men flying? How? Be dey witches?" She looked more concerned than frightened.

"Perhaps. It's of something Jim saw that is said to be over ten thousand years old. Nothing for you to worry about."

"I dunno. Bible say the Earth is only six thousand years old, so how can that be?"

Tilman looked at her and saw a sly person hiding her intelligence, rather than a true believer, but this was no time for a theological discussion. And he had work to do.

"Well, probably not. It's a matter for further investigation. And if you don't mind..."

Sookie smiled, bowed slightly, and retreated out the door, leaving Tilman staring at the chart, trying to align it with what he recalled of the night sky. Finally, after supper, he went outside and looked for himself. The sky was clear and the stars bright, but the chart looked off somehow. He went back and consulted the notes Frazer had left behind. Some of the words seemed unfamiliar, and he wondered if buying a book on astronomy might help him.

Should he visit Kicking Horse, or another wise man of the Apache? He would ask Jesus in the morning about it.

. . .

That same day, Jim Frazer was seated in a brown leather club chair at a certain office in Whitehall, London, England. There were three other men, all Proctors of the Ethnographic Survey, seated in other chairs. All were well-dressed and wore beards, and Frazer was oddly relieved that he'd managed to grow his own back. He'd trimmed it that morning.

The three men, none of whom he'd met before, were all sipping from cups of tea and looking at him carefully. Not staring as if he were a specimen in a laboratory, but openly curious about him. One of them was quite old, about ninety, but still spry and able to move on his own even as his aging body shrank into itself. This just made his head look impossibly large. The other two were about forty. One was a large, robust Scot who wore a kilt of Frazer's own Clan, Clan Lovat. The other was thin, almost reedy, wearing a black suit and a clerical collar, and had a preciousness about him, an effeminate aspect that suggested homosexuality. He stopped admiring his perfectly manicured nails and spoke in a surprisingly deep voice.

"We understand you were attacked last night near your hotel?"

"I was," answered Frazer. He did not elaborate further, waiting to see where this was going.

After a moment of silence, the effeminate man raised an eyebrow, "Your attacker came off decidedly second best. He's now in hospital."

"I must remember to send him flowers," Frazer replied, sending the old man into a short coughing fit. The effeminate man looked annoyed.

"Cheeky bugger," the old man said.

The effeminate man ignored that, and continued, "Are those skills you learned from the Apache?"

Frazer shook his head. "No, on the Glasgow docks when I spent my summers there. An Apache would not have suffered him to live."

"Surprised you didn't think to take his scalp," the old man chuckled.

"Apaches don't take scalps," Frazier said. "That's for lesser tribes. But I have now accomplished another deed required to become a full-fledged Apache warrior. I have touched an enemy without killing him."

The Scot nodded, "A warriors' pride. You touched him rather hard."

The three men looked at one another, smiling.

"Your report is very complete," the old man said; "In fact, I fear it's too much so."

Frazer felt a chill. "Is there a problem?"

"Several," the effeminate man said.

Seeing the stricken look on Frazer's face, the old man leaned forward to reassure him. "We are not rejecting it. I'm sorry, do you prefer to be called James or George?"

"Actually, I've gotten used to 'Jim'," Frazier said, feeling his stomach start to clench.

"Jim it is, then."

" Oh, do relax," said the effeminate man. "You are not in any trouble. Anything but. But we'll get to that later. Let's go over some details. You will have your articles for The Transactions. The parts about myth are just first rate. No one has ever gotten that deep before. But there are some aspects we do not want to see the light of day, and which must be kept from public view."

"Such as?"

"To begin with, it must have occurred to you that your so-called 'Vision Quest' was the product of mental manipulation and some very powerful drugs. Probably cannabis and peyote. These were enhanced by sleep deprivation, starvation and chanting that threw you into a hypnotic state. You cannot think any of it was real."

Frazer considered his answer carefully. "The point of the exercise was to separate my mind from my body. It is a test of manhood for Apache warriors, and some die of it and go into the Other World."

"Yes, the Other World," said the old man. "I would like to hear more about that, since I am close to leaving this one. It would be comforting to know that such a thing exists."

Frazer shook his head. "I don't think it's 'heaven' with angels and the like," he said slowly. "Rather it seems to be simply another, much like this one, with slightly different rules. Apache myth does mention 'Starmen' who came to help them in the past, by teaching them better ways to live. The original Corn Maiden may have been one. Before she came, all they did was hunt game. And often starved. She brought them corn, potatoes and other things to grow. Part of the original tribe became farmers. Those are the Navajo. The Apache, in order to protect the tribe, stayed warriors and nomadic. They are very proud people. Most of the men die young, because they are insanely brave in battle. I met one whose tribe name is 'Always Charges The Enemy'. I was told that warriors like him often go to the Other Side to help the Fanged God with his battles."

The old man sighed. "The Fanged God? No rest for the wicked, eh?"

"And damned little for the righteous. It's a hard life. Yet, never did I feel more at peace than when I was with them. But the Fanged God seems to be fighting evil invaders, and is considered good and benevolent in many ways. This is another thing Cremony got wrong in his book. Their version of the Devil seems to be the god behind the Conquistadors, who ruined them, searching for gold they did not have."

"There was gold," the Scot said.

"Yes, but no cities built from it. That was a fantasy. And the Spanish were also on a quest for souls and brought Catholic priests who burned idols and books, so that they lost their culture, their language, and their science."

"Science?"

"They were wonderful astronomers. They knew how to work gold and copper and other metals. And the Shamanic cures that our scientists dismiss as primitive superstition actually work. Much if that knowledge has survived by being passed down through the generations by word of mouth."

"For a benevolent God, the Fanged deity seems rather bloody minded," the effeminate man said. He shuddered slightly.

"And the Christian one is not? With Christ bleeding on the cross, and all those martyrs? Our religion is soaked in blood."

"So you are still one of us. From what you wrote I'm surprised you didn't stay," the Scot said. He was frowning.

"Oh, they wouldn't let me. I was only there to record their stories. They made that plain enough. When it was time to go, they showed me the way home. I went peacefully, holding them in my heart." Frazer watched as the three of them absorb this.

"You do seem to have thoroughly assimilated," the effeminate man said. "That photograph of you as an Apache warrior, all but naked on horseback, certainly shows that. You can't really hope to publish that. It's indecent, almost pornographic."

"Maybe for you," the Scot murmured; "But going into battle naked is part of our history, as well. Sometimes we still do it. It terrifies our enemies. It says that we have nothing to lose."

The old man was amused. "Let's put that aside for the moment. We can understand that you feel an affinity for them, and feel they have been hard done by. Oppressed. In this, you are perfectly correct. They have, but the American government have made provision for them, if only they will comply."

"Reservations? A patch of bad land no one wants? When they once owned it all? That's like the card shark who, having cleaned out his victim, offers him cab fare home." Frazer felt himself flush with anger.

"True. Very true," said the effeminate man soothingly. "It's worse than that. In most cases, their land was bartered away by people who never even saw it. Their problem was the lack of a cohesive whole, an overarching political organization that could rally enough military power to resist the incursions of the Spanish. Here is what I think: I think that when the Spanish started to invade in their singular and bloody-minded search for gold, the chiefs of whatever tribe they encountered took one look, decided that they would pass the problem on to the next tribe up the river. 'You want Gold? We have none. Try the people we hate over there. They know where there is a city of gold.' And had just enough of it to convince those turds of the lie."

Frazer nodded. "That seems to agree with my own research in Madrid."

"So, the Spanish steal what they can, melt down those beautiful ornaments, and ship the bullion home, some of which we steal *en route*. Maybe there's more where that came from, we think, and start sending our own expeditions. We don't find gold, but we do find land. And tobacco, and slaves to work the land, those that don't run away. The French, Dutch and Portuguese join in the fun, and we go everywhere because we have found work for the nobility's second, third, and fourth sons as soldiers, priests and colonial administrators. They co-opt some of the natives. But there are millions of natives. With quite sophisticated governments of their own and military potential. Sooner or later, they will figure out that a man on horseback can be pulled down and killed."

"This is why the Apaches fight naked and oil their bodies. To reduce that chance," Frazer said. The effeminate man looked at him, irritated. He did not like being interrupted.

"Armor is only as good as the man inside it," he said. "But the Spanish accidentally find an even better weapon than men on horseback. One they themselves had no knowledge of. The pox. And that eliminates native military potential by killing most of them off. Those that remain are too scattered and divided to resist."

"Except they have for over 400 years," Frazer said.

"And now they are done. The Apache are at the tipping point. They will either be assimilated into the whole, or die. Whether or not it is right, or just, is beside the point. It will happen, simply by sheer force of numbers."

"I think they are prepared for that," Frazer said slowly. "My tribe, anyway. They simply do not want to be forgotten."

"And your full report will be held in the National Archives. People will be able to read it forever, but in the short term, the public version must be amended," the Scot said. "Laddie, do ye not think we Scots faced a similar fate 130 years ago? The Glorious Revolution failed, and we exported the trouble makers to North America."

"And lost part of it thirty years after. Short term gain, long term loss," the effeminate man sighed. "We simply cannot permit you to 'go native' and become an advocate for these poor people. We have an Empire now. One that controls about one fourth of the globe. You did this work on a government grant, so, that said, you have a choice. Be one of them, or be one of us, the oppressors, and yes, Britain shares in that sin – glories in it, in fact. It's how we built the Empire."

Frazer saw that his best intentions would not be enough. That he was trapped. "What am I to do?"

The old man smiled kindly at him. Frazer felt a chill go up his spine. "Go back to Cambridge and teach what you have learned, with a lack of natural sympathy if you can manage it, and avoid anything to do with that moment when you felt in the presence of God. That will only provoke imitators and controversy, and Vickie won't like that."

Vickie? thought Frazer. *Is he talking about Queen Victoria?*

"She is the head of our predominant religion, after all. The penalty for heresy is still a traitor's death. So this work of yours must not be passionate, but objective and detached. Skeptical. Like Captain Burton, you made an amazing infiltration and showed us another world."

"But not that Other World," said the effeminate man. "There is a special department that investigates such things, because the laws against witchcraft are still on the books, but it is scientific now, and simply wants to know how such a thing can be. Conveniently, they are at Trinity, and you will hear from them in due time. It is not like the Inquisition. We no longer do that kind of thing." He shuddered. "A nasty way to go, all that disemboweling and such. I wouldn't choose it."

Frazer felt himself swallow hard.

"But there are better, easier ways. Continue your research, and resist the pleas of entrepreneurs to become a public figure. We understand someone offered you a thousand pounds to do a lecture tour?"

"They did. I turned it down."

"As not enough?"

"As something not done by academics. Our work is not for public sensation."

"Very wise," the effeminate man purred. "Very wise, indeed."

The old man smiled kindly, again sending a fresh chill through Frazer's spine. "As it happens, The Prince Albert Trust for Scientific Advancement has taken note of your work, and is awarding you a grant of a thousand pounds to continue your research on myths. That comes with a public letter that calls you the Queen's 'beloved' subject. Do you have any idea of how important that is? That word?"

Frazer's mind was racing. *I've had the stick. Now I get the carrots.* He was not impolitic enough to say that aloud, suddenly aware that the old man must be an obscure member of the Royal Family if he dared to call the Queen 'Vickie'.

"It puts your feet on a path to great success," the old man continued. "Good work is always rewarded."

"Like the Apache mocassin ceremony" Frazer said.

"What is that about?" the Scot asked.

"It's for children. So they will walk through life on a path straight and true."

"May you do likewise," the old man said. "Now, there is another matter."

"Yes?"

"That remarkable hot air balloon you described in such detail, and its operators. Where did it come from?"

"They said, Italy."

"Not true. No trace of it there. Something that large could only be built in a big industrial facility, like the shipyards on the Clyde. It could not fly without being seen, and no ship calling at Matamoros carried such on its deck. Certainly, it is not something the Queen would finance privately, when she has a complete government and empire at her disposal."

"I only know what I was told," Frazer protested, his voice weak.

"It gets better. Rose Greenhow is not a courtesan. She has become a stage actress, according to that notable barrister who still manages the Confederate government in exile, Judah P. Benjamin. She was married for a time to an American army officer but he abused her. Belle Boyd, her mother's old spying colleague, who is now also an actress under the name of Nina Benjamin, took her in and showed her the trade. Judah assures me neither has ever flown in a balloon. Greenhow is notoriously afraid of heights. And Sir Percy Wyndham is once again attendant at King Victor Emmanuel's Court, but preparing to take charge of the Burmese Army for us. He still has those ridiculous mustaches." The old man stared at him, now a bit angry.

The effeminate man cleared his throat, seeking permission to speak. The old man nodded. The Scot just sat there, looking throughly confused. This was apparently something he had not heard before.

The effeminate man spoke softly. "You see, Jim, the whole thing seems made up, like one of Jules Verne's scientific romances that have become so popular. We don't think you are lying. Your text is too specific and there are other witnesses. Many, in fact, and your Mister Deets took photographs from a distance of the thing in the air. We do not know who these people are. Where did they come from, and where did they go, and how is that thing able to move so fast? These are questions we have no answers for yet — and do not want asked."

That part of his report would be suppressed. Frazer was not unhappy about that. *Give a little, get a lot,* he thought. And he wanted nothing more than to be shut of all politics and continue his research.

"Perhaps there is another world," he said. "The Shaman said more than one, laid alongside of ours, all a lot alike and each a little different. I did see Rose, my Rose, someplace, ruling the natives as a Queen. But I was drugged and starved at the time, so I can't say it's real." He shook his head. "What would you have me do?"

The old man shook his head as well. "Live your life. Do your work. Glory in her Majesty's favor in a quiet and unassuming way. You are 'beloved'. Never mistake that for licence. I do have one last question for you."

Frazer, glad that it was over, smiled and said, "Ask me anything you like."

"When you felt yourself in the presence of God – what the Apache call 'the Great Spirit' – what was that like?"

"Why," said Jim Frazer; "It was wonderful. Wonderful."

CHAPTER TWELVE

Blake Tilman stepped from the barber shop next to the new Exchange Hotel, and eyed the bright dusty street warily, blinking at the harsh morning light. It was his habit to have himself shaved daily when in town. This was not vanity, but simply a promise to himself fulfilled. A clean man by nature, he had been dirty before and would be again, but while soap, hot water, and barbers were available, he would, by God, shine.

He also purchased a hot bath whenever he was the first to arrive at the shop. This fastidiousness about staying clean was part of his nature. He carefully brushed his black wool suit every morning, as well. He thought of it as self-respect, setting a style that aided him in his work as a Pinkerton.

He was too well-dressed to be a local. But only a fool took him lightly or for a greenhorn. Men walking toward him tended to make room for him. *That is respect hard earned*, he thought, and always nodded a cordial greeting in return.

His cheeks still smarting from the bay rum, he automatically checked his new Remington .44 revolver, touching it briefly, almost tenderly. Feeling a stiffness as he slid it out of the holster, he sucked at his teeth worriedly. He'd have to work the leather more, so the four-pound weight of it would come more easily into his hand. Always ready, and often alone, his eyes scanned constantly, looking for any sign of trouble. His ears took in every sound above a faint whisper.

Drawing the lapels of his black frock coat together, and fussing with them as his eyes slowly scanned the street, he waited and then drew his silver-plated Raymond Railway watch from a vest pocket. The post office should now be open for business. Purposefully, he walked across the street, unconsciously at the same 120 steps a minute he had learned on the parade ground 14 years earlier, when he had given up the sea for a soldier's life.

William Pinkerton, who shared the management of the growing agency with his brother Robert, now that their famous father had retired, thought that El Paso had a promising future. Tilman was beginning to settle in, and the local Pinkerton enterprise was beginning to feel more like a family affair.

. . .

Harry McLean had brought his family down from Denver, and bought a huge rambling house on the edge of town. He seemed like a man who'd finally found his place in life away from Chicago's savage winters.

He'd said as much at Sunday dinner the week before. And the Pinkerton National Detective Agency was needed here. McLean made the case by stating what everyone here already knew. They could see it with their own eyes.

El Paso was now so lawless that murders and robberies frequently went unaddressed by the authorities, overwhelmed by the task of keeping the city from descending into complete anarchy. Organized less than three years before, the 'city' suffered from the overhang of the great war that had wracked the nation a decade earlier. As a place, it was hundreds, perhaps thousands of years old, and more Mexican than anything else. 'Americans' were the unwelcome newcomers.

"There is great opportunity here, Mister Tilman. Great opportunity. A bonanza awaits us. Our only challenge will be how to manage the onslaught." McLean leaned back in his comfortable chair, at the head of the long table in the dining room of the hacienda that had once belonged to an *Alcade*. Quite the nicest house he'd ever owned, he said more than once.

Tilman wondered if the expansive attitude came from the wine McLean was drinking, or he was just being happily domesticated, basking in the presence of his beautiful wife and three daughters seated on one side of the long ceramic-topped wooden table that had come with the house, and the company of his guests seated on the other. These included Captain John Pershing, of the 9th US Cavalry, and his counterpart from the other side of the border, El Capitan Emmanuel Hernandez y Hernandez DeSilva ("Call me 'Manny'," he said when introducing himself) of the Mexican Federal Police.

Manny and the oldest McLean daughter, Molly, who now ran the day-to-day business of the El Paso office, were eyeing each other cautiously. Not flirting, but interested in each other. Pershing, who Molly also acknowledged, was at that moment more interested in his food. He'd just finished another long patrol into 'Indian country' with his company of Negro troopers.

Also present was William Pinkerton's oldest son, William II, called "Bill" to distinguish him from his father – now assigned to the El Paso office to learn how to run a branch of his own. Not old enough for such a job at eighteen, but quick to learn; tall, slender and itching to go to the field.

His pretty, but dour, new wife Mary sat next to him, looking around, her nose slightly tilted, even more determined than his father to keep Bill close to the office and away from danger. A North Shore rich girl born to privilege, she was a stranger to El Paso and the detective business, and wondered at first why Harry McLean had her going to Mildred's Tea Room to listen to gossip. But she soon realized that this was a better source of business intelligence than any newspaper. So she looked and listened, and got into the spirit of it. She was envious of Emily's and Molly's Pinkerton badges and revolvers, and wanted the same for herself, and was quite put out when Harry McLean told her that these had to be earned in the field. Mildred's was not the field. Being in the field implied risk, skill, and discretion. Emily and Molly had learned these. Mary had not.

Tilman had hopes that young Bill's presence would allow him to go in search of some danger of his own. Being a 'boss' was something he abhorred. He could do it well enough, but it did not give him pleasure. Profit and loss and schedules were not engaging enough for his quick mind. He missed the field, and the challenges that went with it.

As he looked at the people at that Sunday dinner, chatting, he felt even more like a stranger, as if he were on some fresh assignment trying to discern the players in a new case. It reminded him of the society swells he'd mingled with in New York, cordial, but never really friends he could trust.

The business has gotten too big, he said to himself. *Too big for me, anyway.* And he'd come West to escape polite society. He wanted to once more be in the more natural world like Henry David Thoreau in "Walden". He quite envied Jim Frazer for having so successfully infiltrated the Apaches for his ethnographic study.

· · ·

"*I sometimes wish I had never left*," Frazer had confessed in his last letter, responding to Tilman's query about what to do with the star chart and notes that he'd left behind in El Paso. "*Please dispose of those as you wish. I have other copies and have had two papers accepted for The Transactions about Apache myths and customs. But I have been warned off publishing anything that might dispute the accepted cosmology and time line of the King James Bible. Not to be thought of. It would upset the Queen, who is of a delicate disposition since the death of her husband, and who is the titular head of the Church. Nonconformers like myself are barely tolerated now. Heretics are not. My copy of the star chart was confiscated by a mysterious government office that examines such phenomena. It seems that we no longer burn witches and may actually employ some, but the chart and the notes on the Starmen are now held within the bowels of the British Library. My remedy is to seek similar legends in other cultures far away from the Americas. To this end, I have been given another grant, and since I now also teach and lecture, I send other scholars in my stead to do the fieldwork. But I am content. I must be. My star here rises. Please extend my best wishes to everyone. Should you care for a respite from the Detective's life, I might be able to find you something here. You would be quite a novelty.*"

Tilman laughed out loud when he'd read that last sentence. Jim Frazer had been quite a novelty himself. But quickly forgotten and barely mentioned now. Life moved on, and there was work to be done.

. . .

Tilman's Eastern style of dress sometimes attracted bullies. Some in El Paso took Tilman for a drummer when he first appeared on the streets of the town. One drunken fool, misled by his new bowler hat and stiff white paper shirt collar, had called him a 'Bible salesman' as he fumbled out his old cavalry cap and ball pistol, and found himself disarmed so quickly that, for days afterward, he still could not recall the exact sequence of events that left him floundering in a horse trough full of stale water.

Later, sober, he went looking for Tilman, who was having a quiet supper in a hotel. He found him in the dining room, and, with a whine in his voice, asked for his old gun back. Tilman stared at him with cold dark eyes, then produced the weapon from a pocket of his commodious black frock coat. As the man reached gingerly to retrieve it, Tilman's hand fell across his wrist with a painful, almost crushing, grip. The man looked into Tilman's unsmiling face and shivered at what he saw there. There was no mercy in those eyes, and no anger either — just the coldness of death and the grave. His face could have been carved from stone. The pleader felt his bowels loosen just a bit.

"Come at me again," Tilman said quietly, "and I will kill you. You've been warned."

Swallowing hard, the man nodded, and was almost grateful when Tilman released his hand and turned his attention back to his food. He retreated, moving sideways like a crab, afraid to turn his back on this quiet man with the deadly dark eyes. At the doorway, curiosity got the better of him. "Say," he asked, "What is your trade? You some kind of law?"

Tilman looked up, almost surprised. "Used to be," he replied pleasantly. "Railroad detective, nowadays."

The fool gaped at him and nearly laughed, before he remembered those eyes. "Why, there ain't a railroad within three hundred miles of here," he said. "What's a railroad detective doing in El Paso?"

Tilman showed him even yellow teeth under the luxuriant brown mustache. "Been wondering that myself," he said, "But I go where they tell me."

Unable to tell if Tilman was smiling or just baring his teeth, the man touched the brim of his hat respectfully and went quickly away.

. . .

Tilman smiled at that memory. Word got around, and he was no longer troubled by drunks and bullies. He never looked for trouble or acted the bully. He found that a soft voice combined with a stern look won cooperation almost every time. Quick, unrelenting violence won the rest.

Trouble went with the job. His silent, undaunted manner and cold stare when challenged was intimidation enough. But Harry McLean's genial manner, necessary for keeping Pinkerton business, and the comfortable Sunday dinners, were eroding his edge, making him less on his guard.

He looked around the table again. It was very comfortable, but there was a hidden purpose as well, and the men soon rose and went into another room with comfortable chairs, to smoke. Manny and Pershing took chairs next to each other, looking around at the paintings on the wall that had come with the house. Dramatic battle scenes mixed with more pastoral images. McLean and Tilman took chairs opposite with young Bill Pinkerton standing near the door, and Jesus Martinez at the far end, unfolding a large piece of paper. Molly McLean, notebook in hand, sat next to him, ready to take notes. Cigars and pipes were lit and the meeting began.

McLean spoke first: "Several months ago a large quantity of U.S. gold coins and currency disappeared from the offices and vault of the Adams Express Company here. There were twelve wooden chests, bound in brass, that were removed under the cover of darkness. How, we do not know. No locks were broken, and the Adams Express guard had a sudden attack of the trots that took him elsewhere. Last month, the manager of that Adams Express office retired suddenly, and moved to Ciudad Juarez where, it turns out, he owns a large hacienda he purchased several years ago for more cash than his salary would have been over a period of years. This excited our suspicions, and we, as the security and protective agents for Adams Express, decided to inquire further. We had only rumours and supposition, and the man had taken a new identity as Don Francisco DeVega. Again, something he established over several years. He is part of a group of former Confederate officers allied with Judah Benjamin, who proposes to build a second transcontinental railway, this time across Mexico. They are also assimilating into the local Mexican political scene, as a way to gain and hold power.

"Do I have that right, Manny?"

The Mexican officer nodded. "They are part of a Mexican secret society, a Masonic lodge called the Yorkinos, after the York rite practiced mostly in England."

"The bloody Masons again," Tilman muttered, and then remembered that Harry McLean wore a Masonic pin. "That a problem for you, Boss?"

"Not my Lodge," McLean said, "And we don't tolerate criminality."

Manny continued, pausing a moment to absorb what had been said. "I'm a Yorkino myself," he said. "It's one way to advance in government in Mexico, and the reason I am already a Captain, chosen over many more senior men, but that is simply how we do things in Mexico. Favors for friends."

Pershing cracked a smile. "Should I leave now to avoid hearing things I should not hear?"

Manny chuckled.

McLean spoke quietly. "No, Captain Pershing. This is part of our contract for secret service with the U.S. Government, and you are Elmer Washburn's man in El Paso. Our plan will require the participation of you and some of your men. Captain DeSilva cannot participate in the raid we plan."

"The Yorkinos have no knowledge of the stolen gold, which was supposed to be sent on to Fort Bliss," Manny explained. "If they did, they would seize it for themselves as a legitimate prize of war. They consider themselves still at war with the United States. They want their Confederacy revived."

Tilman nodded. "The next presidential election may give them a shot at that anyway if Mister Tilden is elected. Everyone is tired of Reconstruction, and wants it to end."

"Pray for Hayes," Molly said.

"Pray for *los negroes*," Manny said. That earned him a brief smile from Molly.

"I prefer to lead Negro troops here than White ones there," Pershing added, also seeking a smile from her. "They are serious soldiers, grateful for their freedom, and committed to serving the Nation. White ones in the South are now policemen, and often brutal in their enforcement of the new laws. This has caused resistance, not just among former slave owners, but other White men who also want back the myth that has grown up about the so-called 'Lost Cause.' "

Molly favored him with a brilliant, admiring smile, obviously enjoying having two strong military men in competition for her favors. Emily, ever watchful, had her head down, and then looked up, directly at Tilman, in a way that he found a bit unnerving. It was the look a much older woman might give her secret lover.

Yet another reason to get back to the field.

McLean, deciding his daughters' love lives could wait, barged ahead. "Anyway, formal representations to the Mexican government are not going to get us the gold back. So we are going to steal it back."

Jesus Martinez stepped forward with the crude map he'd drawn.

"The house is a big one with many servants, all of whom are fanatically loyal to El Patron, except for one. A serving girl named

Elsa, who used to be his favorite. He recently pushed her aside and has a new favorite."

"Hell hath no fury like a woman scorned," Tilman said.

Jesus nodded. "He was, when he drank, very forthcoming about his embezzlements and other crimes. He was also selling information to some of the hold-up gangs."

Manny smiled. "In Mexico, if this became known, it would increase his reputation. Even the French who did not go home after Maximilian was shot, appreciate a clever man. But a clever man is not a greedy man. A clever man shares his largesse. Gives them a taste. This he has not done. So when the gold disappears, there is no one who he will be able to tell. Not without provoking an investigation."

Captain Pershing looked at the map. "How heavy are the chests?"

"About sixty pounds each."

"And they will need to be carried how far?"

"About two hundred yards. There will be a wagon waiting. Muffled wheels," Manny answered.

Jesus said, "He is planning a fiesta this weekend. All of his people will be drinking, even those who guard the room."

"Describe the room."

"It's at the end of a long hallway, only one door, no windows, full of old furniture. They will take that out to use at the fiesta. The chests are stacked at one side."

Pershing said, "That's a lot of weight. And quite a distance to walk. Can you provide security?"

Manny shook his head. "My part in this cannot be known. I am betraying a lodge brother. They would expel me, and I would lose my patronage and protection. Besides, I will be attending the event." He smiled at Molly, "Perhaps the lovely *señorita* would like to come with me?"

Her head snapped up at the unexpectedness of this. She frowned. "We'll talk later."

McLean frowned as well. He did not like this at all. But Molly was eighteen and her own person now.

Tilman smiled. "Perhaps I should go as well?"

Manny shrugged, "And bring Emily? Why not?"

Tilman thought, *Trapped, hoist by my own petard! You smooth bastard.*

McLean shook his head. "She's only fifteen."

"And you have only yourself to blame if she wants in," Molly said, "You gave her a badge and a gun."

There it was again, Tilman thought, *feminism writ large.*

Harry McLean looked as if he'd swallowed something disagreeable. He moved on. "Table that for later. How many troopers will you need?"

Pershing thought carefully. "About half my unit, but perhaps all of them; security, horses, a wagon, it's a lot to lay on."

"How much will it cost?" Manny asked.

"Silence is expensive," Pershing replied. "At least enough to get each of them that forty acres and a mule they were promised, and never got. What is your end?"

Manny looked up at the ceiling as if seeking divine guidance. "Keep it simple. One chest will stay with me. I will pay some expenses here from that."

"A clever man shares the bounty?"

"It's called '*mordida*'. The bite. One of our finer cultural traditions." Manny smiled and relit his thin brown cigar.

And so it was agreed, even the part about McLean's two older daughters attending the fiesta. The event was a coming of age ceremony for the target's oldest daughter, who was herself turning fifteen. McLean hoped that Emily would not suddenly want such a party for herself, but she never brought it up. She was Scots/Italian, not Mexican, and that birthday had already passed. Nor was she looking for a husband. A lover perhaps, but the only man who attracted her had too much rectitude to engage with her that way. Stiff as a board. The harder she tried, the stiffer he got. She needed a new way to entice him. One that did not invite scandal.

Emily McLean did not know why she was so taken with Blake Tilman. The sight of him made her breathing shallow and her heart beat faster, it was true, but Jim Frazer, especially after his transformation into an Apache warrior, had had similar effect. But Jim still had a boyishness about him, and Tilman had the kind of solid character that she admired in men like her father.

That he was so damaged by the war and the loss of his wife and daughter that he had retreated into his books and studies was a barrier that she would have to surmount. She wasn't going to throw herself at his feet. That he had responded so readily to her long kiss gave her encouragement, but was at best a beginning. The matter was not resolved.

She had grown up with war and tragedy, as a Pinkerton girl from the start. Transcendentalist principles informed her life. Not just the mysterious writings of the Bhagavad Gita and the Kama Sutra and other oriental philosophies, but the quiet radicalism of Emerson, Thoreau, and other giants of the American movement. From that had grown Abolitionism, and from that the Underground Railroad.

From the outside some of it looked quite silly. There had been communes where men and women tried to live without rules about fidelity, breaking social norms. All failed. Conversely, the nudist summer camps sponsored by the poet and building contractor Walt Whitman were where she learned to not be ashamed of her body or repelled by those of others. And to touch and be touched, without excitement or shame of either sex, while maintaining a sense of one's self that protected virtue. Even in that closed society, one had to maintain a distance from those who might take advantage, such as Bronson Alcott, or his lesbian daughter. One learned the signs by close observation, and smiled politely at unwelcome overtures. As for force, Eastern religion had an answer for that, too: fighting techniques that could disable someone in an instant. And Whitman was a bear of a man who would crush anyone foolish enough to break his rules.

Emily missed those summer meetings. In Denver, one had to observe the local mores, and so it was also in El Paso. Dancing at midnight in a moonlit meadow was different. It was Magick. A women's ceremony intended to heal the damage from the war.

Finding suitable lovers, much less a husband to spend one's life with, was a problem. Molly was more eager than she. She took more risks. Emily saw little point in boys her age. Or Molly's. She felt no desire towards most men, even other Pinkerton detectives. Most were too stupid and brutal. The ones with refinement usually preferred other men, something that anyone who knew Walt Whitman could not be surprised at. So this was a quandary for Emily McLean until the day she met Blake Tilman, and felt her face flush and her heart beat faster. Age difference be damned, this was the man for her.

But how to proceed? A question that she pondered as she played her violin or worked on the Branch accounts and billing, or went for long rides in the country alone. Blake was a mystery. Until her mother taught her some spells and meditations that allowed her to see the situation from above and clearly.

In later years, Blake would say that she had bewitched him. He didn't know the half of it.

. . .

The raid went smoothly. Men as black as the night itself entered the huge hacienda, went quietly and invisibly to the target's strong room, removed the chests, left as silently as they had come, without violence, and carried the chests to the waiting wagon.

That rolled away to where a coach was waiting. The chests were transferred by another party of silent black men, and the coach rolled away over the border without any kind of escort. That might have attracted unwanted attention from Manny's men, who patrolled the invisible border that no one recognized.

On the other side, young Bill Pinkerton received, and in front of the new local Adams Express manager, counted 120,000 dollars in gold coins and US currency recovered by the Pinkerton Agency for that company. Ten chests in all. Armed Pinkerton guards now protected the El Paso Adams Express office around the clock.

Young Bill Pinkerton was their supervisor, and they had learned not to take him lightly. Dundee, Illinois, was also a rough town. He had the social polish learned from two years at Princeton College back East, but had also knocked one of them to the ground with a single blow in a dispute over pay. The boy could hold his own, they agreed.

CHAPTER THIRTEEN

Bill Pinkerton was learning the difference between 'legal' and 'right'. Reading his grandfather's accounts of the Agency's most famous cases, educated him in how tedious the work could be. The measures needed to bring even one criminal to justice were daunting. And while he ached to be part of that raid, he also realized it was the last thing a member of the Pinkerton clan could be caught up in. His work with the Agency had begun when he was fourteen as a clerk in the Chicago office, handling the billing of hundreds of hours of guard time for the railroads and other big firms. This, his father assured him, was the future of the company. The detective business, as glamourous as it was, made up a smaller percentage of billings every year, and was retained only for the publicity it generated.

One of the members of the infamous James gang had been killed two years before by two Pinkerton detectives who, rather than storm a heavily defended house, had thrown a hand grenade instead, killing everyone inside. Such ruthlessness was widely appreciated. It drew in more business.

Bill Pinkerton felt himself ready for such adventure. No one else did, and his wife cried openly at the thought of her man in such danger. While he did his present job well, he chafed at the restrictions it carried.

Mc Lean's daughters were detectives now! Except for Kate, who seemed to be learning Indian ways from Jesus Martinez, who actually seemed to be a real Apache brave as well, even though he was just Kate's age.

The two went hunting together sometimes, on ponies borrowed from the Pinkerton contract stable. While McLean seemed bemused and a bit perplexed by this, his sophisticated Italian wife made no objection, and even seemed to approve. "It's part of her education," she told McLean, "And that boy is still very much a boy. Like a brother to her. She's perfectly safe. He will defend her with his life, if he has to."

McLean was, after all, a detective, and his blood had come up when Kate mentioned that, because the day was so hot, the two of them had cooled themselves with a swim in a little creek, and then dried off by sunning themselves on the grass, Apache style. Kate's clothing was dry when she said this in the most casual way, and he realized that she and Jesus were naked with each other.

"You have an evil mind," Sophia said, when McLean brought this up.

"I do. It's how I make my living."

"They are as innocent as Adam and Eve in the Garden" Sophia said.

"And we know how that ended, don't we?"

But Kate had two things in her favor. She was too smart to gossip, and no desire to become an Apache squaw. And her time had not come yet — that monthly ritual of pain and blood all women must endure. She took note of the struggles her sisters had, trying to figure out men, but did not join in, even to tease them. The McLean girls were not amenable to teasing. They knew their place in the world, and were very serious.

Bill Pinkerton knew this, and had a wife to satisfy his own desires. He watched the McLean girls carefully, so he could learn from them. They all seemed to have some mysterious power over men.

Molly had both Manny, and John Pershing, courting her, playing off one against the other in a friendly rivalry. Emily went to the fiesta on Blake Tilman's arm, introduced as his niece, which the Mexicans misinterpreted as the usual term a man might use when introducing his much younger mistress. Tilman was troubled by this, and the winks and nods it produced. Emily simply smiled, looked up at him adoringly, and held his arm tighter.

Bill Pinkerton was also thinking about something else he had seen....or had it merely been a dream? Walking between guard accounts at night, he had cut through a patch of cottonwood trees and seen a remarkable thing in a near-by meadow. A group of women in a circle under the full moon, dancing silently. All of them naked. He stopped to watch and caught the sounds of low chanting as they moved, stepping sideways, arms upraised. And while they were too far away to see clearly, he thought that among the brown and even black faces were white ones; some of them very much like McLean's wife and three daughters. He felt a thrill of fear, certain this was not something he was supposed to witness. It aroused him, and that was even more disturbing.

He completed his rounds, and reflected upon the thought that even six months into his marriage, he had never seen Mary completely naked. Too much the prude, she was, still laboring under the illusion that such things were, of themselves, sinful. Even in bed, she wore a cotton nightgown, and forced him to fumble through it with his hands to find her. This was not how the business was done, he well knew. When he turned fourteen, his father had taken him to the best brothel in Chicago, and turned him over to a lovely, exciting, older woman for 'a course of instruction.'

"A detective had to know these things," William said with a wink, "because you never knew where the Work would take you. A good one was always prepared."

But Mary was still a mystery he had not solved. Her natural modesty and religious upbringing made her regard McLean's wife and daughters with ill-concealed disapproval. They were too free, too easy with men. Not 'proper' ladies.

"Where do you think we are?" Bill asked her. "What do you think we do? We're detectives, and we deal in facts without the shade of false morality. We take others as they are, not as we might wish them to be. Stop judging, and learn to see, really see, what is happening."

And that night Bill Pinkerton, still aroused, went home, undressed not just to his underwear but his skin, pulled his reluctant wife from their comfortable bed, lifted her nightgown over her head, ignoring her protests, until she was naked, too, and admired her generous figure and full breasts. She tried to cover herself. He pulled her hands away, and shoved her back on the bed. She stared at him, dazzled.

"Are you going to rape me?" she cried.

"Never," he replied. "I am going to make love to you properly." And then added a religious twist. "We will be like Adam and Eve in the Garden."

" 'The Song of Solomon' would be a better choice, if you are going to quote scripture," Mary said with a giggle. "What took you so long?"

Of course, Bill Pinkerton said nothing about this to anyone, after a night of furious lovemaking that had Mary singing to herself, and smiling the next morning as she prepared breakfast, still naked. "It was very hot," she said.

He arrived at the office late, and, after writing his report of his rounds the previous night, took Tilman aside and asked about the dancing women. Should that be in his report?

"It's an ancient harvest and fertility rite," the older man said. "None of our business. And anyone you thought was there would deny it, and then hold your intrusion against you. It's the Old Religion, before Christ. Let it go."

And so he did. It seemed to have healed his faltering marriage, and made his stiff young wife more pliable. What the Pinkertons did was not always legal, or what others thought of as moral, but they always tried to do right. The path to that was not always clear, but they did try.

. . .

Entering the post office the following morning, Tilman saw the new clerk on duty: an older man, grey now and wearing a new pair of spectacles, whom he quickly recalled from an earlier life. One of the ring of Maryland postmasters working for the South during the War. It took barely a second for the memory to come back. Tilman never forgot a face, but the War was ten years behind them, and the Amnesty Act was passed in '72. The old fellow looked at him quizzically, as if trying to place him, and asked, "Help you, suh?" An accent more Virginia than Baltimore.

"Any mail for Pinkerton?"

"Got a whole pouch, but you'll have to sign." Shifting the chaw of tobacco in his mouth, the clerk reached under the counter and pulled up a half-full canvas bag. On top of it, he put a large book covered in green canvas, and opened it to a page half filled with entries.

"That third one, there," he said, and offered a pen dripping with ink. Tilman swiped it once on the blotter paper to remove the excess, and signed neatly and precisely.

"Anything for Blake Tilman?"

"Why, yes. Got a package — no, two." The clerk turned aside to a wooden case sectioned with large square cubbyholes. He pulled out two rectangular objects wrapped in many layers of brown paper. "Books, I'd guess."

"Yep," replied Tilman; "That they are."

"You a teacher on the side, Detective?" the clerk asked, "That what the books are for?"

Tilman folded the canvas mail bag over the books. "Nope," he replied. "Why, you writing one?"

The clerk shrugged. "Just making conversation. You're a curiosity to folks here."

Tilman stopped halfway to the door and turned. "And why is that?"

"Railroad detectives where there ain't no railroad? It does raise some speculation."

Tilman realized that the question was not going to go away. It would be worried at and asked again and again, until a satisfactory answer was given. Being of a curious nature himself, he did not resent that quality in others; while he liked to keep his own counsel about business, he saw no harm in devising a reasonable explanation. He spoke politely. This old gossip would repeat whatever he said to the post office's many customers.

"Well, Mr. Pinkerton is a forward-looking sort of man. There's no railway yet, but one day soon, there will be. They're surveying the right of way even now from Amarillo to Lubbock, and the Union Pacific is headed in from the other direction. Besides, the fellows that like to hold up trains tend to head this way, looking to get over to Ciudad Juarez and spend their ill-gotten gains on whisky and loose women."

The clerk nodded, listening carefully. "That Pinkerton fellow was a friend of old Abe Lincoln, I hear."

He spit carefully into a brass spittoon, a big brown glob. Tilman's pleasant smile faded like a snowflake on a hot griddle.

"Some of us are trying to put the war behind us," Tilman said quietly, "and you, Mr. Perkins, would be well advised to follow suit."

The clerk stiffened. He turned pale, and said with a slight tremble in his voice, "My name is Harris."

"No, it's not," Tilman replied. "You're Jebediah Perkins, of Andover, Maryland — and the Amnesty of '72 does not pertain to those who aided and abetted the escape of John Wilkes Booth."

Blood drained from the man's face. "I don't know what you're talking about!" he protested. His voice was high and shrill, as he looked around the office to see if anyone else had heard the deadly accusation.

"Since you want to know everyone's business so badly," Tilman continued, his voice now tinged with anger, "Then you should know that I rode with Luther Baker the night Booth was hunted down. First District Cavalry, Mr. Perkins, under General La Fayette Baker, the scourge of traitors everywhere."

Tilman walked back to the counter and leaned over. "The only reason you didn't hang with the rest, Perkins, is that we found out you were too damn drunk to do anything to help Booth."

The old man staggered backward and leaned weakly against the wall.

"In the future you will not talk trash to me about President Lincoln, or President Grant, and you will mind your own business, and not inquire into mine. Are we agreed?"

The clerk nodded, close to tears now, miserable.

Tilman felt a tinge of remorse. Like a common bully, he had brought a man low for no good reason. Worse, he had broken his own promise to himself to think no more on the War. With a curt nod, he turned and walked out of the post office.

With the same brisk military stride, he walked the two blocks to where the Pinkerton National Detective Agency had its new office over a dry goods store.

He went up the stairs at a rapid pace, the mail pouch over one shoulder and the books under his left arm. Every sense he had strained to detect an ambush, but there was none. He paused, opened the door, and went into the office that took up half of the second floor.

Inside the office were four massive roll-top desks with two wooden chairs apiece, arranged for easy conversation. A rack of rifles and shotguns was mounted near one of the three windows. The arrow that Jim Frazer had shot into the far wall was still there as a sort of memorial. A large wooden table with a green baize cover left by a previous tenant stood near the center of the room.

At the cast iron stove in the center, Harry McLean stood, trying to pour hot coffee into a tin cup without burning his hand. He did not succeed, and swore loudly. Tilman dropped the mail sack on the center table and, fingering out a key from his watch pocket, unlocked his desk.

"Morning, Mr. Tilman," Harry McLean said. "What have you there?"

"Books."

"More books? You are the readingest man. What is it this time?"

Tilman unwrapped the brown paper packages carefully. "Politics, I suppose. Englishman named Marx — except it was originally published in German, and I've had to wait for a translation. Something about capital."

"Sounds dead boring," McLean said, with a slight burr that betrayed his Dundee origins, "Don't even like the kind of politics that they have in Chicago. What's it about?"

"The Money Power, I reckon."

"You a Radical now, Mr. Tilman?" McLean asked lightly, but his eyes were sober and doubtful. The Pinkertons were now employed mostly by very large businesses.

Despite their founder's past as a Chartist in England, they currently favored established institutions, and took the "National" part of their title very much to heart. More men were employed by Pinkerton as guards and detectives than were in the current U.S. Army. In addition to their pursuits of robbers and thieves, they were also engaged in a constant running fight with agents of the International. The communist labor movement that had originated in Germany, France, and England, was finding favor among discontented workmen in the United States.

In one of Tilman's previous assignments, he'd infiltrated several nascent groups forming in the Pennsylvania coal fields. He'd been too successful with one group, and was arrested and beaten by Pinkerton operatives ignorant of his true purpose. Furious, he had resigned — only the intercession of one of Pinkerton's sons, Robert, brought him back. Still, the memory lingered. And then Harry McLean had asked lightly, "You a Radical now?"

Every Pinkerton employee was constantly a probationer, and he and Harry McLean still, after all these months, hardly knew each other. He smiled easily. "No, Mr. McLean, I am not. But I learned when I was in Federal service that one must always know the enemy, and attempt to apprehend his motives."

McLean nodded thoughtfully, "You're a deep kind of fella, Mr. Tilman, that's sure. And the other? Aristotle or the like, I suppose?"

"No, sir. Not at all. It's Mr. Twain's new novel, 'The Adventures of Tom Sawyer'."

"Haw!" McLean exclaimed, and blew on his coffee. "I might enjoy that one meself. Well, enough of this," he said. "What's in the mail?"

"I'll dump it out," Tilman said, carefully locking his desk with the precious books inside.

McLean snapped his fingers. "Damn me! What's the time?"

Tilman consulted his watch once more, "Nearly nine. Why?"

"I found us a new man. He's coming in this morning to get situated. A real Johnnie Reb. Fastest man with a gun I've ever seen."

"Oh?"

"Usual dispute over cards. If a fellow plays well, some drunk will accuse him of cheating and draw down."

Tilman started to sort the large brown manila envelopes inside. They contained wanted posters for men who had robbed trains or otherwise gotten a price put on their head by a Pinkerton client. A fresh batch arrived from Chicago every week.

"So he shot a man?"

"Nay, laddie, he did not, although the other fellow hadn't cleared leather when he found himself staring down this fellow's gun barrel. No, he disarms his man, asks me to hold their sidearms, and then invites him to settle the matter outside with their fists."

"Interesting. Not bloodthirsty, then?"

"Hard to say, Mr. Tilman, because there was blood aplenty before it was over and done. No, the Reb beat him like a dog, and never got so much as a spot on himself while he did it. Fought him like a Chinaman, feet as well as fists. Man cried out for his mother before it was done. He'll not be the same again. Crowd started out boisterous and all, but by the end all you heard was the thunk of meat being beaten, like in a butcher's shop. Got, oh, so quiet." McLean shook his head at the memory, saddened.

Tilman paused a moment, trying to read him. They hadn't worked together before being sent here to open the new branch office. McLean preferred to talk his way through an assignment. In fact, Tilman thought him a bit too fond of the sound of his own voice, and was looking forward to working a case again, in the field, far away. He needed a partner for that, and a suitable hire had yet to appear and apply for the work. McLean's description of the new recruit was less than encouraging.

"Letter here from Chicago, Mr. McLean," Tilman said. "Why employ such a brute, then?"

"Because he's not. Just full of that prickly over-developed sense of personal honor that some Rebs carry around with them. Bought him a drink, and found out that he's not just tough, but smart. Attended college before the War. Rode with Jeb Stuart, and before that Turner Ashby under Stonewall Jackson, and then was in Europe at the end, working for Judah P. Benjamin."

They looked at each other, both thinking that Benjamin's name was coming up a lot lately, and that this man might be one of his active agents for a Rebel government far from dead, sent to infiltrate their office. Likely, McLean's Masonic pin had been seen as something that made his approach easier.

"Secret Service?" Tilman's face was thoughtful.

"Blockade runner, I suppose. Claims he knew Belle Boyd personally."

"Do tell," Tilman said. He did not think much of the South's most notorious spy. He'd read her book, and found it fanciful. General Baker could have told him whether it was all true, but... Baker was dead now, like so many others.

"Well, Miss Belle was a tribulation to us ... "

"That she was," said a soft slow voice behind them. Both Tilman and McLean jumped and sought their weapons in surprise. They aimed them toward the doorway.

A slim, elegantly dressed man with dark hair and deep-set blue eyes stood there. He raised his slender white hands in mock surrender. "Really, gentlemen, I come in peace."

"Jesus!" said McLean, blowing air through his lips like an exhausted horse. "How did you do that? Those stairs creak and give warning. I took this place for just that reason."

"Something I picked up from an Arab I knew in London," the stranger said, crossing the room as he held out his hand to Tilman. "How do you do, suh. I am Ashley Portier and I understand we'll be working together."

Tilman slipped his revolver back into its holster, and accepted the hand, found its grip strong but not oppressive, and smiled easily in return. He looked carefully at the man's knuckles which seemed unmarked by any recent fight. *More feet than fists, then. A dirty fighter who didn't fool around with false courtesies. but just got the job done.* Tilman liked that. He accepted violence as a necessary part of the job, but took no joy in it and avoided it as much as possible.

"It seems so, Mr. Portier. You do make quite an impression on people."

"It's my devil-may-care ways, I suppose," Portier smiled. "But please do not think me unequal to the tasks at hand. After the unpleasantness last night, I have decided to leave off card playing for a bit. Unfortunately, Lady Luck has left me somewhat short of funds, so when opportunity arose... "

He's like a character in a play, Blake Tilman thought, charmed almost against his will. He found himself liking the tall Southerner almost at once. He did not like many people. Portier looked like any other card sharp, down to the fancy gold brocade of his vest and his string tie, but there was nothing shifty in his manner. Tilman noted with approval that his nails were clean and well-trimmed, and his hands bore the calluses of honest work.

McLean handed Portier some papers to fill out and a thick stub of pencil. He and Tilman directed their attention once more to the mail.

"Well, lookee here," McLean said a few minutes later; "Parker Boone has escaped from prison again. Old friend of yours, I believe, Mr. Tilman?"

Portier listened with bright-eyed interest.

"That's true," Tilman looked at the flyer. He glanced over and saw that Portier had stopped writing. An explanation was expected.

"Right after the war, I was a U.S. Marshal for a bit. Parker was with that last bunch who surrendered after Mr. Lincoln was killed. Louisiana boy. One day he decides that the War ain't over and takes a Union payroll meant for the occupation forces. Tracked him down, got most of it back — which was the important thing — and saw him off to the Federal penitentiary up Kansas way. He escaped about two years later, and immediately robbed the southbound Katy to Amarillo. By that time, I'd signed on with Pinkerton, and being familiar with his ways, it fell to me to track him down again. This time he got ten years, on top of the five he was already serving."

"Sounds like quite a rascal," Portier commented. "Is he dangerous, or just stupid?"

"Oh, I don't think that Parker has a mean bone in his body," Tilman replied. "It's just that he don't think things through. I was sorta hoping that prison would settle him some."

"Stupid, then."

"Smart enough to break out of two very tough joints," McLean said sternly, "Don't underestimate him."

"Stupidity, in the absence of an evil and perverse nature, is the inability to learn from experience," Portier replied, and bent to his writing again.

McLean looked at Portier and then at Tilman, sighed, shook his head, and said, "I can tell that the two of you are going to be great friends. You'll have to go after him again, Mr. Tilman. Much of the loot from that last robbery is still outstanding, and he'll undoubtedly go straight to it. I can't say I like the idea of you tracking him alone, so take Mr. Portier along, and show him how we do things. There is a reward to be shared, if you catch him."

He turned over the letter from Chicago in his hands. "There is also this other matter. Mr. Derek Seaton, who is the heir to a considerable Chicago fortune, apparently came down to Texas to get some experience of life after his time at Harvard College, and has inconveniently disappeared. Perhaps he has fallen madly in love with one of the local *señoritas*, perhaps he's in some other difficulty, but William directs that we dispatch someone to find him with all possible speed, the family having paid a sizeable retainer for this service — with more to come if the young man can be delivered home more or less intact."

"How does that fit with hunting for Parker Boone?" Tilman asked peevishly. "We don't need to be lugging a spoiled rich kid along with us."

"Well, Mr. Seaton is of age, can ride and shoot, but — no, if you find him, you are directed to get him to a telegraph so he can send word home, then try to get him to go home. Parker Boone will take second place to this matter."

Tilman shrugged, "As you will, then, Mr. McLean."

"You'd better get some kit for Mr. Portier, and see to the horses. I will handle matters here," McLean said. "And have his photograph taken for our files."

Portier's head came up like an interested hound's.

"Photograph?"

"Company policy. We have hundreds of men and quite a few women working for us as detectives and operatives. Some of the work is secret, and we've a few instances where an undercover operative was arrested and beaten." McLean could not help but look at Tilman when he said this. "So we have everyone's image made and circulated to all the branch offices."

"A very wise policy," Tilman said dryly. How much did McLean know about what had happened to him in Pennsylvania? He was from the Chicago office and claimed to be related to the boss, but had he been told?

Portier nodded and went back to filling out the forms. Tilman wondered if the Southerner might be wanted someplace for some crime. It had happened before. Hiring, especially at branch offices, had been lax. Some fugitives had been found in the ranks, especially among the female staff, many of whom came from the Demimonde: the floating world of prostitution found in every major city during and since the Civil War. Such men and women often had useful connections in the criminal underworld; since the main business was protection of lives and property, rather than rigorous law enforcement, such discoveries were often ignored. Expediency ruled the day.

Tilman did not like it, and resolved not to be too charmed by his new partner. His charm might be simply a mask hiding his true nature. Only after some time in the field would he really know this man. He looked at Portier. "Any questions?"

"Just one. Where do we look first?"

Tilman consulted the papers that had come with Boone's new wanted poster. "We'll ride out toward Esperanza. The information is that Parker was headed that way. Young Mr. Seaton was somewhere in that area as well."

"Could be a long ride," Portier said gravely.

"You game?"

"Always. I took the Queen's shilling, as it were, from Mr. McLean last night to settle my hotel bill." Portier rose gracefully from his chair; "Therefore, lead on."

CHAPTER FOURTEEN

Ten days later, they finally set forth. The time between was mainly spent on gathering supplies, with Ashley Portier trailing along in Blake Tilman's wake like a bright and interested tourist. Ashley's traps were examined and sorted, with much put aside as impractical and unnecessary for the journey ahead.

The agency advanced funds for a new Winchester repeating rifle, and a brace of new Remington Army revolvers in the same .44-40 caliber as Tilman's own guns. Tilman would carry a shotgun as well, for close work. Portier's converted Colt Dragoon would be left behind, as would his fine Arabian horse.

"Indian ponies are what's needed for this job," Tilman advised. "This one'll founder in the heat."

"The breed was made for the desert," Portier objected. Like all Southerners, he considered himself an authority on horseflesh.

"But not this desert," Tilman replied. "An Ay-Rab does his heavy work with camels, I've read, and we've none hereabouts. I propose to travel light, but we'll need to pack our food, for there's no time to hunt game. And if we run into trouble, we'll need mounts that can run all day if need be." Tilman patted the black satin coat of Portier's horse. "He's a fine animal, but the mustang is part mountain goat, and we'll see our share of high ground before this is done."

Portier smiled that easy smile he had, and shrugged. "It seems that I will be well schooled by you, Mr. Tilman. You must have been a sergeant during the War." Portier struck a match and lit yet another one of the thin black cigars he favored.

Tilman looked up, unsmiling, in the measuring way that usually unnerved people. "Aye, that I was," he said, "How did you know?"

"I led a troop of cavalry, suh, and was officer enough to value sergeants. That was in the first part of the War."

Tilman nodded, acknowledging the compliment, and then consulted a pocket notebook. "Then you'll know that I am a great one for lists and the like. We'll take flour, salt, a can of baking powder, coffee, beans, jerked beef, a small amount of bacon, and eight large canteens for water. A pannier of grain apiece for the horses, because often there's nothing for them to eat but sand and rock. A hundred cartridges apiece for the guns, beyond what's in the belts and cylinders. A good knife apiece, a shovel, cooking gear, and a large piece of canvas."

"Ample," Portier commented, reached under his coat and drew forth a Bowie knife of fearsome size. "Made by ol' Jim Black himself. I trust it will do?" He offered it handle first for Tilman's examination.

Tilman hefted it gingerly. It looked wicked and had been well used. "You shave with this?" he asked, deadpanned.

Portier smiled. "When need be, yes, I do." He rocked back on his heels as he took the knife and put it carefully back in its brass-bound sheath. "I would say that we are amply provided for, Mr. Tilman."

"You might not think so if we run into Apaches."

"I thought they'd been rounded up?"

"Well, that's what the Army likes to tell folks, but I've been in the Army. Ain't all that much they can do with just two regiments of cavalry, and the Border is close. Some tribes refuse the Reservation. They doubt the Government's promises."

Portier looked at him thoughtfully. "It promises much and delivers little, either in the North or South. What about bandits?"

"Bandits, Apaches, not much difference between them, except I understand the bandits better."

Here Tilman was running a bit of a bluff, and repeating something he had heard a fellow boarder say at dinner one night. He was, if the truth were told, almost as much of a greenhorn as Portier. His conversations with Jim Frazer gave him context but not experience, and while Jesus Martinez was a useful asset, he was not yet a Pinkerton, and might never be, since he seemed to be scouting them as much as he scouted for them. The boy was a mystery still, and less of a boy now, having shot up several inches in height over the summer. If his grandmother was a Bruja, then what was he? That unasked question troubled Tilman and McLean both.

If Portier had caught on to Tilman's bluff, he was very good at concealing it. Or maybe just too polite to say so. A small silver flask of liquor touched his lips at regular intervals, and that might have taken some of the edge off him. This was an issue to settle before they left.

"I have a Sharp's trap door rifle, .45-70, that may be of use," Portier volunteered.

"If you can use it to advantage," Tilman said, "then bring it."

"Oh," said Portier, "I'm not much good with it beyond a half mile or so."

Tilman smiled, "That so?"

Portier raised an eyebrow, "Do I hear doubt in your voice, suh?"

"I've never known a drinking man to be that steady."

Portier smiled and looked away. "I do sometimes shave myself with that knife," Portier said. "'Tis the drink that steadies me, and sustains me, suh." He wondered if that would be an issue between them. "I note that you yourself do not indulge."

"I'm Temperance," Tilman replied. "It was a promise to my wife."

Portier, for once, did not smile, for he heard the pain behind the words. He waited.

"She died of the fever," Tilman said at last, softly releasing a sigh. "While I was at Gettysburg."

"A Christian lady?"

"She was. We had a daughter, as well. The fever took her, too."
Tilman looked at the ground. Portier found himself liking the man.

"I, too, lost a love," he said softly.

Tilman gazed at him, once more taking his measure. Their male
comedy of manners had suddenly taken a turn towards tragedy.
Tilman shook himself like a cat. He turned away.

"We'll need long linen dusters for the journey. It does blow up
there something fierce and we need to keep our clothes as clean
as we can."

"Yes, of course," said Portier, as they walked back toward the
Pinkerton office. "Perhaps the dry goods place will have such."

Tilman nodded, distracted. He saw Molly and Emily McLean
walking together in the distance, their heads together. They seemed
to be laughing.

"Look here," he said at last; "The drink's your own business, as
long as you keep it in bounds. I won't have a man under me who's
not ready at all times, but — if you feel the need — neither will I
judge you harshly. I do not put my ways on others."

"I appreciate it, suh. I am not a heavy drinker, as these things
are measured, but I am a constant one. It deadens the pain of
my loss."

Tilman stared at him again, but Portier was not daunted.

"If a man neither drinks nor smokes, what consolations does
he have?" Portier asked. "Ladies?" In El Paso that term covered a
lot, from the Demimonde to what passed for high society.

Tilman shook his head, "No. I'm still a married man in my
heart."

"Ah." Portier was genuinely puzzled. He was about to embark
on a long, potentially dangerous journey with this man, and could
not find his measure. "What then?"

"I read." Tilman saw no profit in disclosing his education to
someone he hardly knew.

"Ah," Portier said, understanding at last. "My friend Captain
Burton was a great man for reading. English fellow I fell in with in

London. Went down to Egypt and then into Africa with him once. Damnedest man I ever met, Mr. Tilman. Had the gift of tongues."

Tilman tilted his head quizzically, obviously interested.

"Some men learn a language. Burton inhales them like the air around him. Claims he learned most of them in bed, and I never did see such a man for the ladies. Has some very curious views about them as well. He's by way of being a bit of a spy, you see. Once lived in the Bazaar like a native, and was the scandal of his regiment, but a great man. Went down to Mecca and became a Muslim."

Tilman shook his head. "That's bold. He should write a book on that."

"He did. I may have it still, since he signed one to me."

"I'd like to read that," Tilman said.

"I'll bring it along. If I can borrow your new Mark Twain novel in return."

"Done and done," said Tilman, happy again.

"I did enjoy his 'Innocents Abroad' — quite the wit."

"You might want to bring another as well," Tilman said; "I propose to rest up in the heat of the day. It's easier on the horses, and us. The Mexicans know a thing or two with this *siesta* of theirs."

"Yes, study the customs of the people of the land," Portier commented. "Burton taught me that."

"What became of him?"

"He went off into the interior on a survey. He's the fellow found the source of the River Nile before the War. Invited me along, but I went on to India instead."

"You've wandered far," Tilman said, with a tinge of envy in his voice.

"I have," Portier said. "Didn't seem much point in coming back here after the War. I get down to New Orleans, and I'll have truly been around the world."

"Think oF that!" Tilman exclaimed, excited at the idea. He surprised himself with his unexpected enthusiasm, and felt embarrassed for a moment. Burton's name was one he'd heard before. From Jim Frazer of the Ethnographic Survey. *Should I tell McLean? Portier is a Confederate officer, knows Benjamin, and could be part of some plot of his. Or is he just a wandering soul trying to get home? The only way to find out is to see what happens in the field. That is the true test of a man's mettle*, he told himself; *or am I just anxious to get away from El Paso, and the complication of Emily McLean, who I like more than I should or is proper, even by Unitarian Transcendentalist standards?*

At that moment, Harry McLean came bustling along, carrying the mail. "You fellows haven't left yet?"

"No," Tilman replied, "We'll leave at first light."

"Stop by the office first. You may want to keep an eye peeled for that fellow Harris from the Post Office. Seems he absconded with the petty cash in the middle of the night. Postmaster is real put out about it. Bound to be a reward for bringing him in."

"Really?" Tilman commented, and said no more.

"Already got a flyer done up on him. You take it along with the rest."

Portier took it from McLean, looked at it briefly and folded it up, putting it inside his coat pocket. He touched the brim of his hat.

"I'll meet you in the morning at your boarding house, if that's all right," he said to Tilman. "I have some business to attend to."

He walked off, leaving Tilman and McLean looking at one another.

"Well," McLean demanded; "will he do?"

"I reckon he will," Tilman said. "He's a bit of a mystery, and the drink's a worry, but I've seen worse. Far worse. No, I like him."

"What about that photograph?"

"The photographer is in jail. Got caught making dirty photos of young women. We'll have to see to it later."

McLean stared at him a moment. He didn't like it. "All right," he said at last.

"It will be all right, Mister McLean. This is a good 'un. He's got sand, and depth, and I expect he'll take up the work easy enough."

"How's that?"

"Man's got the eye of a hunter," Tilman said. He touched the brim of his hat and went to get his supper. He hoped McLean wouldn't find out that the photographer had easily made bail. The photo had not been done because Tilman was reluctant to ask Portier questions he might not want to answer. Rather than risk the Southerner quitting and the trip being delayed, he let the matter go. He was bored and eager for action once more.

Tilman avoided hotels when he could, because of the noise and foolishness that so often made them unpleasant places to sleep. In El Paso, he had found and taken a room with Lucy Blunt, an attractive widow with a young son. She had large blue eyes, red hair, and a trim figure. She dressed well, but more like a school marm than one of the Demimonde. Her servant was a young woman of color, Sookie Grimes, who cooked and cleaned. She, too, was slim and attractive: skin the tone of coffee and milk, with dark brown eyes. The two women were easy with one another, which told him that they'd been together a long time, liked each other, and were as loyal as sisters. The house was new, two stories with six bedrooms: four of which they let, with meals in the bargain.

The one Tilman rented was small but comfortable; he did not have to share it with anyone, which was how he liked things. He had his reading and his studies to pass the time when he was not out on a case, and he valued quiet. Since he didn't drink, he had few friends. His work apart, he was unwilling to tolerate the sloppy speech and manners of drunks, and moderate drinking men were simply not the fashion since the War. Most pounded the drinks down until they passed out. He'd been alone, and comfortable with his solitude, for a long time.

Most of the other boarders were lawmen, and they were respectful to 'the ladies' as they called them. Women living alone might be assumed to be following the Demimonde, but the presence of six or so fellows with badges, who acted like over-protective big brothers, soon put that notion to rest. As did the fact that Sookie attended the Baptist church three nights a week as well as on Sunday. There was hazard in talking to her too long, because the conversation always turned to God, or more specifically, Jesus Christ. Men who swore and spit and drank too much soon found themselves asked to find other quarters, and Sookie, who'd been trained in the best homes in New Orleans, was a wonderful cook.

The only flaw in this portrait of rectitude and grace was the fact that the boarding house did not quite produce enough revenue, and, therefore, Lucy also dealt Faro several nights a week, and sometimes poker as well. To guard against annoyance from foolish men, she carried a silver dagger and a Derringer, and often asked one of the boarders to escort her to and from work.

Tilman had performed this service several times since arriving in El Paso. He enjoyed her cheerful manner and light conversation, but was careful to maintain a distance between them by calling her 'Mrs. Blunt.'

One night she surprised him by saying, "Actually, it's Miss Blunt, Mister Tilman."

He turned to see her looking steadily at him, her eyes holding both boldness and concern, with a hint of defiance. He fumbled for the right words, not sure of what she had put in play with this unsought and unsavory confession.

"Then the boy is... "

"Mine and mine alone. 'Bastard' is such an unpleasant word."

Tilman stared at her a long moment, taking her measure. "Why confide in me? This is no business of mine." He found her face unreadable. What did she want of him?

"You're a detective. You'd find out sooner or later." Again, that defiance in her eyes, and something else, as well. He felt uneasy. He was too experienced not to see that she had fond feelings for him. That, somehow, she hoped for a closer relationship.

Tilman felt himself flush with confusion. In fact, he'd found himself admiring her beauty and her calm and cheerful manner. He realized that he now thought less and less about his dead wife and child. They stood there for several moments staring at each other, until she looked away, almost in tears.

"Have I been too bold?" she asked, biting her lip.

Suddenly he wanted to take her into his arms and comfort her. But he couldn't move. It had been too long since he'd been with a woman, or held one. He'd lost the way of it.

"No," he sighed. "I'm not an easy man to know, Lucy. I have ghosts that haunt me and griefs that drag me down. And I work for Pinkerton. It's a solitary life, you see."

"I figured," she said. "But you're clean and mannerly and brave, and very, very smart! All those books! I've been looking for a man like you."

Suddenly he laughed. "Frontier women are bold, I know, but..."

She smiled uneasily. "We have to be. Life is fleeting, and you grab it while you still can." She started to turn away. "I am such a fool..."

Then he did take her into his arms. "No, not at all," he said into her hair, as he felt her warmth flooding into him. "It's been too long. Twelve years... "

She stared up at him. "In twelve years, you never... "

"No. I couldn't. Not once."

"Well, that is the most romantic thing I ever heard," she declared; "and the most foolish! Tomorrow is not promised! Was she so jealous, that she would want this hold on you?" Lucy broke away from him, and smiled nervously.

He shook his head. "Probably not. We had a child, a daughter. My heart aches for her, as well."

"You must let them go. To do otherwise is less than manly." She bit her lip, realizing that she had said too much.

Tilman gazed at her, trying to imagine a life with her. It was too much, too soon, but he was a dullard not to have seen this coming, so he laughed. "Perhaps, but I'm a little rusty at this courting business, so you will have to give me time."

Lucy Blunt nodded. "You're a cautious man. I'm the same way. I have to be here, lest strange men take me for less than I am." A becoming blush came to her cheeks as she looked away, trying for a modesty that never had been hers.

"You seem to be a model of virtue," he said, as they began walking again toward the casino where she worked.

"I am, now," Lucy Blunt said after a bit.

"But not always?"

"How do you think I came to have my wonderful son? I'm hardly the Virgin Mary. Nothing like. I was a woman with needs like any other. I was broken to the trade when I was 13. I have no idea who his father is. Don't much care, either."

Again she had that defiance and spirit that he found so attractive in her, and she was far from plain. He was flattered that she wanted him, but also bound by his natural caution.

He nodded and delivered her to her work. He was not shocked by her confession of having once been a whore. More women in the West than would admit it traded their favors for money, advantage, or shelter. In his work, he often interviewed them and found them more honest than some of their hypocritical sisters — who deplored prostitution and sin openly, but had many faults of their own.

Eight hours later, walking her home, he said nothing more except: "I need to think on it. Give me time."

She simply nodded, grateful that he had not rejected her in horror, and satisfied that he would not shame her. "Take the time you need. I'll be here."

Now he was leaving, but he was careful to sit with her in the parlor and explain it to her. He gave her forty dollars so he could keep his rather pleasant room, and not have to store all of his books and other traps at the Pinkerton office. She was very still and then smiled wonderfully at him.

"You're coming back." She glowed with pleasure. Her gamble looked to pay off.

"Yes. If I can," he said, reminding her that his was a dangerous trade.

She looked down at the two twenty-dollar gold pieces he had given against keeping his room. "This is two months' worth. More if I credit the meals you won't be having here. Do you expect to be gone that long?"

"No. Not at all. The subject of our main pursuit is a man I know well. In an odd way, we're friends, or at least friendly. He won't shoot it out or anything like that. He'll say 'fair catch' and come quietly. The fellow he broke out with is another matter, but there will be two of us against him. He's wanted 'dead or alive' and if he's too difficult, we'll simply take the first path rather than the second."

Lucy involuntarily raised her hand to her throat. "You're a Hard Man."

Tilman nodded. "I want to be straight with you about my work. If we are to follow your plan for a mutual future, then you need to know all of it. You need to be sure."

"I'm very sure."

Tilman favored her with an unexpected smile. "I've never been able to talk any woman out of anything she set her mind to. But I have a dangerous life, and anyone close to me shares that danger. I'm a killer, Lucy. I wouldn't have survived the work this long, if I weren't." He saw fresh doubt in her eyes.

"If I return... "

"When you return," she corrected him, as firmly as a school marm.

"...we can try this out. But I don't want to start anything that can't be remedied."

She stared at him a long moment. "You're too kind, Blake. Too kind. Trying to protect me from myself." Tears came to her eyes. She closed her tiny fist around the gold coins. "So we'll call this rent, and nothing more."

He nodded. "That's right."

"And I should be at liberty to accept other beaus?"

He hesitated. El Paso was full of men, most of them not worth her time, but agreeing put the whole thing at hazard. He wanted her. But... how much?

"That's up to you. But life is uncertain. I have no claim on you."

"The more fool you," she said bitterly. Lucy got up and left him there.

There was such tension in the air that he felt the need to walk a bit, and collect his thoughts. Tilman walked over to Harry McLean's house. Not so much to curry favor as to make sure they were on the same page about Portier. He intended to draw the Southerner out, and determine if his coming to El Paso might be part of a larger plan. Men talked to fill the hours on a long ride. Sometimes they said more than they wanted to.

Standing outside was Emily, staring up at the sky with Jim Frazer's chart in her hands.

"I've decided to take up astronomy," she said as he drew close. "This chart don't quite match what I see up there."

"It's thousands of years old. Things have shifted."

"How do you know that?"

"I used to navigate our boat when I was a fisherman. Even then there were slight variations." He pointed upward. "See there? That is the North Star, and from there down the Big Dipper and the other constellations. If you know them, you can always find your position. A sextant helps, but if you've done a lot of sailing you can get by with the naked eye."

"Damn! You are so smart, Uncle Blake. Why aren't you married?"

The profanity threw him off. He stared at her.

Emily folded the map, and put it back in the cowhide envelope that held Frazer's notes.

"I was..."

"Yes, before the War. Long ago."

"About the time you were born."

Emily shook her head and held out her hand. "Walk with me."

He did so, and soon they were in the little grove of live oaks behind the house.

"You never thought about giving it another try?"

"I had cause to tonight," he said. "Miss Blunt...."

Emily laughed softly. "Really? Instant family, ready made? Home cooking? That does not seem like you. You're a wanderer, Blake. Seriously?"

Tilman paused. "Well, I did explain the nature of our work..."

"And how long do you think it will be before she pressures you to find more 'honest' work like school teaching? Or get herself with child to put another anchor on your boat? You hardly know the woman."

Tilman bridled. "You seem to be a little too interested in my business."

Emily handed him the envelope and raised her hands in mock surrender. "Tell me I'm wrong," she said; "And there's an end to it."

Tilman stared at her. *This is serious*, he thought. *I've been trying to avoid this by thinking of her as a child. It won't do. Many women marry at fifteen, and she's more mature than most. And quite a looker with that classic Mediterranean face, those eyes, long lashes, and full lips that most men would kiss without hesitation. Her father is my boss...*

Emily broke the silence. "Perhaps I should have Mister Deets make me a portrait to give you. You are staring at me like you've never seen me before."

"Perhaps I am."

"And does Lucy Blunt warrant such close attention?"

Tilman shook his head. "I told her I would think on it. Further than that, I promised nothing."

Emily stared back. After a moment she looked away. "Blake," she said softly; "We are detectives, are we not?"

"What does that have to do with it?"

"You should look carefully at what Miss Blunt is offering you. I'm sure, with all of your experience with the Demimonde, you've heard the term 'Boston Marriage'?"

"I'm surprised you have."

Emily rolled her eyes. "You have a lot to learn about women, Blake. Men think about us a lot, but few learn to think like them. We are very different."

Tilman laughed, relaxing. "No honest man will profess any understanding of the fair sex," he admitted.

"Yet you underestimate us at your peril. Traditional attitudes towards women do not serve you well. They keep you from seeing us as we really are."

He saw her earnest face staring us at him, partially shaded from the bright moonlight by the leaves overhead. "I was raised differently, Emily. Transcendentalists favor equality between the sexes."

"You won't get there by making us another species of men."

Tilman was suddenly aware of just how smart Emily and her sisters were. They favored a practical education that included bookkeeping, mathematics, science and languages, rather than philosophy and literature, but were equal to any man mentally, and better detectives than most. Emily's interest in Jim Frazer was as much intellectual as romantic, and now he was gone, she was turning her attention to him. Social convention was against that, but when had a Transcendentalist ever cared about that?

"Where does the servant girl sleep?"

Tilman realized that Emily had seen what he and the other men in the house had not, or just passed over as none of their business. Such pairings were common in the West.

"I take your point. So the offer is not just home cooking, but two for one?"

"If you are trying to shock me... "

"I doubt that I could."

"Thank you. Lucy Blunt is looking for a good man to step-father her boy, and enticing men is second nature for girls like her. They profess love and may even convince themselves they do not lie. But it will all be false and you will be miserable with it."

"How do you know? Maybe I'll grow to like it."

Emily laughed. "I know you, Blake. I made a study of you for Jim Frazer. He is very interested in cultures, and decided he'd better get a brief about detectives when Dad began trying to recruit him."

Tilman, bemused, asked, "And what did you find?"

"Someone I admire and could love in time, whose mind is quick, and who is tough but not brutal. Someone who needs a companion like me."

"Is this a proposal?"

"More like an invitation." Emily looked around the grove. "Do you know what this place is used for?" She looked back at him.

"No idea. Some women's rituals?"

"Nothing like that," Emily giggled. "Too many thorns for that. You'd be scarred for life. No, Molly brings her beaus here for private conversation. And kissing."

"Kissing?"

"Women like to kiss. We judge a man by how he kisses. We're silly females, and always want romance. Real romance, which is not fucking. That's a completely different thing. Care, tenderness, regard: those are what wins a woman's heart."

Tilman was fascinated. "And what has Molly discovered through kissing?"

"That Manny D'Silva is a brute who takes what he wants, and does not give back. He's offered her the life of a Grande Dame in Mexico, but admits to keeping several mistresses already, and is filled with vice and corruption. Very rich, but that could all be swept away by the next revolution. So he will not do. She's told him as much. He offered to abduct her until she reminded him that she's a Pinkerton. Part of a private army fully capable of exacting a terrible revenge. So, he passes off that unfortunate threat as a joke now, to keep the peace. Dad's Masonic connections are another barrier, since he's Catholic. Now, John Pershing is a good kisser, not a great one. And he also has a mistress: the U.S. Army. The life of an Army wife is not easy, and seldom a path to power."

"Power?"

"Women are barred from being lawyers or even voting. We live through our husbands and lovers, and influence them. By me, that's no way to live. But Molly is set on it, and is going back East to attend Vassar College. The daughters of the elite and wealthy old-line Protestant New England families are there. Molly will mingle and may meet a man who meets all of her requirements."

"This sounds very expensive," Tilman said. "How can Harry afford it?"

"He does not have to. Vassar offered her a full scholarship, and she will still be working for Pinkerton's. Robert sent her a letter from the New York office. It's quite an opportunity. Obviously, Vassar has a problem and needs our help. Not our usual line of business, but the Pinkerton sons are always looking for other ways to be of service." There was a sarcastic edge to that last. Tilman laughed.

"Anyway, if you are taking offers, let me advance my own."

"Emily you are less than half my age… "

"Irrelevant, sir, where two hearts truly meet. And speaking of that, have you ever kissed Lucy Blunt?"

"I've been rather careful not to."

"And that says it all, does it not? Her offer is devoid of romance. It's a business merger."

Suddenly, she put both arms around his neck and their lips met. He tried to pull away.

"One kiss, Blake, Just one."

He relented and that kiss went on for a long time as a wave of emotion came over him, and his arms hugged her tightly. She kissed him again. He felt dazed.

She stood back, smiling happily.

"That was very nice. Try not to get yourself killed out there. We can continue this when you return."

He smiled. "Not very romantic."

"Ah, but it was. It's just that Pinkerton's girls are so hard and unsentimental, like the men, that this is the best we can do." Emily frowned and ducked her head. She walked away, back towards the house, leaving Tilman in a stew of his own emotions, doubts and desires.

He found himself even more eager to get out of El Paso, just so he could think! An owl hooted. "Oh, shut up!" Tilman said and began to walk back to Lucy Blunt's.

CHAPTER FIFTEEN

Portier came to Lucy Blunt's boarding house with three mustard-colored mustangs they had purchased the day before on the Pinkerton account, just as Tilman was finishing his breakfast.

The other boarders had already left except for Judd Strong, a tough old Texas Ranger, who was reading a newspaper as he sipped his third cup of coffee. He was a new lodger, the captain of a troop of Rangers sent to El Paso at the request of the mayor to help calm the town. From what little Tilman had seen, he and his men were going to be there a while. Strong expressed mild interest in the question of what railroad detectives would do in a town without any, but also made it plain that he did not care for 'amateurs,' and warned Tilman against trying to recruit any of his men for the new Pinkerton branch.

"In Texas we treat poachers and horse thieves alike," he said, his face solemn – then laughed loudly when Tilman held up his hands in mock surrender.

Lucy's son, Lance, was clearing away dishes before heading off to school. He was twelve, and respectful of his elders. Tilman was looking at him carefully, realizing that if he wanted Lucy, he must also want her boy. That required much thought, and spending time with the lad. How would he even begin? At that age he'd been fishing with his own father for cod, and none of that was pleasant to recall: long, hard days of cold, wet, and stinking fish... and the moments when men and boys were lost to the sea, drowned.

How long ago had the boy's mother given up the Demimonde? Was he already too knowing about things that young boys were never supposed to know? In New York, he'd met boys younger than him employed as pimps and look-outs. Knowing the truth might not be possible. The boy had better manners than most his age. But....

Lucy brought Portier into the dining room, chatting with him.

"I had no idea you were also a woman of property, Missus Blunt," Portier said, as he found a chair. Apparently, she had dealt him cards at her work.

"We have to live someplace," Lucy said, and Tilman saw that she regarded him with awe and a bit of caution. She had been there when he had beaten that other man nearly to death. Behind his high manners, he was a cold-blooded killer: one to be kept at a distance.

"Have a cup of coffee," she urged him. "And I think we have some pancakes and bacon left." Her face was anxious.

"Yes to the coffee, but I've had breakfast. Also, those horses are a bit on the excitable side, so riding on a full stomach does not strike me as prudent."

"Are all you Pinkerton men so refined?" Lucy asked. It was a teasing question, but Tilman saw that she was not being flirtatious, just polite. That she did not really like Portier.

Sookie came in with the coffee pot, and stopped dead in her tracks. She stared at Portier as if she had seen a ghost. Then she recovered herself, placed a white china cup before him, gently poured it half full. She left the pot and started to walk away.

At the door, she stopped and turned back. "Sir," she asked softly, "Do you remember Sookie? I belonged to Miss Alicia. Back in New Orleans before the War."

Portier looked up from his coffee. He froze for a moment. Confusion and doubt washed across his face. He took a long look.

"Yes," he said slowly, his face assuming a charming smile. "I do recall you now. How are you?"

"I'm very well," Sookie said; "And glad to see that you are, too. They said that you had died in the War." Her face was grave.

Portier seemed nonplussed by that. "I tried hard, but couldn't quite manage it," he replied. "So, here I am. Your mistress, how did she fare?"

Sookie shook her head, "I don't rightly know. They said she ran off with some Yankee captain, but that didn't seem likely, as much as she hated Yankees."

Portier shrugged. "She was a bit flighty. It could be true." His pretended indifference told Tilman that whoever Miss Alicia was, she meant a lot to him.

Sookie shook her head again. "Well, fare you well, sir," she said, and headed back to her kitchen.

"And you, miss."

Tilman watched all of this banter with the growing conviction that they had both left much unsaid, and that there was quite a bit of polite lying going on. Portier finished his coffee, rose to his feet, and said, "Well, Mister Tilman, Mister McLean needs to see us before we go, so perhaps we should start." He walked outside to wait.

Blake Tilman and Lucy Blunt shook hands before she ventured a short kiss on his cheek. He rubbed that spot thoughtfully, as he and Portier rode their horses slowly back to their office to confer with McLean. Inside the office, Emily McLean sat writing a report. She smiled easily at Tilman with a sparkle in her eyes, but kept working.

McLean introduced her to Portier as "one of our best agents." Then she rose gravely to shake his hand. She offered Tilman her hand and he took it. Leaning close, she whispered, "I will pray for you, Blake. Much success and a safe return." Conscious of the other two men so close, he simply nodded. Her father seemed too distracted to notice this byplay.

"I got to find us some more men," McLean said woefully, as he again sorted the morning mail. "We got business coming in like you would not believe. Hullo!"

"What is it?" Tilman asked.

"They sent down a picture of that Seaton fellow," McLean replied. "Nice-looking fellow, he is." He handed it to Portier who stared at it a moment before passing it on to Tilman. Tilman looked and saw a well-fed, somewhat callow youth with a faint smirk on his face. Dressed in a formal way, with a thin tie and a wing collar.

Tilman grunted. "Comes from money, I'd be bound."

"Seatons," McLean said with a smile; "Own most of the North Side that didn't go up in the Great Fire. Here's a letter he sent home. Last one, I'd say." McLean squinted at it. "Mailed from Esperanza. Says he's moving on to some place called Apache Wells. Sierra Blanca?"

"The White Mountains, north by northeast from here," Tilman supplied. "I think they're out that way. Over by Fort Quitman. If we follow the trail along the Rio Grande, we'll get there in a couple of days." Tilman looked at Seaton's portrait again and then put it in a leather case with the other posters and flyers. Their trip would be a catch as catch can affair, a hunting expedition. They might find many of the wanted men or none at all. That was what being a detective was about: effort with uncertain rewards.

"I expect reports as you go," McLean said, and opened a drawer in his desk. From it he took a strong box, and opened it with a key worn in lieu of a fob on his watch chain. "Expense money," he said, and carefully made two stacks of twenty-dollar gold pieces. "I want paper on every penny."

Tilman put his in a leather poke. Portier weighed them in his hand and then dropped them into an inside coat pocket. He made a bit of a show of buttoning it.

Very solemnly, Tilman shook McLean's hand, and then went down the stairs. Portier followed suit. McLean watched from the window as they mounted their ponies and rode out, leading the third carrying their supplies, seemingly in no particular hurry. He wondered, as he always did, if he would ever see them again.

Tilman was the smartest man he had ever met. And the toughest. Portier was a bit of a dandy, but hard-eyed as well. He watched them until they turned into the main street, and looked at Emily, who seemed to be lost in thought. Or was it a prayer to gods unknown to him? He sighed and drafted a report for William

Pinkerton. Emily would type the final version for him on the new-fangled machine.

. . .

Tilman and Portier, long linen dusters over their normal clothes, rode out. Tilman had left his bowler behind in favor of a stained, disreputable brown felt slouch hat with a wide brim. They rode quietly together, following a trail that gradually disappeared into open country, usually in sight of the river. The weather stayed fair and neither of them had much to say. They were getting accustomed to the horses and vice versa. That required careful management.

About noon of the first day, Tilman consulted a map and a compass, and then surprised Portier by taking a miniature seaman's sextant from a saddlebag and shooting a position on the blazing sun overhead. After briefly consulting his watch, he marked a spot on the map and started to put the sextant away.

He noticed Portier staring at the instrument. "Never seen one of these before?"

"No, I have," Portier replied. "It's just unexpected. We're a far piece from the sea. Fact is, I worked my passage from Bombay to Singapore as a third mate on a steamer. Learned something of the art of that myself." He lit another one of his thin black cigars. "And you, suh? Where did you acquire your obvious skill?"

"My father's fishing boat, before the War."

"From fisherman to detective. That's quite a change."

"And what was your trade, Mr. Portier, if I may ask?"

"Oh, I had none, suh. Not as such. A bit of a wastrel. I was a lad at college when the War broke out. Went off with some local fellows and joined the Seventh Virginia straight away. Made my father proud, although he would have preferred me in a Louisiana regiment."

Tilman looked away, disturbed.

"Then you did know Belle Boyd?"

"Miss Belle? Oh, yes." Portier blew out a large puff of gray smoke. "Damnedest female I ever did know."

"That's what General Baker said," Tilman grinned. "But he never said much about her otherwise."

"Baker? I thought you were at Gettysburg?"

"I was. That was before. 20th Maine under Chamberlain at Little Round Top. You know the story?"

"I've heard that he carried the day with a bayonet charge, but never understood why he would do something so foolhardy."

Tilman looked up at the sun and checked his watch again. He wondered how to answer Portier's question, and decided that a straight, unvarnished reply was the best one.

"Sheer desperation. Orders were to hold at all costs, and you Rebs were trying to flank us. We were anchoring the whole Union line. Came at us four times, and we were just plain out of ammunition. Well, Chamberlain was a college professor before the War, and no slouch in the thinking department. He figured that the Rebs would be pretty tired and would be greatly surprised, so he called, 'Fix bayonets!' and we went down that hill like the vengeance of the Lord. Rebs lost all heart and just gave it up."

"Been a different matter if there'd been any cavalry," Portier said grimly.

"Heavy woods and steep hills. I doubt if they could have been employed with any profit." Tilman looked at him curiously. "You were there as well?"

"Not that day," Portier said bitterly. "I was off with that vainglorious fool Stuart, who thought more of getting his name in the newspapers than he did of his assigned task to provide a screen for the infantry. Ashby dead, Jackson dead. And Lee got sucked into the meat grinder, although no one would say so then or later. The War was lost on that day."

Tilman had never considered that view of it before. He made a sympathetic grunt.

"Truth is, I lost all heart. Wrote to Judah P. Benjamin and asked for another posting. He was our family lawyer in New Orleans. He sent me over to England to work with the fellows there, who were trying to build us a navy to break that damned blockade."

"Secret Service," Tilman said. "We might have been opposite one another had you stuck here. I was Chamberlain's color sergeant and clerk and runner. Little Round Top got him promoted, and a fellow came around from the War Department looking for men who could read and write. The Colonel put in a word for me, and I got transferred over to the Treasury Department, and Baker's First District Cavalry. He was a hard man, Baker was."

Portier nodded, stubbing his cigar out on a rock. "I heard that. Ol' 'death to traitors'."

"Yep, that's him. I worked with his cousin Luther, who was a bit softer, but not that much. Baker, he'd been one of those Vigilance committee fellows out in San Francisco. Been a sort of tinker or mechanic before that, like Mr. Pinkerton. Truth is, that Pinkerton got in because he was Lincoln's man from the railroads. Made a mess of it, and Baker had done this mission where he'd pretended to be an itinerant photographer. Walked all over Virginia with a broken camera scouting the Reb lines. So Pinkerton stepped aside as gracefully as he could, and Baker took it on."

"With a vengeance," Portier said bitterly.

"Truth. He did. Always did seem to take the whole thing personal-like." Tilman nodded thoughtfully. "Never said much about your Miss Belle, though. Said the newspapers lied a lot."

"Well, yes," said Portier, grinning now; "but you'd have had to have met her to take her true measure. Not a pretty woman. As tall as a man, maybe taller than most, and could ride and shoot better than most, too. Had the heart of a lioness, that girl did. Shot a man who broke into her house, and killed him, and she was what, seventeen? Why, Stonewall Jackson would not have had a Valley Campaign but for her information, delivered in the dead of night after a desperate 15-mile ride. Butter wouldn't melt in her mouth the way she wrapped those Yankee officers around her little finger."

"So her book is true?" Tilman said, somehow gratified by the idea.

"What she told. She got too famous to do much good, wearing that captain's uniform and all — and there was one Yankee officer she was a sight too friendly with."

"Keily."

"You know about that, then?"

"One of those 'wild geese' officers imported from Italy to show us how it was supposed to be done. Mercenary; no real loyalty. It caused some concern on our side. We'd lost one general to Mosby's bunch because of the Ford girl. Got plucked right out of her bed. Keily was no smarter. Belle owned him."

"He got shot up pretty bad. Belle nursed him herself, and put us on notice that we were not to take him. Belle usually got what she wanted, but that was a bit much. So, Mr. Benjamin asked her to go to London as a diplomatic courier. And you know the rest. She up and ruins another Yankee officer, in the Navy this time, but then married the fool."

Tilman nodded. "Baker really did want her hanged, you know, He was just livid, especially when that Reb sea captain took his leave in New York and that young fool the Navy had put aboard as prize-master went and married her. Oh, it went real hard for him."

Portier nodded, "I met him, after he was released. They had this big wedding ceremony at Saint James's Cathedral. Quite a show. Harding, his name was."

"What became of her?"

"Became an actress."

Tilman laughed, and after a moment Portier joined in. "Of course!" Tilman shouted, "What else would she do? Well, Mr. Portier, let's go down by that creek over there and find a place to rest up."

The creek was running full and there was a grove of trees. They tied the horses and broke out the large canvas square so they could rig it for a sun shade. Tilman dug into a saddlebag for a loaf of bread and a packet of roast beef. He started to make sandwiches. When he looked up, he saw Portier was taking off his clothes.

"What are you doing?"

"Thought I'd take a little dip in the creek. Care to join me?"

Tilman frowned, unsure of Portier's intentions. "No. One of us has to stay ready so we're not surprised."

"As you like," the Southerner said. Naked now, he splashed into the cold water.

Is he one of those? Tilman wondered. *A sodomite?* He'd met many during the war and was not upset by the notion. But that vice had never interested him. Walt Whitman might be a 'natural man' and parade naked in the woods, but Tilman did not. Never had. Some men took comfort wherever it could be found. But man-love held no attractions for him. Neither did the idea dismay him. He had seen too much for that. But, if the matter came up, he'd have to be sharp and set a boundary. He wanted no misunderstandings on that score.

Seduction was a natural part of spying. Portier was a former, or maybe present Confederate Agent, and a client of Judah Benjamin. What was his real purpose for hiring on as a Pinkerton Detective? For that matter, was his sudden desire for a bath simply a natural desire to stay clean, or was there a hidden purpose?

Portier rose and walked out of the creek, shivering, shaking water off.

"You seem to have forgotten a towel," Tilman observed.

"I'll be dry soon enough." Portier sat cross-legged on a patch of grass, put his hands on his knees, palms upward, closed his eyes and started humming to himself. Or something very much like it. It seemed to be a chant in something that might be Chinese. Tilman saw to the horses and checked his watch. He ate a sandwich, watching Portier, who did not move nor stop chanting. Bored, Tilman took a book from his saddlebag, sat on a log and read. Sometime later, the temperature cooler, Portier got to his feet and dressed.

"Should be about four," he said. "Are we moving on, or camping here?"

"Moving on. We can put five more miles behind us before it gets too dark to ride safely."

Tilman looked at his watch and saw that it was exactly four o'clock. He untied the canvas square and folded it, secured it on the pack horse, and mounted his own. Portier was already in the saddle, scanning the road ahead. "Will that be a regular thing?"

"What?"

"You going natural?"

Portier looked amused. "Not if you don't want it to be. It's a ritual so I can clear my mind for the task ahead. The real point was the cold bath to shock the body into a higher realm of alertness, and the meditation."

"Meditation?"

"Trying to perceive where I am, where my body is, in relation to the world and the dangers in it. Something I picked up from Captain Burton. Or rather from friends of his."

The horses found the trail again. Tilman looked at Portier and wondered if he had just been the victim of an elaborate prank. Portier saw the doubt in his eyes and decided to explain further.

"When Burton went to India he was surveying the Hindu Kush for signs of Russian influence. Up in the Himalayas there is this other place called Tibet, and these warrior monks who see things that mere mortals can't. We stayed a few months and learned a bit of it, but they doubted our sincerity and threw us out."

"But you still practice it?"

"Some. It relaxes me and makes me more aware. More ready."

"Ready for what?"

"The difficulties to come," Portier said calmly.

The whole thing sounded like mumbo-jumbo to Tilman, who had seen many a short con in New York City when he worked there, but Portier was so sincere, that he let it go. His Transcendentalist upbringing had exposed him to Eastern Religions, but not much of that had stuck. Thoreau promoted them, but Thoreau was a very odd man by anyone's measure.

"Next time, a little bit of warning would be appreciated."

"Yes, suh."

"Now you've made me itchy, but I prefer my baths hot and soapy. And at a barber's, not in a creek."

"Duly noted, suh. Think no more about it. The meditation can be done by itself and often is."

Tilman resisted the impulse to reply and simply rode on.

"Look here," Portier said a few moments later; "Can we drop the formality? I think we know each other well enough by now."

"That's Mr. Pinkerton's idea," Tilman said. "It creates a more professional manner, and lawbreakers find it daunting. It intimidates them." Tilman said this with great solemnity — and then cracked a boyish grin, shaking with suppressed laughter. "But, yes, call me Blake if you like, as long as it's just us two," as he used his heels to gently urge the horse forward.

"Ash is a name I answer to," Portier said happily, following close behind.

"Then let me ask you something man-to-man."

"Certainly."

"That fellow who accused you of cheating at cards?"

Portier eyed him warily, "Yes?"

"Why'd you beat him so hard?"

The Southerner looked away, considering his answer, perhaps not sure himself of why.

"Revenge," he said at last. "He's a cheat himself, but very slick. He and his little gang of friends second deal, and then, if someone complains, turn the accusation back on them. Where I come from, cheating at cards is a crime worse than murder. It was simple enough to get in a game and to lose so I looked like an easy mark." Portier looked away, his eyes cold and distant. "He was their dealer: their mechanic and trickster. So I ruined them."

CHAPTER SIXTEEN

The next morning Ashley Portier woke suddenly, as was his custom. Instantly awake, his hand on one of his new revolvers. He knew himself to be in a strange place by the cold seeping into his bones from the ground underneath, and by the absolute silence that always fell just before dawn. His mouth was dry and his throat scratchy. Absently, he reached for the silver flask of whisky, unscrewed the cap and took a sip, feeling its warmth flow slowly through him, and the dull pounding behind his forehead noticeably recede. He recollected where he was. The new job.

The fire had burned down to coals, giving only a dim glow to the campsite, but first light was spreading across the sky from the east. He could see the silhouette of his new partner, Blake Tilman, sitting hunched against the morning cold, a blanket across his shoulders, a Winchester across his lap, a cup of coffee in his hands.

They had been watch and watch, four hours apiece, all night. Tilman's idea, but Portier, who recalled the life he'd led as a cavalry scout, did not argue its wisdom. Behind him, one of the horses snuffled, browsing for grass. That caused a movement forty feet beyond the other side of the camp. Portier rolled out of his bedroll as easily and quickly as a cat, revolver in his hand, thumbing it to full cock. It was an antelope, a yearling doe, intent on her own breakfast.

"Don't shoot," Tilman said quietly.

Portier eased the hammer down. "Why not?"

"We got food enough," Tilman said, still in that half-whisper, "and I'd rather just admire God's handiwork."

Portier smiled and shook his head. He found the other cup and poured himself coffee, careful not to upset the pan of pinto beans soaking and getting plump. He found a place the other side of the fire, sat atop one of the leather saddlebags and sipped his coffee. They sat that way, silent, for half an hour or more, until the doe, finally catching their scent when the wind shifted, startled and took flight.

"This is the best part of the day," Tilman said, and set to making breakfast, carving bacon into slices and dropping them into the cast iron skillet, and then adding the beans. Portier did his part by taking the loaf of camp bread from its place under the hot rocks next to the fire, and dividing it into several hunks that could be used to sop up the grease.

After eating, they buried the fire, drowning it with the last of the coffee. The tin plates they scoured out with sand. They broke camp, packing up and saddling the horses.

"You're a surprising man, Blake," Portier said at last, as they negotiated their way down a hillside onto flatter land.

"How so?"

"I haven't met many men who were content to just enjoy the natural world, rather than take everything they could from it. And you seem to attract the ladies."

Tilman blushed. "You caught on to that, eh?"

"I did. Is that girl in the office one of McLean's daughters?"

"She is. But don't take her lightly. She's a good detective and works cases. It's not an indulgence."

"And will he indulge her romance with a man twice her age?"

"Not up to him. All of the girls do as they please. How did you figure it out so quickly?"

"Lots of gossip about the very unusual McLean family. Not all of it kind. The older girls are considered 'fast'. The youngest is considered 'wild'."

Tilman shook his head. "I doubt that any of them care. As for Emily, I've tried to dissuade her. But she seems determined, so I have to think about it, don't I?"

"And your landlady? What about her?"

"Again, nothing I started. No promises made."

Tilman frowned, irritated, and Portier decided to drop the matter.

Portier shakily lit a cheroot, shielding the match with both hands. Tilman looked once more at his map.

"We should make Esperanza over that next range," Tilman said. "You should enjoy this while you can, Ash. It's all going to go away."

"How do you figure that?" Portier looked at the vast empty space before them.

"Country's filling up. People coming here from all over the world for land and what the land brings. The buffalo are about hunted out, just feeding the railway gangs. There ain't a whole lot of reverence for nature, which most folks see as something to be taken, the way a brutal man takes a woman."

"That, too, is part of nature, Blake," Portier observed.

"There is a difference between love and rape," Tilman shot back. "We could learn a thing or two from the Indians."

Portier grinned and shook his head, "Now, you're dangerously close to heresy. Since the War of 1812 was settled, we've done nothing but try to crush the Indians, and take their land."

"You don't approve, I take it?"

"I am somewhat sensitive to land," Portier replied. "My family used to have quite a bit of it. Before the War."

"Ah." Tilman looked at him shrewdly; "You were rich?"

"Some might say so. We had plantations. Land that soaked up whatever cash came in. Money was tight and credit scarce, so we always worried a bit."

"And slaves."

"Yes," Portier replied. "But we treated them well. It was not 'Uncle Tom's Cabin'. They never starved, and were never beaten. And were mortgaged to the hilt with a Yankee bank in Boston. The land wasn't worth all that much. But they were also part of our family — at least at the start. We never sold a one of them except for misbehavior. And we gave them money so they could buy things and be happy. They were, before the Abolitionists started agitating them."

There was an awkward silence. The Pinkertons' connections with the Abolitionists and the Underground Railway was well known.

"Freedom is a powerful idea," Tilman said at last.

Portier chewed at his lip. He did not want an argument, nor did he feel that Tilman was being needlessly provocative. "It surely was a devastating tactic on the Union's part to declare them free. That was the beginning of the end for our cause. Gradually, the best ones left, and we white folks had grown too fat and lazy. I think my daddy would have let them all go years before if he hadn't owed so much money to the bank. We took care of them, and they of us, until the Abolitionists began coming around and interfering, and he saw the way it was going to go. But we were trapped, and had to play out the hand. He said as much."

"Lots of them stuck it out," Tilman observed.

"Home is where the heart is, they say. Some of them were very loyal. Like blood kin." Portier looked away and laughed bitterly. "And some of them were... and recorded as such in the family Bible. One of the great scandals that no one talks about. But even without that, they held the family they served as dear as their own. Like a rock, they were — until Abe Lincoln cracked that rock with the Emancipation Proclamation.

"I recall that, when she began, Miss Belle was able to use her servants as spies and couriers, with absolute trust. Slavery was not the issue, but the rights of the States to conduct their own affairs as they saw best. You Yankees certainly didn't endear yourself to the colored folks."

"Really?" Tilman said.

"Oh, some would be all courtesy, but very uncomfortable, but the bulk were rude and treated them badly, not as if they were people at all. They resented that."

"Even more than slavery?"

"Well, they didn't see that changing any, until Lincoln's Proclamation. Then, they thought anew, and became surly and indifferent to our cause. No, it was a brilliant maneuver."

"I recall," Tilman said carefully; "that Lincoln once said as how, to save the Union, he would free all the slaves, or just some of them, or — if need be — enslave everyone."

"Well, he was the man to do it."

They rode together, side by side, and then began their way up a narrow twisting track with Tilman taking the lead. At the top of the pass they paused. Tilman pointed.

"Town there. Might be Esperanza."

"Think they'll have a good hotel?"

"I doubt that. But we can ask around and maybe pick up a trace on Parker Boone. He's known there. Has a sweetheart or two." Tilman referred to his pocket notebook. "Maria del la Villa."

"A woman of the town?"

"Probably not," Tilman said; "Things are a bit different on the border. It's not purely a commercial transaction."

"You surprise me," Portier replied. "Certainly it was in El Paso."

"That's because there are so many American girls — most of them ruined in the War." Tilman was shooting the sun again with his sextant. He checked his watch for the time, marked the map and put everything away.

"What do you mean?"

"Girls — women, rather — who lost their husbands in battle, or who might have been taken by guerrillas or bandits, or stolen, and broken to that life. The agency has a list of missing women whose families want them back enough to pay money."

"Regardless?"

Tilman chewed at his mustache a moment, "No. Usually not. I've found one or two, and they have begged me not to give them up, knowing the kind of approbation that would greet them if they tried to go back to their old life. They wouldn't be able to bear the shame, they said."

"So why'd they do it?"

"Once dishonored, what was left to them? For others, it was simple survival. One of them told me that hunger is a wonderful aphrodisiac. Made me glad I'm a man."

Portier turned away. Tilman regarded him curiously.

"There was a young lady, once," Portier said after a moment. "I've often wondered what became of her. She owned that nigger gal Sookie you board with."

"Some mysteries are better left unsolved," Tilman replied, and urged his horse forward. Portier took a swig from his flask and followed. They rode on in silence, each occupied with his own thoughts.

Tilman wondered, *Does my reluctance to accept Lucy Blunt as a lover have anything to do with her past. She's been refreshingly honest, but, as she herself had pointed out, he's a detective and would find out sooner or later. She's smart enough to get out ahead of it. I don't mind whores; some are charming company. I've liked most of those I have interviewed, even as I pity their plight. Pity, on the other hand, is the last thing that Lucy Blunt wants from me. No frail victim, she. Tough as a boot under that pleasant exterior and pretty face.*

Yet she showed her most vulnerable side just to get my attention. Am I that closed off? That isolated, that I can't see the possibility of love, marriage, and family once more? I have a solitary life now, but I remember all too well what being married was like before the War changed everything. He recalled it as perfection, filled with love and happiness. *I've shied away from a second chance, because I think I will never be able to match it again. But how do I know?* a small voice within asked.

As for the physical side of marriage, he had seen too many men lured into bad ones by their baser instincts. He was a Puritan in his heart. *What Lucy Blunt proposes is more of a business arrangement than a love match.* On the frontier, such things were common, only because they were also convenient.

And Emily McLean is anything but convenient. Beautiful, reserved in manner, and very, very smart. That excited him almost as much as the kiss she had forced on him in the live oak grove. Emily was practical, as well. She knew what she wanted. *The puzzle is my own desires. What do I want? I honestly do not know.*

As they rode down into the valley, things took on a more organized look. Fences appeared, and houses and outbuildings could be seen across the flat plain. The trail widened into a road. Coming from the other direction, they saw a double column of riders, throwing up a cloud of dust in their wake. They came on quite rapidly, and the two detectives pulled their own mounts aside and watched as a troop of U.S. Cavalry trotted by, led by a young, blond-haired lieutenant, followed by a sergeant and a corporal holding a guidon with a fluttering unit flag. Aside from the officer, every other man was a Negro. Some had the look of veterans, with sergeant's stripes and hash marks for service on their sleeves, and others were barely more than boys; all looked, however, entirely professional, sitting erect and alert in their saddles.

Portier stared after them, simply amazed. Tilman said, "The Indians call them Buffalo Soldiers, because of that dense curly hair they have. There are two full regiments of them now, the Ninth and the Tenth. Generally considered the best we have."

Portier shook his head. "Things have changed." A former cavalryman himself, he never would have credited an entire troop of Negroes in that difficult role, had he not just seen it himself. And this was no minstrel show. They were all too real.

"Aye, that they have," Tilman said. He saw that Portier found the cavalry disturbing, but did not know why. *Portier will have to adjust his attitude toward them,* he thought. *Many of the best Pinkerton detectives are black. There is no room for the old thinking.*

They rode on into Esperanza. It being the middle of the afternoon, not many people were on the street, and the place had a rank odor. The buildings were faced with unpainted wood, weathered gray, shack-like, and leaning to one side, pushed there by the fierce winds that blew across the broad plains. There was a sheriff's office close to the center of the main street. A man dressed like a cowhand, wearing a big sombrero, sat on a wooden bench in front of it, his boots resting on a wooden crate. He seemed to be asleep, but they knew better than to trust appearances.

They stopped in front of him. Slowly, with great deliberation, Tilman dismounted and tied his horse to the rail in front. Portier followed suit, and secured the pack horse as well. All three beasts immediately dipped their heads into the horse trough, sucking down the green, slimy water.

Tilman took the leather portfolio with the posters and warrants from his saddlebag, and turned to the man sitting on the bench.

"Howdy," he said; "The Sheriff about?"

The man looked up slowly, sleepily, yawned, and then stretched. "That'd be me," he said, as he rubbed the six-pointed star-shaped silver badge that rode crookedly on his shirt pocket.

"I am Mr. Tilman, and this is my colleague, Mr. Portier. We're with the Pinkerton National Detective Agency."

The man with the sombrero seemed more amused than impressed by this. "Do tell," he said.

"We're after a Federal fugitive named Parker Boone."

"Under whose authority?"

"Pardon?" The normally unflappable Tilman was taken aback by this question.

"You Pinkertons ain't regular law enforcement. So, by what right do you come into my town, looking for this Boone fella?"

Tilman stared at him coldly. "We're bail agents contracted to the Federal Courts, and therefore, given extraordinary powers where fugitives are concerned. Your cooperation would be appreciated. It is also required."

"There's also a reward," Portier added.

Tilman glanced at him sharply, but Portier moved easily onto the porch. The sheriff looked at him warily. The Southerner held up one hand with a golden double eagle between thumb and forefinger. He could smell corruption from far away.

"A reward?" asked the sheriff, his eyes fixed on the coin.

"Yes, indeed, Sheriff...," Portier let the sentence hang there, unfinished.

"Garza," said the man at last. "Antonio Garza."

"And might you know if Parker Boone is in town, Mr. Garza?" Portier said, still smiling his most becoming smile.

Garza looked at the coin again, like a hungry man at a feast, "I might."

Portier looked expectant, waiting.

"He ain't here anymore. Went up to Apache Wells."

"Apache Wells? Where's that?" Tilman asked.

"North a bit, over toward San Cristobal."

Tilman looked at him suspiciously.

"You sure? Nothing shows that way on the map."

"Last map was done before the War. Lots of new towns sprung up since then," Garza said. "Been quite a few men going up to Apache Wells."

"What kind of men?"

"Hard Men. The kind of men that'd I'd just as soon see the back of," Garza replied. "Men like Parker Boone – and like you."

"Friendly fellow, isn't he?" Portier said.

Tilman just stood there, thinking. Portier tucked the coin into Garza's shirt pocket and produced another. "Think you might help us a bit here, Sheriff Garza?"

"I could do," Garza said with a wide grin.

"How about you show us, on my friend's map there, just where this Apache Wells place is? Then take a look at these posters and such, and tell us if any of these other fellows are also up that way."

Tilman went back into the saddlebags, and brought the map over. Garza looked at it and began to trace an old trail with his right forefinger.

"Well, I've never been there myself, understand, but it's only a day or so's ride. Got this high plateau here, and this bit here where it runs to a lot of scrub pine and live oak, and down in that valley someplace is where the town is. Was originally a gold strike, but that played out. Supposed to be some sort of range war going on. Lots of hired guns passing through."

Portier undid the portfolio. "Look at these, and tell us if you see any familiar faces."

Garza leafed through them and pulled out three. "These men have all been here in the last three months."

"They aren't here now?" Tilman was perturbed.

"Nope. Might have gone up to Apache Wells. Might not. I didn't ask."

"What kind of lawman are you?" Tilman demanded.

"One hired to keep it peaceful. I have a set arrangement with these fellows. They keep quiet, and I will, too."

"Most of them got a price on their heads."

"Most of them got friends as well," Garza said. "Money ain't worth anything if you don't live to spend it."

"A practical man," Portier said, tucking the second coin into Garza's shirt pocket. Tilman started to put the flyers back into the portfolio.

"Here!" said Garza, spying the Seaton boy's portrait. "I seen that fellow, too."

Tilman picked it up, and handed it over for a closer look. "You sure?"

"Yes. But this one ain't no *bandito*. Kinda high-toned and mannerly, but no real harm in him. Nice boy. What's he wanted for?"

Tilman took the portrait back and put it away. "Truancy," he said sourly. "Where's he at?"

"Went up to Apache Wells, like the rest," Garza said, then added: "You know, it's a funny thing."

"What?"

"Lots of fellows going up to Apache Wells, but I can't recall that any of them have come back." He frowned. "Now, that is peculiar."

Tilman and Portier looked at one another. "Care to recommend a good hotel?" Portier asked.

"Can't say as we got one. There's Mama Fisk's place, but it ain't exactly a hotel, if you take my meaning. And she only rents by the hour."

"Another time," Tilman said. "How about a post office?"

"Down the street on the left."

Tilman unhitched his horse. Portier did the same with his, and the one carrying the supplies. Together they walked down the street.

"You paid way too much for that information," Tilman said.

"Didn't have anything smaller," Portier replied with a grin. "And it ain't my money, anyway."

"The boss won't like it. That's more than that man makes in a month, I'll be bound."

"Chalk it up to my impulsive nature, and inexperience," Portier said, pulling another little cigar from his coat pocket. "We're pushing on, then?"

"Might as well. I'd rather sleep under the stars than in bedclothes filled with bedbugs and fleas," Tilman said.

"A point well taken," Portier grimaced.

"I just have to write a report and mail it back to Mr. McLean," Tilman said.

Reaching the front of the post office, a building no more distinguishable than any other in town, they tied the horses once more and went inside.

Stepping through the door into the darkened interior, Tilman heard a curse. Without thinking he rolled forward, coming up with his revolver in his right hand and cocking it just as a shot rang out. Portier ducked, very surprised, and blindly fired a shot back. There was the thunder of running feet and the slam of a door at the rear of the building.

Tilman stood there, letting his eyes adjust to the light.

"Friend of yours?" Portier inquired drily.

"Not hardly." Tilman banged his fist on the counter. "Anyone else here?"

From beneath the counter a man's head showed itself, rising slowly. He was a tall, weedy older man with wire-rimmed spectacles and a prominent Adam's apple. With the air of a bewildered exotic bird, he said, "I'm Adams, Postmaster here. Who are you?"

"Tilman, and this is Mr. Portier. We're with Pinkerton's."

"My new clerk seems to have taken exception to you, Mr. Tilman."

"That would be Mr. Harris or Perkins or whatever he's calling himself now. He's wanted for robbing the El Paso Post Office."

"He said his name was Booth."

"Did he?" Tilman responded, with a grin.

"You're not going after him?" Adams demanded.

"Wasn't him we came looking for," Tilman replied.

"The guilty flee when no man pursueth," Portier added gravely.

"He's but a petty crook," Tilman said; "and we're hunting bigger game."

"As you wish. He did seem to know his way about a post office."

"As well he might. He was a postmaster himself once," Tilman replied.

"Now I've got to find another clerk," the postmaster fretted.

"That you do," said Tilman, and set about writing his report, leaning on the rough counter.

Portier passed the time by nailing extra copies of some of the wanted posters to the exterior wall next to the door. Passers-by, all men, stopped to look, but no one volunteered any information, taking note of his badge. One or two hurried away, probably intent on alerting others that the Pinkertons were in town.

Soon after, they rode out of Esperanza and up again into the hills. As it grew dark once more, they made a dry camp and dined on dried beef. Neither said much to the other during the long afternoon ride. Going uphill demanded a man's full attention, especially as the horses seemed unusually skittish. Even now they seemed unsettled, and Tilman took the precaution of putting hobbles on them. Portier was tired and slept first, while Tilman kept the fire burning high so that he could read a bit by its light. At midnight, he woke his partner and poured him a cup of the strong coffee that had been simmering since dinner. Suddenly, there was a flash of light from over the next range of low mountains.

Automatically, the men began counting, expecting the report of an explosion. No sound came. A second flash about four minutes later had the same result.

"That's like nothing I've ever seen," Portier said.

"Me neither," Tilman replied.

"What was it, then?"

"I have no idea. I expect we'll find out. It's from where we're headed," Tilman said, and then rolled over and went right to sleep.

CHAPTER SEVENTEEN

They smelled the dead man an hour or more before they found his blackened, burned body. It was not the odor of putrefaction, but of roasted pork.

"Smells like a damned barbecue," Tilman said, looking about alertly for signs of an ambush. Portier was also eyewise and careful, his blood up. He now appreciated Tilman's savvy and insistence on using the Indian ponies for this expedition. They were strong and sturdy. Portier's mare was a patient plodder as they came down out of the hills onto another flat plain. Not high-spirited but sensible little horses.

In the far distance stood the San Cristobal Mountains. The valley floor was lush with juniper scrub and dotted with grotesquely formed live oak trees. A gentle wind blew the odor to them. Tilman, more out of curiosity than concern, followed his nose.

The bodies lay on the side of dry wash. One was a white horse that now lay on its back, legs extended skyward. The other was a man, and his condition astounded them. Dismounting, Portier knelt, and touched one foot in a boot somehow turned to charcoal. It crumbled, making him jump back slightly.

"I have nevah seen the like," he said. "It's like he was caught in a house fire at this end."

Tilman examined the other end of the sprawled body, thinking that the bald crown and white fringe of hair looked familiar. "Hardly a sign of that up here," he said grimly.

Portier stood up, dusting his hands off. He looked off into the middle distance, pulled another little cigar from his vest pocket, and lit it as a defense against the disturbing odor that assailed their nostrils.

Tilman poked and prodded at the upper part of the body, wrinkling his nose. "This man did not die of burns," he said at last.

"No?" Portier raised an eyebrow.

"No — it's like he was cooked alive. His head and hair are untouched. His middle is red, and the clothes begin to scorch off. His buttocks are browned like a roast — I bet if we cut in we'd find it was like a medium-rare roast — and his legs and feet are burned gradually to a crisp."

"Any idea what could have done it?" Portier asked.

"Nary a one." Tilman's normally reserved face showed how perplexed he was.

"Any idea who he is?"

"I got a suspicion," Tilman replied. "Help me grab his shoulder and turn him over."

They did this, only slightly surprised to see the lower legs and feet crumble to moist black dirt.

"It's Perkins," Tilman said. His voice held no satisfaction or regret at the discovery.

"The fugitive postmaster?" Portier asked.

"Yep." Tilman stared down at the dead man's face. It displayed a rictus of sheer terror. Perkins had apparently been scared to death.

"Whatever killed him damn near scared him to death first," Portier said after a moment, echoing Tilman's thoughts. He took off his hat and scratched his head.

"Aye, that it did," Tilman said. He walked over to where the horses were standing, and took his sextant from the saddlebag. He began to calculate their position.

"What do we do with him?" Portier asked.

"Normally, we'd pack him in to the local sheriff, get an affidavit, and claim whatever reward was offered, but this rascal's crime don't probably merit such."

"He's in no condition to be moved anyway," Portier said pragmatically. "Be real messy. And the horses probably won't abide it, not with that smell."

"Aye." Tilman finished marking the map. "I say we dig a trench and bury him where he fell. We can fill out an affidavit and claim any reward. At least we've cleared the case."

There was no question of just leaving the body there for the carrion birds to pick at. Even the meanest of men deserved a decent burial and a few words said over them. It was a hot, dirty chore that took most of the rest of the day. The horses stamped their feet restlessly, as it was done, anxious to be away from the stink. Already there were black ravens alighting near the dead horse and pecking at it. Insects were crawling on Perkins and flies gathering. Nature was an efficient undertaker. In the end, there was a mound of sandy brown dirt and a crude cross made from two dead live oak branches to mark the grave.

By unspoken agreement, they did not camp nearby, but walked the horses to a spot about three miles further on. There they made a dry camp under a large singleton live oak. Tilman sat and wrote a report, then drew up two affidavits and had Portier sign one.

"Pencil will have to do," he said. "These are field conditions."

They built a fire, a small one this time. The area around them seemed unusually silent, without the bustling sounds of small wildlife that usually prevailed. The silence oppressed them. Portier sipped once at his whisky flask, burped, and, startled at the loudness of this, put it away.

Tilman, more from reflex than any conscious intention, cleaned his revolvers and wiped down the stock and barrel of his Winchester. Using an oiled toothpick, he paid particular attention to the iron sights.

Neither man wanted to talk. Each was extending every one of his senses out into the darkness. As it got truly dark, even the horses left off their browsing and chomping of the scrub.

Portier signaled his intention to sleep by laying out his bedroll. Tilman merely nodded; he'd take the first watch.

The unearthly silence continued without pause. Tilman sat alertly, rifle in hand.

Suddenly, there was a low growling sound from far away, almost like the rush of a locomotive at full tilt. This was followed a few seconds later by a blinding flash that backlit the far horizon, etching it on Tilman's retina with a brilliant afterimage. It woke Portier.

"Wha... ?" he said, instantly awake, body coiled for action.

"I don't know," Tilman replied, slowly and distinctively drawing out the last word; "But I expect we're going to find out."

Portier chuckled. "Of course we are – we're detectives, after all."

That night, Ashley Portier had a strange dream. He saw himself as a knight of old, armored, with a golden sword in his hand, standing astride and protectively over a beautiful maiden. She lay prostrate, in a flowing gown; her long dark hair, a river of gentle curls, covered her face, and she was weeping.

As he knelt to console her, she turned her head, revealing not a fair face but that of a death's head hag — foul and corrupt odors assailed his nostrils. He awoke at once, still gagging. Shaking, he sought his flask, unscrewed the cap and took a long pull. Sitting upright, he lit a cheroot with a coal from the fire, drew the smoke in to kill the foulness in his mouth.

He looked up to see Tilman regarding him cautiously.

"It was but a dream," Portier murmured. "Perhaps I should take a turn."

Tilman nodded and made preparations to lay down. Portier stood, his joints creaking with pain and stiffness, and did one of the stretching exercises he had learned from Captain Burton. Suddenly thirsty, he poured water into his metal cup and sipped at its coolness. His eyes took in the moonlit plain, the half-sleeping horses, shuffling their hooves.

The dream troubled him. Since Tibet, he'd had many such visions, but was usually at a loss as to what they meant. This one was too vivid, almost too real. He doubted their prophetic power, yet this one chilled him. Suddenly he feared whatever lay ahead. His stomach was hollow with dread. He recalled the silent cautious trek he and Tilman had made after discovering Perkins' body, walking the rough ground, leading the horses. It was necessary to keep them from balking and running away.

Twice on the following day, they found circular areas, perfectly formed, blasted to black ash. Ground and brush nearby were barely scorched. Tilman, thinking out loud, worried at the cause of these like a dog at a bone. Greek fire? A meteor? Some strange prank?

Portier had no idea. He had seen enough of the wider world to know that there were more mysteries in it than answers, but this, too, had a dream-like quality. He'd pinched himself to be sure he was awake.

He was content to let Tilman run on, taking the measure of how his detective's mind methodically worked out the problem, sorting through every possible answer. Tilman shot the sun with his sextant and marked his map at several positions. Portier now saw this as more than an affectation or conceit. He saw the science behind it. In the midst of an uncharted wilderness, Captain Burton had told him, it was always important to know where you stood. A metaphor that applied in the salons of the Elite, as much as it did in the wilderness. He smiled, remembering the kindly but rugged British Army officer.

"Perhaps you should visit my friend Captain Burton," Portier suggested. "After this is over."

Tilman, not sure he wasn't being mocked, simply grunted and moved on – but that afternoon as they rested under the shade of an enormous tangled live oak, Portier took his steel-nibbed pen, a cake of ink, and a sheet of clean white parchment from his own brown leather writing case. He inscribed a short letter of introduction to Burton, folded it neatly, and presented it to Tilman, almost ceremoniously.

Tilman stared at the address. He had never thought of visiting London, but something would not let him dismiss the gift. He put it between the leaves of the thick Marx book.

"Thank you," he said. Such a journey would bring him close to where Jim Frazer lived and worked. Emily would like that... and his mind paused. *Yes she would, but what does it mean that I think that? That her proposition is working its way into my heart?* He shook it off. Nothing had been promised. He didn't have the luxury of dreaming about this in the midst of so much uncertainty and danger. He must put it out of his mind. For now. *Just for now.*

Portier, having already put his writing case back in his saddlebag, directed his attention to the horizon.

"Thunder?" he asked, as a low booming sound rippled toward them from the mountains ahead.

"Not a cloud in the sky," Tilman answered, equally perplexed.

The two detectives moved on.

An hour before dusk, they found the second dead man.

There was nothing mysterious about his manner of death. Shot in the back, at some distance, with a large-bore rifle.

".45-70?" Tilman guessed, probing the garish red wound with a piece of mesquite branch.

"Might be," Portier allowed.

They turned the man over and saw that he had been fleeing in sheer terror. A brief scout found his widely-paced leaps in the brush.

Tilman cast about, taking large steps, first in one direction and then another.

"What is it?" Portier asked at last.

"If he was running, who was chasing him?"

Portier scanned the land around them. "No other tracks?"

"Nary a one."

"Perhaps he was shot from a balloon," Portier hazarded.

"I think we'd have seen it, then," Tilman argued. The huge balloon that had brought Jim Frazer to El Paso came to his mind. How high could it fly? A Sharp's rifle could hit a target more than a mile away with some precision. From above? He kept this to himself.

The balloon had left El Paso and seemingly disappeared. It seemed to have Confederate connections and Portier had spied, or perhaps was spying now, for that defeated but hardly dead enterprise. The less he said about it, the better, Tilman decided.

"I know this face," Tilman said at last, and went to fetch the leather portfolio of wanted posters from his saddlebag. He flipped over a few and pulled one out, passing it to Portier. The Southerner grunted, went over to look at the dead man's face once more, and finally nodded.

"Looks like the fellow," he agreed.

"William Hervey, cattle thief, robber, and gunman. Five thousand for this one, Mr. Portier — we'll have to pack him along."

Ashley wrinkled his nose. "He's already beginning to stink. I don't fancy carrying him over my saddle."

"We'll wrap him in the tarpaulin," Tilman replied.

They set about their task, thankful that rigor had passed and the body was pliable, if fragrant. Now it lay wrapped, a silent third companion, visible at the edge of the fire light.

Portier puffed at a cheroot, considering, filled with the grim anticipation that precedes a battle.

"Yet, where are our enemies?" he whispered softly to the dead man. "Where?" Portier posed a question. "Do I have to go back to El Paso to claim my share of that reward?"

Tilman, surprised, looked up from his reading. "Not necessarily. Sometimes men get killed or die before the payment arrives. The agency sends it on to the next of kin. Why?"

"I'd like to get back to New Orleans. Family business. And opportunity. Land is going cheap." Portier looked away.

Tilman sat up. "I thought you were broke?"

"I'm short of ready money, that's true, but I can cure that with poker the next chance I get. I'm very good."

Tilman frowned. "We need to finish this job. You can't just abandon me and run off."

"Wouldn't dream of it," Portier sighed. He motioned towards the corpse. "This fellow is a reminder of how uncertain life is. And how much has changed. The War..."

"Is ten years behind us, and yet you Rebs keep bringing it up."

Portier shook his head. "For a reason. The Yankee boot is still on our necks, and will be as long as Reconstruction holds. It is tyranny, suh!"

Tilman felt a headache coming on. "I will not argue this with you. There is an election next year. Voting rights are restored. Deal with it then."

Portier nodded. "You are right. We should stick to the business at hand. I will not speak of it further."

Tilman put his book away and laid down. He closed his eyes, but stayed wide awake, thinking hard. He'd been wondering why a man who'd pleaded poverty would have a wallet in his saddlebags with a million dollars in bills of exchange drawn on a London bank. Found when Tilman did a quick surreptitious search of the Southerner's gear while he was answering a call of nature. Who did they belong to, and what were they for? Money was fungible and could be used to buy anything: land, influence, trouble. His best guess was that they belonged to Judah P. Benjamin, and that Portier was simply a courier. A trusted agent of the still active Confederate Secret Service. To what end? Benjamin had been the junior Senator from Louisiana before the War, and the old Slidell machine was still politically active. Portier had made a mistake. But Tilman could not see how he could use it.

His mind turned to another distraction. The envelope he had found in with the flyers; sealed, with his name on it in Emily's handwriting. He had not opened it.

Leave me alone, girl, he thought, I'm working. I have no time for you just now.

The next day duty drove them on. They went about it slowly, taking in every sight, sound and sensation, conscious that this day might be their last. As they rode, Tilman could tell that they were approaching 'civilization.' Again, things took on that built-up, organized look, and a semblance of a road appeared, straight and narrow, rather than a meandering trail that simply followed the terrain. Soon they could see distant houses and barns jutting up from the dry brown plains, tinged with the green of new growth on top, but only two or three — yet, there was an eerie stillness about them, devoid of human activity.

"It's green enough," Portier commented nervously, taking a sip from his silver flask. "There should be someone about."

"Aye," Tilman said, completing yet another of his position-finding exercises with the sextant. "I'd at least expect to see a herd of beeves or a horse *remuda*."

The silence was oppressive.

"Town's got to be that way," Tilman said, pointing down the road.

"Likely enough," his partner agreed. Portier looked back at the dead man draped across the pack horse. They had redistributed that beast's load between their own horses.

"Well, we'd best get on with it," Tilman said, but did not move, his eyes scanning the terrain ahead. Portier deliberately pulled out another of his short cigars, bit off the end, spit it aside and, with an almost ceremonial air, lit it.

"There!" Tilman said softly, and pointed.

Portier looked. He could see three vultures circling lazily at a point near the horizon.

"Could be anything," he said judiciously. "Dead cow, horse, something like that."

Tilman looked at him shrewdly. "Problem, Ash?"

Portier inspected the end of his cigar, carefully considering his reply.

"We are detectives," he said at last; "Men of the world, and wise in its ways. Brave, but not foolhardy, yet... "

"Yet?" Tilman prompted.

"Something here fills my soul with dread. I feel that same desire to turn and run that always came over me just before a big battle."

"And did you ever turn and run?"

Portier laughed bitterly. "In front of all my friends and acquaintances? Never! I was not brave enough for that."

"Neither was I," Tilman replied. He nudged his horse, and without another word they went forward. Three hours later, they found what the birds were circling.

It was a dead horse, and its barely living rider. The man, perhaps thirty years old, with the lean looks of a cowhand, and the low-slung gunbelt of a gunfighter about his waist, lay sprawled face upward beside his mount. His face was sunburned, his lips cracked. While Portier held the horses' reins, Tilman went to him with a canteen. He kept a wary eye on the silver-plated Colt's revolver lying near the man's right hand. The man stared at him with crazed eyes. He tried to speak, his tongue probing at his cracked lips.

Tilman, abandoning caution, slid an arm behind the man's shoulders and lifted him to a half-sitting position. He placed the opened canteen at the man's mouth.

The fellow shook, almost with a spasm, and drank eagerly.

"Easy now," Tilman cautioned; "Drink it slow."

Behind him, Portier struggled to keep their horses from bolting, as the wind shifted and carried the scent of the dead animal to their nostrils.

"He's in real bad shape," Tilman called.

"Shot?" Portier inquired.

"Not that I can see."

The man's arm flailed wildly. Tilman tossed the man's pistol away, out of his reach, and leaned over, giving him a little more water. The man beckoned to him urgently, and Tilman leaned closer to hear something he whispered. Suddenly, the man turned his head to one side and vomited a rush of black bile and red blood onto the dusty ground. His entire body shook with a violent spasm.

Tilman, repulsed, got quickly to his feet and jumped back, barely avoiding the noxious fluids that splattered the ground.

"Jesus!" said Portier reverently. "What a horror!"

Tilman chewed at his moustache. "Never seen the like," he admitted. He knelt and placed two fingers on the man's neck, feeling for a pulse.

"Dead," he said after a moment.

Portier bowed his head a moment, and then asked, "What was that he tried to say at the end?"

Tilman shrugged. "Didn't make much sense. I think he's gone off his head with the heat and thirst. He did say 'They ain't people' pretty clear — couldn't make out the rest."

"They?" Portier asked. "Who are 'they'?"

Tilman shook his head. He was studying the dead man's face.

"I don't make him out," he said at last. "But I suppose we'd better haul out the posters and check."

Portier looked upward at the circling carrion birds. "What about our friends up there? We can't leave him like this."

"Soil's too rocky to dig," Tilman judged. "We'd better pack him along."

Portier looked doubtful. "Think we can?"

"Oh, yes," Tilman said. He walked over and got his sextant from his saddlebag. "And we'd better mark this place. I also think that prudence demands that we cache the remainder of our supplies near by."

"Why?" Portier was placing the hobbles on the horses so that he could help Tilman with the body.

"Just a feeling," Tilman replied.

"Not very scientific," Portier jibbed.

"I've learned not to ignore such things," Tilman said. "There's a whole world of knowledge that science doesn't begin to understand."

Portier nodded. "Captain Burton said much the same to me on more than one occasion."

Lacking another tarpaulin, they settled for tying the dead man's hands and feet together.

Tilman examined the body for gunshot wounds and other injuries. All he found was a red mark on the man's stomach. He leaned and sniffed.

"Damn!" he said suddenly, shocking Portier a bit, since it was the first profanity that he had heard from the other man's mouth. "Damn if it don't smell just like a pork roast."

Portier bent to look, probing with his forefinger. "Feels like a cooked steak right there," he commented.

"He's been cooked inside?" Tilman said incredulously. "What kind of thing would do that?"

An examination of the posters yielded a match with the dead man's tortured countenance.

"This one's no loss," Tilman said. "Clete Morgan."

Portier frowned, thinking hard. "That's the fellow that broke out of prison with your old pal, Parker Boone."

"Is it?" Tilman looked at the poster and then at the note on Boone. "You're right. How did you remember that?"

"I play poker for money. One has to pay attention, and try to recall the position of every card in the deck. And the player's habits, and little quirks, and what the previous action was. It's all details." Portier was dismissive, but Tilman, despite himself, was impressed.

"If your memory is always that quick, then you will be a great detective," he commented. "What else do you surmise?"

"That Clete here was running away from something that scared the living bejesus out of him, which is hard to credit for a man with as many notches on his gunbelt as he has. Whatever it was, was a lot bigger and meaner than he was."

"So where is Parker Boone?"

"Alive and well, by this evidence. No other troops of carrion birds circling, so no other bodies extant. They got to town, and then Clete had reason to run away. and got killed for his trouble. Parker is still around."

"Unless Clete murdered him as soon as they were away from the prison and fed the body to the hogs someplace." Tilman said. He had the sextant and map out again, marking the place.

"That's a disgusting image," Portier said.

"Been done more than once. It's why you should never eat pork," Tilman said, with a wink. "Let's find some rope and get him packed for travel."

They got Clete Morgan up on the pack horse, draped behind the other body, and hid the extra supplies under a stunted live oak tree a short distance away. Tilman marked the spot with a pile of stones. A bold black crow landed on the dead horse and began to pick at the rotting flesh.

"We'll be able to find our way back here for the next few days," Tilman said. "These fellows are better than a smoke signal."

Portier nodded glumly. He picked up the dead man's revolver from where it lay on the ground.

"Good condition," he said, and looked at the front of the cylinders. He turned it, ejecting the shells. "All fired out," he said at last. "Empty."

Tilman nodded, unsurprised. "He was a gunman. He would have gone down fighting." He stowed the dead man's revolver in a saddlebag, looked around, and then at Portier in a measuring way, looking for any sign of worry or panic.

Portier shrugged. "Never did have sense enough to run," he said with a smile, and swung into the saddle of his mount. Tilman mounted as well, then looked all about for several moments, taking all the details of the place into his memory.

"It's quiet," he said at last. "Hardly a sound."

"Too quiet," Portier agreed; "like the grave."

They rode on.

CHAPTER EIGHTEEN

Now that they were in the flatlands and on a road, ill-kempt though it was, the going was easier. "All roads lead to someplace," said Ashley Portier philosophically. Tilman grunted agreement, as he marked the track on the map, and took yet another position with the sextant.

After a few miles, which they did at a walk (in respect for the two dead men, and to save themselves inconvenience should either or both be jostled loose and fall off the pack horse), the road curved into a narrow draw.

Tilman looked upward, trying to see if anyone was standing watch — it was a natural place for such a position — but none was apparent, and no challenge issued from the rocky slopes above them. On the other side of the defile, the road sloped down into a town like so many in Texas and New Mexico and Colorado. A single long street, divided at intervals, with mostly plain wooden plank storefronts. At one end, a brown plastered adobe brick building that might be the jail; at the other, a huge red-painted barn that would be, he thought, the livery and hostlers. A three-story building faced with red brick—likely the hotel.

The street itself was laid straight as a die, he observed, and thought that unusual since it did not lay north-south, east-west, or on any other major points of the compass, but an obscure fraction thereof.

Portier took a spyglass from his saddlebag and made a close examination. "Nothing unusual," he reported after several minutes of this survey. "A few folks on the street, most of them obvious hard cases."

Tilman nodded and looked over his shoulder at the pack horse. "Sooner we get these lads under the ground the better."

"Yep," Portier replied, collapsing the little brass telescope.

They nudged the horses with their heels and rode down into the town.

The distance was greater than anticipated; Tilman almost stopped to take another position, but he felt a certain urgency. They weren't more than ten miles from the last fix, anyway. The road led them behind one row of buildings and into a side street. Tilman thought that odd. It was almost as if the main street had been an afterthought. Something about the wooden buildings nagged at him, too. At the corner, Portier pulled back sharply, alarmed.

Tilman, a few feet behind him and unable to see around the corner, asked, "What is it?"

"Gunfight!" Portier said, as he quickly dismounted, moving silently, like a cat.

Tilman followed suit. It was harder for him. His lower back flared with pain, and he suppressed the loud groan that came to his lips. It took him a moment to suppress all the pain and focus his mind. Wrapping the reins carefully around one hand, they both edged their way to the corner and took a better look.

"That's Quick Rick Tracy," said Tilman, pointing to the man at their far right.

"If you say so." Portier seemed amused by the nickname. "And what is his claim to fame?"

"Murdered a Federal payroll officer, and stole over fifty thousand dollars. There's a price on his head that's been growing apace. He's also wanted for cattle rustling, kidnapping, child stealing and rape — the details are on his wanted poster."

"What's his bounty?"

"Ten thousand in gold."

Portier whistled, "Pity we'll miss out."

Tilman grinned. "Let's keep a good thought — he's killed fourteen men in duels like this. Doesn't matter on the reward though — it's 'Dead or Alive'."

"But if he falls, then the other fellow gets that, right?"

"Yep, but there's a fee for service that amounts to a nice day's work, and we'll do all right, even after the Agency cut."

"I'm liking this detecting business more and more," Portier said. "Who's the other fellow?"

"Can't see him clearly from here, but I don't give much for his chances. Ol' Rick is not just one of the fastest draws around, he's known to shoot first, without warning."

"Oh," said Portier; "Seems unsporting of him."

"Yep, this ain't a game, Ash, which is why we Pinkertons never accept a challenge like this. The rule is: take 'em alive, if ya can, dead if you have to, but take 'em any way you will."

Portier saw that there were spectators on both sides of the street. One side he judged to be townsmen, since they all seemed to be dressed much the same, in suits with hats that might have come from the same store. The other side seemed to be gunmen, and a variegated lot they were, dressed in every variation of cowman's attire, including some Mexican *caballeros*.

On the street, the two men walked steadily toward each other, right hands poised over their revolvers. Portier saw that Quick Rick Tracy was white with fear. He nudged Tilman, but before he could say anything, Tracy went for his weapon. It had not even cleared leather when the other man shot, level and true, and blood spurted from Tracy's neck. He spun and fell into the dusty street, dead before he hit the ground. A cheer went up from the side where the townsmen were. They crowded around the victor.

"Let's go," Tilman said, and stepped out of the side street. Portier followed. He saw that some of the rougher fellows were talking quietly among themselves. The sound of their horses' hooves captured everyone's attention. Everyone turned to stare.

"And I thought Miss Belle knew how to make an entrance," Portier chortled, liking the attention. Tilman grimaced. This was not the way he liked to do his work. Too showy, for one thing.

A couple of the townsmen whispered to each other, and pointed at the dead men.

Tilman led his horse, with Portier following with his own and the pack horse on a long lead behind, to where the victor of the recent contest was accepting the congratulations of his fellows.

The man looked more like a banker or school teacher than a gunman. He was wearing spectacles, wire framed with dark glass. Tilman saw that his friends were similarly attired.

"Allow me to introduce myself," said Tilman. "I am Mister Tilman of the Pinkerton National Detective Agency. The man you just killed is a wanted Federal fugitive, and there is a ten thousand dollar reward for his capture, dead or alive."

The fellow gaped at him, and then clapped his hands together, laughing, his head back. "Wonderful! Simply wonderful! You mean I've won a prize?"

"You might put it that way," Portier said easily.

The man clapped one of his friends on a shoulder, and they began to walk off. "I thought I was paying, not being paid," the man said. One of the others shouted a question in a tongue Tilman didn't recognize.

"No," the winner said in perfect accentless English; "I'm not hungry now, perhaps later." He turned and walked on with his friend, talking excitedly.

Tilman and Portier now saw that two other of the men with the dark glasses were looping a lariat around Rick Tracy's ankles and dragging him through the dust. They looked to the other side of the street to see how Tracy's friends would take this disrespectful abuse of the corpse.

No one was there. They had all disappeared.

"Well, if that don't beat all," said Tilman, genuinely surprised.

Portier looked about. "Where'd they all go?"

Tilman looked around also. Suddenly, they were alone except for a small group of gunmen standing on the steps of the big building he took to be a hotel.

He smiled, already feeling himself slipping into the hot water of a bath. "Come on," he said, and they walked further down the street. The men on the hotel steps stood silently, watching them approach.

"Whatcha got there?" shouted one.

Tilman waited until they were close enough to reply without shouting. "Found these men out in the hills," he said at last. "Can you tell me where the sheriff's office is?"

One man extended his arm in the direction of the adobe-brick building.

Tilman nodded.

The man spit into the dust. "Ya didn't kill them, did ya?"

"Nope," Portier said; "Found them on the trail, thought they deserved a decent burial."

The man sneered. "Yeah, right," he said. "Liar!"

Portier stiffened at the insult, and his hand fell to his revolver.

Tilman put a restraining hand on his arm. "Business, Mr. Portier, before pleasure." The look he gave the other man was designed to chill the blood, and did.

The Southerner shook himself, pointed a finger at the man who had insulted him, and said, "I'll deal with you later."

Tilman pulled away, with Portier following.

"Anything about this place strike you as funny?" he murmured.

Portier looked about. "Not a woman or child anyplace. But maybe they're elsewhere 'cause of the duel."

"Maybe," Tilman agreed. "What else?"

"New wood everywhere. It's all been built in the last six months or so. Nothing in that gray color that comes from the weather." Portier walked a bit further on with Tilman, then said, "It puts me in mind of something I saw in Manchester."

"And that was?"

"I went to visit Belle Boyd one time backstage when she was in that first play — she's a passable actress, not surprisingly."

"No surprise there."

"She showed me the set. It had canvas and wood painted to look like a regular room in a house."

"I've seen plays," Tilman said.

"Well, doesn't this street look a bit like that?"

Tilman glanced around. "Could be," he said at last. "What was that lingo those foreigners were talking?"

"Couldn't make it out," Portier confessed. "Captain Burton would know, probably — what he doesn't speak, he can identify, from Polish to Pushtu."

"Ummmm," Tilman grunted. "This is a little strange."

"Not like anything I've encountered," said that world traveler, Ashley Portier. "And I have a feeling we've but scratched the surface for strange."

A gunman charged suddenly out of the hotel, ran quickly down the stairs, and raced to the horse where the unwrapped body lay prone over the pack saddle. He lifted the head by the hair and tears came to his eyes.

"Oh, no," he breathed; "No, no, no, no!" He looked up at the two detectives, who watched him carefully. He began to cry openly and unashamedly. He was, they saw, rather young, no more than fourteen, slender, with blond hair. A boy. Which didn't make him any less dangerous if he was hanging around with this mob. Tilman shifted his feet. This could be trouble. He reached over and gently lifted the boy's revolver from its holster. The boy looked at him, confused and angry.

"I'm just going to hold this a bit until you're yourself again," he said gently.

Portier unscrewed the cap of his flask and handed it to him.

"Here, son. Take a little comfort."

The boy held the flask and tasted it cautiously, then took a healthy swig, and handed it back. "Thanks, mister," he said. He pulled out a big red bandana and dried his eyes, then stuffed it back in a rear pocket.

"Now, I know who he was," Tilman said, as he handed back the revolver, and the kid holstered it. "But who are you?"

"Jeremiah Morgan," the boy replied, "And you? Did you kill my pop?"

Tilman and Portier looked at each other. There had been nothing in the intelligence about Morgan having a son, or a family of any kind. Portier shrugged and Tilman looked at the young man carefully, looking for a family resemblance. There wasn't one, as far as he could tell.

"He was your father?"

Jeremiah shook his head. "Not by blood. Married my mom when I was three. Took care of us. Close to being one."

"I'm sorry for your loss," Tilman said automatically. How many times had he used those tired old words? The boy stared at him. "You know he broke jail, and killed a man?"

The boy nodded. "Read about it. Didn't bother me none. Family is family. I figured he had his reasons."

Portier was lighting one of his cheroots. "Every man has his reasons, son. That don't make them good ones or worth following." He blew out a ring of smoke. "We didn't kill him, if you're looking for payback. We just brought the body in to keep the vultures from eating him, along with that other poor soul."

The boy stared at them out of dark brown eyes, stared hard at their faces, and glanced at the badge on Tilman's coat. A look of recognition came over him.

"You would have, though. Pinkertons. I know about you. You was hunting him!"

"We were," Tilman said. "That's the job."

The boy Jeremiah shrugged. "Better you than them." He looked over his shoulder at the hotel where the men with dark glasses were still laughing and congratulating each other over the shootout. "With them, it's just sport."

Tilman and Portier looked at each other and then back at the boy.

His tears were starting again. "He didn't have a chance!" Suddenly he ran down the street, very fast, away from them without looking back, simply intent on getting away. They watched him go, wondering what had spooked him, and then turned and saw a well-dressed man accompanied by two of the local hard cases walking slowly toward them.

"You men!" the well-dressed man said loudly, as he got closer; "What do you have there?"

Portier didn't like his tone. "Who's asking?"

"Jake Martin. I'm the mayor here."

Tilman looked him up and down carefully. "I'm Tilman and he's Portier. We're from Pinkertons, looking for federal fugitives."

Martin shook his head. "You got no authority here."

Portier and Tilman looked sideways at each other and then back at Martin. The mayor was about fifty years old, in a black broadcloth suit and boiled white shirt with a black string tie, looking very official. Tilman looked around. "Our authority goes anyplace within the United States," he said quietly.

Martin grinned. "You've lost your way, detective. This is Mexico."

Portier looked at Tilman. Tilman just stared at the man who was so confident that this bold-faced lie would pass muster.

"Do tell," Tilman said softly. "Well, we still have two dead men to process and bury. Is there a sheriff or marshal we can talk to and get our papers signed?"

"Sure." The mayor pointed to the old adobe building. "Right over there. I'm sure the sheriff will be a great help." He smiled unpleasantly, and then laughed out loud. The two men standing behind him broke up laughing. Behind them, at the hotel bar's double door, there was a slamming sound as another man walked out.

Tilman didn't pay him much mind because Portier was watching him very carefully. Looking directly into Martin's eyes,

Tilman continued. "We're specifically looking for another fellow who broke out of prison with him." He jerked a thumb toward the late Clete Morgan. "Fellow by the name of Parker Boone."

Martin's genial smile faded. "Didn't you hear what I said? This is Mexico. You got no right to take him here."

"He can go with us of his own free will," Portier said, still eyeing the approaching gunman.

"He could, but he won't. I can't say I know this Boone fellow, but if he's here, he's come to do a job, and can't just go wandering off." Martin had the easy confidence of a drummer or carny pitchman. The approaching gunman pushed past Portier and went to the pack horse. He lifted up Clete Morgan's head, then whirled around and pointed an accusing finger at Portier.

"You son-of-a-bitch. You murdered him. Fill your hand!"

"What did you call me?" Portier suddenly flushed with anger, and reached for his two revolvers, only to stop as Tilman used his Winchester to club the gunman to the ground.

"Business before pleasure, Mister Portier," Tilman said again, holding the rifle in a way that indicated his willingness to serve his partner an equal blow. Portier held up both hands, palms out.

"I forgot," he said, unable to suppress a grin.

Jake Martin shook his head wearily. "Plover! Get your ass out of here before you embarrass us all."

The gunman shook his head, touching it gingerly. He scrambled to his feet, suddenly looking at Martin with great fear. "Sorry, Boss." He walked slowly away, and then turned back. A flood of emotions washed over his face.

"Can I claim the body? Get him a Christian burial?"

Tilman nodded. "Once we're done at the Sheriff's office, and have the paper on him, you can do as you please. You kin to him, too?"

"We were in the War together. With Quantrill. I owe him."

"We understand," Portier said.

Tilman nodded. "We'll pay for a simple pine box and a Christian service," he said.

Plover looked at Martin, again fearful. "That okay, Boss?"

Martin nodded. "He's spoiled meat. Get it done. And sober up!"

Plover stumbled up the stairs and back into the hotel. Jake Martin watched him go, and then turned to them. "My apologies, gentlemen. Not just a drunk, but a stupid mean drunk." He looked at them, and smiled easily. "I presume you'll want rooms for the night?"

"You presume wrong, then," Tilman said. "We'll sleep under the stars tonight. In case either of these men have other friends looking for payback."

Portier looked at him, startled.

Martin shrugged. "As you wish. I doubt any of the others care. They got other things to worry about."

"Another time, then," Tilman said, nodding to Portier to lead all three horses, while he worked the lever of the Winchester, and scanned the rooflines, looking for an ambush.

"Always open to men of the law," Martin said. "Finest liquor, gambling, and whores in a hundred miles." He laughed loudly, showing a mouth of pearly white teeth. "Of course, they're the only ones."

Without another word, Tilman turned and walked quickly towards the sheriff's office, Portier, pulling the horses behind them, had to hurry to catch up. He managed to draw level with Tilman.

"And you were so looking forward to that hot bath," he murmured.

"I'll live," Tilman said. He looked around. "All this is passing strange, don't you think?"

"I do."

"Keep a firm hand on that temper of yours, Ash. The job comes first." Tilman cocked his head to one side and regarded him closely. "Have you read Mister Charles Darwin's work? Survival of the fittest? Nature red in tooth and claw?"

Portier, dumbfounded, simply shook his head.

"Then I commend it to your attention. This is not some gentlemen's exercise in fisticuffs. Put up your dukes and you're most likely to get a good kick in the balls." He took the reins of his own horse in his left hand and carried the loaded Winchester in his right, still watching for any sign of an attack. He began to walk once more, slowly. Portier fell in beside him, pulling the other two horses along. The violence had not much agitated them, Portier noted.

"May I give you some advice?" Tilman asked.

"I'm all ears."

"First of all, never hit anyone with your bare hand. It's actually very fragile. Always use an implement. Secondly, do not let yourself be provoked by fools who use schoolyard taunts. Let yourself be blinded by anger, and you will surely come out the worst for it, perhaps fatally so. Stick to the business at hand. Forget about your Southern Chivalry. There's no honor to be won here."

The sheriff's office was in a very old red clay adobe building with a new sign. They tied the three horses to the railing out front. There was a trough of water, and each horse dipped its head in turn and took a long drink, then made a deposit of fresh horse turds on the ground.

Ashley Portier and Blake Tilman looked at each other, and broke up laughing. Portier patted the nearest horse on its hindquarters, and said, "That does seem to sum up the situation."

Tilman pulled the brown leather portfolio from his saddlebag, then he and Portier cautiously walked over and opened the door.

CHAPTER NINETEEN

It was noticeably cooler inside, despite the bright afternoon sun streaming through the dusty window, casting shadow stripes over the room and its single dark brown wooden desk. There was a rack of rifles behind the desk; at the desk sat a neatly dressed man with a six-pointed silver star on his gray frock coat, smiling absently into space. Tilman startled him by saying, "Sheriff?"

The fellow noticeably jumped. This caused Tilman to look over his shoulder at Portier, who shrugged. Tilman tried again. "You are the sheriff?"

The lawman slowly turned his head, and slowly smiled. "Sheriff?" He seemed to taste the word in his mouth. "Sheriff," he repeated. "Yes, I am. Today I am the sheriff. It's my turn."

Tilman, anxious to get on with the business at hand, said, "I am Mister Tilman and this is Mister Portier. We are from Pinkertons."

The Sheriff frowned. "Pinkertons? Where is that?"

"El Paso. We have, outside, the body of one Cletus Morgan, a Federal fugitive. We need you to verify his identity, sign an affidavit for the Court, and arrange to have him buried."

Tilman fumbled with the leather portfolio.

"We will pay for the funeral, of course," Portier added, with considerably more charm than Tilman had been able to muster.

"Pine box. Christian service," Tilman confirmed.

The Sheriff looked perplexed. "Affidavit? What is... "

Tilman opened the portfolio and spread its contents on the desk in front of him. "We are also seeking other wanted men."

The Sheriff picked up two of the wanted posters and frowned. "These are not very good pictures," he objected mildly.

Tilman, nonplussed, stopped and stared at him, wondering if he was the victim of an elaborate prank against newcomers. He'd have better luck with the village idiot — unless, of course, this was said idiot.

The Sheriff spied Derek Seaton's photograph and picked it up.

"This is a very good picture," he said happily; "Life-like."

Tilman and Portier looked at one another again. Portier smiled kindly. The man was obviously either under the influence of some drug, or a mental defective. He held up his hand as Tilman drew breath for an outburst of temper. He took the photograph from the Sheriff, tapped it and asked, "Have you seen him?"

"Him. Yes."

Tilman jumped in, "How about these others?"

The sheriff turned his head very slowly to look at him. It was apparently a hard question. Finally, he managed a smile. "Yes. Some of them."

"Are they here in town?" Tilman felt his normal reserved manner slipping. He was tired, hot, and dirty, and in no mood to suffer fools gladly. He wondered if a firm slap across the cheek might not focus the Sheriff's mind more.

The Sheriff rose slightly in his seat and maneuvered the posters to get a better look. His hand was covered with a gray linen glove. "Yes. Some of them. I think so."

"We want these men arrested. They are criminals, and there are large rewards for their capture and trial," Portier said, speaking kindly, as if to a child. The Sheriff looked puzzled and then alarmed as he took this in.

"Arrest? Have to talk to the mayor first."

"Why?" Tilman asked. "There are substantial rewards, as my partner said."

"Friends of his. Until they die."

Tilman and Portier looked at each other again, their faces now very still. Tilman licked his lips, his mouth gone dry. Had they stumbled into a criminal hideout? One where the outlaws ran the town?

"What do you mean, 'friends'?" Portier asked.

"You mean, of the mayor?" Tilman added.

"Yes. Until they're dead," the Sheriff said happily.

Tilman pulled his partner over closer to the door and looked out, wondering if a mob was assembling. His nerves were suddenly combat fraught. But there was no one there. Tilman whispered, "I can't make him out. He seems to be an idiot or a fool, but he's packing two new Colt's, and given what we've just seen over by the hotel, I don't plan to irritate him."

Portier looked over his shoulder at the Sheriff, who was still fingering the posters. "He's a strange one, all right. Ask him where he's seen the Seaton boy."

Tilman looked at the Sheriff again, and back out the window. He was giving serious thought to just leaving, abandoning the two dead men and the extra horse and riding out of town as fast as they could manage without attracting attention, but he hated to leave any job undone. It would not go down well with his superiors. William Pinkerton had fired men for far less. He did not tolerate cowards.

Portier picked up on this, and was waiting for some kind of signal. Some hint as to what to do. His hand hovered near his right hand revolver. The tension between them was almost visible, like a fog.

"No," Tilman sighed. He brushed the road dust from his front and smiled easily. "Sheriff..., I'm sorry. I didn't get your name."

The Sheriff looked up and smiled. "Hiram Johnson."

"And how long have you been the law in these parts?" Tilman asked.

Sheriff Johnson smiled even wider, very happy now. "Today. My turn today. Second time, too."

The two detectives look sideways at each other, trying to make sense of this. Both wanted to inquire further, but also did not want to get lost in the conversational weeds.

Tilman squared his shoulders and moved on. He picked up Derek Seaton's photograph and said, "You saw him? When?"

"And where?" Portier added, earning a hard look from his partner.

" 'Bout an hour ago," Sheriff Johnson replied, still smiling his too-wide smile. "Back there."

"Where?"

"There." He pointed at a thick wooden door under a sign that read 'JAIL'. Underneath that, some wit had printed in black crayon: 'Abandon All Hope, Ye Who Enter Here.'

"You have him in jail?"

Sheriff Johnson nodded, smiling no more. "He's a prisoner. Too bad."

"Why do you say that?"

"Nice boy. No harm in him. Everybody likes him."

The Sheriff tried to look properly sad at this, but could not quite manage it. His words were devoid of any real feeling.

"Can we see him?" Tilman asked.

"You going to break him out?"

Tilman was taken aback. "No, sir! We're Pinkertons. We uphold the law."

Sheriff Johnson nodded. "Pity. Been a week since we had that kind of fun."

"You want our sidearms?" Portier asked.

Johnson smiled. "No. No need. Just go ahead."

Tilman gathered up the posters and put them in the portfolio, holding back the photograph of young Seaton. Portier touched the crayon inscription over the door as they passed under it.

"Not funny," he said.

"No. Not at all," Blake Tilman agreed, pushing the door open. "You think the Sheriff smokes opium?" he asked softly as a row of steel bars was revealed.

"I think someone is," Portier replied sourly; "Because this is some kind of dream."

Behind them, a younger man entered the front door and said loudly, "Can I help you, gentlemen?" He was carrying a covered tray in one hand, balancing it as easily as a waiter at a fancy restaurant. He stared at them, and they took immediate note of the sizeable Bowie knife on his belt near his free hand. The two detectives observed his unsmiling face under a high forehead covered with black hair. He had intelligent brown eyes, and was dressed in tan broadcloth trousers and a faded blue denim shirt. A brass badge pinned on his chest said 'Marshal'.

The Sheriff looked at him nervously. "They want to see Mister Seaton."

The other man looked them up and down slowly.

"Pinkertons," Portier said.

He nodded. "Chicago outfit. You friends of his?"

Tilman realized that the man was an Indian, probably an Apache. "We were sent to find him," Blake said, trying to keep his manner easy.

"Why?"

"His mother misses him."

The Indian almost smiled at that. He gestured to the Sheriff. "Keys."

The Sheriff searched in a desk drawer and produced a ring with several large brass keys. He tossed them to the Indian, who caught them handily with his free hand.

"You two better come back with me."

The Sheriff started to rise. "Not you." The Sheriff sat obediently back down.

Tilman and Portier exchanged a look, and Portier held the covered tray while the Indian unlocked the iron gate that led to the cells. Taking the tray back, the Indian escorted them into the jail, glancing only briefly at the holstered revolvers they wore. He seemed oddly unconcerned about a possible escape.

There was a long hallway that passed three empty cells on each side, and then opened up into a larger area with a rough pine table and four chairs. Behind that was a much larger cell, with a fancy brass bed, a smaller table, a comfortable-looking rocking chair with cushions, and a kerosene lamp that cast a bright glow. A barred window looked out at an endless vista of flat desert with mountains in the far distance. The sky was bright blue, and the sun blazing hot and merciless.

A young man was standing, staring out the window. He was in his shirt sleeves but otherwise well-dressed. His boots looked well-worn; the rest of his attire fairly screamed 'dude'. It was the kind of expensive gear that no self-respecting rancher could afford, or would wear.

The Indian set the tray on the table, removed the linen napkin covering the dishes, and set out the china plates and fancy silverware for what looked like a very good meal of roasted chicken, potatoes, and greens.

"You got company, Boss," the Indian said.

"Tell them I'm not in." The young man kept staring out the window. Tilman, having seen many condemned men over the years, thought he had the aspect of doom about him.

"Can't do that."

"Dammit, Hey-zeus." The young man's voice carried a tearful note.

"They're here, Boss," the Indian said.

Surprised, the young man turned around and stared at them. He smiled in relief.

"You're not one of them, are you?"

Tilman ignored the question and looked at the photograph in his hand. "Are you Derek Seaton of Chicago, Illinois?"

He looked at both of them cautiously. "What if I am?"

"I am Mister Tilman and this is my partner, Mr. Portier. We're from Pinkerton's."

He saw the badges now. "Pinkerton;s? Really? You are a long way from home." He walked over to where his food was set out and sat down; picking up the knife and fork, he began to carve the chicken into pieces. He sipped at the bottle of beer, and sighed. "Is there some new crime I'm accused of?" he asked bitterly. He put the knife and fork aside, and said, "I don't have much appetite."

"We're not aware of any crimes you might be charged with," Tilman said.

"But we're new in town," Portier added dryly. "Just here to drop off a miscreant named Clete Morgan, whom we found dead in the desert."

Derek Seaton turned pale. "Clete's dead?"

Tilman was irritated that Portier had given up this information so easily. Information was valuable currency for a detective, to be hoarded like gold until the right moment, and only exchanged at a premium. But it had produced something in return. How had the high-born Seaton come to be on a first-name basis with Morgan, generally considered a very bad man — even by other bad men?

Seaton snapped his fingers. "Pinkerton's. You guard our trains. My mother sent you."

"That is correct, sir. All part of the service," Portier said. "I know that being chased after like a truant schoolboy must be galling to a grown man... "

Seaton managed a shaky laugh. "Not at all. For once I'm happy for her interfering ways." He beckoned the two detectives closer. "I'm in a lot of trouble here," he whispered. He looked over to where the Indian was waiting by the table.

"Would you not agree, my Apache friend?"

The Indian didn't blink. "Yes."

Then he gestured like a *maître d'* in a fine restaurant. "Luncheon is served."

Seaton dug a finger in his vest pocket and tossed him a five-dollar gold piece.

"There you are."

The Indian nodded gracefully.

"What about them?" he asked, pointing to the two detectives.

Tilman, pretending to misunderstand, said, "We'll be responsible for him."

The Indian dropped the ring of keys on the table, turned, and left without another word.

"We have a new Sheriff again?" Seaton sat back down and began to eat once more.

"Your appetite has returned, I see," Portier observed. "As for the Sheriff, he did seem a bit green."

"They trade the job off every week or so. It's very irregular, but then everything here is irregular. Hey-zeus actually runs the jail. Meals are, as you saw, extra."

Tilman said. "This one seemed to be some sort of idiot. Or maybe just foreign."

"He's one of the Strangers."

"The Strangers? You mean the dressed-up dudes with the funny glasses? This one wasn't wearing spectacles."

"They don't, inside." Seaton finished eating and pushed the plate aside. He took another drink from the bottle of beer, and burped.

"My apologies. I have no manners these days, and no real appetite. I was advised to eat regularly to keep my strength and spirits up." He looked at them speculatively. "Prove to me you men are from Pinkerton's."

Tilman showed him his calling card. "We never sleep," he said.

Seaton looked carefully. Satisfied, he nodded. "Neither do I," he laughed; "Not these days. My apologies, but I've learned to take nothing here at face value. Everything here is like some terrible play."

"In what way?" Portier asked.

"The showdowns they have every day. Those men are the fastest I've ever seen in a gun fight, unless they've had too much to drink. Then you have a small chance. But even when it's one of them that falls, they act like they are on holiday. All a big joke."

"That why you're locked up?" Tilman asked. "You kill one of them?"

Seaton shook his head miserably. "I did," he sighed, "but not by design. It was during one of those brawls that seem to break out every night. One of them pulled a knife of considerable size, like the one that Hey-zeus has, and came at me."

"And you shot him?"

"No. You never have time to draw on one of these fellows. They're too quick. He was enjoying the moment a bit too much, which gave me my chance. I hit him with a chair." A puzzled look came over Seaton's face. "He up and died right there. Almost at once, and I did not hit him more than a mild lick. And before I could even explain or make my case, I was hustled off to jail. They accused me of breaking the rules."

"There are no rules in a knife fight," Portier said scornfully. "You win any way you can."

"So when is the trial?" Tilman asked, wondering if there was even a lawyer in a town this small.

Seaton laughed bitterly. "Trial! What trial?! That's not how they do things here."

"Oh?"

"You kill someone here, your only trial is by combat. In a showdown against one of them. It's a death sentence!" Seaton broke down, close to tears. "You've got to break me out, gentlemen. You know who my family is. I'll pay you any sum you name!"

Portier was distressed at this unmanly display. "Come, suh, it can't be that bad."

"I count myself as brave as any other man," young Seaton pleaded; "but I was not made for this. These Strangers are so quick that even the most seasoned gunfighter falls against them." He was pale and sweating now, his eyes wild with panic. "These are not gunfights, they're ritual slaughters. Tougher men than I have fled. Clete Morgan... "

"What about Clete Morgan?" Tilman asked sharply.

Seaton just stared at them, unable to answer.

"Was Clete Morgan here in jail?" Portier asked gently.

Seaton swallowed hard, and nodded slowly. "He was."

"We packed his body in with us," Portier said softly. "Quite dead."

"We found him in the desert. Damned if we can tell what actually killed him either, 'cept part of him seems to be cooked." Tilman shook his head. "When did ol' Clete break out?"

"Two days ago. They left the door ajar and he took his chance. I promised him a thousand dollars if he brought back a posse to rescue me."

"A lot of money." Portier tilted his head, regarding him with curiosity. "Why not just go with him?"

"It smelled like a trap." Seaton looked from one to the other of them as they looked back with expressions that dripped disapproval. "Hey! I told him as much, but he was determined. They'd told him his time was coming."

"Hobson's Choice," Tilman said, sucking at his teeth.

"No choice." Portier produced one of his cheroots from a vest pocket, stuck it in his mouth, found a sulphur match which he scratched against the rough red-brown adobe, and used to light the little cigar. He drew in the smoke and looked thoughtfully at the other two.

"I'd say, Mister Seaton, that breaking jail did Clete Morgan little good."

"I agree," said his partner. "When are you due for your trial by fire, Mister Seaton?"

"Fire?"

"Gunfire."

"You make jokes at a time like this?"

Tilman shrugged. "With all due respect, sir, when I was a soldier we often used humor to sustain us on the eve of battle."

"Stiff upper lip and all that, eh," Portier said in a fake English accent.

Seaton slowly smiled. He chuckled, and then laughed outright. "Yes! Very good. Very good, indeed."

"So when is your date with destiny?" Tilman prompted him again.

"Not sure. No one has said. It's up to the mayor."

"Jake Martin? Owns the hotel?"

"And the bar and the whorehouse." Seaton looked thoughtful. "Maybe the whole town. I mean, there are people here who are not part of his scheme, whatever it is. Hey-zeus is actually the chief of his band. Native to this place. As you saw, he doesn't say much. But despite hating White men with a quiet passion, he is not cruel. He's actually well-educated. Very intelligent. I think he is playing his own game here."

"Can we trust him?" Portier asked.

Seaton looked baffled and hopeless again. He shrugged.

Tilman gazed out the cell window at the bright blue sky and its merciless golden sun. He said, finally, "We seem to be confronted with a number of mysteries here."

"What do we do, then?" Portier asked.

"We're investigators. So we will investigate," Tilman replied. "You sit tight, Mister Seaton. My partner and I will see what we can do for you."

CHAPTER TWENTY

At the same moment, in a room on the second floor of Jake Martin's nameless hotel, a tall, beautiful, slender Creole woman sat almost naked in front of the mirror on her dresser, carefully applying blood-red color with a small brush to her full generous lips. Once she had pressed them carefully together, and blotted the excess color, she repeated the process for each of her large, erect nipples.

"I don't see why you bother," said the shorter, much younger, red-haired Irish girl laying on the day bed a short distance away. She was wearing a fancy dark green corset and stockings held by fancy garters around her thighs. And nothing more. A green linen dress hung nearby, but it was too hot for her to put on until she had to. The room, despite two windows open to the outside, felt like one of those steam baths they had back East. It smelled of sweat and sex beneath the French perfume sprayed in the air.

"My daddy always said that if a thing was worth doing, it was worth doing well."

"Even being a *hoor*? I always thought it a simple job. Just take the money, lay there, and let them get on with business."

"The secret of any successful business is repeat trade, *n'est-ce pas*? The business is giving them something they can't get at home," the Creole said, standing and pulling a gown from the closet next to the dressing table. "You want them coming back for more. You want to keep them interested, Molly."

"Why? In New York or New Orleans I could see it, Mistress. Here, with this lot? What's the point? I'm pagan enough to enjoy it for its own sake. But these Strangers act as if they've never been with a woman before... and the rest? Brutes!" She pulled her silk bustier down under her right breast to reveal a sizeable bruise on her rib cage.

"You'll have to cover that with something," the other woman said calmly.

"It's my own fault," Molly replied. "I slapped him for going too hard at me."

"One of the Strangers?"

"One of the gunfighters. He was drunk, anyway, and spoiling for trouble – which is my middle name."

"So you think you provoked him?"

"Didn't I?"

"I made the rules quite plain to Captain Martin when we arrived. My girls are not to be abused. No violence by word or deed. You did the right thing. You should have called one of the guards."

Molly rolled her eyes, then jumped up off the bed to help 'Miss Kate' into her black silk corset.

'Miss Kate' stood slowly. She looked around the shabby room with its worn-out used furniture and fake French blue *fleur de lis* wallpaper, and sighed.

"I should have never brought us here, Molly. It was a mistake."

"You was misled, Mistress. That man is not to be trusted." Molly began to pull at the laces at the back of the corset, pulling the waist inward; Alicia Sorrell groaned slightly and then exhaled.

"I already knew Jake Martin's character, Molly, so the more fool I. It was he who broke me to this life after the War, in New Orleans. I was too proud: the Colonel's lady — then the Colonel revealed he had another wife in Massachusetts, and the whole thing was a sham, a game. One he turned back on me."

Molly looked at her a long time. This was a part of Alicia Sorrell's story she had not heard. She poured a glass of water from the cut glass pitcher on a side table and handed it to her.

Alicia sipped delicately at it, gazing critically at her image in the big stand-alone mirror by the window. As long as she had her looks, she had value. That made her ambitious, but ambition had tricked her before. She smiled, revealing perfect white teeth.

"It was a marriage of convenience. *You* like it rough sometimes."

"I do," Molly agreed. "It feeds my passion."

Alicia smiled gently. "It feeds my hatred."

Molly cocked her head to one side as she held Alicia's gown so the older woman could pull it on over her head. She possessed a certain native cunning, and knew that information sometimes became power.

"So it was not a love match, then?"

Alicia looked very sad. "He was a Yankee, and we were at war. I seduced him and married him, so I could spy on him. Charmed him to a fare-thee-well. Belle Boyd or Rose Greenhow could not have done it better. I flattered myself it was for my country, and that the way to power and victory was to become a courtesan."

"And?" Molly was fascinated now, hanging on her every word.

"Well, as I was playing him, he was playing me. The papers I copied and handed off to one of Judah Benjamin's spies were false. Months, this went on, while he undertook to educate me in the ways of pleasure that no respectable woman would ever tolerate. Things so vile that I could not even bring myself to confess them to my priest."

Molly blinked. "You mean he turned you into a whore?"

Alicia shook her head. "As he pointed out, I became one by entering into a false marriage. By making my way and my living under false colors, as he called it. I took the Oath of Allegiance to convince him I was true. And I had already promised myself to another: a handsome Confederate Cavalryman fighting in Virginia, while I made light conversation with 'Beast' Butler and his staff. Colonel Soames's offer to make me 'an honest woman' was a fraud and a joke. But the joke was on me. He made sure to shame me, as he cast me aside, so everyone in New Orleans would know."

She sighed and shook her head ruefully.

"Captain Martin, his quartermaster, was there to catch me. He was already a flesh peddler, since he bought horses for the Union Army in great numbers, and then sold a few back on the side along with escaped slaves; selling whores or renting them was an easy step. They not only stole my virtue, they stole my pride. So I went along with it, and made the best of it, working the circuit between New Orleans and New York City. I like the work, which is fortunate; otherwise I might have gone mad."

Molly thought, *You have your moments*, as she helped her on with her boots.

"And you still let him bed you. Why?"

"Because I am a whore, darling. It is 'work for hire'. I set the terms, and they pay me well. I cannot complain without becoming a hypocrite, can I? Those acts I first thought so vile are now part of my repertoire to entice and thrill men and make them mine. I like them now, not just for the thrill, but for the power they give me over men. But Jake Martin cannot be thrilled nor enticed. It is all Commerce to him, and, being Italian, he favors keeping me close. And honest."

Molly was confused. "Martin is not an Italian name," she said.

"He migrated here as Giacomo Martino. He's very adaptable, you see. We all wear masks." Alicia sipped at the water once more, sat in front of the dresser mirror and adjusted the top of her corset so that the rouged nipples barely showed. "You should teach them, you know," Alicia said.

"Teach them? If I'd wanted to be a teacher, I'd have become a schoolmarm. They get me so stirred up sometimes." The little redhead put her hand between her legs.

Alicia reached out and pulled it away. "Save that for the customers. Or for later when it will be sweeter for us."

"You're cruel," Molly groaned. "And servicing this lot gets me no closer to what I'm here for."

Alicia raised an eyebrow. "What would that be, you little Irish tramp?"

The harshness in her tone, so unexpected, took Molly aback.

"Why, why, … " she stuttered. She felt herself blush bright red. It was as if she had been slapped for no reason. She took a deep breath and let it out slowly. Alicia Sorrell's face was the same, but there was anger in her eyes. Molly bowed her head. "I'm sorry, Mistress." Now she feared punishment. Not just the pain, but the other woman's displeasure.

"Why are you here?" Alicia asked again, softly.

"I want a rich husband," Molly said defiantly. "Some fella who has a cattle ranch or a gold mine or owns a railroad."

"True love, then?" Alicia sneered.

Molly laughed. "Not likely. Just more of the same, and lots less of it if I have my way. But I'll live well, and my children will be rich and powerful. Don't you want more than this?"

"I had it. Was born to it on a big plantation that produced a thousand bales of cotton a year. The War changed all of that. The Yankees stole it, and ruined me."

"So you found you wasn't such a grand lady after all," Molly could not keep the satisfaction out of her voice.

"I was your age and just a stupid girl. Like you. A woman will do what she has to do to survive. If you want to profit from my example, here is the lesson." Alicia stood and loomed over her. Molly braced herself for a slap that never came. Instead, Alicia pulled her close into a protective hug.

"One may be a whore, but that does not mean that one must not also be a lady at all times." She reached down and teased Molly between her legs, producing a gasp. "You are selling what's down here." She raised the same hand to her forehead. "I am selling what's up here. That's where the real power is. You plan to give that away to earn a little respectability? The more fool you."

Molly stared at her, so elegant and so refined, and both hated her and loved her at that moment. "So you will never marry?"

"I did not say that. But it did not go well for me last time, and I've learned caution. When the War began, I was engaged to a dashing, brave young man. He fought for the South."

"He was killed?"

"Perhaps. He was in the Army, and then our Navy. Had to go to England for that, and the Union calls them pirates even now. I never saw him again."

"So you're not so proud, now?"

"Of this? Of what I've become? No, of course not. But I make my brave pretense, and expect you to do likewise, or earn a beating for being a lazy slut. Help me finish dressing."

Molly grinned. "Yes, your ladyship. I'll play the maid."

. . .

Portier and Tilman stood at the doorway of the nameless hotel's bar for a long moment, taking it all in, carefully assessing the situation. Jake Martin was behind the bar in his shirtsleeves. He looked at them and displayed a genial welcoming smile.

"Gentlemen. First one is on the house!" he called.

They looked at each other, shrugged, and walked across the room. There was no one else at the bar. A few men sat at tables, playing cards and drinking. Tilman carried the brown leather portfolio under his left arm, leaving his right free to draw his revolver if need be. He placed the portfolio on top of the bar.

Jake Martin placed his big soft hands flat on the bar, still smiling. "What's your pleasure?"

"I'm Temperance," Tilman said, looking at the display of liquor bottles on the back bar.

"How about some coffee then?"

Tilman nodded. Martin poured a cup and slid it across the bar. "How about you?"

"I don't suppose you have any *Cognac*?"

"Don't get much call for it," Martin said, "But I'm sure there's a bottle here someplace." He reached under the bar, came up with a dusty, straw-covered bottle, and blew the dust off of it. He pulled the cork and poured a generous shot into a small glass. "You a Frenchman?"

Portier picked up the glass, smelled the liquor and smiled. "No, New Orleans."

Martin smiled again. "That vest is rather fancy for one of Pinkerton's sleuths. I'd make you for a tin horn gambler."

Portier nodded. "I've been known to turn a card or two."

"You'll have to try our tables. Fresh meat is always welcome."

Tilman cleared his throat, causing Portier to glance sideways at him to see the slight negative shake of his head.

"We Pinkertons never mix business with pleasure," Portier said smoothly.

"And you're here on business?"

"We are," Tilman said, finally sipping at the coffee. "We have the matter of disposing of Clete Morgan's and William Hervey's remains. I presume you have an undertaker in this town? We'll pay for a pine box and simple Christian service, once we have the affidavits."

Martin looked at him, his face very still.

"Affidavits?"

"So our agency can claim for the rewards and our expenses."

Martin looked serious. "That's a job for the Sheriff."

"He seems a bit at sea," Portier drawled. "Not sure if he's up to the job. Seems to lack experience." He took a sip of his drink.

"Said we should see the mayor. That's you, right?" Tilman chipped in.

Martin looked momentarily flustered. "Sorry. I forgot who had the detail today. He ain't regular."

"And the Indian actually runs the jail?"

Martin nodded. "He does. If you need some sort of official paper, he's the one to see. 'Sheriff' is a courtesy title for our guests, so they can savor the Western experience. Hey-seuss was elected by the permanent residents. I'm the mayor, but he's the *Alcalde.*"

"But he's an Indian!" Portier said, surprised.

"That don't matter in Mexico, *amigo*. Everyone is a citizen. Anyone can serve."

Portier felt at a disadvantage. He turned to Tilman, only to see confusion in his partner's eyes. Tilman looked around the barroom and decided to change the subject.

"Nice place," he said. "Reminds me of the Long Bar at Willard's Hotel in Washington."

Martin looked pleased. "Thank you. I did have that in mind. But I thought you was Temperance?"

"I wasn't always," Tilman said, relaxing now. "I came to it after my wife and child died. To honor them."

"That's very laudable," Martin replied, looking at him carefully, trying to gauge his character. "I suppose you see the inside of a few in your line of work."

"I do. You usually work the bar yourself?"

"In the mornings. Before things get busy. It keeps me in touch. I find if you take care of the little things, the big things pretty much take care of themselves."

"Quite a place," Portier joined in. "Everything looks new."

"It is." Martin puffed himself up a little, showing the pride of ownership.

"So it's not really a town?" Tilman asked.

"Nope. More like a resort. I'm in the entertainment business. Imported everything from the linens to the ladies."

"Really?" Portier felt the impulse to turn over a dish that seemed to be fine English bone china and see its hallmark. It was being used as an ashtray. "Seems like a lot of trouble."

"You have to spend money to make money." Martin smiled. "I have these foreigners who want to experience the true Old West before it goes away. They pay very well, and I provide everything you might read about in a dime novel."

"Everything?" Tilman frowned.

"Whisky, women, card games, and more. So you men are a welcome addition to the *ambience*."

"The showdowns, too?" Portier took a cheroot from his vest pocket. Martin struck a match and lit it for him.

"And bar fights on occasion. Everything the best that money can buy." He smiled once more, but his eyes were hostile. "You boys ask a lot of questions."

"It's our nature." Portier smiled, drawing the smoke into his lungs and letting it out slowly. "We are detectives, after all."

Jake Martin looked at them silently. He picked up another glass, and began polishing it with a small white towel. Then he said, "You understand that I will not permit anything that might disturb my guests."

"That include all these gunmen?" Tilman said, easing back from the bar. He opened the brown leather portfolio to reveal the wanted posters.

Martin nodded. "Them are more like employees, but I need them. All part of the *ambience*, you see."

"There are substantial rewards for some of them."

Jake Martin laughed. "I know. That's why they were invited. They are stars. Major attractions for our guests. So them rewards ain't a patch on what I make by having them here."

Tilman and Portier looked at each other, not sure of what to say next.

"Look," Martin said; "it ain't all about the gunfights. We got some of the most beautiful whores you've ever seen. They'll be down in a few minutes."

"I'm not much for the ladies," Tilman replied.

"Then you'll just have to take a cigar, won't you? I'm sure your friend indulges. He has the look of a man of parts."

Portier was nonplussed. This was too much. "You, sir, are no gentleman."

"Never claimed I was." Martin was now a bit irritated. "I'm a merchant, plain and simple. If you don't like what I'm selling, then the door is over there."

Tilman spoke calmly, in very measured tones, so as not to be drawn into a loud argument. "Mayor Martin. We are here to do a job. Some of these fellows are wanted 'dead or alive'. I'm not particular about how we do it, but we are going to bring them in."

Jake Martin looked at him, and muttered a curse in Italian. Then he took a deep breath in and leaned across the bar, beckoning the two detectives closer.

"We got our own form of justice here. If you think about it, the results are going to be about the same, without the inconvenience of confronting these very bad men."

Tilman shook his head slowly. "Call it the Puritan in me, but I like to do my own work. We always give a fugitive the option of coming along peaceably. Most do."

Martin sneered. "Let me put it another way. This is my town. I own it. What Law there is, comes from me. I am not going to do anything to upset my guests... and neither are you. Unless you want to end up like Clete Morgan."

"Now see here," Tilman finally lost his temper, only to feel his partner take him firmly by the arm and pull him across the room and out the front door to the wide veranda.

"Let us confer a moment, Mister Mayor," Portier said over his shoulder.

Tilman shook himself loose from Portier's firm grip. His partner grabbed him by the shoulders, and said, very quietly, "Look here, Hoss. You're playing a losing hand. Time to fold and ante up again."

"He can't do this!" Tilman protested.

"He just laid it out. He can do pretty much as he likes. Who is going to stop him? Unless you got some magical way to call them soldier boys we passed about two days back, we're going to have play this out. We are very outnumbered, and have no friends here."

Portier let Tilman mull this over and recover himself.

"Maybe we can get the Seaton boy released," Tilman said at last.

They walked back in and found Jake Martin putting on his black frock coat and adjusting his string tie. Another man, a tall light-skinned Negro with garters on his shirt sleeves, and a neat bow tie, was behind the bar. Portier noted that he had the long elegant fingers of a card sharp and thought he looked familiar.

Tilman spoke very mildly. "Mayor Martin. We're also here looking for Derek Seaton. You have him over in the jail."

Jake Martin looked thoughtfully upward at the tin ceiling, pretending that he was having trouble remembering this.

"Oh, yes," he said at last. "Seaton. The murderer."

"Seems he was just defending himself. When do you plan to have him formally charged?"

Martin looked amused. "Charged? Like in a court of law?"

"That's the usual way of handling such things," Portier observed mildly.

"We use an older system here. Trial by combat. Seaton will get his chance."

Tilman and Portier looked at each other with growing alarm. "He's no gunman," Tilman protested. "He's a college boy off on a lark."

"Bad luck for him, then. He killed one of my guests. His friends want justice."

"Your 'justice' is organized murder, if I may speak plain."

"My town, my rules," Jake Martin replied evenly. "It's a free country. You're entitled to your opinion." He shrugged. "My guests will be leaving soon. Maybe they won't get to the Seaton boy's case before then. Then I could just let him go... for a small consideration."

Tilman and Portier were momentarily taken aback by this bold play for a bribe.

Tilman thought, *This is an easy solution to the problem. Too easy. And problematic, since the 'consideration' was likely to be more than Portier or I have with us — or Seaton, for that matter, if he is paying close to a week's wages for most people, just for his dinner.*

There is no telegraph handy to wire for more funds, nor is Martin actually likely to allow us to leave, he suddenly realized. *This town is a trap. A man trap. The gunfighters were lured with promises of big wages for showing their skills, but how many would survive to collect the promised rewards?* "Damn few," Tilman said aloud.

"Pardon?" Martin looked at him quizzically.

"I mean," Tilman said, covering; "We will have to consult with our client. We're not authorized to make that deal ourselves. How much consideration did you have in mind?"

Portier shook his head slightly, and Tilman realized that he had made a tactical error by allowing Martin to open the bidding. Whatever amount was named would be impossible to deliver. But Martin turned it back on him.

"I'm a reasonable man. Make me an offer." He looked upward at the sounds from many footsteps. "In the meantime, why not stick around for the festivities? We have some dazzling damsels from the Demimonde." Martin's chest expanded with genuine pride. He waved his hand like an impresario.

The girls began to descend the wide staircase from the second floor in pairs, smiling and waving. They were all extraordinarily beautiful, and dressed in gowns that revealed quite a bit of skin. Nearly bare bosoms, corseted waists, and long legs in abundance. There were twelve in all.

Portier gazed at them with the appreciation of a connoisseur. He had been in many such establishments, from Boston to Berlin to Bangkok, and always enjoyed the beauty parade. He scanned each face carefully — then felt his own face freeze in shock.

CHAPTER TWENTY-ONE

Alicia Sorrell, glancing down the stairs and adjusting her gown so that not too much of the goods she was selling were on display, barely noticed the tall lean man with the fancy vest. Her attention was claimed by Blake Tilman, whom she'd met in New York City some years before. The Pinkerton who was noted for his rectitude in refusing accommodations from members of the Demimonde. What on Earth was he doing here?

Then she took a second look at the obvious tin horn gambler, and felt the room spin. Instantly, she felt sick to her stomach with amazement, shame, and grief. Ashley Portier, suddenly risen from the dead – or not dead at all. Faint and dizzy, she murmured to Molly, "Take over, dear, I'm suddenly unwell." She fled back up the stairs to her room.

Portier, who had been standing stock still, came alive; staggering slightly, he grabbed the bottle of *Cognac* on the counter before him and, without another word walked out the door. The short red-haired whore, as fussy as a border collie herding sheep, got the rest down the stairs and had them line up for the evening parade.

Tilman stared after him, then looked upstairs at the empty place where Alicia Sorrell had been standing. He was not sure what had happened. Jake Martin looked equally baffled. To cover his confusion, Tilman smiled pleasantly and said, "He gets these spells. Old war injury. How much for the *Cognac*?"

Martin blinked. "Twenty dollars. Ten if he brings the bottle back."

It was an outrageous price, but Tilman didn't quibble. He just placed one of the shrinking hoard of twenty-dollar gold pieces on the bar, and went in search of his partner.

He didn't have to look far. Portier sat on the steps of the hotel, taking a generous swig from the straw-wrapped bottle. Tilman sat next to him, watching carefully until Portier lifted it again to his lips, and pulled it away from his hand. Portier stared at him, obviously offended and looking for a fight.

Tilman just shook his head, saying, "I told you that I will not have a man with me who is not ready at all times. Save the bender and the self-pity for another time." Tilman spoke softly, so as not to be overheard, but his words were like a shout in Portier's ears. The Southerner stared, trembling, then looked away, his face and neck growing red.

"So who is she?"

Portier hung his head, unable to speak. Tilman realized that the Alicia Sorrell he'd known in New York, the hardened and cynical Madam and high-class whore, was the woman Portier had obviously once known before the War.

"Who is she?' Tilman prompted again.

"Oh, only the love of my life," Portier groaned. "We were engaged to be married before the War."

Tilman nodded, and handed the bottle back. "One more and then back to the task at hand," he said kindly, like an indulgent but stern father. He did not think mentioning his previous acquaintance with the woman was advisable, or productive, just then. Some things were better left unsaid.

Molly Shannon, carrying a tray covered with a white linen napkin, cautiously entered Alicia Sorrell's private bedroom, half expecting a slipper to be thrown at her, or to be otherwise abused. Her mistress had these moods from time to time, and they always came without warning. To her surprise, Alicia lay face down diagonally across her big bed, her shoulders shaking as she cried real tears.

Molly maneuvered around the bed, put the tray on a side table, and pulled the napkin aside to reveal a big white china tea pot with a blue flower pattern and a matching tea cup. She carefully poured tea into the cup, saying, as lightly as she could, "Here, luv. Tea's just the thing for heartbreak. I'd have brought something stronger, but Mister Martin was giving me that fish-eye look of his, as it 'twas."

Alicia turned over and sat up, repositioning herself against the pillows and headboard. She reached out and accepted the cup of tea, holding it, feeling its warmth before finally taking a sip. Molly looked at her speculatively.

"Now we've seen this before," she said softly; "haven't we? In Amarillo, with Daisy, when her brother showed up out of nowhere. The dashing stranger is kin?"

Alicia shook her head, fresh tears slowly flowing down her face. "Worse. We were to be married."

"No!" Molly gasped.

Alicia nodded. "I was fifteen, and so in love. My father wanted us to wait a year, so I would be my mother's age when they married. He was twenty and at college in Virginia when the War broke out. He was in the Army with Stuart, and then he went to England to join our pathetic excuse for a Navy. Last letter I got from him was ten years ago, before he went on the *Shenandoah* with Captain Waddell. The Union still calls them pirates. No amnesty. I'd heard he was dead! I never thought I'd see him again! Oh, God! What a cruel fate!"

Fifty yards away, Ashley Portier lit one of his cheroots, inhaled deeply, blew out a cloud of fragrant smoke, and continued his explanation. The liquor he'd swilled was beginning to affect him. He spoke slowly and carefully. " ...I wrote her from England, but never got a reply," he said. "Union agents had gotten very good at intercepting our mail and our money; the faithless Brits just looked the other way. Once we lost Vicksburg and Gettysburg on the same day, they thought we were done, and turned their backs on us. We had a different opinion, and kept sending cruisers out in hopes of breaking the blockade. I was assigned to the last ship out, the *Shenandoah*."

"I've heard the name." Tilman looked skyward, searching his memory. "She did some damage. Whaling fleet, was it? Up near the Alaska territory?"

Portier gave a low bitter laugh. "A famous victory, Blake. Fifty whalers we captured and burned. And fifty or so ordinary ships before we made our last port-of-call at Sydney Harbor. We still had an Army and a government when we set sail, and a man from our Department of State had fresh orders for us. Go North, they said, and attack the whalers. Their captains protested that the war was over, but Waddell was too smart to be taken in by that obvious lie – except it wasn't one, as we discovered when we exchanged signals with a British man-of-war sent to look for us. We were suddenly considered pirates, the scum of the earth. The British Navy wanted no part of us, and warned we'd all be hanged if we surrendered. With that in mind, Waddell dismantled the guns, stored them below, and made his daring run for Liverpool. Over seventeen thousand miles without being spotted once. Through the South Pacific and the Indian Ocean, around the Cape of Good Hope, and north through the Atlantic until we arrived at Liverpool in the middle of the night, and our Commander, Captain Bullock paid off the crew with the last money the Confederate government had."

"So you're a pirate."

"I suppose so. Are you going to arrest me?"

Tilman shook his head. "I wouldn't do that."

"No?"

"We're partners, and we're on a job."

"So I get a pass?"

"You do."

Tilman thought to himself that Ashley Portier was either the biggest liar he'd ever met, or possessed of incredible luck – both good and bad. To date, nothing he'd said could be proved or disproved. Tilman enjoyed campfire gossip and tall tales as much as the next man, but the stricken look on Alicia Sorrell's face was better than an affidavit. Five years before, in New York City, he'd proved her innocent of murder. She'd been attacked with a knife by the eldest son of a wealthy and powerful Boston merchant family, and defended herself by shooting him dead. Sent to find and arrest 'the murdering whore' by Pinkerton's on the family's behalf, his investigation had instead proved legitimate self-defense, and implicated the dead man in the bloody and vicious unsolved murders of several other high-class whores.

He remembered her well. She was as honest as any woman in her circumstances could be, and her offer of an erotic recompense had come as close to breaking his resolve to stay true to his dead wife's memory as anyone ever had.

She was the Queen of the Demimonde! What was she doing here? But life was filled with incredible coincidences and long-shot events. His new partner was apparently another.

"So the last time you saw her was when?" he asked Portier, who was looking hungrily at the bottle of *Cognac*.

"Christmas holidays 1860. Before the War started. We pledged our troth then, and published the banns. But she was a patriot, too, and eager to do secret service work. Women in New Orleans went two ways with 'Beast' Butler and his officers. Either total contempt, for which they were severely punished, or gentle accommodation. Judah Benjamin enlisted her as a spy, and she worked to advance the Cause, knowing I would forgive her anything.

"Once we were engaged, a certain amount of intimacy was not only permitted but also expected, as long as we were not public about it. So I knew she had a passionate nature that she would need to satisfy. That did not trouble me; most men are the same way. How could I judge her for doing what I planned to do myself? As long as her heart was mine, and she stayed true to the South, her body was her own to rule. I was hundreds of miles away. How could it be otherwise, else she would be a liar?"

"How indeed?" Tilman said. He decided not to mention his previous encounter with Alicia Sorrell, or why life and circumstance made her so hard. She was not the girl Ashley Portier had left behind, and his reaction to seeing her here was more emotion than shock.

"Tell me how you escaped Yankee justice after you got back to Liverpool." Tilman wanted to buy time to think things through, so he listened with half an ear as another part of his mind sorted through the shrinking list of options available to them if they were to survive the deadly trap of Apache Wells.

"I shipped out again. Our reception committee was from the British Secret Service. Most of the crew were from the British Naval Reserve, so we were not so much a real Confederate Navy, as a proxy for them to destroy the American commercial fleet. It was all about money and power. They didn't care to actually break the blockade, which they could have done at any time with a man-of-war outside of Charleston or Mobile. There was money to be made smuggling, and they are a mercantile nation. So I was handed two hundred and ninety nine pounds and eight pence in an envelope, along with a false passport and seaman's papers, and told I was shipping out to Africa as the third mate on a Cunard steamer the next day."

Tilman looked at him carefully, and saw that every word was true. Portier looked as sad and downcast at the hand he'd been dealt by fate as any man ever had. He sighed.

"I never forgot about Alicia. I always meant to come back for her," he said quietly. "But she's... "

"Not what you expected, eh?" Tilman looked over at his partner, who had pulled another cheroot from his pocket and was trying to light it with a shaking hand.

After a moment, Tilman, choosing his words carefully, spoke. "Mister Portier ...Ash..., that War changed everything, and it put a lot of people in places they never thought of being. I figured I'd be spending my life at sea on fishing boats, and ended up a detective. You made a similar but different journey. And so has she."

"What am I going to do?" Ashley Portier moaned. "How can I even speak to her?"

"I don't know. I don't know you well enough to say. What is it they say in the Good Book? 'Judge not, lest ye be judged'? If it were me, and that was my wife in there, I would not care if she'd been the Whore of Babylon. I would give my immortal soul for just the chance of it. I love her that much."

"You mean that." Portier's hands were steady now. He took a small taste of the liquor and grimaced. Being drunk no longer appealed to him.

"It might be worse," Tilman said. "She might be dead ...or married."

"She was."

Tilman looked at him, surprised.

Portier stared straight ahead. "Some Yankee son-of-a-bitch, who already had a wife back in Massachusetts, married her so he could feed us false information. He knew she was spying. Then he ruined her by making her disgrace public, and denounced her as a whore. A friend wrote me about it. The letter finally caught up with me in Singapore about two years ago, after the Amnesty was declared. I came home to find her. And foul luck that I have!"

Tilman put his hand on Portier's shoulder to comfort him.

"What do I say to her, Blake? 'Fancy meeting you here'?"

"Start with 'hello'." The other part of Tilman's mind spoke then. "I do not think it would be wise to let that Jake Martin, or whoever he is, in on this. I'm sure he noticed something, but let's not have a big reunion."

"No, that would not do," Portier agreed.

"We do not know enough about what is going on here. I'm real curious about this set-up, which don't even begin to look legal. I don't much care about these desperados getting killed off, but we need to get the Seaton boy clear, and we need to make sure that we can leave."

Portier looked thoughtful, and bent his mind to the problem. "Mister Martin's making some money here. Like as not, he plans to continue to do so. You and I are a pair of wild cards. He hasn't figured out how to play us yet, but we're as doomed as the rest, as far as he's concerned. He can't afford to have his crimes known. I'd rather not end the way Clete Morgan did."

"Speaking of Clete," his partner nodded, "We should attend to getting that rascal buried."

"Back to the Sheriff, then?"

"Yep."

Sheriff Hiram Johnson talked like a simpleton, but had an excellent memory and identified several of the wanted men on the posters in Tilman's portfolio as recent visitors to Apache Wells, and some as newly made permanent residents of Boot Hill, the new gunfighter's cemetery at the edge of town.

When Jesus came back in with a sheath of printed forms, the names of the dead gunmen written in, they were surprised. He had Sheriff Johnson sign each one at the bottom, which pleased the Stranger no end. He actually giggled as he finished each elaborate signature with a flourish.

"What do we owe you?" Tilman asked, as he tucked them in the back of the big brown leather portfolio.

The Indian actually smiled. He handed over a printed card. "My tribe has an account at the Bank of New York. Send us part of the reward money."

Tilman looked at the card and could not contain his surprise. He felt his mouth fall open. Portier just stared.

"You're serious?"

"I am," Jesus said. "Your government may be faithless, but those bankers pride themselves on their rectitude. My tribe needs many things now from the White Man's world."

"Such as?" Portier couldn't resist asking.

"Medicine, warm clothing for the winter, lawyers to fight the government, and guns to fight the bandits." Jesus drew himself up proudly. "We will not simply give way to your seizure of our lands."

"You're a rebel, then?' Portier sounded almost hopeful when he said this.

"Hell, no," Jesus scoffed. "That didn't do the South a bit of good, and got a lot of good men killed. It will not rise again ...and shouldn't, since it was founded on an evil principle."

Tilman could not have been more surprised if Jesus had been transformed into the second coming of the Messiah. "You're not really an Indian, are you?"

"I am and I'm not," Jesus said. "The White Man educated me, and tried to turn me into one of them so they could use me against my tribe. It came back to bite them. I know their ways now, and how to fight them."

"You're a dangerous man," Portier said.

"Where did you acquire that obvious education?" Tilman asked.

"Harvard, and then West Point."

"You were in the Army?"

Jesus shook his head. "I would not swear the oath. So I was dismissed."

Tilman nodded slowly, taking it all in. "So you accomplished what you set out to do."

Jesus looked at him a long moment, then shook his head. "Not yet. The tribe is not safe. The town is not safe. No one is safe." He looked over at Hiram Johnson, who had been listening to him with bright-eyed interest. Suddenly he didn't look quite so stupid.

Tilman saw it was time to change the subject. "You got an undertaker here? It's time to get those bodies outside under the ground."

Sheriff Johnson wrinkled his nose, and nodded. "Spoiled meat," he agreed.

Jesus said, "Seamus Corcoran does the burying. I'll take you over."

He nodded toward the door. Tilman and Portier moved to go with him. The Sheriff also got to his feet, but Jesus turned and said sharply, "Guard the prisoner."

The Stranger blinked and did as he was told, sitting back down and staring at the door to the jail. Jesus motioned to the two detectives, and placed one finger over his lips.

They went outside and Portier unhitched the pony burdened with the dead bodies. He handed the set of reins to Tilman. The horse resisted at first, until Jesus said a few soft words in Apache to it. Then it settled down and plodded along.

"You have the gift of tongues?" Portier asked.

Jesus shook his head. "I know animal spirits. I was a boy here, happily so, until they shipped me off to the White Man's school. The tribal elders told me to go learn what I could about their ways, so we could defeat them. When I came back, many were dead, from drink, or disease, or shot down by Rangers. The young braves want the warpath and revenge, but that way lies our death as a tribe and a people. So I became Chief."

"And?"

"If you can't beat them, join them. We have a contract with the Cavalry to provide scouts. That contains the more restless spirits among us. And that was enough to keep the peace until Mister Martin and his friends showed up."

By this time they had arrived at the large open shed that held the undertaker's.

"Seamus is drunk most of the time," Jesus said, as the elderly Irishman came out, and, without a word of acknowledgment, took a cloth tape from his pocket and began measuring the two dead bodies. Finally he turned to face them. He was dressed in a black broadcloth suit. The collarless shirt underneath that might have once been white, but now was gray with grime and sweat. He stared at the two detectives, his facial expression doubtful. His voice was high and reedy.

"So you're the fellows who packed this worthless sod Clete Morgan in?"

"We are," Tilman said. "We're with Pinkerton's, and we will pay for the burial since we was tracking him when he fell. Pine box and a simple Christian service."

"Oh, no need for that, sir." The undertaker grinned sardonically. "It's all on Mister Martin's account. One of the benefits he provides his employees," he said cheerfully. Seamus looked about and spotted a jug of liquor on the ground nearby. He walked over to the jug, picked it up, and took a long pull.

"Clete Morgan was working for Martin?"

The undertaker looked around, a bit angry. "I guess we all is now. Except those guests of his." He held out the jug, but put it down when no one took hold of it, and shook himself. "This used to be a nice quiet little town, with decent folk. He's spoiled it for sure."

"There was a town here before Martin showed up?"

A pair of Mexican workers took the dead bodies and laid them out on a table and removed their clothes. An old Mexican woman came out of the shed with a pail of warm, soapy water. She began to wash the bodies carefully with a rag.

The undertaker said, "*Numero cuatro*" to the two Mexican workers, and they went and fetched two empty wooden coffins, placing them next to the bodies. The undertaker sighed. "There *is* a town, and we all got along. Even the Chief, here, kept his braves quiet hereabouts."

"So he is a Chief?" Portier asked.

"He didn't tell you? Well, no, he wouldn't. Modest to a fault, he is. Jesus Santa Maria Sanchez. Also known as Black Horse, Chief of the Mescalero Apache Band. Most educated Indian you'll ever meet. Some well-meaning fools tried to turn him White, and he came back here more Indian than ever. Didn't you, Chief?"

The Indian shook his head and looked away, his face impassive.

Seamus Corcoran looked at them speculatively, and pulled out his tape measure again.

"Say, gents, as long as you're here, you don't mind me taking a few measurements? I like to work ahead if I can."

Tilman was so startled that he couldn't speak.

Portier simply laughed. "We don't plan on being customers."

The undertaker shook his head. "You say that now, but Mister Martin, he has other plans, I am sure. Him and his guests. None of them that came here figured to die. Real killers, all of them. But Martin has got himself a real unique enterprise. The Old West, complete with saloon, whores, drunken brawls; everything you ever read about in a dime novel. A real honey trap.

"He puts out the word that he needs gunmen at good wages, with free whisky and loose women, and the fools can't wait to get here. They come up from Esperanza, and that's the end of it. They play their part in the show, get killed, and then a pine box and a few words said over them. Some last longer than others.

Most get buried alone. Their so-called friends are too drunk to ride out and see them off, knowing that their turn is coming. As for the words, I do my best or get the Catholic priest out."

Tilman and Portier looked at each other and then at Jesus, who simply nodded.

Corcoran found his jug again and took another long pull. "The Chief and me are in a sort of holding action. Sooner or later, Martin is going to run out of targets for his guests, and as long as you don't threaten them, they leave you alone. Sooner or later, we'll get our town back."

"Don't be so sure." Tilman said.

"Why do you say that?" Jesus asked.

"Because this is a criminal enterprise. Someone will take note, and Martin and his men will be arrested, tried, and hanged. When we get the Seaton boy out... "

"Ain't going to happen," Corcoran said. He walked over to Clete Morgan's body and pointed at his belly, the portion that had been cooked.

"You saw this?"

"We did," Portier said. "What would do that, anyway?"

"Lightning. The Strangers don't need guns. They can throw lightning."

Tilman and Portier looked at each other, greatly surprised. Neither of them knew what to say.

"It's true," Jesus said heavily. Tilman realized that he, too, was bewildered, and more than a little afraid.

"Who are they?" Tilman asked. "Where do they come from?"

"From the depths of Hell," Corcoran declared grandly, reaching for his jug once more.

"No," Jesus said, and pointed upward to the clear blue sky. "From the Other World. They are Starmen."

Tilman's mind went immediately to Jim Frazer's chart and notes. "How do you know?"

"From an old tale from long ago." Jesus turned his head away, not wanting to discuss the matter further.

CHAPTER TWENTY-TWO

Later, the two detectives rode out to Boot Hill with the undertaker, who also doubled as a preacher. The rough wagon that he used as a hearse, with their dead men now in the plain pine coffins, bumped along the rough track to where a line of graves was already dug out and waiting. A crew of four silent Mexicans handled the coffins respectfully. The two detectives, their hats over their hearts, stood by as the coffins were lowered into the earth, and Seamus Corcoran recited a short service from memory.

He'd obviously done this many times, and there was an angry weariness in the way he delivered the words. Here the dead were merely intruders imposed on the town, rather than cherished members of the community – that was why they were buried separately, outside the town limits.

Unlike most Boot Hill events, this one had other mourners. Not just the boy Jeremiah, but the victim's uncle, the famous bandit Black Jack Morgan, who put his hand on the boy's shoulder to steady him as he wept. Two women in black stood by a skinny, pimply-faced boy in his teens, wearing a gunfighter's low-slung holster with a new Colt's revolver in it. Respectfully, to give the family some room, the two detectives stood back from the ceremony. Plover, the gunman who'd offered them violence, was not there.

Portier noticed an old woman, wrapped in a black shawl, standing apart. She looked at him solemnly. After the service was over and the family was walking away, she stepped forward, raised her hands toward the sky and began chanting in a tongue he had never heard before.

He nudged Corcoran. "What's that about?"

"That, me boy, is about making sure the dead stay dead."

Portier was nonplussed. One could not grow up in New Orleans without learning about Voodoo and other such cults. He felt a tinge of fear grip his stomach.

"I don't believe in ghosts," he said.

Corcoran shrugged. "Neither did I until I started seeing some. Thought it was because of some bad liquor, so I stopped drinking for a bit, but they were still popping up here and there. Scared the daylights out of some. So we asked the local witch to intervene."

"And has it helped?"

Corcoran nodded. "I'm a practical man. Some might call us ignorant superstitious fools for hiring a witch to cast spells, and Father Tomas had a real hissy fit over it. But if it works, it works." He turned and went back to supervise the filling in of the new graves.

Tilman had caught some of the conversation. He took out his notebook and a stub of pencil and wrote himself a note.

"I am not putting that in my report," he said. "They would think I'd lost my reason back in Chicago. It's all about Science these days."

"But you have a more open mind?"

"I do. As Shakespeare said, 'there are more things in Heaven and Earth, than are dream't of in our philosophy.' "

Portier wondered briefly what Captain Burton would make of this. *He'd probably write another paper for The Transactions of the Royal Society*, he decided.

Tilman looked around. "Come on," he said. They strolled down the line of fresh grave markers, writing down the names of the recently killed, then mounted and rode slowly back to the Sheriff's office.

"It's almost like a factory," Portier observed thoughtfully.

"It is," Tilman agreed, "and they've got it down to a science."

As they checked off name after name, the two detectives came to understand that the crime rate in the West would shrink simply because there were so few surviving criminals and murderers. Apache Wells was indeed a deadly trap.

When they came to the poster of Parker Boone, which had a recent prison photograph, Sheriff Johnson shook his head.

"Not here."

"No?" Tilman inquired. "Are you sure?"

"No reason. Not a gunfighter. Rancher. Teacher."

Tilman was about to ask further questions when the outer door opened. Jesus came in, holding it wide for the redheaded whore from the hotel. She was wearing a dark green silk dress, a fashionable hat, and a white lace shawl wrapped around her shoulders.

"Hello, boys," she said with a cheerful grin. Portier returned the grin.

Tilman was puzzled. "What is she doing here?"

"Mister Seaton sent for her," Jesus said. His face was solemn and disapproving.

"He can buy that, too?"

"Sure, and why not?" the red-haired girl said, a County Clare lilt in her voice. "A girl has to make a livin', hasn't she?" She winked at him.

"Keys," Jesus said. The Sheriff pulled them from his desk drawer and slid them over. Jesus picked them up, began to move toward the door to the jail with the redhead slightly before him. Portier and Tilman started to follow, but she turned around and shook a finger at them.

"None of that, now! You boys want your turn, you'll see me at the hotel, and one at a time! Like proper gentlemen."

"That was not my ...," Tilman started to protest.

"Eh. I know your type, boyo, and you'll want to have a bath first. Get that trail dust off." Then she turned and looked seriously at Portier. "And you stay away from Miss Kate!"

"Who?"

"My mistress, you gob-struck fool! The fiancée you abandoned to be raped by some brute of a Union captain! Men! Worthless! The lot of you!!" She swept through the door to the jail that Jesus was holding open for her. Over his shoulder the Indian said, "Be right back," and closed the door behind them.

Portier staggered to a chair and sat down.

Blake Tilman shook his head. "Well, if that don't beat all," he said. He turned to the Sheriff. "That don't worry you? She could be taking him a pistol, helping him break out."

The Sheriff shook his head. "She wouldn't do that."

"No?"

"She likes Mister Seaton. Not want him dead."

"But ..."

Portier recovered himself enough to interject. "Blake."

"What?"

"We're forgetting the client here. What he and that girl do is none of our affair. And he ain't going to try anything that will get him killed."

Jesus came back through the door to the jail, locking it behind him. He slid the ring of keys back across the desk to the Sheriff, who put them back in the drawer.

"I'll come back in two hours," he said.

The Sheriff nodded happily.

"Twenty minutes is the usual time," Portier observed. "She must really like him."

"I'll take your word for it," Tilman replied sourly, "Since I don't indulge."

Portier managed a crooked grin. "Do tell." He obviously had a hard time believing this. "Well, sometimes even the most hardened whore finds something or someone to like."

"So these are Romeo and Juliet?" Tilman scoffed.

"I believe in true love, no matter where," Portier said wistfully.

Both men were pensive and quiet for a minute. Then Tilman snapped his fingers. "Or she is playing him," Tilman said. "I never met a whore yet, who didn't want a way out of the Life, and a rich husband."

Jesus was listening carefully. "She tells herself that is what she is up to," he said quietly, "But it's a lie."

The two detectives stared at him. He was as impassive as a bronze statue.

"What do you mean?" Tilman finally asked.

"Seaton may be a rich man, but she stopped charging him days ago. And she can't fake the pleasure he gives her."

"So ...?"

The Indian shrugged. "You White people are crazy, that's all. She loves him, and he loves her. You can tell from the way they look at each other. But neither will admit it. She's been hard used all her life, but he's as tender with her as ..."

"I get it," Tilman said. "Another complication. He won't want to leave her behind."

"No."

"What about Clete Morgan?" Portier asked. "Did he indulge?" He offered the Indian one of his cheroots.

Jesus accepted. They shared a match getting them lit. Jesus blew out some smoke, and coughed. "Until he lost all his money playing cards with the Strangers. No free rides for him. The girls didn't like him much."

"Why not?"

"Dirty. Wouldn't take a bath. He was rough with them, too. Beat one up. She died."

Tilman was shocked. "And all he got was jailed?"

"Well," the Indian said slowly; "I did propose to Jake Martin that we revive another Old West custom and simply lynch the miscreant – but Jake, he wants his guests to have their fun, so Clete was put in the jar so he'd go out in a 'fair' fight."

"Jar?"

"Jake keeps a jar behind the bar with all of the gunfighters' names in it. He draws one or two a day, and that man does a showdown with a Stranger."

"Be kinder to just kill them," Portier said.

"But not as much fun." Jesus smiled, and continued, "The Strangers like their fun."

"Why don't they run for it, all of them?" Tilman shook his head. "Surely they can see what's coming?"

"Because one or two have won, and these killers have too much pride to admit that they are dealing with men of superior skill. So they take their chances. Not that Clete ever had one."

"No?"

"Jake took all the other names out of the jar. Clete's from here, but – that boy Jeremiah and Mister Plover aside – no one liked him. Not one spoke up for him."

"So he ran." Tilman realized that he was feeling something he had not felt since the War: fear. Things were happening here beyond his comprehension.

Portier felt helpless and no longer the master of his fate. He resolved to find a place where he could meditate and recover himself. Seeing Alicia had unnerved him. His mind was scrambled. He needed to find his center once more, and calm down.

. . .

"Do you love me?" Molly asked, as she lay naked across Derek Seaton's chest.

"Not much," the young man sighed; "but I'm getting to like you far too much."

Molly raised herself up and stared at him, at the handsome face with the cocky grin that faded slowly, as she put her hands behind his neck and pulled herself up to his head so that he almost smothered in her breasts. He pushed her away, and sat up. She felt tears come to her eyes.

"Oh, sheet! What can we do now?"

"I don't know," Seaton said. "But the Pinkertons are here. They'll think of something."

Molly started to say something harsh about Alicia Sorrell's long-lost love, but it was too complicated, and Seaton had worries enough. She didn't want to queer what luck he had left.

"Help me dress," Molly said. "I've got to get back."

Seaton laid back and admired her trim figure as she began to pull on her black lace stockings. It suddenly bothered him that she would be with several other men that day, doing the same things with them that amazed and gratified him.

He was no innocent. His father had seen to his initiation into sex at the age of fourteen by buying him a night with the most skilled practitioner in Chicago.

His mother had simply said, "Do not mistake this for love, son. Those women make pleasure their business. They are well paid. Indulge your lusts as you will, but never fall in love with one. And never, for a minute, entertain the idea that you can make one your wife. I will not have it!"

As he tenderly helped Molly Shannon into her corset and dress, he realized that, if he did not die in Apache Wells, he planned to do just that. He kissed her on the forehead and patted her bottom, saying, "Everything will be all right."

She read the look on his face and her heart leapt just a little, but she kept her face faintly scornful, and replied, "You're quite mad, you know."

Jesus walked Molly Shannon back to the hotel. Portier wanted to go as well, but she whirled around furiously and told him once more to stay away from 'Miss Kate'.

Tilman suggested that they go instead to talk to Seamus Corcoran once more. Grumbling, Portier agreed. He sipped at the *Cognac* bottle as they walked.

"Just to clear my head," he said.

Tilman just shook his head. There was no point in delivering another lecture. Come what may, they were in this together.

The undertaker was working on one of the coffins as they approached his open shed, using a plane to shave some of the splinters off the edge of the rough pine boards.

"Who is that for?" Tilman asked.

"No one in particular," the old man said. "It's like I told you, I like to work ahead. And why not, since Jake Martin has already paid for them all?"

"That don't bother you?" Portier asked, as he offered him a pull from his own bottle.

"It bothers me plenty, but since I don't want to end up in one meself, I keep me head down and do as I am told. At least we provide these poor souls a Christian burial." Corcoran took a deep drink, and then wiped his mouth with the back of his hand. "Good stuff. Give Jake Martin credit. He may be the Devil, but he don't cheapen the experience. Miss Kate is a case in point. You never see that kind of quality in the hinterlands. Strictly big city. New Orleans or New York." He peered at Portier. "I understand you've met previously."

Portier flushed red, and started to make an angry reply, but Tilman jumped in quickly. "Yes, I have. In the line of business. But it's an old case, settled long ago." Portier turned and stared at him, astonished. Tilman ignored him and pressed on with the undertaker. "What about the Strangers? They also get a Christian burial?"

"Oh, they're not for the likes of me to see to. It's only happened twice, and both times one of Martin's thugs claimed the body and took it away. Probably to that ranch where they all sleep."

He leaned forward and whispered, "Sometimes they take one of the gunmen's bodies, too. Or part of it."

"Why?" Tilman was genuinely perplexed.

Corcoran shrugged. "Why do they do anything? Why are they even here?"

"Any idea where they come from?"

Seamus Corcoran looked upward, thinking. "I asked Jake Martin that, once. He said something about 'the seacoast of Bohemia', which is from Shakespeare – and his way of telling me to mind my own business."

"The real Bohemia doesn't have a seacoast," Portier said. "I've been there."

Corcoran gave him a sarcastic look. "Do tell." He scratched himself under the chin, thinking hard. "Wherever it is, it has to be someplace dark. They're always wearing them dark glasses, like they got weak eyes, but when push comes to shove they shoot real fast and real straight. Once to the head or the heart. Never miss. And wicked quick. It unnerves the most able shootist, because they know any mistake will be their last. Don't seem sporting, somehow."

"Well, I am advised that the Pinkerton Agency never wants a fair fight neither," Portier said.

Corcoran frowned. "That's neither here nor there. Being from Ireland, and the seventh son of a seventh son, I have the Second Sight and other powers." He beckoned the two detectives to lean closer and lowered his voice, although no one was close enough to hear him.

"I don't think they're really human."

Tilman and Portier exchanged a puzzled look, but said nothing. Was the undertaker merely drunk and rambling, or perhaps mad?

"I think they're demons from Hell. They smell of the pit sometimes. There's a brimstone smell when one dies."

"So some do get killed?" Portier raised an eyebrow.

"It does happen. That Seaton fellow killed one, and I got a close look before they carried him off. There was something very odd about the body. Way too light, and some of the skin on the neck peeled off. There was snake skin underneath."

"Snake skin?" Tilman was writing in his pocket notebook. He didn't want to forget any of this.

"Reptile of some kind," Corcoran replied earnestly. "Gila monster, but not green. More white or light gray." He took another swig from his jug. "I've never seen the like. Thought I was finally succumbing to John Barleycorn, and seeing things that weren't there, but the Chief, he saw it too. And some of the girls have said things about how they look with their clothes off. Puny-like. Very thin. So I'm taking my lead from the Chief. Watch and wait."

"And when do you think young Seaton has his date with Destiny?" Tilman asked, wondering again if the old Irishman was telling the truth, or having a bit of fun at their expense. He didn't think so, despite the high probability of blarney. Corcoran looked genuinely frightened.

"Ah. That depends on when his money runs out. That's the way Martin works. And the boy has expensive tastes."

Tilman shrugged. "Seaton is rich. He can probably last a few days more."

"Not if he keeps seeing Miss Molly. She don't come cheap. None of them does. I could live for a week on what Miss Kate gets for an hour."

Portier groaned loud, causing Corcoran to favor him with an evil grin. "Sorry," he said, insincerely.

"Molly, we are told, no longer charges him. She's gone sweet on him."

"And is making up the difference out of what she gets from the others?" Corcoran laughed out loud. "She's a shanty Irish bitch if I ever saw one. No, she's playing a deeper game. How much money does the boy have?"

"Ever hear of Chicago?" Tilman asked drily.

Corcoran was offended. "Of course I've heard of it. I'm a drunk, not an ignorant fool!"

"Seaton's family owns most of the North Side, and the odd railway or two."

"Ah, so that's her game. Well, good on you, Molly. Gather ye rosebuds while ye may. She always talks about marrying rich." Seamus Corcoran grinned from ear to ear.

"Won't happen," Tilman said. "His mother would never stand for it, and we was sent after him to keep him from falling in love with some Mexican girl."

"Well, she's not Mexican," Portier laughed. "But all things considered, the mother might come to prefer that." The idea of a domineering rich mother being discomfitted by her's son's choice of a bride, made him remember how much Alicia Sorrell's mother had tried to prevent their marriage.

"In any event, if Molly helps him get away, she'll be taken care of," Tilman said, and put his pocket notebook away.

"Are you sure?" pressed Corcoran. "Nothing is certain. We need to find a way to get clear of all this."

Tilman and Portier looked at each other and shrugged at the same time.

"What about us?" Portier asked at last. "How is Martin going to handle us?"

"You've got him stumped," Corcoran said. "Probably, he'll try to set you up, the way he did young Seaton. He knows the Pinkerton reputation, though. If you don't come back, someone will come looking for you, right?"

"And more than two of 'em," Tilman said. "He'd be better off with the Army." He thought suddenly of John Pershing and his company of Cavalry. How would they fare against the Strangers? And could he send them a dispatch that would sound sensible and not absolutely insane? Jesus's band had a contract to provide scouts …perhaps… ?

Jesus shot the idea down. "You don't understand the tactical situation here. If they come riding in, they'll be slaughtered. And John Pershing is a friend of mine. We were at West Point together. He was one of the few who showed me kindness there."

He looked at Tilman and sighed. "Obviously, you are a very smart man, Mister Tilman, so be smart enough to shut up and listen."

Corcoran laughed until tears came to his eyes.

CHAPTER TWENTY-THREE

They needed to eat, and it had to be grub they could trust. Tilman thought of their buried supplies outside of town, and discarded the notion of retrieving them. Too far, and fraught with hazard. He asked Corcoran, "Is there anyplace where we can buy a meal? Anyplace safe?"

"Well, if you don't mind Mex food, my old lady sets a handsome table," Seamus Corcoran said. "I'd be pleased to have you as my guests. You come, too, Chief."

"Let me get Seaton his supper, and tuck him in first," Jesus said. He was more relaxed now. Corcoran watched as he strode away toward the hotel.

"They say 'never trust an Indian', but that's a man I'd bet my life on," Corcoran said.

"Civilized?" asked Portier.

"Not hardly. Cruel as they come when it suits his purpose. Martin tried to get him to do an Indian raid on the town, but he saw the trap. More amusement for the Strangers, but Black Horse ain't nobody's fool, and sent most of his braves off to keep the Cavalry amused."

"That might be even more dangerous," Portier said. "I saw a troop of them on the way here. Never thought I'd see Negroes so employed, but I was Cavalry myself, and I know soldiers when I see them."

"Oh, they don't fight each other anymore. They're working together to scout the bandits that terrorize the border, riding with

Captain Pershing and his troop, and with Manny d'Silva and his *Federales*. Black Horse and Pershing knew each other at West Point before he got chucked out. Pershing is from this big Abolitionist family in Boston. He don't mind working with Blacks. Or Indians." He peered at Tilman. "I seem to remember you Pinkertons had a hand in that, and the Underground Railroad."

Portier sucked his teeth thoughtfully. "Things have really changed since the War." Inwardly he felt rage and confusion. *How did I not know this before I came back?* he thought. *Why was I not told? Have I fallen into a trap?*

He turned and stared hard at Tilman for a long moment, and then looked away, his poker face on. The world had changed so much. Yesterday's enemies were now friends. Or at least partners. For now. He didn't know what to say.

"I told you about that," Tilman said. "Can you cope?"

"You mean not drink myself stupid?" Portier sighed and shook his head. "I can cope. It's just going to take a little time to get used to."

Seamus Corcoran's 'old lady' turned out to be a well-formed, dark-skinned, and rather formidable Mexican woman about thirty years old. She greeted them cheerfully, and, with two younger women, laid out a small feast on a long table. While his hacienda looked like just another old brown adobe house on the outside, inside it was well appointed with rich hangings of colorfully patterned blankets, and well-cushioned chairs and couches.

Tilman was impressed. "This is very nice," he said. "You live well."

"Burying the dead has always provided us a good living," Corcoran said. "Come on, dig in. Stuff don't taste all that good once it cools."

Suddenly an Indian – naked to the waist, wearing moccasins and leather leggings, and a single feather in his hair – appeared as if by magic behind Corcoran. Portier and Tilman scrambled to draw their pistols.

"Relax. It's just Hey-seuss. Or, as he likes to be called when he's an Injun, Black Horse." Corcoran laughed again, enjoying the joke. Black Horse simply sat down and took some food.

Tilman and Portier looked at each other, still recovering from the sudden shock.

The Indian kept his face very still, although there was a glint of amusement and satisfaction in his eyes. The detectives realized they'd been the victims of a prank. Or was it a test, so the Apache could take their measure?

"You got to stop doing that, Chief," Corcoran said. as his women burst into fits of giggles. "Let us say grace," Corcoran said, as the three women found their own seats and everyone joined hands. "Heavenly Father," he intoned in a deep voice, "bless this food. Accept our thanks for the health of everyone here in this time of trouble, and for the deliverance to come, as promised by the presence of these two fine and resolute Pinkerton detectives you have sent to aid us. In Jesus Christ's name, Amen. Pass the butter."

Everyone fell to consuming the heaps of food before them. When he stopped to draw breath, Tilman realized what Corcoran had said.

"I appreciate the prayer and the compliment, sir," Tilman said. "But please understand that we are simply here to make arrests, and to rescue young Mister Seaton. No other work is intended."

"And that's quite enough," Portier added.

Seamus Corcoran winked at Black Horse. "But you are. Your coming was foretold."

"You have the gift of prophecy?" Portier asked, his face very serious now.

"Well, sometimes, but I don't talk much about it because it goes against what the bigwigs in Salt Lake say. They like to claim all that for themselves. For the power, ye see."

Tilman was very surprised. "You're a Mormon?"

Corcoran grinned. "When it suits me, as I was wanting to be sealed in marriage to all three of my lovely brides, but I'm also a lay brother at the other Church, where Father Tomas looks the other way, and call them my nieces and wonders why I never take Confession ...and then there is the witch that services the Tribe. You've seen her. It may sound mad, but it works. Everyone gets along."

The two detectives looked at each other and broke out laughing. Seeing that the others did not join in, they stopped. Portier spoke for the two of them. "Oh. You're serious."

The three women looked at each other, confused, and the look in Corcoran's eyes brought them up short.

"Like Church on Sunday," Black Horse said. He stared at them, stonefaced.

"That savage was once an altar boy. So you can take his word for that," the Irishman added. He frowned and shook his head.

"Then we beg your pardon," Tilman said, suddenly contrite.

"Apology accepted," Corcoran replied with a wave of his hand, that might have been a blessing.

"So you knew we were coming?"

"Well, not you in particular. Someone to smite the evil-doers." The Irishman was very serious now, to show he was not playing a prank. "And not me, but the witch."

"How?" Portier asked.

Corcoran shook his head. "There are some mysteries here I don't explore, and some questions I never ask. Hers is the larger power. She knew. That's enough."

The conversation died off, and the meal resumed with Corcoran's wives acting as though they had heard nothing – which was true in a way, since none of them knew any English.

Everyone ate their fill, talking very little. Corcoran, like a nobleman in the old country, finally pushed himself away from the table, and poured three glasses of whisky.

"I don't indulge," Tilman said. "I'm Temperance."

Corcoran shrugged. "The Chief don't drink either. More for me, then." He tossed one glass off, and picked up another to sip. Portier laughed and took the remaining one.

"Well water for you?" Corcoran inquired politely.

"Yes, thank you." Tilman said. Corcoran made a gesture and one of the younger women hastened to fetch Tilman and Black Horse brown stoneware mugs half full of cool, clean water.

"Well is right in the house," Corcoran said.

"So you have a fortress here?" Portier asked, remembering a similar arrangement he had seen half a world away near the Khyber Pass.

"Until Black Horse decided to make peace, it was the only sensible thing to do, and we still have them bandits to worry about."

Tilman thought about all that had happened that day, and suddenly snapped his fingers, recalling the one thing he had overlooked.

"Parker Boone. We came to get that boy back to his residence in the Federal Pen up Kansas way. Where is he, anyway? He was not out in the desert with Clete Morgan."

Black Horse smiled, and shook his head, "Even Jake Martin could see that boy is no gunman. The Strangers are particular. They want a fair fight with a gunman of great renown. They decline the easy mark."

"Sporting of them," Portier remarked.

"Just so. Now, Martin didn't want Parker Boone wandering off and telling wild stories, so he gave him a job at the ranch where the Strangers stay."

"Say," Tilman said, "Does that mean that Seaton can get off doing a showdown?"

"Nope," Corcoran shook his head. "He killed one of them. So it's personal. Besides, he's not totally helpless. He's obviously been practicing, just in case he needed to use those fancy new pistols he brought with him. His mother may not see much in him, but he's pretty tough and can hold his own."

"He's a man," Black Horse agreed.

"So Parker Boone is out at Martin's ranch house? He can give us the lay of the land there, then."

"A little *recce*, as Captain Burton would say," Portier looked suddenly cheerful.

"Speaking of reconnaissance," Tilman said, "We need to go beard Jake Martin in his den."

Portier winced.

"Come, sir. We're investigators. We must investigate."

"I suppose so," Portier groaned. He stood up, looked around – then asked, very quietly, "Where's the Indian?"

Black Horse was no longer in the room. No one had seen him leave.

Seamus Corcoran chuckled. "Damned if I know how he manages that. If he weren't a friend of mine, it would worry me some. He carries a big blade sharp enough to shave with," Corcoran grinned as he drew his finger across his throat and laughed maniacally.

Tilman and Portier put on their hats and checked their pistols. They looked at each other and nodded, determined to see the job through to the end. Corcoran looked from one to the other and lifted his glass of whisky in silent salute. The situation looked less desperate now that there were Pinkertons on the case.

"Thank you for a lovely meal," Tilman said formally.

Corcoran waved a hand magnanimously. "You're very welcome. Anytime."

Outside, the moon was three-quarters full and shone brightly through the clouds. As they saw to their horses and retrieved their Winchester rifles, Tilman looked up, thinking of his sextant. Portier read his expression as he gazed upward.

"You'd never get a fix," Portier said. "Not a star anywhere."

They set off toward the hotel, walking slowly and carefully, rifles carried in the crook of their right arms, fearing an ambush. But despite the early hour and the bright diffused light that came through the clouds above, no one was on the street.

"Quiet." Portier said, feeling for a revolver with his free hand.

"Too much so," Tilman agreed. "The people who live here are hunkered down in their houses. You can smell the fear."

Even if it had been pitch-black dark, they could have found their way to the hotel simply by following the raucous noise that issued from within. Laughter and shouting mixed with the tinny, badly played piano.

There was no one on the front steps of the hotel; as they paused at the door, the scene reminded Portier of a painting he'd seen in London many years before: an artist's conception of Hell, with devils busily torturing the damned. Miss Kate's girls were standing behind customers who were playing cards, or sitting on the laps of the ones throwing back shots of liquor. There was tension in the air that could have been cut and packaged for a sizeable profit.

Tilman took a deep breath and plunged in, with Portier hastening to follow, going directly toward Jake Martin, who greeted them expansively, with open arms, playing the generous host. He poured two glasses of whisky, neat, and said, "I was wondering when you boys were going to show up. Where have you been?"

Tilman waved away the drink. "Just taking care of business."

"You haven't checked in yet," Martin said, his face that of a reproving parent. "We've got plenty of rooms."

Tilman smiled easily and leaned his Winchester against the bar.

"If you're charging twenty dollars for a two-dollar bottle of rot-gut, I doubt we can afford it, even on Mister Pinkerton's account. How much is a room? A hundred?" Tilman kept smiling. "The man's a Scot and known for his thrift."

"In other words, tight as a tick," Portier chipped in.

Jake Martin looked exasperated. "See here," he said; "I own the place, so it is what I say it is. You can stay for free if you mingle with my guests. They're real excited to meet you. They've heard all about the great Allan Pinkerton and his detectives. It's quite a thrill for them, having two of the genuine article here."

He crooked his head to one side. "Sure I can't offer you a drink, sir?"

"I'm Temperance," Tilman replied. "It was a promise to my late wife."

Martin nodded solemnly. "I can respect that. How about a cup of coffee or a glass of French mineral water?"

"I'm not thirsty."

Martin, nothing daunted, turned his attention to Portier.

"How about you, Mister Portier?"

"I'm fine." He looked over to the noisy crowd. "Y'all play poker here?"

Martin smiled. "Poker, faro, roulette, blackjack. We usually have those later in the evening when things are more mellow. Gives the ladies a chance to do their special kind of entertaining. Are you a card player, Mister Tilman?"

"Not much," Tilman looked away to the crowd.

"Damn me," said Martin, now genuinely put out. "Are all you Pinkertons so straight-laced and uptight? You are a daunting man to entertain."

"He likes a good book," Portier offered with a friendly grin. He didn't quite know what Tilman was playing at, but decided to watch and wait. He was the apprentice here.

Martin gaped at Portier a moment, and then laughed very loudly.

"A good book? Damn! I never thought to put in a library."

"All the best hotels have one," Portier said.

Martin nodded. "I will have to see to that for the next set of guests."

"You're expecting new ones?"

"Next month. Fresh guests, fresh faces."

Tilman turned his head back to stare at Martin. He leaned forward slightly.

"I might want some companionship later," he whispered. Portier had to keep himself from laughing out loud. He understood suddenly what Tilman was about. Investigating.

Jake Martin relaxed, smiling.

"Well, that's a relief, Pard. You kind of had me worried there. I thought I had found a preacher or something. See anything you fancy?"

"That red-headed girl over there. She seems quite lively."

Martin nodded. "Excellent taste. Her name is Molly. Now you'll have to make your own arrangements there. I just provide a venue. I don't have anything to do with that end of it. It's all Miss Kate." He peered at Portier's face, looking for a reaction. "I believe you know each other? A fine piece of Southern womanhood."

Portier shook his head slowly, tasting the lie even as he uttered it. His mouth was dry and sour from the bile that suddenly filled it. There was nothing he wanted more than to smash Jake Martin's leering face in, but he fell back on years of playing poker to control his face and his emotions. "No," the Southerner smiled. "That was my mistake. She reminded me of someone I knew in another country. Besides, the wench is dead."

Tilman listened to this carefully, appreciating how Portier had used the truth to tailor the lie. The Confederacy he had fought for had, indeed, been another country, and the Alicia Sorrell he had been engaged to in her sweet and innocent youth was also long dead, her spirit murdered by Jake Martin and his ilk. He gazed over at his partner, reading him, and thought him filled now with a terrible resolve. There would be a reckoning.

"You should see about that," Martin was also looking at the Southerner carefully, trying to read him. "Miss Kate is the Madam, but she will also oblige a customer. It's her stable; all top rank, but she's by far the prettiest filly in the herd."

Portier simply smiled. "Quality always shows itself. Perhaps I will." He left his rifle and walked away. "I need to piss," he said over his shoulder, and went toward the back. Martin stared after him, his mouth working as he tried to figure the detective out. Tilman had new-found respect for his partner; Portier had answered Martin's provocation nimbly, then gone off to relieve himself, catch his breath, and keep his composure.

He smiled genially at Martin. "That fancy water the kind that comes in green bottles?"

"It is. French."

"Let me have some of that," Tilman said, keeping an eye on his rifle and his partner's. "I want to see why fools will pay good money for something they can get for free anywhere."

"I believe it's all those little bubbles. Coming right up." Martin reached into the cool box and retrieved a small dark green bottle, uncapped it, and made something of a ceremony of pouring it into a glass. He looked expectantly at Tilman, who took a cautious swig.

"Not bad," he admitted.

"On the house."

Tilman nodded.

"Say," Martin said; "I saw those Winchesters you boys brought with you. You planning an arrest?"

Tilman turned and looked at the raucous crowd.

"Don't see anyone I can arrest ...yet."

Jake Martin looked both relieved and disappointed to hear that. Tilman sipped his mineral water, and kept observing the crowd by watching the mirror behind the bar. It was going to be a long night.

CHAPTER TWENTY-FOUR

The room where men relieved themselves was actually right in the hotel, something Portier had only seen in the best hotels in big cities. He went into a stall and did his business, taking his time. He knew that his mental balance was still off.

He was confused and confounded by finding Alicia Sorrell in these circumstances. Even her being married to a damnyankee officer would not have set him back as much. He'd imagined her on a plantation someplace, perhaps struggling to make ends meet, but happy and with several children. As he emerged from the stall, his hands went immediately to his revolvers. The tall thin Negro he'd seen behind the hotel bar that morning was standing there, waiting, slowly raising his hands.

"Mister Portier, sir. I was hoping to have a word."

Portier relaxed just a bit, so the man could lower his hands.

"Simms, isn't it?"

"Yes, sir. Julius Caesar Simms. We've played a few card games together in the past."

"That's quite a handle you wear, Julius Caesar."

The Negro smiled and shrugged. "My former master had an affinity for the classics. He named us all after famous people in antiquity. I might have come off worse."

"True." Portier was trying to remember the man. "What can I do for you, Mister Simms?"

"Oh, it's what I can do for you, sir."

Portier was immediately on his guard, suspecting some kind of trick. He frowned. "Why would you? We're not friends."

The Negro gave him a big smile, showing an even double row of white teeth.

"No, sir. That's true, but you are a gentleman, and a man of demonstrated rectitude and sterling reputation at the table. I heard about how you schooled that cheat in El Paso. And you are polite. Don't talk down to folk like me. Never call us 'boy' or that other word."

Portier nodded in acknowledgment of the compliment.

"The tables are always democratic."

The Negro put away the phony smile and grew serious. "I wanted tell you that all the games here are rigged. Mister Martin is not just a cheat that takes men's money, but also their lives. It's a setup, these games, like a play or a show. Someone spots the cheat, there is a fight, and someone gets killed. Those guests of his are wicked quick on the draw. It's never one of them."

"Except for Mister Seaton. He prevailed."

"Not with a gun." The Negro watched as Portier washed his hands and offered him a clean white towel. "He broke a chair over the man's back. That white boy knows how to fight dirty."

Portier carefully rubbed his hands with the small towel. "He's from Chicago," he said, as if that explained everything.

Simms laughed out loud when he heard that.

Portier found himself trusting Simms. It surprised him. "How do you know the games are rigged?"

"I originally came to try my hand at being a gunman. I gave that up as a bad job the minute I saw one of the Strangers in a showdown; I'm quick, but not that quick. Fortunately, Jake also wanted card dealers, and I know a few tricks – I'm a mechanic. He hired me to teach the other dealers how to cheat."

Portier looked again at Simm's long, elegant fingers. He gave him a hard stare.

Simms laughed easily. "Them tricks is for the rubes, sir. Never for professional play."

"And?"

"Well, sir, just don't sit down to play. Don't buy trouble. The whole place is a trap."

"I've already got enough trouble."

"Yes, sir – Miss Kate? I did hear something about that."

Portier stared at him a long moment, recalling a certain kind of house slave that always knew his master's business as well as he knew his own; that – despite the laws against it — could read, write, and do sums better than most white men. Who always wore the best clothes and never went hungry. He wondered briefly how well this man knew Alicia Sorrell. How intimately? One of the well-hidden scandals of antebellum plantation life was how many respectable white women would take such a man as a lover, not just for his prodigious endowment, but his elegant manners and wit.

But he was oddly untroubled by the notion. Too much had changed. He had seen too much while abroad, and lacked the necessary hypocrisy.

"Well, thanks for the warning, Mister Simms. Is there more?"

The Negro pointed to the brass badge on his coat. "If you could put in a word for me. I would like to join up. Allan Pinkerton is one white man we colored all respect. He helped with the Underground Railroad." He was staring at the White man now, the former plantation owner and slaver, trying to read him.

Portier felt a rush of emotion, indignation as he recalled how many slaves had been stolen away from his father's and other plantations before the war. But then he laughed, and Julius Simms laughed with him. Nothing was really funny, but it dissipated the tension between them. Portier thought, *He's playing his own game, Simms is, and he's a cheat and liar by his own account, but he's warned me away from danger. Why?*

Portier saw no love in Simms' eyes, but no hatred either. Just cold calculation.

"I'm new myself on this job, but I will see what I can do. We are hiring, but you need to speak with Mister Tilman." Portier shook his head ruefully. So much had changed. He actually tipped his hat to Simms as he walked away, a gesture of respect impossible before the War.

He walked back to the bar. Tilman was leaning easily against it, talking with the red-haired whore they'd met at the jail.

"Mister Portier. You may recall Miss Molly Shannon?"

"I do. How are you, Miss Shannon?"

She frowned and turned away from him.

Tilman raised an eyebrow, and said, "I'd be obliged if you would take these Winchesters and put them back with our other gear. Miss Shannon and I are going to take a room."

Portier nodded. "As you will, sir." He hefted a rifle in each hand and moved toward the door, turning once to see Molly Shannon, now chatting gaily, leading Blake Tilman up the long central staircase to the rooms where the whores lived and did their business. To his surprise, Tilman looked perfectly at ease, like a drummer on holiday.

Once they were in the room and she had locked the door, Molly Shannon became brisk and businesslike.

"You can put your clothes on the settee and wash in the basin there."

"Wash?"

"Your parts, man. Clean them." Molly started to undo her own clothing.

"That won't be necessary."

She looked up at him, frowning and irritated. "Oh, but it will, boyo. You don't stick that thing into me dirty."

Tilman eased himself onto the settee, and replied, "That's not why I am here."

Molly pulled her dress over her head, revealing her bare breasts above a black lace corset that supported her black silk stockings. Aside from shoes, she wore nothing else underneath her gown while working, for speed and convenience. She stood there and struck a pose, confident in her beauty and appeal. To her surprise, he looked slightly away, rather than gawking or moving toward her.

"You're serious?"

"I am."

Molly looked a little hurt, pouting. "What, then?"

"A little conversation."

Molly Shannon looked exasperated. Picking up a white lace shawl, she wrapped it around her, covering her generous, well-formed breasts.

"You're not one of those, are you?"

"Pardon?"

"You want to save me from my wicked ways? Or you just want to hear the gory details? How many men have I had today, and what nasty things did they make me do?"

Tilman smiled, and shook his head. "Nothing like that."

"Good. Because I absolutely never talk about it. It's not polite, and it's no one's business. A hoor don't got much, but her discretion is very important."

"Not a business for big talkers, eh?"

"No, Mister Pinkerton Detective, it's not. What do you want to talk about?"

Blake pulled his pocket notebook from a coat pocket.

"The fee's the same, you know," Molly said uneasily.

Tilman smiled and produced a twenty-dollar gold piece. "I expect nothing less, Miss Shannon."

Molly bit the coin to see if it was real.

" 'Miss Shannon' is it?" She smiled and relaxed, slipping the coin under her corset. "Well, truth to tell, I can use a bit of a sit-down. That Seaton lad gave me a fairly vigorous riding. I'm a bit sore."

"I'll tell him you said so," Tilman said, writing in his little brown notebook.

Molly laughed loud and hard. "Haw! And me going on about my great discretion!" She was blushing from head to toe, shaking her head, and smiling at the memory. "Truth is, I'm a bit sweet on the lad, and let him just do whatever he wants to me. He's ..."

She caught the look in Tilman's eyes and clapped a hand over her mouth, rocking with laughter now. Tilman laughed with her, to put her more at ease.

"Well, you caught me out," she said. "What do you want to know?"

"Let's start with you," Tilman said. "How did you end up here?"

"I joined Miss Kate's stable in Philadelphia. Fresh off the boat I was. Just fifteen. She's been like a sister to me, and trained me right. I can be a lazy slut, but she has a wicked hand with a riding crop when I don't measure up. Keeps me in line. And she knows everything about pleasing men and controlling them. Until now."

Molly's face was suddenly full of doubt. She looked a bit scared.

"Until now?" Tilman prompted.

"I think we made a mistake in coming here. Oh, it looked good going in. That Jake Martin is a smooth customer. He tells her he's got these rich foreigners coming to his new resort that he wants to keep happy. So he doesn't want a cut, just courtesy, and we can charge ten times as much as we usually do."

"Courtesy?"

"That's a bit like the 'freedom of the city' back in the ould country. Any girl he wants, any time he wants, any way he wants, no questions asked. Fortunately, he's pretty much a meat-and-potatoes fellow in bed. Nothing too exotic. No Greek or French or anything like that. You know what those are?"

Tilman nodded.

"Lately, he mostly wants Miss Kate and her riding crop." Molly looked thoughtful. "Maybe the old bugger does have a soul someplace." She looked at him shyly. "You know about her and your partner?"

"Some of it. They were to be married, but there was a War."

"She was raped by a Union officer and made to look like a whore."

"And so became one," Tilman added. "It's not the first time I've heard that story, Miss Shannon."

"Molly. Please. You make me feel like I'm in court on a charge."

"Molly, then." Tilman made another entry in his notebook. "What about the Strangers?"

"Now that's a rum lot," the little redhead said thoughtfully. "We're here for them, but they don't have much to do with us. We mostly get those murdering thieves Jake brought in for target practice."

Tilman looked very surprised and stopped writing for a moment.

Molly shrugged. "I mean, it's all the same to me," she said. "The fee's the same. No courtesy there – and a good thing, too. A rough, ugly bunch. Reminds me of my uncles, the way they go at it. The odd Stranger I've had don't seem to know what to do, so you've got to take them in hand ...literally. And it's all very traditional. And quick. The other thing is that it's like hugging an oven. Be nice to have with you on a cold night in Philly, but you're so sweaty when you're done, you've got to go wash off. Funny thing is, they don't sweat at all. Dry as that desert out there."

Tilman was writing all this down furiously.

Molly Shannon shivered a bit. "Their skin is real dry and tough, like a leather glove. It's soft enough, but it don't feel natural. And you never see the same one twice. It's like they've had the experience, but not the joy of it. Like it wasn't all that good for them. They never tip. And, I'm sorry, I may be a hoor, but I'm a damned good one, and I take pride in my work." She sounded indignant.

"As well you should," Tilman said.

"You sure you don't want a tumble?" Molly asked wistfully.

Blake Tilman shook his head and put his notebook away. "I had a daughter who died during the War. She'd be about your age now."

"Oh, what does that have to with it?" Molly said pleasantly. "My father and uncles and brothers started in on me when I was twelve. Sure, and I figured if I was going to be used that way, I might as well get paid for it."

Shanty Irish, Tilman thought, feeling pity for her.

She saw that in his face, and was immediately defiant. "Does that shock you, Detective? You're a man of the world. How do you think that young girls come to do this?"

"It makes me sad, that's all."

"It's a wicked world we live in, Detective, and I'm sure that's no surprise to the likes of you, with all your vast experience. Don't look at me like a judge. You going to help my Derek?"

"*Your* Derek?"

"If I can manage it. It will take more than the Pinkerton Agency to stop me."

Tilman laughed. "We won't interfere. He's a grown man and in his right mind. It's his mother you'll have to get past."

"Are you going to help him?" Molly demanded again.

"Of course. He's the client. We'll get him out."

"That will be no easy task," Molly said.

Tilman suddenly realized that she was possessed of more than just a certain native cunning. She was actually very bright, and thought strategically. If she had half the feelings for Seaton that she professed, she was an asset, not a liability.

A single tear ran down her cheek. Irritated at this show of weakness, she wiped it away and said, "Jake Martin's set a real trap here. I don't think we're meant to leave, any of us."

"What do you mean?"

"He's a greedy, grasping man. I can tell that from having been with him. You know the type: nothing's ever enough."

Tears started again, very slowly. "If we're all dead, there's more money for him. I mean, these gunfighters are the scum of the earth and good riddance to them, but what happens to us girls after? Or the people of this town? Think we'll be left alive to tell the tale? No one is allowed to leave. You saw what happened to Clete Morgan."

"What about the Strangers?"

"Well, aren't we all their playthings, to be toyed with and tortured? I think that ould soak Seamus has got the right of it for once. They're demons from below. This patch of ground is pretty enough, but that's an illusion. If there is a Hell, then we are surely in it."

Blake Tilman watched helplessly as she began to weep. He didn't know what to do to comfort her, that wouldn't wind up with both of them in the nearby bed. But soon she stopped, found a handkerchief, dried her eyes and blew her nose. She smiled at him.

"Sorry, Detective."

"That's all right."

"You're a hard man. A lesser one would have taken advantage, especially having already paid me out. Am I so unattractive?"

"Not at all," Blake Tilman replied, keeping his face still, so she would not see what a close thing it had been for him – to keep from taking her in his arms and letting cruel nature take its course.

CHAPTER TWENTY-FIVE

Ashley Portier had barely gotten back into the big room at the hotel when one of Miss Kate's girls came up with a saucy smile and slipped a note into his hand.

"Let Gayle take you upstairs. We need to talk," the note said in the elegant cursive handwriting Alicia Sorrell had learned at Miss Upton's Female Academy before the War.

Gayle smiled at him nervously. She was a fleshy blonde with big hips and breasts. Probably from Germany.

Portier nodded and said, "Lead on."

Gayle took his hand and led him up the staircase. She chatted gaily, with a Swedish accent, but Portier was too focused on the room around him and all the various games of chance and surly gunmen to pay attention. At the head of the stairs, Gayle suddenly put her arms around his neck and slipped her tongue into his mouth. He stiffened for a moment until she whispered, "Relax. It's just for show. Jake Martin is watching."

Her eyes moved sideways, and when he snuck a glance himself, he saw that she was indeed correct. Martin was behind the bar, staring up at them. Portier leaned over and exchanged a long passionate kiss with her. She came out of the clutch breathing hard and murmured, "Pity that wasn't really for me."

Gayle pulled him into the hallway and shuddered a little bit. "That fellow gives me the creeps," she said. She continued down the hallway, opened the door to a big, well-decorated room, and ushered him inside.

"I'm going on my break," she said, and closed the door behind him.

Portier turned around and saw Alicia Sorrell sitting at a dressing table, peering into a mirror. She was naked. Her beauty took his breath away. She turned and smiled.

"Well, sir, now you see me in all my glory, that this poor estate affords me."

Portier said nothing. Instead, he looked away.

She stood up, walked over to him, and used her hand to turn his chin back. "Look at me, damn you! This is how I would have appeared on our wedding night. I want you to remember this, because it's your fault I've come to this."

"My fault?" Portier was stunned by the accusation.

"You and your Southern Chivalry! You had to ride off and fight the Yankees in Virginia, instead of protecting us in New Orleans! You subjected me and all my friends to the depredations of Beast Butler and his men! It is they who led me to this. I am no better than a slave. Jake Martin owns me, body and soul." She pointed to a scar on her bare hip. Portier leaned over and saw it was actually a brand, burned into her flesh years ago. It was red because her blood was up. 'J.M.' it read.

Portier, horrified, realized that Jake Martin had branded her like cattle to cement his control over her. With that mark, no man would ever want her as a wife; she would always be a whore. Forever his, even if he later sold her.

Alicia turned and walked back to the dressing table and began to apply some red coloring to her nipples. Her breasts were firm, like those of a much younger woman.

"Every night I make a grand entrance, and the girls and I sing and put on a little show. The gunmen seem to like it. The Strangers, not so much. They just stare at us like we're animals in a zoo. I think the high notes bother them. Some of them cover their ears." She sat and began to pull on black silk stockings.

"Why are you here, Ashley? And with Blake Tilman, of all people, and working for that damnyankee Pinkerton!" She reached for a black silk corset, raised her arms, pulled it over her head and started to wriggle into it.

Portier found his voice as last. "I am as surprised to see you, my dear, as you are to see me. This is an awesome trick of Fate. How do you know Tilman?"

"From New York City. He saved my life about five years ago. Got me off from being hanged for murder. How do you know him?" She walked over and turned her back on him so he could help with the laces in the corset.

"Pull hard. They have to be tight."

"Tilman and I met last week in El Paso, when I hired on with the Pinkerton Agency. I needed the money. You take the work available. And I'm not proud, not these days. He's my mentor. And he seems decent enough – for a Yankee."

"They hold him in high regard in the Demimonde," Alicia replied. "He's tough, but fair, and never takes advantage. Never expects to bed us – unlike the city police, who are as corrupt as they come."

"So you never ..."

"Not with him. I cannot be expected to fuck every man in the world. There are only so many hours in a day. That's enough." She turned so her breasts were dangling like overripe fruit right before his eyes and then walked away, but not before he could smell the heat of her body and become instantly aroused.

He blinked in confusion. Had she done that deliberately? Of course she had. He suddenly realized that Blake Tilman's reticence with such women was as much sound policy, as respect for his late wife. Once you were in their power, you were lost. Alicia Sorrell had entranced him as automatically as ordering a glass of wine, with no real thought, and the unspoken expectation that what she desired would be promptly delivered. He watched her pull on her gown over her head.

"May I ask what happened?"

Alicia sat again at the dressing table, facing him this time. "If you play a game with me."

"A game?"

"Come here and kneel before me. I will permit you to help me with my boots."

He stared at her a long moment. Did she want to humiliate him? Of course. It was a petty revenge. And he was not too proud, if it gave him answers. So he did as she asked and kneeled. He had to walk on his knees to get close to her, which made her smile.

"You've heard of Belle Boyd?"

"Heard of her? I knew her in London. You were a spy?"

"Major Alicia Sorrell, at your service ...or Judah Benjamin's anyway. Miss Belle came through on tour, as it were. Several of us young women, all belles in our own right, were invited to meet her. This was in 1863, after she had attained a sort of shabby fame as a secret agent, and before the disasters at Vicksburg and Gettysburg. She was recruiting for the Secret Service, and looked so impressive in uniform. A lieutenant colonel, she was. She told us the story of how she'd made that rank, and how the intelligence she collected had helped General Jackson. And how other young women in Virginia, by letting young Yankee officers pay court to them, were collecting much valuable military information. One girl had just helped Colonel Mosby capture a Union brigadier! It sounded so exciting, and a chance to do something for the Cause. All we risked was hanging – or worse, the loss of our reputations."

"Why that?"

"Consorting with the enemy? Even if they are well-mannered young men from good families, it's considered treason by those not in the know: the unthinking patriots who did stupid things like burn cotton, keeping it from being shipped to Britain where it could earn us much-needed foreign exchange – where Britain could finally grant us official recognition or break the blockade."

Portier reached for one of the short, high-heeled boots next to the dressing table. Alicia Sorrell picked up a riding crop from the table and used it to smack his hand.

It stung quite a bit. Portier stared at her, amazed. "Why did you do that?"

"You need my permission to touch me. I demand obedience."

Suddenly very unsure of himself, he asked, "That is the game?"

"Of course," Alicia favored him with a cruel smile. "Call it payback for abandoning me."

Portier put his hands behind his back, still kneeling. He felt her attitude unjust. "See here, ..."

"Speak only when spoken to, slave." She smiled. "That is also part of the game."

Portier decided he did not much care for this game. It was unmanly. But he needed her to tell the rest of her story. Otherwise, he would never understand what had happened, or why she was now such a cruel bitch. He understood the need for revenge, but not his part in her having such great anger.

"Now you may help me with the boots," she purred.

Cautiously, he picked them up and slid them on her feet, then tightened the laces. She laid the tang of the riding crop against his cheek. Startled, he looked up. Was she going to hit him again?

"Good boy," she said. "Do you want the rest of the story?"

He simply nodded, afraid to do anything that might provoke her further.

"Okay. Go sit back down." She put the crop aside, reached down and tugged at the top of the boots.

"Did you enjoy the game?"

"No. Not much."

"You would be amazed at what grown men of standing and sophistication will pay to have me treat them so. It's quite popular in New York. Such is a whore's life. It comes from a book called 'Venus in Furs' by some German." She stood up, adjusting her gown.

"But you meant it," Portier protested. "You were quite serious."

"Was I? Belle Boyd is not the only Southern belle who became an actress. Truth to tell, all of us played a role before the War. It was expected at every dance, every ball, every social. And I do enjoy this game. Having even the illusion of power over a man does improve my mood."

Portier's confusion must have shown on his face.

She suddenly became tearful. "Really, Ashley. I've been branded like a farm animal. That mark will never go away It will always remind me of my shame, my fall from grace."

Portier shook his head. He was trying hard to understand. "Perhaps you can finish the story."

"Oh, yes. I volunteered for secret service, one of many, and we were schooled. Miss Belle is not a pretty woman, but she has a way with men that is simply amazing, and makes them forget that unfortunate face and big nose of hers. They fall all over themselves to get close to her.

"Unlike Belle's Captain Keily, the man I fell in with was no gentleman. Colonel Soames was chief of staff for a whole division. A rich source of intelligence, but he meant to have his way with me, and one night I succumbed. It was rape, I suppose, but my protests were muted. It seems I like fucking. My protests went unheard. My own fault for taking up with a damnyankee and what did I expect? My family disowned me.

"When I demanded he make an honest woman of me, he laughed in my face, and broke me on the wheel of my own desires. But he went through with it anyway, neglecting to tell me about the wife and six children he had at home. He feared scandal, I suppose. My reputation in New Orleans was not improved when it came out how he had tricked me. So I was cast out. When he went back to Massachusetts, he turned me over to his supply officer."

"Jake Martin."

"Yes, indeed. But I've been able to reclaim some of my own power from old Jake."

"How so?"

"Jake also likes to play that game."

Portier felt his eyebrows climb upward.

Alicia Sorrell laughed scornfully. "Most men are like little boys. They want approval, and fear and love their mothers."

"This is all my fault," Portier said slowly. "You are right. I should have been there to protect you."

"Oh, nonsense," Alicia replied. "You were thousands of miles away. What could you have done? The fault is mine, no matter how much my black heart insists otherwise. I knew I was to be married, and should have kept my virtue safe for you. I just could not stop thinking about how good it felt when you kissed me and felt me up. My breasts ached for your touch ...or somebody's touch, anyway." She stood up.

He stepped closer.

She held up her hand. "Unless you have twenty dollars to match that intention, stop there."

Portier felt that remark like a blow to the stomach.

"You see," she said; "this is who I am now. A whore to the end. This is my work. And I like what I do. So, please, save your pity."

"What would you have me do? I have always loved you."

"Find a way to save me, Ashley. To save us all, because Jake means to kill us all to save himself. He's told me as much."

"What do we do? Have you any ideas about how?"

"None. How long have you been a detective?"

"About a week. I'm more familiar with saloons and card tables."

Alicia grinned. "Aren't we a pair? A card sharp and a whore. Won't our parents be proud?"

"The Arabs say 'It was written' as if God has a big book someplace with everything planned. It's a commonplace in many Christian religions, too." Portier shook his head. "I don't hold with that. By that reckoning, we're already dead, because I can't see how we get clear of it. But I've been in many tight spots, and bluffed my way out of them. Fate is not fixed nor immutable."

He surprised her then by kneeling once more. "I still want you for my wife, Alicia, if you will have me. I've been to a lot of places and seen a lot of things. People start new lives everywhere. We can, too. Forget New Orleans. We'll go to San Francisco. No one knows us there."

Alicia put her hand protectively over her throat, as if he might strangle her. Her lip curled once again in that same cruel smile. "Just like that? You speak as if it were the simplest thing in the world. You may be footloose and fancy free, but I've got a dozen girls who are like sisters or daughters to me – who look to me for protection and guidance. I have to take care of them!"

Portier stood up. He saw that she was perfectly serious. It was a matter of honor with her. She would not abandon her flock.

"Surely ..."

"They are all the family I have now, Ashley. And I have gotten them into a very bad spot. All of these killings, and the Strangers, and then there is Jake Martin himself." Alicia leaned her body into his, seeking comfort. He caught her scent and felt himself aroused, but knew to put that reflex aside.

"What about him?"

"I think the fool has fallen in love with me," she said, laughing bitterly. "He asked me to save myself for him alone. Me! When he broke me to the life himself, and made me what I am! It is not to be believed, and certainly not the arrangement I agreed to!" Her indignation was real, but almost comical.

Confused and unhappy, he moved away from her, shaking his head. "What in God's name should I say?"

"That I made my bed and now must lie in it? That's what all those hypocrites in New Orleans say. All right, I am what I am, but this is a contract and it must be honored."

Portier looked at her, trying to remember her as the sweet, innocent girl he had proposed marriage to in 1860. So many years ago.

Her red lips trembled. "I have never loved any man but you, Ashley. I have known many, but none has ever had my heart; I am not that faithless. Nor have I ever pretended otherwise. Colonel Soames knew he was getting a cold bitch at the altar, and said he preferred it that way. When he cast me aside as damaged goods, because I seduced other officers for their information, Jake Martin took me up; he could get good money for what was between my legs. And he burned his brand into me to make sure of me. But that was strictly a business arrangement. He was never supposed to love me. And I cannot love him, knowing what he is."

"And what is that?"

"Evil. Pure evil."

Ashley Portier looked at her a long moment, and then felt her hand slip into his trousers. She was an accomplished seductress, but he wanted none of it. He gently forced her hand away, even as his body ached for her to continue.

"I said I want to marry you. The consummation will come after that."

She laughed and stepped away. The cruel smile returned to her lips. "A true romantic, like all the Chivalry. You boys ruined us with your romantic notions about manhood and dying in battle. The Yankees were more practical. I entertained a similar romance when I married Soames. I was a spy, and delivering critical intelligence to our Army, but everything Soames was so careless with – that he invited me to steal – was a lie, deceptions designed to mislead and confuse us. He told me this with great gales of laughter when he finally had me arrested, and then had me raped by the guards at the jail. That all my heroics were for naught, a lie, because they had fooled me. That burned far more than the red-hot brand Jake Martin applied to my flesh when he went my bail and then got the charges dismissed."

"That must have hurt."

"Not really. We were smoking opium when he did it. I barely felt it, although the smell made me very ill. Jake is not a cruel man. He never beat me. He never had to. Opium makes me very compliant with his wishes."

The shock must have shown on his face.

"That's another part of the bargain, Ashley. I'm riding the tiger. I must have this. I'm a pathetic wretch."

She stared at him defiantly, full of self-loathing. "Now please go away. I have customers to see to."

CHAPTER TWENTY-SIX

No man ever wanted a drink as badly as Ashley Portier, did as he walked slowly down the big staircase and through the crowded noisy barroom. Jake Martin was nowhere to be seen, so the desire just to shoot him outright for all he had done to Alicia Sorrell went unfulfilled.

A drink was out of the question because he would not be able to stop at one. He could not try to drown his sorrow; no, he must follow his partner's example and keep a clear head. He walked outside past the gunman standing guard, wondering if Tilman was still upstairs with Molly Shannon or had gone back to the jail. Then he heard Molly's distinctive laughter from the room behind him.

He looked up, saw that clouds still obscured the stars overhead. Ground fog was seeping up, making a mist that hid anything more than a hundred feet away. Confused, he tried to remember the way to the jail as he walked several yards toward the dim light of a lantern. He stopped, plucked another cheroot from his vest pocket, and struck a match. The light from the sputtering flame revealed Jesus standing almost next to him. Portier felt his heart stop for a moment, and he automatically reached for his revolver, dropping the burning match. He stayed his hand, as he realized who it was.

"Ahh! You gave me a turn. Have you been there right along?"

"Actually, I followed you from the hotel. You've been with Miss Kate."

"How do you know that?"

"Her scent is on you."

"Really? You can tell? I hardly touched her."

"A White man wouldn't be able to tell," the Indian said; "Especially one who drinks whisky and smokes cigars. Come on. The others are waiting for you." He turned and walked away. Ashley, as if he were drawn on a lead, automatically followed. Black Horse led the detective back to the open shed where Seamus Corcoran prepared the dead for burial, then on to the little shed where supplies were kept.

A single candle provided light for the interior. His partner was there, along with the undertaker and several other men. Two of them looked like the gunmen they had been sent to arrest or kill. The other were obviously locals – ranchers, except for one whose pinstriped suit proclaimed him a tradesman of some kind. In a far corner stood Julius Simms, nervously shuffling a deck of cards over and over.

"It seems that we are forming a Vigilance Committee," Blake Tilman said ironically. "Was your interview with Miss Kate productive?"

"Alicia says that we must all get away – that we are in great danger, all of us. Jake Martin means to sell us out, and dead men tell no tales."

"Nor dead whores neither," Seamus Corcoran added. He was more drunk than usual, and stared at them owlishly.

"But now he can't just murder us all," Tilman said. "The Pinkerton Agency takes very unkindly to that kind of thing, especially when the victims are its own. And then there is the matter of young Mister Seaton, whose family is rich and powerful enough to send an army after him if he does not return."

"Never underestimate a mother's love," Portier commented. "And, speaking of that, Alicia will not leave her girls behind, and just abandon them to their fate. She's like a mother to them."

One of the gunmen laughed. "I've heard that. And they are all scared as hell."

Simms put the deck of cards away in a side pocket of his suit. "Do we have a plan?" he asked plaintively.

"More like a plan to have a plan," the gunman said.

"Who are you again?" Simms asked.

"That's Black Jack Morgan," Tilman said; "Wanted for bank and train robbery. Where's the rest of your gang, Jack?"

"Hello, Mister Tilman," Morgan replied. "I thought that might be you." He was lean and somewhat handsome, with curly black hair and blue eyes. "We lost one to the Strangers in a showdown about a week ago. Some of them decided they would just ride away, and I was hopeful that they would find those nigger cavalrymen and bring them back, but when you packed Clete Morgan and that other poor soul back in, I despaired of them having managed it and decided we would throw in with you."

"You know we have warrants on all of you?" Tilman asked.

"I thought as much, but I've always preferred a few years in prison to the finality of the grave. We get out of this, and we will go with you quietly. My word on that as a Christian."

Tilman wondered briefly how much the word of a Christian wanted in three states might be worth, but reflected that, as far as he knew, Morgan had never murdered anyone. He was a robber, not a killer ...unless his hand was forced as it was now.

"Done." He looked around the small crowded room. "We need to know more about the Strangers. Who are they? Where do they come from?"

"Somebody said Bohemia, wherever that is."

"I'll tell you where!" Seamus Corcoran said. "They're demons from Hell. Jake Martin has sold his soul, and these are demons from the Pit! They stink of brimstone! And we poor sinners better get right with the Lord. We need Father Tomas to do an exorcism."

Everyone stared at him. Most of them had no faith in divine providence or miraculous interventions, but they shared his desperation. They were willing to try anything.

Jesus had been silent until that moment, standing so still that he once more seemed to disappear, but he stepped forward and pointed upward. "Not so. They come from the sky."

"You've seen this?" Portier asked.

"I have."

"Is it like a balloon?" Tilman asked. "I saw the one that Professor Lowe put up for observation during the War."

"More like a wagon or a boat," Jesus said. "But these move through the sky or just disappear entirely. I wish I had a telescope so I could get a closer look."

"Why haven't you said anything before now?" Corcoran was suddenly sober, sweating.

Jesus shrugged. "Would it have helped? You Whites are already scared half to death. I regarded it as White Man's business. I hate you, so if you all kill each other the way you killed all the buffalo... " He paused, thinking it through. "But you just had this big War where you killed more than a half million, and now there are more of you than ever. When I went back East, it was to study the White Man's ways, but not for the White Man's purpose. I wanted to know how to defeat you, but that is not possible.

"There are too many of you; too few of us. And you have no honor. You give us the worst land for reservations – land that no one wants, unless gold is discovered. Then you take it back. You give us blankets infested with diseases to make us sick and die, and liquor to destroy our souls. You have no honor. You do not fight fair. My heart aches over what you did to the Comanches last year."

Tilman, who studied politics and history in his spare time, knew that Jesus, or Black Horse as he was now, was only speaking the truth. He was no advocate for Manifest Destiny, and did indeed harbor some of the radical sympathies that Harry McLean suspected him of. But the Indian's complaint of an unfair conflict simply struck him as juvenile. Surely this very intelligent and articulate man knew the way of the world? Such fights were never fair.

"What is your point, sir?"

"That with White Men, I know what I'm dealing with, and I can do so without fear. If I die, I die. Such is Fate. But the Strangers are not White Men, and certainly not on their side. They smell nothing like the White Men, and only act that way because they are playing a game. It is all pretense and play for them. They really are on holiday. Tourists. At first I thought that a good thing, because they will not stay. They leave and new ones come. It is not land they seek but pleasure. Just like those European royalty that Bill Cody and the other buffalo hunters started bringing over when the railroad gangs stopped needing so much meat. Like Jake Martin, Bill provides everything they might want, from wines and fine crystal to Indian raids they can fight off."

"Sounds risky," Portier commented. "What if one of those Royals got killed?"

Black Horse grimaced. "All for show. Blank ammunition. Didn't even take a scalp or kidnap a pretty girl to hold hostage."

"You played your part, I gather," Tilman said.

Black Horse bowed his head briefly. "My people need money to survive. And that is the other White Man's poison. It also steals the soul."

"Hell," said Jack Morgan. "You don't have to steal mine. It's always for sale. If there was a better way to get a lot of it, the boys and me would turn into honest men in a heartbeat, but any banker can steal more in a day than I can in a lifetime, if he is so minded."

Black Horse nodded. "The Strangers will kill all the White Men. This was my hope when they first appeared. But they only kill a few bad ones, who are stupid enough to fight them. The rest they leave alone. So far. What becomes of us when they stop culling the herd? I can protect my people from the White Men because I have studied them. Of these Strangers, I know almost nothing. They fly through the air, and can throw lightning. How they do that, I have no clue, and the first time I saw that I thought it was a peyote dream. Clete Morgan's body proves it is all too real. How do we fight men who act like gods?"

"I am sure there is a way. Jack?"

"Yes?" answered the robber.

"Can you talk to some of the other gun hands? Maybe get them to help in whatever plan we come up with?"

Morgan shook his head doubtfully. "I ain't too sure that's a good idea. Most of them are drunk most of the time, and going to the whores more for comfort than a fuck; like them girls is their mothers or something. Scared shitless, most of them. And Martin is paying pretty good to the ones who decide just to be hands. They'll back him. It's only the ones with the big reps, who are in the dime novels, or have wanted posters with big rewards, that interest the Strangers. And none of those men wants to become known as a coward. Certainly not me. I'd rather become a clerk in a shoe store, or the like, than be seen to back away from a fight."

"So there's no one?"

"Might be one or two," Simms said; "Once you explain the odds. Leave that with me. Lots of chatter at a poker table."

Tilman and Portier looked at each other.

"I think this meeting is adjourned," Tilman said. "But leave one at a time, so we don't attract attention."

As the men began to filter out, Tilman motioned to Jesus/ Black Horse. The Indian came closer.

"Chief, I want you to show us where you saw the Strangers come out of the sky."

"After the Moon is down, so we can't be seen." The Indian looked at him curiously. "You believe me, huh?"

"You're not the kind of man to make up fancy stories for tenderfeet. Much too serious. Where is it?"

"Martin has a ranch about ten miles out. The Strangers stay out there, and then ride in, or come in an old stage coach he has, to stay at the hotel."

"How many?"

"It varies. Never more than twelve."

"Twelve guests, twelve whores. Logical." Portier tried to keep the bitterness out of his voice.

The Indian shrugged. "That might have been the original idea, but it ain't come out that way, which is why Jake decided to let the gunmen have them, too. The girls was complaining that they wasn't making the money they'd been promised."

Tilman and Portier looked at each other again.

"Seems Jake Martin don't know his customers very well, either. What do the Strangers really want?"

"Gunfights," the Indian said. "Those make them happy. One got so happy last week that, after he had killed his man, he used a Bowie knife to slice open his belly and ate part of his liver."

Tilman just stared at him, trying to comprehend.

Portier asked, "He was trying to capture part of his opponent's spirit? I saw that once in Africa."

The Indian shrugged. "Maybe. Personally, I think he was just hungry."

. . .

There was still enough light to see by, even though the Moon had set. They went slowly, almost at a walk, skirting a trail just below the ridge line so they could not be seen in profile. Two of Black Horse's braves went with them, and the Chief communicated with them in sign language. Portier was surprised that he could understand most of it from an adventure he'd had with Captain Burton and some Sepoys near the Khyber Pass. Some things were universal, it seemed.

When Black Horse signed that it was time to dismount, they all did, slowly, and the two braves took the reins as Black Horse and the detectives started to carefully climb the ridge. Tilman carried the telescope in his left hand, a habit that assured that his gun hand stayed free and ready. There were still too many clouds overhead for the sextant to do him any good. He heard a rustling sound in the brush near his feet.

"Say," Tilman asked; "Are there any snakes here?"

"Probably hundreds," Portier whispered; "But likely all underground, sleeping."

"I just don't want to add snakebite to our difficulties," Tilman said nervously.

Portier was startled, and then amused, that the steely-eyed Blake Tilman had a fear of anything, much less snakes. He chuckled. "You'd have to step on one and wake him up first. Even then, he'd probably not strike. Right, Chief?"

"Not at this time of night. No self-respecting snake would," Black Horse agreed, drily.

Tilman stared at him wildly for a moment, and then grinned. "Very funny."

The three of them crept up the steep hill until they could peer over into the valley on the other side. Below they saw a large hacienda in a flat yard with horses and men standing around. There was a lot of cold white light coming from within the long rambling building, and a lot of noise muted only by the long distance.

"It's the middle of the night," Tilman said. "Don't these people ever sleep?"

"No, it's always busy," Black Horse replied.

"No rest for the wicked, eh?" Portier said.

"And damn little for the righteous." Tilman looked sideways at Black Horse. "What now?"

"Wait. Watch. This is where the Strangers lodge. Not in town. That made me curious, so I decided we would watch them."

"Ever think of working for Pinkerton's?" Tilman asked, perfectly serious.

The Indian turned and stared at him. "No." He seemed almost offended at the idea.

Suddenly, the entire area was flooded by a blinding white light from above that caused pain to shoot through their eyes. Squinting, Portier could see something that looked like a large boat, maybe an ironclad ship from the War, floating down silently. It amazed him; he saw that Tilman was equally awestruck. They had not gone suddenly deaf. The same noises still drifted across the distance to them from the hacienda. But the large floating thing came to rest in front of the building as gently as a falling leaf. The bright light went out in an instant, leaving the three of them temporarily blind. Portier, who had seen many remarkable things in the previous decade, felt a thrill of genuine fear, because he could not comprehend how something so massive could move so silently. He had seen hot air balloons, but this was far too big to be one of those.

Blinking, Tilman also had a thousand questions spring to mind. How was this even possible? He, with all of his experience, was astonished.

"God help us," Portier murmured.

"Is that how they normally arrive? The Strangers?" Tilman asked softly. He was remembering the big hot air balloon in El Paso that had brought Jim Frazer into their lives, and the star chart he'd left behind. This was no Jules Verne fantasy, but all too real.

"Yep," said Black Horse. "New ones come and old ones leave. Ten or twelve. But there's not a hair's difference between any of them. All about the same height, build, weight."

Tilman lifted the telescope and pulled it to its full length. Putting it to his right eye, he surveyed the yard below. "There's a new passel of Strangers," he reported. "All in new duds and boots, looking around. No sidearms, though." He shifted his gaze slightly. "I guess that's the ones that are leaving. And there is Jake Martin!"

Martin emerged from the front door of the hacienda and started shaking hands with the departing Strangers. Then he turned to greet his new guests and lead them inside. Two or three men dressed like cowhands brought out large metal containers and placed them next to the huge conveyance that transported the strangers. Tilman blinked a moment and the containers were gone. Then the departing Strangers were also not where they had been, and were no place to be seen.

"Chief," said Tilman slowly; "Did you see what I just saw? Or rather, didn't see?"

"Like a magic trick?" Black Horse nodded as the detective handed the telescope to his partner, who took it eagerly, and also looked.

"Yes."

"That's how they do it. Damned if I know how."

"Whatever this is, Jake Martin is in it up to his neck," Tilman said, still a bit stunned.

"He's not the only one," Portier handed the telescope back. "I do believe that's your old friend Parker Boone, over to the right of the big door."

The Strangers' big craft began to silently rise into the sky.

"Get down so they don't spot us," Black Horse said urgently. They all lay prone in the dirt, keeping their heads down, as the big white box rose further and further and further into the night sky, until it disappeared into the clouds.

Tilman rolled over and tried to follow it with the telescope to no avail.

"No hot air balloon could go that high," he said.

"No," Black Horse agreed. "Never could."

Tilman pointed the telescope back towards the hacienda. "That's Parker Boone, all right," he said at last.

"Are we going to try to apprehend him?" asked Portier in disbelief. "I don't see us walking in there, producing our warrant, and having him coming quietly."

"Probably not at this time," Tilman said. "But I surely want to talk to that rascal, and find out what he knows." He looked over at Black Horse's impassive face. "Can we get closer?"

"If you follow my lead and don't stomp around like White Men."

Tilman checked his Raymond Railway pocket watch, although he was barely able to see the dial. "We have three hours before sun-up. That enough time?"

"Let's go," the Indian said.

An hour later, they were fifty or so feet from the back of the hacienda, looking at an alert guard holding a Winchester in one hand as he tried to light a hand-rolled cigarette with the other. Parker Boone came out, wiping his hands on a towel, said a brief word to the guard and set out for the outhouse that they were hiding behind. The outhouse was a four-holer, but, at that moment, empty.

They watched Boone go inside and crept closer. Inside, Boone seemed to be in conversation. The three men paused, uncertain, then Black Horse put his hands together and nodded toward the sound. Boone was praying! — Reciting the Lord's Prayer like a child. With a few hand signs, Tilman motioned them to step back. Aware of how far even the slightest sound carried at night, they spoke in very low whispers. There was considerable noise coming from within the hacienda that might cover their conversation, but why take chances?

"Well, this will make it easy," Tilman said.

"You'd catch a man with his pants down?" Portier grinned. "Don't seem fair."

"It's the Pinkerton way," Tilman reminded him. "Parker is actually pretty fast with a gun, and knows how to use a knife as well as our Apache friend here. He's just too smart to try someone he has no chance against."

Black Horse raised an eyebrow at the word 'friend.' His expression said that he doubted that Parker Boone was as skilled as he was with any weapon.

"Still, there's no real harm in him." Tilman looked upward thoughtfully. "Wonder if he's suddenly found God. He ain't a killer. We get the drop on him, and he'll give it over."

"Best get on with it," Portier said.

"This is White Man's business," Black Horse objected. "I ain't no bounty hunter."

"Then you keep watch. Make sure we're not interrupted."

Black Horse looked from one to the other, and finally nodded. He pulled his foot-long Bowie knife from its sheath and suddenly was not there. Tilman and Portier looked around and then at each other and shrugged at the same time.

"You wait outside," Tilman whispered as they drew their revolvers and stepped back toward the outhouse. A slight crunching sound came from the dried sage beneath their boots. As they got closer, they could hear Parker Boone still in earnest conversation with his God.

Tilman hesitated, and then holstered his revolver. He opened the door and slipped inside to find Parker Boone, eyes tightly shut, still repeating the Lord's Prayer. He reached over and placed his left hand over the outlaw's mouth.

Boone's eyes popped wide open. There was enough light from a single candle that recognition came in an instant. Boone was shocked. Tears came to his eyes, and he sobbed. "Oh, thank God! I knew you would come for me!"

CHAPTER TWENTY-SEVEN

It took several moments for Parker Boone to regain his composure after he threw his arms around Tilman, and wept unashamedly like a child on his shoulder. Portier slipped in and witnessed this with great surprise and growing alarm. It was only a matter of time before someone else in search of relief discovered them. Finally, as Tilman disengaged and Portier offered him his pocket flask, the outlaw wiped his eyes with his sleeve and sighed.

"I thought I was a goner," he whispered, and took a short swig. "Take me away, and I will do the balance of my time without a word of complaint. No more wandering for this cowboy."

"Well," Tilman said; "We may get there, but you have to tell us about the Strangers and what Jake Martin does for them. How do they... well... fly?"

"You saw that, eh?"

"Still trying to take it in," Portier said. "That's an enormous device. Is it a balloon?"

Boone shook his head. "Some kind of machine. How it works, I have no idea, and neither do any of the other hands. Even Mister Martin hasn't said. He likes to show off what he knows, and brag, but on that, he is curiously silent. And it's one of many things about them Strangers that no one talks about."

Tilman's eyebrows went up. "Really?" He pulled his watch from a vest pocket and looked at it. "We can't linger, as fascinating as this all is. Make it quick."

Parker Boone's face fell. "You ain't taking me with you?"

"Not this time. This is a scout, and you'd be missed, which would give the game away. You'll have to endure it a bit longer," Tilman said.

"The more we know, the quicker it will be," Portier said, handing him the pocket flask again. Boone looked at it and shoved it away.

"Can't get liquored up. Jake Martin don't like it." He took a deep breath and looked from one to the other. "So I'm stuck, huh?"

"Not for long," Tilman assured him.

"Well, I don't know where the Strangers come from, but when they get here we have to teach them everything — even how to use the outhouse. It's all 'monkey see, monkey do,' but they learn quick, so they're only here for a day or two before they start going to town. What I teach them is gunfighting: how to draw, what the rules are, and like that; after a few hours, though, they are quicker on the draw than I could ever be, and more accurate. We got targets set up in back — straw dummies — and once they get the hang of it, it's right between the eyes every time. I never want to go up against them, which is why I signed on to be a hand instead."

"Are they really that good? We've seen a lot of well-known gunmen and desperados in town. We've got paper on most of them," Tilman said.

"Been to Boot Hill? Because that's where about half of them have ended up, and the rest will, in time. What's left of them."

"What does that mean?" Portier took a cheroot from his vest pocket, stuck it in his mouth, but didn't light it.

"The Strangers eat what they kill," Boone looked at them, eyes going wide, his expression sick and defiant.

The two detectives looked at each other, genuinely surprised. They looked at Boone, suspecting a lie. Cannibals? That notion was hard to accept, but then so were men who flew through the sky and threw lightning. Portier shrugged.

Tilman stared at Boone hard. "Oh, come on!"

"God's honest truth!" Boone whispered. "I seen it myself, in fancy silver dishes with the select bits, like a pork roast. I thought at first it was one, but I don't know many pigs that got a tattoo of a naked lady on their butt."

Portier looked at his partner, his eyes wide with amazement.

Tilman nodded slowly, going through the wanted posters in his mind.

"Rick Tracy," he said at last.

"Jake told me that it's just like those hunting parties that Bill Cody takes out from back East. Except these dudes is from a lot farther away."

Portier fumbled for a match. Black Horse took the cigar out of his mouth and threw it into the open latrine. Offended, Portier said, "Where the hell did you come from?"

"You're making too much noise," the Indian hissed. "Time to go."

"You heard what he said?" Tilman asked.

Black Horse nodded. "Most of it. Not a big surprise."

"No?"

"Bill Cody takes them dudes out to hunt game. Why do you hunt game?"

"For food, and a little sport."

"Well, here the gunfighting is the sport, like hunting puma, and we are the game."

The other three men were silent for a moment, dumbfounded. Boone's mouth dropped open in amazement.

"You are one smart Indian," Parker Boone moaned. "That's exactly what it is. Oh, dear God, what I have I gotten myself into?" He started to tear up again. Portier slapped him firmly across the cheek.

"Be a man!" he hissed. "Get hold of yourself."

Boone, stunned, sat rubbing his cheek and looked at Tilman in silent appeal. Tilman shook his head.

"You're going to have to play the hand out, Parker. These creatures can fly through the air and throw lightning. You go missing, and they'll come looking. Like they already done for your partner when he tried to run."

"Clete's dead?"

"Yep."

Boone sighed. "Well, no loss there. Never did care for the man. Wasn't my idea to cut and run. I was actually doing okay." He looked sadly at Tilman. "Guess I'm in, like it or not. What now?"

Tilman said, "Stay calm, and just watch and wait. Someone will be back when we have a plan." He gestured to Portier. "Give him his gun back."

He started to say something to Black Horse, but the Indian was no longer there.

"And don't try to run," Tilman cautioned Parker Boone. "You can't get away."

"I know." Boone looked miserable and started to tear up again. "They got some kind of damned magic carpet and they shoot light."

"Whatever it is, it burns flesh. Clete was about halfway cooked."

Boone nodded. "One of the other hands made a run for it last week. Didn't get far. They brought him back and left him in the yard as a warning to the rest of us. No one leaves without permission, Mister Martin said, and that's not until the 'season' is over."

"Except that day is never going to come," Portier said.

"I know."

"See here, Parker," Tilman said; "Be a sight easier to overcome these Strangers if the hands stayed out of it."

"Most of them are as dumb as a box of rocks," Boone replied. "They never made this much money, nor were able to buy such beautiful girls to satisfy their lust with. They don't want it to end."

"We have it on good authority that Jake Martin plans to kill everyone, and keep all the money."

Boone looked thoughtful and unsurprised. He nodded. "Sounds like him. He's very 'hail fellow and well met' when he comes out to check on his guests, but it's all a con. Last time I had one of the girls, she was complaining about what a rat he is."

"Miss Kate?" Tilman looked sideways at his partner to see how Portier was reacting to this. The Southerner's face was very still, as if he were in a tight hand of poker.

Boone smiled and nodded his head. "Best filly in the herd. Never had a ride like that. And such elegant manners. Worth every penny."

"Do tell," Portier said tightly. He turned away so Boone could not see the flush of blood that rushed to his face. Tilman put his arm around his shoulders and took him outside, ducking into the brush, as another hand came out of the hacienda, headed for the outhouse. Boone stepped out, adjusting his belt and greeted the man casually, giving them time to get away.

Cautiously, they made their way back to where the increasingly nervous horses and their Apache handlers were waiting. Black Horse was already mounted. When Portier started to say something, he put a finger to his lips, and used sign to indicate the direction of their retreat. The two detectives mounted and walked their horses in line slowly behind Black Horse, with his two braves following. They had just gotten to a gully filled with live oak trees and brush, when there was a high-pitched sound from the direction of the hacienda.

Black Horse and his braves rolled off their ponies and went to ground. Tilman and Portier followed suit. The Indian chief motioned for them to crawl under their horses.

"So they don't see you!" he whispered urgently.

Above, a shimmering light came down and swept over the gully. Portier and Tilman tried to bury themselves in the hard earth. The light moved off, then shone down on another grove some distance way. The process was repeated a few times at increasing distances. Finally, the source of the light, a narrow, pointed vessel shaped like the bottom of a boat, moved back towards the hacienda.

Tilman just stared, trying to understand what he was seeing. It was like something from ancient myths, a chariot ridden by gods.

Portier, his voice unnaturally calm, softly asked, "What the Hell is that?" He stood up to get a better look. Tilman and the Indians did likewise.

"It's the Strangers' sky wagon," Black Horse said.

"Sky wagon?"

"What else would you call it?"

Just then the shiny object in the sky moved with incredible quickness to the next mountain range, which they knew to be twenty miles away: a day's ride.

Black Horse spoke slowly, with awe. "I've never seen anything move that fast. Never. They got big medicine. Too big for Apache."

"How do we fight that?" Hands shaking, Portier started to light the cheroot he had taken from his vest pocket, only to have Tilman slap it out of his hand.

"Not here! We surely don't want to be seen." He turned to Black Horse. "It throws lightning, doesn't it?"

"Something like that, except it ain't a flash. More like a beam from an oil lantern, but much, much brighter. Bright red." Black Horse shook his head. "I've never seen the like."

"And it's what killed Clete Morgan, and that other fellow?"

"Not just them. I've lost a couple of braves to it. They were brave, but stupid. Tried to shoot arrows at it. That's when we learned to hide under the horses and trees. They can't see everything."

"Is it safe now?" Portier was almost pleading.

"Yep. We can go. They've given up for the night. It's like they know we're watching them, but just want us to keep back and leave them alone." Black Horse looked uncertain for a moment. "If they want meat, then any one of us could end up on the menu. The women, too. They like to play at having showdowns, but if they tire of that game, they'll just start killing everybody, like buffalo hunters." The Indian looked around. "It's clear now. Let's get back to town."

Black Horse mounted. He looked away from them, toward the town, reading the way ahead. Portier was struck by how noble his profile was. Like that of a Roman general he had seen in a painting, years ago at the Masonic Lodge in London. Here was a warrior defending his own, as he had himself many years before. It was a counterpoint to the steadiness of Blake Tilman. It gave him hope.

It was almost dawn. They rode down the gully, which was widening out. When the ground beneath them became flat, the five of them dug their heels in, and rode as if their lives depended upon it, until they reached the outskirts of Apache Wells.

Portier was surprised at how indignant Tilman was about the Stranger's dietary choices. Once they got back to town and could talk openly, the detective railed about cannibals for a good half an hour.

Finally, Portier said, "See here, Blake, that argument don't hold water, and you're just blaming them for what you and I do all the time — or do you no longer enjoy a good juicy steak?"

Tilman stopped, dumbstruck.

"You're going on like it never happens. Remember the Donner party in the Sierras during the Gold Rush?"

"That was different," Tilman said.

"Why?"

"They was stuck. It was that, or they all would die. They drew lots for it. Here it's for sport."

"I'm told it happens in Borneo and other places, like Africa. Captain Burton said it has a religious element. Men are hunted to their deaths some places."

Black Horse nodded. "I would not care to fall into Paiute or Pawnee hands. But they would not eat me."

"You sure about that?"

"Well, maybe a little of my liver, to capture my warrior spirit, but that's more from our ignorant savage ways than anything else. Of course, there is that whole 'body and blood of Christ' thing the Catholics have been peddling for hundreds of years." The Indian was amused at their discomfiture. "White Men are such hypocrites. But you're missing the point. To the Strangers, we are simply a game animal. Give them credit, though, they try to take us on our own terms in a fair fight. Not their fault we're not fast enough."

"What happened to those braves you lost?" Tilman asked suspiciously.

Black Horse shrugged. "The Strangers are ethical hunters. They don't like to let good meat go to waste."

Tilman gagged. Portier handed him his pocket flask.

"Take a bit of comfort, Blake. It ain't like they was tortured. We seen worse."

"And my tribe has done worse," said Black Horse; "trying to discourage the settlers. So get a grip, Detective. We got bigger problems than their choice of diet."

"Like not ending up on the menu," Portier said, taking a sip from the flask for himself after Tilman pushed it aside.

They were back in Seamus Corcoran's comfortable great room. It was after dawn. Tilman and Portier were beginning to feel their eyes close, despite their best efforts to stay awake. Black Horse was changing back into the clothes he wore as Jesus.

"About time to give Mister Seaton his breakfast," he said. "You boys want to catch some shut-eye in one of the empty cells?"

"Let's do that," Portier said.

"After breakfast," Tilman said, hearing the sounds of Corcoran's women getting busy in the kitchen. They could smell bacon frying.

"What do we tell Seaton?" Portier asked. "How much does he know?"

"I've kept pretty quiet about the goings-on at the hacienda," Black Horse said. "Didn't want to be accused of telling tall tales, or making things up. He can be a little touchy at times. But now I have two Pinkertons to back me up... "

"But will he believe it? I can hardly believe it myself," Portier replied.

"Seaton likes to talk about himself," Black Horse said thoughtfully; "And he's a very smart man. Someone raised him right, because he ain't like most rich White boys I met back East.

He's serious, not prideful or arrogant, and he didn't actually come down here just to fuck *señoritas* or get mixed up in gunplay."

"No?"

"No. He has a degree in geology."

"Prospecting for gold or copper?"

"He said not. Something called 'petroleum'."

Tilman nodded. "I read about that. Not gold, exactly, but will likely be as valuable in a few years. But it's hard to get out of the ground most places."

Black Horse had completed his transformation back into Jesus. "Well, then, let's eat, and take Seaton his breakfast," he said. "Maybe he has an idea about how to get rid of the Strangers for good and all."

"Time we let him in on all this?" asked Portier, as Corcoran's women, smiling and murmuring in Spanish, brought in platters of hot food.

"He is the client," Tilman said, helping himself to ham and fried potatoes. "He deserves to be informed."

At the jail an hour later, as Derek Seaton finished his own plate of food, Tilman carefully laid out everything they had seen the night before. The young millionaire didn't seem particularly surprised.

"You've seen this, Chief?" he asked. The Indian nodded slowly.

"We all have," Tilman said.

"Why didn't you say anything before, Jesus?"

"Would you have believed it?"

"Not at the first telling," Seaton admitted. "I've heard some pretty tall tales out here. Lying to greenhorns is just sport to most men. Jackalope humor. But I've had a lot of time to think about what I'm going to be facing in that duel. I knew they were from some place other than Earth."

Tilman gaped at him a moment, stunned to silence.

"Excuse me, sir," said Portier; "With all due respect, how could you possibly know that?" He, too, was amazed by what the young millionaire had just said.

"It's the logic of the situation, Detective. They are faster with a gun than any man has a right to be. Are they supernatural creatures from Hell? Maybe, although I don't hold with that kind of thing myself. One thing is sure, they ain't from here, and accounts of such men would have appeared some place before now if they were from anywhere on Earth. My family has a quite good private intelligence service, that sends us reports on new and unusual phenomena. Information is power, and often opportunity. My great-grandfather invested in steam power back when everyone thought it a ridiculous notion. He saw the potential. Petroleum is another one of those. Right now, it's mostly used in patent medicines, most of which don't really cure anything."

"So what does it really do?"

"It burns. Very hot. Tremendous amount of energy once it is refined. We find enough of it, and we'll be able to use it instead of coal in locomotives. Much more efficient."

Seaton walked over to the big cell window that looked out at the vacant desert. "So they don't act like us, and aren't from here. Do they come from Hell?"

"No," said Jesus; "From the sky."

"You've seen this? All three of you?"

They all nodded.

"Then all is not lost," Seaton declared. "Because if it is the Devil, then he's just toying with us, and we are in Hell, but if not — then these Strangers are mortal. We know they can be killed. I've done it, and without much effort. And there are only twelve of them, at most?"

"And Martin and his men. Maybe forty or fifty more."

"Then we need a strategy," Seaton declared. "And we don't need to understand how those flying machines of theirs work to defeat them."

The Indian nodded gravely. "One thing is sure. We ain't going to take them one by one. Because they don't know much about pistols, but they can throw lightning. You try that way, and you'll all die. Maybe the women, too. It will be a slaughter."

Molly Shannon came through the door from the Sheriff's office. She looked at the four of them uncertainly.

"What's all this?"

"A conspiracy," Seaton said, smiling at her.

"Not against me, I hope. Because I'm not the type of slut that takes on more than one at a time."

Seaton sputtered, turning bright red. Tilman and Portier broke into laughter, and even Jesus forced a tight smile.

Beginning to get angry, Molly turned to go. "A girl has her standards, you know!"

"No, no, Molly my love, let us explain," Seaton pleaded.

Molly stopped and was very still.

"Did you just say 'my love'?" she asked quietly.

"I guess I did," Seaton admitted.

"And you weren't just throwing me a bit of the blarney? You meant it?"

The other men looked at Seaton, also waiting for his answer.

He drew himself up, his face solemn. "I did. Every word."

Molly shook herself like a cat. "Well, then," she purred; "Tell me all about this conspiracy and how I can help."

The men all looked at each other. None had thought of her as an ally until that moment, not even Seaton. Women weren't much good in a fight, unless they were an Amazon like Belle Boyd, who could shoot a man's eye out at a hundred feet and possessed the resolve to do so. If they were not in on the plot, then they would be more hindrance than help.

"How much do the other girls know?" asked Tilman slowly.

"Not much. When you're on a play party like this, you just try to stay as sober as you can and get on with business. Miss Kate suspects, but she don't talk much to the girls now. She leaves that to me as her deputy. Some of them ain't too smart. And they whine a lot, because they always have to get their way with men. The Mistress has no patience for that, and she's too eager sometimes to add a little correction with that riding crop."

Portier shook his head. "She was the kindest, sweetest... "

Molly favored him with a sneer. "Like you would know."

The Southerner stared at her. "There was a time."

"I'm sure there was. Before the beatings and the rapes and all the other things they do to you to break you to the life of a whore." Molly looked very sad for a moment. "Me, I came to it naturally, because I have shitheads for relatives. Never expected anything else. But Miss Kate was Quality, born to and brought up on featherbeds. She had much farther to fall. And that drives her. Her anger would kill most people, and I've often wondered why she doesn't just take an ax or a cleaver, and mow down the lot of you men." Molly was crying by this time.

Seaton walked over, took her in his arms and held her. She struggled a moment and then just collapsed against him.

"And you?" he asked softly. "Are you angry, too?"

She looked up at him, and her face softened. "Not with you. Never with you."

Tilman watched this byplay carefully. Seaton was still the client, but he was a grown man. He would have to take his chances with this feisty little redhead, who was anything but naive or stupid. Who was playing whom? Or was it all real, as unlikely as that was?

"We need a plan," he said.

"To do what?" Seaton asked pleasantly. "What is our objective?"

"To get shut of Jake Martin and his 'guests' before they kill us all."

"And is that their plan? It may be Jake Martin's, because he's in way over his head, fears discovery, and wants to get away clean with as much money as he can." Seaton patted Molly absently on the back.

She wriggled free, embarrassed now at her loss of control. "Dead men tell no tales," she said, "Nor dead whores neither."

Seaton nodded. "But the Strangers are more selective. And much more honorable. They only kill the really bad men. The ones that are known to be killers themselves from the posters and the dime novels. They're very moral, if you think about it."

"They eat people," Tilman objected.

"Only those they kill in fights. And if they're not actually human, it may not be a sin nor a crime," Jesus said. "You really have to get past that, Detective. In the end, we're all meat, and we all get eaten eventually, if just by the worms. It's the natural way."

Tilman shuddered. "We need more information." He looked away, thinking hard. "Remember that thing that Parker Boone said, about how the new ones have to be instructed about how to do everything? Even take a shit? How would any natural man need to be taught that?"

"Maybe he just meant how to use one of them fancy toilets like they've got at the hotel?" Portier said, puzzled.

"What if that's the literal truth?" Tilman looked over at Molly, who was distracted by where Seaton had now put his hand, and was blushing a bit with embarrassment. "How are they in bed, Molly?"

She shoved Seaton's hand away. "Leave off!" she hissed, and then smiled at Tilman. "Totally clueless. Like a virgin being taught to fuck the first time. Clumsy. But not embarrassed at all. They just never done it before. It's like... I don't know, when a father brings his son to be tutored. You take them through the motions and they climb aboard and do what they can. But they do it like a chore, like something they got to check off a list. There's no passion, either. All the girls say the same. At least with the gunmen, you get a little emotion, some tenderness. The Strangers in bed? Like fucking a statue."

Tilman snapped his fingers. "Frankenstein! That novel by Mary Shelley. A monster made of bits and pieces and brought to life with an electric shock."

Jesus crossed himself. "Then they are devils. That's witchcraft. Bad magic!"

Portier sighed. "I wish my friend Captain Burton was handy. He knows all sorts of strange and wonderful lore. There are cults that bring back people from the dead, or so he said."

Seaton stared at him a long moment. "Is that Captain Richard Burton of the British Army? The explorer?"

"You know him?"

"By reputation. That intelligence service we own buys reports from him. I've read his work."

"The world is so large and yet so small," Portier marveled.

Tilman thought they were getting lost in the weeds, and cleared his throat. Everyone looked at him while he asked, "Molly, how do the Strangers look when they are naked? Like ordinary men?"

"Never seen one naked," Molly replied. "Long underwear is as far as they go. All the same, that way. Too embarrassed, I suppose. And getting them undressed all the way just slows everything down. There's nothing in it for the girls but the money. Why bother? They're nothing special that way." She smiled at Seaton. "Unlike some."

Seaton had the grace to blush and look away, as the other men chuckled. Tilman thought that if Seaton were able to so impress a professional like Molly, then he must indeed be a man of parts... or that she wanted him very much to think she thought that. But that was nothing to the business at hand.

"So what do we have here?" he continued. "Men who are not men? Men who are, it seems, mechanical?"

"I saw something like that in a museum in Amsterdam," Seaton said; "When I did the Grand Tour one summer. Automatica. It was only clockwork and not very real, but that it worked at all was the impressive part."

"What drove it?" Tilman asked.

Seaton blushed again. "Sorry, I did not take notes. I think it was clockwork — a spring. It was my first time abroad, and Amsterdam had other attractions."

"Whores?" Molly Shannon pretended outrage. "Derek Seaton. You mean I'm not the first girl from the Demimonde you've been with?"

"No." He stared at her a moment. "But you'll be the last."

Molly faltered a bit. "I will?"

"If you marry me."

Molly looked like she was going to faint.

"Save that for later," Tilman said, his irritation plain. "Let's stick to the plan."

"We have a plan?" Portier asked. "Oh, good. I wasn't sure." He paused a moment and fumbled for another cheroot. "What is it?"

"Right now, we need to know more about the Strangers. Molly, can you get the other girls to focus on them? Pay them special attention?"

Portier struck a match and lit his little cigar.

Molly Shannon looked thoughtful. "Jake has said that we need to show them more kindness. He's quite put out about it. But there is just so much a girl can do, if the bloke is a stiff."

"Extra effort is always good for business," Portier observed.

"Right. I'll have a word with them all."

"But nothing about why we want to know."

Molly shrugged. "They wouldn't understand any of it. Not sure I do myself."

"See if y'all can inspire them to passion." Portier said. "Get their hearts racing."

She shook her head. "They're different that way, too. I can get a man's heart racing at a gallop with some of the tricks I know. Not them. Always steady as a metronome. Like a clock ticking away."

The men all looked at each other with amazement, mouths open in surprise.

Molly looked from one to another, and clapped her hands with glee.

"That's it, ain't it! I've solved the puzzle!"

CHAPTER TWENTY-EIGHT

Later that day – after they had caught some much needed sleep – Tilman and Portier went back to the hotel, which was as rowdy as ever. Three of the Strangers were in the barroom, all seated at different tables. All playing cards. All winning, yet as solemn as priests in church. Spotting Julius Simms dealing at one, Tilman tapped his partner on the shoulder and nodded toward the two empty chairs there. Jack Morgan, looking rather depressed, was sitting between the Stranger and Simms.

Portier surveyed the room, starting with the large painting of a nude reclining young woman behind the bar above the mirrors. Two bartenders were pouring drinks and, unlike most of their ilk, carried holstered revolvers high and tight on their belts where they could be cross-drawn and used as clubs if need be. The blonde whore who'd kissed him with such enthusiasm earlier was carrying a tray of drinks to one of the tables. She winked at him as she passed by.

Portier and Tilman sat down at Simms's table. The Stranger smiled at them, as delighted as a child. The other men simply nodded. The poker table was never a place to show emotion.

"You gentleman want to ante in, or wait for the next hand?" Simms inquired, looking from one to the other with open curiosity.

"We'll wait," Portier said, and pulled a folded banknote from his vest pocket. "Chips."

Simms unfolded the crisp new bill, stared at the ornate printing on it, and smiled. "This bank went bust about five years ago," he said, "but I've been told that you're to be accommodated, regardless. One hundred dollar buy-in."

His long elegant fingers pulled a mixture of red, blue, and white clay chips from the rack in front of him, and stacked them in front of Portier before continuing the deal. He then flicked another round of cards face-up to the four players still in the hand. Jack Morgan groaned and folded his cards. He stood up.

"Gotta piss," he said. He walked away slowly toward the back of the room. Tilman also carefully took note of everything and everyone in the room, making a mental map. There were seven tables for cards, but only three were occupied. A whore was leaning over the shoulder of one of the other Strangers, whispering in his ear. Despite the rule about only one player to a hand, none of the gunmen at the table objected. The girl was a pretty redhead, wearing a yellow gown that exposed her shoulders and displayed her large breasts to advantage. Her nipples were erect and painted red, easily seen beneath the white lace top of her gown.

The Stranger bet a few chips and the rest of the players simply folded their cards. The girl laughed, and walked off to find a seat at another table — or rather on the lap of a gunman who welcomed her with a kiss. The Stranger she'd abandoned looked at her curiously, but seemed untroubled by her defection.

Everyone else in the room either ignored this, or waited for something else to happen. Tilman appreciated that the mood was tense but quiet. The 'floor show' had not yet begun. He looked for paths to the exit to be sure he and his partner would not be caught up in it, when the fight broke out.

Portier divided the chips in front of him and passed some to Tilman, who tilted his head, regarding Simms curiously.

"You think my friend counterfeited you with that note, and yet you let us buy in?"

Simms shrugged. "Not my money. Not my game. Just one of the hired hands, so I do what I'm told — and Jake Martin wants you boys at the table. I never defy my betters, you see. Sir!"

The last word had a sharp edge to it, causing Portier to look up. "You're not calling me a cheat, are you, Simms?"

Simms smiled tightly. "I would never do so with a man of your sterling reputation for fair play, and well-considered violence when crossed. It's only a card game; not worth my life to dispute over trifles. Now Mister Johnson here might feel different if he had his mind on the game."

Simms leaned forward, lowering his voice. "In fact, that's part of the larger game: to provoke him to violence, but Miss Dolly was with him earlier, and gave him something new that he finds very agreeable. So he's very peaceable, if you take my meaning."

Portier smiled tightly, as Simms collected the cards and shuffled them for another hand. The remaining players anted up.

"If you persist in talking in riddles... "

"In Frisco, they would say that Mister Johnson was riding the tiger or maybe the dragon."

"Opium?"

Simms nodded. "Miss Dolly is an enterprising sort. Keeps a supply for her customers who indulge. But I believe it's the gentleman's first adventure with the joys of the Orient."

Tilman looked at his hole card and folded a king, his mind racing. Johnson bet without looking at his. Portier was showing an ace and raised. The rest of the players dropped out and Simms shoved the chips toward him.

The game went on silently for a few more hands. Tilman played indifferently, because he was trying to parse what Simms had said. If the Strangers were purely mechanical, then opium should have no effect upon them. Yet this Stranger, another one named Johnson, was acting like a man under the influence. How could that be?

Portier, having won a big hand, assembled a stack of chips and shoved them toward Julius Simms.

"I'd like that note back."

Simms smiled, counted the chips, and said, "One hundred."

He passed the bad bill back to Portier, who carefully folded it and tucked it back in his vest pocket.

"It has sentimental value, you see," Portier said with a smile.

Tilman shook his head, laughing. He'd known many rogues in his time, but few with the bold-faced style his partner had just displayed. One of the other gunmen at the table laughed loudly. The Stranger suddenly startled, looking confused, like an actor in a play who had just missed his cue. He stood up, reaching for his Colt's revolver and slurred out a challenge.

"You should have not done that," he shouted.

But he was uncertain on his feet and in his manner. Jack Morgan came up behind him and plucked the gun from his hand. The Stranger whirled around and then went down like a sack of grain.

The two other Strangers looked up suddenly, but Morgan simply reached down and helped the Stranger to his feet with his free hand.

"There you go, pard," he said kindly, dusting off the Stranger's shoulder. "No harm done." He was careful not to hand the revolver back.

The Stranger sat back down, looking around. At the other tables, everyone stopped looking at him and went back to playing cards.

Simms said loudly, "Ante up!" He slowly dealt the cards, one up and one down.

Tilman threw away his hand again. Portier likewise saw no profit in his, and dropped out.

"Say," he said to the Stranger; "where are you boys from, anyway?"

"Far away," the Stranger replied. "Far, far away."

"Well, I've probably been there. Been around the world these last ten years, I have."

"Do tell," Jack Morgan said, sounding bored. His eyes were quite lively, checking everything and everyone. The revolver he'd taken off the Stranger was nowhere in sight.

He glanced at Simms and then at the two detectives.

"I like a quiet life," he said. "So why don't you stop talking so much?"

"Just being friendly," Portier said, discarding another bad hand.

"Pinkertons ain't exactly known for their charm," Morgan growled; "So shut it."

Simms slapped his hand down on the table. "Manners, gentlemen. Keep it friendly. My table, my rules."

"Or we could take it outside," Morgan said loudly. "You and me, Mister High-and-mighty."

"You don't want to do that," Tilman said calmly.

"Why the Hell not?" Morgan asked angrily.

"Because I might remember that we've got paper on you that says you're worth five hundred dollars. Then we arrest you, and take you down to the jail. We can do that later. Right now, let's just play cards." Tilman was trying to figure out what Jack Morgan was doing. What his game was? He actually seemed to be ahead in the poker game if the pile of chips in front of him were any indication. Morgan looked sideways at the Stranger apprehensively.

The blonde whore came over and said, "Can I get you boys anything?"

Portier smiled. "Why are you doing that? Where are the regular girls?"

"None showed up. Neither did the barmen. Mister Martin said we'd have to pitch in and do double duty." She laughed. "I don't mind. Tips is tips, and I ain't too proud to earn an honest living." She dropped her hand down on Morgan's neck and rubbed. "You're a little tight there, Jackie."

He stared up at her. She leaned over and rubbed her breasts in his face, saying, "Why don't you and me go up to my room?"

"I'd like that, but I'm a little short. All my money is in the game."

"I'll take chips, honey. Three blues."

Jack Morgan pushed his chair back. He stood up, plucked three blue chips from his pile, and handed them to her.

"Mister Simms, if you'll give me a count, I am going to take some time and return later."

"No problem, sir," Simms said, as he efficiently stacked Morgan's chips and counted them. "You have one hundred seventy in the bank."

The Stranger looked at Morgan walking off with the whore toward the big center staircase, and his face filled with confusion and disappointment. It came to Portier that Morgan had just escaped danger.

"Well, that was kind of her," he said.

"Yes, indeed," Julius Simms chuckled. "Delores has a kind and giving nature. Wouldn't you agree, Mister Johnson?"

The Stranger had a baffled look on his face, as if he had been cheated, but could not quite determine how.

"Let's play cards," Simms said. "Ante up."

The Stranger stood up suddenly and went for his gun. It wasn't there. He looked around, eyes blinking, even more confused. The other men at the table, indeed all around the room, just stared at him. Finally, he walked out to the hotel's veranda, shaking his head slowly.

"If you can't beat 'em, then baffle them," Julius Simms said under his breath.

"So that's the game?" Tilman asked.

"Yep. We might live to see morning."

Portier could see the other two Strangers, also waiting like actors for cues in a bad play. Jake Martin came in from a door behind the bar, concern on his face. He walked slowly around the bar and over to the table where Tilman and Portier sat, a tight false grin on his face.

"Everything all right?" he asked.

"Never better," Julius Simms replied easily. "As quiet as a church on Monday night."

Martin looked around the room, perplexed. Another of the Strangers came down the big center staircase, slowly, a beneficent smile on his face. Martin walked over until he was very close, and stared into his eyes. He looked up the stairs and his ears turned red. He was suddenly enraged. He started up the stairs, cursing.

Just then, the piano on the small stage rippled out a chord. Everyone turned to look, and saw the red-headed whore seated there. Another of the girls stood next to her, holding a violin.

They began to play a sweet melody, and a third girl began to sing in German.

Miss Kate appeared at the top of the stairs, dressed in a black silk gown that revealed her shoulders and much of her bosom. She was carrying the riding crop. She began to slowly descend the stairs, revealing her black high-heeled riding boots. Molly Shannon followed quickly, dressed in a dark green gown that contrasted nicely with her flame-red hair and pale freckled skin. Molly was smiling: a tense, false smile, her eyes darting around, seeing who was in the room below.

All the men watched them carefully, and, as they got closer, could smell the perfume they wore. Card playing stopped. Miss Kate walked around the tables, slowly, her hips swaying.

"We've decided that the program for tonight will not be another fight," she said in a rich contralto. "That's hard on the furniture, and it doesn't help us do what we're here for." She laid her riding crop on a Stranger's shoulder.

"And it's boring," Molly added. "We didn't come here for that. We are lovers, not fighters."

She and Miss Kate exchanged a long, provocative kiss.

Portier pushed his chair back from the table, and said tightly, "Cash me out."

Simms looked at his face, and hurried to count his chips and match it with gold and silver coins. Portier scooped them up, turned on his heel, and made for the door.

"Something wrong, honey?" Miss Kate called after him.

Tilman had to admire his partner's restraint, and hoped he would not seek solace in another bottle. Was Alicia Sorrell trying to get herself killed? There was just so much humiliation a proud man like Ashley Portier could take. He saw that Jake Martin was also disturbed by the girl-on-girl act, his face flushed almost a deep purple with outrage.

"Say!" he shouted from the top of the stairs. "None of that!"

Alicia turned and smiled at him, faking a puzzled facial expression as Portier slammed out the double doors leading to the veranda.

"That a little too public for you, Jake?" she asked. "They pay big money to see that in New York or Naw'leans." She turned to the crowd, motioning the girls on stage to stop playing for a moment. "You boys have not seen the full range of services we offer our clients. While we enjoy you individually, there is nothing like a good old-fashioned orgy. But that don't come cheap. So how about trying two for one for openers? Me and Molly together? Let's have an auction. What's your pleasure and what will you bid?"

"One hundred dollars," said one of the gunmen.

"One twenty," said another.

Tilman was amazed. All of the gunmen were bidding, and the Strangers soon joined in, looking anything but bored. He had to admire Alicia Sorrell's enterprising spirit, and wondered, what was the strategy behind her boldness? He doubted that this was entirely about the money. One thing was sure: there would be no bar fight this night, and no one would die. He looked up at where Jake Martin stood fuming, helpless to stop what was happening. The girl at the piano was playing a raucous dance-hall tune now, which simply increased the excitement in the room.

He stacked his chips and motioned for Julius Simms to cash him out.

The Negro leaned over and said, "Suddenly a different game, isn't it?"

Tilman regarded him carefully. "Your idea?"

"Not at all. I'm as flummoxed as you are."

"And will you be a player in that game?"

"No, sir! My presence would not be welcomed by some of those rednecks." He started cashing out the other players. "Besides, it is a point of pride with me that I never pay."

"Me, neither," Blake Tilman said, who pocketed his money and once more went in search of his missing partner.

Back at the jail, Jesus was once more transforming himself into Black Horse. Derek Seaton lay on his bunk, staring at the ceiling.

"Can I just pay a bribe and get us out of this?" he asked suddenly. "I'll pay any amount."

The Indian took a moment to consider this, and then slowly shook his head. "I don't think your money would interest them, Mister Seaton. Where would they spend it if they're not from here?"

"Well, what then? Gold?"

"I doubt it. They like the hunt."

Seaton sat up and swung his legs over so he was looking out through the cell bars. He looked more irritated than scared. "That's insane. Would you hunt something that can shoot back?"

Seaton was not a thrill-seeker, it seemed. He calculated risk as carefully as an actuary.

Black Horse shrugged. "Buffalo or bear will kill you pretty quick if you don't know what you're doing. That is part of the honor in hunting them. The risk."

"As fast as they are, there's not much of that."

"Some of those royal dudes that Bill Cody took hunting wanted it easy, too. Certain arrangements were made so they got their money's worth. Lots of money, but not much honor. Everybody got a prize." Black Horse snorted disdainfully.

Derek Seaton nodded. "I knew boys like that in college. And they were boys, not men. I was raised better. As rich as we are, I had chores and responsibilities growing up. Got a licking if I fell short."

"Then you should realize that there is no easy way out of this. You're trapped."

Seaton nodded slowly. "Perhaps I can use my money to better advantage."

Blake Tilman came in from the front. He looked at the two men, who silently looked back at him.

"Where's your partner?" Seaton asked.

"It got to be a bit rich for him. Miss Kate and Miss Molly upped the ante with some girl-on-girl action, and started an auction for both of their favors. Got everybody excited."

Black Horse laughed outright.

Seaton looked very confused. "They did what?"

"Well, like all great romances, it began with a kiss," Tilman said, watching Seaton's face carefully.

Seaton blushed.

"How much do you know about the Demimonde, Mister Seaton? In Japan, they call it the Floating World because it's all illusion. Such arrangements are very common, for comfort and mutual protection. The illusion is that the girls in that life can ever trust or love a man again. Now, some men marry whores, anyway, because they get what no proper lady can ever deliver, but a soiled dove like Molly is usually on the make. She'll marry you and be true; she'll give you children; she'll even become the kind of grand lady that society demands with ease, because all of them are the greatest actresses the world has ever known. But be aware of what you're buying."

Seaton stood up, furious now. "I'm supposed to thank you for that?"

"Pinkerton Agency, sir. All part of the service. No extra charge."

Seaton slammed his fist into the wall.

Tilman, for the first time in several days, thought of Lucy Blunt waiting for him back in El Paso — and knew that he would not marry her. Emily McLean was... suddenly he recalled the unopened envelope she had tucked in his leather portfolio that held all the wanted posters. Now it demanded his attention. Emily was a mystery he needed to solve.

Seaton sat on his bunk, shaking his head.

Black Horse cleared his throat. "How do you know it won't work for him with Molly? She seems pretty intent on it."

"I don't," Tilman admitted. "It might work. She is keen on it. Already picking out the drapes and china, you might say. Maybe I'm wrong, and the whole thing will be wonderful, blessed with magic and pixie dust. But she's pure Pagan. You won't be able to control her."

"Had to be to survive," Black Horse agreed.

Seaton looked up, fresh hope in his eyes. "Mister Tilman."

"Sir?"

"You have done your duty and given me your best advice, which I have heard."

"Yes, sir."

"In the future you will not talk about my fiancée that way."

"No, sir. I will not."

Tilman's voice was flat. He did not want to argue with Seaton. He let it go.

There was a moment of quiet as Seaton rubbed his scraped and sore knuckles.

"Back to the matter at hand," he said finally.

Black Horse and Tilman looked at one another. There was suddenly something about Seaton that demanded their attention and respect. He was a man who'd been born to be in charge. Now he was very still, abstracted in thought.

"We cannot defeat the Strangers one at a time. They're too fast."

"Right."

"We cannot just run away from them."

"No. No, indeed."

"So it's kill or be killed."

Black Horse sighed. "It took you this long to figure that out?"

Seaton shook his head, very serious now. "Not at all. I'm just restating the problem. I propose we organize the gunfighters and buy their services."

"Most of them are wanted men with a price on their heads," Tilman objected. "They know Mister Portier and I are here to take them in, or failing that, kill them. Jake Martin is the only protection they have."

"Some protection," Black Horse scoffed. "He's letting them be picked off one by one. Wait around long enough, and I'll give you all the affidavits you need to claim those rewards. They will all be in Boot Hill."

Tilman nodded. "And what then? Do they come for the rest of us and just harvest us like a herd of buffalo? They've developed a taste for long pig."

"How much money is in that poke I gave you to put in the safe?" Seaton asked.

"I didn't make an exact count," the Indian replied. "Ten or twelve thousand."

"You carry that kind of money around with you?" Tilman asked, outraged. "Are you insane? You could be killed or robbed for a small fraction of that!"

Seaton shrugged. "If I find land with petroleum on it anywhere, I'll have it on hand so I can buy it on the spot. People in this part of the country ain't real big on taking checks or bills of exchange. Cash is a convincer."

Tilman gaped at him. "It's more than most people make in a lifetime."

"I am not most people," Derek Seaton said. "My family takes in that much from our various enterprises every hour of every day. I personally earn dividends in that amount every day. And it's not that much. If some robber wanted it, I would just hand it over. It's not worth losing my life."

"I don't think I ever understood what it is to be really rich before," Tilman said, amazed. "You don't need to make a living. You can just lie back like an ancient potentate and have anything you want. Why are you here?"

Seaton smiled. "We're Presbyterians. I was raised to be of use, to do good in the world, and with that wealth, comes some big responsibilities. We have thousands of people who depend upon us for their livelihoods, and our investments are to create progress and a better life for us all."

"You're also ruthless bastards," Black Horse observed, without heat.

"Yes, we are," Seaton admitted. "But we mean well."

CHAPTER TWENTY-NINE

Tilman went back to the hotel in search of his partner, who was sitting alone at one of the tables near the bar. The oil lamps had burned down; everything looked brown, as if it were a living version of an illustration in *Harper's Magazine*.

It was quiet, too much so. Most of the gunmen were absent, presumably upstairs with the companion of their choice. Simms was seated alone at the same poker table he'd been at earlier, playing solitaire. He looked up and displayed a wide grin briefly.

Portier had a bottle of whisky and a glass, but did not actually seem to be drinking. Tilman drifted over to where Simms was, and nodded in Portier's direction.

Simms shook his head. "I'd give him a minute," he said quietly.

Tilman pulled out a chair and took a seat. He looked around as one of the whores playing barmaid came over.

"Something for you, honey?"

Tilman looked up at her and saw a young woman of about nineteen with the eyes of a woman twice her age. Green eyes that stood out from her dark brown complexion and the rich black hair that reached halfway down her back. He knew she had a sad story to explain her life. Every whore did. And some of them were true. This one looked as weary as a housewife on Christmas Day.

"From the bar, I mean," she prompted.

"A cup of coffee?"

"Sure." She wandered off. "I'll make fresh," she said over her shoulder.

Tilman looked at the Negro card dealer. "Mister Simms, isn't it?"

Again a flash of the bright white teeth.

"Yassah! Julius Caesar Simms, at your service."

Tilman looked him over carefully, taking in the long elegant fingers, narrow jawline, intelligent black eyes, and well-tailored clothes. Simms met his gaze without flinching, but the smile faded.

"Like what you see?" His voice had a bit of edge in it.

"I'm not sure." Tilman leaned back easily. "How do you know my partner?"

Simms shrugged. "From the tables. He's a man with a reputation for fair play and vigilante manners when it comes to cheats. I would never cross him. I know about you, too."

"How is that?"

"The girls. You have quite a reputation among them for fair play and honesty. They hold you in high esteem, like an honest priest."

Tilman smiled. "Aren't all priests honest?"

Simms stared at him hard, then returned the smile. "We both know better than that. The one we had at the plantation I grew up on was quite a rascal. A secret Abolitionist. Taught me to read, despite the laws against that, and a brave man. Loved the Bible and, like Stonewall Jackson, thought everyone should be able to read the holy word. But he liked little boys, too. So we fell out."

"What did you do?"

Simms shrugged. "Me? Nothing. I was just a boy. My daddy put a dagger through his heart. The Underground Railroad work excused that. He got off because the War had started, and he promised to raise a regiment. Which he did. Got killed at Fredericksburg."

"Your father was your master?"

"My mother is comely. High yellow." Simms smiled again. "Such is the way of the world, Detective. My mistress never held that against me. Made me part of the family. She taught me numbers, and how to keep books. Said I was way too smart to be a field hand. And freed me the day that the Emancipation Proclamation became law. Said that slaves were such a bother, and that she was happy to be shut of us all."

"Did she mean it?"

"Mostly. It ruined her money-wise. She was a widow by then. And we loved her, so most stayed and worked the ground for her on shares, after it was all over. But then she died, and no one wanted to stay after that."

Tilman nodded. "And your own mother?"

"Entered the Demimonde, and later married a free Negro in Washington. Man has a lot of property." Simms swept up the cards and shuffled them again. "Why do you ask? Or care?"

"Mister Portier said you wanted a position with Pinkerton's. We're always on the lookout for men of ability. Women, too." Tilman leaned forward. "We have a situation here, Mister Simms. We are all at hazard and confronted with circumstances that defy description, much less solution. If you help us out, then I will certainly put in a good word for you."

Rather than the expected happy grin, Simms favored Tilman with a slit-eyed suspicious gaze. "How does your partner feel about it?"

"Surprisingly positive. Said if there were Negro cavalrymen, why not Negro detectives?"

"Did he now?" Simms ruffled the cards. "I guess not every cracker longs for the old days." He continued to look at Tilman solemnly.

"He's traveled widely. Seen too much."

Tilman looked up as his cup of coffee was delivered.

"What do I owe you?" he asked.

"Your money is no good here, Detective. Mister Martin's orders." She smiled. "Anything you want." She tilted her head invitingly.

Tilman did not ask the obvious question that came to mind, and sipped at his coffee. "This is enough for now. Thank you."

She dimpled a smile and walked back toward the bar, her hips swaying.

Julius Simms collected the cards in front of him, shuffled the deck, and began to lay out another game of solitaire.

"I wish I had your rectitude," he said. "The problem is that even whores suffer from the green-eyed monster. They are very jealous creatures if you stay with one. And I'm no pimp."

"I would not be offering you employment if that were the case," Tilman said.

"I assume that the offer is provisional, based upon performance and good behavior?" Simms raised a ironic eyebrow.

"Always. We have very high standards."

"Of course, I would be on your side in any event. Jake Martin has no hold on me. And we do have a dilemma. The Strangers have powers and machines that are beyond our ken."

"How do we defeat them?"

Simms leaned back, considering carefully. "Well, I have said to more than one of the gunmen, that if they are outmatched and know that going up against one of them means they die, why not just throw up their hands and surrender?"

Tilman nodded. "That would be the smart thing to do. Criminals aren't very smart — and the ones that get chosen have reputations to consider."

"Pride."

Tilman nodded. "Yep. If you've been a shitheel all your life and are suddenly admired for something — even robbery and murder — you want to protect that hard-won reputation. You'll rather die than surrender. This is why the Pinkerton Agency does not engage in showdowns. Dead or alive, it makes no difference, we are bringing you in. Probably by shooting from ambush."

"Blame Ned Buntline and those other dime novelists for making these miscreants worthy of admiration." Simms frowned. "You know the whole set-up here is terribly romantic."

"What do you mean?"

"Right out of one of those dime novels. Men shooting it out as if they were knights of old at a tournament. The Chivalry sure did take to that kind of manly combat before the War, going at each other with lances from horseback. Sir Walter Scott has a lot to answer for. He damn near trained the South's cavalry himself, by getting those boys to pursue that fantasy. Ever seen that?"

"I'm from Maine. A fisherman's son."

"Imagine, if you will," said Simms, "trying to put the point of a lance into a six- inch wooden ring at a full gallop."

"Why? That sounds very dangerous."

"It is. Part of the thrill. The other, of course, being the favor of your sweetheart or other stuck-up little bitch you are trying to impress." Simms shook his head ruefully. "More than one boy got himself injured or killed for the chance to carry his lady's favor. But them that survived were the best horse riders I ever saw, until I got out here and met Black Horse and his band. Of course, General Ashby made his reputation playing an Indian at tournaments. The Knight of Hiawatha!" Simms laughed harshly. " 'What fools these mortals be.' "

Tilman looked up. "You know Shakespeare?"

"A bit. I also know that ol' Jake has got these gunfighters fooled about how they have to face the Strangers in these duels. For the sake of their honor! Honor! Murderers and thieves, every one of them, and they give themselves such airs." Simms sighed. "So what now?"

"If this is magic, then we need to find a way to break the spell." Tilman looked around. "It is all like a play. Young Mister Seaton said as much."

"Then we need to ring that curtain down. It's a farce. Or an execution dressed up as one. 'Cept there's no trial first. Quick and clean, but legal? — That, I doubt."

Tilman leaned back, regarding him carefully. "You care about the law? Don't you live outside it?"

"Me, sir? No, sir! I'm no robber nor thief, and the only men I've killed made the bad mistake of coming at me first. I was simply defending myself."

"You cheat at cards."

"That's different. I only shear the sheep that present themselves at the table, and there I simply play what's dealt me. I'm never the dealer when I win a hand. That way I can never be accused of cheating. And, let me add, with the level of play and the level of drink I encounter with rubes, I have no need to cheat. They cheat themselves."

Tilman absorbed this. He knew that meant Simms probably worked with other card sharps to rig the game. He'd have to ask Portier about it.

"Clever. You're very intelligent. Have you a solution for this problem?"

"You Pinkertons are some kind of law, ain't you?"

"Agents of the Court. Not policemen. We have to have paper on a man. Otherwise, we can't touch him."

"Unless he commits a crime right in front of you."

"Well, any citizen can do that."

"Ever have a man just give up?"

Tilman nodded. "Embezzlers. Men who've done nothing but clerk in a bank or store usually don't have much sand in them. They ain't violent. They come quietly. Most throw themselves on the mercy of the court in hopes of a lighter sentence. No one hangs for just stealing from the till. Some got families to consider, so they do the time, get off a bit for good behavior. When they get out, they move away, change their names, and hope to live down the disgrace."

Simms flashed his even white teeth in what might have been a smile. "Now if these desperadoes that Jake Martin has collected would only do the same, you and Mister Portier would be saved a great deal of trouble, and make a great deal of money."

Tilman made a mental calculation. "I could retire on that."

"All due respect, sir, you don't seem like the retiring type. You have something of a reputation yourself. I'm surprised Mister Buntline never wrote a dime novel about you."

"I told him I would kill him if he did."

Simms looked at Tilman, his mouth hanging open for a long moment. He laughed again, as if this was the most humorous thing he had ever heard. His mouth shut like a trap when Tilman failed to join in.

He nodded respectfully. "Well, yes, sir. That would put me off as well. Did you mean it?"

"I did. Every word."

"Yes, sir. Man like you has to stay quiet, or the whole detecting thing goes to hell. It don't pay to get noticed." Simms peered at him. "I was surprised, speaking frankly, that Mister Portier was allowed to sign on. He's a bit on the flashy side."

"We take all types," Tilman said; "And it's a new branch."

"So I do have a shot?"

Tilman nodded. "As good as anyone, but I don't do the hiring." He looked around the room at the few depressed and desperate gunmen who remained, waiting for their chance to die. "You might want to take heed of how we get out of this situation, Mister Simms, before you make any big plans."

Simms grinned very wide, and nodded his head. "Yes, sir. Tomorrow is not promised. I take your point, but I live in hope."

As it grew light outside and a new day dawned, Ashley Portier poured himself another shot of whisky and stared at it, knowing his search for oblivion was a futile one. The image of Alicia Sorrell naked, astride a Stranger's body, was burned into his memory — as was her cool expression as she lifted her breasts with both hands and said in a cruel voice, "Want some?"

He turned and fled the room in confusion, outraged and hurt. Yet what did he expect? She had made her position plain. He had failed her, and let her fall. Witnessing her degradation was his punishment. His feeling for her, nurtured by years of remembering her when she was sweet and innocent, clouded his judgment. He needed to borrow some of Blake Tilman's hard-edged objectivity.

Be a man, he said to himself. He longed to find Jake Martin and pound his face in, but that would not serve, either. The pimp was too well protected. So he banked his anger for another time, sipped his whisky, and tried to think what Captain Sir Richard Burton might do if confronted with these bizarre circumstances. He continued drinking. *I may not be able to drown my troubles,* he thought, *but I can make them swim for it.*

His partner came in about two hours later, looked carefully around the room which was almost empty, and walked over to the bar. "Seen my partner?" he asked the tall, redheaded man behind the bar.

"Over there, getting drunk." The barkeep was unable to keep a note of disapproval out of his voice. "I thought you Pinkertons was better than that."

Tilman managed a tight little smile. "He's new, and he's had a hard day." He looked the man up and down carefully. "What's your name?"

"Bob Williams." He did not offer to shake hands.

Tilman shook his head. "I don't believe I know that name. You wanted for anything?"

Williams tugged at one side of his long brown mustache. "We ain't all crooks and murderers, Detective. I was in the War as a scout, and I can handle a gun. I came for the work. As for the rest of this," he gestured toward the big room, "it don't interest me. I got a wife at home, and I took the pledge, same as you. Don't smoke neither, nor play cards."

"You sound like a Christian."

"Deacon. First Baptist, where my homestead is."

"Many more like you here?"

Williams shook his head. "Not that I can tell."

Tilman leaned in a bit. "Say," he said quietly, "what do you know about these clients of Jake Martin's?"

"I know evil when I see it."

"But you're working for Martin?"

"Need the money. I figure as long as I stay away from the cards, whores, and spirits, I'm in the clear. Lots of evil in the world. Can't fight it everywhere. Not until the end times."

"Which may be upon us."

Williams, a peculiar look in his eyes, leaned across the bar and frowned. "Here? Now?"

"Soon," Tilman whispered. "Seamus Corcoran says the Strangers are demons from Hell."

Williams' eyebrows climbed upward toward his hairline.

"They stink of the Pit when wounded," Tilman added.

Williams began to polish the bar furiously with a dry rag, as Tilman related what had been found at Jake Martin's hacienda. When he was done, he went over to where his partner was drinking. Behind the bar, Bob Williams mouthed a prayer as he stared into the middle distance.

Ashley Portier stared up at Tilman with unfocused eyes, and tried to stand up. He failed, and sat down hard on the chair under him.

"Don't get up on my account," Tilman said, his disapproval dripping from every word.

Portier gestured at the empty chair opposite him, and Tilman sat down carefully, observing the almost empty bottle of whisky at his partner's elbow.

"What are you doing?"

His irritation was plain, but Portier just smiled at him in that beatific way of drunks everywhere when they have reached the early stages of unconsciousness. Soon he would be dead to the world.

"Not a damn thing." He peered at Tilman like a curious bird. "Except, maybe, cursing Fate." He poured himself another glass of whisky. "You ever think about Fate, Blake?"

"Now and then." Tilman saw that there was nothing he could do but let his partner ramble on. His present condition made him useless. Portier raised his glass in a toast to Fate.

"I've been thinking about the incredible string of bad luck that brought us here. If I were a religious man, I'd call it divine retribution." Portier stared at something no one else could see in the middle distance. "I've never loved anyone else but her. Years I spent, trying to find my way home, without being hanged by the Yankees for piracy. Against all odds, because I became a detective, I have found her. But she's fallen so far."

Tilman sighed. "What happened?"

"In my eagerness, I walked in on her." Portier turned pale at the memory.

"And she was with someone? She's a whore, Ash. That's what they do. She can't leave off it just like that. It would tip our hand to Jake Martin." Tilman shook his head, disappointed. "What did you expect? She's been with hundreds of men and is famous for her skills. She is not the girl you left behind. Get over it!"

Portier set his jaw, angry again. "She was with one of the Strangers."

"Doing the job she was hired to do. Even if she knew what we now know, what could she do about it? What choice does she have? You can't recapture the past, my friend, and whining about the cruel trick Fate has played you doesn't help you none."

Portier squinted at him and fumbled for a cheroot. Finding one, he got unsteadily to his feet, and said in a solemn voice.

"Mistah Tilman, I wish to resign my position with the Pinkerton National Detective Agency."

"And do what?" Tilman asked sharply. This was not acceptable.

They stared at each other, as Portier sank back down into his chair and dropped the little cigar on the floor. He stared at it, confused. Tilman felt out of patience.

"Are you going to defend an honor she no longer has or wants, and get yourself killed for nothing? Try not to be any more of a damn fool than you already are! We need you alive, and we need you sober." Tilman forced these words out from between clenched teeth. He stood up.

Portier rose once more, as unsteady as a palm tree in a hurricane. "You can't talk to me like that... " and began to swing his fist at his partner's head.

Tilman ducked under his arm and took him over his shoulder like a sack of grain. He expected a struggle, but the Southerner had gone slack, passed out. He carried him out of the big room into a rear hallway.

There he encountered Molly Shannon coming down the back stairs, who stared at him, amazed. Before she could speak, Tilman raised his free hand.

"I need a room."

Molly looked quickly about. "Use mine!" she said.

Two minutes later they were upstairs; Tilman was gasping for breath as he laid Portier's slack body carefully on the messy featherbed in Molly's room. The room was loaded with the odors of recent sex, sweat, and sweet perfume. It needed a good airing.

Molly put her hand on Portier's forehead. "Just drunk," she said. "You'll need to be turning him over."

"What for?" He was still breathing hard.

"As much as he's had? He might puke and drown in it. One of me brothers did that."

Tilman pulled Portier on his side, and placed him so that anything that he regurgitated would mostly land on the floor. He told Molly, "I need you to stay with him. I'll pay for your time."

The little redhead looked sourly amused. "Well enough. I could use some time off me ... feet."

"Can you get some coffee into him?"

"Why would I do that? All that gets you is a wide-awake drunk. And keep your money. It don't mean much if I'm not alive to spend it."

Tilman nodded. "You understand the situation, then?"

"Derek Seaton's idea of pillow talk is to talk and talk and *talk* about every angle of his situation. He has a high regard for himself and his opinions, and worries a problem like a dog with a bone. I abide it, because I don't want to die, either. I'll get your man here back on his feet and ready for what comes. Miss Kate — Alicia to you — told me about him walking in on her and that Stranger. Me being her best friend in all the world, she told me the rest, too. Gives me the creepy crawlies, it does, just thinking about it. I've had men tell me that I was 'quite a dish' or that they 'just wanted to eat me up' but I never took it literally before."

She jabbed a finger into Portier's prone body. He stirred briefly. "When he wakes, I'll tell this fool how she saved his life by keeping the Stranger occupied so he couldn't challenge your man. Keep your money, Detective. Keep my Derek safe. and I'll be satisfied with the bargain."

"Gone sweet on him, have you?" Tilman's face betrayed his doubt.

"Very unprofessional of me, I know," Molly grinned; "But the lad's got a quality about him. Aside from being a man of considerable parts, he's actually kind to me."

"He won't marry you, you know."

"With that mother of his, why would I want that? Oh, I could play the grand lady and ignore the whispers behind my back. But, no, he's too fine for Molly Shannon, silk underwear and all. It's a game we're playing, ain't it? But he's honest, and he'll see me right. Help me better meself. And he's very sweet."

There was a wistful expression on Molly's face, a desire for more, but the words she'd just spoken were her armor against hurt — against the day that Derek Seaton married whatever High Society bitch his mother chose for him. Tilman read history; he understood dynasties. He suspected that Molly did, too. Portier's body began to shake. Molly quickly reached under the bed for a clean chamberpot, and said, "You'd better get on."

"Who is the running boss for all these gunmen?" Tilman asked, as Portier retched into the chamberpot that Molly was holding for him. She, from long experience, caught all the discharge without missing a beat.

"That would be Butch Plover. He's sly enough to stay out of the showdowns, and tough enough to keep the others in line. Being a Mormon, he ain't much for the drink, and respected because he's never robbed nor stolen. He's honest."

"What is his crime, then?"

"Stone killer. What they call a 'regulator'. Told me he was in the pest removal business."

Tilman cracked a grin. "I'm sometimes doing that, myself. We should get on. What's his relationship with the late Clete Morgan?"

Molly shrugged. "They was friends from the War. He owed him, I guess, and Butch is honorable in his own way. They say he's never shot a man in the back."

"More than I can say," Tilman admitted.

"I heard that about you Pinkertons. He might hate you for that." Molly looked upward, thinking. "Butch is sweet on Daisy, the black girl with the red dress. I'll get her to pass the word about meeting up with you," she said after a moment.

"I'll be at Seamus Corcoran's in two hours."

Tilman pulled his Raymond Railroad watch from his vest pocket and stared at it. It seemed to be running slow. Surely more than an hour had passed?

"What will you be doing in the meantime?"

"Getting some money from your lover, and finding Jesus."

Molly tilted her head to one side, confused. "Jesus? What's that odd Indian going to do?"

"You'll see."

"So I can tell Daisy to tell Butch that it's a paid job?"

"You can," Tilman nodded.

"Isn't money a wonderful thing?" Molly smiled.

Portier began to moan, and she rushed to get the chamberpot under his mouth.

"There, lad. Let all the evil humours come up." She looked over her shoulder at Tilman as his partner retched out more fluid from his stomach. There wasn't much, which meant that dry heaves were next.

"Best get on with it, Mister Tilman. I'll tend to your man here. No worry."

"None at all," Tilman replied, already at the door, cautiously looking into the hallway.

CHAPTER THIRTY

III

"Would it surprise you," Rose Green asked in lazy voice; "That I'm bored with being adored?"

She shifted her nude, bejewelled body on the blue velvet cushions of her golden throne. She smiled and waved to the assembled audience kept out of hearing range, in front of her, and was rewarded with a shout of appreciation that became a chant that died slowly.

"Are you bored?" Sir Percy Wyndham asked. He was weary. These parades bored him as did all such formalities, the part of being a soldier he had never liked. Spit and polish over grit and muscle. Uniforms that glittered with stiff formality. This one was at least comfortable. It could hardly be otherwise, since there was so little of it.

He was standing a little way apart, wearing a crested, shining bronze helmet, a loincloth, a shining but otherwise useless silver breastplate, and leather sandals rather than hard military boots, for comfort.

"I am extremely bored," Rose said. "But the job is the job. I feel useless; a ceramic figurine kept wrapped in cotton wool. I pretend to rule, but Lord Chamberlain Koh's minions do all the work. My power is an illusion."

Wyndham smiled. "Back in London, did you never go to Buckingham Palace for one of Queen Victoria's soiree's? Very much like this without the nudity."

"Ah," said Rose; "They would never let the likes of me within a country mile of that place. Secret service has to be secret, and I'm a whore in the bargain. Much too scandalous. That's why I live in Liverpool, and attend daily at Fraser Trenholm's offices until my next assignment."

She pinched her waist critically between her right thumb and forefinger. "I'm getting fat, " she moaned. "I have to take more exercise."

"Come with me on my next campaign," Wyndham said. "I'll soon set you right. Hard marching tones the muscles."

Rose smiled and looked sideways at him. "I might do," she said, "If Doctor Koh permits." She sighed. "Do you think Queen Victoria has these difficulties?:"

"No idea," Wyndham admitted. "King Victor Emmauel is my sponsor as long as I stay out of trouble, but I do not apprehend much difference between his establishment and ours. Different only on the surface. Same nasty little bureaucrats getting in the way."

"How do you get into trouble?"

"Drink." He looked away sullenly. "But you know that."

Rose changed the subject. "Where are you going next?"

Wyndham sighed. "Someplace very much like this, but not this. Ten thousand infantry, two thousand cavalry, and the usual train of cannons and supply wagons. Koh keeps explaining how it is that we will be in a parallel world, but I can't get my head around something that is at right angles with everythng else. It's magic to me."

"So there will be witches?"

"Quantum physicists, whatever that means."

Lord Koh bustled in. Wrapped in humble brown peasant's garb, carrying a portfolio under the left arm. Smiling unctuously.

"How are we today?"

Rose waved to one of her guardians, a six foot tall female soldier in full armor, who stood to one side. She in turn took several steps out to the center of the raised platform and shouted a garbled command that made Rose's admirers utter a huge collective sigh, turn, and disperse into the ancient mud brick city behind them. The audience was over, and they went quietly, clutching small ceramic figurines of her to their bosoms. Koh looked at them shrewdly.

"They seem peaceable enough."

"Hanged the last of the known rebels last week," Wyndham said; "To encourage the others." He stared at Koh. "Are you ready to brief me on the next campaign?"

"Of course," Koh said. He clapped his hands, and four of his minions carried out a large table with a relief map of the next objective. Rose got up and signaled for her attendants to bring her wrap and put it around her. It was thin, and did little to conceal her body, but was magically quite warm. She felt a rush of pleasure.

Wyndham was staring at the map.

"Where is the enemy?" he asked. "Where the devil are their fortifications?" He fixed Koh with a glare.

Koh shrugged. "There are none."

Rose turned and stared as well. "Who are we making war on then?"

Koh looked upward as if he was trying to remember something. Rose knew that for a lie. Koh kept every small detail in that enormous head, and could pull any of them out in an instant. He hadn't said a word yet but was already lying.

"Come on now. Out with it!" Wyndham barked.

"It's a clearing operation." Koh smiled easily. "There will be little resistance. Just natives. Do the usual."

"And that is?"

"Pillage,, rape, kill and burn, preferably in that order."

Wyndham took one long stride and knocked him to the ground. The four minions scattered away from him. Rose's attendants rose as one, and began to draw their swords.

"Stand down," she cried. Obediently, they sheathed their blades but remained standing, waiting for further orders.

"Everyone take a deep breath," Rose said. She turned towards Wyndham and smiled reassuringly. "My General. What has displeased you so?"

"Mum! With all due respect, this job is hard enough without insults from those who never stood a post." He was standing astride the hapless Lord Koh, his hand on his sword's hilt, ready to draw, seething with rage.

"Well, don't kill him yet," Rose said. "Let's talk this out."

"Always the diplomat, my Lady?"

Rose nodded. "It's what I was born to do."

"You do take all the fun out of things," Wyndham said. He took several deep breaths to center his mind and regain self-control. Then he reached down and helped Lord Koh to his feet.

Rose smiled in a becoming way. "Please inform the Lord Chamberlain where he has gone astray."

Wyndham stood erect, and looked past Lord Koh into some middle distance. "You cannot do what I do without a strong moral center. Soldiers routinely kill people and break things… "

"And that's all we ae asking you to do here," Lord Koh interposed. His face was pink with suppressed rage.

Wyndham sighed, and went on. "No, Sir. There are no opposing forces worthy of our battle. No just cause as our rationale. Your 'clearing operation' is not War. It is the slaughter of innocents. Mass murder, if I may make plain."

"And your point is?"

"Soldiers, real ones anyway, do not do murder. We do not kill innocents. We are meant to protect them."

Koh grimaced. "But it was the perfect plan."

Rose shook her head. "I have to side with Percy on this one, Koh. You know how expensive these campaigns are. My subjects pay the costs, do they not? In blood, as well as treasure? I am not willing to add moral stain to that butcher's bill. There has to be a just cause."

She looked up at Percy, her friend now after all their troubles, standing so tall and erect. "Any ideas?"

He glanced sideways at her. "You're the diplomat. Perhaps some diplomacy? Always easier to fight if you have allies. Perfection in war is having your enemy surrender without a fight."

"Really!" Koh scoffed. "How often does that happen?"

"More than you would think," Wyndham replied. He smiled at the memory.

"Where I come from, in what we call the Italian War, I led a brigade of fifteen thousand men for Garibaldi, the politician who ultimately carried the day. We spent more time marchng to and fro, maneuvering, than we did in actual battle. Ultimately, our adversaries saw that they had no chance. They gave up, and peace was restored. Not like that bloody mess in Crimea, or the obscenity of the American Civil War."

"Before my time," Rose said. "Very good. I will send an embassy, or perhaps go myself."

Lord Koh looked alarned. "Your Court is not secure. There are intrigues. You risk being deposed." He rubbed his hands together nervously.

"And are you not the chief intriguer yourself?" Wyndham stared at him again. "I cannot go, can I? I must protect my Queen."

Koh's shoulders slumped. "No. You are right. We must have another plan."

"Oh, this is all such a bore," Rose said. "Why must we have wars anyway?"

"Why Madam," Koh said; "To improve the breed. To encourage the others."

That night Wyndham lay in her arms and wept bitter tears of frustration. She embraced him warmly, but it went no further than that. Not with a dozen Ladies and Gentlemen of the Bedchamber nearby, and no real passion between them. There was no place else he could turn for comfort.

"We have no friends here," he whispered in her ear. "We must get away."

"I know," Rose said. "I'm working on it."

III

CHAPTER THIRTY-ONE

A single candle flickered inside Seamus Corcoran's small shed. Tilman entered and saw that three men were already there, waiting in the shadows. One of them was Williams, the barkeep he'd met a few hours before.

"Plover?" He nodded toward the man he'd clubbed with his rifle the first day in town, and saw a grimace of resentment fill his face. He was the older of the two, and dressed more like a farmer than a gunman, down to the bib overalls and faded red checked flannel shirt he wore. He raised his hand.

"That would be me," he said, spitting a stream of tobacco juice to one side. He was a large man with a big belly, and, rather than a holstered pistol, carried a long rifle with a telescope on the top. *The rifle is unusual*, Tilman thought, *Probably made in Germany. New, the kind that took metal cartridges, and powerful enough to kill something two miles away.*

Plover did not offer to shake hands, nor get to his feet. He simply stared at Tilman, taking his measure. "I understand you want a palaver with us?"

"That's right."

"Where's your partner?" asked the other of Plover's companions, a much younger man. Short, thin, and carrying a double set of holstered pistols, he looked barely out of his teens. His pugnacious face was spotted with large red pimples and sores.

"He's a bit indisposed at the moment."

Plover snorted. "That's a pretty fancy way to say 'drunk as a skunk'."

"Let's move on," Tilman said, with more patience than he felt.

"Say your piece," Plover said, looking sideways at his younger companion. "Shut it, Billy." The younger man stared hard at Tilman for a moment.

Tilman pulled a leather poke from his coat pocket, very slowly, so as not to alarm them and set off a gunfight he did not want and could not win. He deposited it with a clinking sound on the top of a nearby barrel.

"Five hundred in gold," he said.

Plover looked up, staring at him a long moment, and then smiled. "Well, you have my attention. What's the job?"

"To help get us out of this trap with the Strangers. End the gunfights."

Plover choked with laughter. "Why would we do that?"

"To save yourselves. You can't win against them. Why fight them?"

"For the honor of the thing?" Plover's voice was freighted with sarcasm. "We're not fools, Detective. None of us plan to go up agin 'em. I don't even carry a pistol, but I can pull the trigger on this rifle and blow a man's head off before he can slap leather. You know that. That's why you Pinkertons carry Winchesters."

"And shoot men in the back," Billy said, his resentment plain.

"We're not *pistoleros*," Tilman replied. "We're bail agents on contract to arrest and retrieve criminals wanted by the Courts. It's not a game. We take you if we have a warrant. You can come peacefully, or over a saddle. Dead or alive. We don't care which." He squinted at Billy hard. "I don't believe I've seen your face on any posters, young man. Are you wanted anywhere?"

Plover laughed. "No, but he's working on it. He's the terror of Sante Fe, but has yet to make his mark here. But never mind that, Detective," Plover added, as he reached over for the poke and felt its weight, looking inside at the gold coins. "You've overplayed your hand. We've nothing against Mister Martin's peculiar guests, and we've contracted to him for the season. Why should we break faith with him? Why not just shoot you instead, and keep the gold? You aren't fast enough to take all three of us."

He started to put the poke in his pants pocket. A thrown knife grazed his cheek and lodged firmly in the post behind him. Jesus stepped into the light.

"I wouldn't do that," he said quietly.

Plover felt his cheek and came away with blood on his hand.

"You damned half-breed!" he shouted. "Shoot him!"

Billy started to draw one of his pistols, when Seamus Corcoran stepped into the light from the other direction, holding an ancient blunderbuss with a bell-shaped mouth aimed right at Billy's midsection.

"I wouldn't do that," the Irishman said. "I'd hate to clean up the mess."

Billy raised his hands slowly, looking from Plover to Tilman to Corcoran for a chance that was not there. When he started to lower his hands, the Irishman said, "Tut!" and he quickly raised them again.

Tilman took a step and retrieved the poke of gold coins from inside Plover's pocket. "I'm disappointed, Butch. I was told you aren't a robber."

"Who told you a dumb thing like that?" Plover growled. "The whores? Why would you believe anything they say?"

Tilman lifted the poke in one hand, and shook his head like a disappointed father. "Butch, Butch, Butch. You didn't think this through. There's more where this came from. Our client will pay well for your assistance. And you do not want to start a feud with the Pinkerton Agency. There are thousands of us now. Kill me, and the rest will come for you."

Plover shifted his chaw, thinking. He spit again. "And who might your client be?"

"Young Mister Seaton."

"That tinhorn?" Plover scoffed. "He ain't got that kind of money. I seen him eat beans right out of the can. No damn manners at all."

"Mister Seaton's family owns some of those railroads that Pinkerton protects. He came down here to get a taste of how the other half lives." Tilman thought it inadvisable to say anything about Seaton's true purpose, or the word 'petroleum'.

"Another fuckin' tourist," Billy said scornfully.

"You're no one to talk," Plover said, as he backhanded him. "I told you to be quiet!"

Billy, holding his face, stared at him with perfect hatred. It gave Tilman a chill. Billy would wait for the right moment, but he would take his revenge on Plover.

Plover looked at Tilman, serious now. He chuckled, and shook his head, conceding defeat. Bob Williams moved a little apart from the other two, like a man avoiding a bad smell.

"Well, thank him for the kind offer, but me and the boys are contracted to Jake Martin. We ain't really available for other work. Especially going up agin them guests of his. It don't sit right, and Boot Hill is filling up with them that tries."

"Does that contract include being butchered like cattle, one by one?"

"What do you mean?"

"You came to entertain Jake Martin's guests, am I right?"

"Yeah. Strange bunch of dudes. I take them hunting for antelope. They ain't much for climbing up hills, so they usually give it up after a day. Prefer the whores and the gambling, and who can blame them?"

"Ha!" Corcoran said. "If only that were true. You ever wonder why they get into so many showdowns with your – ah – colleagues?"

"Yeah. Never saw men who can draw that fast."

"You seen a Stranger get killed yet?"

Plover frowned. "No," he said.

"Them is long odds, ain't they? As many as three showdowns a day, and Boot Hill is filling up, but not with any of them." Tilman paused to let that sink in. "Ever think they might be hunting gunmen?"

A stunned expression washed over Plover's face.

"What do you mean?" He looked very unsure of himself.

"That they are after the most dangerous game in the world. Us."

"And what's more," Jesus added; "They eat what they kill."

"But they're sportsmen, and decline the easy mark," Seamus Corcoran said in that poetic way he had. "They want the thrill of the chase, or the showdown. I'd say just shooting antelope was too tame for them. They want a bigger thrill."

Plover stared at Jesus. "Did I hear you right, Chief? They're using us for game animals?"

The Indian simply nodded.

"They're cannibals? How do you know that?"

"You know Parker Boone?"

Again the scared, solemn nod.

"Mister Tilman and his partner took conference with Mister Boone last night out at Jake Martin's ranch. He's one of the hands out there. Had an amazing tale to tell. The Strangers have formal dinners where they consume the best cuts of what they kill. He was pretty shook up about it, because one cut was from a friend of his. He thinks we'll all be on their menu in due time."

Plover just gaped at them, amazed, trying to take it all in. His companions were equally gob-struck. Young Billy's eyes were as wide as saucers.

Tilman pushed onward with his argument. "Jake Martin got you here by telling you that these were Dudes who had no experience with firearms, and he sweetened the pot with the promise of honest card games, lots of money and liquor and pretty women."

"And he delivered on that," Plover protested. But there was doubt on his face.

Tilman bore in. "Did he? Mister Simms told me that Jake Martin hired him to show the other dealers how to cheat and not get caught. The women were tricked, too. He's a liar and a cheat." He turned and looked at Billy. "What will you do, son, when your time comes? You going to go up against someone who can draw and shoot before you can even think about it, and who never misses?"

Tilman pointed his forefinger like a pistol barrel at Billy. "Bang! Right between the eyes! And then the best part of you ends up in the stewpot?"

Plover looked again at Jesus. "Chief? This is all true?"

"Yep. I seen it myself, and we lost a couple of young braves who tried their hand." Jesus's face was hard as iron as he said this.

"You boys got a choice," Tilman drawled. "Get picked off one by one, or join with us and try to get everyone out alive."

Plover rubbed his unshaven face, mulling this over. "Money's no good to a dead man," he admitted.

"Oh, you won't be out of pocket. Mister Seaton will match your wages from Jake Martin." He tossed the poke of gold coins back at Plover, who caught it handily.

"Uh, Butch... "

"Shut up, Billy. I'm thinking." Then he tucked the gold into a pocket. The deal was done. After a long moment, he stood up and offered Tilman his hand.

"I got no love nor trust for Pinkertons," he growled; "but if the Chief backs your play, then I'm in."

Tilman took his hand and they shook briefly. "You'd take his word over mine? I'm a White man," Tilman asked. Something seemed amiss. Men like Plover usually clung to their prejudices.

Plover sneered. "White men don't have much credit here. You're well on your way to ruining everything. This is Black Horse, Chief of the Mescaleros. He's an honest Injun. And we're kin on his mother's side."

Tilman felt considerable surprise, but it suddenly made sense. It explained the 'half-breed' jibe thrown at Jesus earlier, and he felt humbled and a little ashamed of himself for not having picked up on that. Some detective he was.

"Look," Billy pleaded suddenly; "Can't we just shoot them all and be done with it?"

The other men looked at each other.

"Not the worst idea I've heard lately," Tilman said.

"Works for me," Plover said, nodding.

"Out of the mouths of babes," Corcoran chipped in. That earned him a hard look from Billy.

"But how?" asked Black Horse. "They bring in that sky wagon and start throwing lightning, it's going to take more than an ambush. We have to take that out first."

Overhead there was a flash of lightning, a loud crack of thunder, and the rushing sound of a sudden downpour of cold rain.

They crowded in the doorway to the outside, watching the rain turn the dusty street outside to mud. Tilman laughed. "Well, I've been wanting a bath."

"How fast can a man draw in rain like that?" asked Billy, in a dreamy voice. "Wearing a slicker and all?" All he wanted was a way to even the odds. He was too young to die.

Tilman saw that he was not a coward nor a fool, but someone who thought things through... and that he had no real honor and was not to be trusted. That he was truly dangerous. The one most likely to be a Judas. Jake Martin's spy.

"I think we're done here," he said.

As the day turned to night the rain increased. Having concluded the deal with Plover, Blake Tilman knew that there was not much else that could be done until the next day. He trudged back to the jail with Jesus, enduring the soaking he got. The Indian seemed untroubled by the cold rain, which slid off his garments. Tilman's black wool suit absorbed enough water to feel like a sponge, and he began to shiver.

"I am going to take you up on your offer of a bunk," Tilman said, as they got into the front office. "I need to get out of these wet clothes, and I need a good night's sleep." He looked around the office. "Where's the Sheriff?"

"Back at the hacienda. Strangers don't sleep in town. In fact, I'm not sure they actually sleep. Never seen one do that. Jake Martin keeps them out there, under guard."

They walked back into the cells, where Derek Seaton was sound asleep.

"Take the first cell," the Indian said. "I'll build up the fire and get you a blanket."

Tilman stripped off, down to the skin, careful to put his revolver within reach, and hung his wet wool suit and underwear to dry. The Indian came back with some lumps of coal, which he added to the fire. He went into another cell, stripped a blanket from the bunk and brought it back to Tilman. The room began to get warmer, so much so that steam began to rise from Tilman's suit. Jesus brought in more coal.

"Where'd you get that?" Tilman asked, wrapping the rough wool blanket tighter.

"There's an outcropping just outside of town. Nobody paid attention until someone discovered it can be burned like wood, only hotter. Seaton was excited when he saw that."

"Really?"

"Yep. Which means that there's money in it, and another reason for White Men to come and steal our lands." Jesus sounded resigned. Tilman decided to change the subject.

"Are you and Plover really kin?"

The Indian nodded. "You can pick your friends, but you can't pick your family, and in this part of the world the Spanish ran things for three hundred years. They ain't particular about color or race or any of that. That's an Englishman's obsession, purity of the blood. You Americans conquered Mexico in 1848, and gave it back because everyone there is an Indian or a Negro or both. No one cares about that. Except those slave owners who were hanging on to that fantasy. Like they didn't rape every pretty black girl they could get their hands on, and sell their own children like cattle. No one there is a slave."

"Some of those girls were willing."

"You think so? Maybe they were accommodating, but if they were property, what did it matter? What's that old saying? If it's going to happen anyway, relax and enjoy it?" The Indian brought over a brown bentwood chair and sat, fanning himself. The room was suddenly very warm.

"Butch and I are cousins once or twice removed. I think his mother was my mother's aunt or something like that. It don't show much, because he favors his father, but there's a lot of Apache in ol' Butch."

"So him calling you a half-breed was a bit like the pot calling the kettle black?"

Jesus nodded. "It's a joke between us, not an insult the way it would be with an outsider. If you grew up here, you would know this, because everybody knows everything about everybody else."

Tilman nodded. "It was like that where I grew up in Maine. Fishing village. We harvested cod, gutted it, cleaned it, salted it, and shipped it all over New England."

"But you don't miss it."

"No. The War changed everything. My wife and daughter died. Typhoid. I just couldn't go back there. It made me too sad, and I'd changed. Outgrew the place. Sure as hell was not going to go back out to sea and net cod. That's very hard, dangerous work, and I hold myself better than that. Colonel Chamberlain made me his clerk and I caught the reading bug from him. Very smart man, taught college. Offered me a spot there, and I like learning. My parents were well read. But that did not appeal as much as being a detective in the real world. La Fayette Baker showed me where the real power lay, and what happens if you abuse it. I never wanted that, but you learn things doing the work that you can't learn from books."

The Indian nodded. "I was like that, too. White enough to pass, but Indian in my heart. The tribe comes first. That is where Butch and I part ways. He's not particular who he kills. Indian, White Man, Mexican, Negro, it's all the same. Just part of the job. Worse than the Cavalry that way. That little shit Billy Bonney fits right in with his band. Stone killer."

Tilman suddenly yawned, his mouth stretching wide. He felt a wave of fatigue wash over him, and sat on the bunk. "Sorry," he said, "I've got to get some rest."

Jesus stood up and moved the chair back to where it normally was. "You do that. I'll keep watch."

Tilman felt his eyes closing. "You worried about an attack?"

"No better time for it. It's what we Apaches would do."

"We Pinkertons, too," Tilman admitted, as he wrapped the blanket tight around his body, and fell into a deep dreamless sleep almost instantly.

He awoke several hours later to the smell of frying bacon. He rolled out of the bunk — feeling bruised from the flat wooden boards he'd been sleeping on — and felt his clothes, which were dry enough to put back on. His boots were still damp. He ran a hand over his face and felt the two-days' growth of beard. He picked up the boots and walked out to where Jesus was frying bacon and beans on top of the black iron potbellied stove next to Seaton's cell. Seaton was sitting at the table, picking at his food. He looked very down-in-the-mouth. Tilman put the boots close to the stove so they could finish drying, took a tin plate, and helped himself to bacon and beans.

"Where's your partner?" Seaton asked suddenly. He seemed angry about something.

Tilman searched for the right words. "He's indisposed. Got sick last night."

"Drunk, you mean."

Tilman saw no reason to deny this. "Yep. But throwing up. I left him with one of the girls."

"Molly."

Tilman looked at him a long moment. Seaton's neck and ears were flushed a bright red.

"This bothers you?" he asked after a moment.

Jesus shook his head. "He asked where she was when she didn't come over for her morning appointment. I made the mistake of telling him."

Tilman couldn't help it. He laughed outright. "Good Lord! You're jealous over a girl from the Demimonde? That way lies madness!"

"I'm not jealous!" Seaton looked confused and foolish.

"No?"

"It's just that I expected her here," Seaton pouted.

Overhead, thunder cracked and a fresh downpour of rain began.

"She ain't coming out in that," Jesus said. "She'd look like a drowned rat when she got here." He shook his head and sat down to eat his own breakfast.

"So we have the place to ourselves. No Stranger playing Sheriff out front?" Tilman asked.

Seaton looked at him quizzically. "Would that be a problem?"

Tilman nodded. "Think about it. We don't know anything about them. How well can they hear? I learned as a scout in the Army that sound carries a long way sometimes. Especially in the dead of night. The rain gives us a mask against eavesdroppers."

"So we can talk strategy," Seaton said.

"As much good as that will do. We need more information. We simply don't know enough about what the Strangers are, or what they can do," Jesus said.

"We need to survey them where they live. The hacienda."

"I can send a scouting party," Jesus said.

"In this?"

"It might be hard for White Men," Jesus agreed; "But for Apache, this is a balmy summer day. And the rain will help. They won't be able to fly that sky wagon."

"Are you sure?"

"No. But they won't be able to see anything on the ground."

"Are you sure?" Seaton asked again. "I am sure that device looks miraculous to most, but there is science behind it. We can barely comprehend what it is, so it looks magical, but there is an answer to those questions. If we figure that out, then we can defeat it."

CHAPTER THIRTY-TWO

There came the distant sound of church bells ringing.

Seaton's face was filled with sudden longing. "Is it Sunday?" he asked. "Is there a church here?"

"Of course there is a church here. Has been since the town was founded by the Jesuits about 200 years ago. And, yes, it is Sunday." Jesus looked at him curiously.

"I would like to go to church," Seaton said, as simply as a boy. "Why did you not tell me that one was here last Sunday?"

Jesus smiled cruelly. "Last Sunday you had your mind on other things. Mostly liquor and whores, as I recall. Before you fell into trouble."

Seaton looked downcast. "It's true," he said; "I am a terrible sinner. But I would like to go to church. May I?" He seemed very upset.

Jesus tilted his head to one side. This was a new side of Seaton's character. Could he trust it? He looked at Seaton's face very carefully.

"You ain't thinking of making a run for it? Because if you do that, I will have my braves track you down and bring you back. For your own protection. Nothing has been said yet about actually having you face one of those creatures in a showdown. But if you really want to go, then Mister Tilman and I will escort you and bring you back."

"You don't trust me on my own? On parole?"

"No," said the Indian.

Nor would I, you spoiled, rich overly-entitled brat, thought Tilman. He saw that Jesus had the right of it. Seaton would run if he had the chance, and if he himself were facing the same odds, against one of the Strangers in a showdown, he might run as well. But that was no longer an option.

"I assume that this is all right with you?" Jesus asked Tilman.

"Not a problem," Tilman said. "We always put the client's wishes first. As long as he's in his right mind."

Seaton frowned. "What do you mean?"

"I mean, sir, you've been under a strain, and might lack a true understanding of our situation. Your demeanor is not that of a man who has all of his faculties. But you are very fit; rather than risk you being able to outrun Black Horse's braves, I will simply shoot you. With luck, it will be just a flesh wound."

Jesus actually smiled when he heard that. "Feeling lucky?"

Seaton pouted like a disappointed child again. "Not really. Not if you are both against me."

"Oh, grow up, Derek!" Tilman said in exasperation. "We're trying to keep you from getting killed. We're standing with you!"

"I would still like to go to church. Please."

Tilman looked at his anxious face and downcast eyes. Was the young engineer on the verge of a crack-up? He had seen many lose their reason under the harsh conditions of combat in the recent civil war. Some for just a day. Some forever. Seaton faced imminent peril. He was brave enough, not a coward, but the waiting was doing him in. He needed the solace of prayer. Tilman looked at Jesus, who nodded.

"Yes, of course, Mister Seaton, if it means so much to you," Tilman spoke in a soothing voice, as if Seaton were a child or a madman, either of which he might be in the moment.

"Thank you," Seaton spoke with uncharacteristic humility. He seemed very soft and tame. Still, Jesus went to the front office and came back with a pair of manacles.

"You'll have to wear these," he said, "so everyone knows you're still a prisoner, but I won't make them fit too tight."

"All right," Seaton said. All of the fight had gone out of him.

"Say," Tilman said; "can we get some slickers or ponchos? I've just gotten my clothes dry."

"Let me see what I can find up front," Jesus replied. He soon came back with a pair of rubber cloaks that had 'USA' printed on them. He helped Seaton slip his arms through the side slits and fastened his hands in front of him, then put a brown beaver hat on his head that looked very new and expensive.

Tilman struggled into the other cloak, and saw there was no easy way for him to draw his pistol. He retrieved one of the Winchesters, checking to see that it was loaded with a round in the chamber, and eased the cocked hammer down so he could fire it from any position with a flick of his thumb. He looked down the iron sites out the window.

"I'm ready," he said — then saw that the Indian had not bothered with rain protection. "Nothing for you?"

"I won't melt," Jesus sneered.

The church bells rang again; the three of them set out. The rain was slacking off and other people, in twos and threes — and even an entire family — were moving toward the brown adobe church a block away. With the Winchester tucked under his right arm, and Seaton's right elbow gripped with his other hand, Tilman took the lead. Jesus, his hand on Seaton's other elbow, walked with them at a steady pace.

People looked, and then quickly looked away, as if they feared contamination. Seaton looked like one of the condemned already, his face drawn and haggard. Others on the street moved away from them as they walked, as if they had some loathsome disease.

To Tilman's surprise, some of the gunmen were among those headed to church. He recalled Morgan's description of himself as a Christian. Not all of them were 'godless'. And it was Morgan himself who was acting as the warden of the open door, and directing people where to sit.

"In the back row, please," was all he said when he saw the three of them. Tilman positioned Derek Seaton between them in the rear pew for better security, and placed the Winchester on the cushion beside him to save a place for his partner.

Looking around, he was surprised to see most of Miss Kate's girls in the front row, all modestly well-dressed in appropriate styles out of *Godey's Lady's Book*. They whispered among themselves, and ignored the whispers between the men and women seated directly behind them. These were obviously townspeople, scandalized at the presence of the Demimonde in their little church.

Occasional flashes of lightning illuminated the images of Christ and his disciples in the elaborate stained-glass window behind the altar. On one side of the altar was a confessional.

Miss Kate herself emerged from the confessional, eyes down and crossing herself, lips moving in prayer. Tilman was a bit surprised to see her. He had always thought her a bold and defiant sinner. From the other side of the confessional, a middle-aged priest stepped out. More Mayan than Mexican, he carried his authority easily. He stopped to confer with two altar boys in grimy white cassocks, and turned to the women in the front row.

"Ladies? A hymn?"

All of Miss Kate's girls rose, as did several women and some men behind them. Someone blew a single note on a penny whistle. Everyone began to sing "Rock of Ages," which Tilman remembered from his own boyhood as a Protestant hymn. Apparently, this priest did not stand on ceremony in this part of the world, where some of his parishioners also worshiped the Black Virgin, and sacrificed small animals in other ceremonies. Who knew what compromises he made to keep his own pews filled every week? Tilman looked to one side and saw that Derek Seaton was mouthing the words, drawing comfort from them.

Behind him, he sensed that his partner came in. He turned and looked to see Ashley Portier, looking worn, speaking with Jack Morgan; Molly Shannon was making her way down the long center aisle to join her compatriots in the front row. Morgan pointed to where Tilman sat. Portier looked and lifted a hand in greeting. Tilman indicated the empty place next to him with a jerk of his chin. Portier's eyes were rimmed with red, and he looked disheveled. He had obviously slept in his clothes and reeked of whisky. Tilman decided to ignore this fall from the standards expected of a Pinkerton. They had other, much larger problems.

When the hymn finished, the priest began to recite prayers in Latin. This took several minutes. As Portier settled into his seat, he whispered, "Why is our client here?"

Tilman shrugged. "Wanted to come." He pointed to the shadows along one wall where three of the Strangers stood, transfixed, their faces almost ecstatic.

"Why are they here?" he whispered.

Portier looked. "Why indeed?" He looked at them long and hard.

The prayers done, the priest looked out over the congregation, the largest he had ever had.

"I am Father Tomas," he began. "This is God's house, and all of his creatures are welcome. We are all sinners on the Way" — he glanced at the row of pretty whores to his left — "some more than others." There was a ripple of laughter from the audience. Tomas held up his hands and looked at them sternly.

"Judge not! Lest ye be judged and found wanting." He sighed. "I see many here I have not seen in some time, and others I have never seen here before. Many are not of this church, but it makes no difference. This is God's house and all of his creatures are welcome." He glanced toward the three Strangers briefly, his face troubled.

"As long you are sincere in your repentance, your sins can be forgiven. But what we cannot abide is Evil. And Evil is here, too, in many forms, and not just the ordinary pedestrian sins of the flesh, but also in the casual dealing in death, cruelty, and degradation." He looked over the crowd, scanning them slowly with his eyes, nodding his head. "We must not just resist Evil, but cast it out. When civil authority fails or is absent, then we must pray for divine intercession. Let us pray now."

He began speaking Latin again. Some of the regular congregation began to pass around small brown woven baskets to collect the offering. They filled up quickly with coins and banknotes. Seaton dropped a twenty-dollar gold piece in.

Finally, the service was over — with a "Go and sin no more" interjection from Father Tomas that would only be observed in the breach.

During the service, Tilman had felt himself relax for the first time in days. Tension flowed away from his body, and he was perfectly calm. He reflected that religion had been no solace to him when his wife and daughter were taken from him, and that he had unconsciously turned his back on his church, seeking only those moments in the wilderness that came his way, for a sense of connection to the Almighty. His work afforded him few opportunities for quiet reflection, that were not connected to a case. *Perhaps I've been missing this?* he thought. He looked over to Seaton, who had a more peaceful countenance. The young man looked over and smiled at him.

"Thank you for bringing me," he said.

"You're welcome."

The Indian looked about, sensing something out of place, but kept silent.

Tilman and Jesus kept Seaton confined until the place emptied out. Tilman took advantage of the pause to watch the three Strangers closely. They all looked very much alike. They were enjoying themselves hugely. He wondered why that was? He tapped Portier on the sleeve, and said quietly, "Follow those three."

Portier got up and made his way to the door. He waited until the three went outside and then slipped out after them. Molly Shannon came up the center aisle with the rest of Miss Kate's girls, and detoured for a moment to come over and put her hand on Seaton's shoulder. He looked up at her and smiled. She smiled back, a genuine warm smile.

"I'll be by later," she said, turned and went out the door, ignoring the outraged expression on Father Tomas's face.

Jesus and Tilman rose, and Seaton struggled to stand with them.

"Back to the jail?" Jesus asked.

"Back to work."

It began to rain harder.

And a notion suddenly crystallized in Tilman's mind, emerging from the depths. "Say, where are all the kids?"

For the first time since he'd met him, Jesus avoided his gaze and looked away.

"Jesus?"

The Indian swallowed hard.

"What's going on?"

"Most were kept home. Some are missing." The Indian shook his head. "We think Martin took them as hostages."

"But you're not sure?" Tilman had seen that scared, frozen look before. Rich men with relatives taken and held for ransom. "Why?"

"He won't say. Talks all around it. 'Maybe he does and maybe he don't know.' 'Maybe we'll see them again when the season is over.' — If we behave and not interfere."

"And you're going to stand for that?" Tilman felt his anger building.

"If we knew where they were, we'd just go get them," Jesus said, miserable now. "But there's no trace anywhere. We think they might be where the Strangers lodge."

"You should ask for proof of life," the detective said.

"How? He's too sly to admit anything, and the Strangers aren't much for conversation. Some of the mothers are half-mad with worry."

Tilman nodded. "They would be." This was another unwelcome complication. Organizing against Martin and his gang was going to be many times harder, as long as there was any chance of seeing those kids again. The townspeople were just too scared.

Sheriff Johnson was back, his feet propped up on the big desk in the front office when they brought Seaton, still in manacles, through the door. His face took on the expression of an interested hound when he saw the prisoner. Then he looked disappointed.

"He did not escape?"

"No, sir. Prisoner desired to go to church, as is his right," Jesus said, glancing over at Tilman. "The detective and I escorted him to make sure he could not run away."

Johnson's eyes rolled upward for a moment and then focused back on them. "Too bad. Mayor says he's next," Johnson twisted his body and stood up very quickly.

"Next?" Seaton's voice quavered.

"For trial," Johnson looked grave for a moment, and then grinned.

"For a showdown?"

"Yep," he said. "Have to wait. Can't do it in this weather. Pardon me, boys, I have to go call off the posse." He walked out the door they had just come in. Tilman was not unhappy to see him go. Tilman looked at Seaton's face. The boy was scared, swallowing hard. The Chief began to unlock the manacles on his wrists.

"Well, ain't this a thing?" Seaton said quietly, sitting down and rubbing his wrists.

Jesus looked out of the door that Johnson had exited. He shook his head. "Damnedest thing I ever saw."

"What?"

"The Sheriff. He was dry when we got here, not a drop on him, and now he's walking in that gully washer out there and there still ain't a drop on him."

Tilman walked over and looked out. "I can't make him out. Where'd he go?"

"Toward the hotel."

"Not there now."

Jesus looked again. "No, he's not."

The three men looked at each other, perplexed.

"You believe in magic?" Tilman asked.

The Indian nodded. "We ignorant savages, being more attuned to the natural world, are not so quick to embrace the logic of White Men's rationalism, nor to deny the supernatural."

"What?" Seaton said. "What? What are you talking about?"

"What he means," Tilman said; "is that when something defies logical explanation, there must still be some reason for it. Some device we cannot apprehend."

"I would like to know how he stays dry," Jesus said. "I'd also like to know how he knew that Seaton had left this building?"

"And who was in that 'posse'?"

"Wouldn't be anyone from here. Everyone knows that he killed that Stranger by accident, and that he didn't start the brawl in the first place. This 'trial' is bullshit." He shut the door and looked at Tilman speculatively.

"What about you, Detective? You believe in magic?"

"I've seen some strange things that defy easy explanation before, and Portier has been to even stranger places. Let's say that we have open minds."

"Well, I don't!" Seaton said. "There has to be science behind it someplace. It just hasn't revealed itself yet."

"Explain," the Indian demanded.

Seaton screwed up his face, concentrating. "Well, hundreds of years ago no one knew much about electricity. Then ol' Ben Franklin proved that it and lightning are the same thing. Now we have the telegraph for sending messages almost instantly across the country. The Strangers must have something similar. Something that does not need copper wires. Something that goes through the air, like lightning does."

Seaton grew very thoughtful. "I'd like to know what that is," he said softly. "The man who invents that will do society a great service."

"And make a pile of money in the bargain," Tilman added.

"That, too, but that ain't the point."

"No?" Jesus looked at him scornfully. "You don't care about that?"

"Oh, I do," Seaton said. "Passionately. But you don't understand why the rich are rich. It's not greed. There is just so much you can consume before you choke on it. It's about resources, and having the means to encourage progress. My family gives millions of dollars every year to scientists who have nothing more than a hunch or a mathematical formula we can't understand. We have a fellow in New Jersey named Tom Edison that works on electricity. He invents things."

"And what do you do?" Tilman was genuinely interested. He'd never much cared for the rich people he was sometimes charged with protecting or serving as a Pinkerton detective, but he was coming to the firm opinion that Derek Seaton's life was worth saving.

Seaton looked at him, puzzled. "What do you mean?"

"What do you do with the things this Edison fellow invents?"

"We make them, and sell them at a handsome profit. That gives folks a way to make a better living, and us money to invest with the next genius we find. It's a virtuous cycle."

"A what?" the Indian asked.

"You called money a poison, Jesus. It can be, in the wrong hands, I give you that. But for me, it's a tool."

"Well, a gun is a tool, too," Tilman said. "And if you're about to face a Stranger in a showdown, we'd better concentrate on getting you ready."

Seaton nodded unhappily. "Not my strong point. I can't draw fast enough to take on an ordinary gunman. I would plead for my life first, without shame."

"Or offer them a big bribe," Jesus said. There was disapproval on his face.

"Call me a coward if you like," Seaton said calmly; "but I was not made for this. I'm not a killer. Fate has played me a rotten hand here."

"Well, you can't run and you can't hide. So what now?"

Seaton shrugged. "I'll make the best of it. Go down with a gun in my hand." He shook his head. "I can't disappoint Molly."

Jesus kept his face perfectly still, as did Tilman, not wanting to laugh at an otherwise intelligent man who'd just confessed that the good opinion of a whore meant more to him than his own life.

Tilman said, "Well, you'd better practice some. Who knows how long this rain will last?"

"I do," Jesus said. "It will be a few days yet. We get this storm every year."

Tilman had a sudden thought, remembering something Butch Plover had said. "Say! Using a pistol means drawing it, cocking the hammer, and pulling the trigger."

"I'm familiar with the process," Seaton said, irritated. "I'm not that green."

"What if you just had to point it and pull the trigger?"

"I might win," said Seaton slowly. "Would they let me? Give me that edge?"

"If you use a Winchester rather than a Colt, they will have to."

For the first time, Tilman saw hope in Seaton's eyes. "How would I win?"

"Point and shoot. It's as simple as that. Line up the barrel with the target and pull the trigger."

"Aim low," Jesus added. "The recoil will pull your aim upward. If you aim for the crotch you might get a head shot."

Seaton mulled this over. "Will they let me change the rules?"

"What rules?" the Indian replied. "Ain't any of this legal. It's a duel to the death."

"That's right," Tilman said. "Duels were outlawed, but not that long ago, and there are dueling codes and laws we can fall back on."

Seaton looked even more unsure of himself. "Really?"

"You read Law, Detective?" the Indian asked.

"Part of the trade I'm in. And we have to know the Napoleonic Code as well as English Common. There's a section about duels in that. So, given these circumstances, I would posit that the Strangers are the offended party and have issued the challenge. That means you have the choice of weapons."

"I should also be able to sue for peace or appoint a champion."

"Not going to happen," Jesus said. "So let's focus on winning the battle at hand. Parker Boone said he was appointed to teach the newly-arrived Strangers gunplay, am I right?"

"He did say that," Portier said. Tilman and Seaton jumped in surprise. Portier was leaning against the wall next to the doorway.

"God! How long have you been standing there?" Seaton exclaimed.

"A bit. Enough to hear the part about dueling and Winchesters."

Tilman was suddenly irate. "You didn't notice or say anything?" he said to Jesus.

"Why would I? I could smell him the moment he got here. I thought you could, too."

Portier sniffed under his arm. "I do need a hot bath." He stepped forward into the room. "As I recall from my salad days in New Orleans, there is quite a bit of ceremony associated with dueling. You're right about the choice of weapons part. You also have the right to appoint seconds."

"So would they," Tilman said. "That will just compound our problem."

"That's true. Best keep it simple." Portier walked over to where Seaton was sitting. "Do not despair, my young friend. There is hope, yet."

"Despair is a sin." Jesus suddenly looked more like his Black Horse persona. "There is no honor in it. Honor accrues to the man who faces danger, and even death, boldly, without reservation. Only such men can be trusted."

Seaton looked unsure and confused.

"Let me put it another way," Black Horse said. "Trust will buy you far more than money ever will. If you want to trade with people here, you need honor. Your wealth means nothing. because we do not recognize its power."

"In other words, be a man," Portier advised.

CHAPTER THIRTY-THREE

The next morning the storm began to howl. Strong winds drove the rain almost sideways. Jesus wondered if this was what Sophia had promised, then realized that she had not had time to form a coven.

Tilman took a hand at preparing breakfast.

Portier cleaned his weapons, including one that Jesus had not seen before. A Sharp's .50-90 caliber buffalo rifle. He held out his hand, and Portier passed it to him. The brass fittings and smooth cherry wood stock gave it a deadly beauty. He wanted to hate this weapon for what it had done to him and his people, and all the other tribes called Indians on the Plains, but could not. It was merely an implement. It was the hunters who had destroyed the gigantic herds of buffalo, and with it the natives' livelihood. Had there been no Sharp's rifles, they would have found other ways.

"Yours? You hunt with it?"

Portier took it back and rubbed the stock with an oily rag, burnishing the glow on the wood. "Only men," he said. "I was a scout and sniper in the War, and had one like it. This one, I won in a poker game from an Easterner who found it too hard to handle. Landed flat on his ass the first time he fired it. It's got range, and delivers quite a punch." He dropped the block by working the lever and slipped in a brass cartridge about four inches long.

Jesus nodded respectfully. "You will need to choose your target carefully. Only one shot at a time."

"Big heavy slug should plow through this rain okay," Tilman said.

"I thought I'd back Mister Seaton's play when his time came," Portier said, smiling. "Maybe my finger will slip, and fire it into the air at just the right moment. Give the boy a bit of an edge."

"You don't think the Winchester will suffice?"

"He said it himself. He's not made for this."

"But he seemed to be getting the hang of it yesterday."

"Dry firing, and working the lever? Not as good as having the experience," Portier said; "And he's going to be out there alone, standing still, rather than dodging and weaving on horseback. He's only going to have one shot. He misses, then it's over."

"So if he uses that, and takes an infantry stance, sideways, you think he has a better chance?" Jesus asked.

"I do."

"Let me work with him once the rain abates," the Indian said. "Maybe I can improve his aim."

Portier looked doubtful. "I only have about twenty rounds for it. And .50-90 cartridges don't grow on trees."

"Well, let's see if he can handle it at all. It's like being kicked by a mule when you fire it," Jesus said.

"You have a Sharp's, too?"

"The tribe has several. Don't use them much. Mostly .45-70s, but there might be one of these. I will inquire. Should be plenty of ammunition."

"Dare I ask how you came by them?" Tilman asked.

"Usually by trade, but some were contributed by dead buffalo hunters," Jesus replied, looking at him steadily. Tilman and Portier looked at each other as if they wanted to say more, but Jesus cut them off.

"You Whites hang cattle rustlers and horse thieves. On the spot, with no trial. You don't want to know what we savages do to them, and buffalo ain't wild animals free for the taking. They are ours."

Tilman nodded, conceding the point. He finished frying the bacon and set out four plates. A pot of beans with a ladle sticking out of it was steaming on the table. There was a loaf of fresh bread on a wooden trivet as well.

"Mister Seaton," he called; "breakfast is ready."

There came a muffled sound from the big cell at the rear, and sleepy conversation.

Jesus and Tilman smiled at each other.

Surprised, Portier asked, "Molly is still with him?"

"Spent the night."

Portier chuckled. "Scandalous."

Seaton, partially dressed, came out of the cell, and looked at the food on the table.

"Do we have another plate?"

Tilman shook his head. "You'll have to share, but there's enough food to go around."

"Molly!" Seaton called. "Breakfast!"

She peeked her head out of the cell and blushed, as if she were a young girl caught out with her first lover. Tilman found it charming.

"Please, Miss, take a seat. A young girl needs a good breakfast."

"Don't tease me," she protested. "I didn't mean to stay over. It was just that the rain... "

Portier laughed. "What will your mama say?"

"Oh, she'll have at me with that riding crop of hers, no doubt." Molly bit her lip, and suddenly the teasing wasn't fun anymore.

"She hits you?"

olly raised up her dress to show two welts on her thighs. "This was her thanks yesterday for me helping you with your... ah... illness. She assumed the worst, which is ridiculous, when you consider why we are here. What if I had? What would it matter, since we're simply whores? But she was all injured wife, right out of her mind with jealousy, and put as much of it on you for doing me, as on me for doing you. Totally mad."

She smoothed her skirt back down and sat at the table, looking at Derek Seaton, wondering if she'd said too much.

"But you hadn't done anything?" Seaton asked.

"Lord, no! He stank of drink and puke, so why would I, even if he could, which, just then, he couldn't, and it would have only been by the way of business, if I'd let him, which I never would with any man in that condition. I have my standards. I'm not some skivvy in a crib in a mining town, taking on all comers for fifty cents each."

Seaton seemed stunned, and his open mouth moved silently as he tried to take it all in. Molly ate bacon and beans, and mopped the grease up with a bit of bread, and then sat back, holding a blue-enameled tin cup of lukewarm coffee. The others also focused on their food. Finally, she looked over at her lover, irritation still plain on her face.

"Detective Tilman," she said; "you are well acquainted with the Demimonde and our curious ways. Can you not give my lad here a proper brief?"

"I did try," Tilman said, sipping his own coffee, and watching Derek Seaton with something close to pity.

"Then he should know that a whore services both men and women, and that most of us prefer the latter. That Miss Kate is also my lover."

Seaton nodded. He stared ahead, trying to not say anything that would make the situation worse. Molly reached out and took his hand, and gently squeezed it.

"You see, lad, with each other, we can be kind and gentle and tender, as you were with me last night."

Seaton flushed bright red.

"Oh, please, don't be embarrassed. It's not all about the fucking that makes a man a great lover. It's having some regard for your partner's feelings, and you had that last night when you just held me, and I slept in your arms. That was so nice. Like being married, I imagine."

Tilman said quietly, "Yes, it is."

Molly turned her smile on him. "Are you married, Detective?"

"Only in my heart. She died."

"Oh." Molly shook her head. "And there I go again, nattering on. My apologies."

"Oh, don't apologize," Portier said. "It has been most instructive."

He lit a cheroot and looked away, trying to deal with what he'd just heard.

Molly looked out the window at the rain, which had begun to slack off and pushed back her mane of red hair. It needed brushing and a comb. "How am I going to get past that without ruining my clothes and hair?"

Portier said, "I borrowed a parasol from one of the other girls. You can take it back to her." He looked around and pointed to where it sat drying in a corner of the cell he'd slept in the night before. "There it is."

"Which girl?"

"Daisy, the black one."

"Oh, I like her," Molly said. "I can't understand half of what she says, with that Caribbean accent, but she is so sweet."

"I have a note for her," Jesus said suddenly, reaching in a pocket and pulling out a carefully folded piece of paper. "She wanted some powders. This is from our local medicine woman."

Molly nodded. "Probably for cramps. It's getting near that time of the month, and we'll all need a potion. Be out of action for a few days."

She took the note and slipped it into her dress. She stood up, walked over and picked up the parasol.

"Best say I was never here," she said, worried now. "Miss Kate is a mad bitch when her temper is up. Maybe she smoked some opium after I left. That would settle her down." With that, Molly Shannon went out the door and ran toward the hotel as she held the parasol aloft.

The four men she left behind were silent for several moments. Finally, Portier said, "Mister Seaton, if you can tame and harness that little wildcat, you will have the undying admiration of men everywhere."

"Indeed," Tilman added solemnly, with a glint in his eyes that indicted he might be laughing underneath. "Indeed."

Seaton was thoughtful. "I may have bitten off more than I can chew," he admitted.

"But you are resolved to have her," Tilman said.

"Oh, yes. More than ever. She is unique. A jewel beyond price."

. . .

The weather began to clear the next day, and Sheriff Johnson came back with a formal note for Seaton from Mayor Jake Martin. His 'trial' would be the next day in front of the hotel. The Strangers were drawing lots to determine who his opponent would be.

The detectives continued to drill their client in marksmanship, using both the Winchester and the Sharp's. The exercise was to point and shoot in one smooth motion without bringing it to the eye and aiming.

"You're an engineer," Tilman said at one point. "Think of this as a geometry problem. You and the rifle as two points of a triangle, and the target as the third."

After that, Seaton did better, and actually hit the mark a few times.

As Tilman was putting Seaton through his paces, Jesus and Portier looked on. Jesus shook his head. "This is a desperate enterprise."

Portier lit yet another cheroot, regarding the Indian sidewise from slitted eyes.

"Tell me, suh, how is this even permitted? It's not a fair trial. Hell, it's not a trial at all. It's simply murder in legal finery. Most of the gunmen are already condemned. When Pinkertons go after them, we know it's a fight to the death, because they're going to hang anyway. Which is regrettable, but necessary. But this boy did nothing but defend himself. A good lawyer would get him off in a regular trial, because he had no intent to murder anyone."

Jesus sighed, "All true."

"So how did Jake Martin, who is not one of you, get elected mayor here? And why don't the people of the town rise up and put a stop to this deadly farce?"

"He bought the office. Actually, he invented it. This town has no government. Never needed it. Never wanted it. We got along fine with everyone doing their part, as neighbors, to share the common chores. If you saw something bad, you took care of it. If you needed help, it was there. Like church, you go to meetings and pay your dues. Between the Catholics and the Mormons, we got it done."

"And your tribe?"

"We're part of it, too. Bandits don't come this far north because of us, and we work with the Cavalry to keep the settlers safe. They need us. One company of Buffalo Soldiers ain't enough for two thousand square miles. We live in two worlds now. Apache is the romantic one. Whites are the reality." Jesus sighed again. "Jake and his gunmen got the drop on us. He threatened us: took some children hostage, and said he would burn the town if we didn't go along with his 'resort'. And then he started bringing the Strangers in, and the whores."

"There was an objection to the whores?"

"There were two. One was that this is a town of decent church-going people, so we never wanted 'the Wild West' here, or that kind of immoral influence."

"What was the other one?"

"For that kind of money, he should have hired locals."

Portier laughed out loud, bending almost double.

The Indian, offended, stared at him. "It's not funny."

Portier tried to put on a straight face. But the hypocrisy tickled him, making him long for the honest corruptions of New Orleans.

Jesus, irritated, went on. "This is why I call money the other White Man's poison. It corrupts the soul. But, of course, the gunmen are the real problem. Jake's private army. They make the whole place a prison, and the Strangers kill anyone who tries to leave and get help, from that sky wagon of theirs." Jesus spit on the ground. "We have to take that out."

"How bulletproof is it?"

The Indian shook his head. "Don't know. They never let it get within range. Keep it high up. And it throws lightning that burns a man to death on the first shot. Even my braves are terrified of it."

"Really?"

"Not an honorable death where you meet your opponent in the field face to face, but a stupid one, like falling off your horse and hitting your head on a big rock. No one wants to die stupid."

"It has to come to ground sometime, right?"

Jesus nodded. "Out at the hacienda. But they keep it under guard. And how would we wreck it? It's made of some kind of shiny metal."

Portier thought for a long moment. He snapped his fingers. "When I was in the Navy, the thing we feared most was fire. In those tight, confined spaces, fire would kill you very quick. Maybe we could burn it."

"With what? It's metal."

"Greek fire. We'd toss bottles of that from catapults into the rigging of enemy ships. It's sticky, hard to put out."

"And where do we find Greek fire?"

"It's not hard to make. Whale oil and soap."

"Soap?"

"That's the sticky part. Tar works, too."

Jesus leaned back against the adobe wall, thinking. "There is a place where black tar comes out of the ground. Hot and stinky. In a little defile about a mile out of town."

Portier stared at him. "Well, there you go. That'll work. Probably burns very hot."

Jesus nodded. "It does, but the stink is too much. No one uses it."

"You know what that is?"

Jesus nodded, unhappy now. "Petroleum. The stuff that Seaton came here to find."

"But you haven't told him about it?"

"And invite another invasion of White Men? Never."

"The Whites are coming anyway, you know that. You said as much. You're like that ancient British king who went to the ocean and commanded the tide not to come in. Wanted to demonstrate how powerful he was. And did the opposite. Damn fool was defying Nature." Portier just raised an eyebrow, and Jesus stared at him until he realized what was being said. Jesus's shoulders slumped a bit.

"You're saying the White Men are a force of nature that we can't stop?"

Portier nodded. "Until I signed on with Pinkertons, I made my living at card tables calculating the odds. My considered opinion is that you should fold this hand and seek a new deal."

"And what would that be?"

Portier nodded to where Seaton was practicing shooting the Winchester from the hip. "That is a very rich man, and a moral one, as much as any of that tribe are. Save his life, and you have a friend for life. One who won't just refuse to take what you have, but will help you turn it into something."

Jesus shook his head, doubt on his face.

"What have you got to lose?" Portier asked.

"Only everything, but I'm already half-way there."

"You're worried about the children?"

The Indian stared at him a long moment. "Of course. They are loved."

The look on his face made Portier choose his next words with great care. "If they were taken by the pox, what would you do?"

"Mourn them. Send them into the next world."

"What if they are already there?"

The Indian nodded gravely. "I take your point. Then Jake Martin no longer has a hold on us. Then we can rid ourselves of him and his 'guests'. But we think that the little ones are still someplace nearby. The Brujas say so."

Derek Seaton had been listening. "Are you open to a suggestion from a stupid white man?" he asked, a serious look on his face.

"Which one?" Black Horse replied. He looked around at the other three. "You are pretty smart for Whites, but still ignorant about Apaches. Jim Frazer was eager to learn our ways, but we never wanted him to stay. He could have become one of us. But it was never his path. He tried hard to learn a warrior's ways, but he's not a killer. We are dealing with killers."

Tilman smiled and shook his head. "How many men have you killed, Ash?"

"In the War. Fair number. Lost count after Gettysburg."

"Me, too. Still see their faces in my dreams."

Black Horse grunted. "You're soft, both of you, like all White Men. Once you send one into the other world, you never think about them. You can't. If they haunt your dreams, you give them power over you. You have not defeated them."

Derek Seaton looked pale. He swallowed hard. "Look," he said.

"Yes?" Black Horse looked at him coldly. He shook his head. His face was as hard as stone.

"As fascinating as this theological discussion is, I think we might consider the problem another way." The other three men waited silently. The Detectives because he was their client, and the Indian because he actually liked the young man, and saw he needed confidence if he was to survive what lay ahead.

"When I was twelve," Seaton said; "I disturbed a nest of hornets. Suddenly, they were all over me, stinging and biting. I ran away, but they pursued me. I ran as fast as I could, but they did not relent. So I got home with hundreds of stings all over my body. I swoll up like a balloon and damn near died. In fact, I think I did at one point, but my mother pounded on my chest and told me I was not allowed to; that it was not part of the plan. So my heart started again. I was packed in ice and was very sick for several days."

Black Horse nodded. "You learned a valuable lesson."

"I did. But look what happened. I was many times the size of those insects, a giant, but they almost killed me because they had a plan to defeat any invader: swarm and sting them everywhere." He looked at the other three men carefully, as they nodded. "What if we swarm the Strangers?"

Black Horse sighed. "What about the kids?"

Seaton looked him right in the eye. "I killed a lot of hornets, swatting them, trying to get them off of me. That did not stop the rest."

"All in, just like a poker showdown," Portier said. "That's pretty ruthless for a greenhorn."

"Runs in the family," Seaton replied. "You should meet my mother. She's said to be mean enough to hunt bear with a switch."

Black Horse burst into laughter. "I would like to meet her," he said.

Seaton relaxed. "We need a plan," he said. "And we need everyone with us."

"Even Jake Martin?"

"No, not him."

"Good," Black Horse said; "Because I am looking forward to showing him how long it can take a man to die."

"No less than he deserves," Portier said.

Tilman felt a bit queasy, but said nothing. Killing was one thing but he drew the line at torture.

CHAPTER THIRTY-FOUR

Jake Martin was relieved when he learned that Derek Seaton was going to try his luck in a showdown. He motioned Portier to take a seat opposite the desk in the tiny office where he did business and kept his accounts. He was courteous but wary. This man was no friend. He placed a Colt's revolver on top of the desk to show that he knew that. Portier ignored this and lit one of his cheroots without asking permission.

"I suspect you've got a trick up your sleeve," he said to Portier; "but that's fine with me. I wouldn't mind seeing one of my guests get a little hurt. It might make them more amenable and less demanding."

"You find them troublesome?"

"They ignore the restrictions I set when I invited them. They are scaring the people in the town. All my waiters and barmen quit. I have to ask Miss Kate to let her girls fill in. And they ain't supposed to be mixing with people at the church. That old priest had a few choice words for me about that. Not about the girls or the gunmen, mind you. Just my guests."

"I was there. They didn't cause any kind of a fuss."

"No? Well, he's pretty upset. Said he didn't mind whores or killers in church, since they were maybe seeking redemption, but those that consort with the Devil are another matter. Cursed me in Latin, he did."

"You speak Latin?"

"Grew up with it in Italy."

So Martin was a Catholic. Portier looked at him closely, at the nervous tic that troubled one cheek, and reflected that he'd seen many a bluff at the poker table in his time, but none as bold as this one. And to what end? He looked around the office, at the unpainted wooden walls and cheap paintings and furniture, and asked, "Tell me, Mayor. You ever think that maybe you've bitten off more than you can chew?"

Martin's face flushed a deep unhealthy red. "You can leave now, Detective. Mister Seaton will meet his fate as soon as this awful rain clears up." His voice cracked.

Portier stubbed out his cheroot, leaving a burn mark on top of the desk, and sneered at him. Martin stared, astounded at his effrontery.

Walking back to the jail, holding a lady's parasol borrowed from one of Miss Kate's girls against the steadily sleeting rain, he reflected that Jake Martin was one of those men too proud and arrogant to admit fault or error. Or perhaps he knew that he had to play out the hand. Anything less would end in his death.

There was now a long line of people who wanted Jake Martin dead, himself first among them. Ashley Portier put himself at the head of that line for Alicia Sorrell's sake alone. It was a measure of his self-control that he had not already done the deed.

Back at the jail, Blake Tilman was writing his daily report and wondering how to get it back to Harry McLean in El Paso, and whether or not it would be believed. It did seem rather fanciful, even a bit mad. As he was putting his writing case away he found the sealed envelope with his name in Emily McLean's handwriting. He opened it and found a letter and a small charm on a thin black ribbon:

Dear Blake:

You may think I am a silly young girl and too young to be a life companion for such a man as you, but I remind you that when I kissed you, you, Sir, kissed me back with great passion. I take that as hopeful. Perhaps you will no longer be immured in your great grief for your wife and daughter and see that life goes on. That said, I promise you nothing but a chance to woo me in the traditional way. I care not if the wooing ends in marriage or seduction. Pinkerton girls are ready to play any role required, and you have already seduced my mind with the considerable depth of yours. As did Jim Frazer. Do I use him as a foil against you? Perhaps, but I am reading Margaret Fuller and the other Transcendentalists. The charm is something that I purchased from the old woman who will not die in the marketplace: Jesus's grannie. She says that you will need it to protect yourself from great evil, so it will please me if you do not dismiss it as a superstition and wear it about your neck. I am prepared to love you and to be loved in turn. I bind your soul to mine....

Tilman stopped there. Was Emily casting a love spell? He found the letter to be very odd. Cold and clinical words mixed with passionate kisses. He held the charm up to the light and saw it was a ceramic disk with a crude drawing on it. He blushed when he realized what the drawing represented. Then he took off his hat and put the ribbon around his neck, and tucked the charm beneath his collar where it could not be seen. He felt the warmth of Emily's presence, but tucked the letter in his pocket to be finished later. There was work to be done. He had to turn his greenhorn client into a gunman.

Behind the jail, Jesus arranged for the wooden cut-out of a man to be set against several bales of hay sheltered under a tarpaulin. It was here that Derek Seaton practiced for his Date with Destiny. Tilman's Winchester rifle was cleaned and oiled, and Seaton, who already shot as well as any other dude on a lark out West, bore down to learn, in his body, how to outshoot an opponent.

Tilman began the first lesson by rapidly firing five rounds, working the lever quickly, tossing the rifle up and down in one hand. Seaton was amazed to see that all five shots landed in a tight group in the middle of the target.

"That's impressive," he said. "Where did you learn to do that?"

`"First District Cavalry. From horseback. Needed the other hand to control the horse when things got tight chasing Mosby's Rangers."

"I see."

Tilman handed him the rifle. Seaton placed the stock on his shoulder in the approved position and took aim. He worked the lever and fired, striking the target slightly below the chin.

"That'll work," he said with some satisfaction.

"You think you'll have time to stand there and aim before that Stranger puts a bullet between your eyes?" Tilman took the rifle, worked the lever to load another round and handed it back.

"One-handed. From the hip. As quick as you can."

Seaton tried, and the shot went wild, missing the target entirely.

"You have some work to do," Tilman said. "Again. Make the rifle part of you — an extension of your body."

They continued until it got too dark to see the target.

Afterward, the detectives took Seaton with them to the town's barbershop to enjoy, one by one, hot baths and shaves. The barber was one of Seamus Corcoran's women. She had the assistance of two young boys who heated and hauled the water needed to fill the large tin tub. Soap and scent were provided, and she shaved them with brisk efficiency while ignoring their naked bodies.

Seaton was resigned now to facing his possible execution. "I was too young to serve in the War," he said. "So, since I have neither the time nor the inclination, will have to substitute this for that experience."

Portier and Tilman looked at each other and choked with laughter.

"Have I said something amusing?" Seaton asked. His face flushed pink from the collar up.

The two detectives grew serious.

"My dear sir," Portier said, "Mister Tilman and I both saw the elephant, as they call it, at Gettysburg and elsewhere. We faced death every day for months without end, for our respective countries or causes. We saw dear friends and companions shot down, blown up, or otherwise fall to the diseases that ran rampant in the camps. Whole cities burning. Women and children starving by the side of the road. Men executed for cowardice and treason. You simply have no idea how offensive that statement is to any veteran. Especially from someone of your class, which was notorious for hiring other — poorer — men to serve their time in the field."

Seaton stared at him a long moment. "You are right. I am a fool and that was a very foolish thing to say, so I beg your pardon. But not every rich man avoided service — my father and uncles raised regiments of volunteers for the Cause and led them in battle."

"Which Cause?" Portier demanded angrily. "The Union?"

"Enough!" Tilman said sharply. The other men turned and looked at him. "Derek — if I may call you that?" Seaton nodded. "Mister Portier also comes from money, and so does Miss Kate, whom he first knew as Alicia Sorrell when they were engaged. The War ruined them. I suggest that we not pull scabs off old wounds. People of our generation have known suffering that, pray God, you will never experience. And — if you listen — you will learn many things to your advantage. What you are facing is a temporary inconvenience. You're a very intelligent man. Too much so to speak so foolishly."

Portier lifted his chin proudly. "When you have lost everything, then talk to me of wars and battles."

"He jests at scars that never felt a wound, as Shakespeare said," Tilman added.

Seaton was contrite. "Again, my apologies. I had no idea."

"Well, now you do. And there is enough misery in the world without you adding to it with careless talk." Portier was looking away, in the mirror. Tilman rose from the now tepid water, took the large cotton towel that one of the boys handed him and began to dry himself.

"I did not know about you and Miss Kate," Seaton said. Tilman shot him a warning look so that he would not say more.

Portier's shoulders slumped a bit. "It's a long story," he said after a moment, "but not mine to tell."

"Molly said nothing?" Tilman asked.

"Not a word. We don't talk much when she visits."

The detectives again both laughed long and hard, which broke the grim mood.

As they walked back to the jail, Tilman noticed that he could see stars overhead.

"It has cleared off. If it stays like this you may be in trouble tomorrow."

"Pray for rain," Portier added, not in jest.

Once they had Seaton secured in his cell, Tilman went in search of his saddlebags and found his sextant.

"What's that about?" Seaton asked as Tilman started back outside.

"A little thing we do for the government. This town is not on any map. This is *terra incognita*. So we try to fill in the blank spots when we can." Tilman looked at his Raymond Railroad watch and then stepped outside to shoot a position with the sextant. He came back, wrote the numbers in his notebook, and then stared at them. Shaking his head, he went back outside to try again.

Portier, yawning, poured the last of the coffee into a tin cup and sipped it.

Coming back inside, Tilman asked his partner, "Any good?"

"Not bad for floor varnish," Portier grimaced.

Tilman checked the numbers he had written before and shook his head. "I'm in a muddle," he said. He handed the sextant to Portier. "Here, you try."

The Southerner did so and came back in a few moments. He looked at Tilman's notebook. "These are correct, as far as I can tell."

Tilman dug in his saddlebags for the map and laid it out. "They can't be," he said. "Look at my previous sightings, which are here and here and here."

Portier looked closely at the pencil marks with the dates and times. He nodded. "I see the problem."

"By dead reckoning, we should be here," Tilman said, and then moved his hand and marked a spot several inches away. "By the sighting I've just taken, we are here."

"Where we have no jurisdiction."

Seaton had been following the conversation. "Where?" he asked loudly.

"Where Jake Martin said the other day. Mexico."

Seaton stared at them, amazed. "How is that even possible?"

Tilman rubbed his head. "I don't know, but I'll bet the Strangers have something to do with it."

. . .

While the detectives and the prisoner were cleaning themselves, Jesus went to see the old woman who lived alone at the edge of town. She supported herself by selling ignorant people potions and charms against Evil. Father Tomas, as a proper Catholic priest, publicly deplored her presence from time to time, but otherwise did not bother her. She was known as Mother Sophia, or Wisdom, and she was suspected of being a Bruja. Jesus knew that she was strong in the spirit world and often went to her for guidance.

"You are troubled, my son?" she asked when she opened the door of her humble hut to him, and beckoned him inside. The interior smelled of burning sage and other herbs. He sat down cross-legged opposite her and placed his hands on his knees opened upward. He closed his eyes and began chanting softly. It was his Death Song.

"Enough," she said quickly. "You will not die for many years. Do not invite it."

He opened his eyes and looked at her aged face and crone-like body, a serape draped loosely about her shoulders, wearing an old buckskin dress with beaded patterns beneath.

"What am I to do, then?"

"What does that false priest Tomas always say? Have faith."

"So you agree with him this once?"

The old woman laughed harshly. "He and I agree more than we disagree. We are simply on different paths to the same destination."

"I don't understand."

"You don't have to. You are not meant to. Why have you come?"

Jesus looked deeply into her brown eyes. "Are the End Times upon us? Are we beset by devils? Is this now Hell?"

She shook her head. "No more than at any other time. You fear the men they call Strangers?"

"Me among many."

Sophia took a small tan leather pouch from her bosom, and from that some colored stones. She cast them on the floor, bent over, swept them up, and cast them again.

"They are men, but not men. From far away."

"From Hell? Are they demons?"

She laughed softly. "Hell is not far away, but here, all around us, every day — and they are not demons as taught by those Jesuit fools you were sent to. That is a Christian conceit. No, these... things... are... "

She stopped and cast the stones again. "I have never seen this pattern. There is danger, but I think it means that while they do evil and delight in evil, they do not mean to kill us all."

"They eat us."

"Only for ceremonial purposes. Our flesh cannot nourish them."

"Why then? Why hunt us like animals?"

"Because they are Evil. For sport. Rich ignorant White men do the same. It gives them pleasure. Our Pain does feed them hugely. They savor it the way some savor a fine wine. This is very bad."

"For the gunmen and the whores?"

"For us all. The emotions from Tomas's church were so strong, so intense, that I felt them here, and was made quite ill for a time."

Jesus was very surprised. "You?"

"I am flesh, same as you, and will soon pass to another world. It stole my strength."

She cast the stones once more. "There is a battle soon. But you have allies."

"Who? The Buffalo Soldiers?"

Sophia frowned, eyes closed. "They are too far away. No, these three knights of the White Man's world. You have been much in their company."

Jesus shook his head. "Two Pinkerton detectives and a faint-hearted rich boy? Not much to work with."

"They are not just strong, but as wily as the fox. And I will send you something from the spirit world to counter those malign spirits that trouble the town. Many will die, but you and yours will not be among them, so be resolved."

Jesus felt himself suddenly relax, and become one with the world again.

"The rich boy," Sophia said; "is more than he knows. He has completed himself, and draws strength from a Druid priestess that knows not her own power. She is his rock."

"You mean Molly?" Jesus shook his head.

"Just so. Those women have several powerful priestesses among them. They simply have never been taught how to use that power, since they know not that it is theirs. Only one among them is self-knowing. You must send her to me so she can bring the rest when the time for battle comes. The black girl they call Daisy follows the Black Virgin."

Jesus felt confused. None of this could be shared with the three men Sophia had just called 'knights.' They would not, being rational men, accept it. "What will you do? You Brujas?"

"We will send you the wind."

"Will it help us find the children?"

The witch shrugged. "If they can be found."

"What do you mean?"

"That no one can know everything, and about this I know nothing."

• • •

When Jesus got back to the jail, the three white men were bunking down for the night. Tilman was sitting up, reading a big heavy book with a black leather cover by candlelight. Seaton was in his cell, lightly snoring. Jesus locked the door between the front office and the cells and said. "Why don't you turn in? I'll keep watch."

Tilman closed the book, marking his place with a slip of paper.

"I will," he said. "Where have you been?"

"Walking the town. I am the Marshal here."

From Seaton's cell came a soft feminine whisper. Jesus was surprised.

"Molly's here?"

Tilman nodded. "Came in about an hour ago. Had a falling out with her mistress, it seems, and is spending the night." He stretched out on the bunk in the open cell he was using.

Jesus shook his head. "That's bold."

"That's Molly."

Outside the rain began again, the sound of the falling drops masking anything the lovers might say or do with each other. Jesus was just as happy. He was no prude, but some White people had few limits on their behavior.

He looked at Tilman's book, which was by some German named Marx, but found it too heavy, after such a long day, to read with any profit. Sitting at the table, he took a small printed poster off the wall and turned it over. With a pencil, he began to draw a map of the town. He knew the layout by heart, having lived there many years, but the 'three knights' were new, and would need to learn it for the battle ahead. With the detectives asleep and snoring, he was enveloped by the steady beat of the raindrops falling. He tried to put himself into the spirit world where the future might be known.

Tilman dreamed of Emily. He had read the rest of her letter:

If you wish to avoid scandal, I suggest that you simply marry me and be done with it. That will add a thin veneer of respectability, even as many question it. Or I can go on pretending to be your "niece" and you can suffer all of those winks and nods you endured at that party. As Whitman said, I contain multitudes, and think that I would be no mean actress should I take that up. But such frivolity does not appeal to me. I do not crave applause or renown. I like having secrets, but will keep none from you. That is my pledge. I will be your partner as well as your lover, and never play you false. Use me as you will but honor my devotion with your own. Respect me and my ambitions. Guide me. Treasure me and I will treasure you.

There was more in this vein, and Tilman was both touched and amazed at this outpouring of emotion. Pinkerton girls were supposed to have hearts made of ice or stone. Molly's was warm enough to melt his own. His mind raced as he considered the possibilities and problems. What would Harry McLean say? Tilman did not much care for the opinions of others, but The Pinkerton Agency was still a sort of big family. Would such an arrangement be accepted within the firm? Emily was a 'Pinkerton girl' in the tradition of Kate Warne. She would not be deterred from this path; social conventions meant nothing to her. She would always try to do the right thing, inside or outside the law.

What was the right thing now? Pinkerton's had changed and become a private army for the Money Power. Allan might still be a Chartist at heart, but Robert and William ran things now. He could not see them entering into a Cause like Abolitionism now. There was no profit to be had there.

As for Emily, his mind told him to go slow, and his heart, once clouded by doubt, said otherwise. She had declared herself. He had to answer. And he recalled the facial expressions of the men at that party who assumed the title 'niece' translated to 'mistress'. Envy. Pure envy.

As he slept, the tension in his body faded. He felt warmed by the thought of her, and that he was once more, loved.

CHAPTER THIRTY-FIVE

Jeremiah Morgan was riding back from Boot Hill when he encountered Billy Bonney riding the other way. The winds had abated, as had the rain. Seeing no way to avoid Billy without giving offense, he stopped to talk. Billy had two Colt's revolvers and a Winchester, and a cruel, unpredictable nature. Jeremiah was unarmed and feeling a bit lonely, so what was the harm in being civil?

"What ho?" Billy said. "Where have you been?"

"Visiting my pop," Jeremiah said. "I know everyone says he was a bad man, but I liked him. He was kind to me and Ma."

Billy nodded. "I feel your pain." He looked away. Jeremiah felt the weight of his loneliness. It was a bond between them. A man had to be careful about the friends he chose, but still... "So you're a Regulator now?"

"Trying to be. Butch has me on probation. Says I have too much temper and not enough patience. My temper is high, that's true."

"He should Regulate some of these damned Strangers," Jeremiah said with feeling. "Where's the justice for my pa with these showdowns of theirs?"

Billy looked away, chewing at his lower lip.

"They ain't what they seem," Billy said at last. "They're ghosts or devils or something, not natural men. The whole thing is a cheat."

"How do you know that?"

Billy drew himself up self-importantly. "Me and Butch and Mister Williams took conference with them detectives. I know all about it. The detectives are trying to save Mister Seaton for killing that one."

"He ain't no gunman, that's sure." Jeremiah reached over and petted the neck of his horse. "But no real harm in him. I'll be sorry to see him shot down like the rest."

"The detectives is working with him. So is Black Horse. With a Winchester."

"Now that will be something to see. Never seen a Stranger use a rifle."

Billy smiled. "He might live after all."

Jeremiah shook his head sadly. "Nope. He ain't no killer. Too kind."

"Maybe he'll have help," Billy said.

Jeremiah looked at him, suddenly suspicious.

"What does that mean?"

"Maybe someone will even the odds."

"You'd shoot someone from ambush?"

"What do you think a Regulator does?" Billy said. "It's all about killing. That's why I like it. And Strangers got no kin to come back at you. They're all here for the killing, too."

Jeremiah nodded sagely. "He who lives by the sword dies by the sword, eh?"

"It's something to think about," Billy grinned.

Jeremiah knew he should not be talking about this with anyone, much less Billy Bonney, who everyone said was a braggart and a liar. But no one doubted his courage... or perhaps he was just a madman. He had it in excess, as much as any Apache. As if he knew the long odds would always be against him. It made him both unpredictable and dangerous. And no one to admire nor copy, since he had no honor, just murder in his heart. Jeremiah had worked all of this out for himself, and wondered if Black Horse might let him join his Apache band. The Apache girls were fierce but very handsome, and the braves bowed down to no one. It would be a fresh start.

Feeling he had lingered enough, Jeremiah flicked the reins of his horse. "I got to git home. Ma's waiting dinner." He smiled apologetically at Billy, whose deep loneliness began to show. His mother was right. Billy Bonney was already a bad man, beyond redemption, and someone to be handled with care, like a rattlesnake. Actually worse, now, because the rattler gave warning, and a Regulator never did. Where was the honor in that?

"Okay." Billy seemed disappointed.

"Where are you going, anyway?" Jeremiah asked, to be polite.

"Up to Boot Hill. See a few friends." Billy was somber for a moment, and then grinned. "And there's a girl."

Jeremiah was appalled. "You'd fuck a girl in a graveyard?"

"Why not? It's nice and quiet, and the dead don't mind. Her daddy already caught us in the hayloft, so that's out."

"You'd be better off with one of Miss Kate's girls."

"I ain't got that kind of money," Billy said; "And I like them fresher than that."

The two almost friends rode on their respective ways, with Jeremiah thinking about the new Sharp's carbine Clete Morgan had given him for his last birthday.

· · ·

As the sun went down, Daisy, Delores, and Molly excused themselves from the nameless hotel and walked into the village. One dark, one blonde, one redheaded, carrying parasols and dressed against the evening cold in dark wool dresses meant for everyday. At the edge of town, they knocked on the door of Sophia's shack.

The old woman opened and greeted them each warmly by name, although she had never seen them before. She motioned them to sit where they would; a young girl half their age came in from the other room, carrying a teapot and cups.

"This is my niece, Mercedes," Sophia said.

Mercedes poured each of them a cup of tea.

Molly cautiously sipped hers, and said, "Bitter."

"Like life itself," Sophia said. "You all know why we are here?"

The three nodded. Delores looked a little scared.

"I've never done anything like this before. Is it Devil worship?"

Sophia smiled, leaned over, and patted her hand. "Nothing to do with that. And women have performed these ceremonies for thousands of years." She looked directly into Molly's eyes.

"Do you know what you are?"

Molly laughed nervously. "I'm a pretty good whore. Why?"

"Oh, so much more," the old woman said. "Drink your tea and think back, not of this life but the many lives you led before. Feel and find your power." She nodded at Delores. "You, too, Miss. Drink your tea."

They did as they were told, watching the flames flickering on the candles, feeling the dream take them. Time went by. When they were ready, she began to teach them the proper incantations.

The rhythms made the three sleepy and they began to dream together. Looking around with wonder, they saw a rock-walled space with a sandy, level floor and rough stone walls that rose so high that they could not see the top of it. It was like a cathedral. Perhaps there was nothing overhead but sky? Little lights twinkled in a far distance, some white, some blue, some red. And the three of them felt the presence of other women: Apaches, mostly, but other tribes as well. How had they come here? Who were they? *Bruja!* The word came as a fierce whisper. The others were faint as they joined the circle, as wispy as a white silk negligee at first, and then became more solid.

Molly thought she was far calmer than she had any right to be. This was serious witchcraft, far beyond the country covens her grandmother had taken her to before the rapes and beatings made her run away. But rather than fear, she felt love being focused for a purpose. There was a war on, and the three of them were now warriors. She saw herself as an Apache warrior woman, riding naked on horseback, feeling the mare's muscles moving smoothly between her thighs, moving as one, with an ax in one hand and a

Colt's revolver in the other, meeting the enemy... Then as a priestess, making an offering to some strange god, and then as a shamanic crone dispensing wisdom. Without fear of dying, because there was no death. The body died and went away, but her spirit would always remain... She was all of these things, and yet none of them. The possibilities were without end: beyond comprehension, in places beyond, beyond... and then the illusions went away.

The old Bruja snapped her fingers. The three girls shook their heads.

"What have you done to us?" Daisy cried. Her dark black skin was covered with lines; silver they were, glowing slightly.

"Only given you the power you always had, that was hidden from you," Sophia said. "Does it bother you?"

"Oh, not much. I wonder what my clients and lovers will say?"

"They will not see them. You have to have the Sight, and few men do. Only women like us. You can wish them away."

Daily closed her eyes, frowning and soon the silver lines went away. Molly looked down and saw that she was marked too, not in silver but in brown. They were mostly circles. One set started close to her left nipple and covered her entire breast. Delores was marked in black.

"I rather like them," she giggled. "Pity they don't show."

"We must keep our secrets," Sophia said, sounding both stern and bored. She poured them more tea, and began to teach them more incantations.

"Concentrate your minds," she said. "We must find the children."

Later, as they formed a circle and began to dance – if a foot stamp and a side step could be called that – Molly felt the presence of other women, many, in circles, too, and dancing in the same way, building the rhythm, and summoning an elemental force from another world, both mystical and physical.

This was outside, under the stars, until they were all exhausted and fell to the ground. Laying under a pine tree, Delores said, "I see something."

"What do you see?"

"It's not so much seeing as knowing," the blonde girl said slowly. "Apaches call themselves 'people of the forest'?"

"That is correct."

"Then we should ask the forest."

Molly, as tired as she had ever been, said, "Sounds mad to me. Talk to a tree? Where, which one, what kind? Must be a million trees out there."

"You've been corrupted by those strong logical men you're seeing. Science blinds them to our craft. It is not one tree but all of them. They are collectively a creature, or maybe just a community, but they are not just the trees, but every other living thing there. They know where the children are." Sophia smiled. "Touched by the great spirit. Rest now. We will look further."

Just before dawn the three of them walked back to the hotel. Saying nothing, not even looking at each other, sated with the big ranch breakfast the old woman served them. As they walked, Delores asked nervously, "You're sure we're not all going to Hell?"

"Darlin'," replied Daisy in that rich island accent of hers; "We are already there. Now we are trying to get out."

"Amen to that," Molly Shannon said. She was shaken by what was revealed to her the night before. While in the trance, she saw her many past lives as a high pagan priest or priestess. This was destiny! To channel the secret forces that controlled the world and this universe for the good of all. With all of that before her, why be a whore? A new path had been revealed.

But she was still filled with doubt. "What's it all about, Daisy? You got us into this."

The Black girl shook her head, and flashed her brilliant white smile. "Damn me if I know. This somthin' different than we practice in the Islands. Stronger. Me old granny taught what she had learned from hers, stuff out of Africa all mixed up with Catholic and Indian stuff. Nothin' like this powerful. Dis the real deal."

Delores was quivering. "It scares me. I never felt anything like it. Did you see what I did? Those other women who looked like ghosts at first. Are they devils? Were we in Hell?"

"No," Daisy reached out and took her hand, "Come on, girl, did not your granny tell you tales of the old ways, the Old Religion?"

"I'm an orphan. Beggar girl before my tits came out, and never could get enough to eat. Then I had something to trade and did better, but I can't even read or write."

"You'll have to learn, then," Molly said. "This world's too complicated to be ignorant."

"What if I can't? I'm just a stupid whore."

"Don't think that way!" Molly said. "You'd not have been invited to that party if you were. Stupid is forever. Ignorance is easy to cure."

"And reading be a wonderful ting," Daisy said. "Like traveling to another world, another place in your mind. You can read novels and take yourself away from all this for a little time. It will ease your mind."

"That sounds nice." Delores shook off her dread. Whatever this was, whatever she had become, what was done was done, and there was no going back. Even a stupid whore knew that.

The rising sun illuminated the street. Sparkling droplets of water on the leaves and needles of the trees began to vaporize, creating a mist that made it all seem magical. Were they still in a dream?

The back door of the hotel was solid enough. They opened it and went inside.

J.C. Simms was at a small green-covered table in the hallway, sleepily dealing hands of poker, flipping them over, collecting the cards, shuffling them, and dealing again. He looked up at the three of them, his smile fading.

"Miss Kate wants to see you," he said. He jerked his head towards the back staircase that led to the second floor.

Daisy smiled her brilliant false smile. "And how is that you're the one to tell us this, Darlin'? Why not one of the other girls?"

"All locked in so they don't run away, too. Jake made noises about the contract, and she accused him of letting you three go freelancing. Me, I just work here. Boss says guard the back door, that's what I do." Simms did not look happy.

The three girls looked at each other apprehensively.

"It's our time of the month," Delores said.

"That's right," Molly added; "We heard the old medicine woman has a cure for the pain, so we went to her. Fell asleep."

"You see, Darlin'," Daisy said, "No worry."

Simms just shook his head. "Don't tell me. Tell her."

Molly bit her lip. She had a lot to tell Miss Kate, and it was not going to be pretty.

The three of them started up the stairs. Molly hesitated.

"What are you thinking about?" Daisy asked.

"That damned riding crop," Molly replied.

• • •

In El Paso that same day, early in the morning, Emily McLean, woke suddenly in the comfortable feather bed she shared for warmth with her sister Molly. But Molly was not there. Rather, she sat in the chair by the window, staring out at the dark clouds blowing in from the southwest.

"Do you feel it?" she whispered.

Emily sat upright, swinging her legs over the side of the bed, and stood, her feet on the cold brown tile floor with red triangular patterns. She shivered but not from the cold. Picking up her wrap, she covered herself and went to the window to watch the clouds.

"I do," she replied softly. "I feel him now, and the other one, and someone else."

"Many others," Molly whispered. "So many others. I see a village. And trouble. They are in great danger."

"I feel him closer now," Emily said. "He's read my letter. He wears the charm. And it warms his heart."

"Is that good or bad?"

"Both. We need to go there."

"How will we manage that?" Molly demanded. "You know that Father will oppose us doing such a thing on our own. That our 'feelings' are not evidence enough."

"Mama will persuade him."

"And who will persuade Bill Pinkerton?"

"Derek Seaton's mama. How much business will we lose if it comes to light we knew where he was, at great peril, and did nothing? If she were here, she would be screaming at us to go rescue her little boy. Even on something as thin as this."

"We need to bring others."

"Hey-seuss?"

"If he's still here. He and Kate were working that surveillance last night, when he suddenly left. Just left her there, and disappeared into thin air."

Emily cocked her head, trying to read her sister's expression.

"I like him well enough," Emily said; "but if he left Kate on her own, I will have something to say to him. I hate it when he turns Apache."

"Kate said he turned into something else. One moment he was there, and then there was this big black crow flying away."

Emily sat down hard on the bed. "Brujo!" she gasped; "That's not right."

"What do you mean?"

"He said Apache witches can fly. He never said he was one himself."

Molly chuckled. "An obvious oversight. Why did he have to? Had you not been mooning around over Blake Tilman, you would have seen it, too."

"Was I that obvious?"

"Mama's already planning the wedding, and trying to think how to break the news to Father," Molly giggled, enjoying the joke.

Emily drew herself up primly. "Surely not. Nothing has been said either way."

"Get dressed," Molly said. "We have much to do."

"Do we have a plan?"

"I haven't even decided which of my lovers will escort us to wherever they are. Are they in Mexico or the U.S.?"

"That is a question, isn't it?" Emily was momentarily distracted by the realization that Molly had not just kissed Manny D'Silva and John Pershing, but gone quite a bit further with both. Most would call that shameless, but they were Transcendentalist Pinkerton Agency girls: detectives wise in the ways of the world, who knew no shame.

Molly played with men, was an outrageous flirt, while Emily desired only one man in her life, and played at being maidenly. It served her well.

Lucy Blunt came to mind at that moment. Two days ago, that tough old Texas Ranger Jud Strong had come to the Pinkerton office with Blake's things and the forty dollars that Blake had paid to keep his room. He was embarrassed by the task. Emily was at a desk near the front, tallying hours of guard service for the week's payroll.

"She said it won't do," Strong told Harry McLean. "She can't stand the worrying about him." His weary lined face folded in on itself.

Harry McLean did not so much as glance his daughter's way, but just nodded. "Best to decide that now," he said kindly. "We are often in the field. Sometimes for months. I am sure Detective Tilman won't mind."

Strong leaned forward, lowering his voice. "I got the impression he wasn't that keen." Again he was hesitant, unsure of himself.

Harry McLean shook his head. "He never said one way or the other. One of those still trying to shake off the War. He had a wife that died. Still carries her picture. You know what that War was like."

Strong leaned back. "Actually, I don't. Spent the whole bloody time here rangering after Apaches, Comanches, Paiutes, and bandits. Protecting the homeland. Thirty years of it. Sitting in that saddle has gotten old. Them hemorrhoids is killing me." He laughed loudly, slapping his knee with his right hand. Harry joined in. He looked at Jud Strong carefully, and saw how weary he was, and sensed an opportunity.

"Ever think of taking up another line of work?"

"What do you mean? I'm a detective, too, you know."

"I understand. But I need someone here to run guards. Young Bill wants to get out in the field more. The job requires someone clean, sober, tough, that the men will look up to and the clients respect. If you were planning on maybe taking your retirement... "

Strong looked at him, thinking. "I do find myself liking the widow Blunt," he admitted. "It's a nice house. Her Negro gal is very sharp, too, and cooks like it was a New Orleans restaurant. I could see myself settling in. I like her boy, and Lucy thinks he needs some fathering. Never had a son of my own, but I been training young buck Rangers for twenty years now." He looked off into some distant scene only he could see.

He stood up suddenly, and offered his hand. "Thanks. Tell Tilman I'm sorry when you see him. I'll think about the job."

Harry McLean rose and took his hand. "We're always hiring."

Strong turned and walked the length of the office and went down the stairs without another word.

"Well, that was surprising," Emily said.

Harry McLean smiled. "Look at you, sitting there like butter wouldn't melt in your mouth."

Emily felt herself flush. "Why, Father, whatever do you mean?"

"Daughter, you are not too big or so old that I might not take you across my lap and give you a good spanking. I may not be into all that mumbo jumbo you and your mother and sisters spout, but I have eyes, and I'm a detective. I see what you're playing at!"

Emily lifted her chin proudly. "I'm not playing at all."

"Oh, I see that. I think everyone does, even poor old Lucy Blunt."

He looked at Tilman's valises and tied bundles of books that Jud Strong had left behind.

"I guess we'd best haul this all home."

"You were wanting another boarder."

"Get that out of your mind. Not him."

"Whyever not?" Emily smiled, and fluttered her eyelids like a comedic actress.

"Jim Frazer was enough of a complication and a worry. And I liked him."

Emily was very surprised. "You don't like Tilman?"

Harry McLean felt himself groping for the right words. "He's not easy to like. Too smart for this trade. A man like him should be teaching someplace."

"He'd be bored silly by that. He needs the challenge our work provides." Emily walked over to where he was sitting and kissed him on the cheek. Harry was very surprised. He rubbed the spot, staring at her.

"You are the best father a girl could want," Emily said. "You should know that."

Harry chuckled. "People say I indulge you girls too much."

"Scandalous, I know." Emily went back to her work.

After a few moments, she said, "Perhaps we should just get our own place."

Harry McLean tried to ignore the provocation, and shook his head. He would not be drawn.

Manny D'Silva and John Pershing both came to the office later that day. Harry McLean watched as his older daughter took charge.

"Since we need to move quickly, and don't know exactly where they are, we need the help of both of you. How do we do that?" Molly was very serious now. The two Captains looked at each other.

"We sometimes do joint patrols to catch bandits," Pershing said after a moment.

Manny nodded. "But this time we keep it small. No more than ten men each, plus an Apache Scout or two."

"What about us?" Emily demanded. "We're going, too."

"Uh, we won't have a wagon... " Manny began.

Emily cut him off. "You think we're too delicate to sleep rough, or can't handle a gun or a horse? We're Pinkertons!"

Manny stared at her, impressed by her passion. Perhaps he had been wooing the wrong McLean daughter?

"No, of course not," he said smoothly. Pershing laughed.

"Give it up, Manny. These are 'new' women. They do as they like, and the Devil take the hindmost. But, seriously, we are getting reports of something untoward happening in those badlands. We should take a look anyway."

Emily started to say something more, but Molly motioned her to be silent. She knew that you could get a man to do anything, if you first allowed him to think it was his own idea.

So the meeting ended with a plan, and money from Elmer Washburn's Secret Service fund to pay for it all. Officially, another expedition to find that missing balloon. That mystery still gnawed at Harry McLean. Where had it gone, and what was its true purpose? Jesus Martinez professed no knowledge of it, but Harry knew he was lying.

As for his older daughters, they were both women grown, and did as they pleased. As hard to predict or control as the weather. Fiercely independent, tough, smart, and ready. He was proud of them, but also ridden with anxiety at the chances they took.

. . .

Miss Kate was sitting at her dressing table, naked. When she saw Molly step through the door, she leapt up and rushed at her, the riding crop raised in her right hand. Molly Shannon decided she had had enough, and forced her back. The riding crop flew out of Miss Kate's hand and across the room to Molly's, who broke it in half over her knee.

Delores stared at her. "How did you do that?" she gasped.

Molly froze. She had not touched her assailant physically. They were still too far apart. Yet, Kate was standing flat against the wall, unable to move or speak.

"I don't know," Molly said after a moment; "I just thought about it and it happened."

"Must be one of those 'powers' the old woman told us about," Daisy said. "Magical fer shoah."

Molly stared at Kate and then stepped slowly across the room until they were face to face. Tears ran down Kate's cheeks. Molly felt tears of her own begin. She reached out and touched the other woman on the cheek.

"I love you, Darling," she said softly. "You know that?"

Kate nodded and found her voice. "I was afraid. So afraid."

"Of what?"

"That you'd run off with him. That I would never see you again."

"Then you're a mad bitch to come at me like that... "

"I know!" Kate collapsed, wailing, her shoulders shaking.

The three women helped her to her bed, where she lay prostrate, still weeping.

Molly looked at the other two. "What now? How do we console her?" At the back of her mind was the thought that her time with Miss Kate, her time as a whore, was coming to an end. That she would be 'running off ' with Derek Seaton if she could.

Daisy, ever the practical one, said, "How about a nice cup of tea?"

CHAPTER THIRTY-SIX

Just before dawn the expedition set off, with Captain Pershing and his nine Black troopers in the lead. Then came the Pinkerton detectives: Bill Pinkerton, and the two McLean sisters. Bringing up the rear was Captain D'Silva and his *Federales*.

To keep from exhausting themselves, they set a moderate pace, and had scouts out, five Apache warriors led by the old Shaman, Kicking Horse. The others were Lone Eagle, Little Crow, Red Flower and Horse Woman. That the last two were female caused some ribald comments among the young Mexican men.

That stopped when Red Flower turned her horse, a grey mare, and rode directly at the lead offender, snatching his hat off, while leaving a thin red cut down his cheek from a ring on her forefinger. Shocked, he slapped his hand over the wound, and broke formation to retrieve his hat, from the top branches of a live oak tree.

"I think she likes you," Manny D'Silva shouted in Mex, as he signaled for a halt.

The other men broke into laughter.

Captain Pershing rode back to see what had happened. He chuckled, but leaned forward in the saddle so only Manny could hear him.

Molly McLean rode up, too, within earshot. She was also annoyed by some of the ribald comments directed towards her and her sister. *Uncalled for*, she thought.

They were dressed for the trail in rough blue denim shirts that clung to their breasts. Hers were growing quite large. Both of the McLean sisters understood Mex quite well now, but kept that to themselves, more interested in what someone might say in an unguarded moment if they assumed they could not be understood. All part of the detective's trade. Molly was learning quite a bit about Manny, that she suspected he did not want her to know. Her respect for him had diminished, and she was in no mood to be charming. She did not like drunks, and certainly would never marry one.

"See here, we can't have these high-jinks. The whole thing will fall apart," Pershing started to say.

"Your men are acting like school boys," Molly scolded. "Make them stop, or I will."

"How will you do that?" Pershing was both irritated and amused. Manny smiled as well. Obviously, they did not take her seriously.

Molly frowned, turned to stare at the young Mexicans, and pointed her right forefinger at them. A sudden wind ripped off all their hats and sent them flying into the dust. All of them turned and stared at her, and whispered among themselves, scared now.

"What are they saying?" Bill Pinkerton asked, trying to control the restive mount he was on. Fighting for dominance with one of the half-wild mustangs from the contract stable. They were still getting used to each other. Bill did not ride much, and his muscles were already telling him that there would be a price to be paid for this.

Emily was next to him. She leaned over and grabbed the bridle of his horse to keep it from bolting. "Bruja. They think she's a witch and sent that wind."

"And is she?" Bill felt a chill of fear course down his spine. "Did she?"

Emily smiled. It was an insolent, cruel smile that slowly faded. "You saw us dance naked in the light of the moon. What do you think?"

Bill was amazed, and shocked that she knew this. He had been so far away, and had not told anyone, much less his gossiping wife.

Pinkertons kept secrets to shield themselves from rumor and unwelcome inquiry from reporters and government officials. Even among themselves, they were closemouthed. He worried that this chance remark might have been overheard. He cocked an eyebrow and gave the slightest shake of his head. Emily looked away, biting her lip. He was right, of course, but it galled her to admit it.

Bill had a sunburn that was beginning to peel. It marked him as a greenhorn. She and Molly had covered their features with a white salve that made them look like china dolls.

The two Captains were looking at a map and seemed not to have heard what she'd said. Emily bowed slightly forward in the saddle.

"Sorry," she said; "That will not happen again."

"Are you a Bruja too?" Bill's natural curiosity overrode his caution.

Emily leaned forward once more, and whispered. "Of course not, Mister Pinkerton, sir. The Pinkerton Agency would never indulge in such native superstitions. Brujas are Indian or Mex. We're Scots, aren't we?"

Bill Pinkerton realized that the teasing was good natured, and strategic, so nothing of that kind would appear in a report going to Chicago or New York.

"But we have them in Scotland, too, don't we? Witches."

Emily put on a prissy face. "I have no idea what you are talking about, sir." Then she laughed. "Give it a rest, Cousin. You wanted to go to the field and have an adventure. Well, here it is. Take it as it comes."

He saw Pershing and D'Silva signal to their men for a rest. There was an attractive grove of live oaks and a little stream nearby. A good place to water horses and have a quick meal. The men had already dismounted, and were leading their horses down the slope. Pinkerton looked around, taking it all in. He breathed in deeply, enjoying the clean air.

"I'd be a fool to imagine I'm actually in charge of anything, wouldn't I?"

Emily's smile was kinder this time. "I do think it is awfully kind of you to organize all of this, just because I thought my lover might be in trouble," she said.

"Not at all. We Pinkertons take care of our own."

He was a serious young man, she saw, trying his best to understand the business that his grandfather had founded, while everything was changing so fast. Adding magic that few understood was no kindness. She was at a loss to explain some of it herself.

She wondered how long it would take Bill to realize that Little Crow was known to him in El Paso as the ever helpful Jesus Martinez, or if he would say anything about it. She thought not. Bill had learned discretion at his mother's knee, and seldom said what he was thinking.

Unlike his North Shore bitch of a wife, who traded in gossip at the marketplace and the tearooms. This was permitted, because it produced some useful intelligence from time to time, but made the McLeans cautious in her presence. Mary felt and resented her isolation, but Bill was more relaxed these days, an indication that their love life had improved. His eye no longer wandered. He regarded Horse Woman and Red Flower with awe. Fierce, brave, and confident, they would have fit well in one of the dime novels he loved. The reality exceeded such pallid imaginations.

The Apaches clustered together briefly, and then rode off in different directions.

"Where are they going?" Bill asked, just as Captain Pershing rode up, Molly by his side. Manny D'Silva broke off from the stern lecture he'd been giving his own men and joined them.

"Scouts out." said Pershing, as if that explained everything.

"We don't want to be surprised," Manny added. "The Apaches own this land, know every rock and tree of it, so they can spot danger way before we do. They are experts at concealment themselves, able to move with great stealth. And Little Crow thinks he knows a short cut we might use, a cleft between two mountains that will take us closer. Kicking Horse and Lone Eagle tried to shush him, but he's eager. I think it's a secret they'd rather not have us know. For strategic reasons. Something that explains how they can get so quickly from one place to another? That would be worth knowing." Manny looked thoughtful.

He smiled hopefully at Molly and Emily. "I have disciplined my men," he said, "there will be no more nonsense."

Molly shook her head. "They must behave. This is no lark. We're on serious business."

Emily frowned and nodded in agreement.

"It is just that the idea of two attractive young women as Pinkertons confounds them. They don't think it's real."

"Would they like a demonstration like the one Red Flower gave them, or shall I send the wind again?" Molly asked.

"That's the other thing they don't believe," Manny said. "They think you got lucky." Manny smiled so politely, they knew he believed this, too.

"We don't care," Emily said. "Brujas do not perform tricks. We're not at a carnival. Just keep them in line."

Manny looked over to where Bill Pinkerton was listening carefully. "Is that your instruction, *Jefe?*"

"Yes, of course," Bill said sternly. "The McLeans are acting for me whenever they give an order. Make that clear to your men."

Manny's agreeable smile faded. He did not like taking orders from an arrogant Yankee, and taking one from a woman was intolerable. "The things I do for love," he sighed.

Pershing laughed. "It's well we settle this now."

"What about your troopers?" Manny sneered. "Are they easy with this?"

"Plantation-born ex-slaves? They know the whip crack of the Mistress's voice," Pershing said. "They never question an order. Never. The Army is not a debating society."

Manny was abashed. "You are correct," he said; "My men should be better trained."

"No time like the present," Molly said.

Manny touched the sombrero he was wearing, and rode away to continue his lecture.

Bill watched him go, reading the resentment in his stiff back. "That went well," he said.

"Men," Molly said. "Still little boys, the lot of you."

"If I may venture some advice," Bill said.

"Of course," Molly said.

"Pull that back in, that attitude. It's not helping."

The McLean sisters looked at one another, perplexed.

"What should we do?" Emily asked.

"What you do best. Charm them." Bill Pinkerton looked around, wondering where the Apaches had gone, knowing that one might be right next to him and never seen until he or she chose to reveal themselves. He looked at the two girls.

"And do me the courtesy of pretending I am actually in charge. It will go easier for all of us that way. I may be a greenhorn here, but I started in the Chicago office when I was fourteen, and worked many cases there. I know what's what."

"Yes, sir," Molly said. "Message received and understood."

Emily nodded.

"Now would either of you care to explain why our office boy is here in full regalia as an Apache brave? Are we infiltrating them, or are they infiltrating us?"

"That, sir," Emily said; "Is a matter for further investigation."

"Our father is fond of him," Molly added; "And he is very useful in many ways, but said he will not be given a badge to wear." Molly and Emily both had Pinkerton brass shields on their vests.

"Why not?"

"His true loyalty is to his tribe. Father said no man can serve two masters."

Bill Pinkerton thought about the way Jesus looked in buckskins and war paint. Pinkertons were famous for their ability to blend in and deceive others to make a case, but he found himself agreeing with Harry McLean. The risk was too high.

Captain John Pershing rode up. "Bill, we are getting ready to move on. Eat something and drink some water."

"I'm okay. Not hungry."

"Do it anyway. You look a little pale. I won't have you getting sick on us. Dismount and walk around a little." Pershing looked over at Molly and Emily.

"Them, too."

The two sisters were only too happy to get down off their mounts for awhile. They had scandalized the Mexican boys by not using side saddles and not wearing the split overskirts modesty demanded over their trousers. This had caused the raucous behavior. Pershing's Black troopers expressed no opinions, except flashes of bright white teeth when they smiled.

So the break continued, leaving the detectives to wonder where the urgency of the mission had gone. The two Captains conferred over the map, which was more of a topographical outline with few details. Bill Pinkerton joined them.

"Where did you get this map?"

"Mexico City." Manny pointed to some of the lettering. "It's copied from the original Spanish survey. Very old."

"*Terra incognita.* If we had time, we'd be taking sightings and measurements," Pershing said.

"No," Manny said. "That's a sore point with *los* Apaches. They still claim the land and don't want it measured."

"I see," Bill Pinkerton said. He had read parts of the Cremony book. "And we need their help."

"The concern is a religious one," Manny said. "Hey-seuss's short cut leads through sacred ground. Past that huge cliff painting where that big balloon disappeared. The one that Jim Frazer was with when it came to El Paso. They say the ancient gods there do not like strangers. The old Shaman is quite put out. He will have to propitiate them with some kind of ceremony."

"So are we going to save any time?" Bill Pinkerton had his pocket notebook out and was making notes.

"At least a day." Manny shook his head. "I don't see how that is possible."

John Pershing gazed at the map, "Me neither. Even if it was flat desert rather than mountains, it's the same distance."

"Is it a trap?" Bill Pinkerton asked, suddenly worried.

"Not with the McLean sisters along. Hey-seuss is very fond of them. Considers them sisters. Goes hunting with the youngest one. Or so I've been told." Manny smiled a charming smile.

"Hopefully, that's all he does." Pershing said.

"Why do you say that?" Bill Pinkerton stopped making notes.

"These are very wild girls, and little Kate is a law unto herself," Pershing said. "Harry McLean does nothing to control them, and they have few boundaries."

"But Emily and Molly are women grown," Manny said. "What should he do? When he gave them badges and revolvers, he gave them their independence. They resist marriage."

"As they should if they want to stay independent," Bill Pinkerton said.

"This is the West, Bill. The rules are different here. More freedoms."

"Sisters, eh?"

"Until the day that Hey-seuss stakes a horse for Kate to water outside his house, Harry does not plan to worry, and Hey-seuss, it seems, has a wife."

"Really? Who?"

"Red Flower, of course. That's why she is here. To make sure that the McLean sisters remain sisters, and nothing more."

"The Green-eyed Monster, eh?" Bill Pinkerton smiled, and shook his head. "Some things never change. Regardless of culture."

Molly was close enough to hear that. "Now you sound like Jim Frazer," she said.

Emily frowned. She wished that Frazer was present, and that Molly would stop teasing her beaus. Theirs was a friendly rivalry. So far.

"Let's get this show on the road." Pershing took a brass whistle from his pocket, blew a loud, shrill note, and then pumped his right arm up and down. The whole party quickly assembled in good order, and the Apache scouts rode in. Kicking Horse and

Lone Eagle seemed to be having some sort of argument, but were stone-faced when they rode up to speak with the two Captains.

"I will go ahead," Lone Eagle said. He rode down the trail towards a narrow cut in the mountainside. Pershing and his troopers followed. The trail was wide, but the steep stone cliffs soon hemmed them in, leaving no room for outriders. Pershing's men looked anxiously up the steep walls of red basalt and granite. It was the perfect place for an ambush.

Emily, taking off her hat, craned her head upward and saw birds' nests suddenly come alive, as black birds with red-streaked wings flew about in confusion, and a great white owl swooped down so close that some of the horses took alarm, and almost bolted. Further on the trail widened and the walls seemed lower.

They rode on, and an hour or so later experienced a tingling sensation, as if they were near a thunderstorm. Electricity was in the air, which became moist as freshets of water poured down on their right, and on their left was the huge wall painting Jim Frazer had seen when the huge balloon had left him there with the Apaches to begin his vision quest.

Molly and Emily reined in their horses and just stared in wonder. Bill Pinkerton was equally gobsmacked. The troopers and the *Federales* were all silent, as if they found themselves in a huge cathedral. There was a reverent silence. The skimming clouds above made the huge painting seem to be alive. The wind came up, blowing dust in their faces.

Lone Eagle appeared some distance before them, his right arm pointing down another wide trail. He rode on. As they got to the intersection and turned to the right, they saw a wide plain with lots of greenery: grasses, small groves of trees, and little hillocks. Such terrain was also rich in opportunities for ambush. Kicking Horse made a motion and dug his heels into his horse's flanks. It trotted ahead. He began a chant, raising both arms upward. Everyone else followed, again feeling the electric tingle pass over their bodies.

And suddenly, impossibly, there was the huge balloon that had arrived that day in El Paso so many months before. The two Captains signaled for a halt. The rigid superstructure that held it up seemed broken in places, the basketwork below ripped, revealing a shining grey metal body below. It looked as if it had not moved in some time. Bird droppings covered the remaining silk and struts.

Some distance away, a tall slender man and a young woman with bright blonde hair sat on a crude wooden bench. Further away, several other men, stripped to the waist, were lounging on the grass. Inside the basket, two older men were looking at some kind of chart or diagram, quite absorbed in a task. Light lit their faces from below: very bright white, unnatural, light.

Molly and Emily spurred their horses and went ahead. The tall slender man got to his feet and put on a military uniform coat, and stood stiffly before them.

As they pulled their mounts to a halt, he said loudly, "Who are you? What do you want?"

Molly leaned forward. "Detective Molly McLean, Pinkerton National Detective Agency, out of El Paso. And you?"

"Colonel Sir Percy Wyndham, British Ethnographic Survey."

Molly and Emily looked at each other, amazed.

"Do you know where we are?" Wyndham asked plaintively.

"Someplace in either Texas or Mexico," Emily said. "Along the Border."

"And who are you?"

"Detective Emily McLean."

By this time Bill Pinkerton had joined them, and the two Captains, having given orders to their men, were riding up as well. Wyndham saluted, and the two captains returned the salute. Wyndham's eyes went from one to the other, assessing them coldly, like a disappointed parent.

"So you finally found us." he said.

"Actually, we weren't looking," Bill Pinkerton said. "Just passing by."

Wyndham looked crestfallen. "Oh," he said. Behind him the young blonde woman laughed and stood up.

"Hallo, luvs. Good of you to stop. Care for some luncheon and a chat? We're absolutely starved for company."

Bill Pinkerton was writing in his notebook. He looked up.

"We're in a bit of a hurry," he said.

"Time stops here," Wyndham said.

"What do you mean?" Pershing asked. He looked sideways at Manny.

"Just what I said. We are in some kind of frozen place. It's very odd. Check your watch, if you don't believe me."

Bill Pinkerton pulled his Raymond Railway watch from his vest pocket and saw the hands were frozen. He shook it.

"Wound it this morning," he said, confused.

Manny D'Silva pulled his own ornate gold watch from a pocket, flipped open its cover and cursed softly. "Mine is dead, too."

John Pershing looked at his. "Same here."

"How is this possible?" Emily asked.

"I presume it has something to do with magnetism," Wyndham said. "Do you have a compass?"

"Of course." Pershing reached into another pocket and pulled out one issued by the U.S. Army. When he opened that cover, he saw that the hands were spinning wildly. He showed it to the others.

Emily and Molly gasped. The men all shook their heads.

"What does it mean?" Emily asked. She felt quite excited.

"Devil take me if I know," Wyndham said. "Do stay for a bit. We have plenty of food."

Manny and John Pershing looked at one another.

"It is a matter for further investigation," Bill Pinkerton said.

"Are those your men?" Pershing asked.

"Of course," Wyndham said. "Our crew for our flying machine."

"Look very fit. Military?"

"Like me, on detached service from King Victor Emmanuel."

Manny frowned. "As a responsible officer of the Mexican Government, I must ask you what a foreign military expedition is doing on Mexican soil."

"Or American soil," Pershing added.

"We have permission," the blonde woman said gaily. "An official letter from José Limantour, Minister of Finance."

"And you are?" Pershing was irritated.

The woman got up and walked over, placing her hand on his. "I'm Rose Green, Luv. Late of Liverpool."

Emily and Molly felt immediately jealous of the blond woman. She had power over men, that was plain. What other powers did she possess?

"Please," said Rose Green, "Stay awhile."

After some back and forth arguments, the men were told to dismount and rest.

The two Captains and three Pinkertons sat at a wooden trestle table set under an outdoor awning, with Sir Percy Wyndham and Rose Green. An informal meal was laid on fine English Bone china with a blue pattern, with silverware and white linen napkins provided.

Molly McLean sat between the two Captains and Emily between Bill Pinkerton and a very dignified Lone Eagle. Rose Green sat at the head of the table with Wyndham and the other two men who'd been working on the balloon next to him. Kicking Horse took the seat at the opposite end from her. There were platters of cut meat and some sorts of yellow vegetables to be shared. Yet no one seemed to want food.

Emily noticed that Rose Green and her party all seemed to have a waxy sheen about them. They looked like dolls in a store. Despite the heat, none of them were sweating.

Rose Green smiled becomingly, and said. "Everyone comfortable? All right then, cards on the table. You lot seem to be some kind of military expedition. How came you here?" She looked not at the Captains, but directly at Kicking Horse for an answer.

Kicking Horse looked away, closing his eyes, and said something in Apache. Lone Eagle cleared his throat. "We are conveying them to deal with a White Man's problem. There is some urgency. We did not mean to intrude."

"Oh, you are very welcome," Rose Green said. "We have been hoping for a rescue." She looked at Wyndham. "Somehow, we got lost and ended up here. Shipwrecked, you might say."

"Or marooned." Wyndham added.

"What is this place?" Bill Pinkerton asked.

"Damn me if I know," Wyndham replied. "Some sort of transit point, or maybe a jail. It seems to go on forever. Me and some of the lads tried to hike out, and ended up right back here after two or three hours. That's when I noticed that the watches had stopped, and the compass couldn't find any direction."

"Well, if it's a jail, it's a very comfortable one. Not much to do, but the weather is nice and we obviously won't starve. Our airship came to grief, but none of us were harmed. Paolo and Justin have been trying to fix it. Bunch of scientific mumbo-jumbo that I can't begin to understand, and that Percy only pretends to."

"Ma'am!" Wyndham said sharply.

"Oh come on, Percy. You're out of your depth. Admit it. Or explain to me why the square root of one-half is so important and what that has to do with the price of eggs."

Wyndham flushed red, and shook his head. He had no answer.

Emily looked around and saw that no one except the scientists seemed to know.

The two Apaches were stone-faced as usual.

Bill Pinkerton wrote in his notebook.

"What exactly happened," he asked. "How did you crash?"

"We had just left Jim Frazer off to meet a party of Apaches in that canyon with that amazing cliff painting. He was going to do something called a 'vision quest'. He studies such things for the Ethnographic Survey, and was also somehow involved with the Pinkertons."

She looked suddenly at Emily and Molly.

"McLean? You're Harry McLean's daughters?"

"Yes, ma'am," said Molly and Emily in unison.

"And Detectives yourselves?"

"Yes, ma'am."

Rose Green absorbed that slowly. "Good to keep it in the family, I suppose."

A wistful look came over her face. "Tell me. How does Jim Frazer fare? Did he survive that fool's errand he was on?"

Emily said cooly, "Very well. Practically an Apache himself now. Learned the language and the customs."

Rose turned her gaze to Lone Eagle. "So he's still with you?" she asked hopefully.

"No," Emily said. "At Cambridge University, teaching and preparing papers for The Transactions of the Royal Society."

Rose laughed. "Of course. A man of great wit and dedication."

"I found him so." Emily said.

Rose raised an eyebrow. "Did you," she murmured.

"We correspond," Emily said; "But as friends. Not sweethearts."

Why had she added that detail?

Rose looked around the table. "So if Jim Frazer is not the object of your expedition, what is?"

"Two Pinkerton detectives, and possibly a client, in trouble," Bill Pinkerton answered. "We thought to save time."

Rose looked at Kicking Horse. "Well we're doing that ain't we? We seem to be in a series of dreams here. I feel incredibly old. Had one where our craft was forced into another world. One like this, but not like this, where we are flying over mountains, with terraced fields being worked by natives.

"Brown, squat little people the likes of which I've never seen. And there is a big square where we are coming to rest because the engines have failed, and there are a lot of soldiers and officials. It's hot, and no one has any clothing on except weird headdresses and breechclouts. We're decently clothed, but when in Rome, y'know, you do as the Romans do. And we were in Rome, or a province of it in South America, The Roman Inca Republic.

"So anyway, it's looking pretty hostile, and Percy has the lads loading the Winchesters so we can all die gloriously, when I say wait, let's trying something else, and I strip off to the buff, shake out my hair and stand on the rail of the basket right out front, and spread my arms and legs like some primitive deity.

"And they buy it. They all bow down. Percy and the lads strip down and form up to escort me to what looks like a temple. And their High Priest comes out and begins speaking to me in Latin! Latin, of all things! I had to let Percy take the lead on that, but the High Priest says that our coming was foretold, even to the Chief Minister and the Twelve Acolytes... and I was Queen of that place for thirty years.

"Gave me a right appreciation for our own Queen. Poor little Vickie. I don't see how she does it, all that detail, and decisions and palace intrigue. But it was just a dream."

"Was it?" Wyndham asked. "I was there, too, and remember. But one day we all woke up back here, and no real time had passed."

The newcomers at the table all looked at each other. The two Captains broke into laughter, that quickly faded when they realized that Rose Green was not inventing a tall tale. Wyndham and the others looked offended.

Rose said smoothly. "Just a dream, but very real. So be kind. We're not entirely off our heads yet."

Percy Wyndham said. "I had one where I was leading a force of some kind of flying machine, being attacked by other smaller craft as we went to drop bombs on a city. Very dangerous work, done by very brave young men. Explosions all around. Never been so frightened in my life. But I woke here once more."

Bill Pinkerton said. "You haven't told us about the crash."

"Oh. Right!" Wyndham frowned. "It was during the lift-off by that very remarkable painting on a cliff, from next to an ancient road you can barely see. Justin had taken an ore sample... what we took to be one... and as we lifted, something began to force us back down. The object turned red hot and dropped, and then burned a hole right through the bottom of the basket. And still we were being forced down.

"Justin and Paolo went to use the emergency power, but flocks of black birds, some kind of swallow or wren, attacked us. Not just the balloon, but all of us, shrieking, and pecking at us. It drove us mad. There was that Mexican boy from your office. Very agreeable young lad. He jumped over the side, I'm sorry to say. I'm sure the fall killed him... "

Kicking Horse grunted. Lone Eagle shook his head.

Or he just flew away, Emily thought.

Bill Pinkerton and the two Captains were completely absorbed by this tale. Pinkerton was writing in his notebook. Suddenly, he turned his head to look at Molly, who laid a forefinger by the side of her nose: the old Pinkerton Agency signal to keep quiet.

Wyndham continued, his brow wrinkled in concentration. He sighed. "From there my memory is a bit fuzzy. It felt like we were pulled into that other world, and if that was a dreamm it was a damned – pardon my language – vivid one, because I remember everything that Rose does. I was her Chief Minister and military commander, and we were at war constantly. Thousands killed every damn year. I was always training replacements, setting forth on new campaigns."

"Which you loved," Rose said. "You live to lead men into battle."

Wyndham's face acquired a confused look. "You see, if we were in that world for all that time, and thirty years seems about right, then we should be dead or dying or very aged. Yet, here we are as we were. Hale and hearty."

Lone Eagle looked over at Kicking Horse, who nodded slightly. Lone Eagle stood up suddenly. "We should go."

The two Captains looked at each other, and Bill Pinkerton also got to his feet.

"Yes," he said; "We're on a mission, Colonel, and should not tarry further."

Emily and Molly started to protest. They had so many questions.

"Now!" Pinkerton said. There was a scramble to mount horses and form up the expedition. Rose Green and Percy Wyndham looked wistful but unsurprised.

"I will report your circumstances," Manny said, exchanging salutes once more with Wyndham.

"If you would be so kind," he replied.

"Miss McLean," Rose Green called.

"Yes?" Emily and Molly replied in unison.

"When you write to Jim Frazer, please tell him that I have fond memories of our brief time together, and hope to renew our acquaintance when I get home to Liverpool, where there is also a very fine university."

Emily and Molly looked at each other, and shrugged. They did not really care, but had manners. Why should they help a whore pursue a romance with Frazer? They smiled in unison.

"If we can," Molly said, and flicked the reins of her horse as the expedition began to move forward. Emily once more smiled a brilliant, false smile.

That Rose Green had enjoyed Jim Frazer in a most intimate way was well known, but Emily thought it rude of her to bring it up. It annoyed her. Why should she care? Jim removed himself back to England, and she chose Blake Tilman instead, and was rushing to save him from a danger she only felt, and that might not be real. It was distracting thinking about Jim Frazer.

She put it aside and looked around. She sensed danger everywhere.

They reached the intersection again,and turned right. They were still sandwiched between two sheer rock walls as they moved forward. The cleft was not laid in a straight line,but bent slightly. Soon the intersection was out of sight and she wondered if it existed at all. She dug her heels into her horse's sides and rode forward until she was next to Lone Eagle.

"See here," she said, and waited for him to turn his large head and scarred face.

"Why did you show us that?"

"Show you what?"

"Please, Mister Eagle. We Pinkertons, some of us anyway, know magics. My sister and I belong to a coven. We can see beyond the physical world."

Lone Eagle actually smiled. "And what else do you know?"

"That Apache witches can fly. One in particular. The one you call Little Crow, and that we know as Hey-seuss Martinez." She cocked her head and smiled her most becoming smile. "So, are you a Brujo as well? Does it run in the family?"

Lone Eagle frowned. "My son is too impetuous. How did you find out?"

Emily smiled again. "I am a detective, sir." She touched the Pinkerton badge on her coat. "This is no girlish fancy or parental indulgence, but hard earned. Please do not take me for a fool. And it is not a hard solve. When you eliminate all other possibilities, then the one that remains, no matter how wild or improbable, must be true."

Lone Eagle nodded gravely, "No flies on you, little girl. You have many powers."

"What I don't understand," Emily said; "Is if you can fly, why you simply do not do that and find out what we need to know?"

"What would we do with our horses?"

Emily stopped and stared at him. She thought for a moment.

"Surely, they can be made to fly as well?"

"They weigh as much as six men. So it is not possible. There used to be a breed with wings, but it died out many, many years ago. And, if you fly, you have to go where the winds take you... and that is seldom where you want to go. And one more thing."

"Yes?"

"It's very tiring. I'd rather ride. As for your first question, White people have been looking everywhere for that balloon. Now it's found. They will leave us alone. End of story."

Up aheadm Manny D'Silva and John Pershing were riding side by side, and trying to look at the map that the intermittent wind threatened to carry away.

"Just where the hell was that?" Pershing asked.

"As Colonel Wyndham said, 'damned if I know'," Manny replied. "Did you see what I saw? In the distance, above those hills?"

"Something flying?" Pershing shook his head. "Biggest damn birds I ever saw."

"Were they? Birds?"

"I have 'artillery eyes'," Pershing said. "I'm far sighted, and pretty good at calculating distances. Those creatures were two or three miles off, and I don't think birds would look that large at that range."

"So they were?"

"Men. Flying men."

Manny folded the maps and put it away. "There's another thing."

"Yes?"

"That valley is not on this map."

"So where the Hell were we?"

The two young men stared at each other, and then broke apart to see to their men. To tell them to be on guard. And to hasten the pace.

Behind them, the earth rumbled, and had they troubled to look, they would have seen that the narrow cleft that had given them such easy passage was no longer there.

CHAPTER THIRTY-SEVEN

At the jail that morning, Derek Seaton and the two detectives sat at the old wooden table, joined by J. C. Simms. Breakfast was delivered by two of Seamus Corcoran's women, who smiled and nodded as they dished out beef and beans but pretended not to understand the questions put to them in English, Spanish and Creole French. Simms shrugged. He watched them leave.

Outside the rain stopped, but water dripped slowly from every limb. They walked quickly away, their heads down, not wanting to be caught when it began again.

"They either know nothing or have been told not to say anything."

"You, sir, have the makings of a detective," Portier said, smiling.

"You think so?" Simms smiled back and then asked cautiously, "You don't mind if I partake of this generous bounty?"

"Not at all," Portier said. "Those days are past, and these are field conditions."

Simms ate a few bites, looking at him for tells. Poker players were always hard to read.

"I recall objections when I was growing up. Special rail cars for the Negro that somehow did not make us feel special."

"But only if you traveled alone. If you were in service, you had to stay close to your owner." Portier brushed away an annoying fly and did not see the quick flash of anger that passed over Simms' face.

"That's right," he replied evenly. "At your beck and call."

"Well, we're all equal now. The law says so. And I do not dispute it."

Derek Seaton looked up from his own food. "Where did you say Molly was?"

"I did not say, Mister Seaton. Truth to be told, I have no idea. I was on the door, when she and two other girls came quickly down the stairs just before dawn with Miss Kate, and carried her away. Where to, they did not say and I'd rather not know."

"Why?"

"Because their absence put Jake Martin in a rage when he discovered it, causing me to dissemble and say that I had not seen them. I suggested to him that it was probably 'female trouble' and that they may have gone for some kind of herbal treatment. Where that is, well, who knows?"

Portier stared at him. "You might have mentioned it."

"Why?" Simms began eating rapidly, as if he expected a fight. "Because you lay claim to her too?"

Tilman looked from one to the other, suddenly alert. Seaton eased his chair back.

"Easy now," Tilman said. "Let's stay friends."

Portier suddenly laughed, his face agonized

He took a deep breath. "No! Of course not. That would be ridiculous. She is not that sweet maiden I left behind. The Yankees ruined her, as they did so much else."

Tilman nodded. "The South invited it."

Portier flushed a dark red and then breathed slowly, letting his air out.

"That is true." he admitted; "But let us talk about something else. To keep the peace."

"Fine by me," Simms said eagerly and pushed his empty plate aside. "What is that tome you are reading, Detective Tilman?"

"Capital. By a German named Karl Marx. Political economy. It's rather dense."

Portier shook his head. "I met him once. Quite a crackpot. A real troublemaker with those wild ideas he has. Like you Transcendentalists, Mister Tilman."

Formality! Tilman thought. *Are we no longer friends?* He stared at the Southerner, who for once seemed to be completely sober, and thought that the matter should be aired now rather than fester. He spoke mildly. "Where was that? The meeting?"

"Paris. What was left of our government landed there. The English were all too anxious to get rid of us because of the Alabama Claims and the fear that Canada might be lost. After I returned from my extended cruise, Judah Benjamin sent me there to help John Slidell pick up the pieces. I studied Law at the Sorbonne. And met Marx there. His theories are the same as yours, theft of other people's property to give to the less deserving."

Seaton looked up from his food. "I'm sorry," he said; "I'm just a dim-witted engineer. Can you explain that?"

Tilman said, "I think he's referring to the fact that Transcendentalists like Emerson and Thoreau began the Abolitionist movement. Mister Pinkerton was also very active."

"Ah," Seaton said. "So the issue was...?"

"The North's hypocrisy," Portier said. "We owned slaves but banks in New York, Boston and Philadelphia lent money on them, and their insurance companies wrote the policies that were part of the deal. Slavery could not persist without them. Slaves were money and credit and cotton was the end product. The English needed cotton for their mills. The South was their plantation. The only reason they backed us was to preserve the supply of cotton. Now they are paying the price."

Simms stared at him, stunned. "I've never heard it put quite that way," he said. He looked away, biting his lip. "What about the land? Did they entail that too?"

"Without slaves to work it, it does not have much value," Portier said. "Worth about ten cents an acre now – if you can find a buyer." He reached into his pocket and produced a cheroot.

"So," Simms said as he produced a match, struck it, reached across the table and lit it, "I could take my winnings, go back to Virginia, and become a man of property."

"How would you farm it?" Seaton asked.

"Not with cotton." Simms looked thoughtful.

"No," Portier said. "Cotton is a peculiar crop. It requires careful management."

"And back-breaking labor," Simms added. "I grew up on a plantation, but that life's not for me." He looked at the burnt match in his hand. "I quit all that."

"We are creatures of the saloon and brothel now," Portier said. He did not seem upset by the notion. Simms stared at him.

"You're a hard man to figure, Mister Portier."

"How is that, Mister Simms?"

"You seem to accept the way things are now, but I see a longing for *quod fuit ante*. And I suspect that if you could turn back the clock, you would."

Portier sighed. "With Alicia – Miss Kate – I certainly would. As for the rest, no. Slavery was the most dreadful trap ever imposed on a people, and I don't mean just your people, but mine as well. They were bound to the land and, despite the lies in *Uncle Tom's Cabin*, content because their lives were ordered and safe. They were employed, sheltered, fed, and petted. They had money. Allowances for buying things they wanted. Money from little side jobs or handicrafts that they could keep. There was a lawsuit about that. Even a Master could not reach into his slave's pocket and take it. It was his alone. And if they had ambition, that way lay freedom. Save enough and buy it!"

"I did," Simms said. "A few could. My master said the worse thing he ever did was to teach me how to play cards. He wept when he handed me the certificate of emancipation."

"Why?" Seaton asked. He was learning something new and listening very carefully.

"Because I was his son as well. He loved me. And I him. He was afraid I would run off up North and join the Yankees."

"And did you?"

"No. He was about to go fight them and they held no attraction for me. They came to save us, they said, but they were ignorant and cruel. Never knew how to even talk to us properly. Called us 'Sambo'. And worse."

Seaton nodded. "I see. So you stuck it out."

"Yes," said Simms. "I became the Overseer and tried to keep it going. The Yankees thought nothing of stealing our animals or using our fence rails for firewood. Ruined the corn we needed to feed our cattle. Like a plague of locusts. I came to quite hate some of them."

Seaton wondered if he should ask his father and uncles about this. If their troops had done such things. He suspected that they had, and would use the war as an excuse.

"Well," he said. "That is most edifying."

"So you would not buy land?" Tilman asked. He closed the heavy book.

"My father liked to pretend that owning a thousand acres made him a man of substance, and lord it over his neighbors, but it was all a lie. The banks owned it. He just managed it for them. He had his horses and his dogs and his mint juleps to ease his pain and the humiliation of being trapped in slavery as well, and we had that peculiar ante-bellum society that produced generations of useless children like myself. It was not until the War that I found my manhood. Until then, it was all vanity and pretense." Portier shook his head. "And if Mister Marx has his way, the State will own all the land and we'll all be slaves. I was in Paris when the Commune of 71 was declared. It was not pretty.

" We had offices there, still trying to figure out the next move for those who still adhere to the Cause. Emperor Napoleon the Third protected us. Then he lost the war with Prussia and was deposed, so we were adrift again. Unwelcome. Strangers in a strange land. Judah sent me to Brazil to talk to their Emperor. Don Pedro has land aplenty, and is willing to welcome us because he wants to produce and export cotton and even import machinery to make cloth. So those who can grow cotton are welcome. Slavery is still legal there. We are recreating the whole rotten system there, complete with all the old manners and customs for those who cannot bear to live under the heel of the Yankee boot. But Don Pedro is no fool. He made us promise to be good. No open Confederate government in exile. No military adventures. He fears the Yankees more than the English do."

"Why would the English fear us?" Seaton asked.

Portier smiled. "Canada."

"Canada?" Simms was surprised. Seaton was likewise dumbfounded.

"The Confederate Navy was the terror of the seas. Commerce raiders. Took and burned hundreds of America ships and whalers. Most of those left, re-flagged so they would not suffer a similar fate, and the English got back the carrying trade and all the income that went with it. Which is why the Confederate Navy was built and based in Liverpool, and crewed almost entirely by sailors from the British Naval Reserve.

"Lincoln had a half a million men under arms when the war ended. It would have been a very simple thing to point them North and take Canada away from them in retribution. Lord Lyons, the British Minister in Washington, was so worried about this that he had a nervous collapse and had to be relieved. This is why the British are paying the Americans fifteen million dollars."

Seaton nodded. "And count themselves lucky. My family owned some of those ships and cargos. We lost a few million." He shrugged. "Easy come, easy go."

Simms laughed. "You are that rich? Millions of dollars gone and you shrug it off?"

Seaton smiled easily. "It's just like poker, Mister Simms. Once the hand is over, you shuffle the cards and deal the next hand. There are more important things in life than money."

Simms laughed again and slapped his knee. "Out of the mouths of babes!"

Portier smiled wistfully. "I thought I was that rich once. The War took it all."

Seaton looked around the room. "Where do you think Molly is?" he asked again.

"Attending to her other lover," Simms said and looked at the expressions on the faces of the others. Seaton and Portier were suddenly angry and Tilman just stared at him, stone-faced.

"Sorry," Simms smiled. "Was it something I said?" He did not want to provoke anyone. The words had just slipped out. And Portier was no stranger to the Demimonde. He was 'a man of the world' and presumed to know 'what's what'. Seaton, on the other hand was learning a new lesson. Those who lived outside the Law, or on its fringes, must be honest. The polite pretenses of social convention had to be discarded.

Portier pulled his flask from a pocket, took a swig, and stepped outside. Simms regarded Derek Seaton kindly. "If I might venture a comment... "

"Oh, do!" Seaton snapped.

"Your problem, young sir, is whether Molly Shannon became a whore because she saw it as a way up, a way to gain money and advantage, and, pardon me, a rich, naive husband, – or because she actually enjoys the work."

Seaton's mouth seemed to be chewing on something. "Say on."

"Well, if the former, then she will always be true to you. There will be no going back. If she has fallen in love with you, so much the better. If it was because she is one who cannot resist those pleasures and strays, then you are better off without her, because she will and laugh in your face for being such a fool."

Tilman nodded. "Judah Benjamin had such a wife. She greatly embarrassed him when he was a Senator in Washington before the war. Such antics, and then she left him to pick up the pieces and ran off to Paris."

"So he divorced her?"

"No. They are married still. I understand he visits her once a year."

Simms pursed his lips. "And people look down on the likes of Molly for just trying to earn an honest living." He took out a deck of cards and shuffled them.

"Something to pass the time?"

"Same game as yesterday?" Seaton asked.

"As you like." He dealt the cards.

Simms consulted his hand, smiled and said, "Do you have any threes?"

"Go fish."

CHAPTER THIRTY-EIGHT

Red Flower lived in two different worlds. In the tribe, she had been a slave, a maiden, an apprentice healer, and a horse thief, and was now the woman of the shaman Little Crow. She would bear his children. This made her very powerful within the tribe; her voice would always be heard.

In town, she was the Mexican, Maria Montoya, whose deep blue eyes contrasted with her dark brown face when she lifted her head far enough for them to be seen. Emily McLean had noticed this only when she and her sister accepted Horse Woman's invitation to share a small cave in a defile near the main camp. Some of the Mexican young men were making noises about seeking them out in the night.

Red Flower said, "We will be safer together." The two detectives, weary from a long day in the saddle, looked at each other and quickly agreed. A small fire was built for warmth and light. An old ceramic bowl marked with triangular patterns of red and black served as a common mess. Into it went corn, beans, and dried beef with a few red peppers. Emily and Molly did not hesitate to dig in, wiping their hands afterward on their trousers. This won them approval from Horse Woman, who noted their practical nature during the journey. During rest breaks, they squatted and did their business like any Apache. Something few White women did.

Red Flower was amused when she finally met Emily's gaze, and was rewarded with a gasp when the Detective saw her eyes and realized she was actually a White girl. Emily bit her lip as she tried to find something to say.

"Who are you?" Emily finally whispered. Molly and Horse Woman were sleeping soundly. "Are you White?"

"Only when I need to be," Red Flower whispered back. "I'm Apache now."

Emily's face showed her confusion.

Red Flower smiled, showing even white teeth. "It's like this," she said. "I was taken in a raid when I was six, but Kicking Horse decided I was too pretty to sell, so I was put to work with other young girls, and had a moccasin ceremony. I was never beaten, and once I was even the Corn Maiden in the spring ceremony. I can read, and my Mex is so good I can walk into a village and become one of them. I scout it and come back, become Apache again, and lead the raid. I'm also a warrior woman."

Emily looked for any sign of deception, and decided that she had been given the unvarnished truth. She could always tell. This was one of the powers that Detectives had. Her sisters and parents had it as well, and Blake Tilman most of all. His unblinking stare extracted information from people very quickly. He had a quick mind, and a powerful memory as well. That was the thing that first attracted her to him. He was so smart.

She looked at Red Flower again. "You never thought of just staying, or running away?"

Red Flower shook her head. "I was the Corn Maiden! I'm Apache now, body and soul."

Emily heard a rustling sound near the mouth of the cave, rolled over and pulled her Colt's revolver from its holster, and said loudly in Mex. "Come any further and I will blow your shit for brains out." She cocked the hammer slowly so the ratcheting metallic sounds could be heard. The rustling resumed but faded quickly away.

Red Flower was shaking with silent laughter. Horse Woman and Molly were now wide awake, staring at her. Horse Woman nodded, and put her head down.

Molly crawled over and said, "Put that thing away before you hurt someone." in English.

Red Flower was still laughing, her hand over her mouth.

Molly pulled her Raymond Railway watch from a vest pocket and squinted at it. "You should get some sleep," she said. "I'll take the next watch."

Emily nodded, feeling fatigue seeping into her now. She started to say something in Mex to Red Flower, who cut her off.

"I heard her," the Apache girl said; "I know English, too,"

Molly looked at Emily. "What were you two talking about?"

"Ask her," Emily yawned, and crawled to her bedroll.

Molly smiled at Red Flower. "Do you mind?"

"Ask me anything."

Molly looked up at the stars visible out of the cave's mouth. "Well, I heard most of it, but there is one thing that bothers me. That place we stopped, with the British people and that wrecked balloon, where was that? Manny and John say it's not on any map."

Red Flower looked away, a bit scared, biting her lip.

"That I do not know," she said after a long moment. "I don't understand it, either. You should ask a Shaman."

. . .

Molly Shannon looked tenderly at Alicia Sorrell's face, relaxed now into a deep sleep. Her mistress was laying on a crude platform heaped with many brightly patterned woolen blankets, naked, as Sophia, eyes closed, passed both hands slowly over her, shaking her head.

"She is strong," she said, "But the wounds are deep."

"Yes,"Molly said. "I can't believe she was so addled as to allow that bastard to brand her. What kind of example does that set for rest of us? Every girl looks for a way to escape the Demimonde. No one wants to keep at it forever."

Sophia turned, her dark wrinkled face impassive. "Why do it then?"

"To escape something far worse," Daisy said, in her Caribbean lilt. "It looks better going in. Men are so easy."

"Until you meet the one that ain't," Delores said. "Then it can be horrid."

Sophia put her hand over the brand mark that Jake Martin had burned into Alicia's hip.

"I have a salve that will make this go away." She looked at the three new witches she'd recruited. "In time, the skin will be as if the branding has never happened. But that will not cure the wound to her spirit. That will take a healing spell, and where do I begin? I don't know... "

"She was born Catholic," Daisy said, "And is marked by the Devil. I know a few things from Santeria liturgy that might work."

Molly Shannon felt a tear run down her cheek. "All those times she came at me with her damned riding crop, as if possessed by the Devil, I always forgave her. I knew that it was not me she hated, but herself – that I was once more standing in for her. Isn't that a daft notion?"

"No," said Sophia; "I think you are right, and that whatever possessed her will have to be cast out."

"So, an exorcism? Will you need the old Catholic priest to perform one?" Delores asked.

Sophia chuckled. "Nothing would delight him more. He would never let me hear the end of it. It would strengthen his hand against us. No, we will find another way."

"Against us?"

"Have you ever heard of the Inquisition?"

Delores shook her head. "No. This is all new to me. Not something my clients speak of."

"It is quiet these days, but still alive, waiting for an opportunity to raise its ugly face. Witches are tortured and burned. The accusation alone is enough. They do not need proof."

Sophia motioned to her niece standing in the shadows.

"We must leave her be, for now. Mercedes will care for her while we begin our work."

The three girls looked around the chamber they were in. It was carved out of stone and lit with oil lamps that burned fitfully, casting moving shadows against the walls.

"Come this way," Sophia said, and led them to a tunnel they had not seen until then, and that Molly thought had not been there the first time she'd looked around the room, giving everything the most careful attention. But the tunnel beckoned, and they followed the old Bruja willingly.

"What if Jake comes looking for her?" asked Daisy.

"He already is. He will not find her. That room does not exist in his world."

"It's hidden that well?"

Sophia led them to a wide, tall chamber carved out of the same stone, with a table in its middle, holding four brown earthenware mugs, and benches where they could sit. She motioned for them to take their places. One of Seamus Corcoran's women entered, with a pitcher of clear cold water, and a brown woven basket with loaves of bread. She placed it in the center of the table and then retreated back the way she'd come.

"Eat and drink. You need strength," Sophia said. "While I tell you why Jake Martin will never find that room." She sprinkled a few grains of fine black sand on the table top, and then laid a piece of thin white chiffon on top.

"What do you see?"

"A piece of cloth?" Molly said.

"Do you see the sand beneath?"

"No. Not really."

"Touch the cloth. Can you feel it?"

All three of them did, nodding.

"So you know it is there, but hidden?"

"Yes."

"Like so much of our Magick. Below the surface. Where your friend is, is like one of those grains of sand: present but not seen.

She will be safe. Jake Martin cannot see her. His power over her cannot penetrate that almost invisible barrier."

Molly Shannon, believing every word of this, felt a great rush of relief.

"Oh, thank the Lord!" she said, and then looked at Sophia. "Am I allowed to say that now?" The old woman smiled kindly.

"The Lord, Jesus Christ, the Great Spirit: it all means the same. That's what White people fail to understand. Many names, one God. 'In my Father's House are many mansions' as Father Tomas says. Jesuits are soldiers for their militant sect. They want to control the world, and have us all sing from their hymnal and no other. This causes a lot of needless bother."

The three women were dazzled. They didn't know what to say.

Sophia picked up the cloth and shook it. A few grains of the black sand were still there. "Imagine," she said, "That a fabric like this, much thinner but very strong, was wrapped around everything in the world, that everything is connected. Everything from the most little insect to the largest animals, to the tallest trees, and that we, as we gain knowledge of our Craft, can sense it all."

"Sounds like a lot of work," Delores laughed nervously.

"No one can see everything at once," Sophia said. "You must not try to do that. You will be overwhelmed and consumed. Eaten alive."

Molly felt scared. Daisy and Delores gasped.

"What do we do, then?"

"Learn your Craft. The spells and chants are guides. They focus the mind. Do the work before you, and learn from that."

Daisy took a piece of bread and bit into it. "Is this connected?"

"Yes. You draw its substance into your body to live. We give thanks for our daily bread, do we not?" Sophia shook her head. "I have more to tell you. Each of you take a mouthful of water. Do not swallow or spit it out. Just listen."

The three of them did so.

Sophia laid the chiffon back down and placed another identical piece on top of it.

"There are other worlds. Many others. Sometimes a grain of sand will go from one to another. That grain of sand can be one person, or an army of thousands. It can be a new disease, like the pox that killed millions of us three hundred years ago. It can be the Strangers with their odd and terrifying machines. We need to make them go back from whence they came."

Sophia laid another piece of chiffon on top of the others, and then another and another, repeating the process until the grains of black sand could no longer be seen at all.

"The problem is, my daughters, where in the infinite number of possible other worlds did they come from? For that, we need the help of the Starmen. You may swallow."

"Who are they?" Delores asked.

"People from the stars who taught us much: how to grow corn, how to weave cloth and work metal, and many other things. How to fly like birds when we must."

"How can they be called?"

Sophia shook her head. "That knowledge has been lost. It was inscribed on golden plates that would last for thousands of years. The Conquistadors stole many of them, and melted them down. And then the diseases they brought killed those few priests who knew the language written on the rest."

Sophia sighed. "We have no way to call them. We barely know where to look for their home. The stars overhead have shifted since they were here. But that is not our quest today."

The other three looked at her expectantly.

"Eat," she said. "You will need your strength." She cast her eyes upward at the flickering shadows. "This will be hard to understand. But think of our world as a single grain of sand on a huge beach, and the home of the Starmen as another grain of sand at the other end of that beach. So far away."

"Why, they'd never get here," Delores said. "How did they manage it before?"

Sophia reached over, took a piece of chiffon and folded it.

"This is how one may go very far very quickly."

"Just like that?" Molly laughed. "It cannot be so easy."

"Oh, it's not," Sophia assured her; "And we no longer know how, thanks to the greedy Conquistadors." She clapped her hands together and wadded the cloth. "Now, go the other direction. Imagine that all the sand is piled together, and going from one grain to another so easily that we barely notice."

The three apprentices nodded.

"Everything is connected, but to get from one particular grain to another, we must find a path. That requires the powers you all have within you. You simply must exercise them, and if you do it together, your powers multiply, and it will go quicker. Your path now is not through the stars but close to us, in the paths used by the trees in the forest to talk among themselves."

Molly thought the whole notion daft, but what did she know? She looked at the other two girls who nodded slowly.

"What are we to do?"

"Jake Martin took some children hostage, to get us to agree to, and go along with, his mad schemes. Before we can rid ourselves of him and his strange guests, we need to find and rescue them."

"Now that I understand," Delores said, tossing her blonde hair and shaking her head. "The rest sounds, well, excuse me, Mother, quite mad. This is simple."

"Yes," said Daisy. "Simple. Keep it simple!"

CHAPTER THIRTY-NINE

After they tired of cards, and Simms made a fresh pot of coffee, they had been quiet, each absorbed in his own thoughts for a time.

Seaton suddenly looked over at Simms. "May I ask you a question, Mister Simms?"

Simms startled, and smiled his usual false brilliant smile. "That depends on the question, and whether or not you want the truth."

That caused Blake Tilman to look up from his reading, suddenly as alert as a hound dog. Maybe things had gotten to the point where honesty prevailed. He watched Derek Seaton lick his lips nervously as he formulated his words.

"Why did you do that? Rush to light Mister Portier's cigar? You did it so quickly and smoothly, that it almost escaped notice, but I think, underneath that smooth veneer you wear, you quite hate that man."

Simms looked a bit stunned. Then he laughed. "No flies on you, are there?"

Seaton smiled, acknowledging the compliment. Tilman was struck with admiration. Seaton was, like a good detective, a close observer. And much smarter than he let on.

Simms sighed, and leaned forward, putting his long elegant hands together to make a church steeple. He choose his words carefully. "It's not him I hate, but the Class he represents: the Slavocracy that held me and mine in bondage so long. He pretends to accept the new facts on the ground, but he and his ilk will fight them to their dying days. Would you not agree, Mister Tilman?"

Tilman nodded. He closed the book and put it aside.

"But you have not answered the question? Why show such immediate unthinking deference?"

The Negro sighed again. He rubbed his forehead and tried to smile.

"Old habits die hard? I was trained to service, and he also expected it. We fell back to our plantation roots. Nothing more. And we are equal, now." Simms grinned sourly at that last.

"You think so?" Seaton looked wide-eyed and innocent, but there was an edge to his voice. "That a piece of paper called The Emancipation Proclamation wiped away more than two hundred years of custom and history? How about you, Mister Tilman? What is the Pinkerton Agency position on this?"

Tilman frowned, and shook his head wearily. "Do not put that on me," he said. "I do not speak for the firm, and I'm not sure I like the new direction we are taking. Too much in service to people like you."

Seaton frowned. "The purpose of business is to make money isn't it?"

"Not entirely. Not while we call ourselves the 'Pinkerton *National* Detective Agency'; there must be some regard for the greater good."

Simms chuckled. "Spoken like a true Transcendentalist. High sounding words, but no more. It encourages people like that Marx fellow, who just want to tear everything down."

Seaton looked at him carefully. "You've read Marx?"

"Just a little here and there, but I know a grift when I see one."

Tilman got up and poured himself a cup of coffee. The conversation was growing very interesting.

Seaton stared at Simms a long moment. "Grift?"

"Slaves were all equal under the law, Mister Seaton, but the house niggers got the best food, and wore new clothes every year. Originally a Master could do as he pleased with one. Sell him, rent him out, whip him, even murder or rape were not out of the question. We were little better than livestock. You cannot do that with a free man. Our defense was to be so useful as to become indispensable. And to always defer and treat them with the affection they craved.

"We have our rights now, and the rule of law. Now Mister Marx proposes to make all men 'equal' in rank and income, except of course for the *intelligentsia*. His version of the house nigger. I can speak with authority on this, having been one myself. Human nature will not admit to such an idealistic arrangement as the one he proposes. Everyone will seek advantage, and a better position."

"Yet the Apaches seem to live that way," Tilman said. "We had a man with the tribe this year and he described it as a very harmonious society."

"Primitive people. Not a fit model for a large industrial political economy," Seaton said. "They are being wiped away. Look what happened to the once proud Comanche nation last year."

"Swept into that 'dustbin of history' Mister Marx describes?" Simms grinned tightly.

Seaton sighed. "I'm not that harsh. I thought it a great waste to kill so many fine horses. Some accommodation could have been made. As much as people like my father and uncles talk about 'Manifest Destiny' and 'the White Man's Burden', they are ignoring the real problem. It was their land before the White Men came, and they will defend it fiercely. Were we in their place, we would do the same with equal savagery. One can't help but admire them for this. This is why I am talking to Black Horse. A deal can be made, and a deal only works if it is fair to all concerned. This is why I am concerned about Mister Portier and his true intentions."

Tilman and Simms stared at him.

"What do you know that I don't?" Tilman asked at last.

Seaton looked upward and to the right, remembering. "I don't 'know' anything. It's something that Molly told me. He was sitting at Miss Kate's bedside, and whispering to her about getting out from our current difficulty. You've heard the phrase 'the South will rise again'?"

Both men nodded.

"Mister Portier is going to New Orleans at the behest of Judah P. Benjamin and the remnants of the old Confederate government."

"He is going to start up that old mess again?" Simms asked. "Didn't they learn anything last time?" His face flushed with suppressed rage.

Seaton shook his head. "Quite a bit actually. It's not that. No one wants another war. But they have a scheme. The old Planter class is to be rehabilitated. There is an election coming up. Everyone is sick of Reconstruction. He is an advance man for someone named Henry Hotze."

Tilman looked puzzled. "Why do I know that name?"

"He was the Editor of something called'"The Index'?"

"Of course. The Confederate paper in London. He was very good at placing favorable stories in other newspapers, even in France. There is a file on him in the Chicago office. We are supposed to keep watch. Let Elmer Washburn know if he comes back. The Secret Service does not take him lightly."

"You Pinkertons do travel in the high cotton," Simms said. "That would be the 'National' part of the title?"

Tilman nodded. "We support President Grant and the Republican Party. Always have."

Seaton sighed. "Portier is supposed to advance the Democratic Party. Buy influence, organize rallies, hire some thugs to break up opposition. But most of all, he is supposed to buy newspapers, so that the news can be slanted, and the Negro made to seem unworthy of his freedom."

"Oh, now!" Simms cried out; "Why do that? Why!"

Seaton looked at him sympathetically. "To get him back on those plantations. To grow cotton. For England and France, so they can make cloth."

Tilman summoned a memory. "Judah Benjamin was always suspected of being in Britain's pocket, even when he was the Junior

Senator from Louisiana. He was born a British subject in the West Indies."

Simms seemed almost on the verge of tears. "And it will work. When the Emancipation Proclamation was announced, my Master... my former Master... said he could no longer support us and hired poor white men to turn us off his land. We did not know where to go! So we begged to return and be as we had been before. A deal was struck, pending the end of the War. And we were happy again." The bitterness in his voice belied his words.

"Really?"

Simms looked down. "No. No, not at all. This is evil! How do we stop him? Stop them?" Tears trickled down his cheeks.

"You can't," Seaton said at last. "It's legal. Protected by the Constitution. Freedom of speech. The only thing you can do is to use the same tools to oppose it. Buy or start a newspaper of your own. Organize your people as best you can."

"And how do I do that?" Simms demanded.

"Ask me after my showdown," Seaton said. "Money is a tool, nothing more. I might back your play."

Simms stared at him, and took a crisp white handkerchief from his pocket so he could wipe away his tears. "Why would you do that?"

"To restore balance. Evil must be opposed," Seaton said. "My family has been blessed with good fortune, so much so, that accumulating more wealth seems meaningless. And we believe that we will be called to account on Judgement Day for what use we make of it. Did we try to better our fellow man once we had enough? Did we lift up the poor or help the sick?"

"There's that 'virtuous cycle' you spoke of again," Tilman said.

"Exactly." Seaton smiled. "If you have a plan, Mister Simms, let me support it. But know that our support comes with the burden of our supervision. Staff will be assigned to assist you. We do not just give money away."

Simms nodded. "No, of course not."

"There is a bright spot in that," Seaton added, a mischievous grin coming over his face.

Simms, wary now, looked him over carefully. "Okay, share the joke."

"We won't ask you to pray to us or for us. That burden we do not impose."

Simms and Tilman laughed until tears came to their eyes.

Later, when Seaton was sleeping, Tilman took Simms aside and spoke in a low voice.

"The key is education," he said; "You cannot advance your people if they cannot read, write, and do simple arithmetic at an early age."

Simms nodded. "Some of us do that now. Despite all the laws against it, some Masters taught their house slaves these things, just to be able to do business. Written notes are a surer form of communication than memory."

"They are also evidence."

"True. But so what? Many laws are never observed nor enforced."

"One of the reasons we Pinkertons sometimes have to work outside the law, if real justice is to be done."

Simms stared at him. "I've met a few of your detectives in the past. Most are not so articulate. You seem to be very well educated yourself."

"I read a lot." Tilman looked away a moment and decided this was not the time to disclose his Doctor of Philosophy diploma. "May I offer some advice?"

"By all means."

"Do not dismiss Mister Seaton's offer of assistance. Rich people with a conscience feel compelled to do such things. There would have been no Underground Railroad without them. You may, as many do, dismiss the Transcendentalists as crackpots, but they founded and financed the Abolitionist movement. Mister Emerson was part of a very wealthy family, and put money behind it. My parents were part of the last link to Canada and freedom. Before the War, when my brothers and I were not harvesting cod, we were carrying escaped slaves to Nova Scotia. Emerson knew wealthy Quakers in Philadelphia, and while they did not approve of some of our other notions, they became the southern terminal of it, and some went to Virginia and bought farms there to extend the line further. Where the law failed, morality prevailed. Frederick Douglass was promoted by them. So was John Brown, until he went too far, and that little book by Harriet Beecher Stowe, most of all. And newspapers were part of it. They founded many in the South. Smart people knew what was going on. Every political faction has a newspaper. Some of those Abolitionist papers had their offices burned or blown up. Their editors had to run for their lives or get lynched."

Tilman looked at Simms carefully. "How White are you?"

"My mother was High Yellow. One eighth. I am half of that."

"A sixteenth. You could pass for White."

Simms frowned and shook his head. "I do not care to do that. Having been brought up Black, it would strain my soul to change over now. No, sir, I will stay as I am. I just need to set up someplace where my color don't matter all that much."

"Ever been to El Paso?"

The Negro looked surprised. "Not to live. Pass through now and then, but, as that cracker says, I am a creature of the saloon, the gambling hell and the brothel. Looks pretty though. What's it like?"

"Mixed. Very mixed, and hundreds of years old. Pinkerton's sons see it as a place with great possibilities. They are also Transcendentalists, at least in spirit. Big election next year. A newspaper could be very profitable."

Simms stared at him. "I never knew this. About the Pinkertons, I mean."

"Most people don't. It is not something we advertise, especially when the Pinkerton Agency is on a new course to serve the Money Power. His sons are in charge now, and more than a little greedy."

"Why?"

Tilman shrugged. "Allan had a stroke, and now just dictates his memoirs. They sell very well. I never heard him use 'Sambo' to describe a Negro back in the day, so I am sure that was something added by his publisher. He hired his first Black detective in 1858."

Simms leaned back, absorbing this, thoughtful.

"To my main point," Tilman resumed; "Do not turn away from well meaning Whites out of pride. They died by the thousands to free you. Become worthy of those sacrifices."

Simms nodded. "You mean this is not a grift?"

"Not this time," Tilman assured him.

. . .

Molly McLean smelled frying bacon and was instantly awake. There were tendrils from some vine touching her face, caressing it as gently as a lover.

She began to sit up, only to encounter the green mat that Red Flower had woven the night before from grass so that she and Emily could conceal themselves in a slight depression in the prairie. It was done quickly. It weighed almost nothing but hid them from the young Mexican men who'd been so annoying. This time, there was no nearby cave.

"I think it likes you," Emily whispered from her place next to her. "I'm quite jealous."

Molly looked and saw that the tendrils had sprouted three leaves. "Just a passing fancy," she said, "A flirtation." Carefully she pushed the mat aside and looked around.

"Where is Red Flower?" she asked.

"She got up a few minutes before. Perhaps for a call of nature?"

"I am here," Red Flower said. "You White girls are so lazy. It's almost time to leave. You can see the Morning Star." She was a few feet away, sitting on her haunches, sharpening a small knife with a whetstone. She barely turned her head when she spoke. Her beautiful smile and ease of posture showed her simple enjoyment of the world around her.

Emily and Molly sat up together and dragged the mat to the side. Both had pains that they were careful to conceal from Red

Flower, who retained a White girl's ability to tease with cutting remarks. They looked around. The camp was beginning to wake up. Molly peeled the amorous tendril from her face, laid it on the ground and gave it a reassuring pat.

"Some other time," she said, rolled over, and got to her feet. Emily did the same.

"Put the cover back," Red Flower said. "It can be used again."

Emily looked around at the flat plain with its endless sea of grass.

"How will you ever find it again?" she asked. She dragged the woven grasses back into place. They blended in almost perfectly.

Red Flower tapped her head with her right forefinger. "I will remember. Apaches remember everything. Especially from the Earth Mother."

Emily and Molly looked down at their clothes, which were damp and had streaks of dirt on them. They brushed some of that away.

"It will dry," Red Flower said; "And the wind will take it away."

A groan attracted their attention. It came from a bundle on the ground that seemed to be a young Mexican *Federale*. He was bound hand and foot with a gag in his mouth.

The two Pinkerton detectives looked at him, very surprised, and then at Red Flower, who shrugged. There was a hint of amusement in her clear dark blue eyes. She reached down and lifted him to his feet with one smooth motion, further surprising the sisters. He was much taller and weighed more. She was very strong, as one must be when dealing with horses.

"Another unwelcome suitor," Red Flower said. "I have been telling him in great detail how Apache women treat prisoners, how we use the most delicate tortures and keep someone alive, and in great pain, for days on end until they beg to be killed. Which we never do."

Emily and Molly stared at her, mouths open.

Red Flower smiled. "Why spoil the fun?"

She reached down with the bone-handled knife and cut the rawhide strips that bound the young Mexican's ankles with one smooth motion.

"Walk," she said, and the young man stumbled forward, trying to lift his head up high. Red Flower and the two detectives walked a bit behind him.

"What are you going to do with him?"

"Return him to his master. Captain D'Silva is not a kind man. I suspect he will get a beating in front of the others, but that's nothing compared to the humiliation he will suffer from the other men. Even *Los Negroes* will shun him." Red Flower shook her head. "I should have just killed him. It would have been kinder, but I do not need my face on a wanted poster, nor a bounty on my head. Maybe the others will take the lesson and leave us alone, so we can get on with the work."

Emily and Molly both realized that, while Red Flower had been born White, she was now pure Apache. She had the religious intensity of a convert. They would have to warn Kate. They could not imagine their rambunctious little sister accepting the role of a junior wife, if that was her plan. But was it? Kate was learning things taught in no other school. They hoped that would be enough.

"What did the Earth Mother tell you?" asked Red Flower.

She was looking at Molly.

"What do you mean?"

Red Flower sighed. "She touched you in the night. That's what the plant was for. Did you dream?"

Molly felt very confused. "The plant? What do you... "

"You think that was an accident? It is a message." Red Flower looked at her scornfully. "I thought you girls were *Brujas*."

"We are White Witches," Emily replied.

"Of course, *bruja blancas*. Very powerful. You should understand this touching."

Emily and Molly looked at each other, feeling helpless. "We're city girls. This is all new to us."

Red Flower shook her head. "We must do something about this. Lone Eagle says we are facing great evil from some Other World. If you can't see the magic, then you are useless to us."

Molly started to say something, but felt Emily lay a hand on her arm.

This is not the time, her sister said in her mind. *This is new. We have much to learn.*

Molly didn't know which surprised her more: that Emily could speak to her that way without actually speaking, or that she was the cooler head of them both at that moment.

"All right," she said aloud, and tried to recall her dreams from the night before. "One thing."

"Yes?"

"There is another Molly mixed up in this and she's no *Bruja*."

"No?"

"From the old country. Some kind of Druid."

. . .

Molly Shannon woke from her dream feeling very small indeed. She was laying in a bed of moss under a huge Live Oak. Her shift had ridden up, exposing her legs and buttocks, but rather than being exposed, she found that she was covered in green vines that had sprouted leaves to preserve her modesty. Something she had never cared about before, since it had no utility in a whore's life, but now wished to reclaim. The night before, she was given a potion to drink, and it caused dreams that awakened her to the true nature of the world.

Delores had asked a question the night before.

"Should we not be in a sacred grove to practice magic? There was a *nemetom* near the village I grew up in. Until the Catholic priests found it and set it afire."

"Why did they do that?" Daisy asked, her dark skin glistening with sweat. The three of them, along with Mercedes and other women from the town, were sitting in a sweat lodge. It was dark. What light there was came from the glowing coals of the fire. Steam rose from hot rocks in the center of the circle they had arranged themselves in. A purification rite that encompassed them in the soft chanting of the other women.

"Hate. No other word for it. They tried to burn it with us still there, without warning."

"How did you escape?" Molly asked.

"Sometimes witches do fly, even in the Lowlands."

Later, Sophia led them out of the underground into a meadow. There were a few trees at its edge. The three young women drank more of the potion, feeling it suffuse every part of their bodies. Molly felt the world itself waver, shimmering slightly. Sophia stepped into the middle of the field, spread her brown withered arms, and said, "Here is your grove. Everything is sacred to the Earth Mother. Find someplace to lay down, and she will inform you."

Molly held out her hands and the other two girls clasped them as they walked across the tall grass to find some soft place to lay under the trees. The sky lost its glow from the horizon, and millions of stars appeared overhead. She gasped at their beauty, and realized how very, very far away each one was, and that rather than being small points of light, that each was also a fiery sun casting off light. That her own planet was merely a speck of dust in the cosmos. Then she fell asleep, and her dream turned to her surroundings, feeling not just nearby woodland creatures, but the grasses and trees, and even the rocks that could be seen here and there in the field. Each of them was also a creature! And even smaller forms, invisible to her eye, were creatures, too, above and under the earth. That they did not live solitary lives, but were a boisterous community, constantly in conversation with one another – and that the forest that held this collective was also a creature – as was the entire planet. She recalled Walt Whitman's line about containing multitudes, and examined her own body, faintly surprised at all the creatures that resided therein. Such understanding daunted her. What was she to do with such immense knowledge? How would she remember it all?

But rather than being alarmed or overcome, she remembered an old General named Marcy, who was a client in New York when she was new to the Demimonde, and part of Annie Jones's stable, and who, like Derek Seaton, was a great talker. He'd once spent the better part of an hour with her one morning, going on about maps and how important accurate ones were in any military campaign.

He was too tired to perform his part of the business, and simply admired her naked form, laying sideways on the rumpled bed as he smoked his pipe and looked downward with regret at failure once more. She basked in the glow of his admiration, and gave herself audible pleasure so that his pride was saved, and his incapacity hidden from the other patrons of that house. It was a simple act of kindness.

"You have to know the ground you're fighting on," he said. "Or you will be lost, and the battle, too." She folded all of her new knowledge into herself, like a set of maps. In the forest one did not look at the trees above the ground but under it, at the roots where most of the conversation took place. And they were quick, those paths. As fast as any telegraph. They led everywhere a plant could go. A wise witch could use them for conversations as well. She felt humbled by knowing this.

After she emerged from her cocoon of greenery, and, with the other two, made her way back to Sophia's hut and had some breakfast, she suddenly smiled.

"I think I know where the children are."

The other two gasped, understanding.

Daisy stood in the center of the room and spun around, pointing her left arm as she stopped. "There. That way!" She froze in place like a statue.

"Yes!" Delores shouted. She laughed with glee, and clapped her hands together.

Sophia stared at them, and then beckoned to Mercedes. "Go find Black Horse. We need mounts and a map." The Indian girl slipped out of the room.

Molly Shannon felt quite pleased with herself, and then thought of Alicia Sorrell.

"My Mistress? How does she fare?"

Sophia smiled. "She will be fine. And she's no longer your Mistress. You are a free woman, now."

Molly Shannon knew this to be true, and felt both sad and elated at the same time.

"Poor Miss Kate. What will become of her?"

Delores and Daisy stared, their eyes hard. No love lost there.

Molly lifted her chin. "She is still my friend. I came to this life on my own. She protected me from the worst of it, until we came here, and still is."

"How do you make that out?" Delores demanded.

"I'm still alive. So are you. No one has made a stew of us, have they?"

"Not yet," Daisy said. "Not yet."

Molly Shannon suddenly realized that she now had a much better opinion of herself. She was no longer a 'whore' or a 'dirty whore' or a 'bitch', but a young woman of substance, who had great power. She was now worthy to be the wife – not the mistress, but the wife – of a man like Derek Seaton.

Did he really love her, or was it just a game? And if he really married her, did any of that matter, as long as she was safe? That was something to ponder.

CHAPTER FORTY

Captain Pershing and Captain D'Silva took a walk together around the camp, checking on the sentries. As they walked, they were careful to observe everything. D'Silva looked upward at the stars. Pershing followed his gaze. There were only a few wisps of clouds, and the air was so dry that even the nighttime sounds came faintly to their ears. Pershing lifted his canteen to his lips to moisten his dry throat. Still, his voice was scratchy and weak.

"Doesn't look right, does it? he asked.

"No," the Mexican officer sighed. "I'm an old campaigner, John. Usually I can look up, find the Big Dipper and the North Star, and know where I am within a mile or so. But this is not a sky I know. So where the Devil are we?"

"And how did we let two young girls talk us into this?"

The two looked at each other.

"Maybe they really are Brujas?"

"I don't believe in such superstition," Pershing said. "I have a warrant to do secret service, and so do the Pinkertons."

"And they are Pinkertons. Fully vetted as detectives. I had it checked."

"Did you? You didn't think that Harry McLean was just an overly indulgent father?"

"What father puts his children at such risk? It's insanity."

"I asked him about that," the American Captain said. "He told me that they are anything but children. Women fully grown, and capable of making their own decisions, and way in the world. By giving them employment, he keeps them close for a while longer. Classic Transcendentalism. Women also have rights."

D'Silva stared at him, indignant. His voice cracked, "A very dangerous idea. Where will that lead?"

"Women having minds of their own?"

"And being wild and out of control!"

"Are they out of control? They seem to be running this show. Even Bill Pinkerton gives them deference."

D'Silva rubbed his forehead. "I can't have a wife like that."

Pershing chuckled. "Did you really think you had a chance? That either of us did?"

D'Silva groaned, "But she took me to that grove behind her house. We were intimate."

"She took me there, too. How intimate?"

"A gentleman would not say."

"You are no gentleman. Neither am I. We are soldiers. We protect the innocent. None of the McLean girls, even little Kate, meet that description."

"You're very cool about this."

Pershing shrugged. "I accepted her on her own terms, and stayed friends. She'd have to be crazy in love with me to accept the hard life of an Army wife on the frontier. She's not. End of story. But answer the question. How intimate?"

"She showed me her breasts."

"Magnificent, aren't they?"

"Yes. Yes they are."

"But she didn't let you touch them or fondle them, or see anything below the waist."

"No." D'Silva sighed; "I was quite annoyed."

"One way to put it. Me, I had to go look up that girl Rosalita from the café."

"I have other resources."

"You admit to two mistresses, and God knows how many others you have in your *remuda*. That is an obvious non-starter for Molly. Whoever she decides on will owe her complete loyalty."

"What about you? You seem willing."

"She said that I'm already married to the Army. And she's not wrong about that. I intend on being a General someday, and that's not easy, when you start out leading Black troops. So we left it at that."

"But we're still under her spell, aren't we?"

"I can't officially endorse such superstition, but that does seem to be the way of it."

The two of them walked on a bit, quietly, each lost in his own reverie.

"What about Emily? What are my chances there?"

"Oh, Manny, that ship sailed long ago. She's decided on Blake Tilman."

"But he's more than twice her age. Far too old for her."

"Really Manny, who decides these things? Even in conventional society, it is not uncommon back East. This is the Frontier, a very different *milieu*, and we are dealing with Transcendentalists, who defy convention. She doesn't think he's too old, and there's an end to it. She's taken, and I would not annoy Mister Tilman. He's a killer."

"With all those books? He always seemed rather soft to me."

"Another Transcendentalist. Looks are deceiving. He's killed a lot of bad men. And she knows it. They are very tough people underneath, and do not play by our rules."

Manny D'Silva sighed. "If I do not make some arrangement soon, it will be made for me. My mother wishes me to return to Mexico City for the 'Season,' where she will trot out a number of promising candidates, all vapid Catholic ingenues with great domestic skills and absolutely no conversation. Molly, for all her wildness, held the promise of being very interesting. I will be bored to tears with the alternative – so much so that I will probably leave her there, and return to the Frontier. That will not help me politically. A man who is not seen in the circles of power soon becomes invisible. I would retire a Captain."

Pershing shook his head. "My Army shuns politics now. We saw the evil of that as we fought each other to a standstill in the

Civil War. Killed off the politicians who wanted to play soldier, or drove them from the field in disgrace. Now we have a professional Army, the equal of any in the World."

Manny chuckled. "You really think that War is over? That the South has been crushed?"

Pershing, slightly alarmed, turned and looked at him. "Don't you? What have you heard?"

"Come now, *compadre*. We both do secret service. Spying and scouting are part of frontier life. The Pinkertons are not in El Paso because there are railroads there. There are none yet. They are part of that Chicago gang that runs the Republican Party, and they seek to operate in Mexico as a kind of transnational police force. But it's all about the money now, so what was the old Confederate government is now buying its way back in. Starting in New York City, with the Copperhead faction, the 12th Confederate state."

Pershing stared at him. "Is this just your theory, or do you have facts to support it?"

"A White Paper shared by the British minister in Mexico City, except that he does not realize we've seen and copied it. We still have a lot of French officials left over from the Maximilian government. They have friends. Governments come and go, but the spies remain and keep in touch with each other. Information is currency. You should know that."

Pershing shook his head. "I'm just a simple calvary officer. This is way over my head."

"Oh, please," Manny D'Silva groaned.

"Truly. I have no idea what you are talking about."

"So what I've just told you will not occasion a long letter to Elmer Washburn?"

"I didn't say that."

"Good. Good. I was beginning to fear that I was wasting my time. You should look to your men. There will be an effort to return their kind to bondage."

"Won't work. There have always been free Negroes. Now there are millions. All free."

As they completed their tour of the camp, they came upon Kicking Horse and Lone Eagle. The sun was just at the horizon, and the first rays illuminated their figures. Something about their stance and absolute stillness directed their gaze towards the nearby creek.

There, Red Flower and the McLean sisters were standing knee deep in the flowing water, arms stretched out towards the sunrise. They were naked. Pershing felt he should avert his eyes, but could not. Such a vision of feminine beauty had never met his gaze before. Manny D'Silva was equally frozen in place. Then all three women slowly lowered their arms and fell backward into the creek, suddenly splashing and laughing.

"People don't bathe where you come from?" Lone Eagle asked drily.

The two Captains suddenly turned in confusion, and stared at him.

"Well, yes, of course," Pershing stammered.

"I've often wondered about that," Lone Eagle said. "You Whites seem to be a particularly dirty lot. Not cleaning yourselves for days, even weeks, on end."

"And Apaches do better?"

"We do. As often as we can. Water is plentiful if you don't mind the cold, and there are also sweat lodges."

Manny turned his head back towards the creek, and saw that all three women were now dressed and walking back to the camp. They were chatting gaily. Suddenly just like girls, rather than Brujas. He looked at Lone Eagle and saw a glint of humor in his eyes.

"Did we interrupt something?"

Lone Eagle nodded, and Kicking Horse said something in a language neither Captain knew. "It is customary to welcome the Earth Mother's companion as the day begins. Brings good fortune. So look to your men. This is a religious ceremony and must br respected."

The two Captains looked at each other.

"Absolutely," they said together. Then they went to supervise the breaking of the camp.

An hour later, with fires drowned or buried, gear loaded, calls of nature taken, the entire party was mounted and moving. The McLean girls let their hair dry naturally, combed it out, and put it up in buns at the back of their necks. They had hats against the sun, and rode easily in between Cavalry and the *Federales*.

Bill Pinkerton, having gotten better control of his horse, fell in besides them. The Apache known as Horse Woman had seen his difficulty controlling his mount, said a few words to it, and calmed it. Then ridden off at some speed, controlling her own horse without reins or saddle, just the pressure of her knees. He shook his head at the memory. He was so green, with so much to learn about Frontier life. But his own mustang was more agreeable now, and his cousins, his Detectives, took note.

"*Hola*, Cousin," said Emily; "How do you fare?"

"I'm very well. You look quite refreshed, both of you."

Molly laughed. "Did you use that telescope to get a closer look?"

"Briefly. Quite handsome, but it struck me as religious in nature, and not something to gawk at. And there was a scramble amongst the *Federales* to find field glasses. Since neither of the Captains were nearby I took it upon myself to quiet them."

"And how did you do that?" Molly asked.

"The cocking lever of a Winchester makes a lot of sound in the clear morning air. They looked around and saw mine pointed in their direction. I really didn't have to say anything more. They all found other things to do. Silly bastards think I'm your lover. Both of you."

Molly and Emily looked at one another. "Really?"

"Such arrangements are common here on the Frontier," Bill said; "Or so I am told."

"I'm sure Mary will be quite amused."

Bill Pinkerton flushed bright red, and looked alarmed. "Oh, dear God. Don't say anything about that to her. She's already jealous enough."

"Of us? Whatever for?"

Both girls looked at him, a pretense of total innocence on their faces.

"Of the freedom you have. The badges and revolvers are one thing, but the attitudes really set her off."

"Hmmph" Emily sniffed; "Just jealous."

"As I said," Bill Pinkerton sighed. "I'm trying to get her to loosen up. But she still has her mother's voice in her head."

Emily and Molly looked at each other. "Well, Boss, what can we do about that?"

"You could be kinder."

"We could," Molly said. "We'll try harder."

"What was that ceremony about, anyway?"

"Connecting to nature. A bit like 'Walden's Pond'. Red Flower was showing us the Apache ceremony, and we were showing her ours. Much alike in most respects."

"We feel more connected to the life force: the Goddess or Great Spirit. So you are right, it was religious." Emily looked around. The peace of their worship followed by the cold shock of the water had energized her, made her more alert and sensitive to her surroundings. She looked across the sea of brown and green grasses that stretched for miles in either direction, and waved her arm in an all-encompassing motion.

"Look at that, Bill. What do you see?"

He tried to follow her gaze. "Not much," he confessed. "Looks pretty desolate."

"There you have it wrong, Bill," Molly said. "There is life there; rambunctious life, an entire community of plants, animals, insects, and other things, all connected. The Apaches and other tribes know this, and cherish it, taking only what they need. Jim Frazer learned this, and recorded it. But he said there are tidal forces in history. And those have been against Nature for hundreds of years. Whites are a plague on this land, worse than the pox or the Black Death. Greed, the piling up of wealth, and Devil take the hindmost, are another. Makes you wonder if we are working for the right people."

Bill looked over and saw the teasing expression on her face. There was also a tide at work within the Pinkerton National Detective Agency that he did not like, but that was best left unsaid. He had learned to swim in the cold waters of Lake Michigan, an inland sea with tides of its own. You had to swim with the tide, not resist it. Otherwise, you would drown. None of them were old enough to change anything, still in their teens, and still on perpetual probation.

He decided then and there that none of the McLean sisters' adventures with Magick would be reported. Either it would not be believed, or it would, and they would all be fired. That would profit no one. So he added a caution.

"Don't tell Mary about that. She'll make a fuss about Pagans and Devil Worship."

"How boring of her," Molly said. "And I don't feel like explaining it to anyone. Much less her." She spurred her horse and rode ahead to find Pershing.

Bill and Emily watched her go. They looked at each other.

"There's one other thing we can do," Emily said after a moment.

Bill Pinkerton said, "And that is?"

"Show her. We can take her to a ceremony, and see if she can feel the life force herself."

Bill shook his head. "That's not likely." It came to him that Mary was essentially a scared little girl trying to escape the mental prison of her upbringing. That she hated the McLean girls because they had something she didn't have. He'd been able to unlock one door on that prison through their lovemaking. Perhaps ... "Let me think about it," he said.

"A matter for further investigation?" Emily asked, and thought about Blake Tilman for the first time that day. What would he make of her now?

. . .

Blake Tilman spared no thought for her that morning. His client seemed ready for the hard day ahead, but his partner was in a sullen mode, nipping at his flask.

Portier looked up from the table at him and said, "Have no fear. I'll be ready."

Derek Seaton, surprised, looked at him sideways, now slightly alarmed. He started to speak, but saw Tilman's slight shake of the head.

"It's just the nerve of that tinhorn, accusing me of hiding her and then lying about it."

"Molly said she's well hid, and won't say where. He threatened her and she just laughed in his face. Miss Kate is not available. And that's that."

Derek Seaton shook his head. "She seems different somehow."

Tilman spoke slowly. "Women in that life depend on each other for aid and comfort. Maybe Miss Kate finally broke down. Putting her back together will take time. Leave that to her ladies. You have no credit with them where she is concerned, Ash. You abandoned her."

Portier nodded slowly. "God forgive me, I did. But Jake Martin brought her into this life, and should be even more repugnant to them." He frowned, and looked at his two Remington .44-40 revolvers once more. They were to be left behind, so that he could focus on the Winchester in his hands.

"Jake Martin is only alive because he owes them money from that big safe in his office. They think him quite mad," Simms said. He was sitting in the corner of the open area between the cells. He was wondering if Tilman would ask him to join them in saving Seaton from what seemed like an inevitable death. He intended to decline that spurious honor. Seaton had made him some big promises, but those were just words, and he'd seen young Masters try their courage before. Some things a young man must do for himself. As for Seaton's odds of success? He didn't take sucker bets.

But all that Tilman said to him was, "Is everything arranged?"

Simms had spent much of the previous evening disbursing small payments from Seaton's stash of cash, with the promise of more to come. His first trial as a Pinkerton. And while he held no faith in honor among thieves, he had a high regard for detectives like Tilman. Having spent years sizing up men at card tables, he had great confidence in Tilman's character. Portier, on the other hand, he knew to be a rascal. A wild card, if there ever was one.

"I've done the best I could," Simms said.

Seaton smiled at him. Tilman just nodded, and continued to look carefully at his erstwhile partner. Portier held his hands out before him to show their steadiness. Tilman picked up his Winchester, and handed Seaton Portier's beautiful, elaborately decorated, single shot Sharp's rifle.

"Load up" he said.

The young man dropped the block to reveal the chamber and slipped in the long metal cartridge. Tilman had cut a shallow cross in the tip of the lead bullet. "When it hits, you will have four bullets instead of one and all the energy will be absorbed by the target rather than travel through. It will be devastating."

"If I hit the target."

"See it in your mind, like a trigonometry problem. Control your breathing. Slow and steady. Aim low to compensate for the recoil," Tilman said softly.

Seaton stood up, took the rest of the cartridges in hand, and dropped them in his left coat pocket. "Will Molly be there?"

"I don't know," Tilman said. "Don't think about her. Don't think about anything but killing your opponent. Focus only on that."

Portier also stood up. He felt a brief moment of panic; a feeling that it was all about to go horribly wrong. He looked at Tilman, who'd also seen the horrors of war, and saw only resolve there. Strength drawn from within, not from the bottle. But it mattered not. The moment was upon them.

"All right," Seaton said; "Let's go."

· · ·

The rescue party was still far away, fighting its way through a dust storm. Everyone had wrapped scarves around their faces to keep out the fine grit that blew at them, and goggles helped a little. They were dismounted and leading their mounts, who also had scarves over their eyes and whinnied in protest at the harsh conditions.

Emily McLean wondered if it was all in vain? Would they be in time?

Suddenly, the wind stopped. So quickly that the absence of its roar made them all think they'd gone deaf. Everyone stopped to shake off the dust, and to take a mouthful – and no more – of water. The wetness cleared their throats so they could speak.

Molly McLean pumped her right arm up and down, the same gesture that the Captains used to signal their men for attention. Curious, the two officers rode over to see what she wanted. Lone Eagle also rode to her, while Emily and Bill Pinkerton looked at each other, both curious and slightly alarmed.

Molly looked at each of them, licked her lips nervously, and said, "You are going to think me quite mad, but we have to divide the party. I suddenly know something that we must do."

No one spoke. She had their full attention.

"There are children being held hostage in a cave. They are being used against the people of that town. I've seen where they are. We must rescue them to break the spell."

Manny D'Silva started to laugh, then stopped when he saw that Pershing and the others took her quite seriously.

Lone Eagle asked gravely, "You had a vision?"

"More like a seeing. It was not a trance, but something sent to me by the other Molly."

"And she is?"

"Another witch. Very like me. A Druid, not a Bruja, but she has great power."

Manny D'Silva felt his mouth fall open, and an electric thrill of fear course down his spine. He looked around again, suspecting he was being made victim to an elaborate prank, but saw that everyone else simply nodded, especially Pershing, whom he knew to be a serious and responsible officer, not given to playing pranks.

"What are we to do?" Pershing asked.

"I can find the place. I know it in my mind, but there are gunmen. The children have not been harmed. In fact they all seem to be sleeping."

Pershing said, "My men are a superstitious lot. They may balk at anything to do with witchcraft. And we are supposedly in Mexico, where we have no right to be."

Manny saw the way that Molly McLean was looking at him, and knew that if he was ever to have a chance with her, he had to go along with this madness. So he swallowed his doubt and said, "Kidnappings are a police matter and *Federales* are military police. So we will go. I will need two scouts."

Lone Eagle made a gesture and Red Flower rode quickly up.

"Two Brujas are better than one," he said. "I will go ahead. Bring my horse."

Red Flower nodded. Lone Eagle suddenly disappeared, and everyone looked up to see a large Bald Eagle floating above, and then digging its wings into the air to go higher and catch the wind that would carry it further. Manny D'Silva and John Pershing, thunderstruck with amazement, just stared. Bill Pinkerton followed their gaze.

"I have it on good authority," he said drily; "That all Apache witches can fly." He turned to Emily. "What about you?"

Emily shook her head. "Not part of our craft," she said.

Molly snapped her fingers to get Manny's attention. "Let's go, Captain."

Manny realized that he was in charge, and owed no one an explanation, and that his written report of the expedition would be very different than the facts. He sighed, crossed himself, and said, "Yes, of course," and called his men to rally to him.

John Pershing rode to reconfigure the line of march, putting half of his men in the advance. Bill Pinkerton looked at Emily McLean.

"So you can't fly?"

"No. I don't know. I've never tried, and haven't the first idea of how to go about it."

Bill nodded. "Well this is becoming quite an adventure. Thank you for including me."

Emily smiled, shook her head, and then said, "We, too, must make haste. Our detectives are also in terrible danger."

By which she meant Blake Tilman, the cold remote man twice her age she had given her heart to. He didn't understand that, but there was so much that he didn't understand and might never. That was all right. From his first days in the Chicago office, he had been told to be silent and apprehend everything about him, as good detectives should. This was no different. Watch and learn.

Little Crow rode up to speak with Pershing. Seeing Pinkerton, he put his right forefinger next to his long nose; the Pinkerton Agency signal for silence. Pinkerton did likewise, as a kind of salute. Soon they rode on, making haste now, with Emily next to John Pershing in the lead.

CHAPTER FORTY-ONE

Black Horse sent fifteen braves out to the hacienda before dawn. Five to throw the Greek fire bombs, and ten to deal with the Strangers and any gunman who decided to resist the burning of the place. Jake Martin had not troubled to buy the land, nor get permission, before erecting the enclosed courtyard where the Stranger's sky wagon sat most days. That made him a squatter, and the tribe was well within its rights, even under the White Man's law, to remove him and remove the illegal building.

Mr. Portier, who had studied law in Paris and knew the Code Napoleon, which was still operative in Mexico, told him as much.

What to do about the missing children was another matter. One that troubled him no end, but Mother Sophia assured him that they had been found, and would soon be rescued by a Pinkerton detective and a dozen *Federales*. When he asked Tilman and Portier about this, they had no explanation. Tilman looked thoughtful, and unconsciously place his hand over his heart where, in an inner coat pocket, he kept the letter from Emily McLean. She was also a Pinkerton, but too junior to organize a rescue party, even if they had some means of communication. Her father was still the Branch Manager, but it was Molly McLean, not her sister, that Manny D'Silva was courting. Was it possible that she was also involved? Tilman turned it all over in his mind, came up with no resolution, and put it aside, clearing his mind for the day ahead. He had enough to worry about.

A young brave, Grey Squirrel, who was about twelve and known for his stealth, was sent to find Parker Boone, and slip him a note that read, *Leave now. Your life depends upon it.* It was left to Boone whether or not to say anything to the other gunmen.

Boone was not very smart, but he knew caution from his years behind bars. And because it had fallen to him to take food and water there, he knew where the town's missing children were being held: at another ranch house two miles away, guarded by three gunmen who had children of their own. Even Jake Martin was not so depraved, nor stupid enough to harm a child. His men would not abide that. Parker reported them all in good health, playing simple games, such as Duck, Duck, Goose, and sleeping a great deal because of some powder added to their food.

Parker, although wood-wise, and moving as cautiously as he could, never sensed the presence of Red Flower until she tripped him, and put the razor sharp edge of her bone-handled knife to the side of his neck. His containers of food were splayed out around him, and Red Flower had her other hand twisted in his long greasy hair. She was sitting on his back.

"Please," he said in a whisper; "Don't kill me. I've done nothing wrong."

"I doubt that."

Parker looked up to see a young White woman, in trousers and a workman's brown coat and hat, squat in front of him. He saw the shiny brass badge she was wearing, and recognized it at once. All of the breath went out of him, and he began to weep.

"Oh my God. I've never been so glad to see the Law in my life! Did Blake Tilman send you?"

Molly motioned to Red Flower, who stood up and sheathed her knife, and then reached down, lifting Parker Boone to his feet. This amazed him, since she was much smaller than he, and did it with one hand under his left arm.

"Blake? No. We came for the children." Molly stared at him, a little disgusted.

"Get a grip, man. Tell me who you are."

"Parker Boone, fugitive, and I surrender. Who are you?"

"Detective Molly McLean."

"You're a Pinkerton? But you're a young girl."

"Not that young. Save the surrender for later. Where are those kids? Are they safe?"

Parker Boone quailed at the look in her eyes. "Oh yes, of course. These are bad men, but none of them would hurt a child."

"Scaring them half to death doesn't count?"

"We never did that. Treated them like our own."

Molly looked at Red Flower, who shrugged. That might be true. Molly McLean looked at Boone carefully, and saw only a very frightened man. She made a signal with her hand. Parker watched, amazed, as several *Federales* emerged from the thick woods behind her, moving silently. They were led by a young Captain. He smiled at Boone, and put an arm around his shoulders.

"We will be *compadres*, no?" he said softly.

"God, I hope so," Boone whispered, his mouth so dry he could feel his tongue swelling up. He looked at Manny D'Silva, who smiled encouragingly.

"Draw us a map," he said; "Where the house is, and the ground around it. What it looks like inside: how the rooms are laid out."

Parker Boone knelt down, picked up a short stick of deadwood and began to sketch. He explained it all, as he went along. When he was done, he looked up and summoned the remains of his courage.

"You don't have to kill anyone, you know?"

Molly McLean regarded him coldly. "What makes you think we are going to do that?"

Red Flower took out her knife and tested its edge with her thumb.

Parker Boone, eyes wide, nodded in her direction. He quailed when she looked at him with her unblinking deep blue eyes.

"Her. Just looking at her makes me ready to piss my pants. What is she? Apache? Mex? I never saw an Indian with blue eyes before." He stopped to draw breath, as Red Flower put a finger to her lips. He was talking too loud.

"We ain't really part of Jake Martin's outfit any more. Told him we could not abide his friends and quit. He said that we'd been hired for the 'season', whatever that meant but if we did this with the kids, we didn't have to be gunmen. It wasn't a hard choice, once we figured out that the hunting party was killing people, not game, and eating what they killed. Disgusting!"

Red Flower shook her head. "You Whites are so squeamish."

"Let me go in and talk to them," Parker said, as his eyes went to her and saw how pretty she was, and how cruel. That alone unnerved him. "I can tell them the game's up, and get them to come out peacefully."

"And the kids?"

"We can send them out first."

He watched hopefully as the young female detective whispered in the Captain's ear. After a bit he nodded.

"All right, Mister Boone, your offer of assistance is accepted. But if any of the children are harmed, we will not take you to answer in a Mexican Court, but hand you over to *los Apaches.*"

Parker Boone looked at Red Flower and saw no mercy there. They would be killed very slowly. He looked to Molly McLean and saw that her face was like a stone idol. The Captain was looking down at the crude sketches he'd made in the sandy brown soil, memorizing them.

"Well," Boone said slowly; "I'd better get it done." He gathered the containers of food and started to walk slowly towards the dilapidated old ranch house again. When he looked back, he saw no one behind him, but he knew they were there.

Derek Seaton felt very calm. He was holding Portier's Sharp's buffalo rifle.

"It may be too much gun," Tilman warned.

"As quick as they are, I won't get a second shot, so I'll take this one and make it a good one. Or die trying."

"You'll be fine," Portier said. "If you hit him anyplace, the shock will kill him."

"That's what I was thinking," Seaton said.

"Great minds run in the same channels," Tilman said. They all laughed. From the way that the detectives looked at each other, Seaton was sure there was a plot of some kind that he was not privy to. But that was okay. He had enough on his mind.

"Doctor Johnson once said that 'when a man knows he is to be hanged in a fortnight, it concentrates his mind wonderfully'," Seaton said quietly. He reached inside his pocket. "I have some letters. I will trust you to see to their delivery if... should this go against me."

Tilman took them and put them aside. "Certainly. My honor."

"And don't let them eat me."

Portier said, "It's time," and the three of them, rifles in hand, went out the door and walked slowly to the main street.

Seaton, never a sentimentalist, thought that his surroundings looked particularly beautiful, as if he were walking in the midst of a fine painting. He took a deep breath and felt particularly calm. If Death was waiting for him, so be it.

Now dressed as 'Jesus', Black Horse watched the stagecoach roll in, that Jake Martin used to transport the Strangers to town. It was very crowded, and held ten of them on top and inside the coach. All dressed in the cheap black suits, boiled white shirts, and black string ties Martin kept for them to play at being lawmen. The lone gunman who drove the coach, watched them disembark, spit a stream of tobacco juice to one side, snapped the reins hard, and drove the rig toward the livery stable.

The ten Strangers milled around, talking noisily in the language that no one else understood. A dust devil whirled down the street and left a fine coat of brown dust on the Strangers' coats. Jake Martin stepped out on the veranda, dressed in a better black suit, and pulled his pocket watch out. He checked the time.

On the level above, Miss Kate's girls crowded the windows, anxious. Molly Shannon was standing still, not moving at all. She took heed of Mother Sophia's soft words that morning. "You cannot save him. Don't even try. Your powers are not meant to alter Fate, and for his own sake he must face this trial alone, as all young men of the tribe must. Failure is death, but cheat death and you face disgrace. Only with such trials can our race survive and grow stronger."

So while her heart ached for Derek Seaton, she knew that Sophia was right. Only in this way would the boy become a man. She must leave him be. Still, it was hard.

The mayor called out, "It's almost time, Marshal. Where is the prisoner?"

"On his way," Jesus shouted back; "Under escort by the detectives."

Martin tapped his foot impatiently. A short gust of wind nearly knocked him off his feet. The gunmen who still worked for him filtered out of the double front door of the bar, and the wind blew harder. Townspeople filtered in from the alleys on either side of the hotel.

"Are you really going to go through with this?" Jesus shouted.

"I have no choice. They want vengeance." Martin looked over to where one of the Strangers was examining a Winchester rifle and working the action. He seemed disgusted with his guests and himself.

"At least you don't pretend it's justice," Jesus said. He looked down at Tilman's Raymond Railroad watch, saw that it was nine a.m.

He raised his hand, and Derek Seaton, with a detective on either side of him, walked slowly from the end of the street toward the hotel. They all carried rifles.

"Only one of them!" One of the Strangers shouted. Was it Sheriff Johnson? They were all named Johnson. He looked for the one with the badge. It was not the one with the rifle.

"We are acting as Seconds under Code Duello. He is entitled to an even chance. We're here to make sure it stays that way," Tilman shouted back. "There are ten of you. About an even match."

Portier laughed, while the Strangers huddled together trying to understand Tilman's brag and the whole idea of 'Seconds'.

The wind increased. Jesus looked at the watch in his hand again. If all went as planned, the Greek fire bombs were being thrown into the hacienda courtyard at that very moment, and the Apache women were rescuing the children, after quietly slaughtering their guards. In the high wind the flames from the Greek fire should spread very quickly. But he couldn't think about that now.

"All right. Mister Seaton will stand at that end of the street, and Mister Johnson at the other. Your places are marked. When I drop the watch, you may fire at will." He snapped the cover shut and held it out.

Tilman and Portier watched the other Strangers for any hint of movement. Some drops of rain fell, making marks in the dust. Seaton felt the wind at his back blowing harder now, and saw the Stranger was trying to blink away the dust in his eyes. It was hard to hear anything.

"What?" he shouted.

"You first," the Stranger taunted. "Take your best shot."

"All right," Seaton replied. He made as if to raise the Sharp's to his shoulder, but pulled the trigger when he had it at waist level, and aimed at his opponent's genitals. The rifle recoil jerked it out of his hands and sent it flying sideways; the explosion echoed so loudly that all of the other Strangers, and some of the people watching, clapped their hands over their ears. He was sure his shot had gone wild, but his opponent fell slowly forward, the top of his head gone.

Seaton picked up the Sharp's and dropped the block for a reload, but the fired cartridge was too hot to touch.

Portier and Tilman faced the other gunmen down. They were in shock. One drew and fired at Portier, missing him.

Tilman shot him in the groin. This produced a high-pitched keening sound that caused the other Strangers to clap their hands over their ears, dropping their Colt's revolvers.

Another shot came from behind him. The sharp bark of a pistol, but neither Seaton nor Portier had one with them.

"Are you all right, Ash?" Tilman asked, looking around while keeping his rifle trained on the Strangers. They were raising their hands slowly in surrender. One dead and one wounded was all they could take, it seemed.

"I don't think so, Pard," Portier said, and then fell face forward into the dusty street.

Alarmed, Tilman handed Seaton his Winchester.

"Cover me," he said. Seaton dropped the elegant but now useless Sharp's in the street, worked the lever on the Winchester to be sure there was a live round in the chamber, and watched as Tilman went to his fallen partner.

Portier had a small round hole in the back of his head, blood matting his carefully combed hair as it trickled out of the wound. Tilman sighed and turned him over to see the Southerner's eyes staring upward, blank, as his life drained away.

He suppressed the rage he immediately felt, and drew the Remington revolver on his right hip. Turning, he saw Jake Martin, a mean little smile of satisfaction on his face, with his own revolver, a Colt's, in his hand, the barrel smoking. Somehow he had gotten behind them. How? He'd been on the veranda just a few seconds before.

Behind Martin stood Simms, with a Winchester. He tapped Martin on the shoulder. When Martin turned and started to cock the hammer again, Simms knocked him to the ground and kicked the revolver away.

Tilman nodded. "Marshal?" he called.

"Sir?"

"We have a complex crime scene here. Can you get some help? I want all the witnesses held for questioning."

"I'll try," Jesus looked about wildly. Jake Martin's men might try to rescue him, if only because he still owed them money. He spotted Butch Plover and Billy Bonney.

"Butch!" he called, "I need you to be a deputy again. Your friend, too."

Butch shook his head.

"Hey, I'm stuck. For the tribe."

Plover sighed. "Okay, then. Where do you want us?"

"I ain't no kind of Law," Billy whined.

"Shut up, and do as you're told," Butch said.

"Yes, sir," Billy replied, looking up once more at the roof of the feed store, where he could see Jeremiah Morgan retreating, his new Sharp's carbine in his hands. No one followed his gaze, and he turned his head quickly, to keep from giving his friend away. There were secrets that even Billy Bonney could keep. This one he resolved to take to his grave.

Tilman was standing over the wounded Stranger. Plover came over to help. He looked down and saw something in the Stranger's hand. He stepped over to Tilman and handed him the object he had found. "What do you make of this?"

Tilman felt it. "Kind of a soft rock. Soft outside. Hard inside. I've never seen anything like it. Mister Seaton?"

Seaton, still dazed, and not sure he was not in some afterlife dream, started. "What is it?"

"Come look at this thing that Mister Plover found."

Seaton walked over and took it from Tilman's hand. He examined it carefully and then held it to his ear. Shaking his head, he said, "No idea. It's manufactured, but I'd say it's not of this world."

Jesus joined them. He looked at the object and shrugged. Seamus Corcoran walked up with two of his men.

"Told you I should have measured earlier," he said. "What are your arrangements?"

Tilman stared at him, unable to comprehend for a moment. Then he nodded.

"You can't move him yet," he said with a calm he did not feel. "There are some measurements I must make." He turned to Seaton. "Will you assist me, Derek?"

Seaton nodded gravely. "I'd be honored."

Tilman nodded, fighting back emotions he had not felt in a long time.

"What will you need?' Seaton asked.

"Nothing much. A long surveyor's chain, and a pole about six feet tall. The rest is geometry and sketching."

"No doubt about the cause of death is there?" Corcoran asked.

"It's not the cause but the manner that concerns me," Tilman said, and beckoned Simms to come closer.

"Hand the prisoner over to the Marshal."

Simms, did so. Jesus took a still stunned Jake Martin off towards the jail.

"Let me see your revolver," Tilman said. Simms, amused, handed it over.

"You think I would shoot a man in the back?"

"You have a lot to learn about being a detective. I do that all the time, and you had a certain animus towards the deceased."

He took Simms' weapon and examined it, discharging the cartridges. There were five, all unfired. Tilman handed them and the empty revolver back. Simms, looking at him warily, began to reload.

Tilman sighed. "I'm now a man short, J.C. Here is your chance to become a Pinkerton. Help Mister Seaton and me measure the crime scene as your first lesson in the craft. You may take Mister Portier's badge and wear it. Also his revolvers, which will serve you far better than that ladies' gun you have now. Those are also company property, as is the Winchester. It's probationary, of course."

Just then Molly Shannon came up and hugged Derek Seaton fiercely.

"I was so scared and I am so proud of you," she said. She whispered in his ear. He looked momentarily delighted, and then frowned. "Not now. I have work to do."

"Oh," Molly said, "Well, excuse me!" But from the sway of her hips as she walked away, he knew she was not really displeased.

Then he looked at Tilman and saw the gleam of approval in his eye, and felt that he'd passed some kind of test, one far better than besting or killing a man in combat. Simms was also smiling at him and then shrugged.

Seaton, now a free man, walked back to the jail to retrieve his surveying kit. As he walked, he look about, admiring the town, and wondered what it would be like to live in such a place. Would Molly be happy here? Would he? And did that matter when he had responsibilities in Chicago? He felt no remorse over the Stranger's death. It had been a game, a deadly one he'd been forced to play, and he wondered what madness made Jake Martin throw away all he had gained to kill his rival for a whore's affections. Not that he was one to talk. He'd risked his own life to make Molly Shannon proud, and now she was his. How was he going to tell that to his mother? What fictive tale could he devise that she would not see through at once? Better to tell the truth, and let her worry about what was told to the Public. But what would Molly say? Did she truly love him, or was she simply, as the detectives suggested, looking for a way out of the Life?

He got his gear and returned to the main street, passing several of the Strangers under escort by Butch Plover, and some of the other roughs towards the jail. They looked around curiously, unsure of what was happening. This was not part of the experience they had been promised.

Seaton and Simms worked with Tilman, who made measurements and drew a fairly accurate picture of the street and the murder scene in two and three dimensions. Seaton, who had learned mechanical drawing as an engineer, marveled at his skill and ability to do so in freehand, without tools. Tilman's face showed his complete attention to the task. Seamus Corcoran was finally allowed to remove the bodies.

A column of riders appeared at the far end of the street. *Federales*, and eight of them carried a small child in the crook of an arm, speaking softly to them in Spanish. The children, all less than four years old, looked around sleepily, understanding where they were. A great cry went up, and people from the town who had hidden themselves in fear for so many weeks, were crying and crowding around the horsemen, reaching up to retrieve the little ones.

Behind them came another set of riders, and Tilman suddenly felt the charm around his neck grow warm. He handed the sketch pad to Simms, and turned to see that the lead riders in that column were the McLean sisters, Bill Pinkerton, and Captain John Pershing. Emily McLean spurred her horse and rode up until she was next to him. She looked down and gave him a relieved smile. Her face was flushed under its new tan, and beads of sweat were on her long graceful neck and her forehead. He thought she looked very beautiful.

"Mister Tilman. Are you well?"

"I am very well. What are you doing here?"

"I got this silly notion that you and Mister Portier were in trouble, so I organized a rescue party."

The notion stunned Tilman, and set many questions racing through his mind. How had she known? How had she convinced the others?

"Of course, it's officially on Mister Seaton's account. His mother gave us *carte blanche* to find him and get him back home to Chicago."

Seaton, who was close enough to hear this, groaned.

"Hello, Mister Seaton," Emily said cheerfully; "I thought that might be you. I'm Detective Emily McLean, and I'm so pleased to see that you are all right."

Seaton waved at her weakly.

"Where is Mister Portier?" Emily asked.

Tilman shook his head. "Murdered. We are working the case right now. The colored gentleman is Mister Simms, whom I have hired, on probation, as his replacement. It's a long and very complicated tale."

"Then help me off this horse, and save that for Bill Pinkerton, who came with us because he wanted to experience the field. Got more than he bargained for by a country mile."

Tilman reached and put both hands on her waist, and lifted her from the saddle as her arms went around his neck, and she planted a long passionate kiss on his mouth. The scent of her instantly aroused him, and he could not help but respond in kind. He was very aware that people were watching. There were whistles and cat-calls from some of the *Federales*. He was also aware of the heat from her body. Tthe scent of her was mixed with sage and lavender.

Finally, he broke it off, and looked over to see Bill Pinkerton, Manny D'Silva, and John Pershing, all looking at them with ill-concealed amusement.

Emily whispered in his ear, "Everybody knows, Blake. Seems some secrets cannot be kept." She smiled and kissed him again. Blake Tilman felt tremendous relief wash over him. He would no longer be alone.

"Did I hear you correctly?" Bill Pinkerton called; "Portier is dead?"

Tilman looked at him carefully, a man much younger than he, but with much more authority because he was Allan Pinkerton's grandson. He was anything here but a tourist. A vetted Detective with years of experience, and there was nothing arrogant nor prideful in his expression, just distress at the loss of a brother operative. So Tilman broke free of Emily, stood apart and nodded respectfully.

"Yes, sir. Shot in the back by a jealous rival for the love of a woman."

Pinkerton whistled softly. He dismounted, and walked over, stopping to shake hands with Seaton, and looking at Simms, who was holding one end of the surveyor's chain.

"Excuse me, sir. Who are you?"

"Julius Caesar Simms," the Negro looked back at him carefully, sizing him up.

"I've just hired him as Mister Portier's replacement," Tilman said.

"Have you? That was fast."

"Exigent circumstances. I had no idea you were coming."

"It's a long and complicated story," Derek Seaton said; "But the Pinkerton service has been extraordinary."

Bill Pinkerton looked around. "Ours is also quite a tale. I will take statements tonight. In the meantime, what is left to be done here?"

"Witness statements. And we have some unusual prisoners."

Pinkerton turned to Emily and said, "It seems you were right, Detective. We were needed. Frankly, I had my doubts."

Emily smiled. She took Tilman's arm.

"If you will excuse me, sir, I want to take conference with Mister Tilman for a few moments." Tilman looked at her, feeling something bloom within him that he'd thought lost forever. The adoration in her eyes was like an balm to his heart.

Bill Pinkerton laughed. "Take all the time you need, but I expect to be invited to the wedding."

Emily blushed. "Must there be a wedding? I was so looking forward to being a shameless hussy for awhile."

"As a Pinkerton girl, you already were that. Up to you, but Chicago will expect it. We're a big company now. Thanks to Grandfather's books, we have a public image to nurture. One of sterling rectitude."

Emily looked up at Blake Tilman. "I have not been asked yet."

Tilman laughed. "I have to ask? So far this has been like a Sadie Hawkins Day dance. You've been very bold."

Emily frowned. "Have I? Perhaps, but I had to get your attention."

"You have it now."

"And?"

"Yes, of course. But we have work to do, first."

Emily smiled happily. "Yes, sir." She took his hand and led him away.

Pinkerton looked around. "Mister Simms. What is left to do here?"

"Nothing, sir."

"Then let us go examine the bodies." Simms walked with him down the street towards Seamus Corcoran's shed, talking quietly, trying to make a good impression, and wondering how much he could tell without compromising Tilman. Pinkerton looked young, but had the air of an exceptional man, the kind he'd seen read Law and lead cavalry raids when he was growing up, rather than waste themselves with drink and women. Derek Seaton was still earning his maturity. Bill Pinkerton already had his.

CHAPTER FORTY-TWO

Ashley Portier was laid out in a large side room. When Derek Seaton and the two detectives arrived, they were ushered in by one of Corcoran's male assistants. It was noticeably cooler in that room, and the ambience was much more formal than the exterior shed. The room was lined with dark wood paneling. Religious paintings hung on the wall. Father Tomas was bending over the body, administering last rites. Candles cast a soft light.

"So he was a Catholic?" asked Bill Pinkerton.

"From New Orleans with a Cajun name? Not a hard guess," Tilman said.

Seamus Corcoran looked up from his work. "Found a cross in his pocket on a chain with a Star of David and a Masonic doo-dad."

"A man of many allegiances, then," Bill Pinkerton said.

"Or none at all," Tilman murmured.

"He was a true Son of the South," Alicia Sorrell said from the doorway.

They all turned and saw her standing there, as erect and stiff as a statue, already dressed in black widow's weeds, that clung tightly to her lush body.

She always knows how to attire herself for every occasion, Tilman thought. Her face was pale and drawn, as if she was recovering from a long illness. Molly Shannon and another of her girls, whose name he did not know, stood on either side of her.

"And that, Blake Tilman, is all you need to know. All any of you need to know. I would like him buried under that flag."

Corcoran looked surprised, then mystified. "Excuse me, your ladyship. Are you his next of kin? By what right…"

"He and I were engaged before the war," Alicia said; "And he came here to find me and rescue me from… whatever I am now. A romantic, foolish gesture, I grant you, but he fell as a soldier in its cause even to the end."

"Blake, is that true?" Bill Pinkerton asked.

"It seems so, Mister Pinkerton," Tilman replied. "I say so on information and belief. He may have signed on with us to conceal his true allegiance to the so-called Confederate Government in Exile. He admitted to me that he sailed on *The Alabama* and *The Shenandoah* both, so there's paper on him somewhere. Wanted for treason and piracy. I was going to discharge him when we got Mister Seaton safe home."

Out of the corner of his eye, he could see Seaton bridle slightly at the notion that he needed such care, recent events notwithstanding. Others edged into the little chapel to hear more: the McLean sisters and Simms, who now wore Portier's Pinkerton badge.

"You weren't going to arrest him?" Simms asked, an edge in his voice.

"Just him and me, J.C. Why would I do that? The whole situation is very problematical. I had no idea that the cavalry was coming, and still have not sussed out exactly what is going on here. Despite his deficits, I had confidence in his loyalty to the task."

"Well you had that right," Alicia said. "He rather liked you, and said that no man of honor would desert a friend in need, so he would have to play out the hand here first. Said Mister Seaton was very likeable for a damnyankee callow rich boy. Was pretty sure you were all going to die out there." She looked around with red-rimmed eyes, staring. "So which of you betrayed him? Shot him in the back?" Her gaze fell on Simms. "Was it you, J.C.?"

Simms shook his head slowly. "You know me. I'm a lover, not a fighter." He stared back at her, wondering if she had a weapon someplace on her. She looked half-mad to him.

"It was Jake Martin. He was driven mad by jealousy," Tilman said.

Alicia laughed bitterly. "Of course. He made enough fuss, trying to find me. Upset the whole town, didn't he? And for what? The most infamous whore in New York and New Orleans? To what end?"

She walked slowly, alone, to where Portier's body lay. "Ashley loved me once, in the most romantic way possible. He would read old poems to me, and write new ones himself about how beautiful and innocent I was back then. I was just sixteen. But he became a man of the world and a habitué of the Demimonde himself. So my transformation held no surprises for him. None at all. And while he said he loved me still, he was quite intent on dragging me and my ladies into secret service work, not just for his Lost Cause, but the British and the French as well. Sorry, says I, but I signed the Oath of Allegiance, and I may be a whore, but I'm an honest one."

She looked over to Tilman who was listening to every word. "I trust you will put all that into a letter to Elmer Washburn?"

Tilman just nodded. Alicia Sorrell leaned slightly and placed one hand on Portier's chest, and then bowed to place a kiss on his forehead. "Farewell, my love. It would have been better to never have met again but..." She left the thought unfinished, turned and walked back to where Molly Shannon and the other girl waited. "Where is Jake Martin? I have a few words to say to him."

The three of them went out the door together. Simms followed. Molly and Emily McLean looked at Bill Pinkerton. "So, Boss. What do we do now?"

"Witness statements. If you can find any, and they've not all gone to ground."

Seamus Corcoran cleared his throat. "One of my wives will help with that, sir. Make the proper introductions."

Bill stared at him just a moment, and then said very smoothly, "Thank you. Very kind of you."

"I presume that Pinkerton's will foot the bills for the burial and plot?"

"Miss Kate might claim that privilege," Tilman said.

A young Mexican woman appeared at the door. Corcoran motioned to her. She immediately went to the McLean sisters, smiling, and took one of each of their hands in hers. Emily and Molly went out the door with her to try and find witnesses.

"Mister Pinkerton," said Seamus Corcoran; "You are being very thorough, I see. Perhaps too much so."

Pinkerton blinked. "Why do you say that?"

"We're not much for formalities here. Really too small to garner notice from outsiders, and we like it that way."

Tilman looked up from the little table where Portier's effects were laid out. "With all due respect, that neglect is how you fell into this dilemma in the first place," He said. He picked up Portier's notebook and examined it carefully. It had several pockets holding papers. He spread them out. Some of them were blank.

Seaton watched him feel and then smell one of the sheets. "Damn near got me killed," he remarked without heat. "What are you doing?"

"Looking for treasure." Tilman held the paper up to the light and then near one of the candles. The flame flickered as he held it closer and brown writing appeared. He passed the sheet back and forth until it was all revealed.

Seaton's mouth fell open in amazement. "How did you know?" he asked, his voice high from excitement.

Tilman handed the message to him. "Feel that corner there? There are five pinholes you can barely see."

Seaton did so and nodded. He stared at the brown letters.

"What does it say? I can't make it out."

"That's because its in code," Bill Pinkerton said. He took the sheet of paper and looked at it closely. "Or it could be a cipher."

"Why did you sniff it?' Seaton asked.

"Secret ink is usually one of three things: egg white, lemon juice, or piss. Once I smelled that, I knew it concealed something important."

Bill Pinkerton tried not to show how impressed he was. He still had so much to learn.

"So how do we crack the code?" Seaton asked eagerly.

"We don't. Not now. That could be the work of days or even months."

Tilman put the paper aside and went to work on the other pages. The candle's warmth soon revealed five more coded messages. He nodded with satisfaction as he felt the corners for pinholes. "It's a letter of some kind. The number of pinholes give it an order."

Father Tomas approached cautiously. "May I?' he asked, and held out his hand for the pages.

Tilman handed them over. The priest looked at them, murmuring to himself, and then said shyly, "Codes and ciphers are a hobby of mine. This looks like something done with a Vigenère table. Not hard to crack if you can find the key. I have some books in the parsonage..."

"Could I help?' Seaton asked. Tilman looked at him, and saw that he was unwilling to let Portier's papers out of sight. A sentiment he agreed with. The man was a Jesuit, and therefore a soldier and probable spy for the Pope.

"That's all math, right? Decoding something? Mister Seaton is an engineer by trade. I am sure he can be helpful. How much mathematics do you know?"

"Trigonometry and calculus were my best subjects," Seaton said, looking at the old priest like a young boy anxious for approval.

"Well, then of course," Father Tomas said. "Come along."

Seaton gathered up the papers as the priest walked towards the door. "Let me know," the priest said to Corcoran; "When you want me to officiate at the detective's funeral."

Seaton caught up with him just outside the door, and those still inside could hear Father Tomas say, "Perhaps the *Señor* would like to discuss with me the deplorable state of our church's roof... "

Corcoran chuckled, "He already got Jake Martin to pay for a new roof. You should catch wise your client."

Pinkerton started to say something, but Tilman held up his hand.

"Mister Seaton needs no advice from us. I've gotten to know him over these past days and, with the exception of a certain redhead, he seems to be a man of sound judgement."

Corcoran chuckled again. "Any young man has the right to be a fool for love at least once. And Molly Shannon seems equally smitten. Talks of giving up her life in the Demimonde. Fool asked her to marry him."

Bill Pinkerton, very surprised, turned to Tilman. "How could you let that happen?"

"Jesus H. Christ, Bill! He's a client! I didn't take him to raise! The whole thing was a forgone conclusion when Ash and I got here. She wasn't even charging him anymore."

"True. All true," Corcoran agreed, a sardonic grin on his face; "But he was looking at being shot down and killed, so that might have made him less cautious. They was like a couple of rabbits." He looked around. "I got a couple of things to attend to. Can you stay with him a few minutes?"

"Of course," Tilman said. He watched Corcoran exit and then turned to Bill Pinkerton. There's another thing."

Bill Pinkerton looked at him warily. "What now?"

"When Harry McLean hired him to partner with me on this journey, he said he signed on because he'd lost all of his money at the tables. He'd beaten another gambler nearly to death for cheating, and while that kind of thing passes for Justice in less formal towns like El Paso, there was the possibility of payback from his victim's friends. He wanted the protection of a Pinkerton badge."

"I can see why. But why hire him?"

"We needed someone. And I thought he was basically a good man underneath all that glamour he wore. 'Give him a try,' I said. I was restless and wanted to get back to real work. So some of it is on me. I did, while he was sleeping, search his saddlebags for any surprises, and got a big one: a million dollars in Bills of Exchange."

Bill Pinkerton gaped, shook his head, and looked over at Ashley Portier's body. "Why hide them? He could buy a small army for that. From us."

"Naturally, I thought about that," Tilman said. "I stayed quiet to see what would happen. Sometimes you just have to let the hand play out. When he found that his long-lost love was now Kate Singleton, the most famous madame in New York and New Orleans, rather than Alicia Sorrell, it broke his heart, and to win her back he told her things he should not have. That's Confederate Government money, Bill, intended to buy newspapers and politicians to sway the next election so that the South can rise again, not as an armed force but as a civil one, to overthrow Reconstruction."

Bill Pinkerton sighed. "Politicians come cheap these days. Buy them by the dozen, if you like. President Grant is a good man, but hardly the master of his own house. Sick, maybe even dying, so the whole thing's gotten away from him. I'm sure that Mister Seaton can give you chapter and verse. His family are big reformers, but the tide is running against them."

"And us? What about us? Are we in the pockets of the Money Power now?"

"So it would seem. Dad and Uncle Rob have stars in their eyes... or maybe it's just dollar signs... about all the opportunities out there. They are no longer particular. And I know that it goes against our Transcendentalist roots, but, dammit, Blake, someone has to do that work! Why not us? Maybe we can keep it all from becoming an open sewer of vice and corruption."

Blake Tilman looked at young Bill Pinkerton for a long time. Not yet nineteen, and still determined to do good in the world. Maybe there was hope yet.

"What happens to those Bills of Exchange?"

Tilman considered carefully. "Well, they do not go to New Orleans. And we can't assume they are Confederate money and just hand them over to Elmer Washburn. Seizure is a legal process that requires evidence we do not have. Doubt if Adams Express would handle them. Derek Seaton could, and has already promised to assist Mister Simms with any projects he might undertake for the Negro race. But no matter where they go, they are going to be a stone in the shoe for someone."

"Maybe we should just burn them?"

Tilman laughed. "An expensive bonfire. Unfortunately, that won't destroy the money they represent. It just sits in that London bank ready to do more evil."

"Let's hope Mister Seaton and the *Padre* can crack that code."

Tilman brushed away some of the flies that were beginning to gather on Portier's body. "We need to find him a better resting place than Boot Hill," he said. "He does not deserve to lay among criminals."

Bill Pinkerton nodded. Privately he thought Boot Hill very appropriate, but was not prepared to debate the issue. The manner of death was very important to those of Tilman's generation. They obsessed about it. Honor the fallen. So, with wisdom beyond his years, he simply said, "Let's ask that *Padre*. A generous contribution... "

"Yes, of course."

At the jail, Alicia Sorrell walked in to find Butch Plover, wearing a Deputy's badge on his vest, in charge. He looked at her, his steady gaze an inquiry.

"What do you want?" His tone was not friendly.

"I want to see that bastard who shot Ashley Portier in the back, and killed him."

Plover, being a Regulator, wanted to observe the regulations.

"You seem to be upset, Miss Kate. Do you intend to do the prisoner harm?"

"I want him dead. But I'll let the Court decide his fate," she said, staring back at him, her eyes wild. He tried to find an excuse so he could send her away.

"You don't have a knife or a gun on you do you?"

"No. Would you like to search me? Run those big rough hands all over my body?" She grinned at him sardonically. Plover flushed bright red. He was a Deacon, and not someone who thought lustful thoughts about anyone other than his wife before he met Daisy.

"No," he stammered. "I couldn't do that."

"You rubes. You don't know what you're missing. But let me show you." And with that, Miss Kate slowly unbuttoned her black dress and pulled it over her head. She had nothing on underneath, and stood there like a statue, in only her boots. She turned slowly around. "Do you see any weapons, sir?"

Plover looked away, as embarrassed as he had ever been. "All right. Put your clothes back on."

"I don't think I will," she said. "Take me to Jake Martin. I want him to see me like this. So he thinks about what he lost. I have a purpose." Then she took a moment to read Plover. He was genuinely embarrassed by her nudity.

"Do you act this way with Daisy? Like a little girl?"

"That's different. It's Bible study."

"Bible study?"

"The Song of Solomon. She is the Queen of Sheba. We act out the parts. 'Thou art Black but comely'," Plover said. And he was dead serious, she saw.

She looked around the dingy office, spotted the sign over the jail door, and laughed. "Abandon all hope! How appropriate. This is hell, *n'est pas*?" She folded her dress over her left arm and walked over to the door. So as to not lose all authority, Plover rushed over, and opened it for her. She smiled politely.

"Thank you, Butch." She walked further to see Strangers crowded against the bars of one of the cells, and Jake Martin sitting alone in the one opposite, downcast and miserable.

"Look at me, sir!" she said in an imperious voice. His head slowly rose and she saw he was very confused. "It is I, Jake. The woman you enslaved and branded. Look at me, you miserable worm! You poor excuse for a human being!" She handed her dress to Plover, who took it and averted his eyes once more.

Alicia Sorrell turned slowly around, giving Martin a full view and thrust her right hip in his direction.

"It's gone, Jake. The mark you burned into me that you thought would bind me to you for life. The old witch woman took it away. So your crime was for naught. You killed Ashley for nothing. I wasn't going with him, either. Why, as I am now, would I enslave myself to any man? You fool. You nothing. You no-account bum."

She retrieved her black dress from Plover's hands, and shrugged back into it.

Jake Martin broke down and wept.

The Strangers took all this in avidly, almost ecstatic to the point of drunkenness.

She ignored them. "Help me with the buttons, Butch. I won't tell anyone."

As he did so, she looked at Jake Martin again, and then spit in his direction.

"When are you going to hang this fool?"

Plover finally looked at her. "Have to try him first."

"Why? Everybody knows what he did."

"It's the law. Try him, fair and square. Then hang him."

She looked at him curiously. "I hear you are not so particular on the range, with that fancy rifle of yours. How many have you killed from ambush?"

Plover shrugged. "That's a horse of a different color. There I am smiting the evildoers, like an Angel of the Lord."

It was not a joke, she saw. He was a madman under his pose of decency. For the first time, she feared him. Fanatics might do anything. Logic did not enter into their decisions.

So she smiled politely and left him there.

Molly Shannon left it to the other girls from Miss Kate's stable to attend to her needs, while she went to view Ashley Portier's body. Having cared for him in his drunken state, she felt a small measure of responsibility for his death, as if she had failed him in some way.

He had been kind to her, despite her open intimacy with Alicia Sorrell. Or was it Miss Kate? She was two very different women in the same body. And the intimacy was merely part of a whore's bag of tricks, rather than something she sought – a refuge from the brutality of the male sex that had been her lot before she met Derek Seaton. Someone had trained that boy well. Act like a whore, and you'll be treated like one, Miss Kate said, and used her own refinement and high manners as an example.

She had tried, but her body's affection for the act itself too often defeated her. That was another secret of the Demimonde: most whores did not like sex. How could you with a dozen or more clients a day? It was just hard work with a lot of acting.

Derek had taken his time with her, and rather skillfully shown her a true path to pleasure. And wanted to make her his. But what did she want? Really want, now that she'd been shown her true nature, and given these new powers?

She sensed a presence. She turned and saw two young women standing a little distance away, dressed in men's clothing, with suntanned faces, wearing gunbelts and big Remington revolvers, and each with a brass badge that was engraved 'Pinkerton National Detective Agency'. The taller one smiled at her and said, "Hello, Molly. I'm Molly, too."

Molly Shannon nodded, and smiled, "I know you, don't I? From the dream, or whatever that was, I'd know you anywhere." She looked curiously at the other young woman who held out her hand.

"I'm Emily McLean. Her sister."

"And you are both detectives?"

Emily and Molly McLean nodded together. With badges and guns, what else could they be? Then Molly McLean leaned forward. "And we are also like you. We're White Witches," she whispered.

Molly Shannon was taken considerably aback. How would they know that, when she was so new to the Craft? Was the change in her demeanor that obvious?

"Be easy. We only came here to rescue our fellow detectives," Emily said; "And Mister Seaton, whose family is paying for it all."

Molly Shannon thought, *so my Derek spoke true when he told everyone how rich and powerful they are.* She smiled at the McLean sisters. "Then you know Detective Tilman?"

"Quite well. We are to be married." Emily smiled modestly, looking slightly away.

Well, that's bold, Molly Shannon thought. *He must be twice her age, but she's anything but a silly young girl. Tough as nails under that sweet expression. And her sister, who I've only just met, but feel I've known all my life, likewise. Smart girls, too, and they have powers.*

"You must meet Mother Sophia."

"Who is she?"

"Our local healer. A leader in the Community."

"A Bruja?"

Molly Shannon nodded.

The McLean sisters looked at each other. "They say we're Brujas, too."

"*Bruja Blanca.* White Witches," Emily added.

Molly Shannon smiled. "We have a Druid and a Santeria. And local girls from the tribes."

Emily turned to her sister, and said, "Red Flower said that our journey did not end here,"

Both Mollys nodded together.

"This is all so new to me," Molly Shannon confessed. "I was called to it by Sophia. I'm very green."

"So are we," the other Molly said. "We will sort it all out later. Let us go say our goodbyes to Mister Portier."

They walked into the crowded chapel. Emily went to stand next to Blake Tilman, but Molly Shannon stayed near the rear next to the other Molly. Alicia Sorrell was in the front row of mourners, but so was Derek Seaton. Choosing one over the other could cause an ugly scene.

All of Miss Kate's girls were there, and one began to sing a hymn. The others, as well, seeking to transport Ashley Portier's restless spirit to a place far away.

After the service, Molly Shannon led her new friends to Mother Sophia's cottage. They brought the Apache scout Red Flower with them; Molly Shannon thought her quite interesting, obviously born Mexican, but her affect never gave that away, only her deep blue eyes did. When Sophia saw her, she was only slightly surprised, and greeted her warmly in Apache. Red Flower looked happy for the first time since the McLean sisters had met her. The five of them ate from a common bowl at the big table, and Sophia served them a green viscous drink called *pulque*.

When their hunger was satisfied, Sophia led them to a place in the nearby grove to a circle of white stones, and invited them to make a circle of their own. Other women joined them until they were thirteen in all. Two of the newcomers were Delores and Daisy.

Molly Shannon looked up as they approached. "How is our Mistress?" she called.

"None of that," Sophia said. "I have freed her, and in doing so freed all of you. Think differently about her. Do not give her her power back."

This was said without heat, and Molly Shannon knew it was correct. "I will do better," she promised.

The old witch smiled at her briefly. "Of course you will." Sophia looked around and then spoke clearly.

"Now my daughters, tonight we do not dance. This is not a power ceremony but one of inquiry. Something has upset the Earth Mother, and the fabric of our world. There are great evils that are not native here. War, Famine, Disease. They are leaking in through tears in the fabric that hold our world apart from others like it. We must find the holes and mend them, or everything will continue to get worse. We no longer have the Starmen to help us with this, and have lost the power to call them. One of the many calamities the Conquistadors imposed on us. I think we can no longer plead with the Moon and the Stars, but must look deep within the Earth, so we can revive the Earth Mother."

Molly Shannon and the McLean sisters thought it the most remarkable speech they had ever heard, but the other women just nodded. It all made perfect sense.

"What are we to do, Mother?" asked Red Flower.

"We now have detectives among us. They know how to find the truth of any matter. And we have our friends of the forest: all of the plants, birds, animals and other creatures, to assist them. So stick your hands in the soil so you can sense them, and they sense us, and combine the power of our minds and every sense to the task."

Emily wondered briefly how she would report this, and dismissed the idea. It could not be done. Red Flower was next to her, and she felt the absolute savagery of her. The Apache scout was a powerful Bruja. She reached out and let her thoughts grow and mix with Red Flower's.

All of them quickly apprehended what Mother Sophia was planning: a ceremony where their powers would not just be added together, but multiplied to such a degree that the Earth itself could be moved. Despite the cold damp seeping into their clothes, the newcomers felt quite warm.

Red Flower began to chant in a language none of the White girls knew, yet somehow understood perfectly. She was leading them on a quest into the depths.

CHAPTER FORTY-THREE

The next morning Molly Shannon, feeling the need for his affection, found Derek Seaton seated at a large table in Jake Martin's hotel with several other men. Two were military officers, one American, one Mexican. Another was a tall, lean young man wearing a Pinkerton badge, and then there was Detective Tilman, and finally, Jesus, who seemed different somehow. She was still half asleep. Only later did she realize he was dressed as an Apache warrior.

"What's all this, then?"

"A council of war," said Detective Tilman. He introduced each of the other men, and Molly saw that it was indeed a serious business. As the men rose and each gave her a slight bow of respect, she also saw that there were plates of food and cups of coffee on the table. Whatever was happening was too important for her to take her lover away. He would lose the hard-won respect just earned in his showdown with the Stranger. The other men stared at her. This was men's business. A female presence was unwelcome. She looked around for an excuse to stay and find out what they were planning.

"Breakfast!" she said. "It was a long night and I'm famished. May I have some?"

"Certainly," said Tilman. A chair was brought from a nearby table and placed next to Seaton's. A small silver bell on the table was rung. One of Miss Kate's girls came out of the kitchen with a plate of Mexican food that smelled of beans, chiles, and eggs.

Hobson's choice for a menu. It was on a tray with a linen napkin, silverware, a small pot of coffee, and a clean, empty cup. The waitress was Hannelore, the big Swedish blonde girl. She looked sideways at Molly.

"My, look at you now," she murmured. There was envy in her voice.

Molly dug in, and then became aware that all the men were watching her. She stared back, slowly chewing her food, and swallowing it. She poured herself a cup of coffee, sipped at it, trying to read their expressions.

Finally she said, "Please. Don't stop on my account. Continue what you were doing." She reached out and took Derek Seaton's hand, seeking reassurance. He squeezed it briefly. He picked up a black oblong object from the table.

"The question is, what are these things? Each of the Strangers had one. So did Jake Martin. It's some kind of machine or device. But what is its purpose?"

Molly took it and looked at it, turning it over in her hands, and put it next to her ear. "I hear a clicking sound, like a telegraph. Remember what you said about them being able to send messages through the air? It's one of those."

Everyone stared at her.

"How did you remember that?" Derek Seaton asked, looking a bit stunned.

"Darling, I remember everything you say. And since I've begun studying with Mother Sophia, my memory and my senses have only increased. That has given me a wonderful apprehension of the world around me."

The men looked at each other in open amazement. They might have gone all day, and never found that answer. Now they had to look at Molly Shannon very differently. Smarter than she looked didn't even begin to describe her now.

Derek Seaton was filled with a mixture of pride and stomach-clinching fear. Who was she really? What had she become?

Looking around the table, he saw that the other men shared his unease.

Blake Tilman cleared his throat. "Yes, well then, the question now is what has happened to the Strangers' skywagon. Parker Boone said that when he and the other hands ran away, it was still there. But when Black Horse's braves burned the ranch house, it was gone, and that was about the same time that Manny and Red Flower and his men rescued the children. They no longer have hostages and now we do. So the shoe is on the other foot, but anything that flies and throws lightening is a threat. How do we prepare?"

"It's the Prisoner's Dilemma," said Captain John Pershing.

"What is that?" asked Derek Seaton.

"An exercise in Strategy," Manny D'Silva said. "You have someone who wants something from you, but you don't have all the information. If you get it wrong, someone dies. Maybe you and all your men. How do you decide what to do next? Failure is not an option."

"We use it in interrogations when we have more than one suspect in a crime. The one that tells us the truth first escapes hanging," Bill Pinkerton said.

"Precisely," Derek Seaton said. "So what do the Strangers want? And why haven't they come? They could burn the town or threaten to."

"And we can execute their friends, if they do," Manny D'Silva replied. "It is, you should pardon the expression, a Mexican standoff."

A ripple of laughter went around the table.

Molly, full now, and growing sleepy, pushed herself back from the table and stood up. She had heard enough.

"I will leave that to you. I have to get some sleep." She reached over and squeezed Seaton's hand. "You know where to find me, Darlin'." She walked towards the grand staircase. They watched her go up, slowly, weary from the night before.

"Do you believe in witchcraft?" one of them asked.

"I do now."

John Pershing sipped his coffee, and regretted it was too early in the day for something stronger. A thought came to him. "Has anyone read Jules Verne's novel 'Twenty Thousand Leagues Under The Sea'?"

"I'm not much for romances, even scientific ones," Tilman answered.

"I have," said Derek Seaton. "Tom Edison sent it to me with a letter. He said that everything in it was quite fanciful because we do not yet have the technology, but that within twenty years it could be done if we started the research now."

"Sounds like he wants money," D'Silva said.

Seaton laughed. "He always wants money, Tom does, but he has a big laboratory and over a hundred men on staff, and notebooks full of crazy ideas. Except some are not so crazy. Some could change the world. So my family pours money out, so he can make them happen. And some of them we turn into products. He began as a telegraph operator, and knows a lot about electricity. He wants to know more. Verne's idea in that novel is unique, a craft that travels under the sea, and can sustain itself and its occupants indefinitely. It seems to me that the Strangers have the same sort of thing that goes through the air. I would love to have sketches or photographs so I could begin to build one. Think of the potential."

"They do not belong here," said Black Horse. He looked at them, stone-faced and angry.

"Having read Mister Cremony's book, I see why you think that way," Tilman spoke in a soothing tone. "White men especially. But here we are. Why do these creatures so offend you?"

"Because they are not of this world. Not men at all. Lizards under that shell they wear. We need to expel them." His anger was growing.

"Hold fast there, Chief," said Pershing. "Cool down. It is a mistake to hate the enemy. It keeps you from seeing them clearly. That way lies error and defeat."

Manny D'Silva nodded. "Very wise."

"Something we were taught at West Point," Black Horse sighed.

D'Silva looked at his elaborate gold pocket watch. "Time to change the guards. Will you come with me, John?"

"I will," said Pershing, standing up and buttoning his collar, and then checking his weapons. Together they walked to the hotel's front door and went out and down the steps.

Tilman watched them go. He looked around. Black Horse was nowhere to be seen. Pinkerton was writing in his notebook.

"Molly seems different," he said cautiously.

"Yes," said Seaton softly. "Not as jolly as she was before that old Bruja got her involved in magical practices and devices." He looked over his shoulder and up the staircase.

"Well, we're done here," Tilman said; "Why don't you go up?"

"All right," Seaton said, as if he were mesmerized, and did just that.

They watched him go and looked at each other. As he got to the top of the stairs and turned right towards Molly's room, Pinkerton said, "Interesting the hold she has on him."

"A man in love cannot be reasoned with. I think it's the way she smells," said Tilman. "She holds the whip hand with her clients. Seaton may have fallen into her trap, but she wants him, too, and that is rare in the Demimonde."

"Have you spent a lot of time there?" Pinkerton looked up from his notebook.

"A fair amount, but only as an observer, I assure you. Leaving that alone was a way to build trust with those girls. It helped get some of our clients out of difficulties."

"Think he will really marry her?"

Tilman shrugged. "He's a man of sterling rectitude. But he may think anew. Have you met his mother?"

"I have. That's a conversation that will not be pretty."

Upstairs he entered Molly's room cautiously. It was infused with the faint scent of expensive French perfume and past sexual encounters, an unpleasant reminder that when she was not with him, there was a parade of clients who also enjoyed her favors. Molly was laying face down hugging a pillow. She had only a filmy black silk negligee on. That made her very desirable. He started to undress.

"Don't expect much," she murmured; "I am totally worn out."

"Should I go?"

She turned over, blinking at him. "No, I want you here. But just to hold me, like it would be if we were married. Make me feel your strength. Love me rather than make love to me. Can you do that?"

"Of course," he said, and in his long underwear laid down beside her. She moved into his arms and fit herself to him, sighing, and then tilted her head far enough to kiss him on the lips.

"You're the only one, you know?"

"What do you mean?"

"You are the only man I've ever kissed. It's a rule. Whores don't kiss clients on the mouth. Elsewhere, sure, but the mouth is for lovers, or husbands, or pimps. It's saved for them. So we don't sell everything, and forget why we are here."

"For the money?"

"For the money. It's a business, you see – an entertainment, like a play or a comedy. The first time I kissed you, I knew I was lost, and you could do anything you wanted to me or with me. I was in your power."

"What about Miss Kate?"

"She's a pimp, Derek. A Madam is a pimp. With her, it was a game, a way to get ahead in the world, and become something better."

"But you kissed her?"

"Many times. But that was different."

"How?"

"I'll tell you later. I have to sleep now. Just hold me tight so I feel safe."

She snuggled against him, and within a minute he heard the sounds of her soft gentle snores. He hugged her gently, and soon fell asleep himself.

It was mid-afternoon when they awoke. She was fresh and alert. He looked at her and smiled. "Better now?"

"Yes, but I have to save my strength for tonight. It's a hard thing we're trying to do. Like moving a mountain."

"Are you that strong?"

"Not by myself. None of us are. Sophia has us combining our power. There are thirteen of us in all. So our combined power is that strong."

"Thirteen times as much."

"Much more. It multiplies. Two of us are four times as strong, and three are two times that, and four of us are two times that, and so on."

Derek looked at her thoughtfully. "So it is actually two to the twelfth power. That's a very big number."

"How big?"

"Four Thousand Nine Hundred and Six." Derek felt queasy. That much power *could* move mountains. This was not some silly pagan ceremony that the old witch had arranged. Molly peeled off her negligee and put on a robe and slippers.

"I have to go take a long hot bath," she said. "I'm surprised you can stand to be with me, smelling like this."

"You smell fine to me," he replied; "Intoxicating, in fact."

Molly grimaced. "And that's part of the problem, Darlin'. As long as you're not thinking with your brain, but with that other big thing you have, you don't see me clearly. You can't. I'm your plaything, not a person."

Seaton was taken aback by this, suddenly unsure. "How do you want me to see you?" He began to dress himself.

"If we are to be married and I am to be your wife, your partner, then everything changes. Not that the fun goes away, but there will be much less time for it. I will have responsibilities, and I will be dragging my reputation around like a wagon. I can handle that. But can you? Think about it."

She began to walk out, and he followed. Into the hall and down the steps they went, and he was thankful no one was in the big room below the grand staircase. As they walked out the door, she continued to speak. "I knew who you were the moment I met you. My clients in New York talk a lot about your family; mostly about how to get money out of them for various schemes that they're promoting. Now all of these men, and some of their wives, have enjoyed my favors, or had me pose naked at their naughty little pantomimes, and make no mistake, I was enthusiastic about most of it. As a whore, I am only slightly less famous than Miss Kate. When you marry me, you marry scandal, so big you can't control it."

They were walking down the street now. Seaton heard rustling up above. He looked and saw sentries on the roofs. Most of them had their eyes skyward, but some of the *Federales* were looking down as they passed. The word '*puta*' floated down.

Molly extended the middle finger of her right hand upward, causing a ripple of laughter. Seaton took off his hat and was recognized at once, and all commentary died away.

"*El patrone*," Molly said. "No one wants to offend the boss. But when you are not with me, I am naked again." She adjusted her robe and walked on. "You see? I love you, Derek, but I must decline your kind offer to make me your wife."

Derek felt sad and relieved at the same time. He shook his head slowly. "But what will you do?"

They were at the door of the barber shop. She smiled sweetly at him. "A good question," she said. "Let me think about it."

As they waited for the big white tin tub to be filled, she sat on a wooden bench and stared upward. "What shall I do?" she said. "I'm too smart and mouthy to be a whore now, and too kind to be a Madam, so I am quit with all that. I suppose I could go to work as a detective for the Pinkertons. Many girls who escape the Life find a position there, and they are always hiring, but I'd have to change my name and try to look different, and there again, my fame gets in the way. We might continue on with me as your mistress. That would actually enhance your status with other men, like owning a famous race horse, but that's just more whoring, and, as I just said, I am quit with that."

"Really?"

She kicked off her shoes and let the robe fall, before she climbed into the tub. Derek watched her. It was beautiful, like a painting, and he thought of having one done, if she would agree and pose. A way to keep that memory fresh.

The bathtub was full of steaming hot water and a lavender scented soap. She sighed and relaxed. He watched her use a sponge to wash herself. There was nothing erotic about this. It was not a show.

"I can give you money," he said; "You will never be in want."

"Very kind of you. I have quite a lot put by, you know. Bought railway shares on the cheap. I won't starve. I don't want to be kept. And I don't want to be quit of you. I love you. That's why I won't marry you. But since you are so free with the Green, you could set me up." She looked at him with a mischievous smile.

"I thought you were done with whoring?" Seaton frowned. His family would never countenance such an enterprise. Illegal, immoral, and they kept track of every dime.

"I am," said Molly. "No, I heard what you said to Mister Simms about newspapers and how important they are. Help me start one of those. We have a big Presidential election coming up. We need more voices singing for the nation, and not those bastards who want to turn back the clock so we have another war. That's just evil."

"But how... "

"I'm actually very literate now. Unlike Annie Jones, who just wanted to rent me out by the hour, Miss Kate wants to prepare all her ladies for life after the Demimonde. Most retire at thirty, and then what? So we are taught things that make us more attractive to clients, not just reading and writing, but literature and politics, so we can engage in conversation with educated men. Sometimes they just want someone they can talk to. The sex is extra.

"Not important. So politics and a bit of science and business we just pick up from the talk of the men in the lounge, as they smoke their cigars and sip their whisky. I learned bookkeeping and a bit of law, so I'm ready to be respectable now, but on my own, as an independent woman."

"Sounds like some of Mister Tilman's Transcendentalist ideas."

"Oh, I had those long ago. I read Margaret Fuller and others. I think men have too much power, and get a lot wrong. Like you lot downstairs, making a plan without reading us in. Rather rude if you ask me. Time to let women take a hand. That's what the Indian tribes do. Very progressive."

Seaton nodded. "But that reputation you spoke of...?"

Molly laughed. "Move away, change my name, and hope to live it down? Not a bad idea. Let my hair grow back in its natural color, and use my other name."

"Other name?"

"I was born Molly Maureen Shannon. So I shall become Maureen, with mousy brown hair tied up in a bun, and wear black framed spectacles like a librarian. And sign my letters "M.M." Few will catch wise. Will my disguise make me less attractive to you? I won't be that wild creature that won your heart... or was it something else?"

Derek laughed. "A little of both, but it was your wit and charm that captured me. You are as smart as you are beautiful. A man like me needs a smart wife."

"But not this smart wife."

"No. You are right about that. But the other arrangement appeals to me. Where will you go? You will need printing presses, workers, editors, and reporters."

"I know." She rose from the tub dripping, and let him wrap a large fluffy white cotton towel around her. She looked up into his eyes and smiled ruefully. "Like Romeo and Juliet aren't we? Doomed star-crossed lovers."

"Without the poison, I hope. Where will you start this enterprise?"

"Well, I wasn't going to do this in a big city. Too much competition. I think some little town that doesn't have a newspaper. The other Molly, Detective McLean, was telling me about El Paso. Have you been to El Paso?"

"Passed through. Was not impressed."

"It sounds real nice, Derek. I could start my life over there. It's the West. People go there to do just that. Become someone new. And it's a power center for my other occupation."

Seaton's eyebrows rose slightly.

"I will have friends. The McLean sisters are part of a coven."

"That's a surprise. Do the Pinkertons know?"

"They do, and they don't. Bill Pinkerton does, but figures the news would not be well received in Chicago. So, officially, no. And they are not put off by the Demimonde. Just part of the landscape for detectives. They don't judge me. And that is such a relief!"

Molly was laughing, but there were tears in her eyes. Seaton wrapped his arms around her and held her tight. She looked up at his handsome face and sighed. "I hate to lose you, lover."

"You haven't. You won't. No matter what, we'll be friends."

"Seriously?"

"You got me through a very tough time, Molly. You stood by me. I'll stand by you, come what may."

"But not as a husband."

"Don't put that on me. You're the one who backed out." Seaton laughed.

She laughed, too. She put her robe and slippers back on. "Ready to run the gauntlet?"

Seaton smiled again. "Wither thou goest, so go I," he said.

"How is it that you are so rich and yet so decent?"

"I can't afford to be otherwise," Seaton said.

As they walked back down the empty street she said, "I haven't time to make love to you today. Another session tonight."

"I'd rather not do it in your room anyway," he said.

"Why? Oh, because it's where I entertain other men?"

"Full of ghosts. I like my jail cell better. But not today. Too many Strangers around, caged like they were in a zoo. We'd be another specimen,"

As they walked, he savored how beautiful she was. Her light green eyes set off her fair complexion perfectly. A spray of freckles ornamented her cheeks and nose, and she walked proudly, her chin elevated, oblivious to shame. She knew herself and defied criticism.

They were silent until they were back in that room and she was dressing. "We worked at it so long last night, and found the problem, but it's – well I don't know what it is. Mother Sophia says there are other worlds parallel to ours, and one of them is jammed into the fabric of ours, and leaking into it. That's where all the evils are coming from, the wars, the disease, famine, hatred." She was putting on ordinary clothes, like a housewife. "Does that sound crazy?"

"No more than you suddenly turning into a witch." Seaton felt very relaxed. He was simply happy to be in her company.

"Well, no one was more surprised than me when that happened," Molly said solemnly. "Never in a thousand years... Oh, there is so much I want to tell you, Derek, but I fear you'll take me for a lunatic. Society is not ready to accept us. They still burn witches. But El Paso is different. We've been there for thousands of years. I know all of this, now. My new powers let me see far into the past, and a little into the future, and...," her voice trailed off.

"Tell me about the ceremony," he said.

"Oh, that," Molly said; "Not really sure what it is. A bit like rowing a boat. Takes awhile for everyone to find the rhythm, and the chanting helps, but it's all in our minds, so we have all of our powers combined. And we are burrowing deep into the Earth to find something. Dreadfully hot. Seems there is a Hell with fire and brimstone, but we went right past it and saw no devils there, and we worked down to the center where Red Flower, our scout, finds something from the other world impinging on ours. Very tiny. Too small to see, but too heavy to pull apart and set right. The geometry is like nothing I've ever seen, with part of it at right angles to everything else, a fourth dimension. It makes my head hurt just seeing it, because it makes no sense. How can it be? But there it is." Her face was filled with wonder.

Seaton felt his mouth fall open. He could not even imagine such a thing, but now wanted to see what she was talking about.

"So it's mechanical? One world jammed into another?"

"So it seems."

He felt a hollowness of fear in his stomach, but spoke anyway. "That's the kind of problem engineers tackle," he said.

"And where would we find one of those?" Molly said sarcastically. "Are you inviting yourself to the party?"

"If I can be of service."

Molly sighed and shook her head. "You'll have to convince Mother Sophia and the others. And we applied all the force we could muster, and it would not budge."

"Sometimes it's not how much force you apply, but how you apply the force. At the proper angle, a little can do a lot." Seaton was excited now. Here was a real problem for him to solve.

"Well, why not?" Molly said. "You come along with me and meet the girls. Of course, you've already met some."

So he walked out with her again back down the stairs, where two of Miss Kate's ladies fell in with them, and then out the big front door where, at the bottom of the stairs, the McLean sisters seemed to be waiting. Through the town and out towards Sophia's cottage, where Red Flower rode up, with Black Horse. They had been on a scout, and from their affect perhaps something else had happened. Something intimate.

Seaton tried not to stare. "What's that about? I thought she's Little Crow's woman."

"Apaches are polyamorous," said Emily McLean. "She saw him, fancied him, and tried him on for a bit of fun. Nothing more."

"It is the women who decide these things," Molly McLean added. "But they keep it within the tribe. No outsiders. It has to be that way. Not enough men. Some of the braves have more than one wife. In fact there is one who is called 'Many Wives'. He has seven. No one goes hungry in Apache society. For anything."

Seaton nodded, absorbing this. "A different kind of political economy. Many would envy that kind of freedom."

"It's not freedom, Darlin'," Molly Shannon said. "It's desperation. The men keep getting killed in battle or by White Men's diseases like liquor. They used to own all of this. All of it, them and the other tribes. They are at war. Never think otherwise."

"How do you know this?"

"Listening to the detectives talk when you were asleep, and I was not. At the jail. Detective Tilman is very knowledgeable. Some kind of professor, and while I have no regard for Mister Portier or Mister Simms, they were full of information, as well. I took it all in. Most of my education has been simply listening to men talk."

"I should be more careful around you ladies."

"Oh, why start now?" Delores laughed, and Seaton realized with a shock that he had heard her and the others only in his mind. None of it had been said aloud.

They were at the cottage now. Mother Sophia stood outside, and greeted the women one by one while looking at him warily. She looked surprised.

"Why are you here, *Señor*?"

Molly Shannon took his arm to hold him closer. "He thinks he can help, Mother, as an advisor, not as part of the circle."

"But he has no powers."

"He's very receptive, and he knows things."

"What things?"

"Mechanical things," said Derek Seaton. "I'm an engineer. If you need something moved, I can probably devise a way to do it."

The old *Bruja* was still very doubtful. "You have to believe."

"I believe wholeheartedly, Ma'am. Molly has made me so."

Sophia nodded slowly. "All right. But don't touch anything, and speak only to me."

Several hours later, a massive earthquake roiled much of Texas, New Mexico and the Mexican states nearby. Aftershocks continued for several days afterward.

ɯ

In another time, another place, not of this world but another like it an incalculable distance away, in a hall where soldiers trained, Sir Percy Wyndham adjusted the stiff collar of his new uniform, stood at attention, and saluted General Koh. Koh sat at a long table littered with maps, charts, manuals, weapons, and strange devices who purpose he did not yet know. Koh stood and returned the salute and smiled.

That immediately put Wyndham on his guard. Koh never smiled unless he/she/it was about to deal out some assignment that would be unpleasant, onerous, and dangerous to life, limb, and sanity. One that he could not refuse because, as Koh reminded him from time to time, what else were soldiers for?

"Sorry to pull you from your leave so soon," Koh said; "But a situation has come up." Koh frowned. "Rose is not with you this time?"

Wyndham felt his face redden. "She had to remain behind. She is with child."

Koh looked baffled. "How is that possible? You are... "

"Yes, yes," Wyndham replied briskly. "I am not much interested, but it seems I am fully capable of fathering a child. And that woman could seduce a stone statue"

Koh giggled. Then laughed loudly. Wyndham looked upward. Koh laughng was outside his experience, but didn't strike him as a good thing.

"Let's get back to the matter at hand," Koh said.

"Of course," Wyndham pulled at his collar again. "What is the plan?"

"Not sure. We seem to be dealing with a very rare instance of intradimensional trespass, by some very juvenile spirits."

"Naughty children?"

"Something like that. There was an impingement of one universe on another that the locals found a way to move. It has not quite closed yet, and some are still present, wild and making trouble."

"Trouble is my middle name," Wyndham joked.

Koh just stared at him.

Wyndham looked upward. "Sorry."

"Yes, well. There is no time for the usual preparations... "

"You could make time," Wyndham interjected.

"No I can't!" Koh said. "It would throw everything else off. Chaos everywhere."

Wyndham sighed, "So I have some kind of scratch mob with no discipline to lead?"

"No," Koh said; "I managed to borrow the 3rd Bengal Lancers. They will have to be returned intact, of course."

"Cavalry? That means horses. How are we to transport... "

"Not a problem." Koh picked up a small brass bell and rang it. An aide led a huge stallion into the hall.

"You are a pilot, right?"

"I have been," Wyndham admitted. "Why is that important?"

The stallion stamped its forefoot restlessly, and Wyndham watched, amazed, as huge wings unfolded from its sides, stretching the width of the hall.

"Because you know how to fly," Koh said.

Wyndham was non-plussed. "Only in bombers. Where did you find him? I thought this breed died out eons ago."

"Not everywhere. When you manage an infinite number of worlds within an infinite number of possibilities, all things are possible. Some are just more difficult than others."

"I don't see how you keep track of everything."

"I don't,." Koh said. "I can't seem to manage it. That's why these little episodes keep occurring." Koh shrugged. "That's why we have you."

Wyndham groaned. "When will it end?"

"Longing for Death again are we? Please Percy. You may have rest, but you will never die. You cannot. You are the Eternal Soldier."

CHAPTER FORTY-FOUR

Bill Pinkerton was sitting on the hotel veranda sipping a cup of excellent coffee, and looking down the street at what remained of the false facades that Jake Martin erected when he built the hotel.

The earthquake had brought them all down in a thundering crash, and a broken kerosene lamp set fire to one. That blaze was quickly extinguished by an onslaught of heavy rain. What remained was a muddy mess.

Most of the store fronts were laying flat in the street, face down, their raw wooden backs exposing the lie that had drawn so many gunfighters and other bad men to Apache Wells. The old adobe buildings behind them had simply shrugged off the shaking. Some of them had been there for hundreds of years. They weren't going anywhere.

Wagons were drawn up, with teams of bullocks and mules, not to restore them, but to complete their dismantling. Armed with iron pry bars and hammers, men were extracting nails and sorting boards and timbers into like-sized stacks, and then loading them into the wagons.

Pinkerton saw Derek Seaton and Seamus Corcoran directing the work, trying to decide what lumber might be safely dried and reused, and what would become firewood. The big hotel had also suffered some damage, and inside J.C. Simms was directing that clean-up.

"Hello, Boss."

Pinkerton turned to see a short thin Apache in just a breechclout and belt standing next to him. He was armed with a large bone-handled knife and a Colt's revolver on his belt, and had a red and white painted face. It made an odd picture. Pinkerton started to reach for the revolver in the cross-draw holster at his waist, and then realized who this was. He looked him up and down, noting how muscular he was, and the headband with two black raven feathers that implied some rank or status within his tribe.

"Hello, Hey-seuss," he said; "Or is it Little Crow now?"

The young man squatted next to him, looking past him at the workmen. Pinkerton took note of his profile. Pure Apache.

"I answer to both, but here Little Crow will serve you better. Many Apache use that Jesus Martinez moniker."

"Isn't that confusing?"

"Only to White men, and some Mexicans. Those who don't see us plain."

"What do you mean?"

"When you look at me, what do you see? An ambitious Mexican boy, or an Apache brave?" Little Crow turned his head slightly.

Pinkerton considered carefully. "Both, I suppose, but I'm a detective, and we are trained to notice small details. Either way, I know it's you by the shape of your ear."

"My ear?" Little Crow smiled. "I thought only Indians knew that trick."

"It's one that my grandfather discovered twenty years ago when we started using photographs to identify criminals. Part of our training now. There was a crackpot theory about the shape of the head that did not prove out."

"I enjoy being a detective," Little Crow said.

"Do I hear a 'but' behind that?"

"You're a detective, too," Little Crow sighed. "I won't be coming back to El Paso anytime soon," he said. "I have responsibilities."

Pinkerton felt some relief. He would not have to tell the young Apache that he'd decided not to keep him on. To be polite, Pinkerton said, "That's too bad. We will miss you."

Little Crow nodded, as if he believed him. "It is time for my Vision Quest. All Braves must make one, and I'm also a Shaman. I have to take one. Kicking Horse is not well, and about to pass into the other world. So I am to help lead the tribe. Also, I'm taking a wife."

"Red Flower?"

Little Crow looked at him sharply. "How did you know?"

"She mentioned it a few times on the journey here. Very happy and proud. Which makes the thing with Black Horse... "

"Diplomacy," said Little Crow; "A way of bringing our tribes closer together."

Pinkerton's confusion was plain on his face, but he was too smart to say what he felt.

Little Crow laughed. "You're thinking like a White Man, Boss. We trade mates fairly often within the tribes, and among them, and we bring in new people all the time. This is why we steal children like Red Flower, and let even a stuffy Englishman like Jim Frazer into our campfire. Our numbers have been shrinking for hundreds of years. Black Horse went back East to learn the White Man's ways, and came back to find all of his band's elders sick or dead from the White Man's poison, whisky. Now he has to deal with this other problem that Jake Martin imposed on the town. Maybe the Brujas can fix that. Maybe they just did, when they made the mountains shake." He looked sideways at Pinkerton. "I didn't know that Pinkertons had Brujas."

Pinkerton tried to keep a poker face on. "I don't know what you are talking about."

Little Crow laughed. "Your detectives were there, Boss. So was Mister Seaton, but why, I don't know. Red Flower told me all about it."

Pinkerton drained his coffee and stood up. "Pinkertons is a respectable Christian business, Hey-seuss, and would never engage in occult practices, nor hire anyone that does. You should know that. Just as you know that Apache witches can't really fly."

"You're right," Little Crow said. Pinkerton turned his head to look at the workmen, and when he turned it back Little Crow was no longer there. There was the sound of flapping wings overhead. Bill Pinkerton didn't dare look up, for fear that he'd bust a gut laughing.

Detective Simms came out of the hotel with a pot of hot coffee. He refilled Pinkerton's cup and turned up an empty one for himself. He poured it half full, sipped, and grimaced. Then sat and gazed at the work going on.

"Most of the glassware, crystal, and fine china went to flinders last night, Boss. I think we're pretty much out of business there. I got some of the local women to come in and clean, but I don't know if the hotel's a viable proposition now."

Bill Pinkerton looked at him. "Not our problem, Mister Simms. We're not in the hotel business. We're here to finish what Tilman and Portier started."

"Serving warrants and taking men into custody? Good luck with that."

"We'll accept paroles for them that come peacefully, but the main job was always getting Mister Seaton home safe."

"Good luck with that, too." Simms gestured towards the ongoing work. "He seems to have settled in. Currently acting as the town's building commissioner. Already tagged some of the newer buildings to be torn down and rebuilt. And to that end has promised to pay for the work himself."

"Very generous of him, I'm sure."

Simms made a sour face. "That comes easy when you've never been in want yourself. Money has lost its basic purpose for him. It's numbers in a ledger, nothing more. No, generous is me having twenty cents, and giving you a dime because you will go hungry if I don't. That counts for something."

"Sounds like you've been talking to Mister Tilman."

"The man's a philosopher, that's sure, but not all of it comes from reading. He grew up hard, and was an Abolitionist back before that became the passion of the moment. And still is, even though the tide is running against it. Money sure don't matter to him. Handed me a million dollars in Bills of Exchange that Portier was carrying for the Confederate Government to buy influence against my people, and challenged me to use it for them instead. Who knew that there was still even a Confederate Government? I sure thought that died at Appomattox."

"No, it's rising from the grave even now. You've heard of the Ku Klux Klan, I'm sure?"

Simms made a disgusted sound. "The slave patrols reborn. I would think that also died."

Pinkerton shook his head. " 'The South will rise again'. I take note of what Tilman has to say, not for his big brain but the way that he is able to use it to see the whole board like a fine chess player. It's what makes him such a great detective. And he pointed me to the other battle: the one for truth. There is this group called The Southern Historical Society, determined to retell the story of the War their way. Their way is full of lies. Not big ones, but a pack of little ones that twist what happened, to make them look like noble warriors, like heroes in a Sir Walter Scott novel."

"That should be suppressed," Simms was quietly angry now.

"Can't be. Legal as church on Sunday. Part of the same part of the Constitution. A man has the right to his opinion." Pinkerton looked at him ironically.

"So that's where the real war will be fought?" Simms was thoughtful now. "They are going to buy newspapers, Seaton said. And said I should do likewise."

Pinkerton nodded. "I grew up hearing my grandfather talk about the old cases the firm had before the War. His books are about the easy ones. The hard ones, the ones his publisher won't touch, include the ones where Abolitionist newspapers were bombed or burned out, and their editors murdered – and that happened in the North as well as the South."

"So Pinkerton's is still in the fight?"

Bill Pinkerton frowned, his face troubled. "Not so much these days, and I am too young to have any influence. Not even a Branch

Manager yet. No, that, too, is a battle to be fought out, but one better conducted from within. You understand?"

Simms nodded slowly, taking it all in. "You can only do what you can do." He looked around slowly. "How do I turn that paper into cash? I can't just show up with them, and not have them call the police."

Pinkerton pointed down the street to where Derek Seaton was working.

"If I have a banking problem, I usually go to a banker. Mister Seaton's family owns several of them."

"I thought of that. Can I trust him? It's a lot of money."

"To most. Not him. His family calls it a 'rounding error'. And we've done business with them for more than twenty years. No cause for complaint on either side."

Simms laughed, relieved. "Okay then! Well, I have more immediate concerns." He started to walk back into the hotel.

Pinkerton said, "One more thing."

Simms turned. "Yes?"

"The Pinkerton Agency has no knowledge of any Bills of Exchange. We never found any, and as far as we are concerned, they don't exist." Pinkerton said this without expression.

Simms started to smile, and then remembered his poker face. "I understand."

Simms turned again and Bill Pinkerton got to his feet and fell in beside him.

"There's one last thing, J.C. Miss Kate, or Miss Sorrell, or whatever her real name is, has asked for an escort for her and her girls to get back to New York. If you still wish to be a Pinkerton detective, that will be your next assignment. It's a bit soon, but I'm short-handed here, and since you know the client, and the Demimonde, you are the man for the job."

Simms looked at him to make sure he wasn't joking. "You sure that I can handle this, and will not be seduced?"

"Come on, J.C, you don't like women that way. I see that."

Simms stared at him a moment, and then nodded slowly, "Yassuh. I was interfered with as a child. It left its mark on me. I'm not really interested in any of it. I might have become a priest, except it was a priest that did that to me, and I also lost my Faith."

Bill Pinkerton nodded slowly. "I'm glad you told me that, J.C., but it won't be written down anywhere in our records. You will be judged on your performance. Get those women back to where they belong, and then report to my Uncle Robert at our New York office. I will write to him."

Simms shook his hand, turned, and walked away, leaving Bill Pinkerton wondering if he had done the right thing, or thrown temptation into the path of a man flawed by his own history.

No, Simms was no pimp. He had too much pride. Or at least so Pinkerton hoped.

A short time later, John Pershing, at the head of a column of some of his men and some of the *Federales*, came riding in. With them were the scouts Lone Eagle and Horse Woman.

Pinkerton was still sitting on the hotel veranda, a notebook in his lap, trying to draft a report that would pass muster in Chicago, and yet raise no alarms.

When he saw that all of the horses were restive, and that even Horse Woman was having difficulty calming them, he stood up. The street was clear now, the detritus from the earthquake and rainstorm having been cleared away.

Pershing called out in a loud clear voice, "Dismount!"

All of the troopers and *Federales* did so, some hanging on to their mounts' heads so they would not bolt and run away. Horse Woman rode up and down the line, chanting something.

"Walk them. Then feed and water them," Pershing shouted. He handed the reins of his own mount to one of his troopers, and then walked, a bit bowlegged, towards Pinkerton.

"What happened?" Pinkerton yelled.

"We found the Strangers' skywagon," Pershing said, as he walked up the stairs. "But I only want to tell it once. We need another Council of War, so get everyone together – and include some of the women this time." He sat in the chair that Simms had used and fanned himself with his hat, looking weary.

"Yes, sir," said Bill Pinkerton. He walked back into the hotel to organize the meeting. That did not take long, because everyone wanted to have a look, so on fresh mounts, they rode out to see what was left of the Strangers' amazing flying machine. It was spread in many small pieces along a red tear in the bright green forest.

"That's about a hundred yards long," Pershing said. "Keep the horses upwind if you can. There is a terrific industrial smell that upsets them."

"I don't see any sign of survivors," Manny D'Silva said.

"Smashed with the rest," said Molly McLean.

"So now what? Have we seen the end of them?" asked Derek Seaton.

Black Horse shouted at one of his braves in Apache. Grey Squirrel jumped off his horse and was about to climb up the hill. Lone Eagle made an unmistakable negative gesture at him. Confused, he remounted, and rode over for instructions.

"That's right, Boyo. Stay clear. There's great evil there," Molly Shannon's eyes were focused on what no one else could see. "It's an invisible fire that burns you from within. More than a few minutes will sicken or kill you."

"What should we do with it, then?" asked Seaton.

"Nothing. Leave it be. Put barbed wire all around it to keep others away." She looked at Seaton, whom she saw had his doubts. "And don't you be picking up any souvenirs to send to Tom Edison. It could kill him as well as you."

Bill Pinkerton looked from one to the other. "With all due respect, Mister Seaton, this might be a good time to let your lady have her way."

Seaton shook his head, and said, "Alright. Just this once." That caused everyone to have a good laugh. Seaton gazed at the spot. "How far back for the fences, Molly?"

"At least a hundred yards," she said; "All around. And clear it all."

"That's a lot to burn."

"You can't do that either. It will just spread the poison."

Seaton looked over at Lone Eagle, and then the two Captains. "I can survey it. Can you handle the rest?"

"Have to get some of the men in town to help. That okay with you, Chief?"

Lone Eagle looked solemn. "Normally, I would protest this measurement and desecration of our sacred forest, but I always listen to a Bruja. Even a Bruja *Blanca*. And here we have two."

"So let's get on with it," Derek Seaton said happily. Molly Shannon saw how young and innocent his spirit still was, filled with enthusiasm for yet another project. She was going to regret her decision to let him go, she knew.

Bill Pinkerton looked at the clear blue sky and felt sweat roll down his neck. "So is that the end of it with these Strangers?" he asked.

"No," said Black Horse. "They were coming and going every two weeks or so. They will be back. Very soon."

The two Captains looked at each other. "How far up can a Winchester shoot?" asked Manny D'Silva.

"Not far enough," said Black Horse; "Not when they can throw lightning."

"Indulge us here, Chief," said John Pershing. "Maybe we can wait until we can see the whites of their eyes."

"Probably about five hundred feet at most," Derek Seaton said. "It's not just distance but gravity. A Sharp's would go much farther. I'll have to do some math."

"What's 'gravity'?" Molly Shannon asked.

Seaton and the two Captains looked at her. Seaton licked his lips nervously. "The force that holds everything together," he said.

Molly, heedless, said, "Oh, that thing we were playing with last night that touched off the earthquake," she said cheerfully, and then became aware that everyone except Molly McLean was staring at her, mouths open.

Bill Pinkerton quickly closed his, and, to change the subject, said to Molly McLean, "Say, where is your charming sister this morning?"

"On her honeymoon, I think." There was an undertone of resentment in her voice.

That created a second wave of surprise, and gave everyone else something else to think about, rather than the idea that thirteen women could summon such destruction. Derek Seaton looked away, hoping that no one would know his part in it. One little nudge. That was all it took. Like a house of cards.

He felt a little guilty about it because of the destruction. But Pinkerton's question served its purpose. Everyone else was now thinking about Emily McLean being married to a man old enough to be her father.

There was no hiding the fact that they were now lovers, and Emily would not have had it any other way. She felt and looked like the proverbial cat with a dish of cream. That morning, she woke up in Blake Tilman's arms, both of them naked, still amazed at the intensity of their lovemaking – and they were married!

They had been quietly debating the matter the day before, when Molly Shannon had happened by, looked at them, and approached the quiet alcove where they sat, saying, "My advice, should you want it, is to seize the moment and worry about the others' feelings later. Sure, now, her mother wants that big church wedding, and your sister will be pissed that you got a husband ahead of her, but that's on her. You are ready, and she is not. And you, Mister Tilman, will preserve your reputation for sterling rectitude by following the popular prejudice in such matters. You don't want to be accused of seducing a young girl half your age, do you?"

Tilman was bemused. "No," he said; "Not something a Pinkerton would do, even with another Pinkerton."

"Actually, Molly Shannon, t'was I who was seducing him," Emily said, a bit indignant. "And how do you know my mother's feelings on the matter?"

"Sure, and it's what they all dream of, isn't it? And you really do not want to wear the label of shameless hussy. Take it from one who has borne that for many years. It never goes away."

Tilman slapped his hand on the table. "That settles it, Emily. I will not have you shamed. You must marry me forthwith."

Emily looked at him wide-eyed, and felt her stomach drop and heart explode at the same time. She suddenly felt faint. The game was over.

They stared into each other's eyes for a long moment. Molly Shannon smiled.

"Oh, alright. If it means so much to you." Emily smiled.

"It does."

"Then I accept your proposal, Blake Tilman."

And, as it turned out, Seamus Corcoran was, among his many other occupations, a Justice of the Peace. With Bill Pinkerton and J.C. Simms standing at his side, and both Mollys at hers, the deed was done that afternoon. A civil ceremony. The religious ones could come later.

So now here she was, sitting in the hotel lobby with her husband. Husband! People immediately saw the change in her. She had the morning-after glow and relaxed manner of a woman who had been taken to new heights of pleasure.

It was beyond anything she had imagined. Once they were alone, he had asked her to disrobe and did likewise. Most of her clothes were quickly on the floor around her. Then, as she came to him and started to climb him like a tree, wrapping herself around him, he had smiled and lifted her with big strong hands on her bottom until their eyes were level with each other. He kissed her tenderly.

"You only have your first time once, Emily, so let's us go slowly and savor each other."

She felt herself flush with desire. She wanted him so badly!

"What did you have in mind?" she gasped.

"Something from the Vedic tradition, common in India and Tibet. It's called Tantra." He walked over, and then sat on the bed with her legs around his waist and their faces still a short distance apart. Her skin felt on fire everywhere it touched his.

"Now place your hands upon my chest, and I will do likewise. Slowly, softly."

"Mister Tilman, sir! Can't we get on with it?" Her breaths were coming short and quick.

"Breath slowly. Deep breaths. We will get there. All good things come to she who waits." Passion shook her entire body, a minor earthquake of its own. She thought she had passed out.

"Sorry," she said; "I couldn't wait."

"I could," Tilman said; "So now we begin again."

Emily felt her body shake again at the thought.

"How many times?" she gasped.

"As many as it takes," he said, laughing.

"Yessir. Whatever you like."

So, the morning after, Emily's mind was in a pleasant fog, and she felt as happy as she had ever been. Her instincts had been right. Blake Tilman was the man meant for her by Destiny.

Tilman, too, was in an extraordinarily good mood. He was actually smiling. When they were dressing that morning, and he was admiring her slender body, he said, "You were in fine form last night. Not that I care, but are you sure it was your first time?"

Emily smiled. "In the flesh. I did rehearse it in my mind many times, when I decided to pursue you. I even imagined some of what we did. When Lucy Blunt had your books and things returned, I did find a copy of 'The Kama Sutra' among them. Very instructive. Had she read it, she might have hung on to you."

"So you were reading up?"

"I was, but no amount of reading could have prepared me for the actuality."

He leaned over and kissed her softly. She responded, but then wanted to put the matter to rest.

"No," Emily said. "I've had no other man than you, my dear. But I have thought about you making love to me many times. I saw it in my mind. But only you."

"What about Jim Frazer?" Tilman teased.

Emily waved her hand dismissively. "A girlish fancy. One put to rest by his liaisons with Rose Green and Horse Woman."

Tilman nodded. "Well, we have other things that demand our attention."

"Shortest honeymoon on record, eh?"

"I'll make it up to you. We'll take leave. Maybe go to England. Ashley gave me a letter of introduction to Captain Sir Richard Burton, whom he claimed to have traveled with. The great adventurer, and also the translator of 'The Arabian Nights' and 'The Kama Sutra'. The British Ethnographic Survey is his sponsor. So I should like to know how much of what Portier said was true, and how much was moonshine. Was he also working for the Brits?"

Emily felt very surprised. "So this would be a working vacation?"

"Only in part. We will take at least a month for ourselves." Tilman smiled, and shook his head, very pleased with her and himself. "The inquiry may lead to nothing. So your pleasure will come first."

Emily gave him a becoming smile, "I will hold you to that, Husband."

Emily felt sad when Molly Shannon told her that she would not marry Derek Seaton.

"It's nothing to do with the Craft is it?" Emily asked.

"No. He seems quite easy with most of it. The adventure last night threw him a bit, but me as well. I had no idea that we could combine our strength so. No, if he was not who he is and is going to be, and I were not who I am, and damnably famous for that, then we would give it a shot. We do love each other. But Society and his family will not permit it. He is going to help me to a different kind of life."

"What would that be?"

"Is there a newspaper in El Paso?"

"No."

"Then I will start one. A good Republican newspaper."

Seeing that Emily was staring at her, a bit amazed, she added, "There are stupid whores and smart ones, Emily. You know that. I'm one of the smart ones."

Having practiced Magick with Molly Shannon, Emily knew that she had an open and generous nature, tempered by a hard life. She could make a go of anything, even a newspaper. With Derek Seaton's help, she could make that dream happen, if they could all get out of Apache Wells alive. Her husband was right. There was work to be done.

"As Ralph Waldo Emerson said, 'Knowledge is power'," Emily said.

"And did he not say also that a little of it was a dangerous thing?" Molly Shannon replied.

"I think that was someone else, but that's why we have detectives: to brave the danger and find the truth."

Simms had a free lunch laid out. People congregated in the hotel's bar room. Miss Kate's girls were busy upstairs packing. Simms had no desire to continue their services. He was not a pimp. Nor did he have time to run the gambling properly, and thought it best to avoid conflicts. To that end, he also stopped serving liquor. Beer, wine, coffee, tea, and well water in moderation only.

Manny D'Silva and John Pershing, running short on field rations, started sending their men to eat at the hotel instead. Suddenly, the place was making money again. Not wishing to be sucked into a new life so far from 'civilization', Simms hired Bob Williams to run it all, so he could walk away clean, and fulfill his assignment as a Pinkerton.

Everyone waited for the next incursion of Strangers. Soldiers and *Federales* stood watch on the roofs of the hotel and church, with badly concealed firing positions that no one expected to survive a lightning strike. An informal, leaderless civilian militia collected around them, and Black Horse's braves rode patrols into the countryside, equipped with signaling mirrors that they could use to send alerts in Morse code.

When the ever-inquisitive Molly Shannon asked the purpose of all this effort, when the Strangers would probably just descend from above, Captain John Pershing said, "It gives everyone something to do. Keeps them sharp. Boredom erodes alertness and there is nothing more boring than standing watch. Moreover, we can't assume the direction of their attack. Build a wall to the North and they will come from the South, or the East and any other direction. We must mount a fluid defense."

Molly Shannon, impressed, said, "That sounds like witchcraft."

"No, ma'am. We call it tactics."

CHAPTER FORTY-FIVE

Miss Kate and most of her ladies left that morning in the old stage coach and two carriages, escorted by Detective Simms, and a mixed lot of gunmen who'd given their paroles and citizens determined to enforce them. Two Apache scouts rode with them, to negotiate safe passage with any wandering bands they might encounter.

"Where are you going?" Molly Shannon asked Miss Kate, as they walked together to have a final goodbye. The girl who had been Alicia Sorrell so long ago, smiled back at her from behind the Madam's hard face that Miss Kate wore.

"Matamoros. Mister Simms says that it's better to book passage from there to Bermuda, and then to New York, for the Fall Season. No need to mention us having been here, or even in El Paso." She tilted her head and looked at her former protegee curiously. "You look so different now. Not the same girl at all."

"I'm not that girl anymore. I'm no longer a whore, for one thing." Molly smiled to soften the remark.

Miss Kate sighed, "Well, I shall miss you, of course. You were the best of the best. But you caught the brass ring, and landed a big one. As for this other thing, these 'powers', I know nothing about that. Can't have witches in my stable. So I've asked Daisy and Delores to seek other employment. And I would have done with you, too, but you beat me to the punch. Mister Simms did the divvy, and your share of the profits from this disaster are waiting for you. You know to have a little put aside for emergencies. Use it for that, and don't give it to the poor because you want to prove how virtuous you are now. We both know that for a lie."

Molly shook that off. Miss Kate had to be cruel. It was part of her style, and what made her so desirable to some prominent men.

"Fare thee well, Alicia," Molly Shannon said, and held out her hand. Miss Kate took it, held it briefly to her cheek for a moment, kissed it, and then turned and walked away. She did not look back.

Molly watched her climb up on the driver's seat of the old stagecoach next to Simms. Over her dress she wore a long linen duster and a broad brimmed canvas hat. She took the double-barreled shotgun from its boot, broke it open to make sure it was loaded, and then put it back. Simms cracked the reins, and the little convoy moved on down a road that had existed in one form or another for thousands of years.

Molly was surprised that she felt nothing at seeing her leave. That part of her life was done, and moving away from her. Now she looked at Derek Seaton, the man she loved too much to disgrace him in the eyes of others by becoming his wife.

Detective Tilman had told her of a part in The Kama Sutra that mentioned 'public women' and how they were respected and powerful, and she had immediately set him straight. "Maybe in India, but not here," she said. Then he'd told her of how Pinkertons created new identities for their agents, and with that, she saw a path forward. Surely that could be done for the 'special friend' of a big client such as the Seaton family? Of course it could, Blake Tilman assured her.

And, as El Paso was to be her new home, she'd already chosen a name for her newspaper. It would be called "The Evening Star". Magical, that name.

Molly McLean sometimes viewed Manny D'Silva as an irritating itch that she could not scratch. She found his strong body desirable, even though too much food and alcohol were turning parts of it to fat. She found his opinions and worldview deplorable, and retrograde to a time when all women were chattels. It was that argument that kept her virtue intact. Why would any woman of sense, much less a Pinkerton girl raised as she was, submit to such domination?

Where the Mexican Captain was concerned, she did not know her own mind and could not figure it out. Did she want to be married at all, much less to him? Why did she tease him so with long kisses? Or by exposing her breasts? Why not complete the act and resolve the question?

Now they were rising from the bed where they had spent the night together, fully clothed with his sword laid between them to protect her virtue. A romantic notion that made her laugh outright.

"This is something that Knights did in the Middle Ages to protect the virtue of a noble bride they had under escort," Manny said, before they lay down.

"You've been reading Sir Walter Scott again," Molly McLean scoffed. "It's a ridiculous idea." She was very tired, and simply wanted to sleep. This bed was the only one available unless they wanted to sleep rough, and Molly, fresh from a hot bath at the barber shop, did not want that. Pinkertons suffered in the field, but always got clean as soon as they could. It was doctrine that few in the firm ignored. She could send Manny away, but feared taking her teasing too far. Being admired by two handsome, strong men pleased her, but she could play the Belle for just so long before she lost both of them. John Pershing had already withdrawn. She had to decide.

"Do you love me, Manny, or just desire me?"

Manny looked perplexed. "What a question. I am prepared to do both."

Molly stared upward at the rough, badly plastered ceiling, and sighed. It would be easy to roll over on top of him and begin kissing him, but where would that lead? She must exert a little self-control.

"If I marry you, I give up what few rights I have," she said; "What do you give up?"

"Half of everything I own. You become part of the most powerful family in Mexico."

"I barely speak the language," Molly lied. "And political intrigues pale in comparison to what I do now. I do not handle boredom well. And would that 'half' include your mistresses?"

Manny stared at her. "Probably not. They are very innocent girls. Not creatures of the Demimonde. I made them mine to save them from that."

Molly smiled. "Very noble. So you saved them... for yourself."

Manny shook his head. "I saved them from starvation or worse. If they wanted to express their gratitude, well who was I to deny them?"

"And you lavish presents on them, and give them houses?"

"Strictly for appearances sake. A man in my position cannot be cheap or mean. Appearances matter."

"So, they are merely trophies. Demonstrations of your power."

"Yes. I suppose so."

"And I would be another?"

Manny sat up, and stared at her. "No. Not at all. You would be my wife, and give me children. You will have your own power."

"And the power I have now? The hidden world?"

"You would have to give that up. For appearances sake."

"I cannot. It's who I am."

Manny lay silently beside her for so long that she thought he 'd fallen asleep.

"It's not going to work, is it?" he said at last.

"Would it ever? Your people expect a pure untouched virgin, who will take instruction. I am not that person. I've had lovers. You must take me as I am."

They lay there together all night, and the sword never moved. Molly thought it was time to move on. But there was that itch of desire she dare not scratch. It would be to surrender as Emily had, and she was not ready for that. Not now. Perhaps not ever.

"It's just through here," Seamus Corcoran said, as he pointed the beam of his reflecting oil lantern at yet another opening in the rough stone wall of the tunnel ahead. Derek Seaton used his own lantern to illuminate the ceiling overhead.

"No visible cracks," he said, hoping the old man had not gotten them hopelessly lost.

Corcoran had come to him that morning, and asked him to 'take a look' at a network of tunnels that ran under the town.

"I fear that the quake may have shifted something important," Corcoran said. "We never let outsiders know about them. The Shamans claim it's 'sacred space' and warn of horrible consequences, if it is violated. Pagan superstition, I say. It's an excellent place to raise mushrooms, and I want no part of their ceremonial places meself. That said, I would like to keep the town from falling into a pit. Seems to me that you're just the lad to take measures against that if they are needed."

Seaton knew that Corcoran had paternal feelings about Molly Shannon, and was disappointed that his marriage to her was now not happening. Molly's assurances that the decision was hers, were accepted grudgingly, and Seaton's puppylike eagerness to help the town was poor recompense.

Molly came with them to make sure that Corcoran did not abandon him there from some twisted desire to avenge an honor she had never had. She was wearing boy's clothing under a linen duster, and a canvas hat with a wide brim to keep falling bits out of her hair. She also thought that her new powers would give her a better sense of conditions than could be found with weak beams of flickering oil lantern light. She sensed rather than actually saw the limestone walls. So far, she was at ease. Nothing was going to fall on them.

"What are these paintings?" she asked.

"What paintings?" Corcoran stopped, and threw the beam of light around, searching.

"There," said Molly; "Up above?"

Both beams of light climbed up the wall to the ceiling.

Corcoran's mouth fell open. "Never saw that before," he said. "They have them in the big Kiva where they have ceremonies, but

I don't remember any out here. And why put them there, up where you'd get a bad cramp in your neck trying to read them?"

"Maybe it's a secret," Molly said.

"What secret?" Corcoran ran the beam along the ceiling slowly. "It's some kind of story. Probably of a hunt or battle, or maybe instructions for conducting one. What do you think, son?"

Seaton shook his head. "I'm an engineer, not a bard. Sussing that out is more in Mister Tilman's line. He's studied literature. Might be some myth retold for future generations. Something secret. Some ceremony."

"Not sure I want a Pinkerton knowing about this," Corcoran said. "Might bring more attention. They ain't the Government, but close enough to it that it worries me. Too fond of public attention these days."

"At the moment," said Seaton; "They are working for me."

"For your family, you mean."

"Same thing."

"You said 'at the moment'. Excuse me if I don't put a whole lot of trust in that," Corcoran sniffed. "What about later? The Shamans want anything like this close held, because they don't trust the White Man, and given what has happened lately with all Indians, I can't blame them. You heard what they did to break the will of the Comanches last year?"

"I've heard nothing about it," Seaton said. He hoped that Corcoran would take the hint, and leave it at that. He wanted no distractions. He'd studied geology in depth but not as an engineering problem, and wondered why these tunnels, obviously man-made but very old, existed at all. There seemed to be no rationale for their existence. He was still looking at the paintings, trying to construe their meaning.

Molly Shannon was applying her other senses.

Corcoran rattled on. "It would be a scandal t'were it known. That tribe had a lovely refuge where they could hide from the Cavalry, and that brigade from the East had no regard for any

Indian. Comanches are the best horse breeders on the Plains. It's what makes them so powerful. Horses to ride into battle, to trade for guns and blankets, and anything else they need. The Brigade commander, he finds a Judas among them, who shows him how to enter that huge canyon, and where all the secret places are, especially the meadows where the horses are raised and fed. The Comanches are too tough to fight and too wiley to catch, so this Colonel rounds up all the horses he can find, and has them all shot dead. Over twenty thousand of the most beautiful animals you ever saw. Slaughtered and left to rot."

Molly gasped.

Seaton said, "That is the most disgusting thing I ever heard."

"Given the love that the Comanches had for those beasts? Like their children they were. It broke them. Even the Braves were weeping. They gave up, and agreed to go on the Reservation."

Seaton nodded slowly. "Wiped them out, too. If the horses were their source of wealth, then that campaign turned them into beggars."

"And you don't think that they wouldn't serve women and children likewise? They have, more than once. Surrounded a camp when the men and warrior women were out hunting or fighting another tribe, and killed as many as they could, from babes in arms to old men?"

"Why is this not known?" Seaton felt his own anger growing. "It's a disgrace."

"Who's going to tell?" Corcoran jeered. "All of the big papers are owned by people like you, and the little ones look the other way, too scared to say anything, or bought off."

"My newspaper will be different," Molly declared.

"Will it now? How can you say that?"

"I have a powerful patron."

Corcoran looked at Seaton and laughed. "Working against your own? Is that the way of it? True love!"

"Just policy," said Seaton, still looking upwards at the pictures.

"How is that?"

"Not all wealthy people are greedy monsters. Some of us swim against the tide, and give back, by supporting worthy causes."

"Oh, pshaw. Show me one!"

"Ralph Waldo Emerson."

"The poet? You're having me on, ain't you?"

"Not at all. Emerson was a very rich man, and helped start the Transcendentalist movement."

"A bunch of airy fairy crackpots."

"Not true. They started the Abolitionist movement and the Underground Railroad. Supported Frederick Douglass, and made him famous. Allan Pinkerton is also one. At least so Mister Tilman said."

"So why are they not trumpeting that to the heavens, then?"

"Because they also supported John Brown and Harriet Beecher Stowe, and that went places they never wanted to go. Death and destruction."

Molly Shannon whistled. "Oh, I see why they don't want that remembered. Oh my, yes."

"The thing of it is, that you can never predict the outcome of a good deed. Like a pebble thrown into a pond," Seaton said. "And I know someone who says he can prove that mathematically."

"Now you are pulling my leg," Corcoran said.

"Perhaps. Turn about is fair play. You've pulled mine often enough."

Corcoran laughed out loud, acknowledging the point.

They were making their way down the tunnel again. Going slowly in the dim light.

"What's behind this wall?" Molly asked suddenly.

"Behind it? Why nothing. It's a wall. Rock, like the rest."

Seaton reached for the geologist's hammer on his belt, and began tapping on the stone. The sounds were solid and low until he hit one point that returned a higher, more hollow note. He felt the wall.

"Here it is rough," he said; "And here it is also rough but less so, and crumbles when I tap it. It's stucco!" He looked at Corcoran severely, and said, "If you are hiding something, it does no good to have me look for problems. I can't see behind walls."

"I can," said Molly Shannon, sounding quite surprised. She felt up and down the wall and then stopped. "What is this?"

Seaton felt where her hand was. "I'm not sure," he said and pulled.

Part of the wall moved away, into the side of the tunnel. The three of them stood there absolutely amazed, unable to speak. A gush of cool air hit them in their faces. Derek Seaton and Molly Shannon looked at each other, and then at Corcoran, who seemed to be murmuring some kind of prayer.

"You didn't know about this?" Seaton asked.

"As God is my witness, I hadn't a clue. I doubt anyone did," Corcoran declared. "This passage is not much used. It doesn't lead anywhere. Well, to the Kiva, of course. But only the Shamans go there."

"And, of course, one has nothing to do with the other," Molly said sarcastically.

Corcoran looked like he'd eaten something particularly disagreeable.

Seaton shone the flickering beam of his lantern into the dark room. He coughed. "Lots of dust."

It was about ankle deep. The three of them stepped cautiously inside. Dust flurried up around them. Molly used her hat to whisk some of it away.

"What is this?" She went to something that looked like a row of closets or tall cabinets. She touched one, rubbing dust off to reveal yellow metal underneath. Suddenly there was a whirring sound. The room was filled with soft white light.

Seaton cleared more dust, and rows of colored lights appeared on the cabinets or, no, within them. Corcoran stood in open-mouthed amazement, while Seaton looked for the source of the lights, peering into the smooth hard surface.

And a mellow voice that could have been of either sex, inquired, "Do you need assistance?"

"Well, yes, I rather think we do," Molly Shannon replied with some spirit. "What the Hell is going on?"

"Distress noted," said the voice. "Remain calm. Help is on the way."

It was only later that they realized that they had heard the voice, not with their ears, but their minds.

Further inquiry on their part was stopped when Kicking Horse and Lone Eagle appeared, seemingly out of nowhere. Kicking Horse began a chant. The lights on the cabinets flickered and went out.

Lone Eagle, looking very disturbed, even fearful, whispered, "You have disturbed the Old Ones. You must leave."

Seaton started to say something, but Molly grabbed his hand and said, "We're so sorry, sir. T'was nothing intentional. We will go now." And pulled Seaton out of the room with her, back down the tunnel the way they had come. Corcoran followed, moving slowly, like a man in a dream.

Once they were back on the surface, Corcoran came to himself, and said, "You can't tell anyone about this." His eyes were wild.

"Whyever not?" Molly Shannon asked.

"It's magical. Bad Juju. And you set something off bad enough to get those two scared."

"I can't unsee what I just saw," Seaton said. "It's an amazing find."

"And what was it anyway?" Molly asked, her eyes bright.

"Some kind of machine," said Seaton. "A machine that talks."

"I think so, too," Molly said; "And if it's mechanical, then it's not magical."

"How would you know?" Corcoran challenged.

Molly simply raised one eyebrow.

"Oh," he said; "That's right. You're a Bruja now."

Molly shook her head. "Not exactly. But close enough. Magic can move mountains, and that device can move voices, but there was no magic there."

"What then?" Seaton felt relieved when she said this. Anything mechanical he could understand. "What drives it then? There has to be some kind of force. That voice came from somewhere."

"You heard it, too?" Corcoran asked. "I didn't hear sound. There was no echo."

Molly pointed to her head. "I heard it in here. My mind."

Seaton nodded. "Me, too."

They were outside now.

Corcoran took a deep breath of the clean air. He looked around. "Hundreds of years the Apaches have guarded that secret, and now it's out in the open."

"I wasn't going to tell anyone," Molly said.

"I won't," said Seaton.

Corcoran looked at both of them, a sour expression on his face. "You say that now, but can you hold to it? Ben Franklin said it best. 'Three may keep a secret if two of them are dead.' Not an option with you two. Too well connected, you are. There would be inquiries, and Molly's mind is shared with the other Brujas in her circle... and two of them are Detectives!"

"You had no idea it was there?" Seaton asked.

"Heard rumors over the years, but dismissed them as tall tales. The Apaches keep a lot of secrets. They don't even tell you their true names, so they can't be used against them in a curse, or other dark magic."

"Well this won't be a secret long," Molly said. "Remember the last part of that speech?"

Both men looked at her, puzzled. She smiled.

"Help is on the way."

CHAPTER FORTY-SIX

Of course the thing could not be kept secret.

Others sensed it at once, especially Emily and Molly McLean. Emily was debating with her sister whether or not to continue to style herself as McLean, or adopt Tilman as her surname when Tilman himself added confusion.

"What makes you think my name is really Tilman?" Tilman asked.

Both sisters looked across the luncheon table, their faces frozen in shock.

"It's not Tilman?" Emily asked her voice trembling.

Tilman shrugged. "It is in El Paso, but different in New York and Pennsylvania."

"Why is that?" Molly McLean demanded.

"Because in New York, there is a price on my head. Not by the government, but by certain parties that want revenge upon me for my testimony. Robert sent me out here, over my strong objections, for my own safety. Also because your father needed at least one experienced man. It was that, or give up the trade entirely. They already tried to kill me twice."

Emily was still staring at him. "But Miss Kate knew you as Tilman in New York."

"That was a different case, and a different work name." Tilman brushed off the breadcrumbs from his vest and smiled. "As you gain experience, my love, you too, will use other names and identities. Part of our investigative repertoire. Allan even mentions it in his books."

"I did that once," Molly McLean said. "It was my first case, in Denver."

Emily turned and now stared at her. "Do tell," she said sarcastically.

"Well, I was just fourteen, so you were way too young to know, and where else was Daddy to find a young girl that age to be a detective? It was at that big gambling hell on Market Street. Enormous place with all kinds of bad things going on. There was this counter that sold slices of various cakes and pies. Gamblers, especially men, have a sweet tooth, but there was also competition, so I wore a very tight thin tan silk dress, and no bustier, so my most obvious attractions would draw many customers every day. I might as well have been naked. I was also paid a commission on the sales, and there was quite a bit of traffic. In between, I pretended to be doing my schoolwork. What I was actually doing was writing down everything I could see that looked untoward or suspicious. At night, Mama would copy it all out and hand it over to other detectives on the case. All of the owners had an association, and feared infiltration by criminal gangs. Pinkerton's is their police force."

Tilman raised a glass of lemonade in salute. "Sounds like good work to me."

"I never knew," Emily said.

"You were just too young, dear one. You were still playing with dolls."

"Was it dangerous?" Emily asked.

"It could be. One night, one of the roughs cornered me in a hallway and demanded my virtue." Molly smiled and shook her head.

"What happened?"

"You remember that little two shot Derringer Kate carries now?"

Emily and Blake Tilman nodded.

"It used to be mine. So I shot the brute in the obscene member, he's just shown me, and he goes stumbling out, screaming, holding what's left. Birdshot. Lots of blood. The crowd sees him, sees me, understands the situation, and descends upon him with a vengeance. I am the heroine of the moment. Sold every cake and pie I had that night. Made over a hundred dollars in tips as well. But the job was over. I was known now, and would be watched myself. So I changed my appearance, and went back to school."

Tilman, Emily, and the others at the table had a good laugh. It was a tale that would become legend, and add luster to the Pinkerton name as it was told elsewhere. It had Manny D'Silva shaking his head and looking at Molly with new eyes.

"You are the most dangerous woman I have ever met," he said.

Tilman laughed. "You said the same about Red Flower."

Emily nudged him, "So am I Tilman or not? Are we actually married?"

"Do you care? I seem to recall this very aggressive letter that showed up in my portfolio, that said that you were mine under any condition I might choose."

Molly was actually shocked. "Emily!"

Emily smiled at her coolly. "I had to get his attention, and I don't have big teats."

Raucous laughter went up around the table.

Tilman leaned over and kissed her. She looked at him, dazzled.

"Well, sir," she said softly. "Are we married?"

"Yes, we are." He kissed her again. Her toes curled.

Just then Bill Pinkerton came in the front door of the hotel, walking fast. He spotted them at the table and rushed over. "I thought one of you was going to stay close to Mister Seaton."

"Then who?" Tilman asked.

"Maybe you?" Pinkerton suddenly realized that it was indeed his turn to be Seaton's bodyguard. He blushed with embarrassment.

"That's okay, Boss. Molly, the other Molly, is with him. I'd know if anything had happened. No, wait. There is something. Nothing dire, but something quite extraordinary."

So the secret was out, and another meeting had to be convened.

And once the tale was told, Mother Sophia hit the wooden floor with her cane three times, commanding everyone's attention. She pointed a withered finger at Kicking Horse and Lone Eagle, and said bitterly, "All these children have done is what you should have done long ago. They have called the Starmen. Why have you not done so many, many moons ago?"

"The place for that was lost. The Starmen made its cabinet from gold. When the Conquistadors came, and started to steal all the gold they could find, we had to hide it. The texts on how to use it were also written on gold, and those they took and melted down. The machine was walled up to save it for later. You know what happened next."

Sophia nodded. "The pox. That sickness burned down all Indians like a prairie fire. Some tribes were entirely wiped out. Even White Men died of it." The old woman seemed shrunken.

"The Starmen rose us up," she said for the benefit of the Whites listening. "They taught us language, and how to grow corn and squash and other good things. How to make ourselves strong by fighting one another, and bringing new blood into our campfires. Promised to return, but never did, because we never called. Because the device was hidden and forgotten! The original language lost. The Conquistadors destroyed that, too. Melted it down. Burned it all as pagan superstition. Destroyed the star charts we used to find other worlds. How can they help us now? Too much time has passed."

"They can rid us of the Strangers," Molly Shannon said.

"You're sure of that?"

"I'm sure of nothing. They may not come at all. They may go to the wrong place because of what we did last night. But why worry about it? Let's see what happens, and act then."

Mother Sophia smiled, showing her blackened teeth in a horrible grin. "Out of the mouths of babes," she said proudly. "So we wait."

They did not wait long.

III

Sir Percy Wyndham turned to Koh. "What recce has been done?"

"None. It's an emergency. You will have to take it as it comes."

"Make it up as I go along, you mean? That's very sloppy procedure. It will distort the fabric, and cause endless questions and lies."

"How do you think myths and legends are born?" Koh smiled. "Off you go."

Wyndham saluted and walked out to where his troop of winged horse waited. His squad of angels were all mounted, helmets on, weapons laid handy across their laps. He swung into the saddle.

He held up his right hand and pumped it up and down, signaling the advance. The troop moved forward at a walk until they were clear of the huge hanger overhead and well into the cloud covered surface outside. A long grassy track lay before them.

Wyndham clicked his communicator. "Spread."

The horses moved apart into three widely spread files.

"Wings."

Each horse unfolded huge wings and flapped them slightly.

"Okay, Lads and Lasses, here we go. Advance."

Hooves thundered, and wings grabbed air, as a dozen riders disappeared into the night, and then just disappeared. Behind them other squads followed.

III

The first message came from twenty miles away, in flashes from a signaling mirror used by one of Black Horse's braves. That was a day's hard ride over rough ground, but Lone Eagle disappeared for a time and then reappeared. "Some kind of balloons," is all he said.

Then he and Kicking Horse went underground to the Kiva. When questioned, all Seamus Corcoran would say was, "If you believe in the power of prayer, now is a very good time."

599

It was getting close to nightfall. The sky was clear overhead. The stars were a blinding smear of white light. Stranger skywagons zipped around overhead, apparently searching for something.

The two Captains sent all of their men to the rooftops. Below, they stood with Bill Pinkerton and Lone Eagle and Mother Sophia in front of the hotel. Black Horse and Seamus Corcoran stood a little distance apart, while Tilman and the two other detectives sat, apparently relaxed, but with revolvers near to hand, in the big chairs on the hotel's veranda. Seaton sat with them, holding Molly Shannon's hand.

Father Tomas walked up the street from his church to see what all the commotion was about, since his chapel had suddenly filled with loudly praying parishioners. The informal civilian militia milled about near the jail, determined to keep the Strangers confined.

What happened next was debated for many years. Stranger starwagons and mysterious crafts that looked like flying men on horses engaged in battle. Explosions shook the earth from above and starwagons crashed to the ground.

Those in Father Tomas's flock saw something entirely different: a host of Devils From Hell, engaged and defeated by a host of Angels.

Others saw a spectacular meteor shower, the likes of which had never been seen before, and still others, too frightened to look up, saw and heard nothing.

As that noted philosopher, William Blake Tilman, said, "People see what they want to see."

So most also missed what followed the next morning. Another balloon was reported by the Apache scout Grey Squirrel and the sentries sent back to the rooftops.

The balloon was close to the town's edge, and they could see that it was festooned on both sides with the American flag, the Mexican flag, the British Union Jack, and from poles sticking out from both sides, the white flag of parley.

Captain John Pershing looked at Captain Manny D'Silva, and asked, "What do you think?"

"Always better to talk than fight," Manny said, and shouted in Mex for his men to put their weapons down, but keep them handy. Pershing repeated the command in English. He looked sideways at Lone Eagle and saw him make a gesture with his right hand.

All of the tension in the air, so thick that it could have been cut with a knife and sold in the marketplace, began to float away. The air seemed suddenly clearer, the sun a little brighter, and people were happy again.

"Don't be too relaxed," Tilman murmured to Emily and Molly McLean. "All may not be as it seems."

As the balloon gradually touched the ground in the middle of the street in front of the hotel, part of the bottom vessel became a short ramp. From it, emerged two tall men, wearing the attire of British diplomats. They looked around, and then made their way over to the group standing directly in front of the hotel.

"Good day. We are Mister Anderson and Mister Clay of the British Ethnographic Survey. Apparently, something untoward has happened here that requires our attention. To save time, please identify the wisest person among you."

All eyes, even Lone Eagle's, went to Tilman. The Shaman pointed at him. Tilman swallowed hard, and stood up. He looked sideways at Emily, who was smiling radiantly at him. Squaring his shoulders he walked slowly down the steps and over to the two.

"Blake Tilman, Pinkerton National Detective Agency. How can I be of service?"

"Blake Tilman? *The* Blake Tilman? I certainly did not expect to meet you here."

"Anderson," said the other man, a warning in his voice.

"Oh. my bad. It's just, in our world, Blake Tilman is a very famous man."

"Your world?" Tilman asked.

"Oh, now I've done it!" Anderson said. "But play along, will you? Surely after that adjustment you made... "

Seeing the confusion in Tilman's eyes, he stopped. "You have no idea of what I'm talking about, do you?"

"Not a whit," Tilman confessed. Emily had drifted along behind him and heard everything.

"I think he means the earthquake." She smiled at the two diplomats. "That was a group effort, and can't be repeated. Mister Seaton, who is young but wise beyond his years, can tell you about that. He saw it. But the one who organized it is... "

Mother Sophia stepped forward. "Me."

Anderson and Clay looked at one another, then her, and back at each other, and then again at her.

"Oh, it's you," said Clay.

"Took you long enough," Sophia grumbled.

"You've been out of touch."

"Not wilfully. Come sit down, I'm an old woman now. I tire easily, and you need to hear it all, not just from me. I don't know everything."

Emily began to have an inkling of why Sophia, and those like her, were known as 'the old woman who does not die.'

Mother Sophia nodded towards the hotel. "Let's gather everyone there. These folks need sustenance."

So, within a few moments, all of the principal actors were together, and one by one, with others offering commentary, everything was described that had occurred, the Strangers and their terror most of all.

"Well that is a very bad business," Clay said. "Those people are criminals, and will be dealt with. We will remove them at once."

"They are vampires," Anderson added.

"Oh, not blood. That would just make them sick," Clay said into the silence that now pervaded the room. "They suck up emotions. Especially fear and anger. Then they regurgitate it back where they are from, and upset the balance of nature there. Pollution of the worst kind."

Anderson took a device from his vest pocket, stared at it, and then pressed something. "There. All done. Apologies for all the trouble."

As Deputy Butch Plover described it later, he heard a series of bangs, like Chinese firecrackers, went back into the jail, and found that all of his prisoners had escaped. As had Jake Martin.

"We will also clean up that mess outside of town," Anderson promised, and a day later, the site where the Stranger's skywagon had come to grief was green again, covered with new grass.

"You've let a lot of evil into this world," Mother Sophia complained.

Clay looked at her as if he did not understand the comment. "Adversity is part of the plan. You know that. How else will improvement be possible? It seldom comes on its own. There must be a problem, a contest, a movement... "

"A War," Tilman finished, with a veteran's bitterness.

"Well, yes. Sometimes entire populations must extirpated to make room for others. There are waves in society, as well as in nature. There is one building here. You have one part of this world that is overcrowded, and here you have vast amounts of empty land. That population is shifting even now. Join or die."

"That's very cruel," said Molly Shannon.

"That's life. Adversity has been your friend, hasn't it? Look how you've risen above it."

Molly felt tears come to her eyes. She nodded to concede the point, and held her hand out towards Seaton, who was quick to come to her and take her in his arms.

"But it's all very random," Anderson said. "None of it is planned. None of it is intended. "It's not 'God's will', or whatever mythical deity some use to comfort themselves or buy power. It just happens. And the variations are complex and fascinating. In our world, Blake Tilman is elected President of the United States, and leads the great Confederate Restoration."

Anderson stopped, because everyone was staring at him.

Clay sighed. "Once more, you have put your foot in it. That's Samuel Tilden, not Blake Tilman. Really!"

Anderson looked contrite. "Oh, dear. I am sorry. Please forget I said anything."

"Could that happen in this world?" Bill Pinkerton demanded, his voice cracking.

"Could. Might. Might not. Depends on too many variables to calculate. One little nudge one way or the other and ... well, who knows?"

He looked at his pocket watch, a Raymond Railway pocket watch, all the detectives noted, and said, "Well we must be getting on. Unfortunately, there are other calls for service we must attend to."

Clay smiled at Mother Sophia, and said, "Lovely to see you again."

She pulled her shawl around her thin shoulders, and said, "Wish I could say the same."

Both of them acted as if they had been slapped. Anderson and Clay walked back to their balloon, walked up the ramp, talking furiously to each other. The ramp went back to make the bottom whole, the balloon rose gently into the sky, higher and higher, until it could no longer be seen.

Townspeople began to bring chairs, tables, large umbrellas for shade, cooking grills and baskets of food and drink. Seamus Corcoran and his wives seemed to be organizing things. He turned to the Pinkertons and said, "You lot could help out, instead of just sitting there like bumps on a log."

"What's all this about?" Bill Pinkerton asked.

"Fiesta! We're going to have a party, Father Tomas will offer Absolution for the timid."

It was an epic celebration, so much so that most could not remember what had happened during it, or the weeks before.

But Tilman, as was his wont, stayed sober, and Bill Pinkerton made careful notes for the report he would never deliver. Not everything was lost.

Molly Shannon thought long and hard about the burdens of running a newspaper, between lovemaking sessions with Derek

Seaton, and Seaton thought about how he was going to propose certain ideas to Tom Edison without being dismissed as a madman.

The following morning the detectives and their clients sat around the big table in the hotel lobby eating breakfast, and trying to sort it all out.

The two Captains were elsewhere, trying to get their hung-over men into sufficient condition to ride back to El Paso, while Lone Eagle and the other scouts tended to the horses. They had not indulged, and were clear-eyed and sober.

Back at the hotel, Bill Pinkerton said, "Who the devil is Samuel Tilden?"

"Senator from New York," Molly Shannon said. "I met him a few times. Big drunk. Very corrupt. I imagine he'd be a straw man for the real power." No one bothered to ask how she'd met the Senator.

Pinkerton looked around. "The Great Confederate Restoration, eh? Not if I have anything to say about it."

Everyone nodded.

"How do we proceed?" Emily asked.

"Ask your husband. He's the wise man."

Everyone turned and looked at Tilman.

"Well, first of all, we need a plan, but one that can be changed. The political conventions have not been held yet. It may not be him, but another reptilian creature risen from the swamp. Elmer Washburn may not want to send money to support such an investigation..."

"I will," said Derek Seaton. "And buy a few newspapers as well."

"We need to get to the bottom of this. Who is behind it?" Tilman asked; "Judah Benjamin or the British Government?"

"Why not both? He was always their man, and the Confederate treasury was never found. Something like four million dollars in gold." Bill Pinkerton looked thoughtful. "If that was sold into the spot market in 1864, it could have brought a hundred times as much in British pounds."

"Which is why it was never found." Derek Seaton whistled. "They are going to try and buy the election."

Bill Pinkerton looked at him carefully. "Sir. I can not accept this as a case for the Pinkerton Agency. I don't think we should even mention it to them. My father and uncle are all about the money now. It grieves me to say so, but they can be bought."

"That merely gives me first mover advantage," Seaton reminded him. "We're all good Republicans. It will stay that way."

Tilman looked at Emily.

Her face was lively and flushed with excitement. "What is our next move?"

"Well, my love," Tilman said; "You and I are going to take a long leave and go to England, and maybe some other parts of Europe."

She batted her eyelashes at him, "You mean a Grand Tour?"

"Why not? Been years since I've had a proper vacation. I have that letter of introduction to Captain Burton, and we might drift down to Cambridge to see Jim Frazer. I might even give a lecture or two, while we try to find an English detective who can help us look at Mister Benjamin's operation."

"Isadore Polacky," Bill Pinkerton said; "He worked with us on the Alabama Claims. Big firm. Lots of resources. No love for the South."

"How did you pull that one out of your hat?" Molly McLean asked, a bit dazzled.

"I used to file the foreign correspondence in Chicago. I told you I know what's what."

"So you did, Boss. I apologize for ever doubting you, Cousin. What about me? What's my part in this scheme?"

"Robert asked me to find someone for the Vassar College operation. There is a chance to get to know the daughters of the rich and powerful in and around New York. I thought about you, but then, there was Manny."

"Not going to happen. I was leading him a dance. I don't suit him anyway."

"Yet he is drawn to you like a moth to the flame," Emily teased.

"All the more reason to pursue my education elsewhere."

Everyone laughed. Blake Tilman leaned back, and looked around, happy now for the first time in years.

Everything had turned out all right. Of course, tomorrow was another day.

THE END

SELECTED BIBLIOGRAPHY

Books Consulted

Life Among The Apaches, John C. Cremoney, Roman & Company, San Francisco 1868

Six Years With The Texas Rangers, 1875-1881, James B. Gillet, University of Nebraska Press, 1976

Thirty Years a Detective, Allan Pinkerton.

The Spy of the Rebellion, Allan Pinkerton.

The Molly McQuires and the Detectives, Allan Pinkerton.

The History of the United States Secret Service, by La Fayette C. Baker, 1868 (privately published)

Lecture Series From **The Great Courses** Viewed

Emerson, Thoreau and the Transcendentalist Movement, taught by Ashton Nichols, Ph.D., Dickenson College

Native Peoples of North America, taught by Daniel Cobb, Ph.D., University of North Carolina, Chapel Hill

Conquest of the Americas, taught by Marshall G. Eakin, Ph.D., Vanderbilt University

Superstring Theory, The DNA of Reality, taught by S. James Gates, Ph.D., University of Maryland

Quantum Mechanics, The Physics of the Microscopic World, taught by Benjamin Schumacher, Ph.D., Kenyon College

Many others viewed as well.

Online Resources

Wikipedia, of course. Entries on many topics related to the story. Too many to list.

Documenting The American South, University of North Carolina, Chapel Hill

The Making of America, The University of Michigan Libraries

ABOUT THE AUTHOR

FRANCIS HAMIT has been a professional writer since 1969, and came to the craft through six years in Theatre. He is a playwright, screenwriter, novelist and journalist who has won many awards and believes in "Kaisan" or continuous improvement.

His writing is informed by his service in the US Army Security Agency, and by graduate studies at the Iowa Writers Workshop where he earned an M.F.A. in Fiction.

He has published three previous novels, a memoir, non-fiction books about Virtual Reality, and about Industrial Security, as well as over a thousand magazine articles. He was a Contributing Editor for **The Encyclopaedia Britannica**, *Advanced Imaging* magazine, *Security Technology and Design*, and many other magazines and newspapers.

He is also a film producer and a consultant. He is a Vietnam veteran. He and Leigh Strother-Vien live in Los Angeles, with Tobias, a cat.